# A WILD PURSUIT

&

# YOUR WICKED WAYS

*Also by Eloisa James*

FOOL FOR LOVE
DUCHESS IN LOVE

# ELOISA JAMES

# A WILD PURSUIT

&

# YOUR WICKED WAYS

AVON BOOKS
New York

This is a work of fiction. Names, characters, places and incidents either are the product of the author's imagination or are used fictitiously. Any resemblance to actual events, locales, organizations, or persons, living or dead, is entirely coincidental and beyond the intent of either the author or the publisher.

AVON BOOKS
A *Division of* HarperCollins*Publishers*
New York, New York

Copyright © 2004 by Eloisa James

ISBN 0-7394-4096-9

Printed in the U.S.A.

# Contents

# A WILD PURSUIT

# 1

## In Which Scandal Brews in Wiltshire

*Shantill House*
*Limpley-Stoke, Wiltshire*

It is a truth universally acknowledged by women that it is far easier to dress when the point is to cover one's body, than when one desires to leave expanses of flesh delectably uncovered.

In the days of Esme Rawlings's reign over London society, it took her hours to clothe herself. She would emerge as a caterpillar from its cocoon: silky black curls gleaming over pearly shoulders, bodice miraculously suspended in air at the very moment of dropping to her waist, delectable curves swathed in a fabric so light and revealing that many gentlemen weakened at the knees at her very sight. Other gentlemen stiffened. It was all a matter of constitution.

These days it took precisely twenty minutes to throw on enough clothing to cover herself, and gentlemen in her vicinity never showed reaction beyond a sharpish discomfort at the apparition of a woman with a stomach the size of a large cannonball.

"I am plump as a pork pudding," Esme said, peering at herself in the mirror over her dressing table.

"I wouldn't say *that,*" her aunt said with her characteristic drawl. Viscountess Withers was seated in a small chair, riffling through her reticule. "Drat, I cannot find my handkerchief."

"Stupendously stout," Esme said disconsolately.

"You *are* carrying a babe," Arabella said, looking up and narrowing her eyes. Clearly a pair of pince-nez would have come in handy, but spectacles were inconceivable, given the dictates of fashion. "I never liked the look of it. But you, my dear, might go far to changing my mind. How dare you look so delightful? Perhaps your example will finish the ridiculous habit of women *confining* themselves. Such a punitive word, *confinement*."

"Oh pooh," Esme said, rather rudely. "I am reaching elephantine proportions. No one would wish to see me on the streets of London."

"I believe that your size is normal, not that I've had much to do with childbearing. In fact, this is the first time I have seen a woman so close to her time. So when do you expect it, my dear? Tomorrow?"

"Babies aren't like house guests, Aunt Arabella. They choose their own moment, or so I gather. The midwife seems to think it might be a matter of a few weeks." Privately, Esme thought the midwife had to be mistaken. If she grew any larger, she'd be confined to a bath chair, like the Prince of Wales when he had the gout.

"Well! Here I am, ready to help in every way!" Arabella threw out her hands as if she expected to catch the baby in midair.

Esme had to grin at that. Arabella was her very favorite relative, and not only because her reputation was as scandalous as Esme's own. "It's very kind of you to visit me, Aunt Arabella. Not to mention positively self-sacrificing in the midst of the season."

"Nonsense! One can have just as much pleasure outside of London. Even in Wiltshire, if one applies oneself. I knew that you would be quite dreary in the country all by yourself. Always struck me as a foolish habit, women rusticating themselves in the wilderness merely because they're carrying a babe. The French are much more sensible. Marie Antoinette was dancing up to the moment she gave birth."

"I suppose so," Esme said, wondering whether a black gown would diminish the look of her waist. She was no longer in full mourning, and the idea of returning to blacks was dispiriting. But then, so was her girth.

"I took the liberty of asking just a few persons to follow me tomorrow," her aunt went on briskly. "We shall dine alone tonight, unless Stephen Fairfax-Lacy joins us in time. I suppose you know that your friend the Duchess of Girton is *enceinte*? If she births a male, obviously Fairfax-Lacy will lose his title. Mind you, it was only an honorary one, but having had it for eight years at least, the man will probably feel as if he's lost his hair. We'll have to cheer him up, won't we, darling?"

Esme looked up, startled. "Fairfax-Lacy? I am not in a position to entertain a house party, particularly one which includes a man I have only the slimmest acquaintance with!"

Arabella ignored her. "And of course I've brought my *dame de compagnie* with me. Why be on our lonesome when we needn't? It *is* the season, but I fancy that my invitation outweighs any tedious little parties that might be occuring in London."

"But Aunt Arabella, this is not entirely suitable—"

"Nonsense! I shall take care of everything. In fact, I already *have*. I brought some of my staff with me, dearest, because there are such terrible difficulties with people hired in the country, are there not?"

"Oh," Esme said, wondering how her butler, Slope, had taken this news. The extra footmen might come in handy if she was reduced to being hoisted about in a chair.

"As I said, a very few persons will follow tomorrow, just to enliven dinner, if nothing else. Of course, we won't hold any public gatherings, or perhaps only a very, very small one, because of your condition."

"But—"

"Now darling," Arabella said, patting her hand, "I've brought you a basket absolutely full of the latest creams and soaps made by that Italian man, the one with the funny little shop in the Blackfriars. They are all absolutely efficacious. You must try them immediately! Your mother's skin was disastrous when she was carrying you." She peered at Esme's face. "But yours appears to be remarkable. Ah well, you always did take after me. Now, I shan't expect you downstairs until dinner. You do remember that Fairfax-Lacy is a Member of Parliament?"

Esme was starting to have an odd feeling about the presence of Stephen Fairfax-Lacy.

"Aunt Arabella," she said, "you wouldn't be thinking of matchmaking, would you? My husband died only eight months ago."

Her aunt raised her exquisitely shaped and dyed eyebrows. "If you call me *aunt* again, my dearest, I shall scream! It makes me feel quite ancient. Arabella to you, thank you very much. We are family, after all."

"I would be delighted," Esme said, "but—"

Arabella was never one to respect another's sentence. "It's a dreary business, being a widow. I know, as I've been one three times over." She lost her train of thought for a second and then continued. "Now, I'm not saying that I couldn't be married if I chose, because I could."

"Lord Winnamore would marry you in a heartbeat," Esme agreed.

"Precisely," Arabella said, waving her hand. "I've invited Winnamore as well; he should arrive tomorrow. But my point is, darling, that being a widow is rather—daunting. Fatiguing, really."

"Oh, dear," Esme said, thinking that her aunt did look rather more tired than she had seen her in the past. "You must make a long visit."

"Nonsense," Arabella said smartly. "I shall stay with you for the time being. But where's the excitement in living with a woman, hmmm?"

Her wicked smile made her lose at least twenty years.

Esme grinned back. "I'll take your word for it. Miles and I only lived together for a year, and that was years ago, so I can hardly speak from experience."

"All the more reason to marry again," Arabella observed. "Now I've been thinking about Stephen Fairfax-Lacy. He's just the man for you. Lovely laugh lines around his eyes. That's important. And he's strong too. Apparently he boxes regularly, so he won't keel over in the act the way your late husband did."

"It wasn't *in* the act," Esme protested. Her husband had suffered an attack in their bedchamber. The fact that it had occurred during the first night they had spent together in years was not relevant.

"Close enough. Not that we can fault poor Miles too much. After all, he got the deed done, didn't he?" She waved vaguely in the direction of Esme's belly.

"Yes," Esme said, dismissing the thought of another possible contributor to her situation.

"Fairfax-Lacy is not a man to leave you in the breech, so to speak." Arabella almost choked on her smirk.

"I'm glad you're enjoying this discussion," Esme said pointedly. "It's nice to know that my husband's demise affords someone pleasure."

"For goodness' sake, Esme, don't start taking on airs like your mother. The way Fanny wept over your father could hardly be believed. And yet she couldn't stand the fellow. Well, who could?"

Arabella began opening the jars on Esme's dressing table and sniffing each of them delicately. "*This* is the best of the lot," she said, holding up a small jar. "Almond paste, straight from Italy and ground by nuns. Has a glorious perfume to it. Rub it on your chest every night and it will keep your skin as white as snow!" The viscountess had never been acclaimed as a beauty, but she didn't let that fact get in her way, any more than she was allowing age to dampen her flair. Her hair had faded slightly from a fiery mass to a gingery pink, but it was swept up in an exuberant mass of curls. Her face paint could not have been more exquisitely applied: it alone took some ten years from her true age.

She put the jar down with a little thump. "Now, let's see. Fairfax-Lacy has a good strong leg, and I like his buttocks too." She rubbed a little of the miraculous almond cream into her neck. "He has plenty of blunt, not that you'll need it, since Rawlings left you well established. The point is, Fairfax-Lacy is a good man and he won't give out in the long term. Stamina, that's what you want in a man. Look at me: married three times, and not a single one of them survived past a few years."

Esme sighed. Clearly poor Mr. Fairfax-Lacy was about to be thrown in her direction until his head spun.

"We're dreadfully awkward numbers tonight, with so few men," Arabella said, patting the almond cream into her cheeks. "Yourself and I, of course, and your friend Lady Godwin, and my *dame de compagnie*."

"Who is she?" Esme asked without much interest.

"Well, poor duck, she's really my goddaughter. I don't suppose you know her. She debuted four years ago."

"But what's her name?"

Arabella fidgeted with the glass jar for a moment, looking uncharacteristically hesitant. "I shouldn't want you to—well, I can trust you to be kind to the gel. It's not as if you've a puritanical past yourself."

Esme looked up at her aunt. "Her name?"

"Lady Beatrix Lennox."

One of the most irritating things about pregnancy, to Esme's mind, was that she seemed to have no firm grasp on her memory anymore. "I'm afraid I know nothing of her," she said finally.

"Yes, you do," her aunt said rather brusquely. "Beatrix is one of the daughters of the Duke of Wintersall. In her first season, unfortunately—"

"*That* daughter?" Now Esme remembered. She raised an eyebrow at her aunt. "I suppose you consider her your protegée, so to speak?"

"You're hardly one to talk, my girl," Arabella observed, patting her curls in the mirror. "You've made quite a few scandals yourself in the past ten years, and I'll have you know many a person considers *you* my protegée. Including your mama. Lord knows, Fanny has complained of my influence enough."

Esme was trying to remember the scandal. "Wasn't Lady Beatrix actually caught *in flagrante delicto* at a ball? *I* never did that."

"Naturally, I would never inquire about such a delicate subject," Arabella said, raising an eyebrow, "but perhaps you were merely never caught?"

Esme suddenly remembered a certain drawing room at Lady Troubridge's house, and kept a prudent silence.

"I'm never one to approve of the pot calling the kettle black," Arabella said, favoring her niece with a smug smile. "Poor Bea was only a baby, after all, and no mama to take charge. The duke had found some doddering old cousin to act as chaperone, and naturally Bea was lured into a closed room by Sandhurst. Happens to girls all the time, but the father generally hushes it up. Instead Wintersall decided to make her into an example for his other five daughters, or so he had the impudence to tell me. Apparently, he told Bea she was fit for nothing more than a hothouse and gave her the address of one!"

"Oh, the poor girl," Esme said. "I had no idea." At least she herself had been safely married when she'd embarked on a life that had earned her the sobriquet Infamous Esme.

"Well, don't go thinking that she's a wilting lily. Bea can hold her own among the best of them. I'm glad that I took her after her father disowned her. She keeps me young."

Esme had a sudden thought. "You didn't do this simply to irritate Mama, did you?"

"It did have a miraculous effect on your mother's temper," Arabella said with a smirk. "Fanny wouldn't have me in her house for at least six months. Lately, I have contemplated a major renovation of my town house, if only because I could insist on staying with my sister for a time, and naturally I would bring my *dame de compagnie* with me."

Esme couldn't help laughing. "Poor Mama."

" 'Twould do your mother good to be around Bea for a time. The gel has a backbone of steel, and she enjoys putting people in a stir. Thinks it's good for them. Wait till you meet her, my dear. She'll go far, mark my words!"

"Oh my," Esme said, suddenly remembering her Sewing Circle and their likely reaction to Beatrix Lennox. "I forgot to tell you, Aunt Arabella, that I've become respectable."

Arabella blinked and then snorted. "*You?* Why on earth would you wish to do such an odd thing?"

"I promised Miles before he died that I would avoid any sort of notoriety. He wished to live in Wiltshire, you know. I've been establishing myself among the local people, and—"

"I thought it was deuced odd that you, Esme Rawlings, were whiling out your confinement in Wiltshire like some sort of milk-and-water country miss! So you've decided to change your wicked ways, have you?"

"I have," Esme said, ignoring her aunt's smirk. Arabella could smirk all she liked; Esme was determined to live the life of a respectable widow and mother from now on.

"So how are you effecting this miraculous transformation, then?" Arabella asked, having the impudence to appear utterly disbelieving. "The information might be useful in the unlikely event that I'm . . . I'm . . ." Arabella clearly couldn't think of any circumstances that would drive her into respectability.

Esme shrugged. "It's not so difficult. I joined the local Sewing Circle and—"

But when Arabella was in the room, it was always difficult to finish a sentence. *"You? You've joined a Sewing Circle?"*

She needn't hoot with laughter like that. They could probably hear her in the next county.

"I have," Esme said with dignity. "It's a very worthy cause, Aunt Arabella. We sew sheets for the poor."

"Far be it from me to get in your way! Just let me know when the ladies are descending on the house, and I'll make myself scarce," Arabella chortled. "I'll have a word with Bea as well. I daresay she'll flee into the village rather than be trapped with a bunch of seamstresses."

Esme scowled at her. "There's no need to mock me."

"I'm not mocking you, love . . . well, not entirely. Would you prefer that I return to London and left you to the worthy matrons?"

"No!" And Esme found she really meant it. "Please don't go, Aunt Arabella. It is truly wonderful having someone here, at the moment. Not that I wish Mama could, but—"

"There's nothing wrong with wishing your mama wasn't such a stiff-rumped old chicken," Arabella put in. "My sister has always been a fool. Docile as a sheep. Let you be married off to Miles Rawlings without a by-your-leave, although anyone could tell that the two of you would never suit. Fanny never did learn to say no to your father, but what's her excuse now? Your father went his way these two years, and has she come out from his shadow? No. Just as prissy as he was. The only thing that woman thinks about is her reputation."

"That's quite harsh," Esme protested. "Mama has had a most difficult life. I know she has never recovered from the death of my little brother."

"That was a grievous sorrow, to be sure. He was an enchanting lad."

"Sometimes I'm terrified for my babe," Esme confessed. "What if—what if—" But she couldn't finish the sentence.

"That will not happen," Arabella stated. "I won't allow it. I do wish to point out, Esme, that while your mother has experienced tragedy, she needn't have responded by becoming so highty-tighty."

"Just don't turn into her, with all your plans for propriety. Promise me that. Poor Fanny hasn't had a day in years in which she didn't find some impropriety to turn her mouth sour. That's the problem with caring overmuch about your reputation: it leads to caring overmuch about other people's reputations as well."

"I would never do that," Esme said. "I merely promised Miles that I wouldn't be a scandalous mother to our child."

"Deathbed promise, eh? I've made a few of those myself." Arabella was silent for a second.

"It wasn't exactly a deathbed promise. We had discussed how we would raise our child a few days before he died."

Arabella nodded. "It's difficult to ignore the wishes of a dead man. I agree with you." She seemed to shake off a melancholy thought. "Hey-ho for the Proper Life! Your mother will be pleased, I suppose. Actually, your ambitions are all the more reason to consider Fairfax-Lacy as a husband. He's proper enough to suit your mama, and yet he's not tiresome.

Which reminds me. Such a hen party tonight. The only man in the lot will be Fairfax-Lacy, if he arrives, and even I can't see the point of dressing for a man half my age."

"He's not *half* your age," Esme pointed out. "He's just slightly younger. You're only fifty, and he must be in his forties."

"Too young," Arabella said firmly. "Do you know, I once took a lover who was ten years younger, and it was altogether an exhausting experience. I had to dismiss him after a few days. Too, too fatiguing. The truth is, darling, I'm getting old!"

Esme gathered her wandering thoughts just in time to answer properly. "No!"

"Surprising, but true." Arabella looked at her reflection, but without a trace of melancholy. "I find that I don't mind very much. In fact, I rather like it. But your mother complains endlessly about her aches and pains." She turned around and fixed Esme with a fierce eye. "You are my favorite niece—"

"I'm your *only* niece," Esme put in.

"Just so. And what I mean to say is, I want you to take life on the hilt, rather than sit back and complain about it. Not that I don't love your mama, because I do. But you've more of my blood, and you always have done."

She turned back to the mirror. "The only thing I regret about age are the wrinkles. But I have high hopes for this new almond cream! Do you know, that Italian apothecary promises the cream will make one's skin as soft as a baby's cheek? Once your child arrives, we'll have a viable comparison. Not having seen a baby in years, how would I know what its skin looks like?"

"I'm glad my condition will prove to be of use," Esme said rather tartly.

# 2

## A Hen Party... Plus One

Stephen Fairfax-Lacy straightened his cravat and wondered, for the hundredth time, what in the world he was doing attending a house party while Parliament was in session. It wasn't just any house party either. No, in joining a flock of degenerates at Infamous Esme Rawlings's house he was missing indubitably important speeches on the Corn Laws. Castlereagh was expecting him to keep an eye on things in Parliament while the foreign secretary was off in Vienna, carving up Europe like slices of woodcock pie. There were problems brewing between the Canadian frontier and those cursed American colonies—correction, former colonies—not to mention the ongoing irritation of possible riots due to the Corn Laws. He had a strong feeling there would be deadly riots soon, protesting the increase in food prices.

But he just couldn't bring himself to care. He'd spent the last ten years fighting for the good of the common man. He had never used the honorary title he held as heir to his cousin Camden, the Duke of Girton. No, he'd been elected to the Commons on his own merits. Due to his own convictions.

And where were those convictions? Ten years of battling back and forth about Corn Laws and Enclosure Acts had drained the passion out of him. Years of trying to convince his own party to reconsider its position on Enclosures. Six years ago he'd put up fevered opposition to a proposed Enclosure Act. Now another such act was presented every week. He could barely bring himself to vote. No matter what he did, more and more families were being forcibly evicted from their farmland so that rich men could build fences and graze herds of sheep. He was a failure.

He threw away the cravat, which was hopelessly creased. Generally he could make a simple *trone d'amour* in under eight minutes, but this evening he had ruined two cloths already. "Sorry, Winchett," he said, as his valet handed him yet another starched cloth.

He stared at his reflection for a moment as he deftly tied the neck cloth. Even if this go at the *trone d'amour* finally seemed to be going well, nothing else in his life was. He felt old, for one thing. Old at forty-three years old. And, damn it all—he felt lonely. He knew exactly why that was. It was the visit to Cam. His cousin and wife had just returned from a visit to Greece. The duchess was radiant, intelligent, and expecting a child. And Cam—Cam who had been forced into a marriage, and then spent ten years hiding in Greece rather than acknowledge it—Cam was bursting with pride.

It was Gina and Cam's sense of companionship that underscored Stephen's loneliness. He'd distinctly seen Gina, the Duchess of Girton, tell her husband to close his mouth, and without saying a word! And Cam had done it. Amazing. Cam was *friends* with his wife.

Stephen's mouth took on a grim line as he folded the last piece of linen. There were no women like Gina wandering around London. Not as intelligent and yet untouched, with that bone-deep innocence. Naturally, one had to have that quality in a wife. But he was—just to repeat—all of forty-three. Too old for a debutante.

Finally Stephen shrugged on a coat and walked down the stairs. Perhaps he would plead work and return to London first thing in the morning. He might even attend a ball at Almack's and acquire some fresh young thing who didn't mind what an old man he was. After all, he was a good catch, to put it vulgarly. He had a resoundingly good estate.

Of course, he hardly remembered what the property looked like, given that his work in Parliament had taken virtually all his time in the past ten years. He had a wash of longing for the lazy days of his youth, sitting around with Cam, whittling boats and fishing for trout they rarely caught. These days he fished for votes.

What I need, he thought suddenly, is a mistress. It's a lengthy business, fishing for a wife, and likely tedious as well. But a mistress would offer an immediate solution to his malaise. No doubt life had a plodding sensation because he hadn't had a mistress in a donkey's age.

He paused for a moment and thought. Could it really have been a year since he entered a woman's bedchamber? How could that be? Too many smoky late nights, talking votes with whiskey-soaked men. Had it truly been a year since Maribell had kissed him good-bye and walked off with Lord Pinkerton? Over a year ago. *Damn.*

No wonder he was always in a foul mood. Still, Esme Rawlings's house would be an excellent hunting ground for a mistress. He walked into the salon with a surge of enthusiasm and bowed over his hostess's hand. "I must beg your forgiveness for my importunate arrival, my lady. Lady Withers assures me that she treats your house as her own. I trust she didn't prevaricate?"

Lady Rawlings chuckled, that deep, rich laugh that had entranced half the men in London. Of course, she was great with child and had presumably curtailed her seductive activities. Beautiful woman, though. She was even more lush than he remembered, with breasts that gave a man an instant ache in the groin. In fact . . . Stephen caught himself sharply before he formed the image. I must be getting desperate, he thought, kissing her hand.

There was something about the way Lady Rawlings's eyes met his that made him think she could read his thoughts, so he turned quickly to the lady next to her. It was shameful to be entertaining such thoughts about a woman on the verge of giving birth.

"This is Lady Beatrix Lennox," Lady Rawlings said. There was an odd tone in her voice, as if he were expected to recognize the girl. "Lady Beatrix, Stephen Fairfax-Lacy, the Earl of Spade."

"I do not use the title," he said, bowing. Lady Beatrix was clearly unmarried but equally clearly not eligible to be his wife. A wife had to have an angelic air, a sense of fragility and purity, whereas Lady Beatrix looked like a high-flying courtesan. Her lips were like a pouting rosebud, and that rosebud never grew in nature. Given that her skin was as pale as cream and red curls tumbled down her back, those velvety black eyelashes were obviously false too.

A beauty, a seductively false beauty. He almost laughed. Wasn't she exactly what he hoped for? A woman the precise opposite of his future bride. A woman who would likely be unrecognizable in the morning, were he ever foolish enough to spend a night in her bed. Too bad she was both well-bred and unmarried, and thus ineligible for an affair.

"Mr. Fairfax-Lacy," she said, and her voice had the practiced, husky promise of a coquette. "What a pleasure to meet you."

He brushed a kiss on the back of her hand. Sure enough, she wore French perfume, the sort that a certain kind of woman considers akin to a night rail.

"The pleasure is all mine," he said. She had high, delicate eyebrows, and the fact that she'd colored them black somehow suited her face.

Lady Arabella appeared at his side. "Ah, I see you've met my *dame de compagnie*," she said. "Bea, Mr. Fairfax-Lacy is quite a paragon of good works. Just imagine—he's a Member of Parliament! Commons, you know."

"At the moment," Stephen heard himself say and then wondered what on earth had led him to say such a thing.

Lady Beatrix looked bored by this revelation, so he bowed again and left. He'd just caught sight of Countess Godwin on the other side of the room. Now *she* was a distinct possibility, given that she hadn't lived with her husband for years. Moreover, she was beautiful, in a pale, well-bred way. He liked the way she wore her hair in a nest of braids. It showed a flagrant disregard for the current fashion of dangling frizzled curls around the ears.

Unfortunately, Lady Godwin's reputation was damn near irreproachable. She would be a challenge. But wasn't that what he needed? A challenge? He strode across the room toward her.

In the kind of serendipity that happens only too infrequently betwixt the sexes, his companion was thinking along precisely the same lines.

Helene, Countess Godwin, had watched Stephen enter the room and had been instantly struck by how remarkably good-looking Mr. Fairfax-Lacy was. He had the long, narrow face and high cheekbones of an English aristocrat. Moreover, he was immaculately dressed, a quality she considered to be of the highest importance, since her point of reference was her husband. He was bowing over Esme's hand and smiling at her. He couldn't be interested in a flirtation with Esme, could he? Under the circumstances? Men were always flirting with Esme, Helene thought with a dispirited pang. But the next moment he walked across the room directly toward her.

Helene felt a blush rising in her neck. Of course she shouldn't have been caught staring at the man, for all the world like a debutante. But it would be a pleasure to make his further acquaintance, if only because he was such a conscientious member of Parliament. Her own father said he was the best man in London on grain. More to the point, he was remarkably good-looking. His hair just brushed his neck, whereas her husband let his hair wave around his shoulders like some sort of wild animal. Oh, if *only* she'd married someone like Mr. Fairfax-Lacy instead of Rees, all those years ago!

But of course Stephen Fairfax-Lacy would never in a million years have eloped with someone as young and foolish as she had been. In fact, it seemed unlikely he'd ever marry. The man must be in his forties.

She sank into a curtsy before him. "I am delighted to meet you again, Mr. Fairfax-Lacy. What are you doing in the country? I thought Parliament was in session. And you, sir, are known to be the House's most determined whipper-in!" She allowed him to place her on a settee and sit beside her.

He smiled at her, but the smile fell short of his eyes. "They can spare me for a week or so," he said lightly.

"It must be rather difficult to keep up with all those issues," Helene said. He truly had lovely blue eyes. They were so respectable and clear, as opposed to her husband's muddy, scowling look.

"I don't find it difficult to follow the issues. But I'm finding it difficult to care about them as much as I used to." Stephen was feeling more cheerful by the moment. What he needed was a woman to purge this sense that the world was gray and fruitless. Lady Godwin's bashful charm was a perfect antidote.

"Oh dear," Helene said, touching his fingers with her gloved hand. "I am sorry to hear that. I sometimes think that you are a remarkable voice of clarity in the midst of the Tories. I, sir, seem naturally inclined to Whiggery."

"I find that alarming. What is it that draws you to the enemy side?"

His eyes crinkled in the corners when he smiled at her. Helene almost lost track of their conversation. He had very long, lean fingers. Didn't that . . . hadn't Esme told her something about a man's hands? She snatched her mind away from that vastly improper subject. "I have not found the past years of Tory government satisfactory," she said hastily.

"Oh?"

His eyes actually looked interested in what she was saying. Helene made a conscious effort to sound intelligent. "To tell the truth," she said, "I believe the government is making a huge mistake by ignoring the numbers of unemployed men in the country. The homeless, jobless soldiers wandering the roads are a reproach to all of us."

Stephen nodded and made a conscious effort to sound like a scrupulous and sympathetic politician. "I know. I wish I were convinced that a change of government would shift people's perception of the discharged soldiers." She was so slender that one really had to wonder whether she bothered to wear a corset. He'd never liked those garments, although women seemed to find them obligatory.

"I should not berate *you* of all men," Helene said. "Didn't I just read a speech of yours on the subject, transcribed in the *Times*? And you were quite eloquent on the state of the hungry laborers."

It was appalling, how tired he was of thinking of the plight of the poor. "Thank you," Stephen said, "but I am afraid my speeches are like water on stone; they seem to have little effect."

She leaned forward. "Never say that! If good men such as yourself did not stand up for the poor and downhearted, well then, what should become of them?"

"I've told myself the same, time out of mind, but I must admit, Lady Godwin, that I find the counsel far more engaging when spoken by such an intelligent woman." She *was* wearing a corset. He could tell by the way she moved toward him rather stiffly, like a marionette. It wasn't as if she had extra flesh to confine, so why on earth was she wearing that garment?

Helene pinked and realized that in her excitement she had picked up Mr. Fairfax-Lacy's hand. Blinking, she made to draw hers away, but he held it for a moment.

"It is a great pleasure to meet a woman interested in the political life of the nation."

He had a lovely voice, she thought. No wonder his speeches were so closely attended! Luckily (because she really had no idea what to say), Slope brought them both a sherry, which broke the oddly intimate feeling of the moment.

But they sat together for a moment in silence, and any reasonable observer could have noticed that Lady Godwin was slightly pink in the cheeks. The same observer might have glimpsed Mr. Fairfax-Lacy stealing a look at Lady Godwin's face, while she examined her sherry with rapt attention.

An acute observer—the kind who can see into human hearts—could have perceived speculation. Rampant speculation that led to a few conclusions.

Countess Godwin decided that Mr. Fairfax-Lacy had beautiful lean cheeks. She rather liked his thighs too, although she would never have formulated that thought into words. She was also still trying rather desperately to remember what it was that Esme had told her about men with long fingers.

As it happened, Mr. Fairfax-Lacy's attention was also caught by the question of fingers. Countess Godwin's fingers were slender, pink tipped and strikingly feminine. Being male, that formulation turned directly to self-interest. He liked the little flush the countess got every time she looked him in the eyes. And those fingers . . .

One thought prevailed: how would those slender fingers feel on my body? The image brought neglected parts of his anatomy to attention. Perhaps corsets weren't such an impediment, a thought supplanted by an image of a Norse goddess, pale hair swirling over her slender shoulders, unlacing her corset with delicate fingers. . . .

# 3

## So Young and Yet So Diabolic

*L*ady Beatrix Lennox was inclined to think that she had wasted her efforts dressing. She had expected more excitement from a house party being given by the scandalous Lady Rawlings. But Countess Godwin was the only guest other than those Arabella had brought with her, and the countess didn't interest Bea. First of all, she was female. Secondly, she was prudish, proper and a strange choice of friend for the infamous Lady Rawlings. Thirdly, Bea had little patience for the martyred wife role.

Were I foolish enough to marry, Bea thought, wandering toward the windows, and were my husband as flagrantly unfaithful as is Earl Godwin, I'd take a fork to him. Outside there was nothing to see but a few stone walls with rusty ferns growing from them. She took a sip of sherry. It had a smoky sharpness that went with the gray afternoon.

A husband who invited an opera singer to reside in his wife's bedchamber obviously deserved violence. Shattered china came to mind. *She* would have quickly taught the man better manners.

When someone tapped on her shoulder, Bea was far away, imagining a confrontation with her imaginary husband's imaginary mistress. She spun around with a suppressed gasp. The countess herself stood before her.

They curtsied and exchanged the usual trivialities, and then the countess turned and stared at the same rusty ferns Bea had been looking at. After a second, she said, "You looked so absorbed by the view that I thought it must be magnificent. I forgot that this window looks only into the back courtyard."

Bea was feeling that pulse of wicked boredom, the one that always got her in trouble. "I was meditating on unfaithful husbands," she said, looking at the ferns and not at her companion.

"Oh?" the countess sounded startled, but not appalled. "I have one of those. I hope you're not planning to follow my example."

Bea laughed. "I have no plans to marry, and so hopefully I shall avoid that conundrum."

"I eloped," the countess said rather dreamily. "That was the problem, I do believe. Elopement is about the intoxication of acquaintance. And acquaintance is hardly a solid basis for marriage."

"I always thought elopement was rather romantic," Bea said curiously. It was hard to imagine anyone wishing to elope with Lady Godwin, to be honest. The countess was a slender woman with stark cheekbones and a good deal of braided hair, not a look that Bea admired much. It made her look positively medieval. Plus, she was hideously flat-chested. Bea's own undergarments were cleverly designed to enhance every inch of flesh she had, as well as suggesting many inches that she didn't have, and she maintained a lively scorn for any woman who didn't avail herself of such garments.

"I must have thought elopement was romantic as well," the countess said, sitting down. "I can hardly credit it now. Of course, that was years ago, and I was a foolish girl."

Bea's mind had jumped back to her bloodythirsty fantasies. "Do you ever think of taking your husband in hand?" she asked.

"Taking him in hand?" The countess looked up at her, one eyebrow raised.

Bea's streak of mischief grew larger. Surely, listening to the countess's marital woes would be more fun than examining rusty ferns out the window. She sat down as well. "Why haven't you evicted the opera singer from your bedchamber?" she asked, precisely as if she were inquiring the time of day. This was a deliciously improper conversation, even given that Bea rather specialized in unsuitable topics. Surprisingly, Countess Godwin didn't turn a hair at her impropriety.

"Absolutely not," she said, gazing into her glass of sherry.

"I would *never* allow another woman to sleep in my bedchamber."

"To evict the woman in question would imply that I had an interest in entering that bedchamber."

Bea waited. She had discovered that silence sometimes inspired interesting confidences.

"If she weren't in my bed," the countess continued, "who *would* be there? I think of her as a necessary evil. A nuisance because everyone is so aware of her presence. Along the lines of a bed warmer."

Bea choked. She had just discovered why the notoriously proper Countess Godwin was friends with the equally notoriously *im*proper Lady Rawlings. "A bed warmer?"

The countess nodded, looking as serene as a dowager discussing a baptism.

Bea could see her point. If Lady Godwin didn't want to bed her husband, the opera singer might as well do the chore for her. But all the world knew that Lady Godwin lived in her mother's house, rather than in her husband's house on Rothsfeld Square.

"That's not equitable," she pointed out. "You should be able to sleep in your own house. You *are* married to the man."

The countess cast her a sardonic glance. "Have you found that life is fair to females, then, Lady Beatrix? I think we would both sum it up as deplorable."

Until then, Bea hadn't been quite sure whether the countess remembered her scandalous past. "I don't consider my situation a deplorable one."

"If my memory serves, you were caught in an indiscretion with Sandhurst. His reputation was untouched by the scandal; yours was ruined. You were forced out of your childhood home, and"—she paused, looking for the right word—"ostracized by a great many people you once knew."

"But I didn't want to marry Sandhurst," Bea pointed out. "Had I married the man, I suppose it would have all blown over. I refused him."

"I admit, I thought the offer had not been made," the countess admitted. Then, after a moment, she added, "Why didn't you wish to marry him?"

"I didn't like him very much."

The countess swirled her sherry, then drank it in one gulp. "You are wiser by far than I, Lady Beatrix. I didn't discover a similar dislike until I was already married."

Bea smiled at her. "They should outlaw Gretna Green weddings, perhaps."

"Perhaps. Do you really think that you'll never marry?"

"Yes."

"And did you always feel that way?"

Presumably the countess knew as well as Bea did that no respectable man would wish to marry a person like her. Bea didn't say anything.

"Of course you thought to marry," the countess said to herself. "Otherwise, you never would have refused Sandhurst's offer. I'm sorry."

Bea shrugged. "This is a case where dreams have been supplanted by reality. I could not tolerate a husband such as yours, my lady. I'd probably take to him with a blunt instrument. Truly, I am better off in my position."

Lady Godwin was grinning. Bea was surprised to find how enlivened her face was by humor. She didn't look boringly medieval anymore, but sparkling and quite lovely, in a slender kind of way.

"And just what would you do to my husband?" she asked with some curiosity. "And by the way, you must call me Helene. This *is* one of the most intimate conversations I've ever had with a complete stranger, after all." In fact, Helene was surprised at herself. There was something about Beatrix Lennox, some sort of mischievous sparkle, that reminded her of Esme. Which must explain why she, Helene, was being so uncharacteristically indiscreet.

"I would love to, as long as you call me Bea. I gather that you do not wish for your husband to . . . play an active role in your life," Bea said, trying for a delicate tone. Subtlety wasn't exactly her strong point.

Helene laughed, a short, rather bristly laugh. "No."

"I would make him sorry, then. I would make him very, very sorry that he ever thought to leave my bed. At the same time that I made it clear he hadn't the faintest hope of returning."

"Revenge is mine?" Helene asked, eyebrow raised again. She rather liked the idea of revenge. There were whole days—such as the one when Rees appeared in the Godwin opera box, doxy in tow—when she thought of nothing but doing Rees serious injury.

"Precisely," Bea nodded. "Besides, revenge is not only sweet in itself, but enjoyable. You, Lady Godwin—"

"Helene."

"Helene," Bea repeated obediently. "You have the kind of reputation that the three other women in this room could only dream of. That is, if we had the desire for such dreams."

Helene looked around. True enough, Bea, Lady Arabella and Esme herself could hardly be called champions of propriety. "Esme is turning over a new leaf," she pointed out. "I believe she does indeed dream of being a proper matron, or widow, rather."

Bea shrugged. "Lady Rawlings may be aspiring to a chaste reputation, but I certainly am not. And I've seen no signs of such ambition on Arabella's part either. The point is, though, that you are the one of us who has been most flagrantly slighted by a man, and yet you are the most prudent of all of us. If I were you, I would be flaunting my affairs before my husband."

"Perhaps if he cared, I would. But Rees wouldn't give a hang, to be honest."

"Nonsense. Men are like dogs: they want the whole manger, even though they don't eat hay themselves. If you have an affair, especially one in the public eye, it will curdle his liver." Bea said it with a certain relish. It was gratifying to see how closely the countess was listening to her. "Not to mention the fact that you will enjoy yourself."

"My goodness," Helene said. Then she smiled again. "Naturally, I like the idea of curdling his liver."

"Your husband has the best of all worlds," Bea insisted. "He has that opera singer, *and* he has you. The world and all knows that you're faithful to him."

Helene chewed her lip for a moment. "The problem is that I'd have to have an affair in order to flaunt one," she pointed out.

"Precisely!" Bea said, grinning at her. "You have nothing to lose but reputation, and what has that got you?"

"Respectability?"

But Bea knew she had her. She paused and looked at Helene from the top of her tightly coiled braid to the tips of her slippers. Her gaze spoke for herself.

"I think they warned me about women like you when I was in the schoolroom," Helene observed.

Bea fluttered her eyelashes. "So young and yet so diabolic?"

"Something of the sort." But Helene had come down to earth with a thump. She looked back into the depths of her sherry. "It hardly signifies, because I haven't the faintest hope of attracting a man with whom to have an affair, if you must know. No one has made me an indecent proposal in years. In fact, I think my husband may have been the first, and the last, to do so." She felt a crawling mortification at the admission.

"Nonsense. Available men are everywhere," Bea said, giving her an encouraging smile.

From Bea's point of view, Helene thought glumly. She was likely propositioned every other day.

"Men do seem a bit thin on the ground at this particular party," Bea continued. "What about that—that politician Arabella dragged out here? I've forgotten his name." She nodded toward him.

"Mr. Fairfax-Lacy?" Helene asked. "I'm not sure that—"

"I know, I know. I thought just the same: Church fathers, propriety, honor, Old Testament . . . A boring old Puritan!" *Puritan* was Bea's worst insult.

"I didn't mean that! I actually find Mr. Fairfax-Lacy quite attractive, but he is unlikely to make imprudent love to me. Let alone in front of my husband. Men simply do not think of me in those terms."

Bea hesitated. She could hardly inform a woman whom she had just met that she needed a new wardrobe. "Sometimes those Old Testament types are longing for a diversion," she said. "If not, why on earth did the man take up Arabella's invitation? This is not the house party for a prudent public servant. Arabella is not interested in him for herself; she would have told me. Besides, she dislikes younger men."

They both stared across the room at Mr. Fairfax-Lacy, who was talking to their hostess.

"Do you think he knows anything of music?" Helene asked dubiously.

"What's that got to do with the price of oranges?"

"I couldn't—I'm very fond of—that is, I couldn't spend my time with someone who didn't like music."

At that very moment, Mr. Fairfax-Lacy turned to the pianoforte in the corner of the room, sat down with a twinkling smile at Esme, and began to play a lively tune.

"Does he pass muster?" Bea asked. She herself had been trained on the harp, since her father considered tinkling little tunes to be indicative of ladylike thoughts.

"Not in terms of taste," Helene said a bit sourly. "He's playing one of my husband's arias. You do know that my husband writes comic operas, don't you?"

Bea nodded, even though she hadn't had the faintest idea. Helene was married to an earl. Did earls write comic operas?

"The piece he's playing comes from an opera called *The White Elephant.* Drrread-ful," Helene said. "Overall, the opera wasn't bad. But that particular song was absolutely dreadful."

"What's the matter with it?"

"The soprano has to sing an F in alt. The poor girl nearly strangled herself trying to reach it, and the audience thought her stays were pinching," Helene said, gazing across the room. "And the overture had so many dissonances that the orchestra sounded as if it were sight-reading the piece. Disaster. It was an utter disaster. The fact that Mr. Fairfax-Lacy liked it enough to memorize the piece doesn't say much for his taste."

But Bea had already made up her mind that Helene and the politician were a possible match, and she wasn't going to allow his inadequate musical judgment to influence Helene. "I'll walk you across the room, and you can improve Mr. Puritan's musical taste," Bea said encouragingly. "Men love it when a beautiful woman corrects them. Meanwhile we can assess whether he is worth your time and effort. He's old enough to be going soggy at the waistline, which is far worse than a lack of musical ability. Trust me on this."

"It hasn't been my experience that men enjoy correction," Helene said, "and I'm hardly—" but Bea was pulling her across the room like a determined little towboat.

Stephen looked up to find the glorious bit of disrepute, Lady Beatrix, and the graceful Lady Godwin peering over the pianoforte. His fingers almost stumbled when he realized what a mistake he'd made in choosing a piece of music, and he leaped to his feet.

But the countess was smiling at him, and there was amusement in her eyes. He gave her a wry grin.

Lady Beatrix also smiled at him, but damned if she didn't turn a normal greeting into a shamelessly wanton invitation. It was something about her eyes, the way they melted into a sultry little examination of his body and lingered around his middle. Luckily his stomach was as flat as the day he left Oxford—or was she looking lower? But the last thing he needed was a flagrant affair with an unmarried lass who already had the reputation of a highflier.

He wrenched his eyes away and looked to the countess. "Lady Godwin, I had the pleasure of hearing a *canzone* of yours at a musicale some years ago. Will you honor us with a composition?"

Lady Godwin gave him a reserved but genuinely friendly smile and took his place at the keyboard. "I'd be happy to play something else for you, but I rarely play my own compositions in public."

To Stephen's surprise, Beatrix Lennox didn't seem to have realized that he had snubbed her; perhaps she was so ready with her invitations that they weren't even personal. She leaned over the pianoforte, looking like a schoolgirl, an absurd comparison given that her bodice was so low that her breasts almost touched the glossy surface of the pianoforte.

"I didn't know you wrote music, Helene!" she said. "What a wonderful gift. Will you play us something you have written yourself?" And then, when Lady Godwin hesitated, *"Please?"*

Stephen had to admit that Lady Beatrix was pretty damn near irresistible when she pleaded. Lady Godwin blushed and nodded.

"Would you like to hear something polished or something quite new?"

"Oh, something new!" Lady Beatrix exclaimed.

Naturally, Stephen thought to himself. That sort of flippery young woman would always be looking for the very newest attraction.

Lady Godwin smiled. "All right. But I have to ask a favor of mine own, then."

He bowed. "For the pleasure of your music, my lady, anything."

"I'm working on a waltz at the moment, and it is so difficult to maintain the rhythm during the transitions. Would you and Lady Beatrix dance while I play?"

Stephen blinked. "I'm afraid that I haven't had much practice in waltzing."

Lady Beatrix was looking at him with one slim black eyebrow raised.

"One Christmas I taught my grandfather, who is quite unsteady on his feet, to waltz," she put in, with a sweet smile that didn't deceive him for a moment.

She thought he was akin to her grandfather. Stephen felt a stab of pure rage.

"It's not a question of skill," Helene said earnestly. "I'm quite certain that you will be nimbler than my music, Mr. Fairfax-Lacy." She called to their hostess. "Esme, may I employ your guests for a practical purpose? Mr. Fairfax-Lacy and Lady Beatrix are kind enough to attempt one of my waltzes."

"I only wish I were capable of dancing myself," Lady Rawlings said cheerfully, hoisting herself from a chair and waving at her butler. A moment later the footmen had cleared a long, polished expanse down the center of the Rose Salon.

Stephen eyed it with distrust. Holding a seat in the House of Commons hadn't left him a great deal of time to spin women around the dance floor, especially in this newfangled German dance. Damn it, he'd probably only waltzed three or four times in his life. And now he had to try it before an audience. He stalked to the floor. *She* flitted out before him, the better to display that round little body of hers. Well, she wasn't so very little. He was a quite tall man, and yet she wasn't dwarfed by his height, as so many women were.

He glanced back at Lady Godwin. Truly, she was very attractive. She looked like a cool drink of water.

"This is *so* kind of you," she called. "You must tell me precisely what you think."

Stephen snapped a bow in the direction of Lady Beatrix. "May I have this dance?"

"My pleasure," she said demurely.

If demure was the correct word. That sleepy, sensual smile of hers ought to be outlawed. It said everything, without saying anything. And yet it was more a matter of her eyes than her mouth. Why on earth was she bothering to give him, a man her grandfather's age, apparently, such an invitation? Naturally his body didn't understand that it wasn't personal.

"There's a small introduction before the waltz proper starts," Lady Godwin said. She nodded, lowered her hands and the music splashed around them.

The waltz had none of the ceremonial pacing that Stephen vaguely remembered from the waltzes he'd encountered in the past. No, it leaped from the keyboard.

For a moment he was frozen in place, already behind in the beat.

Then he literally grabbed Lady Beatrix's waist, pulled her hand into the air, and plunged into the cleared space.

They galloped down the center of the room. Stephen didn't attempt a twirl; it was all he could do to keep them on time when the music suddenly broke off.

"I'm so sorry!" Lady Godwin called from the pianoforte. "I've set it far too fast. I see that now. One minute—"

His companion was giggling. "You were far more agile than my grandfather." Her face was pink and her chest was heaving.

There was always the chance that her dress would fall to her waist, Stephen thought with a flash of interest. She had glorious breasts for a schoolgirl. Not that she was a schoolgirl, except in relation to his years.

"You don't seem at all out of breath," she observed.

"We'll start again, please," Lady Godwin called.

Stephen settled his hand more firmly on his partner's waist. This time the music began more slowly, so Stephen ventured a turn. He suddenly remembered that he had once considered dancing a delight, but that was long ago, before he'd discovered politics. Now he had no time for such frivolity. The melody drove them on. It was beginning to speed up again. *One* Two Three! *One* Two Three! Faster and faster they circled and spun. Lady Beatrix was grinning like the schoolgirl she wasn't, her eyes shining with delight.

"May I offer you my compliments?" she said, obviously rather out of breath. "You keep to this rather rapid pace extremely well."

Was her compliment in respect to his age? "I should say the same to you," he said stiffly. It was annoying to realize that his hand on her waist was tingling. That he was taking huge pleasure in holding such a ripe piece of womanhood in his arms . . . and all the time she was thinking that he was fit for the knacker's yard. It was repugnant.

Yet any man would feel a pang of interest. For one thing, he could tell from his hand on her back that Lady Beatrix did *not* wear a corset. His leg brushed hers as he turned her again. If this dance had been in vogue when I was young, Stephen thought suddenly, I'd be married by now. It was intoxicating to hold a woman in one's arms. No wonder all the old biddies thought the waltz was too scandalous for Almack's. This was the closest he'd ever come to lovemaking by music.

The waltz reached out and pulled them forward. It suddenly grew slower and rather melancholy, shifting to a minor key. They floated down the room on the sadness of it. That deep curve to her bottom lip was not something that could be enhanced by art, he thought absentmindedly.

"She must be putting her marriage into the music," Lady Beatrix said, meeting his eyes. "The music is so sorrowful now."

It was extraordinarily imprudent to remark to a perfect stranger about the countess's marriage! She spoke as if they were acquaintances of old, as if he were her uncle, or her infernal grandfather. And she was waiting for a response. "I would disagree," Stephen said, rather stiffly. "I'm not sure the music is sad as much as resigned."

"That's even sadder," Lady Beatrix observed.

Stephen dropped his hand from her waist the instant the music stopped. He didn't want her to think that she'd enticed him, with all her uncorseted beauty. "That was indeed a pleasure, Lady Beatrix," he said, with just the faintest touch of irony.

She caught it. Her eyelids flickered, and she gave him a langorous look that drifted down his front and made his private parts shoot to attention. "The pleasure," she said, "was entirely mine."

Damn it, she was *worse* than a courtesan!

Lady Godwin was rising from the pianoforte. The countess would never be so indecorous. Stephen felt his blood cool to a steady beat just watching her. The fact was, he had neglected that part of his life for too long. Now he seemed to have the unruly enthusiasm of an adolescent, lusting after every woman who crossed his path. Steady, he told himself. Steady ahead.

He strode over to Lady Godwin, took her hand and raised it to his mouth for a kiss. "That was a delightful performance," he told her softly. "Your waltz is exquisite."

"No, it isn't!" she protested. "It is far too fast. You must be quite fatigued." But she was smiling.

Stephen decided to take a chance. He turned her hand over and pressed a kiss into her palm. "Nothing you could do would ever make me tired," he told her, looking straight into her eyes.

She truly had a delightful blush.

# 4

## The Garden of Eden

*R*egular reading of the *Tatler* would convince anyone that English gentlewomen seduced their butlers and their footmen on a regular basis.

"This journal is a disgrace!" Mrs. Cable said, dropping the offending paper to the table. "If Lady Syndenham were indeed foolish enough to run away with her footman—and I see no reason to disbelieve the report—the information ought to be suppressed, so others don't follow her lead!"

Her companion's response was as frivolous as her nature. "Reading of Lady Syndenham's adventures is not likely to prompt one to cast a lascivious eye at a footman," Esme Rawlings pointed out. "At least, not unless one's footmen were better looking than those in my household."

"There'll be no end to it," Mrs. Cable snapped. "Before we know it, impressionable young ladies will be marrying footmen—nay, even *gardeners*! You may laugh, Lady Rawlings, but 'tis a serious concern." She stood up and gathered her reticule and shawl. "I myself am starting a campaign to weed out incorrigible sinners from my staff, and I sincerely hope you will do the same."

Mrs. Cable made a point of visiting Lady Rawlings, since the poor woman was widowed with a child on the way, but she often found her efforts unrewarding. Lady Rawlings's inclination to levity was disturbing. Mrs. Cable found herself all too often reminded that Esme Rawlings was considered something of a fast woman. Infamous Esme, that's what they used to call her in London.

All the more reason for Mrs. Cable to make frequent visits and impress the wisdom of the Bible on Lady Rawlings. Even looking at her now made Mrs. Cable uneasy. Lady Rawlings was entirely too beautiful, despite carrying a child. There was something about the color of her cheeks that looked feverish, as if she were ill. And that smile curving her lips . . . Mrs. Cable could only hope the woman wasn't thinking about one of her footmen. Surely not! Even Esme Rawlings would never smile at such a sin.

Mrs. Cable couldn't quite articulate her thoughts, but she knew what she saw, and if Lady Rawlings were one of her maids, she'd turn her off without a reference. She herself had never smiled like that in her life. She must remember to drop off some improving tracts on the morrow.

Mrs. Cable was right.

Esme had not been thinking of her butler, a worthy man by the name of Slope. Nor had she thought of her footmen, a callow group of country lads who suffered mightily under Slope's tutelage. It was worse. She had lost track of the conversation for a moment because she was thinking about her *gardener.*

Esme bid farewell to Mrs. Cable. Then she sat down in her sitting room and tried to remember all the good reasons she had to be respectable. Mrs. Cable wasn't one of them. She had a sharp nose, the beady, inquisitive eyes of a swallow, and a flock of acquaintances that rivaled that of the Regent himself. Mrs. Cable considered propriety next to godliness, and if she ever discovered the truth, Esme's reputation would be blackened the length and breadth of England.

Normally, Esme wouldn't be caught within ten yards of such a woman. But these days, she didn't have that luxury. Mrs. Cable led the Sewing Circle, an inner sanctum of ladies dedicated to the virtuous and charitable life. When the Sewing Circle was not hemming acres of coarse sheets for the deserving poor, it monitored the reputations of everyone within five counties. Manuevering her way into the circle had taken the diplomacy of a reformed rake aspiring to a bishopric in the Church of England, and Esme found the idea of forfeiting her newly acquired virtue galling.

Yet what was she to do? The gardener refused to leave her employ. Presumably, he was roaming around her garden at this very moment, although it was noon. He had likely retreated to the hut at the bottom of the apple orchard and was sitting there without a care in the world, reading Homer and not even considering the deleterious effect his presence might have on her reputation.

Of course she wouldn't visit him. This was her new life, a principled life, a life in which she would conduct herself in a respectable fashion. She had promised her husband, Miles, as much. Before he died, they agreed that *he* was going to give up his mistress, Lady

Childe, and *she* was going to become the sort of woman who wore little lace caps and sewed sheets for the poor. And never, ever, thought about gardeners.

She bundled herself into a pelisse two minutes later, explaining to her maid that she wished fresh air. It wasn't as if her child was born yet, she told herself as she headed down the slope into the apple orchard. Once the child was born she would never see the gardener again. In fact, she would have her butler terminate his employment. Esme's pace quickened.

The hut was a small, roughly built structure at the bottom of the garden. It had one of everything: one chair, one bench, one table, one fireplace. One bed. And one gardener.

He was standing by the fireplace with his back to her when she pushed open the door. He didn't turn until she closed the heavy wood door with a thump. Then he whirled around so suddenly that the pot over the fire tipped and its contents cascaded across the wood floor. What appeared to be lumps of carrot and beef dripped into the cracks between the boards. Esme's stomach growled. Pregnancy had the unfortunate effect of making her always hungry.

He looked at her without greeting, so she tried a jaunty smile. "Never tell me that you're learning to cook?"

He still didn't say anything, just took a step toward her. Her gardener was big, with a rider's body, tousled blonde curls, and eyes the blue of a patch of sky in summer. His features were as regular as if they were chiseled from marble. No man had a right to be so beautiful. He was a danger to all womankind, perhaps even to Mrs. Cable. "Did you cook that stew yourself?" she insisted, waving at the pot.

"Rosalie, in the village, brought it to me."

Esme narrowed her eyes. "Rosalie? Who is she?"

"The baker's daughter," he said, shrugging. He took another long step toward her. "Is this a social call, my lady?" Something had sparked in his eyes, something that made her heart skip and her knees feel weak.

She opened her mouth to inform him that he was shortly to be discharged from his position, and found herself saying something entirely different. "How old is this Rosalie?"

"Rosalie is a mere lass," he said negligently.

"Ah," Esme said, realizing that there was nothing she could say to that. She herself was no lass. No, she was all of twenty-seven years old, and huge with child in the bargain.

He was just in front of her now, all golden and beautiful in his rough workman's shirt. He'd rolled it to the elbow, and his forearms swelled with muscle. He was everything the smooth, delicate gentlemen of her acquaintance were not: There was something wild and untamed about him. Esme felt a shock of shyness and couldn't meet his eyes.

"My lady," he said, and his voice was as smooth and deep as that of any marquess. "What are you doing in my humble abode?"

She bit her lip and said nothing. Embarrassment was creeping up her spine. Hadn't she told him last time that she would never visit again?

"You are responsible for the loss of my meal," he said, and his hand pushed up her chin so she had to meet his eyes. He loomed in front of her, the sort of man all young girls are warned to stay away from. The kind who knows no laws and no propriety, who sees what he wants and takes it.

"It was purely an accident," Esme pointed out.

"Then *you* must provide me with another." She barely caught a glimpse of the hunger in his eyes before his mouth closed on hers.

It was always the same with them. There were no words for it, really. Esme had been married. She'd had lovers. But she clung to Baring, her gardener, as if he were the first man on earth, and she the first woman. As if a smoky little hut smelling of charred stew were the famous Garden itself and she, Eve shaking in Adam's arms. And he held her with the same desperate hunger and the same deep craving.

It was a good ten minutes later when Esme remembered why she'd come to the hut. By then she was tucked in his arms and they were sitting on the bed, albeit fully clothed. "You're sacked," she said against his shoulder. He smelled of woodsmoke, and Rosalie's stew and more, strongly, of a clean, outdoors smell that no nobleman had.

"Indeed?" His voice had a husky, sleepy tone that made her breasts tingle.

"Mrs. Cable is beginning a campaign to stamp out all incorrigible sinners in the village, and surely you qualify."

"Is she a little woman who wears her hair scraped into a bun?"

Esme nodded.

"She's already tried," he said with a chuckle. "Came around to The Trout and handed out a lot of pamphlets to the lads last week. They were all about God's opinion of the Ways of the Wicked. I gather she forgot that reading is not a strong point in the village."

"Wait until she discovers that my aunt Arabella has arrived and brought a houseful of guests with her. Not a one of them has a decent reputation. Are you listening?"

"Of course." He was dropping small kisses on her neck.

"It's not a laughing matter," Esme said crossly. "You of all people should understand how important it is to be respectable. Why, only last year you were thought of as the most proper man in all the *ton*."

At that, he did grin. "Yes, and you can see how much that affected me. Here I am, living in disgrace on the Continent, and a very small Continent it is," he added, glancing around his hut.

"Entirely your fault!" she snapped. Esme was starting to feel a wicked temper. "If you hadn't lurched into my bedchamber in the middle of the night, you'd still be in the judgement seat, pronouncing verdicts on all the poor disrepectable souls like myself." She brooded over that for a moment. "I used to feel as if you were always watching me."

She glanced up and found he was indeed watching her. His eyes were a darkish blue form of periwinkle.

"I was."

"Not just watching. *Judging.*"

"I had to," he said cheerfully. "I was so utterly miserable about your married state that it drove me mad."

Esme felt a slight cheer in her heart. No woman in the world would dislike hearing that. "Truly, Sebastian, what am I to do? I know you think it's foolish, but I did promise Miles that I would become a respectable wife once we had a child. I can't have one of Arabella's scandalous parties in my house. I'm in confinement! All Arabella will say is that Marie Antoinette was dancing a minuet up to the moment she gave birth."

"Why don't you just accept my proposal? I'll make an honest woman of you, and we'll turn up our noses at the gossips."

Esme's heart skipped a beat and then steadied. She scowled at him. "To begin with, I can't marry you because you are even more scandalous than I am. Half the world believes you seduced your fiancée."

"*Former* fiancée," he put in.

"But that is nothing to the scandal if they discovered your current whereabouts. Arabella, for one, would instantly recognize you, and she's invited any manner of persons, all of whom could also identify you."

"Mmmmm."

He wasn't paying attention. "I don't understand why you consider my wishes to be so insignificant!" she said sharply, pushing his hand off her breast.

He just grinned down at her, all thick golden hair and laughing eyes. "Because I've given up all that respectability you want so much, Esme. I don't have it anymore. And I don't give a damn. Do you know that I once actually scolded Gina for trying to kiss me in public?"

Esme pursed her mouth. She didn't like to think about Sebastian kissing his former fiancée, for all Gina was one of her closest friends. "That sounds just like you," she observed. "Holy Willy, always standing on your consequence."

"I'd still have my Sir Sanctimonious credentials if I hadn't gotten mixed up with you," he observed. "My mother will likely faint when she hears of my new position."

*"You didn't tell your mother!"*

He grinned. "No. But I'm going to visit her tomorrow, and I shall."

"Noooo," Esme wailed. "You can't. You absolutely cannot do that!" She tended to keep well away from the more stiff-rumped members of the *ton,* such as Marchioness Bonnington. Sebastian's mother was one of those women who prided themselves on the fact that they needn't be magnanimous to lesser mortals. And her son, at least before he'd become a gardener, had been an unexceptional successor to her manifold virtues.

He shrugged. His hand was stealing up toward her breast, and his eyes had that look again.

"It will be a terrible shock for her," Esme said, trying to find a shred of sympathy and instead finding an evil ray of pleasure in her heart. "Aren't you rather old to be growing rebellious? I sowed my wild oats a good ten years ago."

Sebastian snorted. "And your mother still hasn't recovered. She's a bosom beau of my mother's, you know."

"I wasn't aware of their friendship." Esme didn't feel it necessary to add that she and her mother hadn't spoken except in passing for three years. She had no idea who Fanny's friends were. Her mother communicated only by letter, and that infrequently. "My mother has decided not to attend my confinement," she admitted. Why on earth was she relating that pitiful fact? She hadn't even told Helene.

"Your mother is as foolish as mine, then," he said, dropping a kiss on her nose.

"Fanny is not foolish," Esme felt compelled to defend her. "She simply cares a great deal for her reputation. And I've—well, obviously, I've been a great disappointment to her. I am her only child."

"So you are," Sebastian said. "All the more fool she, not to be here when her grandchild is born."

"I'm afraid that my mother has . . . has quite discarded the idea of our further acquaintance." It was absurd to find that she had a lump in her throat. She hadn't even had a cup of tea with her mother for some three years. Why should she miss her now?

"Is that why you have such a fierce wish to become respectable?" Sebastian inquired. "So that your mother will accept you again?"

"Of course not! It's only because of Miles, as I told you."

"Hmmm." But he wasn't really listening. He was kissing her ear.

"I don't think my mother likes me very much," Esme said dolefully.

To Sebastian's mind, her mother's behavior had made that clear for years, but it didn't seem politic to say so. "I expect she has some affection for you," he said in as comforting a manner as he could manage, given that he had Esme's delicious body on his lap. He felt like a starving man at a feast. "I am almost certain that my mother has some affection for me, although she would never acknowledge such a thing."

"You were a perfect son to her. And you will be again. Once you return from the Continent, everyone will forget the scandal, and you can return to being the very proper Marquess Bonnington. Snobby old sobersides."

"Never again. *Never.*"

"Why not?"

"I shall never again believe that it matters a bean whether I kiss the woman I love in a garden or my own bedchamber. All that propriety, respectability, it's nothing but a trap, Esme, don't you see?"

"No," she said. Secretly she was a bit shaken by the vehemence in his voice. "I wish—oh, I do wish—that I hadn't been unfaithful to Miles in the first year of our marriage. Perhaps if I'd been more respectable, we could have found a way to be married again. To live together and raise a family."

She was startled by the look in his eyes. "Why? Why, Esme? Why *Miles?*"

"Because he was my husband," Esme said earnestly. This was at the heart of all their arguments. "I should have honored our vows," she explained.

"You vowed to love him forever. Yet you didn't even know him when you married him. He was weak, charming but weak. Why on earth are you harboring the idea that the two of you could ever have been happy together?"

"Because it would have been the right thing to do." She knew she sounded like a stubborn little girl, but he had to understand.

"Ah, the right thing," he said, and there was a dark tiredness in his voice. "I can't fight with that. But if you, Esme, were able to fall in love with your husband because it was the right thing to do, you would have been a very unusual woman indeed."

"I could have tried!" she said with a flare of anger. "Instead I flaunted my affairs before him and the rest of London."

Esme was missing the point. The trouble was that Sebastian wasn't sure how to make himself clear without risking her stamping out of his hut in a rage. He tried to put it delicately. "Your husband, Miles, didn't seem to take much notice of those affairs."

"Yes, he did."

My God, she was a stubborn woman. "You began flirting with other men in an attempt to get Miles's attention," Sebastian said. "Fool that he was, he simply concluded that the marriage was not successful. And to be honest, I don't think he cared very much. He was in love with Lady Childe, these many years before he died." His voice was calm but merciless.

Esme was silent for a moment. "We could have tried," she said finally.

"You did reconcile just before Miles died," Sebastian pointed out. "To my knowledge, you had one night together." He drew her even closer against his chest. "Did it pass in a blaze of passion, then?"

Esme turned her face into his rough shirt. "Don't laugh at Miles," she warned. "He was my husband, and I was very fond of him."

"I would never laugh at Miles. But I would never make the mistake of thinking that the two of you could have had a successful marriage, either."

"Perhaps not. I suppose not. It's just that I'm so . . . so ashamed of · myself!" It burst out of her. "I wish I hadn't done all those things. I just wish I *hadn't*."

Sebastian was beginning to kiss her again, and his kisses were drifting toward her mouth. Suddenly Esme was tired of whimpering about her miserable marriage and her reputation. "You know when you used to watch me so crossly?" she said huskily. Sebastian's large hands were leaving tingling paths in their wake. He was a beautiful man, with his honey skin and tumbling hair. She couldn't tear her eyes away from him. Why was she even *thinking* about Miles?

"Of course," he drawled. He was watching her now too, except his eyes were below her chin. He was watching his hand on her breast.

"You had the most arrogant, sulky look," she said. "You used to lean against the wall and frown at me, and I knew you were thinking that I was an absolute tart."

The corner of his mouth curled up. "Something like that, I suppose."

She was getting breathless because of what he was doing, but she wanted to make herself clear. "I used to do some of it for you," she said, pushing his chin up so he met her eyes.

"Do what?"

"Flirting." She smiled and put all the seductive joy she felt into that smile. "You would be frowning at me from the side of the ballroom, with that gloriously sulky mouth of yours, and I'd play for you."

"Play for *me*?"

She nodded, giggling. "Be even more wanton. Do you remember when I kissed Bernie Burdett on the ballroom floor at Lady Troubridge's house party?"

"Of course," he growled, and he nipped her bottom lip with his teeth. He used to feel half mad, watching Esme Rawlings flirting with her latest conquest, allowing that intolerable Burdett to partner her in dance after dance. While he—he'd rarely danced with her. She'd been married, and he'd been engaged to her best friend. The very memory made him take her mouth with a growl of desire.

"Even as I kissed Bernie, I was wondering what you would do if I simply waltzed up to *you* and kissed you," she said after a little while, and with a catch in her voice. "I decided you'd probably be up in arms about it, prig that you are, so I kissed Bernie instead."

He raised his head for a moment. "You deliberately—"

"Exactly," she said smugly. Then she ran her lips along the strong, sun-browned column of his neck. "You were so disdainful of me and yet—something—I thought I saw something in your eyes."

He growled again, that deep male sound that made her thighs tremble. "So you were longing to kiss me, were you?"

It was frightening to hear it aloud. Esme chose to keep silent, turning her cheek against his shoulder so he couldn't see her eyes.

"So kiss me now, then," he said. And his voice had that dark, insistent throb that she couldn't disobey. It made her feel ravishing rather than pregnant. She didn't know why she'd ever thought he was priggish: He kissed her like a wild man. With one last gasp of rational thought, she said, "But Sebastian, I meant it when I said you have to leave. Tomorrow. It's too dangerous now that a house party is arriving."

"And what shall I do for a living, eh?"

"You'll have to go back to what you did before."

"Before . . ." His voice was dark now, velvet dark, muffled against her skin. "I spent all my time *before* arguing with a certain lady."

"You were extremely vexing," Esme said. "You were always scolding me because I was brazen, and—"

He bent and kissed her shoulder. "Brazen," he agreed. "Improper." He dropped another kiss on the little juncture between her neck and her collarbone. "Strumpet. I'll have to lend you that pamphlet on the Ways of the Wicked."

"And all because I was having a wee flirtation with Bernie Burdett," she said, grinning up at him. "Ravishing man that he was. How I miss—"

"That Bertie," he said against her mouth.

"Bernie!"

"Whatever," he growled. "The pain he caused me!"

She reached up and put her hand to his cheek. "Bernie and I never had an affair. It was a mere flirtation."

"I know that." He smiled down at her then, a lazy, dangerous smile. "Bertie would have made a tedious lover." He dragged his lips over the sweetness of her cheek and the long delicate stretch of her neck. "And you, my darling Esme, are not a woman to tolerate tedium in your bed-chamber."

"And how would you know, sir?" she said, sounding a little breathless. "You have something of a lack of experience in these matters, wouldn't you say?" It was one of the most joyous memories of her life when the beautiful Marquess Bonnington threw off his cravat in Lady Troubridge's drawing room, announced he was a virgin, and proceeded to lose that virginity.

"It would be no different if I were Adam himself, and you Eve," he said. His eyes were burning again. "No one can make love to you the way I do." His hands slipped from her shoulders to her breasts, shaped their exuberance in his hands. She arched up with a gasp. His knee nudged her legs apart, and with one swift motion, he pulled her to the end of the bed, where he would put no weight on her belly.

Then he was *there*, bending over her, and she was laughing, and to him, it felt as if there were only the two of them in the world. He and his intoxicating, ravishing mistress, his very own Esme, his infamous lover . . .

As if his garden were the first garden itself.

As if his Esme, with her plump mouth and her seductive wit, were the very first woman in the world. She moaned, and he shook with desire. Took up a rhythm that he knew drove her to distraction, made her whimper and grow incoherent. Standing there, making sweet, slow love, he was the only man in the world . . . or the first . . . it didn't matter.

Marquess Bonnington was well and truly ravished.

# 5

## *Anticipation*

Stephen had made up his mind to approach—not *seduce*—Lady Godwin. One couldn't use a disreputable word of that sort in respect to such a delightfully ladylike woman. He organized his campaign in the same orderly fashion with which he approached all important arguments undertaken in Parliament.

First, Helene Godwin had eloped at age seventeen, which surely indicated a certain unconventionality, even if she showed no signs of it now. Second, the lady's husband proved to be a reprobate, tossing his wife out the front door and establishing a changing show of young women in her bedchamber. Nonetheless, third, the lady had maintained an irreproachable reputation. She would not be an easy woman to win. But, finally, he fancied that he did have a chance of winning. A long shot, perhaps, but that blush. . . . She blushed whenever she saw him.

Stephen grinned to himself. He was used to assessing the odds of any given victory in the House. He gave himself a forty percent chance of victory over Helene. Sufficient odds to make it a challenge. Already he felt much more himself than he had in the last few months. Enclosure Acts just weren't enough to keep a man's interest. He had been suffering from a healthy dose of lust.

A deliciously bashful countess, intelligent, musical and neglected by her husband, would solve all his problems.

He strode into Lady Rawlings's Rose Salon and paused for a moment. The house party had apparently been augmented by neighbors of Lady Rawlings; country gentlefolk drifted around the room in little groups. The countess was sitting next to the fireplace, talking to their host. Her skin was so pale that it looked translucent. Frosty, almost. Like snow or ice. Stephen loved ices, sweet and cool to the tongue.

He was far too adept a campaigner to approach Lady Godwin immediately. Instead he walked over to greet an old friend, Lord Winnamore,
whom he knew well from various skirmishes between the Houses of
Lords and Commons.

Winnamore was as amiable as ever. "Another escapee from matters
of business, I see," he said, greeting him.

"I should be in London," Stephen admitted. Come to think of it, what
was Winnamore doing in the deeps of Wiltshire?

"Life has a way of creating distractions," Winnamore said. He was
watching Lady Arabella.

"Thank goodness!" Stephen was startled by the vehemence of his
own exclamation. It certainly wasn't as if he ever would consider desert-
ing the House before his term was up. Or even at that point. There was no
threat to his reelection, after all.

"This isn't the sort of party where I'd have thought to meet you,"
Winnamore said, giving him a shrewd glance over his spectacles.

"I am finding it quite enjoyable," Stephen said, checking to make certain that Lady Godwin was still in the corner. In another moment, he
would stroll in that direction.

"Enjoyable, yes. Respectable, no. Have you met Lady Beatrix yet?"
Winnamore said cheerfully, looking at the door to the salon. Stephen
looked as well. Lady Beatrix was making what she clearly considered a
spectacular entrance. Apparently the curls of yesterday had been compliments of a curling iron; today her shining copper hair was straight as a
pin. Yesterday, her skin had been sunkissed; tonight it was pale as snow.
Yesterday her lips had been ripe as a cherry; tonight they were a pale, languid pink. Even her pert expression of the previous night had been replaced by a faintly melancholy gaze—except if one looked very, very
closely, mischief brewed.

"That young woman is a work of art," Stephen said, not without admiration.

"A lovely child, in fact," Winnamore said. "She is a great comfort to
Lady Arabella."

Stephen could think of no reason why Lady Arabella, known far and
wide for her three marriages and various other dalliances, would have
need of comfort, but he kept prudently silent. Besides, Lady Arabella herself swept up to them that very moment.

"Mr. Fairfax-Lacy," she cried, taking a grip on his elbow, "I must *insist* that you greet my niece. Dear Esme is not as nimble as she is normally, and so I have appointed myself the duty of bringing sufficient
conversationalists to her side."

It was suddenly quite clear to Stephen why he had been invited to this particular house party. Lady Arabella had selected him as a prospective husband to her niece. Well, there was nothing new in that. Matchmaking mamas had been chasing him for years.

He bowed to Lady Rawlings but sought Lady Godwin's eyes as he did so. She was just as lovely as he remembered, pure and delicate as a— he couldn't think. Poetry was hardly his forte. She was blushing again and looking rather adorably shy.

*Too* shy. A moment later she jumped to her feet like a startled gazelle and fled across the room. He'd have to go even slower than he had planned. He didn't look over his shoulder at the countess, but sat down next to Lady Rawlings.

For her part, Esme was watching Stephen Fairfax-Lacy with a good deal of interest. Unless she was mistaken (and she was *never* mistaken when it came to men), the man was attracted to Helene. Marvelous. Poor Helene had suffered so much from the cruelties of her careless husband. A kindly, handsome, respectable man such as Mr. Fairfax-Lacy would do wonders to restore her sense of confidence and allow her to hold her head high before that reprobate of a husband.

"Are you enjoying yourself?" she asked, remembering rather belatedly that she was nominally, at least, a hostess. Arabella had taken over all the duties of running the house, the better for Esme to concentrate on her supposed confinement. "Is your chamber acceptable?"

"Truly, it has been all that is comfortable," he said. And then changed the subject. "I much enjoyed Countess Godwin's waltz. Her husband is not invited to this gathering, I presume?"

*Yes!* Esme felt all the exuberance of an old friend. Helene appeared to have made a remarkable impression on Fairfax-Lacy. "Absolutely not," she hastened to say. "Helene and Rees have had little to do with each other for years. He has other interests. She and her husband have an entirely amiable friendship," she added. One wouldn't want the M.P. to be frightened off by the notion of an irate husband.

Stephen was watching Helene talk to Bea on the other side of the room. Esme didn't quite like the contrast that conversation presented: Bea was such a vividly colored young woman that she made Helene look pale and washed out. "If you'll excuse me," she said brightly, "I must confer with my butler." She allowed Fairfax-Lacy to haul her to her feet and then trundled off toward the door, stopping next to Helene and Bea.

"He was just asking for you!" she whispered to Helene.

Helene looked adorably confused. "Who was?"

"Fairfax-Lacy, of course! Go talk to him!"

Helene looked across the room, and there was Stephen Fairfax-Lacy smiling at her. But she felt a strange reluctance; it was all she could do to hover next to the door and not flee to her bedchamber. Her life, to this point, had not been easy. In fact, although she only admitted it to herself in the middle of the night, sometimes she felt as if she must have been cursed at birth. It had only taken one foolish decision—the foolish, foolish decision to elope with an intoxicating man by the name of Rees—to ruin her entire life. But in the last year she had realized that if she didn't do something about it now, the rest of her life would follow the pattern of the past seven years. The years hadn't been unpleasant: She lived with her mother and she was welcome everywhere. But she had no life, no life that mattered. No *child.*

She glanced again at Fairfax-Lacy. He looked like a gentleman, not like that savage she had married. Perhaps, just perhaps, she would even like having intimacies with him. It wouldn't be terrifyingly messy and embarrassing as it had been with Rees. It would be . . . proper. Acceptable. He was quite lovely: all rangy, lean, English gentleman. And without a doubt it would curdle Rees's liver to see her with such a man. If anything *could* curdle her husband's liver, given the qualities of brandy he drank. So why wasn't she walking straight into Mr. Fairfax-Lacy's arms?

Suddenly a pert voice spoke just at her left elbow. "Shall I walk you across the room again?"

Helene blinked. Bea's eyes were sparkling with mischief. She repeated, "Shall I walk you across the room, Helene? Because I believe you are expected."

"Ah—"

"This way," Bea said efficiently, taking her elbow and strolling toward the far end of the room, where Stephen waited. "He *is* quite lovely, isn't he?"

Helene was so nonplussed that she couldn't quite bring out an answer. "Who?" she finally said lamely.

"Mr. Fairfax-Lacy, naturally!"

"I thought you found him Old Testament."

"That too. But it seems obvious to me that the two of you are perfectly suited," Bea said in a coaxing voice, as if she were taking a mare over a high jump. "There he is, a perfect specimen of the English gentleman, and here you are, exactly the same in a female form. Both impeccably virtuous too, which must add luster to your friendship. And I think he's quite, quite interested in you," Bea said confidentially. "He looked straight in your direction when he entered the room. Whenever I speak to him, he simply glances around the room. Normally"—her smile grew—"I am used to complete attention."

Bea had on a dinner dress that had neither a front nor a back. One could only guess how it stayed above her waist, given that her plump little breasts threatened to escape her scrap of a bodice. Men must simply slaver over her, Helene thought enviously. She herself was wearing a gown of Egyptian net over a dark blue silk. She had felt very *a la mode* in her chamber, but now she felt dismally overdressed, like a dog wearing a sweater.

But Bea seemed to follow her train of thought perfectly. "I'm certain that he doesn't like my gown," she said. "Last night at dinner he kept looking at me as if I had something stuck between my teeth. Come along!" She jiggled Helene's arm. "You don't want to wait too long, do you? What if Arabella manages to convince the man that he should wed Lady Rawlings? You could hardly have a liaison with your friend's husband!"

Helene thought about that as they moved across the room.

"You see," Bea said, not quite as softly as Helene would have liked, "he's looking at you right now!"

But when Helene looked up, it seemed to her that Stephen was watching her companion, although with an expression of deep annoyance. She swallowed and curtsied before Stephen Fairfax-Lacy. "Sir," she said. Bea had glided away without even greeting Mr. Fairfax-Lacy.

He smiled down at her, and Helene realized again what a good-looking man he was. There wasn't a whisker on his face, not like her husband, who always had a shadowed jaw by evening.

"How are you?" he asked.

"I'm quite well."

There was a moment's silence while Helene thought desperately of a conversational tactic. "Did you read this morning's paper?" she finally asked. "Napoleon has escaped from Elba and is in France again! Surely the French army will not support him."

"I believe you are quite correct, Lady Godwin," Stephen said, looking away. He had decided to play this game very, very slowly, so as not to startle her.

Helene felt a crawling embarrassment. How on earth could she have ever thought to seduce a man? She couldn't even carry on a simple conversation.

"What do you think of the fact that Catholics cannot sit in Parliament?" she asked.

He blinked, not prepared for philosophical reasoning. "I have long felt that the prohibition should be rethought," he said finally.

"I believe it has to do with the wordings of the oaths they would have to take. Wouldn't it violate their religious vows to take Parliamentary oaths?"

"Most of the men I know don't give a fig for those oaths," Stephen said.

Helene heard a faint bitterness in his voice and wondered about it. Why *was* Mr. Fairfax-Lacy in Wiltshire rather than sitting in the House of Commons?

"Why should we expect Catholics or Jews to be more circumspect than Anglicans?" he continued.

"Surely to establish oneself as a Catholic in this country, given its Anglican past, implies a deeper fidelity to religion than one might expect from an ordinary gentleman," Helene said. She was quite enjoying herself now. He wasn't regarding her in a lustful fashion, just with the sort of normal engagement one might expect during a conversation.

But she waited in vain for a reply. He appeared to be looking over her shoulder.

"Mr. Fairfax-Lacy," she said, with a bit of sharpness to her voice.

He snapped to attention. "Yes, Lady Godwin? Do forgive me."

"Is there something interesting that I should see as well?" Helene said, deciding on the basis of his really quite charming smile that she wasn't insulted after all.

"It is merely that impudent little chit, Lady Beatrix," Stephen said. "I truly can't imagine what Lady Withers is thinking, allowing the girl to dress in that unseemly fashion."

Helene turned as well. Bea was sauntering across the room toward them.

Stephen felt as if the girl were some sort of irritating gnat. Here he was, having a remarkably informed and intelligent conversation with the woman who might well become his future mistress, and there *she* was again. About to interrupt their fascinating discussion of religious oaths. Lady Beatrix seemed to have dropped the melancholy pose with which she had originally entered the room. She looked strikingly exotic and utterly unnatural. And potent. Too potent.

"Do you know, I don't think that is the true color of her hair?" Stephen said. He could hear the rancor in his own voice. Why on earth did the girl get under his skin in such a fashion? "Look at that bronze. Have you ever seen such a color in nature?"

"But why would she color her hair?" Helene asked with some fascination. "She can hardly be showing gray."

"Of course not!" he agreed. "She's barely out of the schoolroom."

Helene didn't agree with *that* pronouncement. Beatrix Lennox was obviously far too ripe for a schoolgirl, and besides, hadn't she debuted some three years ago? That would put her at about twenty years old.

"I expect she colored her hair merely to shock people," Stephen said with a shrug. "She's obviously artificial." He turned back to her. "Not like you . . . a true English gentlewoman, bred to the bone."

Helene felt a pang of envy toward Bea. It wasn't high on her list of wishes to be described as a well-bred filly at Tattersall's. Naturally, she ought to be pleased by the compliment. But it would be fun if just once, she were considered dangerously attractive. Able to shock someone. Helene had never shocked anyone in her life. Well, perhaps her husband. There was that time with the chamber pot . . . Helene wrenched her thoughts away from the unsavory topic.

"Thank you for the compliment," she said, opening her fan. Esme always flirted with her fan to great effect. Unfortunately, Helene hadn't the faintest idea how to do the same thing. She waved it gently, but the only result was that she was unable to see Stephen at all. She snapped it closed.

At that moment Bea joined them. "We have been discussing poetry," she said with a twinkle. "And I am sent to discover each person's favorite poem. Arabella has had the splendid idea that we shall have a poetry reading on Friday evening."

"I haven't read any poetry in years," Stephen observed.

Bea looked up at him from under her lashes. "We'll have to do something about that. Perhaps I'll lend you a book from my private library."

To Helene's amazement, a ruddy tone appeared in Stephen's lean face. "That won't be necessary," he said brusquely. "I was quite fond of poetry as a boy. I'm certain I can remember something."

"Have you a favorite poem?" Bea asked Helene.

"I am acquainted with Shakespeare's sonnets," Helene said uncertainly. "But some of them are hardly suitable for reading aloud."

"I'm sure you will find something you deem appropriate," Bea said, and Helene was unable to dismiss the idea that the girl was laughing at her.

"And *your* favorite poem?" Stephen asked her.

"A love poem by Lord Byron," Bea said, drifting away. "It's quite, quite beautiful."

"That girl is trouble," Stephen said, rather unoriginally.

But Helene had had enough of this torturous flirtation. She was exhausted. "If you'll excuse me, Mr. Fairfax-Lacy," she said with a curtsy, "I will join Lady Rawlings."

Helene had hardly sat down next to Esme when Bea plumped herself on Esme's other side. "Disastrous!" Bea announced.

"What?" Helene asked, but Esme seemed to know precisely what she was speaking about and responded with a choked giggle. Helene narrowed her eyes. "What are you discussing?"

"You, darling," Esme said, with such fondness in her voice that it removed the sting. "Bea and I have been conspiring to bring you together with that estimable gentleman on the other side of the room, but you're not doing your share."

Helene already felt tired; now she felt obstinate as well. "While I much dislike the idea of my affairs being discussed in public," she said, "I also resent the imputation that I have not attempted to . . . to sway Mr. Fairfax-Lacy's attentions. I am wearing a new dress, and I allowed myself to be walked over to him, like a lamb to slaughter. It is not my fault that the man has no conversation."

"You must have discussed something," Esme said.

"Topics *I* introduced," Helene snapped. "First I brought up Napoleon's escape and then the position of Catholics in the government. He had nothing to say to either issue. Really, if this is what he's like in Commons, it's no wonder the government never gets anything done!"

Bea sighed. "He doesn't want to talk about legalities, Helene. The man is bored with the House. He wants to talk about frivolous things. Men always pretend that they want intelligence in their mates, but it's not really the case."

"What sort of frivolous things?" Helene asked.

"I don't agree," Esme put in. "I think Bea has the wrong end of the stick. In my experience, it doesn't even matter what you talk about. The man is burnt to the socket. Look at those circles under his eyes. Unless I miss my guess, he's rather desperately hoping to find a warm body to curl up with. All you have to do is indicate that interest, Helene."

"You make it sound easy," Helene muttered.

"It *is* easy," Bea said. "You watch, and I'll do it right now. He's utterly uninterested in me, so there's no threat to your future."

Helene grabbed her arm. "I can't let you do that!"

"Why on earth not? I do it enormously well," Bea said with some satisfaction. "In fact, I think one could fairly say that I am an expert." She sauntered off, and sure enough, even the very sway of her hips was a promise.

"I do believe that girl is more outrageous than I ever was," Esme said thoughtfully. "She must be quite unhappy."

"Nonsense. She's having the time of her life," Helene said. "Look at her now!"

Bea was laughing up at Stephen, waving her fan gently before her face. Her piquant little face was glowing, her eyes sending the man a speaking invitation. Her bosom brushed against his arm, and even from the other side of the room, Helene could see him start.

"I can't possibly do that sort of thing," Helene said flatly. "I just couldn't." She felt positively riddled with embarrassment at the very thought.

"Bea is not doing much," Esme said. "There's only one important thing, and that's to let your eyes tell Stephen that you're available. That's all. It's easy."

"Easy?" Helene said in an appalled voice. "That's not easy! *Available?* How on earth does one indicate such an unseemly thing?"

Across the room, Bea was laughing up at Stephen. She seemed to be vibrating with desire. Then she turned around for the merest moment and grinned at them. The desire wiped from her face and was replaced by pure mischief. She looked like a girl just out of the school room. The next second she turned around and threw Stephen another languishing look.

"Ah," Esme said with some satisfaction, "she can still be herself."

"I have no idea what you're talking about," Helene said, feeling just on the edge of tears. "I can't do this. I must be missing the ability. Rees always said—" She snapped her mouth shut. She didn't want even her own best friend to know that she was a frigid woman who would never enjoy bedding a man. Her own husband had said so, and she was fairly certain he was right.

"Don't despair, darling. Mr. Fairfax-Lacy doesn't like what Bea is doing. See?"

Sure enough, Fairfax-Lacy was frowning at Bea and clearly growling some sort of reproach. "He's just the man for you," Esme said with satisfaction. "Not Bea's type at all."

A fact which Bea exuberantly seconded a moment later. "He told me to go wash my face," she reported with some glee. "I do believe that Mr. Higher Than Thou M.P. doesn't like my *maquillage,* even though it is imported all the way from Paris."

Helene felt a little steadier. She had never worn rouge in her life and couldn't imagine why she ever would. Perhaps she and Stephen were suited after all.

Just look available, she told herself. "So, I simply look . . . look—"

"As if you want to bed him," Bea said.

"I'll try," Helene muttered. Never mind the fact that she didn't wish to bed *anyone,* and couldn't believe that any woman would wish to do so voluntarily. Except for reasons of revenge.

"Or you could just tell him," Bea suggested with a wicked grin.

"I most certainly could not!"

"I have an idea! The poetry! We'll use the poetry."

"What do you mean?" Esme asked her.

"We are each supposed to read a favorite poem on Friday, remember? If Helene reads the right kind of poem, and looks at Fairfax-Lacy while she does it, it won't fail! That way you need not embarrass yourself," she told Helene. "The poem will do it all. And I'll warrant he'll visit your chamber that very night."

"An excellent idea," Esme said, nodding.

"But I don't know any love poetry," Helene pointed out. "Besides that of Shakespeare."

"Good," Bea interjected, "because we don't want *love* poetry, silly!"

"We don't?"

"Do you love him?"she asked.

"Well, no."

"Precisely my point. This is an altogether different type of poetry. And not to worry, I never travel without my favorite authors."

"You are remarkable. You travel with . . . with this sort of poetry all the time?" Helene asked Bea.

"Naturally," Bea said, opening her fan.

Helene watched with fascination as Bea shook the delicate, lacy confection slightly. She held it just below the level of her eyes, and somehow she looked ten times more delectable. I shall practice with my fan tonight, Helene thought. In front of the mirror. If I read the poem with a fan covering my face, no one can see me blush. Helene loathed the fact that she blushed constantly, like some sort of green girl.

"Don't forget that your friendship with Mr. Fairfax-Lacy will curdle your husband's liver," Bea said with relish.

"Of course I haven't forgotten that!" Helene said. Why on earth would she even consider doing such an immoral act otherwise?

"Just remember to look at Stephen while you read," Esme advised. "I shall put the two of you next to each other at supper so you can practice giving him desiring looks. Naturally I'll have to be on his other side, since Arabella is determined that we should marry."

"I rather agree with Arabella," Helene said. "He would undoubtedly make a good husband, Esme. I was just thinking how very much I wish that I had married someone like him, rather than Rees."

"He's not for me," Esme said, shrugging.

"Nor me," Bea said, with the little yawn of a cat. "He's all yours, Helene. If you can stomach all that virtue and pomposity, that is."

"He's not pompous!" Helene protested, and then realized that her two friends were laughing at her.

"Not pompous—perfect for you. We'll confer over poetry tomorrow, shall we?" Bea said, a twinkle in her eye.

"Better not," Helene said, biting her lip. "If I have to read something shocking, and"—she narrowed her eyes at Bea—"I have the feeling that your choice will be along those lines, I'd much rather not know the worst before the moment arrives."

Esme put an affectionate arm around her shoulder. "I'll be there, cheering you on."

"As will I!" Bea put in brightly.

Helene looked at Stephen Fairfax-Lacy again. He was leaning against the mantelpiece, deep in conversation with a stout lady from a neighboring estate. He was the very picture of a timeless kind of elegance. The kind of elegance that her husband didn't even dream of. Rees didn't give a toss what coat he drew on in the morning. He'd never tied a cravat in such intricate, snowy folds in his life. And since no decent servants would stay in his employ, he didn't have a gentleman's gentleman to tie it for him.

Stephen Fairfax-Lacy was just what she needed: an antidote to her loathed husband. Rees's antithesis. Helene's hands curled into fists at her sides. She *would* do it. She would do it, and then she would tell Rees that she had. And when he looked stricken with jealousy . . .

The smile on Lady Helene Godwin's face reflected pure feminine glee.

When Rees was stricken with jealousy—and suffering from a curdled liver—she would just laugh and walk away.

# 6

## The Contrariness of Men Hardly Bears Repeating

*Bonnington Manor*
*Malmesbury, Wiltshire*

Marchioness Bonnington was not accustomed to opposition from the male sex. She had ruled—and survived—two husbands and fourteen male lapdogs. To her mind, there was no question as to which group had provided the better companionship. And as for logic . . . her own son was an excellent example of the worthiness of lapdogs over humans.

"Did I understand you to say that you are living in a garden hut, Bonnington? A garden hut?"

Her son nodded. The marchioness let silence fall between them. She had not invited him to sit, since she considered sons to be inferiors, along the lines of a butler: willing to take advantage, and needing to be continually reminded of their place. Not that her only son Sebastian had ever shown much proclivity for rebellion. He was a quite appropriate example of his sex, if she said so herself. Never caused her a moment of worry, until she had heard he had been courting the Duchess of Girton and persuading her to seek an annulment of her marriage.

That had ended in disaster, as she had known it would. In the end, her only son had been exiled to Europe, labeled unmarriageable, tarred as a liar and deceiver. The only thing that had sustained her in the past eight months had been a lifetime's knowledge that the sins of young, very wealthy men seemed to dissolve after a year or so. She had fully intended to recall him to England in the summer and rehabilitate him in the eyes of the *ton* by marrying him to an upright young woman, perhaps someone who reminded her of herself at an earlier age.

Except here he was. Back in England without her permission.

She placed her hands carefully on top of her walking stick, which was planted in front of her chair. "May I ask why you have chosen such an insalubrious location in which to lodge?" she asked gently. Neither of them was deceived by her tone. The marchioness tolerated insubordination in no one.

"I am living in a garden hut, Mother," her son said now, smiling at her for all the world as if he were a natural rather than a marquess, "I am living in a garden hut because I am working as a gardener on the estate of—"

She raised her hand. "I do not wish to hear her name spoken out loud."

He looked at her and said, "On the estate of Lady Rawlings, Mother, the woman whom I shall marry."

Of all possible outcomes to her son's disastrous impudence, this was the worst.

"I cannot fathom it," she said, punctuating each word with vigorous disapproval. "I understood when you were courting the Duchess of Girton last year. I was as aware as anyone that Ambrogina Camden's marriage was not consummated. She was a respectable woman, an excellent choice for marchioness, if one could disregard the unfortunate annulment that would have had to occur." She paused and gripped the carved top of her walking stick even harder.

"As I say, I understood your wish to marry her. Marriage to a duchess, even one who has annuled her previous marriage, can never be seen as a mistake. But marriage to Esme Rawlings is—is beyond my—I cannot fathom it. The woman took lovers under her husband's nose. Everyone in London knew what she was up to. Her own mother has publicly expressed horror at her behavior. I was never so surprised as when I heard that Lady Rawlings was actually entertaining her husband in that bed of hers; Lord knows all of London had been there at some point or other."

"If you repeat that comment one more time, you'll never see me again." His voice was calm, but the fury there made the marchioness blink.

She rallied quickly. "Don't be a fool!" she said sharply. "In my estimation, the gossip probably didn't cover half of what she did. I know for a fact—" Her eyes widened, and Sebastian saw that she had only just grasped the full ramifications of the situation.

"*You* to marry her! *You*, who killed her husband?"

"I did not kill her husband," Sebastian said, standing taller. "Rawlings's heart failed him on my unexpected entry to the chamber."

"You killed her husband," his mother said. "You entered that room looking for the bed of your duchess—oh, don't give me that folderol about a false wedding certificate. I don't believe common gossip. You had been bedding the duchess, but you crawled into the wrong bedchamber and encountered a husband. I call that killing the man! In my day"—she said it with grim triumph—"a man ascertained whose door he was entering *before* he did so."

Sebastian suppressed a grimace. "I mistook the room," he said stolidly, "and it had an unfortunate effect."

"Then why in the name of blazes should you marry the woman? A mistaken notion of paying for your crimes? If so, I shall have the vicar speak to you. Because one can overemphasize the doctrine of reconciliation, and marrying a doxy simply because one killed her husband is Going Too Far."

Sebastian sighed and looked about him. He was tired of standing like a schoolboy before his mother. She was perched on a thronelike chair in which the Regent would have felt comfortable, fitted out with claw feet and serpentine arms. He spotted a reasonably comfortable chair in the corner and strode over to fetch it.

"What are you doing?" his mother barked. "I didn't give you permission to sit down, Bonnington!"

"My name is Sebastian," he said, putting down the chair with a decisive thump and seating himself directly before her. "My name is Sebastian, and I am your son. Your only son. It would make me feel a great deal more comfortable if you did not refer to me as having killed Lord Rawlings. He had a weak heart, and the doctor had given him until the end of the summer. It was truly unfortunate that I was the cause of his seizure—and I would give anything to have not instigated that episode. But I did *not* kill him."

The marchioness blinked. Her ever-courteous, ever-proper, almost boring son appeared to be showing a little backbone for the first time in his life. She didn't know whether to be pleased or horrified.

She chose horrified.

"The only man with whom I have ever been on a first-name basis was your father," she said with some distaste, "and that only in the most intimate of situations. You, Bonnington, are my son, and as such should offer me only the greatest respect."

He inclined his head. "And that I do, Mother." But he stayed seated. He had her looks, that son of hers. When she was young, men wore their hair powered and women wore patches. But it would be a pity if Sebastian powered his hair. He had her hair, the color of sunshine, that's what Graham called it. Of course, Graham hadn't been bad-looking either. Those were his deep-set eyes looking at her. After her first husband died, she had married the most handsome man in London, and if Graham Bonnington wasn't a lively conversationalist, he knew his place. He listened to her. She said enough for both of them.

She thumped her stick on the floor. The stick made some of the younger servants quite ill with anxiety, but her son merely glanced at the floor, as if checking for scuff marks. She decided to stay with the most crucial point.

"You cannot marry a doxy out of some misplaced sense of obligation. The Bonningtons are an ancient and respected family. Make Lady Rawlings an allowance, if you must. The estate can certainly bear the cost."

"I intend to marry her," Sebastian said. "But not out of obligation."

"No?" She invested the word with as much scorn as she could.

"No. I love her."

The marchioness closed her eyes for a moment. The day had begun with the unpleasant shock of seeing her son in England, and it was rapidly turning into something truly odious.

"We don't marry out of love," she sat flatly. "Marry a decent woman, and you can always see about Lady Rawlings later."

"I love her, and I will marry her."

"I believe I have fallen into a comic opera. And I detest musical theater. Are you planning to break into song?"

"Not at this moment."

"Let me see if I understand you: you feel yourself to be in love with a doxy who has shared her bedchamber with half the men of London, and whose husband you didn't kill, but certainly helped to his grave?"

"This is your last warning, Mother." He said it through clenched teeth. "You speak of the woman I intend to marry, who will be marchioness after you. Speak so again, and you will have no part in our life."

The marchioness rose with some difficulty—the gout in her left foot was growing worse by the moment—and thumped her stick for good emphasis, although it seemed to have little effect. She was pleased to note that her son rose when she did. At least he hadn't discarded all manners.

"The day you marry that doxy, I shall disown you," she said, as if she were commenting on the weather. "But I am quite certain that you knew that would be the outcome. I may remind you that my portion is not inconsiderable. Any child you—"

Sebastian groaned inwardly. The other shoe had dropped.

"By God, the woman is *enceinte*! I'd forgotten that trollop is carrying a child. Tell me you are *not planning to marry Esme Rawlings before that child is born!*"

Sebastian toyed with the idea of threatening to marry Esme tomorrow, an action that would make her unborn child his heir. But he didn't want to be responsible for his mother having heart palpitations. Miles Rawlings's death already weighed heavily on his conscience. More to the point, Esme still refused to marry him at all.

"Lady Rawlings has not accepted me," he admitted.

A look of grim satisfaction crossed his mother's face. "Well, at least someone is showing intelligence. Of course she won't accept you. You killed her husband." She began to stump her way toward the door. "I don't know where you got this devilishly self-sacrificing side to you. Your father didn't show any penchant for that sort of nonsense."

Suddenly Sebastian felt his temper, which had been growing at a steady rate, flare into life. He walked around his mother and stopped before the door.

"Move aside!" she said.

"I will make Esme Rawlings marry me. She *will* accept me because she loves me as well. Moreover, I shall expect you to attend the wedding and behave in a respectable fashion."

"There won't be a wedding," his mother replied calmly. "I felt a momentary anxiety, true. But from what I know of her, Esme Rawlings is as intelligent as she is dissolute. She won't marry you. She won't even think of it. I've no doubt but what Rawlings left her warm enough in the pocket, and a woman like that doesn't need a protector, or yet a husband either. Now if you'll excuse me, I will return to my chamber."

And she walked past him.

Sebastian spun on his heel and walked over to the other side of the room. He looked down at his clenched fist, pulling it back on the point of putting it through the window. His mother had said no more than Esme herself had done, although she had never said he wasn't the one to father her child. But she probably thought it. How could a man serve as father to a babe when the whole world—his mother included—thought he'd killed the child's true father?

Sebastian Bonnington had faced few obstacles in his life. Thanks to his mother, he was both remarkably beautiful for a man and rigidly aware of proprieties. When other men strayed to mistresses and gambling, losing their estates and their minds in dissolute activities, he had watched and not partaken. Before he'd met Esme, in fact, he had never even felt the urge to commit an indecorous act.

He shook his head, staring blindly at the garden. Oh, he loved Esme's delicious curves and her beauty, but it was her eyes that he found irresistible. There was no other woman in the world with eyes at once seductively enchanting and secretly sad. They had taken his head, robbed his heart, and stolen his senses. Something about her made him love her, willy-nilly.

And if to love her and to marry her was indecorous or foolish, he had no choice in the matter. All he had to do was convince her of the same.

# 7

## A Saint, a Sinner, and a Goat

*L*ady Beatrix Lennox was bored. There wasn't a man to flirt with in the entire house. Lord Winnamore was eligible, but he was hopelessly besotted with Arabella. Too old, naturally, although he was curiously attractive in a ponderous kind of way. But Bea would never, ever take a man from her godmother. She wasn't proud of many of her characteristics, but she had always been loyal.

Bea drifted over to the mirror and practiced a seductive pout. She had dressed herself for a walk, but she didn't know why: there was nothing she found more tedious than the countryside. In fact, the very idea of traipsing through a meadow, gazing at cows, filled her with boredom.

Yet here she was, dressed up like a trussed turkey. In fact, distinctly like a turkey, given that she was wearing a walking dress of Austrian green, exuberantly adorned with ribbons. Little bows marched all the way up her bodice, the better to emphasize her bosom (amply padded with cotton). But there was no one in the house to enjoy it.

Except, of course, Mr. Fairfax-Lacy.

Mr. Fairfax-Lacy had one of those lean, well-bred faces that would have looked as attractive in an Elizabethan ruff as it did in fashionable garb. His grandfather probably wore one of those huge collars. Still, Elizabethans in portraits always seemed to have slightly piggish, avaricious eyes, whereas Fairfax-Lacy had—

A curt voice made her jump. "Lady Beatrix, your godmother is going to the village for a brief visit. Would you like to join her?"

Talk of the devil. She turned around slowly and gave Mr. Fairfax-Lacy a smouldering look, just for practice. The one that began just at the edge of her eyes and then turned into a promise.

He looked unmoved. Indifferent, as a matter of fact. "Lady Beatrix?"

A pox on his well-bred nature! He really *was* a Puritan. Or perhaps he was simply too old to play. He had to be forty. Still, the combination of her reputation and personal assets had made Bea widely admired by the male gender, irrespective of age.

She sauntered over to him and put her hand on his arm. His eyes didn't even flicker in the direction of her bosom, something she found quite disappointing, given the amount of cotton she had bundled under her chemise. "I would rather take a walk," she said. He was much better looking than a cow, after all; his presence might make a country stroll palatable.

"It has been raining on and off all day. Perhaps tomorrow would be a more pleasant experience for you."

"Oh, but I love rain!" she said, giving her sweetest smile, the one that always accompanied outrageous fibs.

Sure enough, he responded like a parrot: "In that case, I would be enchanted to accompany you." But was there a trace of irony in that *enchanted*? Did the Boring Puritan have a little bit of depth to him after all?

Bea thought about that while the footman fetched her spencer. Luckily her walking costume came with a matching parasol, because the idea of allowing even a drop of rain to disorder her face or hair made her shiver.

It was appalling to see how wet it was outside. Bea could hardly say that she didn't want her little jean half-boots to touch the ground, given as she'd squealed about loving rain. So she picked her way over the cobblestones in front of the house, hanging onto Mr. Fairfax-Lacy's arm so that she didn't topple over and spoil her spencer with rainwater.

At least *he* seemed to be enjoying himself. She sneaked a look, and he was smiling as they started down a country lane—a messy, dirty little path guaranteed to ruin her boots. Oh well. Bea had had lots of practice saying good-bye to people and things—her sisters, her father—what was a pair of boots? She let go of Fairfax-Lacy's arm and tramped along on her own. The path was lined with sooty-looking, thorny bushes with nary a flower to be seen.

He wasn't exactly the best conversationalist in the world. In fact, he didn't say a word. Bea had to admit that the landscape was rather pretty, with all those sparkling drops hanging off branches (waiting to destroy one's clothing, but one mustn't be squeamish about it). And the birds were singing, and so forth. She even saw a yellow flower that was rather nice, although mud-splattered.

"Look!" she said, trying to be friendly. "A daffodil."

"Yellow celandine," her companion said curtly.

After that, Bea gave up the effort of conversation and just tramped along. Helene was welcome to the Puritan. In the city there was always someone to look at: an old woman peddling lavender, a dandy wearing three watch fobs, a young buck trying to catch his whip. Bea found the street endlessly amusing.

But here! This lane had only one inhabitant.

"Hello, there," Fairfax-Lacy said, and he had a gentle smile on his face that she'd never seen before. He had nice creases around his eyes when he smiled like that. Of course, it would all be rather more attractive if he weren't scratching a goat.

The man ignored her cotton-enhanced bosom and saved his smiles for a goat! Still, the goat seemed to be the only object of interest, so Bea poked her way across the lane. The animal stuck its wicked-looking face over the gate and rolled an eye in her direction.

"He looks quite satanic," she said. She'd seen that face before, in the grandest ballrooms in London. "Evil, really."

"He's just an old billy goat," Fairfax-Lacy said, scratching the goat under his chin. The goat had a nasty-looking beard, as if it had been partially eaten while he wasn't watching.

"Aren't you worried that you will catch fleas?"

"Not particularly, given that goats don't carry fleas."

Well, that was an exciting exchange. Bea was just standing there, thinking about how hairy the goat's ears were, when the beast suddenly turned its head and clamped its yellowing teeth on the sleeve of her spencer. Luckily it was belled, in the Russian style, and he didn't manage to chomp her arm, although that was undoubtedly his intention.

"Help!" she shrieked, tugging at her spencer. The goat rolled its eyes at her and bared its teeth but didn't let go of her sleeve.

Instead, he began to back up, and a second later Bea found herself plastered against an extremely wet fence, desperately trying to pull her sleeve away from the monster's mouth as it tried to back into the field.

"Do something!" she bellowed at Fairfax-Lacy. She was shocked to see that he was trying to conceal the fact that he was laughing. Quite overcome by laughter, in fact.

"You bloody beast!"

"Me or the animal?"

"Either! Get—this—animal—*now*!"

"At your service!" He hopped over the fence and approached the billy goat. But for all the fact that Fairfax-Lacy had been on the very best of terms with the animal a moment before, it wasn't very loyal. As soon as Fairfax-Lacy got close, the goat's rear leg shot out, caught him on the hip, and tossed him into a mud puddle.

Bea was trying to get her left arm out of her spencer. It was difficult trying to squirm out of the garment while hanging onto a fencepost. But even with such pressing business at hand, she stopped to have a laugh at Fairfax-Lacy's expense.

He shot her a level look and got up. He was plastered with mud from his shoulders to his knees. Even his hair was flecked with brown.

Bea was laughing so hard that her stomach hurt. "What sort of mud is it?" she called out, breaking into a fresh storm of giggles.

"The kind women slap on their faces to improve their complexions," he growled over his shoulder. "May I bring you a handful?" This time he managed to avoid the goat's kick, but he couldn't get close enough to grab her spencer. Every time he approached the animal, it bared its ugly yellow teeth and kicked at him again.

Finally Fairfax-Lacy turned back to her. "Take it off."

"What do you think I'm trying to do?" Bea cried, all laughter disappearing from her voice.

"He's eaten the sleeve already."

"Bloody hell!"

"You swear far too much," the Puritan said.

"I swear just as much as I wish to," Bea retorted, starting to unbutton. The goat hadn't given an inch; it just stood there chewing on her sleeve as if he was making a supper of it.

"You're going to have to help me," she finally said sourly. "I can't unbutton the rest without letting go of the fencepost. And if I do that he'll undoubtedly drag me straight over the fence." She eyed Fairfax-Lacy. "Not that I want you anywhere near me. Does that mud smell as potent as it looks?"

"Yes," he said, sauntering over to her.

He was the most infuriating man. This was literally—literally!—the first look he'd given her that acknowledged her as a woman. In fact, it was as if he were seeing her for the first time. He didn't look Elizabethan at all. He looked . . .

Bea's stomach took a funny little hop, and she felt a wave of unaccountable shyness. So she kept her eyes down as he unbuttoned the rest of her spencer. It was all very romantic, what with the odoriferousness of his person and the grinding sound of a goat munching her extravagantly expensive garment.

Once it was unbuttoned, she managed to squirm the rest of the way out of her left sleeve, and then quickly shed the right. One could have sworn that the goat had been waiting for that moment. The very second her body was free of the spencer he took a bigger bite and then bared his teeth in a smile.

Bea felt a wave of anger. "Go get him!" she ordered the Puritan.

He laughed. He was still looking at her as if she were a person, rather than an annoying insect, but Bea didn't let that distract her.

"Then I shall do so myself," she said, unlatching the gate and pushing it open. There was a ghastly squishing noise as her boot sank into brown muck. Bea ignored it.

*He* closed the gate behind her and leaned on it with a huge grin on his face. She thought about sticking her tongue out at him and rethought it. She was twenty-three, after all.

"Goat," she said, in the low, threatening tone she had perfected on her four smaller sisters. "Goat, give me that garment."

The goat stopped chewing for a second and looked at her, and Bea knew she had him.

She walked over, ignoring the Puritan's shouts. Apparently Fairfax-Lacy had realized she was serious and seemed perturbed that she might get injured.

"Don't even think about kicking me," she told the goat. "I'll tie your ears in a bow and you'll look so stupid that no lady goat will ever look at you again."

He stopped chewing. Bea took another step and then held out her hand. "Drop that coat!" she said sharply.

The goat just stared at her, so she used the meanest tone she had, the one she reserved for little sisters who were caught painting their cheeks with her Liquid Bloom of Roses. "Drop it!"

He did, naturally.

Bea cast a triumphant look over her shoulder and bent to pick up her coat. Fairfax-Lacy was tramping across the field after her, no doubt impressed by her magnetic effect on animals.

Time has a way of softening memories. Yes, her meanest tone had been successful. But how could she have forgotten that her wicked little sisters often found retribution?

The kick landed squarely on her bottom and actually picked her off her feet. She landed with a tremendous splash, just at the feet of Mr. Stephen Fairfax-Lacy.

"Ow!"

At least he didn't laugh at her. He squatted next to her, and his blue eyes were so compassionate that they made her feel a little teary. Or perhaps that was due to the throbbing in her bottom.

"You've still got your spencer," he said reassuringly.

Bea looked down at her hand, and sure enough, she was clutching a muddy, chewed-up garment. The goat may have got his revenge, but she'd kept his supper. She started to giggle.

A smile was biting at the corners of the Puritan's mouth too. A splatter of warm rain fell on Bea's cheeks, the kind that falls through sunshine. Water slid behind her ears and pattered on the leaves of a little birch. Bea licked her lips. Then, as suddenly as it started, the shower stopped.

"I didn't realize how much you treasure your clothing," he said, touching her cheek. For a moment Bea didn't know what he was doing, and then she realized he was wiping mud from her face.

Without even thinking, she leaned against the Puritan and just let laughter pour out of her. She howled with laughter, the way she used to, back when she and her sisters would lark around in the nursery. The way she did when the world was bright and fresh and new.

She laughed so hard that she almost cried, so she stopped.

He wasn't laughing with her. Damned if the Puritan didn't have the sweetest eyes in the whole world. He scooped her off the ground and then strode over to the birch and sat down, back against its spindly trunk. Bea found it very interesting that when he sat down he didn't put her on the grass, but on his lap.

"You have triumphed," he told her. Sunlight filtered through the birch leaves in a curiously pale, watery sort of way. It made his eyes look dark blue, an azure bottom-of-the-sea type of blue.

She raised an eyebrow. Actually, now that she thought of it, all the color she'd put into her eyebrows and lashes had probably made its way down her cheek. Oh well, he likely thought it was just mud.

"A goat conqueror."

"One of my many skills," she said, feeling a little uncomfortable.

"I just want to suggest that you rest on your laurels," he said, and his eyes had a touch of amusement that made Bea feel almost . . . almost weak. She never felt weak. So she leaned against him and thought about how good that felt. Except she wasn't quite following the conversation.

"What do you mean?" she finally asked.

There was a definite current of laughter in his voice. "Your bonnet."

Bea shrieked and clapped a hand to her head, only just realizing that she had felt rain falling on her head as well.

"There." He pointed to the right. The damned goat was chewing up her very best hat. The green plume hung drunkenly from his mouth, and he seemed to be grinning at her.

Bea started up with a shriek of rage.

"I think not!" The Puritan had arms like steel. He didn't pay a bit of attention to her wiggling, just picked her up and turned her around. When she looked up at his face, she suddenly stopped protesting.

He didn't kiss like a Puritan. Or an old man either.

He kissed like a hungry man. Bea's first sensation was triumph. So the Puritan had pretended that he didn't notice her charms. Ha! That was all an act. He was just . . . he was just like . . . but then somehow, insidiously, she lost her train of thought.

He was kissing her so sweetly, as if she were the merest babe in arms. He didn't even seem to wish to push his tongue into her mouth. Instead he rubbed his lips against hers, danced on her mouth, his hands cupping her head so tenderly that she almost shivered. She quite liked this.

Oh, she felt his tongue. It sung on her lips, patient and tasting like raspberries. Without thinking, her own tongue tangled with his for a second. Then she realized what she was doing and clamped her mouth shut. There was nothing she hated more than a man pushing his great tongue where it didn't belong.

But he didn't. His lips drifted across her face and pressed her eyes shut, and then closed back on her lips with a ravenous hunger that made her soften, ache deep inside.

He probably thinks I'm a virgin, Bea thought in a foggy sort of way.

His mouth was leaving little trails of fire. He was nibbling her ear, and she was tingling all over. In fact, she wanted—she wanted him to try again. Come back, she coaxed silently, turning her face toward his lips. Try to kiss me, really kiss me. But he didn't. Instead, his tongue curled around the delicate whorls of her ear, and Bea made a hoarse sound in her throat. He answered it by nipping her earlobe, which sent another twinge deep between her legs.

He tugged her hair and she obediently tipped her face back, eyes closed, and allowed him to taste her throat, all the time begging silently that he return, return, kiss her again . . . But he seemed to be feasting on her throat. She opened her mouth to say something, but at that moment he apparently decided he had tormented her enough, and his mouth closed over hers.

She could no more fight that masculine strength than she could rise to her feet. He didn't coax this time; he took, and she gave. And it wasn't like all the other times, when she'd tolerated a moment or two of this kind of kissing. The Puritan's kiss was dark and sweet and savage all at once. It sent quivers through her legs and made her strain to be closer. His hands moved down her back, assured, possessive. In a moment he would bring them around to her front, and her breasts were aching for . . .

That was the thought that woke Bea. She hadn't been thinking of grappling in the field when she'd dressed in the morning. These particular breasts weren't meant to withstand a man's hand. There was more cotton than flesh. She tore her mouth away, gasping, and stared at him. She didn't even think about giving him a seductive glance. She was too stunned.

"I like you when you're like this," he said, and there was that sweetness to his eyes again. He reached out and rubbed a splatter of mud from her cheek. "You look rain-washed and very young. Also rather startled. It seemed to me that you've been inviting kisses. Was I wrong?"

"No," she said, trying hard to think what to say next. All her practiced seductive lines seemed to have fled from her head.

"Alas," he said, even more gently, tucking her hair behind her ear. "I can hardly offer marriage to a woman half my age. So I'm afraid that I shall have to leave your kisses, sweet though they are, to some younger man."

Bea's mouth almost fell open. Marriage? Didn't he know who she was? "I don't want—" she began, but her voice was hoarse. She stopped. "As it happens, I am not interested in marriage either," she said quite sedately. "I find that I am, however, very interested in *you*." She twisted forward and kissed his lips, a promise of pleasure. And she was absolutely honest about that. With him, there would be no boundaries.

But it was he who pulled back. She had been so sure he would lunge at her that she'd smiled—but the smile faded.

He *was* a Puritan. His eyes had gone cold, dark, condemning. "I thought you played the lusty trollop for fun."

She raised her chin. "Actually, no," she said, and she was very pleased to find her tone utterly calm and with just a hint of sarcasm. "I play myself."

"Yourself? Do you even know who you are, under all that face paint?"

"I assure you that I do."

"You play a part you needn't," he said, eyes fixed on hers. "You are young and beautiful, Beatrix. You should marry and have children."

"I think not."

"Why?"

"You simply want to make me like everyone else," she said sharply. "I like wearing *macquillage*. I would rather not look like *myself*, as you put it. And I find it incalculably difficult to imagine myself sitting by the fire wearing a lace cap and chattering about my brood of children."

"I think *yourself* is beautiful. All your paints have washed away at the moment. You never needed them."

"I didn't say I needed them. I enjoy them," she retorted, and then added, deliberately, "just as I occasionally enjoy the company of a man in my bedchamber."

For a moment they just looked at each other, Puritan to trollop. "Am I to understand that you are not interested in taking a mistress?" she asked, meeting his eyes. She was no child to be whipped by his condemnation.

"Actually, I am," he said. "But I have little interest in one so . . . practiced."

Bea got to her feet, shaking out her skirts. Then she bent over and picked up her mangled spencer, shaking it out and folding it over her arm, taking a moment to make absolutely certain that her face wouldn't reveal even for a second what she felt.

"I have often noticed that men of your years seem to overprize naiveté," she replied calmly.

He showed no reaction, but her quip was so untrue that she gained no joy from saying it. He wasn't old. Suddenly, she decided to be honest. Looking him in the eye, she said, "That was cruel, and quite shabby, Mr. Fairfax-Lacy. I would not have expected it of you."

"I'm sorry."

She nodded and began to turn toward the gate. After all, she'd had much worse things said to her, mostly by women, but then there was her dear father. So when he caught her arm, she turned toward him with a little smile that was almost genuine.

"Don't you think we should take our bedraggled selves home?"

There was real anguish in his eyes. "I feel like the worst sort of bastard. Kissing you in a field and then insulting you."

At that, she grinned. "I gather you wish I were an innocent, Mr. Fairfax-Lacy. But I am not. I truly enjoyed that kiss." The smile she gave him was as wicked and lazy as any she'd ever bestowed on a man. "And I would very much have enjoyed your company in my bedchamber as well. But I have never forced myself on a man. I fully understand that you are looking for a far more respectable mistress." Helene was an altogether perfect alternative.

At that moment, Bea made up her mind. Helene would never be able to lure the Puritan on her own. She, Beatrix, would have to help, if only to prove that she didn't hold grudges, even when rejected. She would give him to Helene as a present.

She turned and made her way across the field, and when the goat rolled his wicked eyes and snapped his lips over a Pomona green satin ribbon, all that remained of her bonnet, she just smiled at him.

Which startled the animal so much that he galloped off to the other end of the field, leaving her hat behind.

# 8

## The Sewing Circle

To Esme's great relief, Mrs. Cable swept into her morning parlor on the very strike of ten o'clock. Esme had been putting crooked stitches into a sheet for at least five, perhaps even ten, minutes and hadn't got further than two hands' lengths. She hastily bundled the sheet to the side to greet her guest.

"My goodness, Lady Rawlings!" Mrs. Cable said. "How very becoming that cap looks on you! You are verily an illustration of the good book of Timothy, which says that women should adorn themselves in modest apparel, with shamefacedness and sobriety rather than gold and pearls."

Esme touched her head self-consciously. It was the very first time that she had ever worn a cap, and she felt like a fool. Like one of those Renaissance fools, with bells hanging off their caps. It felt like rank hypocrisy, as if wearing a trifling bit of lace on top of one's head would make up for the fact that two days ago she'd reveled in indecencies with her gardener. One could only imagine what would happen if her guest knew the truth!

Esme pushed away that thought and offered Mrs. Cable some tea.

"I would be grateful," Mrs. Cable said, plumping herself onto the settee next to Esme, and showing no inclination whatsoever to pick up an unhemmed piece of cotton. "For a body must have sustenance, and that's a fact!"

"I quite agree," Esme said, pouring tea into a cup and ruthlessly repressing visions of other kinds of bodily sustenance, types of which she doubted Mrs. Cable would approve quite so heartily.

Mrs. Cable sipped and raised her eyebrows. "She is like the merchants' ships; she bringeth her food from afar."

Esme was not someone with a facility in biblical verses. Oddly enough, contact with Mrs. Cable seemed to be increasing her irritation rather than her piety. "Indeed?"

"Proverbs," Mrs. Cable said briskly. "This *is* India tea, is it not? An expense, a dear expense, but quite delicious. I have brought with me six sheets, which I managed to hem in my spare time this week."

"How marvelously industrious you are!" Esme gushed. She herself couldn't seem to sew anything except under the direct supervision of the Circle itself, so she never participated in the weekly count of completed sheets.

"You must have a great deal of time on your hands these days, Lady Rawlings."

Esme resisted the temptation to tell Mrs. Cable that having a houseful of dissolute guests made for rather a lot of work. "So one would think."

Luckily Slope opened the door. "Lady Winifred," he announced, "and Mrs. Barret-Ducrorq."

"What a pleasure to see you, Mrs. Barret-Ducrorq," Esme exclaimed. "And here we thought you were enjoying yourself in London and we wouldn't see you until the season ended!"

"We are all assembled," Mrs. Cable put in, "as when the good book says that the elders were assembled."

"I'd take it as a personal compliment if you'd not refer to me as an *elder,* Mrs. Cable," Mrs. Barret-Ducrorq snapped. "Lucy and I have fled London for a week or so. The poor girl is quite, quite worn out by all the festivities. As am I," she added, looking remarkably robust. "Sponsoring a debut is a quite exhausting business." Mrs. Barret-Ducrorq's sister had recently died, leaving her to administer her niece's debut.

"And by all accounts, Lucy is having a particularly exciting time," Lady Winifred said with a good-natured chuckle. Lady Winifred had three grown daughters living in London; while she no longer traveled to the city for the season, she seemed to know of even the tiniest event.

Mrs. Barret-Ducrorq leveled a glare at Lady Winifred, who was demurely threading a needle. "I expect that, as always, accounts of the incident have been grossly exaggerated."

Mrs. Cable's eyes were bulging out with pure excitement. "Never tell me that something happened to sweet Miss Aiken! Your niece could not create a scandal. There must be some mistake!"

Mrs. Barret-Ducrorq's mouth twisted. She was a rather corpulent woman, whose body seemed to have focused itself in her bosom; it jutted below her chin like the white cliffs of Dover. Generally, she had an air of victory, but today she looked rather deflated.

Esme put down her sheet. "What on earth has happened to Miss

Aiken?" she asked. Lucy Aiken had always seemed a pallidly unimaginative girl and certainly not one to achieve notoriety.

"It's her father's blood coming out," Mrs. Barret-Ducrorq said heavily.

Mrs. Cable gasped. "Never say so!"

"I do say so! If my sister hadn't married beneath her, none of this would have happened!"

"It didn't sound particularly outrageous to me," Lady Winifred observed, turning the corner on her hem. "After all, many girls do foolish things in their first season. It's almost expected. And it's not as if she created some sort of true scandal!"

Aha, Esme thought to herself. That would have been my role . . . in the old days. She was astounded that neither Mrs. Barret-Ducrorq nor Lady Winifred had mentioned her cap. Did they really think she was old enough, stodgy enough, widowed enough, to wear one of these? Even Arabella didn't wear a cap!

"My niece insulted the great Brummell himself," Mrs. Barret-Ducrorq said heavily.

"What on earth did Miss Aiken say to him?" Esme asked, fascinated despite herself. She'd often wanted to insult Brummell.

"He did her the inestimable honor of complimenting her complexion, and then asked what preparation she used on her freckles." Mrs. Barret-Ducrorq shuddered. "Lucy was rather tired, and apparently she did not entirely understand the breadth of Mr. Brummell's importance in the *ton.* Or so she tells me."

"And?" Mrs. Cable said.

"She snapped at the man," Mrs. Barret-Ducrorq admitted. "She informed him that any preparations she chose to use on her complexion were her business, and no one else's."

"The snare of vanity," Mrs. Cable said darkly.

"The vanity is all Mr. Brummell's," Esme pointed out. "The man takes a spiteful delight in pointing out the faults that one most wants to hide."

"She loathes her freckles," Mrs. Barret-Ducrorq said. "I blame them on her father's side of the family. We have nothing of the sort in *our* family, and so I have told Lucy, time out of mind."

"Vanity—," Mrs. Cable put in.

Everyone ignored her. "You were right to bring poor Lucy to the country for a week," Lady Winifred said. "Everyone will have forgotten by next Monday."

"True enough. More importantly, has she met any gentlemen whom she finds acceptable?" Esme put in.

Mrs. Barret-Ducrorq looked slightly more cheerful. "Several gentlemen have paid her marked attention. I am hopeful that they will overlook both her slip of the tongue and the freckles."

"Poor Lucy just didn't understand that we fairly beg Mr. Brummell to be discourteous to us," Esme said. "He's a horrid little beast, and so I shall tell Lucy when I see her."

"Lady Rawlings!" Mrs. Cable said with a gasp. "Mr. Brummell is a leader of the *ton!* It would never do for Miss Aiken to insult him yet again."

Esme bit her lip before she retorted that she too was a leader of the *ton,* and knew better than Mrs. Cable what a song and dance one was supposed to make before the great Brummell. Or the *penniless* Brummell, as was rumored.

At that moment the door opened, and Arabella swept in. "Ah, this must be my niece's group of virtuous laborers," she said, laughing. "I thought I'd join you and bring a little frivolity to lighten your exertions!"

"How kind of you," Esme said, giving Arabella a pointed look. If she undermined Esme's new respectability, Esme would have to flay her, relative or no. She had sewn too many sheets to give up her place in the Circle now. "Ladies, may I present my aunt, the Dowager Viscountess Withers? Aunt, this is Mrs. Cable, Mrs. Barret-Ducrorq, and—"

"Winifred!" Arabella crowed. "How are you, dear girl?"

Esme watched, rather stupefied, as Lady Winifred came to her feet with a great creaking of stays and Arabella bounded into her embrace. Lady Winifred was a florid woman with a bewildering range of acquaintances. Still, Esme wouldn't have put her aunt among them, given that Lady Winifred spent a great deal of her time impugning the reputations of women with far fewer sins than had Arabella. Perhaps Lady Winifred was losing her memory.

"I haven't seen you in an age!" Lady Winifred boomed. "It's all my fault, of course. I've grown as large as a horse, and as lazy as one too. Nowadays I loathe London."

"I know just what you mean," Arabella said, patting her hand. "There are days when I feel every bone in my aged body and I can't think of a single activity that might please me."

Esme just stopped herself from rolling her eyes. Arabella was wearing an utterly charming and provocative morning gown made of a cotton so light it floated on the breeze. If she didn't look precisely youthful, she did appear to have a good twenty years before she'd feel even a touch of rheumatism.

The look on Mrs. Cable's face made it clear that she, at least, was having no trouble remembering the kind of activities for which Arabella was famed. "How unusual to find such a distinguished personage in Limpley-Stoke," she said with a titter. "I'm afraid that you'll find our little village quite drab!"

Esme suddenly saw Mrs. Cable through her aunt's eyes. Mrs. Cable's small, dark eyes were glistening with dislike. Her mouth was thinned with contempt. The worst thing of all, from Arabella's point of view, would be the fact that Mrs. Cable was wearing a dress of pomona green poplin, just the color to emphasize the sallow color of her cheeks.

"No place that contained my niece could be tedious!" Arabella replied, whisking herself into a chair. "I do believe I would even travel to America to see her. And that's a profound compliment, as I'm sure you all know how sea air can ruin one's complexion."

"I am honored," Esme said, pouring Arabella a cup of tea. "Thank goodness you needn't go to such lengths, dear aunt. At your age," she added.

Arabella narrowed her eyes at her. "I see you've taken up wearing a cap, dearest niece. At your age."

Lady Winifred had settled herself back with a length of cotton. "I won't offer you a piece of this, Arabella," she said with a booming laugh. "I don't think of you as a needle-mistress!"

"But of course, you're right," Arabella agreed. "I can't sew to save my life."

"Sometimes these sheets are all that come between the poor and the cold floor," Mrs. Cable said pointedly. "Whoso stoppeth his ear at the cry of the poor, she also shall cry herself and not be heard."

Rag-mannered, Esme thought to herself. Could Miles truly have wished her to spend time with the likes of Mrs. Cable?

Apparently Lady Winifred agreed with Esme's assessment. "I have been meaning to mention to you, Mrs. Cable, that there is something just slightly vulgar about quoting the Bible, unless, of course, it is the vicar himself who ventures to recite."

Mrs. Cable thrust back her head, rather like a rooster preparing to battle an impudent hen, and said, "I fear not, but testify unto every man."

Arabella raised one eyebrow and said pleasantly, "My goodness, you do seem to have the Bible at your fingertips. I do congratulate you. It is such an unusual skill to find among the gently bred."

Mrs. Cable turned a deepish puce color. Arabella turned to Mrs. Barret-Ducrorq with her charming smile. "I don't believe we've met. But as it happens, I did meet your delightful ward, Miss Aiken, just two weeks ago, at Almack's. Sally Jersey introduced me. We both thought her manners were remarkably engaging, with very little of that strident awkwardness that seems rampant this season, and I certainly applauded Sally's decision to give her a voucher to Almack's."

Mrs. Barret-Ducrorq had silently watched the skirmish between Arabella and Mrs. Cable to this point, but she was instantly wooed and won.

"That is tremendously kind of you, Lady Withers," she said, putting her sewing to the side, "and I must ask you a question. I have been longing to know the truth behind the Countess of Castignan's extraordinary marriage, and I expect you know all about it."

Arabella laughed. "Well, as to that, Petronella is one of my dearest friends. . . ."

Esme risked a look at Mrs. Cable. She was sitting like a dour crow, stitching so quickly that her needle was a blur. Even for the sake of Miles, her departed—if not terribly dear—husband, could she contemplate a lifetime in Mrs. Cable's company?

# 9

## *Prudishness... That Coveted Quality*

*B*ea woke in the morning feeling rather ashamed of herself. Of course, there was nothing new in that sensation. Her father had often bellowed his amazement that he'd never managed to teach her a single thing, but she secretly thought he had had no difficulty imparting shame. She'd simply refused to reveal it, to his everlasting fury.

But she should never have kissed Stephen Fairfax-Lacy in the goat pasture. Never. He was singled out for Helene, and if there was one thing that Bea did *not* do, it was steal men from other women.

I'll dress in such a way as to make it absolutely clear to Mr. Puritan that he's not to kiss me again, Bea thought. Then she remembered that the Puritan didn't want to kiss her, now he knew of her *experience*. If that pang in the region of her stomach was shame, Bea refused to acknowledge it.

"I'll wear the new morning gown," she told her maid, Sylvie. "The one with blonde lace."

"But, my lady, I thought you had decided that gown was entirely too prudish," Sylvie lisped in her French accent.

"It is rather prudish, isn't it? Wonderful. I'm in a Puritanical mood."

"If you say so," Sylvie said resignedly. She was rather hoping that her mistress had taken a permanent dislike to the gown and would hand it on to her.

Sometime later Bea looked at herself in the glass with some satisfaction. She looked—as her grandmother might have said—as if butter wouldn't melt in her mouth. The dress was made of the finest jaconet muslin in a pale amber, trimmed with deep layers of pointed blonde lace. It had long sleeves, and while the bodice clung to every inch of her bosom (and several inches that weren't hers at all), it was so high-necked that it practically touched her ears.

"No Spanish papers," Sylvie suggested, as Bea sat herself at the dressing table. Once she'd gotten over the disappointment of having her mistress actually wear the coveted gown, she'd started enjoying the dressing, as always. Truly, she was lucky. Her mistress was lovely, invariably cheerful, and, most importantly, took clothing very, very seriously.

"You're absolutely right," Bea said, nodding at her in the mirror. "The papers are far too red. My cheeks should be just the palest pink. Didn't I buy something called Maiden's Blush at that shop in Bedford Square?"

Sylvie was rummaging through a smallish trunk that stood open to the right of Bea's dressing table. "Here it is!" she said, holding up a small bottle. "Although you may wish to consider the Royal Tincture of Peach," she added, handing over another bottle as well.

Bea tipped both colors onto a bit of cotton and considered them carefully. "Maiden's Blush, I think," she decided. "The Peach is lovely, though. Perhaps I'll use it on my lips."

"Don't you think it will be rather pale?" Sylvie asked doubtfully.

"No, no," Bea said, deftly applying a translucent layer of rouge. "I'm nothing more than a seedling today. Utterly missish." She ignored the little voice in the back of her mind that kept insisting on the contradictory nature of her actions. Why shouldn't such an experienced trollop as herself dress any way that she pleased? Illogical or no.

"Ahh," Sylvie said. She loved a challenge. "In that case, I shall change your hair, my lady. Perhaps if I twisted a simple bandeau through it? These beads are entirely too *knowing.*"

"You are a blessing," Bea told her with satisfaction. "What on earth would I do without you?" A few moments later, she grinned at herself in the mirror. Her hair had the simplicity of a fourteen-year-old. She looked utterly milk-and-water. A mere infant!

She refused to think about the perverse impulse that was driving her to demonstrate to Stephen Fairfax-Lacy that she was not as experienced as—well, as she was. For a moment she almost deflated. Why on earth was she pretending to a virtue she didn't possess and had never before aspired to, either?

There was a knock on the door, and Sylvie trotted away. Bea delicately applied kohl to her lashes. Not even for the sake of innocence would she emerge from her room without coloring her lashes.

"May Lady Rawlings visit for a moment?" Sylvie called from the door.

Bea hopped up, slipping her feet into delicate white kid slippers. "Esme! Do come in, please!"

Sylvie opened the door, but Esme just stood there for a moment, blinking. "Bea?" she said weakly, "is that *you?*"

"Do you like it?" Bea said, laughing.

Esme dropped her considerable girth into a chair by the fireplace. "You look like a green girl, which I gather must be your aspiration."

"Precisely," Bea replied triumphantly.

"I do like the color you're wearing on your lips, although I could never wear something so pale myself. Where did you buy it?"

"It was the perfumer on St. James Street, wasn't it, Sylvie?" Bea said.

"Indeed it was, my lady," Sylvie replied.

"I haven't been to London in over six months," Esme said, wiggling her toes in front of the fire. "I hardly remember what the inside of a perfumer looks like!"

"How appalling," Bea said, tucking herself into the chair opposite. "I suppose that carrying a child does limit one's activities." She felt very pleased at the idea that she herself would never be banned from London for that many months. Being unmarried had definite advantages.

"Actually, it's this respectability business," Esme answered.

"Lady Godwin did mention that you are—" Bea stopped, unable to find a tactful way to phrase Esme's ambitions.

"Aspiring to be above reproach," Esme said.

"We all aspire to something, I suppose," Bea said, rather doubtfully.

"Did you buy those slippers from Mrs. Bell?" Esme inquired. "I adore the daisy clocks on the ankle."

"Mrs. Bell tried to convince me to buy a shawl with the same daisy pattern. But I thought that might be too kittenish."

"You're risking kittenish now, if you don't mind my saying so, but you somehow manage to look delightful instead. At any rate," Esme said with a sigh, "I came to warn you that although my Sewing Circle has *finally* departed, I was maneuvered into asking them to return for a late luncheon. So please, feel free to eat in your chambers unless you wish to be showered in Bible verses."

"Sewing Circle?" Bea repeated rather blankly.

"Did Arabella forget to tell you?" Esme said, standing up and shaking out her skirts. "I've joined a local Sewing Circle. We meet every week, at my house, due to my delicate condition. Arabella joined us this morning, which caused great excitement and led to the luncheon invitation."

"Never tell me that Arabella is able to sew!" Bea said with fascination.

"Absolutely not. But her tales of the Countess of Castignan certainly kept everyone awake. The problem is that the most repellent of the seamstresses, Mrs. Cable, and my aunt have taken a fervent dislike to each other. So there is more than a slim possibility that lunch will be a demonstration of gently bred fury."

Esme paused at the door. "I have been trying to come up with a seating arrangement that will keep my aunt and Mrs. Cable apart, and I have decided to scatter small tables in the Rose Salon." She gave Bea an alluring smile. "If you feel sufficiently brave, I would love to put you at a table with Mrs. Cable. She has a marked tendency to punctuate her conversation with ill-chosen Bible verses. Given your current appearance, she will deem you among the saved and be cordial."

Bea managed to simper. "Actually, I am quite well versed in the Bible myself."

"Oh goodness, how wonderful! I *shall* seat you just beside Mrs. Cable, if you don't mind. You can quote at each other in perfect bliss."

"Mr. Fairfax-Lacy seems quite sanctimonious," Bea put in before she could stop herself. "Mrs. Cable would likely approve of him. All those good works."

"Do you think so?" Esme asked with some doubt. "I believe that the man is undergoing some sort of internal upset. He doesn't appear to be interested in Parliamentary doings at all. And that *is* his reputation, you know."

"All work and no play?"

"Precisely." Bea thought about Stephen's activities in the goat pasture and rather agreed with Esme. The man was not thinking about Parliament. No: he was on the hunt for a mistress. Or perhaps a wife.

"But he must be accustomed to tedious speeches, so I shall put him at your table," Esme continued. "Helene can sit there as well and rehearse dallying with Mr. Fairfax-Lacy. You must prompt her if she neglects her practice. Although I must tell you, Bea, it's my opinion that your poetry will have to do the trick if Helene and Fairfax-Lacy are to become intimate. I've known Helene for years, and it simply isn't in her nature to play the coquette."

"But she *did* elope," Bea said, wondering how on earth that had happened. Who would elope with a woman who had all the sensual appeal of a matron of sixty? Yet when Helene laughed, she was surprisingly captivating.

Esme shrugged and opened the door. "Her husband, Rees, effected that miracle somehow, and they've both spent the last ten years regretting it. I do believe the marriage ended before they even returned from Gretna Green, although they resided together for quite some time.

"I am counting on your bravery at luncheon, then." She paused for a moment and looked at Bea. "Amazing! I would hardly have recognized you. I suppose you are revisiting the artless Lady Beatrix Lennox of age sixteen or thereabouts."

Bea gave her a rather crooked smile. "I hate to disillusion you, Esme, but I was fourteen when my father discovered that I was coloring my lashes with burnt cork. He never recovered from that initial shock."

"Oh, parents!" Esme said, laughing. "You should hear my mother on the subject of *my* innocence! Or the lack thereof. According to my mother, I sprang from the womb a fully fledged coquette—shaped in my aunt's image, as it were."

Bea grinned. "You could do worse."

"Much," Esme said with an answering grin. "At luncheon, then!"

When Bea slipped into a chair next to the redoubtable Mrs. Cable, her mind was not on the meal. She was wondering precisely how a Puritan gentleman greets a woman he vigorously kissed in the goat pasture the previous afternoon. Would Stephen pretend that they had never grappled with each other? That his tongue hadn't slipped between her lips? That she hadn't—

Bea could feel that rare thing, a real flush, rising in her cheeks, so she hurriedly pushed the memory away. She hadn't spent a good twenty minutes painting herself with sheer layers of Maiden's Blush only to find herself blushing.

The gentleman in question was rather exquisitely dressed himself, if the truth be told. Bea watched under her lashes as he strode into the room. He was wearing a costume of the palest fawn, with a severely cut-away jacket. For a man who spent his time roaming about the House of Commons, he seemed to have unaccountably powerful thighs.

"Oh Lord, there he is," Helene moaned, sitting down next to her. "This is such a foolish idea."

"You've no reason to worry," Bea said to her encouragingly. "The poem can do the work for you."

"Countess Godwin," Mrs. Cable announced, snapping her napkin into her lap, "we have met, although I expect you have no memory of the event."

"I remember perfectly," Helene said. "And how pleasant to see you again."

"It was a dinner that Lady Rawlings gave some few months ago," Mrs. Cable told Bea.

"How lovely that must have been!" Bea said breathlessly. She was rather enjoying playing the role of a virtuous maiden. It was a new experience, after all, since she'd spent her youth trying to infuriate her father with less-than-virtuous antics.

"It was not lovely," Mrs. Cable said darkly, "not at all. Countess Godwin, I daresay you have formed the same aversion as I to even thinking of the occasion. Quite scandalous."

Bea clasped her hands and widened her eyes. Stephen was on his way to their table, and she wanted him to see her in the midst of full-blown girlishness. "Oh, what could have happened!" she cried, just as Stephen arrived.

Helene, who had just noticed Bea's transformation, gave her a sardonic look. "Nothing you couldn't have topped, Bea."

The Puritan created a diversion by bowing and introducing himself to Mrs. Cable, who seemed enraptured at the idea of sharing a table with a Member of Parliament.

Somewhat to Bea's disappointment, he didn't even blink when she gave him a girlish smile and a giggle. Instead he bowed just as one would to a damsel still in the schoolroom, then turned readily to Countess Godwin and kissed *her* hand.

"Earl Godwin was there, of course," Mrs. Cable said in her sharp voice, returning directly to the subject. "Mr. Fairfax-Lacy, we are discussing an unfortunate dinner that I and Countess Godwin attended in this very room, some months ago. I won't go into the details in present company." She cast a motherly look at Bea, who bit her lip before she could grin, and then looked modestly at her hands.

Stephen caught a glimpse of Bea's downcast eyes and felt like bellowing with laughter. She was a minx. It wasn't only that she was dressed as primly as an escapee from a nunnery. Somehow she had managed to make her whole face look as guileless as a babe in arms. Gone was the mischievous twinkle and the lustful glances. She had the aura and the innocence of a saint, and only that one dimple in her cheek betrayed the fact that she was enjoying herself mightily. Other than that dimple, she was the picture of a naive duke's daughter. If there was such a thing in England.

"I daresay your husband told you," Mrs. Cable was saying to Lady Godwin, "that he and I exchanged some pointed words on the subject of matrimony. Not harsh, not at all. But I think I made my point." She smiled triumphantly.

Helene smiled weakly and took a sip of wine. "It would appear to have slipped Rees's mind."

Bea felt a surge of admiration. She herself would likely have lost her temper by now and started screeching at that harpy.

Mrs. Cable shook her head. "A man shall leave his father and mother, and cleave unto his wife, and so it says in the Bible."

"Alas, Rees is notorious for his defiance of authority," Helene replied.

Bea watched Helene trying to defend herself and felt a surge of fury. Who was this old harridan, and what right had she to say such an unaccountably insulting thing to Helene?

Mrs. Cable looked at Stephen. "I'm certain you won't mind if I act as if we are all old friends," she informed him. "I have given much thought to Lady Godwin's situation in the ensuing months since I dined with her husband." She paused for a drink of water.

Bea saw that Helene's slender hand was clenched so tightly on her napkin that her knuckles were white. "Were you not quoting Genesis just now, Mrs. Cable?" Bea cooed.

Mrs. Cable gave her the approving look of a headmistress with a promising student. "Precisely, Lady Beatrix. It's a true pleasure to meet a young lady with a proper education. Now, Lady Godwin, if I might offer a few—"

"My father puts great faith in religious instruction," Bea interrupted.

"Quite right," Mrs. Cable rejoined. "Now I think that I can bring some wisdom to bear on the situation." And she turned back to Helene.

That old snake can see that Helene is defenseless, Bea thought in a fury. "Why, when I fell in love with one of my father's footmen," she said in a high, ringing voice, "my father made me memorize the entire Book of Maccabees in punishment."

"Indeed," Mrs. Cable said, obviously taken aback at this information.

"Yes," Bea said, favoring her with a dulcet smile, "I offered myself to the footman in question, you see, and my father truly did think that I should not have done so."

Mrs. Cable's eyes widened.

"But I don't agree," Bea continued blithely. "Because, of course, the Gospel of John counsels us to love one another. That's chapter thirteen," she told Mrs. Cable. "But I expect you know that." Stephen was shaking with suppressed laughter. Helene's hand had relaxed, and she was biting back a smile as well.

"Yes, I—"

"Even if my love was unconventional," Bea said with a soulful tremor in her voice, "I'm quite certain that it was ripe with virtue."

"Ripe would be the word," Stephen said dryly.

Bea ignored him. "After all, while it is true that a footman would have had difficulty supporting *me* as a wife"—she glanced modestly at her gown, which cost more than a footman earned in six months—"Proverbs does say that where love is, a dinner of herbs is better than a stalled ox. Although I always wondered what a 'stalled ox' is? Mr. Fairfax-Lacy, perhaps you have come across the term in your many years in Parliament?"

Alas, Stephen didn't have a chance to deliver his opinion because Mrs. Cable sputtered into life again, like a candle that found itself briefly in the path of a rainshower. Now she was viewing Bea with the acute horror of someone who has discovered that an exquisite pastry is rotten in the center.

"Lady Beatrix," she said on an indrawn breath, "I am quite certain that you do not realize the impression your little story might create on the assembled company." She swept a glance around the table.

Helene met her eyes blandly. "Lady Beatrix never fails to surprise me, for one," she said. "A footman, did you say, Bea? How very adventuresome of you!"

"I don't know that I agree," Stephen drawled. He felt a thrill of danger when Bea's eyes met his, especially since the thrill went right between his legs. She was a glorious, impudent piece of womanhood, and he liked her defense of Lady Godwin. If only she knew, she had utterly ceased to look sixteen years old. Her face was too alive for all this nonsense she affected. "I, for one, would like to know how the footman answered Lady Beatrix's overtures," he put in. "Didn't you notice, Mrs. Cable, that while Lady Beatrix apparently offered herself to the footman, she said nothing of his response. Can it be that the man in question refused her?"

Mrs. Cable huffed. "I cannot fathom why we would even discuss such a repellent subject! Surely Lady Beatrix is merely seeking to shock us, for—"

"Not at all," Bea said. "I would *never* do that, Mrs. Cable!"

Mrs. Cable narrowed her eyes. "And where is your father, my lady?"

"At his house," Bea replied, suddenly reverting to her maidenlike docility. "I'm a sad disappointment to him, Mrs. Cable. In fact I make my home with Lady Withers now."

Mrs. Cable huffed. "And the footman—"

"Oh, it wasn't due to the footman," Bea said blithely. "Father moved the footman to a house in the country. It was—"

"I'll not listen!" Mrs. Cable said shrilly. "You're making a May game of me, my lady, and it's not kind of you. I could take one look at you and know that you aren't one of those scandalous women you're pretending to be."

Helene threw Bea a warning look and put a gentle hand on Mrs. Cable's wrist. "You're absolutely right, of course," she said. "I do keep begging Lady Beatrix to be less frivolous, but I'm afraid that she's quite a romp. But, naturally, it's all in fun, Mrs. Cable."

"I knew that," Mrs. Cable said, blinking rapidly. "I'm a fair judge of character, to which Mr. Cable agrees. Now Lady Beatrix, you may attempt to shock us, but your true purity of character shines through. It's written all over your face. What did you say that was?" she asked the footman. "A regalia of cowcumbers? Indeed, I'll try some."

Stephen looked at Bea for a moment, and she had no trouble deciphering his thoughts. He was thinking of the goat pasture, and the true purity of her character.

## 10

## *The Heights of Pleasure*

*B*y the time that Esme finished luncheon, she was resigned to the fact that the house was gradually filling with her aunt's friends, not one of whom was precisely respectable. Her Sewing Circle was doubtless scandalized by her guests, since the said guests substituted cynical wit for gentility. And since they delighted above all in displaying that wit, the house rang with laughter.

Or perhaps it was more accurate to say that the house simply rang with noise. Lady Arabella had taken charge of the housekeeping from top to bottom and seemed to be bent on proving her mothering ability by cleaning from the attics to the cellars. Mind you, it wasn't as if she touched dirt herself.

"I've instructed the maids that we want this house to shine from top to bottom," she announced to Esme. "This is what a mother would do. Remove all worries! You have enough to think about. When *will* that child come?"

Never mind the fact that Esme had no interest in the attics at all. She was hardly the matronly sort, even in her current respectability. But Arabella didn't stop with the attics. "And I've sent men up on the roof to fix the slate. I've no tolerance for gardeners simply sitting about, and there's nothing to be done outside at any rate." March rain was taking fitful turns with sunshine.

Esme had been listening rather absentmindedly, but she snapped awake at that one. "You sent the gardeners up on the roof?"

Arabella blinked at her. "Haven't you heard the hammering? They started first thing this morning. I noticed that the slate had practically evaporated from your roof in several parts. Without repair, we shall have leaks in short order. No doubt the task will take a few weeks or perhaps a month. But it needs doing."

"It's not safe!" Esme said. Panic surged into her stomach, and she suddenly felt a little dizzy.

"Of course it's safe," Arabella said. "They won't drop slate off the roof. Most of the work's being done in the back of the house. But perhaps I'll station a footman at the front door so he can check that the coast is clear before anyone leaves the house. In fact, darling, that is an excellent idea. We have far too many footmen as it is. I seem to have overestimated the difficulty of hiring staff in the country."

"It's not safe for the gardeners," Esme said, trying to calm her racing heart. Sebastian was up there. Up on a slippery roof, likely on the verge of falling to his death. She could not bear it if that happened. Not—not after Miles.

"Gardeners? Gardeners? They're likely ecstatic to be up in the air," Arabella said, waving her beringed hands. "*Much* more engaging than digging up weeds, believe me."

She left before Esme could say another word. Perhaps she should tell Arabella the truth about Sebastian. There was probably no one in the world who would be more receptive to the idea that Esme had her former lover installed in the bottom of her garden. Panic beat in her throat. Sebastian had to come down from the roof this very moment.

She went downstairs, bundled herself into a mantle, and slipped out the side door. The sound of hammering bounced off the neighboring hills. Starlings were converging on the elms at the side of the house, pirouetting against the grayish sky. Every blade of grass bent with rain. Now and then she heard the echo of male voices, but she walked all the way to the back of the house without seeing a soul.

And then, as she rounded the house to the west, there he was. Sitting with his back to a chimney, eating a hunk of bread as if he hadn't a care in the world. Marquess Bonnington wasn't hanging from the gutter by one fingernail. He wasn't spread-eagled in the rainy grass, face drained of color. He was—he was *fine!*

In fact, Esme could hardly believe that Sebastian was a marquess. Not this great muscled man, wearing a rough white shirt and sleeves rolled up to show great muscled forearms. No gentleman had muscles like that. Nor thighs, either.

She pulled herself together. What was the point of staring at Sebastian like a lovesick cat? The man would probably roll off the roof in a moment. He wasn't trained for this sort of activity.

"You!" she shouted. Her voice evaporated into the air. He tipped his head back against the chimney, turning his face up to the sun. It turned his neck to honey, kissed his hair with gold . . . that hadn't changed. He was just bigger . . . stronger. There was more of him.

What was he calling himself these days? She couldn't remember. But she could hardly shout "Bonnington!" either. If any of her guests discovered that Marquess Bonnington was snugly living on her estate, they'd dine out on it for days. Her name—and her child's name—would be mud. The thought gave her backbone.

She picked up a rock and threw it at the roof as hard as she could. It skittered across the sandstone. She tried again and managed to get up to the level of the slate roof, but all the rock did was ping gently and fall to the gutter.

"Drat!" Esme muttered, eyeing the ladders that were braced against the house. Of course she couldn't climb a ladder.

At that moment a voice spoke nearly in her ear. "May I be of service, madam?"

Esme jumped into the air. "Slope!" she gasped.

Her butler bowed. "I noticed your progress from the Rose Salon, my lady, and I ventured forth in the hopes of being of service."

Esme's cheeks burned. What was she to say? What the devil was she doing out here, anyway?

But Slope didn't wait for a reply. "Baring!" he bellowed at the roof. "Her ladyship wishes to speak with you. Be quick, man!"

Baring—or Marquess Bonnington, however one wished to think of it—looked down the roof with such a sweet smile that Esme felt her stomach turn over. He pulled on a cap and descended the ladder. Esme watched for a moment as he climbed down, but she found her eyes lingering on muscled thighs, so she turned to Slope.

"I simply wished to ascertain if the gardener—" she began.

But Slope raised a finger. "If you and the marquess were to retire to the rose arbor, my lady, you would be less likely to be seen from the house."

And with that astounding statement, he bowed and retreated.

Esme stood staring after him, mouth open. But here was her gardener, doffing his hat and fingering the brim, for all the world as if he were indeed an outdoorsman, planning to give his account to the lady of the house.

"How dare you climb my roof!" she snapped, turning her back on him and walking toward the rose arbor, which had so many ancient rose trees growing up its latticed sides that it was impossible to see in or out.

"I wish I could take your arm," Sebastian said, his voice so low that she could hardly hear it.

She didn't bother to turn around. It was quite difficult to pick her way down a slope slick with rain. The last thing she wanted to do was slip off her feet; Sebastian would likely strain his back heaving her back up.

"What the devil are you doing up on that roof?" Esme snapped, turning around the moment they entered the arbor.

Sebastian smiled, that easy smile that never failed to make her feel—*greedy.* The very thought made her indignation rise. "You have no right to risk your life on my roof! I want you off my property, Sebastian. Today!"

He strolled toward her. The rain had dampened his shirt and it clung to his shoulders, outlining a swell of muscles.

"What do you have to say to that?" she demanded, feeling her advantage weaken. Damn him for being so beautiful.

"I say," and his voice was as slow and deep as the rest of him, "first I say hello to your babe, *here.*" He walked just before her and cupped his great hand over her belly. "Hello," he whispered, looking straight into her eyes, not at her stomach. As if he could hear, the child stirred under his hand.

Sebastian laughed. "He must be rather cramped in there these days." He dropped to his knees and cupped her stomach with both hands. "Hello!" he said against the cloth of her gown. "Time to greet the world."

He looked up at Esme, and there was such wild joy in his eyes that she shivered all over. Then he stood up, and his hands slid around her body to her back.

"First I say hello to the babe," he said, and his voice was as slow and wicked as molasses, "and then I saw hello to his mother."

There wasn't even a thought in her head of avoiding that kiss. He bent his head and his hands pulled her against him, lips settling to hers as gently as the kiss of the sun. "Oh God, Esme, I've missed you," he groaned against her lips. And when she opened her mouth to reply, he plundered.

His tongue was rough and warm and God help her—a woman with child, a widow, a mature, respectable widow—Esme leaned into his kiss and wound her arm around his neck. He tasted like farmer's bread and he smelled like rain. He didn't move his hands. They stayed, huge and powerful, on her back, making her feel as delicate as a bird. He didn't even twitch a finger toward her breasts, and yet they melted toward him and longed, and other parts of her too . . .

That wave of longing brought her hands from his neck to his shoulders. It was more than longing: it was exquisite relief. He was whole. He hadn't fallen from the roof. The very thought brought her a measure of rationality.

"What were you doing up on the roof?" she said, frowning.

He ignored her. His warm, rough tongue plunged into her mouth, stole her words, brought that melting weakness to her knees. Willy-nilly, she curled her fingers into his hair, returned his kiss fiercely, until—

"You could have broken your neck!" Her voice sounded weak, a thread away from silence.

"No," he said. His hands were starting to roam now. He cupped her stomach again, kissed her so sweetly that tears came to her eyes. "Hello there," he whispered, "mama-to-be."

He scooped her up without even seeming to notice what an elephant she'd become and sat on the wrought-iron bench, holding her on his lap. She could feel his welcome stiffly, right through her pelisse.

It had never seemed to matter to Sebastian that her breasts were now so large that she couldn't wear the delicate gowns in fashion. His hands ranged, not roughly but possessively, over the front of her gown. It was almost embarrassing. Her nipples were so tender these days that he merely drew a thumb across her gown and a low moan hung in the air between them.

He looked at Esme's eyes then. They had lost all the fierceness. They didn't snap at him like a mother lion. He pulled her head against his shoulder, brushed a silky black curl from her ear and whispered, "What's the most beautiful mother in the world doing out in the rain, then?"

Her head popped off his shoulder before he'd had a chance to kiss her ear. "Rescuing you!" she said, and her eyes were snapping fire again. "What in the bloody hell were you doing up on the roof?"

He couldn't help it; a smile curled the corner of his mouth. She wouldn't be so fierce if she didn't care for him.

"Mending the slate," he said, knowing it would drive her mad. But he liked her furious, those gorgeous eyes blazing at him, breasts heaving, focused on *him*.

She jerked her head away from him. But she didn't move to stand up, so he kept his hands exactly where they were. One on her narrow back and the other cupping the swell of her breast. His fingers longed to move, to caress, nay to take her breast and—

He pulled himself back to a state in which it was possible to listen. She was scolding him for being reckless, heedless, brash, daring, inconsiderate . . . His fingers trembled, and so he allowed himself to take her breast more snugly in his hand. He imagined its glorious weight on his chest.

He was imprudent, unwise and altogether foolish. . . .

He was maddened by the desire to push off her pellisse, sweep a hand under her gown and claim her as his. Again. Every time. Those few times she had visited his hut, he'd found that his sense of ownership, of a primitive she-is-*mine* feeling had lasted only an hour or so after she'd left. She'd returned to the house, and he'd stayed in his hut and dreamed of her.

His hand closed on her breast, and his thumb rubbed over her nipple again. The flow of words stopped and there was a tiny gasp. He did it again, and again, and then bent to her mouth. Those lips, so dark, cherry dark, were his. She whimpered and trembled against his chest. He memorized each quiver.

"You are *mine*," he said, and the growl of it surprised him.

She leaned back against his shoulder, silky curls falling over his shirt, her eyes closed. Her breathing grew shallow, and she clutched his shirt as his thumb rubbed again and again with the roughness of desire, with the roughness with which he wanted to plunge between her legs.

But he couldn't. They were in a rose arbor, after all. Slowly he eased her back against his shoulder and let his hand cup her breast, sending a silent apology to the nipple that begged against his palm.

He knew instantly when she returned to herself. It wasn't that she sprang to her feet. It was an imperceptible change in the air, in the very air they were breathing.

"No," she said, and the anguish in her voice struck him in the heart. "I don't *want* this!"

"I know," he said, as soothingly as he could, tracing with one finger the graceful curve of her neck. "I know you don't."

"Obviously, you don't care for my wishes! Otherwise you would have returned to the Continent by now. What if one of my guests decides to take a breath of fresh air?"

"I *do* care for your wishes. You wish to be respectable. You wish to remain a widow. You also"—he dropped a kiss onto the sweet cream of her neck—"you also wish to bed me."

"I can live without the latter."

"I don't know that I can," he said, his mouth glazing her neck. Her perfume was surprisingly innocent for such a worldly lady. She didn't smell like some sort of exotic inhabitant of the East Indies, but like an almond tree in flower.

"I admit that I find you—enticing," she said, and he spared a moment to admire the steadiness of her voice. "But the game is over. Slope, my butler, knows who you are. In fact, he must have known from the moment you applied for a position. While he is unlikely to gossip about the matter, it is a matter of time before one of my house guests finds out your identity. The house is full of people who know you, Sebastian. I'll be ruined. And I can't bear that, not when so much is at stake.

"And I don't want you to fall off my roof either!" she said, her hand gripping his shoulder. "I cannot bear it if something happens to you, Sebastian. Not after Miles. Not after—Don't you understand?" Esme felt as if her breath caught in her chest at even saying it aloud.

Oh, he understood all right. He'd probably have five little marks on his shoulder, one love mark for each of her fingers. The smile that grew on his face came from his heart, and if she didn't recognize that . . . "You want me to leave?" he said, and he had to steady his voice because she might recognize the rough exaltation there.

She nodded fiercely. "No more Baring the Gardener," she said. "You must go."

Much to his regret, he rather agreed with her. It was time to say good-bye to his disguise, much though he loved the simple life. "Do you really, truly wish me to return to the Continent—or, to be specific, France?"

She nodded again. But Sebastian noted the way she swallowed, and he had to bite back another growl of triumph.

"If you truly wish me to go," he said into her hair, "you'll have to grant me a wish."

"A wish?"

Another curl of her perfume caught him, and he had to stop himself from licking her face, simply drinking her. She was so beautiful, in all her silken, sulky anger and fear for him. "One wish." His voice sounded drunken.

"I wish for you to go," Esme said primly. "It is certainly—"

He cut her off. "One night," he said. "I want one night."

Her backbone straightened. *"What?"*

"I'll come to you tonight. I'll come to your bedroom," he said into her ear, and his tongue lingered there for a second. "I'll take you in my arms, and put you on the bed—"

"You certainly will not!"

He smiled into her curls. "Do you truly wish me to leave your property?"

"Immediately!" she snapped.

"Then I demand compensation." He let his hand spread on her breast again, warm and possessive on the curve. He felt the quiver that rolled through her body as acutely as she did. "One night," he said hoarsely, and he couldn't keep all the lust and love from tangling together in his voice. "One night and I'll leave your employ and retire as a gardener."

She was silent, likely worrying about whether they'd be discovered, fretting about her respectability. Only he, whose reputation was absolutely ruined, seemed to understand how very little respectability mattered in life.

His hand trailed over the fabric of her dress, touching the roundness of her thigh. "Oh God, Esme, give me this." But she was holding something back. He could tell.

"Are you sure that you would want to make love to me in this state?" Her eyes met his, direct as ever. "I've grown even more ungainly and—"

He caught her silliness in his mouth. "I want to devour you." That seemed to silence her; her cheeks turned pink. "In fact, you should take a nap this afternoon, because there won't be much sleep tonight. I mean to have you every way I can. I mean to intoxicate you and torment you so that you know precisely how I feel about you." His finger trailed down her cheek and tipped up her chin.

"Don't mistake what is going to happen tonight." His voice was sinful, dark and hoarse. "You will never forget the imprint of my skin after tonight, Esme. Waste your life chitchatting with ladies in lace caps. Raise your child with the help of your precious Sewing Circle. But in the middle of all those lonely nights, you will never, ever, forget the night that lies ahead of us."

Esme's heart was beating so fast that she could hardly speak.

"Tonight." He held her gaze. "And then I'll leave for France because . . . because that's what you want, true?"

At the moment she couldn't quite remember what it was she wanted. Besides the one thing, of course. That *thing* was pressing against her backside as they spoke.

And the Sewing Circle. She mustn't forget the Sewing Circle.

## *The Delights of Poetry*

*T*onight Helene was going to seduce Stephen Fairfax-Lacy, otherwise known as the Puritan, and Bea was perfectly reconciled to that fact. In fact, she was the instigator. She herself had selected an exquisitely desirous bit of verse for Helene to read. Not only that, but she, Helene and Esme had had an uproarious time trying to teach Helene to use a fan and various other flirtatious tricks.

The only reason I feel a bit disconsolate, Bea thought to herself, is that I have no one to play with. If only Arabella had invited sufficient gentlemen to this house party, she wouldn't have had the slightest qualm while assisting Helene to use the stodgy M.P. in order to curdle her husband's liver. If there was a dog in the manger here, it was Bea herself. Because of course *she* would never want Mr. Fairfax-Lacy, not really.

I merely feel, Bea instructed herself, a mild anxiety at the upcoming performance of my protégée. For it was *her* poem Helene was reading and *her* idea to use Mr. Fairfax-Lacy to make Helene's husband jealous. Thus Helene's success or failure reflected on Bea. And why she didn't just keep her mouth shut when she had the impulse to meddle in the lives of perfect strangers, she didn't know.

Lord Winnamore had elected to be the first to read. He was standing before the fireplace, droning on and on from Virgil's Second Eclogue. Whatever that was. Bea didn't care if it had been translated into English by Shakespeare himself; it was as boring as dirt.

"Well, Winnamore," Arabella said briskly, the very moment he fell silent, "that certainly was educational! You've managed to put my niece to sleep."

Esme sat up with a start, trying hard to look as if she hadn't been daydreaming about the way Sebastian would—might— "I'm not asleep," she said brightly. "The eclogue was utterly fascinating."

Arabella snorted. "Tell it to the birds. I was asleep, if no one else was."

But Lord Winnamore just grinned. "Do you good to hear a bit of the classics," he told her mildly.

"Not if they're that dreary. I've no need for them. Am I right in thinking that the whole thing was praise for a dead man?"

When Lord Winnamore nodded, Arabella rolled her eyes. "Cheerful." Then she turned to the company at large. "Let's see, we'll just put that painful experience behind us, shall we? Who wants to go next?"

Esme shot Helene an encouraging look. She was sitting bolt upright on a wing chair, looking desperately uneasy. As Esme watched, Bea handed Helene a small leather book, open in the middle.

Helene turned even paler, if that were possible. She seemed terrified. "Helene!" Esme called across the room. "Would you like to read a poem, or shall we save your performance for tomorrow?" But Esme saw in Helene's eyes terror mixed with something else: a steely, fierce determination.

"I am quite ready," she answered. She stood up and walked over to the fireplace to stand where Lord Winnamore had been. Then she turned and smiled at Stephen Fairfax-Lacy. Esme almost applauded. No one could call that a lascivious smile, but it was certainly cordial.

"I shall read a poem entitled 'The Shepherdess's Complaint,' " she said.

"Lord, not another bloody shepherd!" Arabella muttered.

Lord Winnamore sent her an amused look. "Lady Godwin did say shepherdess, not shepherd."

Helene was starting to feel reckless. It was too late for second thoughts. Fairfax-Lacy would come to her bed, and then she would flaunt—yes, *flaunt*—him in front of Rees.

She threw Stephen another smile, and this one truly was warm. *He* was going to make it happen. What a lovely man!

"Well, do go on," Arabella said rather impatiently. "Let's kill off this shepherdess, shall we? Lord, who ever thought that poetry was so tedious?"

Helene looked again at Stephen Fairfax-Lacy, just to make certain that he realized he was the benefactor of her poetry reading, and began:

> *If it be sin to love a sweet-faced Lad,*
> *Whose amber locks trussed up in golden trammels*
> *Dangle down his lovely cheeks with joy—*

"Trammels?" Arabella interrupted. "Trammels? What the devil is the poet talking about?"

"The man in question has his hair caught up in a net," Winnamore told her. "Trammels were used by fishermen—" Helene cast him a look as well, and he fell silent. She felt rather like a schoolmistress. One kind of look for Stephen, a look that said *Come to my room!* Another kind of look for Lord Winnamore—*Hush in the back, there!* "I shall continue," she announced.

> *When pearl and flower his fair hair enamels*
> *If it be sin to love a lovely Lad,*
> *Oh then sin I, for whom my soul is sad.*

Helene had to grin. This was perfect! She looked down at Bea with thanks, but Bea jerked her head almost imperceptibly at Stephen. Obediently, Helene looked at Stephen again. It was getting easier to smile at the man. And all this talk about *sin* had to make it clear what she had in mind.

> *O would to God (so I might have my fee)*
> *My lips were Honey, and thy mouth a Bee.*
> *Then shouldst thou sucke my sweete and—*
> *    and my—*

Helene stopped. She could feel crimson flooding up her neck. She couldn't read this—this *stuff!*

"That's a bit of all right!" Arabella called. "Lady Godwin, you are showing unexpected depths!"

But Esme was crossing the room and taking the book from Helene, who seemed to be frozen in place. "It's too deep for me," she said, giving Helene a gentle push toward her chair. "I am a respectable widow, after all." She glanced down at Bea and then decided not to ask that minx to read. "I think we have time for only one more poem tonight." It wasn't that she was particularly anxious to retire to her room . . . except that Sebastian might be waiting for her. A lady never kept a gentleman waiting.

"Mr. Fairfax-Lacy," she said, turning to him, "did you find a poem that you liked in my library?"

"I did. And I'd be most pleased to read it," he said, getting up. "Now as it happens, mine is also supposedly written by a shepherd."

"Who would have thought," Arabella said in a jaundiced voice, "that sheepherders were quite so literary?"

Helene's heart was racing with humiliation. How could she have read those words aloud? Why—*why*—hadn't she read the poem before accepting it from Bea? She should have known that any poem Bea chose would be unacceptable. Finally she drew a deep breath and looked up at Stephen.

She met his eyes. They were utterly kind, and she felt imperceptibly better. In fact, he grinned at her.

"I'm afraid that my poem is far less interesting than was Lady Godwin's," he said with a little bow in her direction, "but then, so am I."

That's a compliment! Helene thought. Mr. Fairfax-Lacy had a lovely voice. It was deep and rolled forth, quite as if he were addressing the entire House.

> *Ah beauteous Siren, fair enchanting good,*
> *Sweet silent retoric of persuading eyes . . .*

He paused and looked directly at Helene. She felt an unmistakable pang of triumph. He'd understood her! She stopped listening for a moment and wondered which of her night rails she should wear. It wasn't as if she had any luscious French confections such as Esme presumably wore when she embarked on an affair.

But slowly she was drawn back into listening, if only because Stephen's voice was truly so beautiful. He made each word sound as if it were of marvelous meaning.

> *Such one was I, my beauty was mine own,*
> *No borrowed blush, which bank-rot*
>  *beauties seek,*
> *The newfound shame, a sin to us unknown,*
> *The adulterate beauty of a falsified cheek . . .*

"I'm not sure I like this one any more than the first poem," Arabella said grumpily to Lord Winnamore. "Feel as if I'm being scolded. Falsified cheek indeed! And what's a *bank-rot beauty*? We've none of those in this room."

"It was not so intended at all, Lady Arabella, I assure you," Stephen said, glancing down at Bea to make sure she was listening. She was curled up on a stool like a little cat. He could see a bewitching expanse of breast. Naturally her bodice was the size of his handkerchief.

> *The adulterate beauty of a falsified cheek,*
> *Vile stain to honor and to woman also,*
> *Seeing that time our fading must detect,*
> *Thus with defect to cover our defects.*

"Enough of that!" Arabella said briskly. "Last thing I need is a lecture about what time is doing to my face, and you'll be lucky, Mr. Fairfax-Lacy, if I don't take it amiss that you've even mentioned *fading* in my presence!"

"I'm truly sorry," Stephen said. "Naturally I viewed this poem as utterly inapplicable to anyone in this room." He bowed and kissed Arabella's hand. "I certainly detect no fading in *your* beauty, my lady." He gave her a look of candid repentance, the one he used when his own party was furious because he had voted for the opposition.

"Humph," Arabella said, somewhat mollified.

He'd made his point; he was fairly certain that he saw a gleam of fury in Lady Beatrix's eyes. Now he intended to pursue the more important goal of the evening.

Helene found with a start that Stephen Fairfax-Lacy was drawing her to her feet. "May I show you a volume of poetry that I discovered while searching for a suitable text for this evening?" he said, nodding toward the far end of the room.

Helene rose lightly to her feet. "I'd be most pleased," she said, steadying her voice. She put her fingers on his arm. It was muscled, as large as Rees's. Were all gentlemen so muscled under their fine coats?

They walked across the room until they reached the great arched bookshelves at the far end. Once there, Helene looked up at Stephen inquiringly, but he didn't pull a volume from the shelf.

"It was merely an excuse to speak with you," he said with an engaging smile. "You seemed startled by the content of your poem, and I thought you might like to escape the company for a moment."

Helene felt that traitorous blush washing up her neck again. "Well, who wouldn't be?" she said.

"Lady Beatrix Lennox?" he said, and the note of conspiratorial laughter in his voice eased Helene's humiliation.

"She did give me the poem to read," Helene admitted.

"I thought so." He took her hand in his. "You have lovely fingers, Lady Godwin. Musician's hands."

Her hands looked rather frail in his large ones. Helene quite liked it. She never felt frail.

"And I thought your waltz was truly exquisite." He was stroking her fingers with his thumb. "You have an amazing talent, as I'm sure you know."

Helene's heart melted. No one ever praised her music. Well, she rarely allowed her music to be played in public, so no one had the opportunity. But she melted all the same. "It's rather a daring piece," she murmured, watching his fingers on her hands.

"How so?"

"Because it's a waltz," she explained. He truly didn't seem to understand, so she elaborated. "The waltz is considered unforgivably fast, Mr. Fairfax-Lacy. You do know that it hasn't been introduced to Almack's yet, don't you?"

He shrugged. "I haven't been to Almack's in years, and I count myself lucky."

"Respectable women seldom dance the waltz, and they certainly don't write them."

"I enjoyed it." He was smiling down at her, and she felt a little thrill all the way to her toes. "Was that the very first waltz that you have written?"

"No." She hesitated. "But it is the first to receive a public airing."

"Then the fact that I danced it is truly one of the greatest honors of my life," he said, with another elegant bow.

Mr. Fairfax-Lacy was truly . . . truly all that was admirable. "Would you consider," she asked impulsively, "coming to my chamber tonight?"

He blinked, and for one dreadful moment Helene had an icy sense of error. Horror swept up her spine.

But he was smiling and bowing. "You anticipated my own question," he said, kissing the very tips of her fingers. "May I pay a visit to your chambers later this evening?"

"I'd like that very much," Helene managed. His smile deepened. He really is handsome, she told herself.

"I believe it is time to retire, Lady Godwin. Our hostess appears to be taking her leave."

"Yes, lovely," Helene said breathlessly. So this is how it was done! How simple, really. She invited; he accepted. She almost pranced back across the library on his arm. Esme twinkled at her. Bea kissed her cheek and whispered something Helene couldn't hear. Probably advice. Arabella frowned a little; she had probably only just realized that her scheme to marry Esme to Mr. Fairfax-Lacy was in danger.

Helene felt a surge of triumph. She had just taken the most eligible man in the house and summoned him to her room! She was *not* a frigid, cold woman as her husband had told her.

She had a lover!

## 1 2

## Beds, Baths, and Night Rails

He wasn't in her chamber when Esme opened the door. Of course, she was glad of that. What would her maid think, to find the gardener in her bedchamber? It sounded like a tidbit from a gossip rag: *"A certain lady widow, in the absence of a husband, seems to be relying on her staff."* Tomorrow she'd start her new life as a respectable mother. Of course she wouldn't take lovers once her baby was born—for one thing, she could never risk having another child, since she had no husband.

But she couldn't seem to concentrate on her future respectability. Her whole body was humming, talking of the night to come. She felt almost dizzy. She and Sebastian had never had an *assignation* before. They'd made love once in a drawing room last summer. Then she had visited him in his gardener's hut a few times, but always on the spur of the moment. He had never come to her. Well, how could he?

She had never known beforehand that he would enter her room at night. That she would watch him undress. That he would lean over her bed with that smoldering look of his. Her inner thighs pricked at the thought.

"I feel particularly tired," Esme told her maid, Jeannie. "A bath immediately, please, with apricot oil." Jeannie chattered on about the household while Esme tried to ignore the fact that merely washing her body was making her feel ripe . . . aware. . . .

Suddenly a tiny movement caught her eye. Her windows were hung with long drapes of a rich pale yellow. And under one of them poked the toe of a black boot. Not a gentleman's boot either. A gardener's boot.

A great surge of desire sank right to the tips of Esme's toes. He was watching. Her whole body sung with awareness of those hidden eyes. Jeannie had bundled her hair atop her head to keep it dry; Esme reached up as if to ascertain that no hairpins fell. Her breasts rose from the bath, drops of water sliding over her sleek skin. The curtain moved again, just the faintest twitch.

Esme smothered a grin and lay back against the edge of the bath. "My skin is so dry these days," she said to Jeannie, hoping that the maid didn't notice that her voice seemed deeper. "May I have the oil, please?"

Jeannie poured some into her hand and slowly, very slowly, Esme opened her hand and let the sweet-smelling oil trickle first down her neck, and then down the slick curve of her breast. Jeannie was darting around the room, folding up clothes and talking a constant stream as she did so. Esme spread a hand across the swell of one breast. The oil sank into her moistened skin, turned it satiny smooth. The curtain moved again, and Esme smiled, a smile for him. For the man waiting for her. Those unseen eyes made a simple bath feel scandalous, forbidden . . . made her feel sensuous and erotic. She raised her arms to her hair again, a ballet of tantalization.

The curtains swayed. He *was* watching . . .

"Now, that's odd," Jeannie said, starting toward the windows. "I could have sworn I shut that window, but there must be a draft."

"There's no draft!" Esme croaked.

"I'll just make certain, my lady."

"No!"

Jeannie stopped short of the windows. "My lady?"

"I think that I shall take a longer bath than I expected. Why don't you go downstairs and"—her mind was utterly blank—"help Mrs. Myrtle with something?"

Jeannie looked utterly astonished, but at least she turned away from the windows. "But my lady, Mrs. Myrtle doesn't need my help! She's far too grand to ask *me* to do aught for her!"

That was likely true enough. Esme's housekeeper was a formidable sort of woman. "I would like to be alone," Esme said bluntly.

"Of course, my lady! I'll just return in ten minutes and—"

"No! That is, I shall put myself to bed tonight."

Jeannie's mouth actually fell open. "But my lady, how will you rise from the bath? And if you fall? And—-"

Jeannie had a point, but Esme could hardly say that she had an assistant at hand. "Help me up," she said, reaching out a hand. Jeannie brought her to her feet, and Esme stepped onto the warm rug next to the bath, grabbing the toweling cloth Jeannie held out. The last thing she wanted to do was give Sebastian a good look at the enormous expanse of her belly. He'd probably run for the entrance. Then she waved toward the door in dismissal.

Jeannie was obviously bewildered. "Shall I just return in—"

"I will be quite all right," Esme said firmly. "Good night."

Jeannie knew a command when she heard one. She stood blinking for a second and then curtsied. She ran down the back stairs, utterly confused. She was that distracted that she actually told Mrs. Myrtle what had happened, although in the normal course of things she would never share an intimacy with that dragon of a housekeeper.

Mrs. Myrtle raised her eyebrows. In the old days, of course, such behavior would have meant that the missus had other plans for the evening. But obviously that wasn't the case. "Pregnant women are like that," she advised Jeannie. "Irrational as the day is long. My own sister ate nothing but carrots for an entire week. We all thought she'd turn orange. Never mind, Lady Rawlings will be as right as rain in the morning."

If Jeannie had but known, the very experienced maid, Meddle, who attended Helene, Countess Godwin, was just as bewildered. Her mistress had also ordered a bath. And then she had tried on all four night rails she'd brought with her, seeming to find fault with each. One wasn't ironed correctly, another had a pulled seam . . . Obviously her mistress had an assignation that evening. But with whom?

"It's plain as a pig's snout," Mr. Andrews said, waving his fork about. "She must have an assignation with my gentleman, Lord Winnamore. He's had no success with Lady Withers, and he's decided to cultivate greener fields." Andrews was a boisterous Londoner who had only served Winnamore for a matter of days.

"I do not agree," Mr. Slope said magisterially. As the butler, he never allowed even the mildest discussion of their mistress, but he had been known to lend the benefit of his expertise when it came to the foibles of other gentlepersons. And his expertise was considerable; everyone had to agree to that. After all, as butler to one of the most notorious couples in London for some ten years, he'd seen every sort of depravity the peerage got up to.

Mrs. Myrtle raised an eyebrow. "You're not suggesting Mr. Fairfax-Lacy, my dear Mr. Slope? And do have a bit more of this pickled rarebit. I think Cook has outdone herself."

Mr. Slope chewed and swallowed before replying; his manners were an example to the understaff. "I am indeed suggesting Mr. Fairfax-Lacy."

"My gentleman a partner to adultery? Never!" Mr. Fairfax-Lacy's valet was on the naive and elderly side. Mr. Fairfax-Lacy had rescued him from near destitution, when the poorhouse had been staring him in the very face.

"It would be an act of kindness," Meddle pointed out. "What's poor Lady Godwin to do, then? Her husband left her ten years ago. If the stories be true—it was before my time—he put the missus out on the street. Made her take a common hackney to her mother's house. Didn't even allow her to take the carriage with her when she left! That's evil, that is."

"Ah, if it's an act of kindness you want, then Mr. Fairfax-Lacy is the one to do it," his valet said, leaning back satisfied.

"I think Lord Winnamore is an excellent choice," Andrews said stubbornly. "My master is known the breadth and length of London. And he's rich as well."

"He's known for faithful courtship of Lady Withers," Mr. Slope pointed out. "Now you, Mr. Andrews, have admitted to all of us that you are still green in service." A few of the younger footmen looked blank, so he explained, "Mr. Andrews has not served as a gentleman's gentleman for a great period of time."

"That's so," Andrews said. "Came to the business from tailoring," he explained. "I finished my apprenticeship and found I couldn't stomach the idea of twenty years of sewing. So I found this position."

"When you are further along, you will learn to read the signs. Now Mr. Winnamore . . . where is he at this very moment?"

"Why, he's in bed, I suppose," Andrews said. "In bed with the countess!"

"You undressed him?"

"In a manner of speaking." Andrews had found to his great relief that his master didn't need any personal assistance. He didn't think he was up to pulling down another man's smalls, even for the sake of a steady wage.

"That proves it," Mr. Slope said with satisfaction.

"Why?"

"A gentleman doesn't undress before he visits a lady's chamber. What if he were seen in the corridor? He makes pretense that he is fetching a book from the library or some such." He chuckled. "There have been nights in this house when the library would have been empty of books, if all the stories were true!"

Andrews had to accept that. It sounded like the voice of experience. And Mr. Winnamore certainly hadn't looked as if he were planning an excursion down the hallway when Andrews left him. He'd been reading in bed, the same as he always did.

"Mr. Fairfax-Lacy, eh? He's a Member of Parliament, isn't he?" Andrews said, throwing in the towel.

"That's right," Mr. Slope nodded. "An esteemed one at that. Lady Godwin couldn't have chosen better. I wouldn't mind another bite of that shepherd's pie, Mrs. Myrtle, if you would be so good. Now, perhaps we should all discuss the proper manner of exiting a room during dinner, because I happened to notice this evening that young Liddin barged through that door as if a herd of elephants were after him."

# 13

## In Which Countess Godwin Learns Salutary Lessons about Desire

*H*elene was battling pure terror. If she could have thought of a way to send Mr. Fairfax-Lacy a note without creating a scandal in the household, she would have done so in a second. The note would have said that she had come down with scarlet fever and couldn't possibly entertain callers in her chambers.

She felt like . . . like a bride! Which was incredibly ironic. She remembered distinctly waiting for Rees to walk into their room at the inn. They hadn't even married yet; they'd still been on their way to Gretna Green. But Rees had guessed, correctly, that her papa wouldn't bother to follow them, and so they'd stopped at an inn the very first night.

If only she had had enough character to walk out of that inn the very next morning and return, unmarried, to her father's house. She had waited in that chamber just like any other giddy virgin, her eyes shining. Because she'd been in love—*in love!* What a stupid, wretched concept. When Rees had appeared, it had been immediately clear that he'd been drinking. He'd swayed in the doorway, and then caught himself. And she—fool that she'd been!—had giggled, thinking it was romantic. What was romantic about a drunken man?

Nothing.

The very thought steadied her. Stephen Fairfax-Lacy would no sooner appear in his bride's doorway the worse for liquor than he would appear in Parliament dressed in a nightshirt. Which made her wonder whether he would come to her room in a nightshirt. If she simply pretended that he was no more unexpected than Esme paying her a visit . . .

There was a knock on the door, and Helene almost screamed. Instead she tottered over to the door, opened it, and said rather hoarsely, "Do come in." He was fully dressed, which she found daunting. She was wearing nothing more than a cotton night rail. Helene straightened her back-bone. She had survived marriage with Rees; she could survive *anything*.

He seemed to see nothing amiss, though. With a little flourish, he held up a flagon and two small glasses.

"How thoughtful of you, Mr. Fairfax-Lacy," she said.

He put the glasses on the table and walked over to her. "I think you might call me Stephen?"

His voice had that rich, dark chocolate sound that he must use to mesmerize the House of Commons.

"And may I call you Helene?"

*Helene* on his lips sounded French and almost exotic. She nodded and took a seat by the fireplace. He sat down next to her and poured a lit-tle glass of golden liquor. Helene tried to picture what would happen next. Would he simply disrobe? Should she turn to the wall and allow him some privacy? How was she to take off her night rail? Luckily Mr. Fairfax-Lacy—Stephen—seemed perfectly content to sit in silence.

"I've got no practice with this sort of thing," she finally said, taking a gulp of the liquor. It burned and glowed to the pit of her stomach.

He reached out and took her hand in a comforting sort of way. "There's nothing very arduous to it, Helene. You and your husband have not lived together for years, have you not?"

"Almost nine years," Helene said, feeling that inextricable pang again. It was just that she hated to admit to such a failure.

"You cannot be expected to go to your grave without companion-ship," he said. His thumb was running gently over the back of her hand, and it felt remarkably soothing. "As it happens, I have never met a woman whom I wished to marry. So I am also free to take my pleasure where I may, and I would very much like to take it with you."

Helene could feel a little smile trembling on her lips. "I'm just wor-ried about . . . about . . ." But how did one ask bluntly when he was going to leave? If he spent the night with her and her maid found out, she would die of shame.

"I am perfectly able to prevent conception," he said. He moved his hand, and her fingers slipped between his.

Helene's heart skipped a beat. She wanted a child—desperately, in fact. But not this way. "Thank you, that would be very kind," she said, feeling the ridiculousness of it. Oh for goodness' sake, perhaps they should just get it over with, and then she could begin the process of cur-dling Rees's liver. "Would you like to go to bed now?" she asked.

He stood looking at her for a moment and nodded. "It would be a pleasure, my dear."

Helene crawled into her bed and pulled the covers up. "I shall close my eyes so as to give you some privacy," she said. Surely he would be grateful for that small kindness. After all, there was no reason why they had to behave like wild animals simply because they were embarking on an affair.

A moment later she felt the bed tilt slightly as he got under the covers. She opened her eyes and hastily shut them again. He was leaning over her, and he hadn't any shirt on. "You forgot to snuff the candles," she said in a stifled voice.

"I shall do so immediately," he replied.

Stephen was so different from Rees. His voice was always calm and helpful, ever the gentleman. Would Rees have snuffed the candles on her request? Never. And Rees's chest was all covered with black hair, whereas Stephen's was smooth. Almost—almost feminine, except that was such a disloyal thought that she choked it back.

He returned to bed, and she made herself turn toward him. Thank goodness, the room had fallen into a kind of twilight, lit only by the fireplace off to the side. She took a deep breath. Whatever happened, she was ready.

Except that nothing happened for a few moments.

If the truth be known, Stephen was rather perplexed. Helene clearly wanted to have an affair. But she wasn't exactly welcoming. That's because she's a true English lady, and not a trollop, he told himself, dismissing the image of Bea's creamy breasts that popped up, willy-nilly, to his mind. He had doubts about those breasts anyway. They'd seemed slightly skewed to the left after she'd wriggled herself out of her spencer in the goat pasture.

With a start he realized that he was in quite a different bed and should be thinking very different thoughts. He bent over and kissed Helene. Her lips were cool and not unwelcoming. He slipped his hands around her shoulders. Her husband must have been something of a boor; the poor woman was trembling, and not with passion.

But Stephen was nothing if not patient. He kissed her slowly and delicately, each touch promising that he would be a gentleman, that he would be slow, that she could take her pleasure as she would. And slowly, slowly, Helene stopped trembling. She didn't exactly participate, though. He kept having to push away fugitive thoughts about the way Bea had made little sounds in her throat when he kissed her in the goat pasture.

Twenty minutes later, he judged that they had reached a point at which she wouldn't mind being touched. He ran a hand down her shoulder and edged toward her breasts. Helene gasped and went rigid again.

"May I touch your breast?" he whispered. A small voice in the back of his head was saying quite obstinately that this was all extraordinarily unexciting. The last woman he bedded who'd shown as little initiative as Lady Godwin had been his very first. And she was all of fifteen, as was he. But Lady Godwin—Helene—was clearly trying.

"Of course you may," she whispered.

It was the whisper that did it. The very small trickle of desire that had crept into his veins died on the spot. She was being polite, and she was being brave. Neither emotion did much for Stephen's desire. The desire he had wilted, in all senses of the word. He slid his hand very carefully around her back and pulled her close. She felt rather like a fragile bird, nestled in his arms. Then he rested his chin on her hair and said, "I thought I knew why I was here, but now I'm not sure that I do."

There was silence. Then: "Because we are beginning an affair?"

He couldn't even tell where all that desperation was coming from. From the idea of bedding him? In that case, why on earth was she putting herself through such an ordeal?

He chose his words very carefully. "Generally, when a couple embarks on such a . . . a relationship, it is because they feel a mutual attraction. I certainly think you are a beautiful woman—"

Helene chimed in with the exquisite manners that accompanied everything she said or did. "You are *extremely* handsome as well."

"But do you really wish to sleep with me?" He ran a coaxing hand down her arm.

When she finally spoke, it sounded as if she were near tears. "Of course!"

"I've never been so attractive that a woman felt she *must* bed me," Stephen said teasingly, trying to lighten the atmosphere. It didn't work. He could feel his chest growing damp from her tears. Damn it, the whole day was a fiasco, from beginning to end.

"I should never have done it," Helene said shakily, wiping tears away as fast as she could. "I simply thought . . ." Her voice trailed off.

Stephen was struck by a sudden thought. "Did you think to use me to prove adultery?" That would destroy his career in two seconds flat—a notion that didn't seem to bother him as much as it should.

"No," Helene sobbed. "I would never have used you in such a way. I thought we might—we might enjoy—and then I could tell my husband, and—" Her voice trailed off.

They lay there for a while, a lanky English gentleman and a sniffling countess. "I'm sure my face is quite red," Helene said finally.

Her wry tone told Stephen that she had regained control. Her face was indeed all red, and her hair was starting to fall out of its braid into wisps around her face. For some reason, he found it very sweet that she hadn't even known enough about an assignation with a man to loosen her hair.

"Helene," he said gently, "this isn't going to work."

"Why not?"

He blinked and realized her surprise was genuine. "Because you don't truly wish to make love to me," he pointed out.

Helene could have screamed with vexation. How stupid could the man be! If she didn't want to make love to him, would he be in her room? Would she have humiliated herself by appearing in dishabille before a man? Would she have allowed an unclothed man anywhere in her vicinity? "I do wish to make love to you," she managed.

He reached out and rubbed away a tear. "I don't think you do," he said, and there was a sweet look on his face.

A sweet, condescending look.

A whole flood of naughty words—the words she had been taught not to use, and indeed, had never even used in thought—came to Helene's mind. "That's *rot*," she said. "You're a man. Men *always* want to make love to women under any circumstances. Everyone knows that."

Stephen bit his lip, and Helene had a terrible feeling he was trying to keep back a smile. "They generally like to feel that the lady they are with is willing."

"I am willing!" Helene said, hearing her voice rising. "How much more willing can I be?"

He looked embarrassed now. "Perhaps I'm not phrasing this correctly."

"I'm willing!" Helene said. She reached up and wrenched open the buttons that ran down the front of her night rail. "Go ahead. Do whatever you wish."

For a moment they both just stared at Helene's breasts. They were small in comparison to Esme's, but they had a nice jaunty air to them. At least that's what Helene thought until she forced herself to look at Stephen. He looked absolutely mortified. But Helene was starting to enjoy herself. It seemed that she *was* capable of shocking people!

She wriggled her night rail back over her shoulders so it pooled around her waist. "Now if I remember this whole procedure correctly from my marriage," she said, feeling a slightly hysterical giggle coming, "you should be overcome by lust at this point. At least, my husband always was."

Stephen looked almost goggle-eyed. "He was? I mean, of course he was!"

At this point one obviously laughed or cried. Helene chose to laugh.

There was only so much humiliation a woman could take in one evening. She folded her hands over the top of the sheet and grinned at Stephen, quite as if they were at a tea party. "I suppose we could have an old-fashioned game of 'you show me, I show you,' " she said. "Or we could simply give it up."

His eyes flew to hers, and the relief in them was palpable.

"I gather that I need more practice before I can induce a man to actually *stay* in my bed," Helene said. "I have to tell you, Stephen, that it is quite a personal triumph that I lured you into my bedchamber at all."

He reached over and pulled the sheet up above her breasts, tucking it about her, quite as if he were tucking a child in at night. Then he said, "Now you'll have to explain to me, Helene, exactly why you lured me up here. After all, your husband is not a member of this house party."

Helene swallowed. But he deserved a real explanation. "I want a divorce. But when I asked my husband whether we could simply manufacture the evidence of my adultery, he laughed and said no one in the world would believe that I was adulterous. It has to be a woman's adultery that dissolves a marriage, you know. It's grotesquely unfair, but the letter of the law."

"I agree with you," Stephen said, nodding. "Especially in cases such as yours, there ought to be other provisions. And I'm sure there will be changes to the law, in time. So . . ."

"So I thought perhaps you and I . . . we . . . might . . ." Helene trailed off and then stiffened her backbone. For goodness' sake! She was half naked in bed with the man; she might as well be frank. "I like you very much," she said, looking into his eyes. "I thought perhaps we might have an affair, but I see now that I was mistaken. There's a great deal I don't understand about bedroom matters."

Stephen pulled her snug against his side again. "There's time."

Helene couldn't help grinning. Here she was in bed, half naked, and snuggled up to a naked man! If only Esme could see her now! Or Rees, for that matter! "It was a lowly impulse," she said, feeling more generous now that the acute sense of humiliation was gone. "I just wanted revenge. Rees laughed when I asked him for the divorce. He says I'm frigid, and no man would ever want me." Her tone had a bitterness that she couldn't hide.

Stephen's arm tightened. "That's cruel nonsense," he said firmly. They sat for a moment, Helene tucked against Stephen's shoulder while he thought about beating Rees Godwin into small pieces.

"Are you absolutely certain that it wouldn't work between us?" she asked.

Stephen looked down at her. "Are you trembling with desire because my arm is around you? Are you secretly wishing that I would push down your sheet and take your breast—"

"No! No, I'm not," she said hastily, tucking the sheet more firmly under her arm. "All right. I accept that it won't work between the two of us. It's just such a shame, because you are quite perfect, and I'm not sure I have enough . . . enough bravery to go through this again."

"Ah, but if you truly desired the man in question, it wouldn't take that much bravery."

Helene didn't agree at all, but she bit her tongue.

"It seems to me," Stephen said slowly, "that you're not quite certain that you wish for the affair itself, Helene. You are more interested in the appearance of an affair."

"True. At the heart I'm terribly prudish about marriage. I *am* married. Or perhaps," she added, rather sadly, "I'm just prudish. That's what Rees would say."

"If only your husband could see you now," Stephen said, a mischievous glint in his eye.

"Yes, wouldn't that be wonderful? Because I do like you more every moment."

"The feeling is entirely mutual." He gave her a little squeeze.

"And there's no one else at this party whom I could even consider inviting to my bedchamber," she continued. "There's no hope for it. I shall have to wait until I can return to London, and that won't be for quite a while. I just *wish* that Rees knew where I am, right now!"

"Invite him," Stephen said, a wicked lilt in his voice.

"Invite him? Invite him where?"

"Here. Invite him to the house. We can make certain that he sees you in a compromising situation."

Helene gasped. "With you?"

"Exactly."

She started to giggle. "It would never work."

"I don't see why not. I've never met your husband. But I don't like what you've told me about him. So why not fashion a comeuppance for the man?"

"It would be wonderful," Helene breathed, imagining it. All the revenge without having to go through with the unpleasant bits. Could there be anything better?

"Unless there's a chance he might grow violent," Stephen said, thinking of various nasty stories he'd read over the years about irate husbands.

"Rees wouldn't bother. Truly. He lives with an opera singer, you know."

"I have heard that," Stephen admitted.

Helene clutched his arm. "Would you do it, Stephen, really? Would you do it for me? I would be *so* grateful; I can't even tell you how much."

He looked down at her and laughed, and the joy of it came right from the heart. "Do you know what I do with my days? I try to win votes. I count votes. I bargain for votes. I beg for votes."

"That is very important work."

"It doesn't feel important. *This* feels more important. So, summon the philandering husband!" Stephen said magisterially. "I always wanted to play a part in a romantic comedy. Sheridan, Congreve—here I come!"

Helene broke into laughter and he joined her, two proper, half-clothed members of the English peerage.

## 14

## Because the Library is
## Not Yet Emptied of Books

*B*ea was creeping down the corridor toward the main stairs and library when the laugh rumbled through a door just at her shoulder. She would know that laughter anywhere. There wasn't another man in London with such a lovely, deep voice as Mr. Puritan Fairfax-Lacy himself.

It wasn't that she didn't want Helene and Mr. Fairfax-Lacy to find pleasure in each other. Of course she did. Why, she was instrumental in bringing them together, wasn't she? She headed directly down the stairs, trying to erase all thoughts of what might have brought on the Puritan's delighted peal of laughter. What had Helene done? Did she know as much as Bea did about pleasuring a man? It seemed unlikely.

Probably that was the sort of laughter shared by people who don't know everything, who discover new pleasures together. She couldn't remember laughing while in bed with a man. She mentally revisited the three occasions in question. There had been a good deal of panting and general carrying on . . . but laughter? No.

The thought made her a little sick, so she walked downstairs even faster. Once in the library she wandered around the shelves, holding her candle up high so she could read the titles. But it was no use.

The idea of returning to her cold bed was miserable. The idea of pretending to read one of these foolish books was enough to make a woman deranged. Instead she plunked down on a chilly little settee, drew up her feet under her night rail (a delicious, frothy concoction of Belgian lace that was far more beautiful than warm) and tried to think where things had gone wrong in her life.

The world would have said, without hesitation, that it was the moment when Lady Ditcher walked into a drawing room and was paralyzed with horror to see one of the Duke of Wintersall's daughters prostrate in the arms of a gentleman. Not that her arms were a problem, Bea thought moodily to herself. It was the sight of long white thighs and violet silk stockings. That's what had done the trick for Lady Ditcher.

But the truth was that the trouble started long before. Back when she was fifteen and fell in love with the head footman. Never mind the fact that Ned the Footman must have been thirty. She adored him. Alas, she wasn't very subtle about it. Her entire family knew the truth within a day or so. Finally her father sent the overly handsome footman to one of his distant country estates. He didn't really get angry, though, until he discovered she had been writing Ned the Footman letters, one a day, passionate, long letters . . .

That's where she went wrong. With Ned the Footman.

Because Ned rejected her. She offered herself to him, all budding girlhood and thrilled with love, and he said no. And it wasn't to preserve his position, either. Ned the Footman wasn't interested. She could read it on his face. After her father transferred him to the country, he never answered a single letter. With the wisdom of time, she realized Ned may not have been able to read, but honesty compelled her to admit that he wouldn't have wanted to write back. He thought she was tiresome.

Ever since then, she seemed to be chasing one Ned after another . . . except all the Neds she found were endlessly willing, and therefore endlessly tiresome.

She curled up her toes and rocked back and forth a little. She was certain that she wasn't merely a lusty trollop, as her father characterized her. She truly did want all those things other women wanted: a husband, a baby, two babies, love. . . . Real love, not the kind based on breasts propped up by cotton pads.

You've gone about the wrong way of finding *that* sort of love, she thought sourly. And it was too late now. It wasn't as if she could let her hair down and put away her rouge, and swear to never utter another profanity. She liked being herself; she truly did. It was just . . . it was just that being herself was rather lonely sometimes.

"Oh damn it all," she said out loud, rubbing her nose hard to stop the tears from coming. "Damn it all! And damn Ned too!"

A slight noise made her look up, and there in the doorway was Mr. Laughing Lover himself, looking tall and broad-shouldered and altogether aristocratic. He could never be a footman. Not even Ned had looked at her with that distant disapproval, that sort of well-bred dismay. Of course, the man *was* sated by his midnight excursion. That alone would make him invulnerable to her charms, such as they were.

"Ned?" he said, eyebrow raised. "I gather the gentleman has not joined us but remains in your thoughts?"

"Precisely," she said, putting her chin on her knees and pretending very hard that she didn't mind that he had been with Helene. "And how are you, Mr. Fairfax-Lacy? Unable to sleep?"

"Something of the sort," he said, looking as if butter wouldn't melt in his mouth.

Why on earth was he in the library instead of snuggling beside the skinny body of his mistress? Uncharitable thought, she reminded herself. You're the one with a padded bosom. The reminder made her irritable.

"So why are you in the library?" she asked. "I thought you had other fish to fry."

"A vulgar phrase," he said, wandering forward and turning the wick on the Argand lamp. "In fact, I came to see if I could find the book of poetry *you* gave to Lady Godwin."

"Why, are you having a private reading?" she asked silkily.

The minx was nestled on the settee, little pointed chin resting on her knees. She was curled up like a child, and with her hair down her back, she should have looked like a schoolgirl. It must be the dimple that gave her such a knowing look. That and the way her lips curled up, as if they were inviting kisses.

He walked over to her. "Why on earth did you give Lady Godwin that particular poem to read?"

"Didn't you like it?"

Close up, she didn't look like a child. Her hair was the color of burning coals. It tumbled down her back, looking as delectable and warm as the rest of her. "You've washed your face," he said. Ignoring the danger signals sent by his rational mind, he crouched down before her so their eyes were on the same level. "Look at that," he said mockingly. "I do believe that your eyebrows are as yellow as a daisy."

"Pinkish, actually," she said. "I absolutely loathe them. And in case you're planning to comment on it, my eyelashes are precisely the same color."

"It is rather odd. Why aren't they the same red as your hair?"

She hugged her knees tighter and wrinkled her nose. "Who knows? One of my sisters has red hair, and she has lovely eyelashes. But mine fade into my skin unless I color them."

"They're very long, though." He just stopped himself from touching them.

"And they curl. I should be grateful that I have material to work on.

They look quite acceptable after I blacken them. Naturally, I never allow a man to see me in this condition."

"And what am I?" Stephen said. She was actually far more seductive like this than when she was *being* seductive, if only she knew. She smelled like lemons rather than a thick French perfume. Her lips were a gloriously pale pink, the color of posies in a spring garden.

"I suppose you are a man. But sated men have never interested me."

"What an extraordinarily rude person you are. And how unaccountably vulgar."

"I can't think why it surprises you so much," she said, seemingly unmoved by his criticism. "Surely you must have talked once or twice in your life to a woman who wasn't as respectable as yourself."

"Actually, brothels have never interested me. I have found ready companionship in other places."

Bea shrugged. He wasn't the first to imply that she belonged in such an establishment, although to her mind, that signaled his stupidity. There was a vast difference between taking occasional pleasure in a man's company and doing the same thing for money, and if he couldn't see the difference, he was as stupid as the rest.

"Where did you find that poem, anyway?" he said, getting up and walking toward the bookshelves.

"I brought it with me."

He swung around. "You travel about the country with a collection of libidinous poetry?"

"I have only just discovered Stephen Barnfield, and I like his poetry a great deal. The piece Helene read is by far his most sensuous. And it worked, didn't it? Called you to her side like a barnyard dog!"

"Not just a dog, but a barnyard dog?" he said, wandering back and sitting down next to her. His rational mind told him to stop acting like the said barnyard dog. And every cell in his body was howling to move closer to her.

"If you'd like to read the poetry yourself, I believe Lady Godwin left it on the table."

He grabbed the book and then returned to the settee and sat down again. He didn't want to look at Bea anymore. Her thick gold eyelashes were catching the firelight. "I shall borrow it, if I may," he said, leafing through the pages.

"I was surprised to find that *you* knew Spenser's poetry, for all you chose an unpleasantly vituperative bit to read aloud. You should have known that Lady Arabella would take it amiss if you read aloud poetry criticizing women for growing old."

"I wasn't criticizing age," he said, reaching out despite himself and picking up a lock of her hair. It was silky smooth and wrapped around his finger. "That poetry was directed at you and all your face painting."

"I gathered that." Bea felt as if little tendrils of fire were tugging at her legs, tugging at her arms, telling her to fall into his arms. She lay her head sideways on her knees and looked at him. He had dropped her hair and was reading the book of poetry. Who would have thought he liked poetry? He looked such a perfect English gentleman, with that strong jaw and elegant cheek. Even after (presumably) shaking the sheets with Helene, he was as irreproachably neat and well dressed as ever. Only the fact that he wore no cravat betrayed his earlier activities.

"Where's your cravat?" she asked, cursing her own directness. She didn't want to know the answer, so why ask?

"I've found the poem." His eyebrows rose as he read. "Goodness, Bea, you are a surprising young woman."

"Only in my better moments. So where *is* your cravat?" He'd undoubtedly left it on the floor of Lady Godwin's room, lost as he'd wrenched it from his throat in his urgency to leap into bed with the chaste—or not so chaste—countess. "Did you leave it on Helene's floor?" she asked, jealousy flooding her veins.

"No, I didn't," he said, looking at her over the book. The somber look in his eyes, that disapproval again, told her she was being vulgar.

She threw him a smoldering invitation, just to make him angry. It worked.

"I hate it when you practice on me," he observed, his eyes snapping. "You don't really want me, Bea, so don't make pretenses."

She threw him another look, and if he weren't so stupid, he would know—he would see that it was real. That the shimmer of pure desire racing through her veins was stronger than she'd ever felt.

But he didn't see it, of course. He merely frowned again and then reached into his pocket and pulled out his cravat.

"Oh, there it is," she said, rather foolishly.

"A gentleman is never without a cravat," he said, moving suddenly toward her.

Bea raised her head, thinking he was finally, finally going to kiss her. A moment later he had tied the cravat neatly over her eyes. She felt him draw away and then heard the crackle of pages.

"Let me know when you wish to return to your chambers," he said politely, although any idiot could hear the amusement in his voice. "I think we'll both be more comfortable this way."

For a moment Bea sat in stunned silence. She didn't even move. She still had her arms around her knees. But she couldn't see a thing. Her senses burst into life. His leg was a mere few inches from hers, and her memory painted it exactly, since she couldn't see it: the way his muscles pulled the fine wool of his trousers tight when he sat. The way his shirt tucked into those trousers without the slightest plumpness. Even—and no good woman would have noticed this, obviously—the rounded bulge between his legs that promised pleasure.

Bea wiggled a little. It was worse than when she *could* see him. Sensation prickled along every vein, pooled between her legs. Perhaps if she leaned back against the couch and pretended to stretch? Her night rail was fashioned by Parisian exiles and made of the finest lace. Perhaps it could do what she could not seem to do: seduce him. At least make him feel a portion of the yearning desire she felt.

But she'd tried all of that before. It was a little embarrassing to realize how much she had tried to create a spark of lust in his eyes. She had rubbed against him like a cat, leaned forward and showed her cleavage so often he must worry she had a backache. None of it had created the slightest spark of interest in the man. Only when she'd been rained on and covered with mud had he kissed her.

Bea chewed her lip. Maybe she should just return to her room. Except honesty told her that she would no more leave his presence than she would stop breathing. Not when he might kiss her, when he might change his mind, when he might—

Oh, please let the poem excite him, since I don't seem to be able to, she prayed to any heathen goddess who happened to be listening. Please let it work for me as well as it worked for Helene.

*"If it be sin to love a sweet-faced Boy,"* he read.

His voice was so dark, so chocolate deep that it sent shivers down her spine. The poem certainly worked on *her*. Bea felt him lean toward her. She didn't let herself move.

*"Whose amber locks trussed up in golden trammels, dangle down his lovely cheeks . . ."*

A wild shiver ran down Bea's back as his hand rested on her head.

"Your hair is darker than amber, Lady Beatrix. Your hair is more the color of—"

"Wine?" Bea said with a nervous giggle. She felt utterly unbalanced by her inability to see. She was used to directing the conversation.

"Not rust. Beetroot, perhaps?"

"How very poetic of you. I prefer comparisons to red roses or flame."

"Beetroot has this precise blending of deep red and an almost orange undertone."

"Marvelous. Bea the Beetroot."

"Mellifluous," he agreed. "Of course, it might look less beetlike if you had pearls and flowers entangled in it like the boy in this poem. After all, his amber locks are—let me see if I've got this right—enameled with pearl and flowers."

"Flowers are not in style," Bea said dismissively. "A feather, perhaps. Pearls are so antiquated."

"*If it be sin to love a lovely Lady,*" he read, "*Oh then sin I, for whom my soul is sad.*"

Bea almost couldn't breath. She wanted to drink that voice; she wanted that voice to drink her. She wanted that voice to tell her—"You've changed the poem," she said rather shakily. "The line reads, 'If it be sin to love a lovely lad.' "

"There's no *lad* in my life whom I love," Stephen said. He couldn't not touch her for another moment. He closed the book and put it to the side. She was still curled like a kitten, strangely defenseless without those flashing eyes that seemed to send invitations in every direction. He rather missed them.

Dimly he noticed that his fingers were trembling as they reached toward her. He lifted her head and just rubbed his lips across hers. She sighed—could it be that she wanted his kiss as he longed to give it? Her arms slipped around his neck.

But he didn't like the fact that those magnificent eyes of hers were covered. So what if they sent him a message they'd sent a hundred other men? He pulled the cravat off her head in one swift movement and then, before she could even open her eyes, he cupped that delicate face in his hands and kissed her again, hard this time, demanding a true response: one that she hadn't given another man.

Her lips didn't taste of the worldly smiles that so often sat there. They tasted sweet and wild, and they opened to him with a gasp of pleasure. He invaded her mouth, only meaning to tell her that he felt desire when he wanted to, not when she willed it.

But she tasted like lemons, sweet and tart, and her mouth met his with a gladness that couldn't be feigned. Nor could the shiver in her body when he pulled her against him, nor could the tightness with which she wound her arms around his neck. Oh, she was—she was glorious, every soft, yielding inch of her. He longed to lick her whole body, to see if she tasted as tart and sweet behind her knees, and on her belly, and between her legs . . . aye, there too. Because she would let him: he knew that without a doubt. All the respectable women he'd slept with, wives and widows, none of them had even dreamed of such a thing.

He had never even tried, knowing one can only take such liberties with a courtesan, a woman paid to accept the indignities of sensual activity. But Bea . . . sweet, unmarried Bea . . .

God, what was he doing?

He tore his mouth away and she leaned back toward him, her mouth bee-stung and her eyes closed. He went back for one last taste, just licked her mouth, except she opened to him and then her lips drew his tongue into her mouth. His hands turned to steel on her shoulders, even as his lower body involuntarily jerked toward her. Lust exploded in his loins at the precise moment that rage turned his vision dark.

"Where the devil did you learn that trick?" he said, pulling back.

She opened her eyes, and for a moment Stephen was bewildered: her eyes were so velvety soft, innocent seeming, dazzled looking. She must have looked dazzled for many a man. Even as he watched her eyes focus. But she didn't lose her languorous, desirous look.

"Do this?" she said softly, leaning forward. She almost took him by surprise, but he jerked back.

Bea sighed. Obviously the rake had turned back into a Puritan. She might as well infuriate him since he clearly wasn't planning on further kisses—or anything else, for that matter. "I believe that was Billy Laslett," she said. Now she really wanted to return to her bedchamber. How excruciatingly embarrassing this was. "Lord Laslett now, since his father died a few months ago."

"Laslett taught you that kiss and didn't marry you?" Stephen asked, feeling as if he'd been pole-axed.

"Oh, he asked," Bea said, standing up. Her knees were still weak. "He asked and asked, if that makes you feel any better."

Stephen felt sour and enraged. He stood up and towered over Bea. "At least you remember his name," he said with deliberate crudity.

Bea rolled her eyes. "There haven't been that many, Mr. Fairfax-Lacy. I'm only twenty-three. Ask me again when I'm fifty. But may I say that I am quite impressed with *your* stamina? After all, it's not every man in his forties who could frolick so gaily with a countess and then prepare such an . . . impressive welcome for me." She let her eyes drift to his crotch.

Then she smiled gently at the outrage in his face and walked from the room, leaving Stephen Fairfax-Lacy alone in the library with a libidinous book of poetry.

And an impressive welcome.

# 15

## The Imprint of a Man's Skin

$\mathcal{E}$sme was having second thoughts. Her heart was still pounding from the pure terror of seeing Jeannie move toward the windows. She wrapped the towel tighter around her shoulders. "This is a foolish idea. The babe is due any day now."

"Oh, I know that," he said with some amusement. "I can count as well as any, you know. Last July, when you and I met in Lady Troubridge's drawing room, is almost precisely eight and a half months ago."

"This is Miles's baby," she said, fully aware of just how obstinate she sounded. But it was terribly important to her that Miles have the child he wanted so much.

"Surely it has occurred to you that your certitude that this child is Miles's may be an error? After all, you had not yet reconciled with your husband when you and I enjoyed each other's company."

"Miles and I reconciled the very next night," Esme said hastily. But she knew it was of no use.

"This may well be my babe. Mine and yours. In fact, mathematically speaking, I believe that Miles and I are in a dead heat, given that we each had the pleasure of one night, and one night only."

"It is surely Miles's. He wanted a child so much!"

"Unfortunately, wishes have never influenced paternity in the past."

Esme had to acknowledge the truth of that statement. "Do you remember when I told you about my mother's letter? The one in which she told me that she didn't feel she could attend my confinement?"

"Of course." He began unbuttoning his shirt.

"She added a postscript saying that she hoped I knew who the father was. That was the worst of it. Because I don't *know*. If only we hadn't slept together, I could have written my mother an indignant letter, and perhaps she would have attended my confinement. Perhaps she would be here at this very moment."

"I trust not in this particular room," Sebastian said, pulling her into his arms. He smelled gloriously male and windswept. "I wish your mother felt differently."

His hand was so comforting on her back. It was no wonder that Esme kept blurting out every humiliating secret she had.

"I love you, do you know that?" he said.

She chose her words carefully. "I believe that you *think* you love me, Sebastian. But I know the guilt you feel because of Miles's death as well. There is no need to compensate for what happened, truly."

"Compensation has nothing to do with what I feel for you."

"How could it not?" she asked, looking into his clear blue eyes.

"Because when I fell in love with you, Miles was alive and sporting with his mistress," Sebastian said, watching her just as steadily. "I loved you all the time I was engaged to your friend Gina. I watched you dance; I watched you flirt; I watched you think about an affair with that abominable idiot, Bernie Burdett."

Esme turned away, wrapping her towel tighter around her shoulders. She *would* cry in a moment, and she needed to keep her head.

"Esme," he said.

She sat down heavily in a chair, heedless of the fact that her damp towel was likely to spot the pale silk. "I know you think you love me. But there's lust—and then love. And I don't think you know the difference."

He watched her for a second. She bit back tears. Why couldn't he just see that it was impossible? She couldn't marry the man who had caused her husband's death. The scandal would never die, and she couldn't revisit that scandal on her child.

He walked over and picked her up.

"I must be straining all your gardener's muscles," she whispered, turning her face against his shirt.

"Not you," he said, carrying her to the bed. "I think we've talked enough, Esme mine. The night is long."

She felt the breath catch in her chest. But Sebastian was as methodical in seduction as he was in every other part of his life. He turned down the wicks and poked the fire before he returned to the bed. She watched the long line of his thigh and tried to remember if his legs had been so muscled last summer when he'd been a mere earl. Before he was a gardener. She didn't think so. His legs had been muscled, but not with the swelling sense of power they had now.

"Oh, Sebastian," she said, and the aching desire was there in her voice for anyone to hear.

He strode to the other side of the room to snuff yet another light. Firelight danced on his back. He must have done some work without a shirt because his skin was golden to his waist, and then it turned a dark honey cream over his buttocks. There were two dimples just there . . . Esme found herself moving her legs restlessly, and she almost blushed. He had snuffed the candle and seemed to be inspecting the wick.

Finally he turned around. Esme's mouth went dry. He stood there with just a whisper of a smile on his face. He knew what he did to her. Firelight flickered over his thighs, over large hands, over golden skin, over . . .

And still he smiled, that wicked, slow smile that promised everything.

"Was there something you wished?" he asked, mischief dancing in his eyes.

Esme felt nothing more than liquid invitation between her thighs. How had she survived even a single night without this—without him? How could she survive another moment? "You *are* beautiful," she said, and the hoarseness in her own voice surprised her into silence. He sauntered over toward the bed, looking like Adonis and Jove all rolled into one: golden boy and arrogant king, sensual devil and English aristocrat.

It was no time to worry about what *she* looked like. If a woman is lucky enough to lure such a man into her bedchamber, it would be a true waste to let an enormous expanse of belly get in the way. So she sat up and reached for him. When he stood just before her, she wrapped her legs around his so he couldn't escape.

"I have you trapped," she said, smiling a little.

"And what will you do with me?" he said, and he wasn't smiling at all.

She reached up and ran her fingers over his nipples, felt the tiny tremor that rippled through his body, right down through his legs. Her fingers drifted south, touching muscled ridges, skin kissed by the sun, drifted around his bottom and pulled him even closer. He seemed to be holding his breath, silenced.

Whereas she . . . she felt greedy and loving all at once. She wanted him never to forget her. In fact, had Esme admitted it, the thoughts she was having were hardly generous. Distilled, they ran like this: she couldn't marry him herself, but she could make it very, very hard for him to marry someone else.

And besides, she wanted *him*, every sun-ripened inch of him. There was no better place to start than the hard length of him, straining toward her even as he stood still. She bent forward and he said something, strangled in his throat, drowned by her warm mouth. She pulled him closer, hands on his muscled rump, and he arched, not pushing forward, simply a body exalting in pleasure.

The pleasure she was giving him. A shiver of delight pulsed down Esme's body, and she leaned even closer, torturing him, loving him. He arched his back again and groaned, a deep pulse of need that made Esme's heart pound.

But then he reached down and pushed her back onto the bed. She resisted for a second and then melted under the pressure of his powerful hands. She felt like the merest wisp of a girl, lying back on the bed with Sebastian towering over her. "I can't wait," she said, her voice revealingly hoarse. But there was no room for embarrassment between them.

Powerful hands pulled her to the edge of the bed. He leaned over her, cupping her face in his hands, kissing her until she was senseless, delirious, but not so lost that she didn't feel him there.

Asking.

"You do remember," he said some time later, and now that wicked grin was back, "that I'm a virgin, don't you?"

She couldn't help laughing.

"Not anymore."

Sebastian's voice was an amused, dark whisper against her skin. "Do you remember the night when you took my virginity, Esme?" His hand was on her womb. "This child might well be mine," he said into her hair.

"Or Miles's," she said, but the shrillness of her tone was wearisome even to her. She closed her eyes and leaned back against his shoulder, letting him continue his gentle caress.

"It makes me very happy." She could hear the joy in his voice. "The very thought of the child."

"And what if we married, and the child was Miles's? You would never know."

"I would love him or her as my own," he said. "I would never do otherwise, Esme."

"I know," she said, humbled by the look on his face.

"If you allow me to have a place in this child's life," he said, cupping her belly in his warm hand, "propriety will not be foremost on my mind. I'm not criticizing Miles's wish that you become a respectable woman. But I don't think it's the most important aspect of raising a child either." She couldn't see his face because a lock of hair had fallen over his eyes.

He leaned forward and dropped butterfly kisses on her stomach. "You have to understand that I don't want to imitate my father, for all you wish to imitate your mother. He was quite respectable. I have trouble remembering his first name."

She reached out and pushed the hair back so she could see his eyes.

"You'll be a wonderful mother, Esme."

She bit her lip hard. It was that or cry, and she had firmly resolved not to cry. "I worry," she said, and her voice cracked.

"Nothing to worry about. The child is lucky to have you."

"I couldn't . . . I didn't . . ." The tears were coming anyway. They blinded her.

"Why on earth are you worried, sweetheart?"

"Benjamin," she said, "just my brother Benjamin. You do remember that he died as a baby? I'm afraid. I'm . . . I'm just afraid."

"Of course I remember that you told me of Benjamin." He folded her in his arms then, and rocked her back and forth. "Nothing will happen to your baby. I promise you."

They fell asleep together, she curled in his arms as if he could protect her from all the evils that life could offer. When she woke, hours later, Sebastian was still holding her against his chest. The fire had burned out, and the room had taken on a pearly, luminous light. He was sleeping, lashes thick against his cheeks. His hair gleamed as if it were gilt. All her fear seemed to have been burned away.

"Sebastian," she said, and his eyes opened immediately. They looked black in this light. She licked her lips and tasted salt tears and desire.

"How are you?" His voice was deep with sleep.

It set off a quiver between her thighs. "I don't think that I have the imprint of your body on mine yet," she whispered.

"Oh?" He raised one eyebrow. How had she ever thought he was a priggish Holy Willy? She must have been blind.

"Not at all." She shook her head sadly. "I'm sorry. All your efforts don't seem to have succeeded."

"You'll have to excuse my failures." His voice purred with seductive power. "I *am* practically a virgin." One hand brushed over her nipple, returned, returned again.

A strangled little sigh came from Esme's throat.

"I need practice." His voice was dark, gutteral, possessive. A shiver of ecstasy jolted Esme's spine. "You will have to give me another chance."

She couldn't answer. His lips had replaced his hands, and his hands had drifted lower. He was fierce and possessive, and he left no space for words. All Esme could do was try to stop the broken moans that came from her chest. But she had his smooth skin to put her mouth to, all those muscles to shape with her tongue.

It was around an hour later that he asked her a question. "Did you ever read *Romeo and Juliet*?"

"Well, of course. I only read it once. She was daft to kill herself for the sake of that lovelorn boy, that I remember."

"My hardheaded Esme," he said, dropping a kiss on her nose. "That's the sound of the lark outside your bedchamber window. I must leave soon."

The light filtering in her window was a watery yellow, filtered through spring leaves. Esme didn't want to acknowledge what those greenish ribbons of light meant. "Would you massage my back?" she asked, ignoring the whole exchange.

Sebastian pushed his thumbs into the very base of Esme's spine. She seemed to have forgotten that mornings always come. That she had told him to leave at the very first light. The sun was pouring under the curtains, and her maid would arrive any moment. She moaned like a woman in ecstasy. Her gorgeous hip rose from her waist like a creamy wave.

"My back hurts more than normally this morning," Esme said in a fretful voice. "You don't suppose we did it any injury, do you?"

Sebastian rolled her over on her back and grinned down at the huge mound of belly that reared between them. "Not the slightest," he said, rubbing a little hello to the babe. His babe.

"I suppose you should make your way out of here," Esme said, eyeing him. She had a distinctly jaundiced and irritable air. "Where are you planning to travel, anyway?"

"I've always enjoyed France," he said rather evasively.

If he didn't wish to give her his direction, that was quite all right. "Well, drink some champagne for me," Esme managed.

"Don't you wish to give me a weeping farewell?"

"I'm not up to hysterical farewells at the best of times," Esme snapped. She struggled up on her elbows and then Sebastian helped her to her feet. "You'll have to leave, because Jeannie will appear soon."

Sebastian smiled to himself. Esme was protecting that vulnerability of hers, the heart she hid amidst all her seductions and flirtations. The heart she had never given to anyone—but him, he thought. Although she didn't seem to know it.

He bundled a dressing gown around her and pushed her glorious tumbling locks back over her shoulders. "You're beautiful in the morning," he said, cupping her face in his hands.

"I am not," Esme said, pulling away. "I have a perfectly foul taste in my mouth and my back hurts like the devil. I am *not* in the mood for sentiment, Bonnington, and so I'll thank you to find your way out before the household awakes."

Sebastian obediently pulled on his trousers and shirt as she watched. He was buttoning the last button on his placket when he realized that tears were sliding down her face. "Sweetheart." He pulled her into his arms. "Don't cry."

"I can't help it," Esme said, sobbing. "I know you have to go—you *have to go!*—but I'm so lonely without you. I'm a fool, a weak, silly fool. I'm just . . . I'm just—"

"I love you, Esme," he said, finally. "If you need me, just ask. I'll always come to you."

"I need you to leave! I can't have an earl hiding as a gardener on my estate. Everyone will know in a matter of minutes, and my reputation will be blackened, more than it is already."

He handed her a handkerchief.

"Thank you. And I wouldn't even mind my reputation being ruined," she wailed, "except for the baby. But you know all this, Sebastian, you know it, and I know it, and—and there's nothing to be done. So please, *go*."

He didn't move.

*"Go!"* She looked at him, face shiny with tears, eyes red, a handkerchief balled in her hands, and Sebastian knew that he would never love anyone so much as he loved her.

He leaned forward and kissed her quite simply on the lips. "Goodbye," he said. Then he put his hands over her belly. "And good-bye to you, little one."

"Oh God, I can't bear it!" Esme said, her breath caught on a sob. "You have to leave, or I'll lose my resolve. Please go."

He slipped through the door and looked to the right and left. He'd entered Esme's chamber by means of one of the ladders being used to fix the roof; he had never actually been in the upper reaches of her house before.

Suddenly there was a polite cough, almost at his shoulder. "If I might help you, my lord?"

He swung about to find Esme's butler bowing before him. "Slope, isn't it?" Sebastian asked.

"Just so, my lord."

"I know your mistress trusts you implicitly. I trust her loyalty is not misplaced."

"Absolutely not," Slope replied, with just a tinge of offense in his voice.

"A workman, Rogers, is stealing slate and selling it in the village," Sebastian told him. "You might want to tell the foreman such. And I am leaving Lady Rawlings's employ, so you'll have to find a new gardener."

Slope bowed again. "I am most grateful for the information, my lord. May I direct you toward the side door, under the circumstances?"

"Thank you," Sebastian said, walking into the light of dawn.

# 16

## The Unexpected Pleasure of Your Company

Esme placed compresses on her eyes for a full hour, but it didn't reduce the swelling in her eyes. When Arabella entered her room, she advised a cucumber mask, but that didn't help, either. Esme suspected there wasn't much one could do to plaster over a broken heart. *I sent him away because I had to,* she told herself fiercely. The only problem was that he'd actually left. That was the worst of it: the petty, mean, screaming little voice in the back of her head that kept saying, *He wouldn't have left if he really loved you! If he really—*

And then the tears would well up again, because why should Sebastian be any different from the other men she'd known? Miles never really loved her. Sebastian said he loved her, and perhaps he did. But it felt like a stab in the heart. If he loved her, really loved her, he wouldn't have left, no matter how many times she commanded. Didn't he know how many women died in childbirth? Didn't he care?

The ache in her chest answered that. He did care. He just didn't care as much as she wanted him to care. *You chased away Miles by creating a scandal,* Esme thought dully. *And then you chased away Sebastian in order to avoid a scandal.* But it was all the same, really. If either man had truly loved her, he wouldn't have left. He would have fought for her. But Miles had just smiled politely and slipped away to other pursuits, other bedchambers. . . . Sebastian smiled painfully and slipped away to the Continent to protect her reputation. It was exactly the same situation. Apparently she was the kind of woman whom men found easy to leave.

The tears welled up so fast and furious that Esme felt she would never stop crying. But she did, finally. More cucumber compresses and an hour later, she even thought drearily about going downstairs. The only reason she would consider it was to talk to Helene. She was faintly curious about the outcome of the previous evening.

Any questions were answered when she entered the sitting room. Helene looked happier than Esme had ever seen her, sitting across from Stephen Fairfax-Lacy and playing chess. An utterly suitable game for such an intelligent couple. She herself didn't even know how to play.

"Hello," she said, standing at Helene's shoulder. Stephen immediately jumped to his feet and gave Esme his chair. She sank gratefully into it as Helene waved Stephen away with a smile. He bowed and pressed a kiss into her palm before strolling off. They certainly seemed to have got themselves on intimate terms in a hurry. Well, a shared bed could do that.

"Esme!" Helene said with a huge smile, "would you mind terribly if we invited Rees to make a brief visit?"

Esme blinked. Had she heard correctly? "Rees? Rees, your husband, Rees?"

Helene laughed. "Of course, that Rees."

"Naturally you may invite anyone you wish," Esme said. She looked around a bit sourly. Winnamore and Arabella were practicing a duet on the harpsichord. Bea seemed, rather surprisingly, to be embroidering something. "No one else is taking notice of the fact that I am in confinement, so why should you?"

For her part, Helene suddenly brought Esme's face into focus. For goodness' sake, what was wrong with Esme? She looked utterly haggard and was obviously out of sorts. "I am being utterly thoughtless," she said repentantly. "Of course I won't invite Rees to the house. Esme, what's the matter?"

Esme ground her teeth. Her nerves were on the edge of total distraction. "I didn't say you shouldn't invite him!" she snapped. "Clearly there is a house party occurring, so why not invite one more? At least it would go toward evening out our numbers, and that will make Arabella happy."

Helene hesitated. "I don't know if he will come."

"More to the point, why on earth would you wish him to? I can assure you that these friendships are better conducted away from one's husband." Lord knows, she was an expert on that subject.

"Not in my case," Helene whispered. "Esme, we are going to *flaunt* ourselves in front of Rees!"

"Flaunt yourself?" Esme repeated. Her back felt as if a carriage had driven over it. That was Sebastian's fault. Last night had obviously been far too energetic for a woman in her condition. Perhaps she would be permanently crippled.

"He's agreed to it," Helene whispered.

"Agreed to what?" Esme asked.

"Flaunting!"

"Oh for God's sake," Esme snapped. "What on earth are you talking about?"

"Stephen and I are going to demonstrate to Rees that I am not undesirable and frigid," Helene said. There was a high, startled color in her cheeks, but she looked straight at Esme.

"Rees never said that!" Esme narrowed her eyes. "That reprobate *dared* to say such a thing to you!"

Helene nodded.

"It's a good thing he's not here," Esme said through clenched teeth. "I'd tear him limb from limb. Men are all the same. Lechers and knaves, all of them!"

"You seem to be in a less than excellent humor," Helene said, examining her closely. "Didn't you sleep last night, Esme? You have marked circles under your eyes. How do you feel? Is the baby on the way?"

"No. Once a day the midwife emerges from the kitchen, prods me, and announces that nature must take its course. I'm so tired of that phrase!" Esme put her head on the back of the chair. On the ceiling of the salon, overindulgent-looking gods and goddesses shaped from plaster were eating grapes dangled in the air by cupids. The goddesses were all slim. Very slim. Probably Esme would never be able to shed the extra weight she'd gained.

"What do you think of my plan?" Helene asked.

Esme blinked at her. "Plan? What plan?"

"Esme," Helene said firmly, "you are not yourself. Would you like me to accompany you to your chamber?"

Esme was trying to think about whether that would make her feel worse—indeed, whether *anything* could make her feel worse—when Slope appeared in the doorway.

"My lady," he said, and there was a warning note to his voice that made every head in the room turn. "The Marchioness Bonnington has arrived to pay a brief visit."

Esme straightened up as if she'd heard the last trumpet itself. She clutched Helene's arm. "It can't be!"

Helene obviously sensed danger. "What on earth is Lady Bonnington doing here? Her son is on the Continent. I certainly hope she is not planning to call you to account for his actions last summer! I shall rout her instantly, if that's the case," Helene said, bristling like a mother goose sensing danger.

All the blood was draining from Esme's head, and she felt a curious airiness in her knees. "I'm going to faint," she whispered.

But there was no time to faint. Lady Bonnington herself was standing in the doorway and surveying the room. Esme forced away her dizziness and stood up. "My lady," she said weakly, "what a pleasure to welcome you to Shantill House."

The marchioness was wearing a carriage costume of straw-colored sarsenet lined in white satin. Her gown was trimmed with black and finished with two of the French ruffs that had just come into fashion. She looked formidable and, to Esme's eyes, utterly terrifying.

"The pleasure is mutual," she said, surveying Esme from head to foot through a pair of pince-nez with an air of vigorous and personal condemnation. That seemed to be the extent of her polite conversation. "Lady Rawlings, I daresay you're within a day or so of giving birth. And yet by all appearances you are hosting a house party. How very peculiar."

"That would be my doing," Arabella drawled, drifting over. "And what a surprise to see you here, Honoratia. My goodness, how long it has been since we were in school together. And yet when I see you, the years melt away!"

"I suppose that's a compliment," Lady Bonnington replied acidly. "One can so rarely tell exactly what you mean, Arabella."

"Such a failing," Esme's aunt replied, smiling. "Whereas one always knows precisely what point you wish to make. So kind of you to clarify your every thought. Now why on earth are you here? Not that your presence isn't a remarkable pleasure."

Lady Bonnington humphed and banged her stick for emphasis. "I merely wish to speak to your niece for a moment." She gave Esme a pointed glance. "In private, if you would be so kind."

"Of course," Esme said, leading the way to the door. "If you would accompany me to the library?" She desperately wanted to remove Sebastian's mother from the vicinity of her closest friend and aunt, both of whom looked likely to burst from curiosity. It was just her luck that Arabella had been at school with Lady Bonnington. Be brave, she counseled herself, walking into the library.

"You'd best sit down," Lady Bonnington said, waving her stick at the couch. "Good lord, you look as if you're about to birth a water buffalo."

"One assumes not," Esme managed. What an extraordinarily rude old woman. She sat down without waiting for the marchioness to do so.

"I've come for my son," Lady Bonnington said, lowering herself into a chair.

"Am I to assume that you hope to find him here?" Esme said, with an air of disinterest.

"To my vast regret, yes."

"I am sorry to disappoint you. He is not here. To the best of my knowledge, he is on the Continent."

"I have information to the contrary. He told me himself that he was working in a menial capacity in your household. I don't approve, Lady Rawlings. I cannot approve. You may have led a rather imprudent life before this date, but I assure you that this current escapade will result in complete exile from the *ton*."

"Escapade?" Esme cried. "He took the position without my knowledge. And then he refused to leave!"

"I thought as much," Lady Bonnington said, with an odd tone of satisfaction. "I've been thinking of nothing else for the past few days. It's the blood coming out."

"Indeed? To what blood do you refer, madam?"

"My father's blood. My father was not a man to be crossed. He had a streak of obstinacy that ran a mile wide. I never thought my son had the least touch of him, but I see it now. Of course he won't leave. My father wouldn't have either."

"Be that as it may, your son is no longer in my employ," Esme pointed out.

"He tried to pull the wool over my eyes," Lady Bonnington said. Now her satisfaction was unmistakable. "Gave me fluff and such-and-such about *love*. I didn't raise him to pay attention to that kind of nonsense. Naturally, I paid that no mind. I stayed up half the night wondering whether he'd gone mad as a March hare due to guilt over killing your husband. But it didn't ring true."

She leaned forward, gray eyes as piercing as an eagle sighting a rabbit. "You're carrying his child, aren't you?"

Esme opened her mouth, but nothing came out.

"Aren't you!" the marchioness thundered, stamping her stick for emphasis.

Esme narrowed her eyes. "No, I am not," she said coolly.

"Poppycock," Lady Bonnington replied, and there wasn't even a speck of hesitation in her voice. "My son is no fool. The more I thought about it, the more I knew that he would never have entered the wrong bedchamber. He entered yours because you were carrying on an affair with him. Your husband was likely just paying you a courtesy visit. All the world knows they could have found him in Lady Childe's bedchamber, if they wished."

"I am carrying my husband Miles's child!"

"I've no doubt but that you wish you were. I expect we all wish you had kept that bedchamber door a bit more securely fastened."

Flaming circles crept into Esme's cheeks. "I *beg* your pardon?"

"The important point is that my foolish son has taken the quixotic notion that it's his child about to be born, hasn't he? And he wants to marry you on account of that."

"The child is Miles's, and his birth as a Rawlings is utterly appropriate." Esme's words bristled with rage.

"Think clearly, girl," Lady Bonnington snapped back. "Even if you managed to lure Rawlings into your bed, that child was more than likely fathered by my son. Miles Rawlings was as weak as a cricket; everyone knew that. I expect you know as well as I do that Rawlings's doctor gave him naught more than a few weeks to live. How could he have fathered a child? It takes strong red blood, you know."

"Miles's blood was quite red enough for the task," Esme retorted. "It is unfortunate that Miles died before his son or daughter was born, but this babe will not be the first nor the last posthumous child. May I remind you, Lady Bonnington, that for Miles's child to be born a Bonnington would be just as much an affront to Miles's name?"

"So you admit that the child could be my grandchild," the marchioness said with grim satisfaction.

Esme opened her mouth to reply, but Lady Bonnington thumped her stick.

"In my day, we didn't spend as much time as your generation does worrying about whose bedroom door was open. I'll put my cards on the table. I would greatly dislike my son to marry a woman with your reputation. And I want my son out of the woodshed, or wherever he is, and back in the drawing room where he belongs." She pursed her lips. "Surely I need not articulate my position further?"

Esme felt as if rage were bursting under her skin. "Your son is not here," she said, punctuating each word with deliberation. "I sent him away. This is my husband's child, and under no circumstances would I marry your son. You do realize, don't you, that Marquess Bonnington is responsible for taking my husband's life?"

"You know as well as I do that Rawlings could have popped off at any time."

But Esme could see just the faintest hesitation in her face. "If your son hadn't entered my bedchamber uninvited and grappled with Miles in the dark, my husband might still be alive," she said flatly. "I cannot marry a man under those circumstances. I could *never* make that man into my child's father."

"It always surprises me that the most flamboyant hussies are the most missish at the core," Lady Bonnington observed. The whole encounter didn't seem to have ruffled her sensibilities at all. "Mind you, your own mother is one of the most punctilious women in the *ton*." She stood up, leaning heavily on her stick. "But it's all well and good that you refuse to marry him, no matter your reasons. My only remaining concern is the parentage of that child. Don't underestimate my son, Lady Rawlings. If he feels the child is his, he'll likely take you to Gretna Green without permission or delay. It's my father's blood coming out."

"I won't marry him," Esme said. "Neither in Gretna Green nor in St. Paul's Cathedral. And may I point out again: he *did* leave my estate, Lady Bonnington. He shows rather less resolution than you give him credit for."

"Miss him, do you?" Lady Bonnington asked.

Esme colored. She was hideously observant, this awful old woman. "Not at all!"

"In his absence, I shall remain until the birth and ascertain whether the child is indeed a member of my family," the marchioness said. "If the child is Rawlings's, this whole debacle will be quickly forgotten by all of us."

"How on earth are you going to know that? Newborn children look remarkably similar, you know," Esme said, nettled beyond all patience. "From what I've been told, they're all equally red and wrinkled."

"If he's a Bonnington, he'll have a spangled mark at the base of his spine."

"No!" Esme gasped. Sebastian did have a small brown mark at the base of his spine.

Lady Bonnington gave a little cackle of laughter. "Don't be a fool! My son has a blemish, but it's his alone. What do you think this is, a fairy story? I'll look at the child and see whether it resembles our side of the family or your huband's. And then I will inform my son of my observations. Since you do not wish to marry him, you might hope for red hair. We have *no* redheads in our family."

She stumped to the door and then turned. "You're not the daughter-in-law I would have chosen, as I think I've made clear."

"The feeling is mutual," Esme said with scathing precision. "I would prefer that you put the notion from your mind immediately."

"But you're surprisingly acceptable," the marchioness said, not heeding Esme at all. "Mind you, you're related to Arabella Withers, and she and I have been at loggerheads since we were at school together. And that *was* a donkey's age ago, for all she tries to act as if she's got no more than thirty years to her. You may have the reputation of a coal scuttle, but you seem to have some backbone too."

Esme literally saw red. She dropped into a faint excuse for a curtsy. "If you'll forgive me, I shall retire to my room in order to recover from that compliment. I can occupy myself by praying for red hair."

The corners of Lady Bonnington's mouth curled upwards. "I am rather reminded of myself, as a matter of fact."

And that comment, as Esme later thought to herself, was the cruelest stroke of all.

# 17

## Playing at Billiards

There are certain times in a man's life when the only thing he wants is the company of other men. After a dinner marked by an incomprehensible female subtext and a ballet of barbed comments, Stephen wanted nothing more than an evening of hard drinking, cards, and bawdy jokes. Alas, the sole male in the household other than himself, Winnamore, rambled off to his bed directly after the meal. Still, there were two places in the house likely free from women: Stephen's own bedroom and the billiards room.

But when he pulled open the door to the billiards room, he saw a trim little bottom lean over the woolen cloth covering the table as Beatrix Lennox stretched to make a shot. Stephen decided on the spot that perhaps *one* female was acceptable company.

"Good evening, Mr. Fairfax-Lacy," she said, glancing over her shoulder as the shot caromed one of the red balls off two walls and directly into a pocket.

He paused as if transfixed. The oil lamps suspended above the table turned her hair into a flaming gold. She straightened with exquisite grace and deliberation, as if she were conscious of precisely what that little movement had done to his loins.

"Do you play billiards?" she asked, pulling balls from the corner pockets.

Stephen nodded. Blood seemed to be thundering through his body, every beat speaking to the sultry rhythm of her body.

She pulled the fifteen balls together. "Pyramids?"

He nodded. "Where did you learn to play?" Stephen said, walking over to pick up a cue stick and trying to appear utterly natural.

Bea shrugged. "I found one of the footmen secretly playing on our billiards table when I was no more than twelve. He would have been instantly dismissed had anyone found out. I'm afraid that I coerced him into giving me lessons."

"Do take the first turn," Stephen said, wanting her to bend over again.

She looked at him, and there was a little smile playing around her mouth that made his face burn. Then she slowly, slowly bent over the table. She was wearing an evening dress so slim that it reminded him of a chemise. It was a faint pink that should have looked awful with her hair but didn't. Around it billowed an overdress of transparent washed silk, embroidered with fleur-de-lis. All that transparent cloth emphasized the trim curves of her body every time she moved.

She broke the triangle, and balls scattered in all directions like drops of water falling on a plate. Three caromed into corner pockets.

Stephen looked at the table. "That footman must have been a remarkable player."

"Why do you say so?" she asked.

"Because you are obviously an excellent player," he said, trying to decide which ball to take down.

"The implication is that a woman can only reflect the skill of her teacher. As it happens, Ned was a mediocre player. I could beat him within four months."

"There," Stephen said, indicating the far right pocket.

He bent down and chose a ball. With casual precision he sent the ball on a voyage from one side to the other, into a collision with another ball, and finally into the pocket he designated.

"You would seem to be a much more formidable opponent than my footman," Bea observed.

He straightened. "I apologize for the inference regarding female skill. You are, as a matter of fact, the first female player I have encountered."

She shrugged, and a few of the loose red curls that tumbled down her back fell forward onto her creamy shoulder. "I might point out that it is difficult for women to demonstrate a skill that no one offers to teach them. I'll take that ball." She whipped the ball off another ball and into a corner, sending it directly into its pocket.

*"Le coup sec,"* Stephen said, admiration leaking into his tone. He walked over to stand just next to her. Her French perfume reached him, a promise, a smoky promise of reckless sensuality.

Bea smiled at him over her shoulder, and he wanted to bend her backwards on the table. Push the balls to the side and take her there. Anywhere.

"I thought I'd take that ball," he said, pointing. His voice was a husky question.

She moved slightly to the side and then peered down at the ball. "Were you planning a low stroke?"

He nodded. He had just noticed that for all her calm, there was a pulse beating madly in her throat. In her beautiful creamy throat that he longed to lap, to kiss, to taste. "If I may," he said, and even to his ears, his voice was deeper, slower, lazy. He put a hand to her back and moved her oh so slightly to the side. Then he bent over, just as slowly and deliberately as she had. He could feel her eyes on his body, on his legs.

He straightened. "This is a difficult shot," he said, looking down at her. There was a faint, faint crimson stain in her cheeks that didn't owe its color to art. "I'll remove my jacket, if it wouldn't offend you, Lady Beatrix."

"Bea," she said. "Please call me Bea."

She watched as he wrenched the jacket from his shoulders and rolled up his sleeves. He knew he had a muscled body, a body a woman would admire, even a woman who had presumably enjoyed more than a few male bodies. The only way he could dispel the tension of hours spent in Parliament was to visit Gentleman Jackson's boxing salon. He'd never resorted to deliberately exhibiting it before, but for Bea—

He bent over again, lining up the shot with elaborate care, his hip nearly touching hers. By some miracle his fingers were steady. The shot went into a gentle reverse spin, glanced at another ball, danced by a third, spun sedately into the designated pocket.

"Your turn," he said, straightening.

"Hmmm. You do have skill."

He threw caution to the winds and let a reckless grin spread across his face. "In many areas, Lady Bea."

"Just Bea," she said. But there was a sparkle to her eyes.

She walked away from him, and it took all his strength not to pull her back to his side. "I believe that I shall take . . . that ball." Her lips pursed. It was torture. Would she—How experienced was she? Would she do things that ladies never did? Already she had kissed him like a wanton. Would she—Images danced through his mind, tormenting him.

She was on the opposite side of the table now. She bent down, focusing on her stick, and Stephen could see directly inside her bodice. Her gown was low, and her breasts were cradled against the hard pad lining the table, resting as they might in the palm of his hand.

Stephen made a hoarse sound in his throat, and she glanced up for a moment. Her cheeks were flaming now. But, "I shall try a jenny in the middle pocket," she said.

"You could better your grip," Stephen said, just as she was lengthening her arm to take a shot.

She straightened, and he saw amusement in her eyes. "And I gather you know a better posture?"

"A better grip," he corrected.

She looked at him through her lashes, a smile playing on her lips. "Mr. Fairfax-Lacy, naturally I would be quite pleased to learn a new *grip*. I'm not a woman who chooses ignorance over knowledge. But I must point out to you that you presumably have a busy night before you."

He raised his eyebrows. Something about her, about the way she looked at him, made him feel recklessly gorgeous, decadent, lustful, wild—all the things that a thoughtful man of words never felt. "I would never be too busy for you," he said. "And my name is Stephen."

She perched a rounded hip on the edge of the table. Stephen watched her, feeling another surge of animal lust. He felt *in* his skin, *in* his body, in a way he hadn't since he was a restless, lustful adolescent. He put down his stick deliberately, and then stretched, letting his chest draw the fine linen of his shirt tight against his chest muscles.

Her eyes darkened. "Alas, I would guess that the duties of a man with a brand-new mistress leave no time for lessons."

"I can be the judge of that," he said easily, coming around the table to her. He felt like a tiger, stalking his prey. She stood absolutely still and let him come up to her. So he moved to stand behind her, just as if they were about to make love, as if he were going to bend her over the billiards table. Then he brought her body into the curve of his, tucking her sweet little bottom against his groin, and leaned down.

"If you straightened your right shoulder, your aim would improve." It was quite a triumph that his voice sounded much as usual. He tucked her fingers back against her stick.

But Bea was no tender lamb, to be driven by a tiger. She slowly straightened, and his body moved with her. Then she turned within the circle of his arms, reaching back and bracing herself on the table.

"Mr. Fairfax-Lacy," she said softly, "I assume that's not your pool cue at my backside? What precisely are you playing?"

He didn't look a proper Englishman now. There was an open male swagger about him, a masculine vigor that she had never seen before.

"Seducing you."

"And if I don't choose to be seduced?"

"Don't you?" He bent his head and brushed her lips. "Don't you, Bea? Because I thought you told me that you were—seduceable."

"I don't invite married men into my bed," Bea said gently, but there was steel in her voice.

"But I'm not married!"

She shrugged. "You are Helene's. I do not betray other women."

Stephen picked her up and seated her on the horsehair pad lining the pool table. Her lips were pale cherry again. The color had worn off. As soon as she allowed him, he would run his tongue along her mouth, bite her round lower lip. "As of yet, I belong to no woman," he drawled. Then he lowered his head, finally, finally, burying his mouth against her, raking his lips against her rosy mouth.

For a second she relaxed against him and her mouth opened slightly, just barely yielding to his hunger. And then she pushed him away with all the determination of a pure-as-the-driven-snow duke's daughter.

"Behave yourself!"

"Bea," he said, and the word had all the hunger he felt in it. "Loyalty in matters of marriage is an entirely commendable emotion. But Helene and I have taken no vows. We are merely *friends*." He looked directly at her. Her eyes were a warm brown, with just the faintest tinge of exotic green, just enough to make them tempting beyond all resistance.

"Friends?" There was an edge to her voice. "You offer euphemisms with practiced ease, Mr. Fairfax-Lacy."

"I am a politician," he said with a sardonic grin.

"I thought you didn't care to take mistresses from women with experience. Too much experience," she clarified.

He looked at her, cursing his own stupidity. "That was cruel, and rather shabby," he said, echoing her own comment. "My excuse is that I want you so much that I—"

"I'll take it into consideration," she said, standing up.

Longing spread through him, coursed down his legs and made him tremble from head to foot. Dimly, he wondered what in the hell was happening to him. Why would this woman—this small, impudent, less-than-chaste woman—drive him into a fever of lust?

"We haven't finished our game," he said hoarsely.

She grinned at that, and the way her rosy lips curled sent his heart dancing. She had a way of smiling that made it look as if her whole body was dancing with joy. "There's no need to finish." She nodded toward the table. "You cannot win after my last shot."

He jerked her against his chest and swallowed her laughter, taking her mouth again and again, driving his tongue in a rhythm his whole body longed to repeat. "You," he said hoarsely, "I want you, Bea."

Her eyes slowly opened, and now they had that slumbrous interest he remembered. She melted against him and silenced him with her mouth, with a trembling sweetness, a speaking silence.

"Might I seduce you with poetry? I gather it is a method that you recommend." His voice was dark and slow, and his hands ran down her back with unsteady promise. She looked at him, and her eyes seemed more green than brown now, all exotic beauty and one dimple. But there was something in her face. . . . She had *expected* him to react this way. What he glimpsed now was not an aching lust akin to his but the faintest hint of satisfaction.

Men no doubt wooed Lady Beatrix all the time. Her beauty and her reputation would bring them like moths to a flame. She dressed to please, to attract; she made up her face so that she looked even more exotic—and approachable. She dared them all to come to her, and Stephen had no doubt but that they came.

Yet he sensed that Bea didn't succumb herself. She found pleasure, but not delirium. He wanted to bring her delirium, or nothing. "On second thought, perhaps I won't seduce you after all," he said, dropping his arms from about her and rolling down one sleeve. He watched her through her lashes.

She looked surprised but not particularly heartbroken.

"I shall wait for you to woo *me*. After all, I shall be quite busy in the next few days, as you kindly pointed out."

"I don't woo," Bea said, her small nose in the air.

He leaned back against the billiard table and looked at her. He had never, ever, felt as if his body were so valuable. Deliberately he spread his legs and watched her glance catch for a second and then fly away. "Did you *never* see a man whom you wanted rather desperately?"

"I have been fortunate in that—" and she stopped. Clearly something—or someone—had occurred to her.

He let his eyes glide over her breasts, linger where she was most sensitive. "It will depend, of course, on whether you think that I am worth competing for."

A corner of her mouth turned up wryly. She was no green girl to be brought directly to heel, that was clear. "I shall have to consider the matter," she said gravely. "You see, I am not altogether certain why Helene desired to summon you to her side. You, a sober party official, seem an unusual choice."

"Can you think of nothing?" The question hung in the air between them.

"I suppose there's your voice," she said.

Mentally, Stephen cheered. She liked his voice! He walked over to her, and his words came out in the dark, liquid language he had used to convince reluctant politicians but never a woman before. "I shall have to hope that this voice is potent enough so that you enter the fray."

She stared at him, eyes dark. He tipped up her chin and saw in her eyes the expectation of a kiss. So he bent and kissed her hand instead. "Lady Bea," he said. "I wish you good night."

She was surprised, he could see that. He doubted any man had ever left her company without begging for greater liberties. He hooked his coat with a finger and slung it over his shoulder. Then he walked to the door, feeling his body in an unfamiliar masculine swagger, in a walk so unlike him that he almost laughed.

"Stephen?" Her voice was so soft that it was no more than a whisper in the night air.

But of course he stopped. Whether she knew it or not, she was a siren, and he would follow her anywhere.

"Are you certain you're worth it? Two women vying for your attentions?"

His smile was as proud as a sultan's. "I've no doubt of that, Bea. To my mind, the only real question is—which of you will win me?"

She shrugged. "Not me. I don't woo."

"A pity, that," he said, and turned on his heel to go.

Bea stared at the closed door in blank astonishment. No man since Ned had ever walked away from her. In fact, she saw her role in society as a fairly simple one. She adorned herself; they came.

He was infuriating, if intriguing. But she'd be damned before she would chase a man, she who already had the reputation of a demimonde. That was one thing that was quite clear in her mind. She might have taken lovers—although far fewer than Stephen appeared to believe—but she had never, since Ned, allowed one of those men to believe that she was desperate for their company. Because she never was. She enjoyed male company. That was all.

And if Mr. Fairfax-Lacy wanted some sort of vulgar exhibition of interest, he was bound to be disappointed.

## 18

### In Which Curiosity Runs Rampant

Rees Holland, Earl Godwin, was in a pisser of a mood, as his butler put it belowstairs. "Got some sort of note from his wife, he did," Leke confirmed.

Rosy, the downstairs maid and Leke's niece, gasped. "I saw a pantomime on my last half-day where the husband poisoned a love letter and when his wife kissed it, she died. Maybe the countess saw the pantomime as well and she's poisoned him!"

"He deserves it then," grunted Leke. He found Earl Godwin difficult to work for, and he didn't like the irregularity of the household. On the one hand, his master was an earl, and that was good. On the other hand, the man had a dastardly temper, not to mention the fact that his fancy piece was living in the countess's quarters.

"And there's something to clean up there as well, so you'd better get to it."

"Don't tell me he spilled coffee on all them papers again," Rosy said, scowling. "I'm finding another position if he doesn't pick up those papers. How can I clean with that much muck about my ankles?"

"Don't you touch his papers," Leke said. "It's worth your life. Anyhow, it's not coffee this time. 'Twas a vase of flowers the strumpet was foolish enough to put on his piano."

"It's a wicked temper he has," Rosy said with relish. "How the strumpet puts up with it, I don't know."

*The strumpet* was Alina McKenna, erstwhile opera singer and inamorata of the bad-tempered earl. The term *strumpet* wasn't truly pejorative; both Leke and his niece rather liked Lina, as she called herself. Not that one could truly like a woman of that type, of course. But she wasn't

as hard to work for as a great many more virtuous ladies, and Leke in particular knew that well enough.

He shrugged. "Thank the Lord, the master's taken himself off, at
least."

"Where'd he go?"

"How could I know? Something in response to that letter from his
wife, I've no doubt. Time for you to go about your duties, Rosy, before the
strumpet makes her way home." The only reason Rosy's mum allowed
her to work in such a house of ill repute was due to her uncle's presence.
He took his responsibilities seriously and did his best to arrange her duties so that she rarely encountered one of the inhabitants of the house.

"I'd best go clean the sitting room then," Rosy said. It was a rare moment when the master wasn't in there pounding on one of them three pianos he had. And now there was likely water all over the floor.

A moment later she flew back downstairs, finding her uncle polishing
silver. "I found the note," she said. "The note from his wife. He'd crumpled it up and left it right there, on the piano." She stuck out her hand.

Leke hesitated.

"Go on, Uncle John! You've simply got to read it—you know you do!"

"I oughtn't to."

"Mum will just murder you if you don't," Rosy said with relish. And
that was true enough. Rosy's poor mum, Leke's only sister, was stuck in
the house caring for Rosy's little sisters. She lived for stories about the
goings-on at the earl's house that Leke and Rosy brought from the great
house. That and the discarded gossip papers that the strumpet read and
threw to the side.

Leke pursed his lips to indicate disapproval and then flattened the
piece of paper. "It's from the countess all right," he confirmed. "Looks
like she's staying in Wiltshire somewhere." He peered at the direction.
"Can't really make it out. Perhaps Shambly House? That can't be right."

"Never mind where she is!" Rosy said, dancing with impatience.
"What did she say? Where's he gone to, then?"

" 'Rees,' " Leke read, " 'I've contracted pleurisy. If you wish to see
me alive, please come at your earliest convenience.' "

Rosy gasped. "No!"

Leke was reading it again. "That's what it says, all right. I'm thinking
it's a bit odd—what is pleurisy, anyhow?"

"Likely some awful, awful disease," Rosy said, clasping her hands.
"Oh, the poor countess! I only hope she's not deformed by it."

"You've never met her. Are you crying?"

For Rosy was wiping away tears. "It's just *so* sad! Here she's probably been pining away for her husband, and longing for him to come back to her, and now it's too, too late!"

"Use your head, girl. If you were the earl's wife, would you be pining for him to return?"

Rosy hesitated. "He's very handsome."

Her uncle snorted. "Like a wild boar is handsome, maybe. Face facts, Rosy. You wouldn't like to be married to the man, would you?"

"Well, of course not! He's awfully old, and so messy, too."

"The countess was better off without him. Funny, though, about that pleurisy. Pleurisy. What is pleurisy?"

"Mum would know," Rosy said.

"Neither of us has a half-day for another fortnight," her uncle said dismissively.

"But you could go over this afternoon, Uncle," Rosy pleaded. "You know you could. The master's gone to Wiltshire, to his wife's deathbed!" Her eyes were huge with excitement.

Leke hesitated and looked at the paper.

"That's our own mistress dying. We must needs know why. What if people ask?"

"I don't see what difference it makes. If she dies, the only thing we need are blacks. That is, if the master even sees fit to go into blacks for her death. Mayhap he and the strumpet will carry on just as usual."

"Oh no, they wouldn't!" Rosy clasped her hands again. "Perhaps this will be enough to reform him. He'll—"

"You're dreaming, lass. Now up you go to the sitting room, and I'll see how I do with the polishing. If I can finish this lot, I'll nip over to your mother's."

It wasn't until that evening that Rosy and her uncle met up again. Theirs was a small household, due to a combination of the earl's unconventional habits and the reluctance of decent servants to stay in a house of iniquity. Supper in the servants' dining room was merely Cook, Rosy, Uncle, and three footmen, not one of whom was quite as intelligent as he might have been. The scullery girl and shoeblack ate in the kitchen.

Rosy had filled Cook in on all the details of the afternoon before Leke made his way to the head of the table.

Rosy waited while he said a brief grace, and then burst out, "What is it, Uncle? What is pleurisy? Did Mum know?"

"Your mum is a keen woman," Leke said, taking some roast beef from the plate handed him by James, the third footman. "Tuck your hand under the plate, James. You don't want us to have to stare at your fingers, do you? Put us right off our food, it would."

James curled his fingers under the plate, and Leke nodded at him.

"She did know what pleurisy was, and that's a fact."

"I thought pleurisy was some sort of thing children caught," Cook said. Cook was a sturdy woman with bright red cheeks and a generous smile who had once cooked for the Prince of Wales and never forgot it. She was a genius in the kitchen, or so the prince had said. Earl Godwin had to pay her one hundred guineas a year to keep her in his house.

"That's right," Leke said, nodding. "You're another shrewd one, just like Rosy's mum. It's a disease children catch. In fact, my sister had never heard of an adult with it."

"But the countess isn't a child," Rosy said, perplexed.

"I do know someone who caught measles and it killed him," Cook said. "Mr. Leke, what do you think of this lamb pie?" Frustrated by the complete lack of visitors to the house, Cook had taken to serving up dishes for the staff as if Prinny himself were expected to sit down with them. "Have to keep my hand in, don't I?" or so she justified it. And it wasn't as if the master noticed anything wrong with the household bills. Rich as Croesus, he was.

"I'm liking it," Leke said, chewing with proper gravity. "There's just a touch of allspice, is it?"

"Correct," said the Cook. "I like a man with a knowing mouth, that I do." She beamed at him and then turned to Rosy. "People die in the strangest ways. There's no telling what might happen to a soul. Why, I just heard the other day that a man was riding his horse across the moors, right in the daylight, mind, and . . ."

# 19

## Yours to Woo

It took two days—two whole days—for Esme's heart to form a hard little shell that stopped her from thinking about the marquess. He was gone. That story was finished. True, his mother was still in the house, sparring with Arabella and occasionally flinging an insult at Esme, but her presence was irrelevant. Sebastian was gone, as Miles had gone, and as men always went. She decided to stop thinking about him. Forever. Of course, that didn't stop her from waking at the first light of dawn and brooding. It's a very good thing that Sebastian took himself off to France, Esme told herself, because I was in danger of believing his protestations and vows of love. More fool I. He didn't love me enough to defy me when I told him to leave. He just left. Probably thinking she'd be waiting when he returned from a leisurely exploration of French vineyards.

Why on earth cry for such a man? A potent, useful rage was filling the empty spaces in her heart. It was *his* fault that she was forced to entertain his mother. And it was *his* fault that she was carrying an elephantine child (never mind the irrationality of that). And it was *his* fault that she was husbandless and in the awkward position of not knowing who'd fathered her own child.

All together, her situation was all *his* fault, and the only pity was that he was no longer there so she could blister his ears with the truth of it. And if Sebastian were standing in my bedroom at this very moment, Esme thought, I would tell him that his attempt to imprint himself on my skin didn't work. That the only result of his exertions was an aching back and a desire to never see him again. She set her jaw to stop hot tears from running down her cheeks.

Of course, if his memories of that night were anything like hers, Sebastian might have trouble believing her. The solution would be to flirt madly in front of him. Perhaps do more than flirt. Why should he think—as he clearly did—that she was some sort of light-skirt who would allow him to waltz in and out of her bedchamber at will? Marriage would be the perfect solution. Especially if she married long before he wandered back from France and thought to pick up where he left off.

Perhaps she would marry Fairfax-Lacy, since her aunt had been kind enough to bring him to the house for precisely that purpose. Helene wasn't acting at all loverlike toward Fairfax-Lacy, and Esme had seen enough surreptitious lovers to recognize the signs. Or the lack thereof. So there was nothing—*nothing!*—to prevent her from taking such an eligible husband. Moreover, her mother would appreciate her marriage. Esme suspected that the only way on earth Fanny would receive her in public again would be if Esme remarried a man of the highest character. Sebastian certainly wasn't in that category. Not that she ever considered marrying him.

Fairfax-Lacy had a reputation for high moral fibre. And he was handsome too, in a sort of well-bred fashion. He didn't have Sebastian's raw beauty. But Fairfax-Lacy would make a perfect husband. A perfect, respectable husband whom her mother would *adore*. He would never leave her on the verge of giving birth.

That was the crux of it: Sebastian didn't seem to realize how frightening it was to give birth. He just didn't care enough to be frightened for her. Esme cried over that for a while and then, infuriatingly, found herself crying over her mother's similar lack of concern. Nobody cares, Esme thought savagely, conveniently forgetting Arabella and Helene. Not Sebastian, not Miles, not her own mother.

She didn't make it downstairs for luncheon, having dissolved into a humiliating, childish pit of despair. But by late afternoon, the hard little shell was back in place. Of course she wouldn't die in childbirth. She would be just fine. There was nothing she could do about the fact that Sebastian didn't love her as much as she wished. Better to forget it, push that fact away, not think about it. She rang her bell and asked Jeannie to prepare yet another cucumber poultice for her eyes.

By the time Esme descended the stairs in the evening, she had managed to channel an ocean's worth of rage and grief into one question: was Stephen Fairfax-Lacy indeed appropriate husband material? She didn't think he had Sebastian's ability to overlook her belly. He was unlikely to be attracted to her in her condition. But she could certainly make up her mind whether he was suitable for a life's worth of dinner conversations.

And so it was that Stephen Fairfax-Lacy, who strode into the dining room hoping against all hopes that a certain lady had decided to woo him, found, to his utter surprise, that his hostess appeared to have made that decision instead. And Lady Rawlings, nine months with child or not, was a formidable wooer.

Naturally, she was seated at the head of the table, but she placed him to her right. And Stephen had no sooner seated himself than Lady Rawlings leaned toward him with a very marked kind of attention. There was a sleepy smile in her eyes that would make any man under the age of seventy think of bed—nay, dream of bed. Yet it wasn't until Lady Beatrix Lennox was ushered into a seat across from him that Stephen began enjoying himself. As Bea sat down, Esme—as she'd asked him to call her—was showing him the intricate figures on the back of her fan. And he glimpsed something in Bea's face. Just enough to make him draw closer to Esme and bend his head over her fan.

He was, after all, an old hand at campaigning.

"Romeo and Juliet, are they?" he asked Esme, peering at the little figures painted with exquisite detail on the folds of her fan.

"Exactly. You see"—one of Esme's curls brushed his cheek—"there's Romeo below the balcony, looking up at Juliet. Bea, would you like to see it? The workmanship is quite elegant."

The Marchioness Bonnington was sitting at Stephen's right. "Goodness, what a hen party!" she said briskly. "Why on earth didn't Arabella even out the numbers when she issued her invitations?"

Esme looked up, and her tone evened to a polite disinterest. "I can't say, Lady Bonnington. I believe that Earl Godwin will arrive tomorrow. His presence should ameliorate the situation."

"Humph," Lady Bonnington said. "Least said of that reprobate, the better. So what's on that fan you are regarding so closely, Lady Beatrix?"

Bea blinked down at the fan. "Romeo and Juliet," she murmured. There was something odd happening here. She glanced across the table while pretending to examine the fan. Esme's impending child was hidden beneath the tablecloth, which meant that she looked like any other gloriously beautiful woman in London—except there were very few women who could match Esme. And to all appearances Esme had decided to seduce Stephen Fairfax-Lacy. *Her* Stephen. In fact, Esme presumably had decided to follow her aunt's advice and *marry,* not seduce, Stephen. Of course she wasn't thinking of seduction, given her delicate condition.

The realization gave Bea a most peculiar sinking feeling. Esme's hair was caught up in a loose topknot; fat, silky curls caressed her shoulders and cheeks. She wore a gown of French violet silk cut very low in the bosom and very short in the sleeves. But more importantly, she was burning with a kind of incandescent sensual beauty.

"Romeo and Juliet, did you say?" Lady Bonnington barked.

"The balcony scene," Bea explained, pulling herself together and handing over the fan. She didn't want to woo Stephen. Therefore, it hardly mattered if Esme decided to do so. "I've always thought it was an absurd scene."

"How so?" Stephen asked, one dark eyebrow raised.

Bea blinked, trying to see what it was about the man that drove all the women in his vicinity to hanker after him. He was handsome, but she'd seen better. Somewhere. He was waiting for a reply, so she shrugged. "Romeo stands below, wailing up at Juliet like a pining adolescent."

"That seems a bit harsh. He is in love."

"He only met the woman twenty minutes earlier. But you're right, he thinks he's in love. The funny part, to my mind, is when Juliet suddenly says: do you plan to marry me, and if so, where?"

Esme grinned. "How extraordinary. I read the play, of course, but I never realized that Juliet proposed to him."

" *'If that thy bent of love be honorable,'* " Bea quoted, " *'thy purpose marriage, send me word tomorrow.'* " Juliet bluntly asks him to marry her, although he hasn't said a word on the subject previously."

Esme's eyes flicked to Stephen with a meaningful laughter that made Bea's stomach twist. She was *so* beautiful! It was almost too much to bear. Bea could paint her cheeks the color of the rainbow, but she could never reproduce that flair of raw sensuality that Esme had just tossed in Stephen's direction.

"I saw a hilarious parody of the balcony scene once," Esme was saying, her voice a glorious, husky alto.

"Oh?" Stephen bent toward her, his eyes bold and appreciative.

Naturally, Bea thought. Given the pick of the three women in the house, Helene, herself and Esme, what man wouldn't choose Esme?

"This Juliet almost threw herself off the balcony in her eagerness to join Romeo," Esme remarked. Her eyes seemed to be speaking volumes. Bea considered pleading a sick stomach and leaving the table.

The Marchioness Bonnington had been examining the painted fan; she put it down with a little rap. "That sounds very unlike Shakespeare."

"Do share it with us," Stephen said.

If he got any closer to her shoulder, he could start chewing on her curls, Bea thought. Just like the goat.

"I only remember a line or two," Esme said, and her crimson lips curled into a private smile for Stephen, so seductively potent that Bea felt it like a blow.

"Romeo stands below the balcony, bellowing at Juliet," Esme continued. "And she says 'Who's there?' "

Stephen had just caught a tantalizing glimpse of Bea's eyes. She looked . . . pained. Stricken? That was too strong. He deliberately returned Esme's smoldering gaze with one of his own. "And what does Romeo reply?" He pitched his voice to a deep purr.

Esme flashed a smile around the table. "I do hope this won't embarrass any of you."

"I doubt it," Lady Bonnington said sourly. "After the astonishments of the last month, I consider myself fairly unshockable."

"The scene takes place in the early morning, if you remember. Juliet says, *'Who, Romeo? O, you're an early cock in truth! Who would have thought you to be so rare a stirrer?'* " Esme said it with dulcet satisfaction.

There was a moment of silence and then Stephen roared with laughter. "I'll warrant you Romeo clambered up the vine as fast as he was able!"

"She wouldn't allow him to do so," Esme said. Her eyes were sparkling with mischief, and she had a slim hand on Stephen's arm. "The next line was something like this: *'Nay, by my faith, I'll keep you down, for you knights are very dangerous if once you get above.'* "

Stephen laughed again, and then tilted his head toward Esme and murmured something in her ear. Obviously, it was a comment meant for her alone. Likely something about *getting above*. Bea chewed very precisely and swallowed her beef. Perhaps Arabella would allow her to return to London on the morrow. It wasn't that she was jealous, because she wasn't. It was just that no man could resist Esme, and certainly not Stephen, who had frankly told her that he hoped to marry. Slope was bending down at Esme's shoulder, interrupting her tête-à-tête with Stephen. Bea looked back at her beef. She liked Esme. She really did.

"My lady," Slope said quietly into Esme's ear. "We have an unexpected guest."

"All right," Esme said, only half listening. She'd forgotten how much fun flirting was. She was actually enjoying herself. She hadn't thought about wretched, wretched Sebastian for at least a half hour. Arabella was right. Stephen Fairfax-Lacy was charming, and he had a ready wit. He was fairly handsome. She had almost decided to marry him. Of course, first she had to make certain that Helene didn't want him for herself.

Slope, seeing that the unexpected guest in question had followed him into the dining room, although his mistress hadn't yet noticed, straightened and announced, "The Marquess Bonnington."

Esme's head jerked up. There he was.

No gardener ever wore a pearl gray coat of the finest broadcloth, with an elaborately tied cravat of a pale, icy blue. He looked every inch a nobleman, from the top of his elegantly tousled hair to the tips of his shining Hessians.

There were murmurs all down the table. The scandalous marquess had returned from the Continent! Or from the garden, if only they'd known.

She met his eyes, and there was a flare of amusement in them that made her smoldering rage burst into flame. No doubt he thought to simply return to her bedchamber. Without giving a thought for her reputation, for her child's reputation, for her future.

"Ah, Bonnington," his mother said. "There you are." She sounded as if he'd been to a horse race rather than exiled to the Continent.

But he waited, as polite as ever, for his hostess's acknowledgement. Esme's hands clenched into fists. How *dare* he think he could simply come and go in her house, just as he had walked into her bedchamber at Lady Troubridge's house?

"Lord Bonnington," she said, inclining her head. "How can it be anything other than a pleasure to see you, after so many months." She reached over and put a hand on Stephen Fairfax-Lacy's shoulder. He had broad shoulders. She was almost certain that he would be as good a lover as Sebastian. He certainly would be less exhausting.

Fairfax-Lacy looked up, and Esme smiled down at him brilliantly. "Marquess Bonnington has joined us just at the very moment I was to make an important announcement. May I introduce my fiancé, Mr. Fairfax-Lacy?"

There was a moment of utter silence in the dining room.

Then Sebastian went into a low bow, the kind with a flourish and a good deal of gloved violence. His eyes were pitch black in the candlelight, but Esme wouldn't have been surprised if they'd burned straight through her. "I seem to have arrived just in time for a celebration," he said, and the sardonic note in his voice was clear for all to hear.

Esme swallowed and tightened her hand on her new fiancé's shoulder. She had always been impetuous, but this was without a doubt her wildest moment yet.

"What a delightful surprise!" the Marchioness Bonnington crowed. Obviously, she saw her son's freedom within reach.

"Yes, indeed," Helene chimed in, giving Esme a darkling look that said, clear as day: *I have use for that man, remember?*

Even little Bea seemed shaken, although she said nothing. And to Esme's endless relief, her brand-new fiancé also refrained from expressing his surprise.

## 20

*Twenty Minutes Later... Privacy at Last*

"You needn't really marry me. After all, it's not as if you asked me."
"My thought precisely."
"In fact, no one need even know that we were engaged—"
"We are not engaged!"
"Would you mind terribly if we just *pretended* that we are?"

Stephen Fairfax-Lacy was perplexed. Even after some twenty years of being an eligible bachelor, he seemed to have reached an unexpected peak of desirability. "Lady Rawlings—"

"Oh, please, you *must* call me Esme! After all, we're—"

"Engaged," he put in. He couldn't help smiling a little. "In that case, you must call me Stephen."

"Thank you," Esme said, with evident relief.

"But I insist, Esme, that you tell me *why* we are engaged."

Esme fidgeted and rearranged her fingers. Stephen had seen that look before, many times. It was the look that a Member of Parliament wore who had been courted away by the other party, who had to disclose that he'd already given a crucial vote away.

"Esme?"

"Perhaps you are aware that Marquess Bonnington and I—uh—" She looked agonized, so Stephen came to her rescue.

"Of course, I am aware that you had an unpleasant experience at Lady Troubridge's house party last year, during which your husband unfortunately suffered a spasm and died."

Esme nodded. "You put it remarkably concisely."

Stephen waited. Esme looked at him and then away again. "I was having an affair with him. With the marquess," she clarified.

Stephen thought for a second. "In that case, I believe I understand why the marquess has returned from the Continent. He has just discovered that you are carrying a child?"

"He wishes to compensate for what happened last summer. Marquess Bonnington believes that marrying me will ameliorate his guilt."

"Guilt is an interesting concept," Stephen said. "I wish I could induce guilt in more of the men I deal with on a regular basis."

"But I don't wish to marry a man who seeks to assuage his guilt. And when I saw him, I panicked."

Stephen was beginning to enjoy himself. While he had never begged for any woman's attentions, they had never stood in line and begged for his either. "I gather I appeared to be a useful solution to your problem?" he suggested.

"I'm truly sorry to have used you so. But would you greatly dislike pretending to be my fiancé, merely until Marquess Bonnington returns to the Continent? I'm certain we can arrange it so that no one outside this small party discovers our brief engagement. His mother is, naturally enough, anxious to turn his thoughts in another direction; perhaps she will manage to convince him to leave by tomorrow morning. He need feel no further guilt when he thinks I am marrying such an estimable man as yourself."

"I bow to your greater knowledge of Marquess Bonnington. I must say that I would not have judged him as one to easily give up. I would describe him along the lines of a terrier with a bone."

"I don't want to be that bone," Esme said despairingly. "I know I'm not looking my best, and I'm not a very appealing fiancée under the circumstances, but if you would play a devoted future spouse in front of the marquess, I would be endlessly grateful."

His laughter echoed around the room. Stephen stood up and kissed Esme's hand, and then helped her to her feet. "Since you are my future wife, perhaps I could take the liberty of telling you that you look exhausted. May I escort you upstairs?"

"Oh, thank you!" Esme said, taking his arm. They encountered no one, and Stephen saw his presumed wife into her chamber with an unmistakable sense of relief.

In fact, he actually leaned his head back against the corridor wall, closed his eyes, and wondered if he'd been caught in a dream. It seemed impossible that he—a staid, proper, boring member of the House of Commons—was pretending not only to be carrying on a flagrant affair for the benefit of one woman's husband but also to be passionately in love with another woman, a drama to be played out before her lover.

He heard a rustle of silk. Of course it was Bea. She seemed to be everywhere, with her painted eyebrows and her red mouth. And the rest of her: those far too intelligent eyes, curved little body, and sultry looks.

"Time for bed?" he said, and he let a deliberately suggestive tone slide into his voice like cream.

"Good night, Mr. Fairfax-Lacy." She appeared to be walking toward her chamber. He stretched his leg out so that she would have to step ungracefully across him to continue down the corridor.

"Sir?" she asked. The very tone of her voice had changed. Where was the impudent suggestion? Where were the smoldering looks that she practiced on him so regularly? (Because he knew quite well that she didn't feel desire; she issued such invitations as a matter of course.)

"Will you let me pass, please?" She was getting nettled now.

But Stephen was surrounded by women begging him to *pretend* to be their lover. What he wanted was just one truthful request. And the fact she had refused to woo him for two days bothered him more than it should. "I should like to read more of that poetry you brought with you," he said.

"I can lend you the book, if you wish. Or you can find it yourself. I left it in the library, since it seems to have become an object of curiosity for all." Her eyes were shadowed, and he couldn't read them.

He reached out and slipped his hand under her elbow. God, but he was consumed with lust. Even the sleekness of the bare skin of her arm made him leap to attention.

She shook her head, frowning. "I think not, Mr. Fairfax-Lacy."

"A further introduction to poetry," he said, his voice as persuasive as he could make it.

"I gather you wish me to accompany you to the library?"

He nodded. Not that he had actually thought it out.

"Why?" She stared at him, and for once her eyes were neither sultry, nor inviting, nor even particularly friendly. "You, a newly engaged man, must have many places to be."

"Because," he said, through clenched teeth. "Because of *this*." He folded her into his arms, and his whole body throbbed with gratitude. She smelled like an exotic perfume tonight, some thick heavy flower of the Nile.

He spread his fingers through her hair, cupping the back of her head and pulling it gently back so he could reach her lips. He could see the perfect oval of her cheek in the dim light. He could see the darker glowing red of her lips. Black lashes fringed her eyes. But none of it mattered, because he couldn't see those eyes well enough to read them.

Did she feel even a fraction of the desire that pulsed through his body? Was she almost trembling? Or was this all the fantasy of an aging man, caught off-guard by a young woman's seductive beauty? Believing—

He refused to think too hard. Instead he pulled her head closer to his, closed his mouth on hers, plunging inside. He never kissed like this. He prided himself on consummate expertise, on dancing over a woman's lips, coaxing her to give him her inner sweetness, to reward him with her lips, her mouth. It was all a foretaste of his future treatment of her body. He was a thoughtful lover, cherishing his partner's pleasure as his own.

Not with Bea. His heartbeat pounded with the same rhythm as his tongue. As for technique . . . what technique? It was all he could do to stay upright, to control his hunger.

Yet she melted in his arms with a fervor he had never awoken in a lover before. If he was rudely plundering her mouth, she certainly wasn't fainting at the intrusion. Her arms were around his neck, and she was— she was offering herself. Yet after a second she stepped back in a swish of silk, and he released her. "Where are you going?"

She smiled over her shoulder, and it was the same smile Cleopatra gave Antony. Antony had no hope of escaping; why should he?

"I'm not interested in wooing you, Mr. Fairfax-Lacy, as I think I've made clear. And I might add that my lack of interest is all the greater since you are now engaged to marry."

"I'm—" But he stopped before he said *not*. Instead he smiled at her, an imitation of all those smiles she gave him, a sexy dance in his eyes. "Too much competition?" he asked softly.

Bea paused and turned her nose in the air. "I don't compete."

He leaned back against the wall, and it was happening again: around Bea, and only around her, he felt *in* his body, if only in fragile control of it. He deliberately spread his legs. They felt muscle hard . . . as did other parts of his body. Her eyes widened slightly. In one stride he had her pinned against the opposite wall. God, he loved the fact that she was tall enough for him. So many women felt like fragile little dolls in his arms.

"Bea," he growled, looking down at her.

"Mr. Fairfax-Lacy?" she said pertly. But she didn't try to move away. Not even when he brought his mouth down on hers, without apology, without warning, without pleading. Instead she just gasped and shuddered in his arms as his mouth drank from hers, came to her again and again with savage tenderness.

He kissed her until he knew she couldn't pull away and give him that Cleopatra smile. Gone was the seasoned beauty, wise in the ways of the world and quick with her seductive invitations. If he didn't know better, he'd have said she was a pure innocent. It was in her eyes, in the way she trembled in his arms, in the way she clutched his shoulders.

"I do wish you'd change your mind," he said. His voice didn't come out that siren call of the polished politician. No, it sounded deep, dangerous. The voice of a man who would seduce a young unmarried girl. Who instructed *her* to woo him. The kind of man who had a mistress, and a fiancée, and wanted yet a third woman.

Stephen reveled in it. He ran a slow hand down her side, and then swiftly, before he or she could think better, slid that hand around her sweet little bottom and pulled her hard against his legs. She gasped, and her arms spun tighter around his neck.

For one blissful second he pressed her into the wall, letting her know just how primitive their joining would be.

Then he snapped back and dropped his arms. "Because should you decide to compete," he said, "I think you would find it worth your while."

His smile was wild and tender and utterly unpolished. It was all Bea could do not to gasp yes, plead, beg . . . *woo.* Whatever he wanted. Her body was throbbing, liquid with desire, beating through her legs. Even her toes tingled. He wasn't like the gentlemen she'd toyed with in the past. He was a man. More: he was a dangerous man, the sort of man who didn't think twice about taking on a fiancée and a mistress in the same week. What would she be? The third woman?

She couldn't drag her eyes off him though, off his broad shoulders, and off those wicked, wicked laughing eyes. How had she ever thought he was proper? He was some sort of a satyr! She licked her lips and watched his eyes narrow. If he reached for her again, she would do—whatever it was he wanted. The *wooing* he demanded.

How humiliating. If she did *that,* begged him in so many words, there would be no escape from all the words her father flung at her. No escape in her own mind. They all crowded together: *wanton, short-heeled, soiled, doxy.*

*No.* Bea swallowed hard, pushed herself from the wall, and started down the corridor without a backward glance. She couldn't look back.

## In Which a Marquess
## Pays a Call on a Lady

*A*s Esme prepared for bed, she wondered exactly how much time she had to herself before Sebastian Bonnington joined her. Because he would, not matter how many future husbands she pretended to have.

She didn't have to wait long. She was barely tucked into bed, with Jeannie sent back to the nether regions of the house, when her door opened. Esme was propped up against the pillows, wide awake. She was unable to sleep very much these days; her back and her belly seemed to be competing to make her uncomfortable.

Sure enough, he had that disapproving look that he always used to have, back when she was married to Miles and flirting with Bernie Burdett. Esme frowned. She never liked it when he played the Holy Willy then, and she didn't appreciate it now, either.

"What are you doing in my room?" she demanded.

He walked slowly over to the bed. "Thinking about corporal punishment," he said, staring down at her. "Hell-born brat. I can't leave you alone for two days without finding you've attached a male to your skirts."

Esme held on to her anger. *She* was the angry one. He had left her when she was on the verge of having a child (but he did come back, a little voice reminded her).

"I could have died while you were gone," she said. Her voice sounded petulant and childish. "In childbirth," she qualified.

"I talked to your midwife before I left, and she had no expectations that you would give birth before a week at least," he said, still staring down at her. There was something in his eyes that made her feel uncomfortable. As if she'd disappointed him.

"Midwives don't know everything!" she said shrilly.

He folded his arms across his chest. "I sent my mother to look after you."

"Your mother!" she gasped. "Your mother is here to make certain that I *don't* marry you!"

"I told her I was a gardener here because I knew she wouldn't be able to resist calling on you. I had to visit my estate, Esme. I've done as much work as I could from afar, but I needed to be there, if only for a day." He ran a hand through his hair. "I stayed up two nights so I could return to you as soon as possible. But it seems you had no trouble occupying yourself."

Esme shot him a swift glance. Sure enough, there were weary circles under his eyes. And a bleak note in his voice that clutched her heart.

"I thought you'd left me," she said, pleating the linen sheet with her fingers. "That you—"

"That I'd obeyed you?" he lifted her chin. "Because you did tell me in no uncertain terms that you never wanted to see me again, Esme. That I would ruin your reputation."

"And so you will!" Esme managed.

"Not with my mother here," he said.

There was nothing she could say to that. Of course, he was right. The very presence of the formidable Marchioness Bonnington would stop all gossip about his presence on her estate.

"But I see I didn't need to worry," he said ironically. "It seems you made other plans for the protection of your name."

"I can't marry you, Sebastian," she said in a low voice. "I want respectability. Our marriage would be the greatest scandal to reach the *ton* in years. Your mother said that, and she's right. I don't want to be Infamous Esme anymore. Please understand!"

"I understand all right," he said.

That was definitely disappointment in his voice. Esme swallowed hard. Her back was aching, and he was angry at her. And he was right. She shouldn't have made that pretense of an engagement with Fairfax-Lacy.

Suddenly he pushed her over a few inches and sat down on the bed. "Back hurting?" And at her nod, he said, "Roll over."

Esme rolled to the right, and those big hands started rubbing her neck and shoulders. The relief was so great that she literally forgot everything else for a few moments. Sebastian had miraculous hands. Somehow he was ironing away all the pain that crouched in her spine.

A half hour later she rolled back, propped herself up against the pillow, and eyed Sebastian. He had to leave her bedchamber. Women in confinement did not entertain gentlemen to whom they were not married. But she had to try to explain her own stupidities first.

"I thought to marry Mr. Fairfax-Lacy because—"

He interrupted her. "Are you sure that you remembered to warn poor Mr. Fairfax-Lacy of his impending marriage? Of course, I would never suggest that he looked disagreeably surprised, but he seemed to me . . . disagreeably surprised."

Esme raised her chin. "He was merely startled by my public announcement. We had thought to wait until after the child's birth."

Sebastian didn't seem angry anymore. "I haven't even said hello to that child yet." He spread his hands on the soft cambric of her night rail. "He's all lumps and bumps. I don't think there's any room in there."

"The midwife told me today that he is . . . well, ready," Esme said. She felt a pulse of worry. The child seemed impossibly large to her.

But Sebastian looked up and grinned. "Don't worry. He'll slip out like a greased pig."

"That is *so* vulgar!" Esme scolded.

"Look at this!" he said, disregarding her. "If I push on his little foot, he pushes back!"

They watched for a second and then burst into laughter.

"Oh, no!" Esme said, clapping a hand over her mouth. "My goodness, I hope no one heard that."

"They'll think you're entertaining your future husband," Sebastian said, shrugging a bit. "Although no one here would give a bean who you were entertaining. I have to say, Esme, I've heard about your aunt's house parties for years, but this one takes the cake. Who's that extraordinarily luxurious-looking girl with all the paint on her face?"

"Lady Beatrix Lennox," Esme said, "and don't say anything cruel about her, because I like her hugely."

"The scandalous one? Daughter of the Duke of Wintersall?"

"Exactly."

Sebastian gave a little whistle. "Quite a gathering. You were certainly right when you thought it might endanger your reputation."

"My aunt invited a few of her friends without my knowledge, and one thing led to another. And what about *you*? If anyone finds out you've returned from France and are attending this gathering, the *ton* will dine out on it for days."

"Not with my mother here. And I don't give a hang if they do," Sebastian said, rubbing her tummy all over. "Face it, sweetheart. You're not made for the respectable life. You collect scandals the way other women collect china. I have some trouble envisioning you as a dutiful wife of a party member."

He leaned over, his face just an inch from hers. A dark blonde curl fell over his forehead. She could smell him . . . all that potent, clean-smelling male body.

"What are you doing in my bedroom?" Esme asked, quite annoyed to find that her voice was breathless.

"Paying a respectable visit to my future wife." His eyes were the blue of a mountain lake. Except no mountain lake ever had that smoky look way down deep that made her want to squirm. "Surely you aren't expecting your estimable fiancé to visit your chambers this evening. Since I intend to be your *next* fiancé, I have every right to be here. Besides, I feel a certain discontent with my performance. I must not have imprinted myself on your skin, given that you leaped directly into another man's embrace."

She couldn't squirm because he was hovering over her. "Certainly not," she said, pulling herself together. "Return to your own room, if you would be so kind. I'm sure you did a very good job of—of imprinting yourself on my skin. More than adequate. Now I'd like to ask you to leave."

She put her palms on his chest to push him away. He was warm and big, and somehow her palms just stuck and forgot to shove him off the bed.

He lowered his head and just kissed the top of her ear. "I'd rather stay with you." His lips slid to her mouth. He tasted of cognac and Sebastian.

Just a kiss, Esme told herself as his tongue touched hers. She couldn't help it; her mouth opened with a gasp. He tasted so good, so male, so comforting and intoxicating, all at once. He moved so they were lying side by side.

"We're not going to make love again," she managed to say. "My back hurt all day after you left."

"I'm sorry about that," and he actually sounded sorry. Except he had his hands under her night rail, and that wasn't her back he was stroking.

Esme gave up. Her body melted the moment his fingers slid up her thighs. So she buried her hands in his hair and let herself stroke circles down his neck with her tongue.

He pushed her leg up to give him better access, and she didn't protest, just jerked at his shirt so that he reared back and stripped it off, giving her all that honey-sweet skin to kiss and lick and touch.

They didn't say much for a while, there being no need for speech. Esme was gasping and moaning, and when she absolutely *had* to make a point, her voice came out in a husky mixture of a moan and a squeak. "Sebastian . . . please!"

"We can't," he said. "Your back." His voice sounded strangled, deep and hungry. He repeated what he was doing, and Esme clutched him feverishly.

"I don't care about my back!"

But he knew her, he knew her body, he knew everything . . . she couldn't stop now, not when he was stroking her like that, hands so smooth and rough at once. It took his mouth to stop the scream that tore from her chest.

The shame of it, Esme realized in the early dawn, was that she'd promptly fallen asleep in his arms, having given no thought to his pleasure. When was the last time she'd slept straight through the night, without waking over and over because her back hurt?

His tousled hair was the color of guinea coins. He was lying on his stomach, and the sheet was pulled to his mid-back. All Esme could see was the flare of his shoulders.

The babe seemed to be asleep. Sebastian was definitely asleep. As she watched, he gave a little humph, almost a snore, and lapsed into deep breathing. He'd stayed up at night so that he could come back to her . . . She had to push down the fierce joy she felt. Respectable widows didn't feel this sort of thing.

It was too much temptation for any woman to endure, even a widow bent on the respectable life.

She scooted the linen sheet down onto his legs. His back curved down to a sweet spot with two dimples and that little brown mark that wasn't hereditary, according to his mother. It looked like a small star. She would have leaned down to kiss it, but an awfully large stomach was in the way. So she contented herself with finger kisses, walking her way over all those muscles, circling his dimples, climbing back up that taut pair of buttocks.

He shifted under her fingers and groaned a little in his sleep. Sebastian made her feel more sensual than she ever had in bed with a man. As if her mere touch were enough. Before, it always seemed that men were interested in her breasts, in her legs—in all the parts of her that she'd been born with. Not in the way she touched, or kissed. Not in what she thought they ought to do next.

The very thought had her heart racing. She spread her hand and cupped one of his muscled buttocks.

Suddenly he made a noise in his throat and turned onto his back. Her fingers slid away and ended up on his stomach. He was still sleeping, lashes dark against his cheek. It was almost frightening how much she desired him. A lady shouldn't feel such a dark pounding wave of lust. That was certain.

What she should have done was wake this slumbering god and sent him on his way. Because she needed him to scoop up his terrible mama and leave her house, so that she could have her baby and begin her life again. Despite herself, her fingers trailed downwards. He was magnificent.

When she looked up, he was looking at her. And he didn't seem to be sleepy anymore.

## 22

## The Infernal Circle

When Dante was writing *The Inferno,* making up all those circles of hellish occupants—the gluttons, the adulterers, the . . . the whatevers—he should have included the Sewing Circle. To Esme's mind, they deserved a circle all their own. Admittedly, her memory of *The Inferno* was rather foggy, but weren't the gluttons sitting around eating and eating as punishment for a life of overly rich dining? In Esme's version of hell, overly righteous women would have to sit on small, upright chairs and sew seam after seam in coarse white cotton while Mrs. Cable read improving literature aloud.

They had been sewing for about fifteen minutes when Mrs. Barret-Ducrorq smiled genially at Esme and said, "That child of yours won't want to wait much longer."

Esme looked down at her vast expanse of stomach, suppressing a wince as a foot made its presence known just under her ribs. "The midwife has suggested that it's only a matter of a few days."

"They don't know everything," Lady Winifred said comfortably, putting down her sheet.

Esme had noticed that everyone except Mrs. Cable took every opportunity to stop sewing.

"The midwife for my first child told me every day for a month that today was the day," Lady Winifred continued. "Consequently I refused to actually believe that I was in labor when the time came. Is Lady Withers going to join us today, my dear? Arabella is such an amusing woman. And so brave. I know the loss of three husbands has been a true source of grief in her life, but she never seems disheartened."

Mrs. Cable said, very frostily, "I doubt that Lady Withers has risen at this hour."

But Arabella pranced through the door at that very moment, blowing kisses in every direction. "Ladies!" she announced. "I come to you on an errand of mercy."

Arabella took a few moments to seat herself. She was wearing a morning dress of celestial blue muslin, which opened down the front and pulled back to reveal an underskirt of sprigged muslin. She looked charming, effortlessly elegant and, to Esme's eyes, unmistakably mischievous.

"Surely you heard who arrived at this house last evening!" she announced, once she had arranged her gown to her satisfaction.

Even Mrs. Cable looked up from her seam.

"The most disreputable man in all England!" Arabella trumpeted.

Esme groaned inwardly.

"The Duke of York!" Lady Henrietta exclaimed.

"No, no, slightly lower in rank," Arabella said, obviously enjoying herself hugely. "It seems quite overheated in the morning room, Esme my dear. Perhaps that fire is too high for the season." She took out a small blue fan and began fanning herself.

"I'm having trouble keeping myself on the cool side as well," Lady Winifred said, eyeing the fan. "We've entered that time of life, I suppose."

Arabella dropped the fan as if it had bitten her.

"Who is it?" Mrs. Barret-Ducrorq said eagerly. "Who arrived last night?"

"Bonnington," Arabella said after a magnificent pause, "has returned."

It was a good line. And if it weren't for the fact that Esme's own life was being paraded before the gossips, she would have applauded Arabella's dramatic turn of phrase.

There was a collective intake of breath. Lady Winifred was obviously amused; Mrs. Barret-Ducrorq was shocked; Mrs. Cable was so horrified that she covered her face with her hands, as if she'd been faced with the devil himself.

"He's reformed," Arabella dropped into the silence that followed.

"I doubt that very much!" snapped Mrs. Cable, seemingly unable to contain herself.

"Astounding, yet true." Arabella picked up her fan again and glanced significantly at the ladies. "He's come back to England to prostrate himself at my niece's feet!"

"As well he might," Mrs. Barret-Ducrorq said rather sourly. "After all, he did . . ." But her voice trailed off when she realized that mentioning the fact that Esme's husband had died grappling with her latest guest wasn't entirely well mannered.

Esme looked down at her sheet and very precisely put another crooked stitch into the hem. That foot was still in her ribs. Oddly enough, she didn't feel the pinched sensation that she usually got at the very mention of Miles. Poor Miles. She placed another stitch. Dear Miles.

"Prrrrostrate himself," Arabella said with pleasure. "As you say, Mrs. Barret-Ducrorq, Bonnington is at least partially responsible for the death of poor Lord Rawlings. Although his doctors had said that Esme's late husband was liable to die at any moment. I lost a husband to a weak heart myself; it's a terrible circumstance. At any rate, Marquess Bonnington is overcome with contrition. Quite beside himself."

Everyone looked at Esme, so she tried to look like a grieving widow. Far be it from her to diminish Arabella's performance. Why was it that whenever she was supposed to look miserable, she felt cheerful? "The marquess has certainly expressed his repentance," she agreed, placing another stitch so as to avoid Mrs. Cable's piercing glance. Really, sewing had its uses.

"How can Bonnington possibly think to alleviate Lady Rawlings's situation?" Mrs. Cable demanded. "What's done is done. The man should stay on the Continent, where he is less likely to corrupt others."

"Unless he's asked for her hand in marriage?" Lady Winifred said, giving Esme a shrewd look.

"A revolting proposition," Mrs. Cable said tightly. "Lady Rawlings is not even out of a full year of mourning! Only think of the scandal!"

"Oh, one can always think of the scandal," Lady Winifred said. "But it's so seldom worth the effort. The marquess, after all, has a very fine estate."

"My thought precisely," Arabella said, beaming. "I do believe the man is genuinely overcome by penitence. He wishes to mitigate the evils he visited on her in any way possible."

"What makes you believe that his intentions are honorable?" Mrs. Cable wanted to know. "After his behavior last summer!"

Esme felt a pang of guilt. She was hardly innocent when it came to the loss of Sebastian's sterling reputation, since he had fabricated a story of depravity in order to protect her reputation. "His mother accompanied him to this house, which seems to bode well for his sincerity," she noted. "The Marchioness Bonnington is also staying with us."

"My goodness!" Lady Winifred exclaimed. "If Bonnington persuaded his mother to accompany him, the man must indeed be serious. Lady Bonnington is as stiff-rumped a lady as I've ever met!"

"I sincerely hope that you informed him that marriage was impossible," Mrs. Cable told Esme.

Esme suddenly remembered her supposed engagement to Fairfax-

Lacy. There was more than one reason why marriage to Sebastian was impossible. Rather than answer, she started sewing again.

"After all, the man forged a marriage certificate in order to take a lady's chastity!" Mrs. Cable continued. "The poor Duchess of Girton might well have been taken in by his depravity, if it hadn't been for the happenstance of his stumbling into your bedchamber rather than hers. And that's not to mention his hand in your husband's death."

Arabella leaned forward. From the look of pure pleasure in her eyes, Esme could see her aunt had prepared herself for just this moment.

"A woman of mercy does not spurn a geninely remorseful soul," Arabella intoned. "By doing so, *she* would be responsible for any lapses in judgement that followed. No, Esme's path is clear. She must aid and succor the poor unfortunate sinner in his moment of contrition."

"The devil is full of all subtlety and all mischief," Mrs. Cable snapped. "Acts."

"By mercy and truth, iniquity is purged," Arabella retorted, without even pausing for breath. "Proverbs."

Esme bit her lip so she wouldn't ruin the moment by laughing. Mrs. Cable was flattened, trapped between the Bible and her abhorrence of iniquitous behavior.

Lady Winifred jumped in at this point. "I quite agree with you, Arabella dearest. It takes a truly charitable heart to recognize where the path of goodness lies."

Arabella was obviously trying to look as if she had a charitable heart. To Esme, it looked as if she had wind.

"I don't support it," Mrs. Cable snapped. "The man is a poisonous influence. You'll have to watch the young women in the house very carefully, Lady Rawlings. He may besmirch them, corrupt them, deprave them!"

No, Esme thought ruefully, he's only interested in besmirching me. Although she wouldn't argue with the idea that Sebastian was depraved. He had *no* sense of propriety in bed. Esme's cheeks grew hot at the very thought of the liberties he had taken the previous night. She wrenched her attention back to Mrs. Cable.

"A man like that is more than likely to seduce the maids," she was saying. "There'll be no woman in the house safe from him."

Too tired, Esme thought. He's definitely too tired for the maids.

Arabella giggled. "It's a pity I'm too old for the man."

Mrs. Cable gasped, but Lady Winifred chuckled. "Handsome, isn't he? I remember seeing Bonnington riding to the hounds, last year it was, before all the scandal broke. He looked as regal as a prince. A prince in a fairy story," she clarified, "not one of our own." Everyone accepted that. The royal dukes were more easily described as fat and friendly than regal.

With pressed lips, Mrs. Cable backed down. "Well, you won't accept Bonnington's proposal, of course," she instructed Esme. "But I do acknowledge Lady Withers's point about improving his soul. It is not ours to question why the Lord places a sinner at our doorstep. We must simply endure while we aid in the cultivation of a better life."

"I must try saying that to my husband," Lady Winifred murmured to Arabella. "I endure, and he never seems to cultivate. Perhaps I could bore him into virtue by reading the Bible aloud."

But Mrs. Cable heard her, and the Sewing Circle disbanded on an acrimonious note.

## 23

### *Various Forms of Advertisement*

*Lady Rawlings's Rose Salon*

"*I* suppose your mother felt she couldn't attend you," Lady Bonnington said to Esme with her usual lack of finesse. "Fanny does have strict notions of propriety."

"My dear sister is very preoccupied by the fate of the poor," Arabella said, with a little snap of her teeth. "She cannot be in as many places as she would wish."

"She wrote me as much," Esme put in. Though why on earth she always defended her mother, she didn't know.

The marchioness's expression showed exactly what she thought about Arabella's fib. "Yet during the confinement of her only daughter!" Lady Bonnington said. "Quite dismaying. You must find her absence painful," she said to Esme.

Esme smiled tightly. "Naturally I am proud of Mama's unfailing attention to those less fortunate than ourselves."

To her surprise, Lady Bonnington's eyes were not scornful; Esme could see a gleam of sympathy there. "As you undoubtedly know," she announced, "I am close friends with your mother. Perhaps the combination of my presence and your entirely acceptable engagement will be enough to change her mind. I fancy I do have some small authority in society, you know." She bent toward Esme with the fanged smile of a leopard about to spring. "If *I* champion your reentry into society upon your marriage to Mr. Fairfax-Lacy, I feel quite certain that the *ton* will quickly dismiss the foibles of your youth."

Esme gave her a weak smile. Obviously Lady Bonnington was offering her a pact. Marry Fairfax-Lacy instead of her son, and the marchioness would reinstate Esme in the good graces of her mother and society. She nodded, meeting Lady Bonnington's eyes. "That would be most kind."

At that moment the rest of the party entered the room. Sebastian strolled over to Esme. "How are you?" he said, leaning over her sofa and speaking in her ear with unmistakable intimacy.

"Stop that!" she scolded, trying to avoid Lady Bonnington's glare.

Sebastian followed her glance. "Ah, my dear mother is here. Now where's your inamorato? Mr. Fairfellow. What is his name? I loathe double-barreled names, don't you?"

"Hush, you monster!" she said, pinching his arm. Under his laughter she caught a spark of something—jealousy, perhaps? She decided that her plan wasn't a failure after all. So she held out a languid hand to Fairfax-Lacy. "Ah, *there* you are!" she cried. "It seemed ages since the men retired for port!"

A few moments later, Bea entered the salon to find that Stephen Fairfax-Lacy was dancing attendance on Esme in a manner that could only be called lavish. They were snugly tucked into a small couch together, and as Bea watched, Stephen tenderly rearranged the cushion behind Esme's back. She felt a prick of jealousy. Apparently Esme and Stephen had discovered a shared affinity for bawdy jokes; Stephen kept murmuring things into Esme's ear that made them both roar with laughter.

They certainly *looked* like an affianced couple. But Bea couldn't work out what exactly had happened the previous evening. Why had Esme announced that she and Stephen were marrying? Presumably because they had agreed to marry, a sensible little voice in the back of her head insisted. But—and this seemed the crucial question to Bea—what was Marquess Bonnington doing in the house, and what was *his* relation to Esme? As Bea watched, the marquess strode over to join the lovebirds. Esme began sparkling like a tree decorated with candles, and laughing (Bea thought uncharitably) like a hyena.

Bea herself was dressed for attention, and she wasn't going to get that if she kept hugging the fireplace like a debutante wearing too many ruffles to dance. So she drifted over to the group and paused for a second until they looked up.

Esme's face lit with pleasure. "Bea, darling! Do join us. Mr. Fairfax-Lacy is telling me abominable jests about codpieces."

"Codpieces?" Bea inquired, walking toward her. She was wearing a gown of slate-gray silk. Slate-gray was the kind of color governesses wore, but this gown was cut with cunning precision to make it appear that she was a governess hiding the soul of a Jezebel. The bosom was as low as an evening gown's, but the addition of a trifling bit of lace gave the bodice a faint claim to respectability. "What is a codpiece?"

Naturally, the gentlemen stood at her arrival, so Bea nimbly slipped next to Esme, taking Stephen's seat.

Stephen himself answered her question, one dark eyebrow raised. "Have you not heard of codpieces, Lady Beatrix? Gentlemen wore them in the sixteenth century. Rounded pieces of leather sometimes decorated with ribbons."

"Wore them? Where did they—" Bea broke off, suddenly guessing where they wore them. Now she thought of it, she had seen portaits of men wearing codpieces over their tights. It was wicked of him to laugh at her in such a fashion, though.

"Life must have been so much easier for women in those days," Esme said, her voice spiced with mischief. "One could presumably choose a man by the number of ribbons he wore. Bea, we must sit together all evening. Our gowns suit each other extraordinarily."

Esme was dressed in a dark silvery crimson gown whose bosom was as low as Bea's but didn't include any disguising lace. Given the fact that Esme was approximately twice as endowed in the chest area, Bea figured that the contrast was personally unfortunate. But it was better than watching Stephen nestle up to Esme's curves.

"So, would you insist your husband match his daily ribbons to your gown?" Bonnington asked Esme. There was a sardonic twist to his lips. To Bea's mind, something smoldered in the marquess's eyes when he looked at Esme. And the same could be said for the way her lips curved up at his question. If she laughed a great deal while talking to Stephen, she got a husky undertone when she spoke to the marquess that was utterly suggestive.

"Ah, what a dilemma!" Esme said. "I doubt my fiancé would agree to wear rosy ribbons, were I to wear a pink costume." She threw Stephen a languishing look.

Stephen sat down in a chair beside the settee. He was suffering from awareness of the fact that if he were indeed an Elizabethan gentleman, wearing little more on his legs than some thin stockings, he'd be grateful for a codpiece, because his body's reaction to Bea's outrageous gown would have been all too obvious. "For you, Lady Rawlings, I would wear the colors of the rainbow," he said, pitching his voice to a velvety earnestness.

"How fortunate that you, rather than I, are marrying Lady Rawlings," the marquess drawled, leaning back in his chair and crossing his legs. "Lady Beatrix, would you demand that a man make an ass of himself?"

Bea could feel Stephen watching her. She gave the marquess a look of liquid promise. Bea had a distinct preference for dark hair, but the marquess's tawny golden-brown hair could well nigh change her mind. "I do believe I would insist on the removal of all ribbons."

"Oh?" he asked. He had lovely blue eyes. If only she weren't so fond of dark eyes. "You prefer a *naked* codpiece, Lady Beatrix?"

"I would prefer that my husband not advertise," she said. "Don't you agree, Esme? If a man wore too many ribbons, he might become the target of many women's attentions." Bea looked at Stephen, her face as innocent as she could manage. "And the next thing one knew, one's husband would have virtually turned into a peacock, thinking that every woman within eyesight is longing for his attentions."

Vixen, Stephen thought. "Do you mean *his* eyesight or *theirs*?" he asked.

"I shall have to take the idea of naked codpieces into consideration," Esme put in. "Perhaps we should have a game of charades. There must be some Elizabethan clothing up in the attics."

She turned to Stephen and said, with a simper, "But, darling, wouldn't you mind dreadfully if I stripped you of ornamentation?"

Bea thought Esme was playing a dangerous game. There was something wild about the marquess, something ungentleman-like, that made Bea a trifle nervous. And yet Esme was toying with him as if he were a mouse and she a kitten. But it was closer to the truth to see him as a tiger, and Esme a mouse.

For his part, Stephen was fairly certain that his courtship of Esme was piquing Bea's jealousy. There was a stormy something in her eyes that he liked. So he picked up Esme's hand and told her, "I would strip myself naked, if you wished."

"Even in this state?" Esme said, gesturing toward her nonexistent middle.

"If carrying a child made every woman as beautiful as you, Lady Rawlings, England's population would be growing by leaps and bounds." Stephen kissed Esme's hand as he watched Bea out of the corner of his eye. Her hands were clenched into fists. Stephen felt a burst of cheer. As long as he wasn't knocked into a corner by Bonnington, his plan was a success.

"I do believe that most women would faint at the idea of gaining such a waistline," Esme was saying.

"The most beautiful things in nature are those about to burst into flower: a bud on the verge of becoming a rose, a tree dripping with ripe apples. And you are more beautiful than a rose, Lady Rawlings."

"Quite the dandy, aren't you?" Marquess Bonnington said to

Stephen. There was a dangerous gleam in his eyes. "I wouldn't have thought a politician would have so much address. You could do much worse for a husband, Lady Rawlings."

"I merely speak the truth when I feel pressed," Stephen said promptly, hoping that Bonnington wouldn't lose control and floor him. Clearly the man had a prior claim. "Lady Rawlings is so beautiful that one can hardly stop oneself from singing her praises. It was the most surprising moment of my life when she agreed to marry me." He sighed, a languishing expulsion of breath. "The keen pleasure of that moment will never leave my memory."

Esme blushed faintly, and Bea realized that Esme had, indeed, decided to marry Stephen, no matter what her previous relationship with Marquess Bonnington might have been. Who could possibly choose to raise a child alone when she might have Stephen as a father? To Bea's annoyance, Stephen began kissing Esme's every fingertip. Now her stomach was churning with jealousy.

"Your eyes are the color of sapphires," Stephen said, his voice a low croon. "And your lips are finer than rubies."

Bea cleared her throat. Stephen looked around in a faintly irritated fashion and then said, "Forgive me, Lady Beatrix, Marquess Bonnington. You must forgive the flush of early love, the delight with which one greets his bride-to-be. . . ."

"I've never met a woman whom I wanted to compare to sapphires," the Marquess Bonnington said with an easy shrug of his shoulders. "What appeals to me is a kind of willowy grace . . . an elegance of form."

Esme stiffened slightly.

"Isn't it the poet Petrarch who compares his lady to a slender willow, swaying in the breeze? That appeals to me much more than comparing my lady to flinty little gems."

"Petrarch loved a woman who was only twelve years old," Stephen said dismissively. "I leave the younger set to you, Lord Bonnington. I find young women tiresome. A woman who *is* a woman is the most appealing." He carefully didn't even glance at Bea. Unless he was much mistaken, a pale pink nipple was just visible through the lace of her bodice. One more look at her chest and he would pick her up and stride right out of the room, and it wouldn't be *his* decoration that was stripped.

Bea was having trouble biting back an unpleasant comment. Clearly she was a member of the *younger set* whom Stephen professed to find tiresome. And presumably Stephen expected her to compete with Esme, though how she was supposed to do that, short of stuffing her corset with all the cotton in Wiltshire, she had no idea. The least she could do was to help the cause of true love.

"Lord Bonnington," she said rather jerkily, "I brought the most exquisite book of poetry with me. And you had not yet joined the house party when we read some of it aloud. Would you like me to introduce you to the work?"

"I would be more than pleased," he said, rising and giving her an elegant bow.

Bea didn't look to see what Stephen thought. He was probably grateful. After all, if she took Bonnington off of Esme's hands, he had no competition to worry about.

They walked into the corridor together. She took a deep breath and gave Lord Bonnington the full benefit of one of her smoldering looks. There must be something wrong with her. He looked no more impressed than had Sebastian. Bea blinked to hold back sudden tears. Was she . . . was she losing her attractiveness to men? That was inconceivable. It was all she had.

The library was just down the corridor from the Rose Salon. Esme's library was a snug nutshell of a room, all lined with books that gave off a sleepy, satisfied smell. Bea felt better immediately. The library had been one of the few places in her father's house where she'd felt happy.

Lord Bonnington walked away from her and looked out one of the arching windows that faced into the garden, so Bea followed. She still could hardly believe that he hadn't shown her the faintest interest. Perhaps—perhaps it had been too dim in the corridor. Perhaps he hadn't seen the expression in her eyes.

It had rained all day. A silver layer of mist crept over the garden, drifting down to a blocky structure that Bea knew was the rose arbor.

"I gather you think that Lady Rawlings should marry Mr. Fairfax-Lacy," Lord Bonnington said abruptly, looking at the garden, and not at her.

"I—"

"And you brought me here to give them breathing space."

Bea swallowed. She could hardly say that she'd brought him to the library in a weak effort to make Stephen Fairfax-Lacy jealous. Or to prove that she was still desirable.

"I do think that Lady Rawlings would be happier if she were married," she said, steadying her voice.

"Married to *him?*"

The scorn in his voice lashed her into speech. "Esme would be extremely fortunate to marry Mr. Fairfax-Lacy!"

"He's a stick," Bonnington said, still gazing out into the garden.

"No, he's not. He's quite handsome, and he's funny, and kind. And he . . . he seems to care for her," Bea said.

"So do I."

What could she say to that? She stood next to him, feeling the chill that breathed off the leaded window panes.

"Did she tell you to take me away? Did she send you some sort of signal?"

"No, no," Bea said. "It wasn't like that at all! I merely . . . I merely . . ."

He turned and looked down at her. After a moment, he said, "We're in the same boat, then."

She couldn't ask what boat that was because she was afraid that she knew. "Absolutely not," she replied stiffly.

"Are you saying that you don't wish to marry that proper M.P. in there?" The touch of disbelief in his voice made her raise her head.

"I do not."

There was a skeptical curl to his lip.

"I don't wish to marry anyone." She walked over to the couch and sat down, not bothering to tilt her hips from side to side in the walk she had perfected at age fifteen. The man was not interested in her. That slow fire she saw in his eyes was for Esme, not for her.

But he did follow her, throwing himself down on the couch. "If I thought jealousy would help, I would have a go at pretending to be in love with you. But it wouldn't make any difference," Bonnington said flatly. "I'm sorry to say that the man appears enamored of Esme Rawlings. And once she draws you in, it's damn hard to look at another woman."

"I am not interested in Mr. Fairfax-Lacy," Bea insisted, more for the sake of her pride than anything else.

He didn't even answer her. "I expect he thinks you're too young."

"Too scandalous," Bea put in, unable to pretend any longer.

"Scandalous, hmmm?"

She nodded. She knew Marquess Bonnington by reputation; well, who didn't? He used to be considered one of the most upright men in the *ton*. There'd never been a whisper of scandal about the man until last summer. Not even a shred. If he knew her past, he would spit at her and leave the room immediately. But he didn't seem to be reacting with condemnation.

"Didn't you side-step with Sandhurst? Why on earth did you choose that odious mushroom?" he asked, and she couldn't hear any censure in his voice. Just a kind of lazy curiosity.

She shrugged. "He had a lovely bow. He complimented me."

He looked at her without saying anything.

"And my father loathed him," she added.

"I expect the noble public servant holds it against you, though." The marquess's eyes were kind, too. As kind as Stephen's. What was it with these men? They didn't react to her best overtures, and then they made her feel like crying.

"Actually, Mr. Fairfax-Lacy said that he wanted a mistress with less experience," she said, her wry grin crooked.

He stared at her. "Fairfax-Lacy said *that?*"

She nodded.

"You're better off without him. Why on earth would you wish to be a mistress to such an intolerable lout? Or a mistress to any man, for that matter?" He was looking at her so intently that Bea wondered whether he'd suddenly noticed she was a woman. Was he going to offer her a consolatory kiss? For all she'd drawn him to the library, she didn't want him to touch her.

"I suppose I don't wish to be a mistress," she said, dismissing the memory of Stephen's kisses. "Nor a wife either."

"Humph," he said, looking unconvinced. "Well, then, where's that poetry you brought me in here for? I shouldn't like to go back to the salon without having read some of it. Lord knows what they'll think we were doing."

Bea smiled back, feeling an unwilling pulse of friendship. He got up and threw another log into the fireplace and then walked back to the couch.

"Here it is," she said, plucking the book off the end table.

He started reading and his eyebrows rose. "I suppose this is from Esme's personal library?"

"No." She blushed. "I brought it with me. Truly, some of the poetry is quite . . . quite unexceptional."

Bea liked his chuckle. She drew up her legs and curled into her favorite position—the one she would never assume before a man because it didn't emphasize how slender her limbs were.

"I like this," he said. ' "*O faire Boy, trust not to thy beauty's wings.*' "

She nodded.

He looked over at her with a wry grin. "I spent a great deal of my life trusting the wrong things. My title, for example."

"Your beauty?" she said daringly.

"Not so much . . . I was convinced that I had to live up to the dignity of my title. I suppose I trusted my reputation too much."

Bea's smile mirrored his. "Whereas I simply threw mine away."

"Then perhaps you are the one who trusts your beauty overmuch." He put the book to the side. "Shall we return to the salon, Lady Beatrix?"

She put her feet down and rose. He looked down at her, and Bea felt a faint blush rise in her cheeks. "If I hadn't met Esme first, you likely would have been the making of me, Lady Beatrix."

"I'm not suitable for someone who honors their reputation," she observed, starting toward the door.

A large hand curled around her hand, drawing it under his arm. "Ah, but it wouldn't have taken long for you to convince me of the worthlessness of reputation. Esme didn't even try, and I was ready to throw it away as soon as I met her."

She looked a question as they walked through the corridor.

"She was married at that point."

"Now she isn't," Bea observed.

"And therein lies my trouble. I am of the fixed opinion that Esme should marry me and no other." He glanced down at Bea. "I am telling you this merely because I wouldn't want you to worry if I have to take out your darling Fairfax-Lacy."

"Take out?" Bea said sharply. "What on earth do you mean by that, sir?"

He shrugged. "I doubt it will come to violence. But no one is going to marry Esme but myself."

## 24

## *Waltzing on One's Deathbed*

*T*rying to not feel guilty because one's wife is dying is a difficult task. Damn near impossible, Rees finally decided. After all, they'd been married for years—nine or ten, he estimated. He'd married Helene when she was barely out of the schoolroom. They were both too young to know better. Yet it wasn't entirely his fault the marriage failed, no matter what she said about it.

But he never, ever thought of her as not being there. Not there to send him nagging letters, or curl her lip at him as they passed. Not there to send him horrid little notes after he debuted a new piece of music, putting her finger directly on the weakest spot, and not saying a word about the best of it.

Damn it, she couldn't die.

He'd been to Lady Rawlings's house a mere few months ago, and Helene had seemed perfectly healthy then. A little too thin, perhaps. But she was always thin. Not like Lina's overflowing little body, all curves and fleshy parts. Rees frowned. Surely it wasn't correct to think about one's mistress while riding in a carriage to greet one's dying wife. And was *greet* the right word?

It was with a great sense of relief that Rees realized his carriage was finally pulling up in front of Shantill House. It wasn't that he cared for his wife, of course. He didn't. Hadn't the faintest feelings for her of that nature. It was merely natural anxiety that had his chest feeling as if it were clamped in a vise. His fists kept curling, and he could bellow with rage. At what? Helene, for growing ill? No!

He had to be sweet, calm, tell her loving things. Because she was dying. His bitter-tongued, frigid little wife was dying.

God knows, that should probably have given him a sense of relief. Instead he couldn't seem to swallow, and he actually had to support himself on the side of the carriage when he descended, because his knees felt weak for a moment.

He could tell by the butler's minatory gaze—Slope, wasn't that his name?—that he probably should have changed his garments before leaping into a carriage. Instead he ran a hand through his hair, doubtless disheveling it more than before. "I've come to see my wife," he said brusquely, heading past Slope and up the stairs. He knew where Helene stayed when she was at Lady Rawlings's house. Not that he visited her bedchamber, naturally, but he'd noted the room.

Dimly he realized that Slope was calling after him. Impatient, he stopped and glared down the stairs. "What is it, man?"

"The countess is not in her chamber. She can be found in the Rose Salon."

Rees blinked. Seemed an odd place to stage a dying scene, but who was he to cavil? Perhaps she wouldn't die until tomorrow. He all but galloped down the stairs, brushed by Slope—and stopped.

A typical scene of English country life greeted him. A stout peer was dozing in a low chair by the fire. A beautiful little tart of a girl was leaning over her embroidery, her lips painted a fantastic red. And there were a few other remnants of English nobility strewn around the room.

But it was the piano that held his attention.

He'd know her playing anywhere, of course. She was seated at the pianoforte, and not by herself, either. They were playing one of Beethoven's sonatas in E-flat major. And she was laughing. As he watched, her companion leaned over and kissed her on the cheek. Kissed Helene! True, it was just a brush of a kiss. But Helene blushed.

Rees's body went from cold to burning hot and back to cold again, in the mere moment he stood in the doorway. Suddenly he was aware of the butler standing just at his shoulder, of the wintery morning sunlight making Helene's pale hair look like strands of silver. Of the very—aliveness of her. They started playing again and she was swaying slightly, her shoulder just bumping her partner's arm. Her face was glowing with joy, as it always did when she played. Always. Helene and he had only lived in the same house for a matter of months, but he'd never forgotten the way she looked when she played the piano.

It was that joy that had made him fall in love with her. The very thought shocked his senses back into movement. Fall in love? Ha!

"I see that the report of your demise was overhasty," he drawled in the nastiest tone he could summon. And Earl Godwin was pretty much an expert at giving offense.

Helene looked up, and he saw her mouth form a little Oh. But the next moment she turned to her partner and said saucily, "I'm so sorry; I almost lost my place, Stephen." And her fingers flew over the keys again, just as if he weren't there.

Stephen? Who the hell was Stephen?

Rees had a vague sense he'd seen the man before. He was handsome, in a pallid, English sort of way. Damn it, he'd been rooked. Although it wasn't clear to him why he had been called as audience. Why in the hell had his wife wanted him to jump to her bidding? He wasn't going to stand around and give her the satisfaction of gloating over his presence. For tuppence he'd turn around and head straight back for London. But he'd been on the road for two days, and his horses were exhausted.

"Excuse me," an amused voice said, just at his elbow. Lady Withers smiled at him. She was a quite lovely woman of a certain age and Esme Rawlings's aunt, if he weren't mistaken.

"Lord Godwin," she said. "How splendid to have you join us. The countess did mention that you might make a brief visit." For a moment her eyes danced over to his wife, cozily tucked against her piano partner.

"Who the hell is that?" he snarled, jerking his head backwards, dismissing the fleeting thought that he might actually greet Lady Withers.

She blinked as if the room were so filled with gentry that she might have trouble identifying the pallid Englishman. "Mr. Fairfax-Lacy is the Member of Parliament for Oxfordshire, and such an intelligent man. He also holds the honorary title of the Earl of Spade, although he chooses not to use it. We are all enjoying his company."

Rees was pulling himself together. He'd be damned if he showed any sort of husbandly emotion before a smirking viscountess. And since he wasn't feeling any of those husbandly feelings, that should be simple. Unless murderous was considered a husbandly emotion.

Then Helene was before him, holding out her hand and sinking into a curtsy. "Rees. I must apologize for my letter," she said, as tranquil as ever. "While the midwife in the village *did* suggest I had pleurisy, it turned out to be something far more innocent."

"Oh?"

"Well, you see pleurisy starts with a red rash. But I had beard burn, as it turned out," she said, laughing slightly. "Aren't I the naive one, then? I suppose you were so young when we married that I never encountered this problem."

Her laugh was breathy, perhaps a sign of nerves. But Rees wasn't going to give her the satisfaction. *Any* satisfaction. He just looked at her, and the giggle died on her lips. "You are still my wife—" he began.

She put a hand on his arm. This was not the naive girl he'd married. Not the Helene he woke up with the day after they returned from Gretna

Green, a girl who veered madly between shrieking tantrums and sullen tears. She was poised, cool, and utterly unapproachable.

"Only in name, Rees. Another woman shares your bedchamber now."

He looked over her shoulder. Fairfax-Lacy was practicing chords. He played well. Presumably she wasn't sleeping alone in her bedchamber. "A gentleman who planned to be at your side during divorce proceedings wouldn't sit at the piano while you face an irate husband," he said, his tone polished steel.

"You are hardly an irate husband," she said, shrugging. "I asked Stephen to remain where he is. I hardly think you are interested in making his acquaintance. And who said anything about divorce?"

"So you've taken a lover," Rees sneered, on the verge of crashing his fist into that sleek bastard's face. "What is it all in aid of, Helene?"

"Pleasure," she said, and the smile on her face burned down his spine. "*My* pleasure, Rees."

He turned on his heel and then back at the last second. "Who did that arrangement of Beethoven for four hands?"

"I did. I've been rearranging all of them."

He should have known that. The sonata sounded half like Beethoven and half like Helene, an odd mixture.

"Now we have that little discussion out of the way," Lady Withers said brightly, coming up from somewhere, "why don't I show you to your room, Lord Godwin? I do hope you'll make a long stay with us."

Rees turned like a cornered lion and snarled at her, then strode out of the room. As Arabella described it later to Esme, who hadn't been in the Rose Salon at the time, Earl Godwin acted precisely like the Wild Man of Deepest Africa whom Arabella had seen once in a traveling circus.

"All hair, and such a snarl, Esme!" Arabella paused, thinking about it. "Honestly, Helene, your husband is quite—quite impressive." There was reluctant respect in her voice.

"Oh, Rees is very good at snarling," Helene said. She, Arabella and Esme were cozily seated in Esme's chamber, drinking tea and eating gingerbread cakes.

Esme looked up from her plate, her eyes sparkling with laughter. "The important thing is he snarled because *you* managed to tangle his liver—or whatever that phrase is that you keep using, Helene."

"Curdle his liver," Helene repeated, and there was a growing spark of happiness in her eyes. "He *did* seem chagrined by our conversation, didn't he, Lady Withers?"

"Chagrined is not the word," Arabella replied, stirring a little sugar into her tea. "He was incensed. Absolutely incensed. Purple with rage."

"I hope he's not feeling *too* violent," Esme said. "I can hardly have

A Wild Pursuit 179

my future husband mangled by your present husband, Helene. It would all be such fodder for gossip if the servants shared what they know."

Helene thought about the difference between what the servants thought they knew about her and Stephen, and what the truth was. "I do think you could have left Stephen to me," she told Esme somewhat peevishly. "What if Rees discovers that you have claimed my lover as a future husband?"

"I doubt very much that your husband will raise the subject with Stephen," Esme replied. "Rees already announced that he will stay one day at most, so Stephen only has to briefly juggle a fiancée and a mistress. He'll not be the first to do so. I can't tell you how many times I found myself at a table that included Miles *and* Lady Randolph Childe. Miles always acted with the greatest finesse, and if my husband could do it, so can Stephen."

Arabella chortled. "Supper will be an interesting meal. Mr. Fairfax-Lacy will face quite a difficult task. You, Helene, wish him to impress your husband with his devotion, and you, Esme, wish to impress the marquess with Mr. Fairfax-Lacy's devotion. Hmmm, perhaps I could ask Bea to create a diversion by flirting with Earl Godwin?"

"There's no need to go as far as that," Helene said hastily. "And do you know, I have the strangest feeling that Bea might be having some feelings for Mr. Fairfax-Lacy herself? There's something odd about the way she looks at him."

Esme laughed. "That would make three of us chasing the poor man. Arabella, are you certain that you have no use for Mr. Fairfax-Lacy?"

"Quite sure, thank you, darling," Arabella said, carefully choosing a perfectly browned gingerbread. "It seems to me that the poor man must be growing tired. I dislike fatigued men. Still, it seems to be quite enlivening for him," she continued rather absently. "The man was getting hidebound. He looked so cheerful this morning. And that, of course, is your doing," she said, beaming at Helene.

Helene hid a pulse of guilt. She was hardly enlivening poor Stephen's nights, even though the whole house believed she was. Now Esme was smiling at her too. Her sense of guilt grew larger.

"I'm very proud of Helene," Esme said. "Arabella, you can't imagine how impossibly rude Rees has been to poor Helene over the years, and she's never staged even the slightest rebellion until now."

"Now that you've rebelled," Arabella asked Helene with some curiosity, "what will be the outcome? Are you wishing to continue your relationship with Mr. Fairfax-Lacy? That is, if Esme gives up her rather dubious claim to him?"

"I wouldn't call it *dubious*," Esme put in. "Merely unexpected."

"No," Helene admitted. "I don't wish to remain his friend."

"I knew that," Esme said. "I watched the two of you. Otherwise, I would not have claimed him as my own future husband, I assure you, Helene."

"Stephen Fairfax-Lacy is good marriage material," Arabella said. "I am never wrong about that sort of thing. All three of my husbands were excellent spouses." She finished her gingerbread and added, meditatively, "Barring their short life spans, of course."

"I have to tell you something," Helene said rather desperately.

"I do hope you are going to tell us intimate details," Arabella said. "There's nothing more pleasurable than dissecting a man's performance in bed. I believe it's my favorite activity, perhaps even more fun than actually being *in* that bed." She looked faintly appalled. "I surprise myself," she said, picking up another cake. "Ah, well, that's the benefit of being an elderly person."

"You're not *elderly,* Aunt Arabella!" Esme said. "You're barely out of your forties."

"I'm not really bedding Mr. Fairfax-Lacy," Helene blurted out.

Arabella's mouth fell open for a second before she snapped it shut.

"I thought so," Esme said with some satisfaction. "You don't have the air of a couple besotted with each other."

Helene could feel her face reddening. "We didn't suit."

"I had that happen to me once," Arabella said. "I won't bore you with the details, my dears, but after his third attempt, I called for a truce. A laying down of arms," she clarified with a naughty smirk. "Well, who would have thought? Fairfax-Lacy looked so—"

"No!" Helene cried, horrified by the conclusion Arabella had drawn. "It truly was all my fault. I'm just not—" She stopped.

To her horror, she felt tears rising to her eyes. How could she possibly admit to a failure in bedroom activity when she was seated with two of the most desirable women in the *ton*?

"You know, I find him quite uninteresting as well," Esme said quickly. "It's something about the Englishness of his face. And his chest is quite narrow, isn't it? Moreover, I never liked a man with a long chin."

Helene threw Esme a watery smile. "It's not that I don't like the way he looks. I do. It's just that I found myself unable to countenance the prospect of bedding him." Her voice dropped. "He was very kind about the whole thing."

Arabella nodded. "There are always men whom one simply cannot imagine engaging in intimate circumstances. Unfortunately, I felt that way about my second husband. But what really interests me," she said, turning a piercing eye on Esme, "is what exactly *you* are doing, announcing your engagement to a man with an overly long chin? Or, to put the same question another way, what *is* Marquess Bonnington doing in this house, Esme?"

Esme almost choked on the gingerbread she was eating. "Expressing his repentance?" she said hopefully.

"Don't repeat that poppycock story that I fed your Sewing Circle!" Arabella cried. "You managed to evade my every effort at a confidential talk last night by clinging to your new fiancé's arm, but now I would like to know the truth. Why has the marquess arrived in your house?"

Helene leaned forward. "I would like to know that as well, Esme. I accepted that his mother was likely here due to the circumstances of last summer, although it seemed extremely odd—"

Arabella interrupted, naturally. "Odd? There's something deuced smoky about Honoratia Bonnington's arrival."

Esme sighed.

"You sound like a bellows," her aunt observed. "Out with it!"

Esme looked up at her aunt for a moment. Arabella looked as delicate and sensual as if a wisp of wind would blow her away, and yet she and the formidable Lady Bonnington were certainly forged of the same steel. So Esme told. "But I don't wish to marry anyone," she finished. "Least of all Lord Bonnington. It wouldn't be fair to Miles, or to the babe."

After a moment of stupefied silence, Arabella burst into a cackle of laughter. "Want to just keep Bonnington around for those lonely nights, do you? And you had him working in the garden during the day? Here I thought you were bent on a sober widowhood! Lord, Esme, even I never created a scandal akin to this one!"

"What scandal?" Esme demanded. "You stopped the Sewing Circle from even considering the possibility with all your quotations."

"Which took me a good hour of poring over a Bible, I'll have you know!" Arabella said.

"Esme, do you think it might be time to give up the Sewing Circle?" Helene asked tentatively. "Things *are* a trifle . . . complicated in your life. Perhaps it would be best if you weren't under quite so close surveillance."

"It's part of my new respectability," Esme said stubbornly. "I rather enjoy it."

"Not that I noticed," Arabella commented. "You sewed a miserable seam. Some people are simply not gifted in that department."

"You know, Mama makes shirts for the poor," Esme said. "The whole shirt, even the collar and cuffs."

Arabella was silent for a moment. "Lord, Esme, I never like to think of myself as someone who could say ill of my own sister, but Fanny is dim-witted. She's spending all that time making up collars for people she doesn't even know, and her own daughter is alone in the country. She's got her priorities in a tangle." She reached over and gave Esme's hand a little squeeze. "Don't go changing yourself into your mother. You have always had a merry soul. But Fanny has grown into a rather dreary adult, if I say so myself."

"That's not fair," Esme objected. "Mama has had a great many disappointments in life." Obviously her daughter was foremost on the list.

"She's dispirited," Arabella said firmly, "although it's good of you to defend her. Fanny spends all her time gazing at the world and pursing her lips. I've always been glad to have one relation with a grain of sense in her head. I can't afford to lose you to the ranks of straitlaced matrons."

"Your aunt is right," Helene put in. "I have only the slimmest acquaintance with your mother. But the idea of you growing as prim and prissy as that Mrs. Cable is simply dispiriting. She's not a very nice woman, Esme."

"I know," Esme said. "Believe me, I know."

Arabella took a look at her niece and judged it time to change the subject. But while she and Helene chatted about the Venetian lace points that adorned Helene's sleeves, Esme sat in silence. She had promised Miles that she would be a respectable mother, yet Miles was gone. She thought never to make another scandal, and she could think of no scandal with the explosive force that her marriage to Marquess Bonnington would have.

# 25

## A Taste for Seduction

The next morning Bea stamped down the lane to visit the goat. She'd taken to visiting the devilish creature every morning, from the pure boredom of life. Of course, she could have spent her time flirting with the Puritan. But annoyingly, irritatingly, hatefully, he and Helene were learning to play a four-handed piece. The sight of Helene's pale braids bent close to Stephen's dark head as they whacked away on that pianoforte gave Bea a strange kind of longing, the kind that pinches your heart. It wasn't an emotion that Bea was familiar with at all.

The one time they had been alone together after breakfast, for the merest moment, he had looked down at her with a rather wintery smile and said, "I gather that you have decided not to woo me?"

She had answered, "I never woo," hoping that he would kiss her or smile at her the way he did at Esme *and* Helene. But all he'd done was bow and walk away. Bea had realized in that very moment, watching his back, that there was nothing in the world she wanted more than to woo the man. But Stephen showed little desire to secure any sort of relationship with her. How could he, in truth? He had no time. When he wasn't playing an instrument with his mistress, he was exchanging bawdy jests with his fiancée. Lord knows where he was at night. Bea ground her teeth together. She was making a regular occupation out of thinking about Stephen Fairfax-Lacy and then admonishing herself for doing it. She held out a branch she'd brought the goat and watched him chew it into kindling.

In fact, Lady Beatrix Lennox was suffering from a mighty loss of confidence. First Mr. Fairfax-Lacy had refused her as a mistress and taken Helene instead. And Marquess Bonnington hadn't shown the faintest interest in her from the very beginning. Bea had to blink very hard to hold back tears.

The goat was chewing so loudly that it was no surprise that Bea didn't hear anyone approaching her. "Aren't you afraid to approach that spencer-eating beast?" said a voice at her ear.

She was like some sort of trained dog, Bea thought miserably. All she had to do was hear his voice and her knees weakened.

"The goat doesn't bother me," she said, not turning to look at him. What was the point? He was leaning on the stile next to her, seemingly unperturbed by her graceless welcome.

"We should introduce the rest of the party to this fascinating creature," he said idly. "I don't believe that Esme even knows of his existence. Whereas I find myself compulsively visiting the beast every day."

Bea's heart hardened. "I thought you and Lady Godwin were spending your time together," she said, being deliberately rude. "Or is it Lady Rawlings who occupies more of your time?"

"Not every moment. And never tell me that *you're* jealous." His voice took on that dark, sweet note that drove Bea to distraction.

"Absolutely not!" she said, turning and facing him for the first time. He was—He wasn't so fabulously handsome. He had wrinkles on the edges of his eyes. And his chin was too long. God, how she hated a long chin!

"I'm glad," Stephen said. She couldn't read his eyes. Was he making fun of her? No, that was a look of concern. Damn it all.

"Because Esme and I . . ." He hesitated.

"You needn't tell me," Bea put in. "I can see the truth for myself. And I assure you that I haven't the slightest feeling about it except happiness for the two of you."

"I'm glad to hear that." It was so unfair that his smile could make her stomach clench. Long chin, long chin, long chin, she thought to herself.

"Esme and I seem to have so many interests in common." Apparently he was feeling quite chatty now that he'd cleared away any misconceptions Bea might have had. "I had forgotten how much I enjoy word play and jests."

"Lovely," Bea said listlessly. She had been routed by a fleshy woman nine months with child. The fact that Bea genuinely liked Esme (and Helene, for that matter) didn't help.

Stephen looked aside at his little Bea. Unless he was quite mistaken, his campaign was working. She was lurid with jealousy. "Do *you* enjoy jests?" he asked.

Apparently she was supposed to engage in a contest of bawdy jests in order to obtain the great honor of being yet another woman in Mr. Fairfax-Lacy's life. Of course she wouldn't do such an ignominious thing. "I know a few," she said, despite her best intentions. "Do you know the ballad that begins: *'He's lain like a log of wood, in bed for a year or two, and won't afford me any good, he nothing at all would do?'* There are quite a few verses."

He laughed. "Perhaps men don't care to repeat that particular ballad amongst themselves." His eyes warmed her to her stomach, sent pangs of warning to her heart.

"I am thinking of returning to London, Mr. Fairfax-Lacy," Bea said, making up her mind on the spot. "I must visit my mantua-maker. After all, my favorite garment was eaten by this animal." The goat rolled his eyes at her.

"Oh," he said. And then, "Are you then determined not to woo?"

"How many times must you ask me?" Bea snapped. The arrogance of the man was incredible. Incredible! Bea peeked a look at him from under her lashes. He looked almost—well—anxious.

"My besetting sin is arrogance, it would seem," he said. "Although I had not realized it until recently. I truly apologize if I misinterpreted your interest in me when we played billiards together."

"No, you didn't!" she wanted to shriek. Why wasn't he wooing her? Why wasn't he trying to seduce *her?*

She peeked another look. It was no use. He had the longest chin in Christendom, perhaps, but she wanted to kiss him desperately. Or rather, she wanted to *be* kissed by him. And it seemed that there was still a chance, before Esme scooped him into a forty-year waltz. But she couldn't quite bring herself to give him one of her seductive looks. She was feeling paralyzingly shy, and there they were in front of the goat, and—

"I'll think about it," she mumbled.

"What? I'm sorry, I didn't quite catch what you said." He was leaning slightly against the fence. He looked like the most respectable, prudish, Puritan in the world. Not her sort at all. Too old, for one thing. And too opinionated. And too—too desirable.

"I said, I'll decide today whether I wish to woo you," she said painstakingly.

"Oh, good."

The infuriating man acted as if they were discussing a trip to see a Roman monument. Bea couldn't think of anything else they had to say to each other, so she made her farewell and then walked listlessly up the lane, swinging her parasol at a rock with the misfortune to be in her way. It was only in front of him that she pretended there was a decision to be made: and that was merely because of an instinctive feminine wish to protect herself.

Tonight she would spent an hour bathing, two hours dressing, and even longer painting her face, and she would seduce that man, by God, if he were seducable.

# 26

## The Experience That Divides the Ladies from the … Women

*E*sme stared out the window of the drawing room. They were having a late spring flurry of snow. The white flakes were making the yellow crocuses on the side of the house look pale and betrayed. Or perhaps it was she who was betrayed. Or was it she who was betraying?

The comedy of errors that made up this particular house party was astonishing. She and Mr. Fairfax-Lacy, to all eyes, were apparently planning to marry. Equally well known to all was the fact that Helene was having an affair with the said Mr. Fairfax-Lacy, although it didn't seem to have given Helene's husband even a qualm. The earl was leaving the next morning, but as far as Esme could determine, he was thoroughly enjoying bickering with Helene over her reformulations of Beethoven and had paid no attention whatsoever to Stephen Fairfax-Lacy's lavish compliments to his wife.

Today the pain in her lower back was even worse than usual. She could hardly stand up, it hurt so much. The door opened behind her.

"Hello," she said, not bothering to look around. It was amazing how closely her ears were attuned to the sound of his step, rather than those of the other two dozen persons thronging her house. He stood just behind her and, without even being asked, pressed his thumbs sharply into the base of her spine. It felt so good that Esme's knees almost collapsed.

"Steady there," he said. "How is that babe this morning?"

"I received a letter from my mother," Esme said, turning around and looking up at him. "Fanny is coming to visit, thanks to your mother's persuasive powers. Much though I loath it, I am going to have to express gratitude to Marchioness Bonnington."

Sebastian narrowed his eyes. Didn't Esme have any idea why his mother would have done such an act of benevolence? "My mother didn't do it out of the kindness of her heart," he pointed out.

"I know, I know." The smile that spread across her face was genuine. "But I am glad that Mama is coming. It must be because I'm having a child myself. And because Miles is dead, of course."

Of course, Sebastian thought cynically. He was getting sick of Esme referring to her husband as if he'd ever played a significant role in her life.

"Don't you see that your mother is coming here solely to ensure that you do indeed marry Fairfax-Lacy?" he asked harshly. "Once you disappoint her again, she'll drop you like a hot potato."

"There's always the *small* chance that I won't disappoint her," Esme replied icily.

Sebastian snorted. "Your mother is the sort of woman who would find something to criticize if you had taken on a nun's habit."

"I mean to be respectable, and I shall be," Esme said. But her heart wasn't in the argument: her back hurt too much.

"You are pretending not to be in love with me. You're a hypocrite, Esme, and you're making a terrible mistake."

"I don't feel very well," Esme mumbled. It wasn't only because she didn't want to think about Sebastian's offensive comment. Her back hurt so much that she seemed to be hearing his voice through a fog, as if filtered through cotton wool. "Perhaps I ought to go to my chambers."

At that moment the door opened and a flood of chatting houseguests swept in. Lady Bonnington took one look at Esme and announced, "I do believe Lady Rawlings is having that baby now."

"Well, you've done this sort of thing before," Arabella said to her with a tone of mild panic. "Tell the poor girl what to do."

"Don't be more of an idiot than nature made you!" Lady Bonnington snapped. "Obviously she needs to retire to her bedchamber."

"I see no occasion for rudeness," Arabella replied, bristling.

Esme took a deep breath. She was surrounded by a ring of faces. A second later Arabella was pushed to the side, and Sebastian bent over Esme.

"Up you go," he said to her, with a tone of unmistakable intimacy. Before she could protest, he picked Esme up in his arms and started carrying her up the stairs, looking for all the world as if he knew directly where he was going.

"Oh!" Esme gripped his arm as her entire body shuddered and seemingly attempted to turn itself inside out. She dug her fingernails into his arm.

"Call the midwife!" Sebastian yelled over his shoulder. A moment later he had her in one of the spare bedrooms, on a bed specially prepared for just this occasion. But Esme didn't let him put her down.

"Wait!" she gasped. He started to lower her to the bed. "Wait, damn it!" She hung on for dear life as another wave swept through her body. Just then the door popped open, and in streamed Arabella, Helene, Marchioness Bonnington, and three maids.

"All right, Bonnington," Arabella said importantly. "If you could just put my niece on the bed, we'll carry on from here. The midwife will be here directly; the silly woman had taken a walk to the village. Just try to keep that baby where it is until she arrives, all right, Esme?"

"Don't be a widgeon!" Lady Bonnington said, marching over to the side of the bed. "The babe will not arrive for hours."

"God, I hope that's not the case," Esme gasped.

"That's the way of it," the marchioness said. Her tone was not unsympathetic.

Esme let go of Sebastian's hand. He bent over her for a moment, pressed a kiss on her forehead, and then he was gone. She felt a bit like crying, except another pain rushed up from her toes and stole her attention away. "Bloody hell," Esme said in a near shout, reaching out and grabbing Arabella's hand. The pain receded, and she flopped back on the bed, drained.

"Profanity will not ease the pain," Lady Bonnington observed. "My own mother told me that what distinguishes a lady from a lower being is that a lady accepts pain without rebuke."

Esme ignored her. "How many of these pains will there be?" she demanded of the midwife as she entered the room.

Mrs. Pluck was a thick-set woman who was cheerfully confident about the "course of nature," as she called it. "I expect you're in some discomfort," she said, bustling about with a stack of towels. "But you've got the hips for a quick one." She chuckled in a wheezing sort of way. "We must let nature take its course, that's what I say."

"My niece will dispatch this business with . . . with *dispatch*," Arabella announced, surreptitiously examining the red patches on her hand where Esme had squeezed her. "Bring me a wet cloth," she snapped at one of the maids. "Esme, darling, you're rather unbecomingly flushed. I'll just bathe your forehead."

"Took me all of six hours," Lady Bonnington trumpeted.

Esme immediately decided that she was going to birth her baby in less than six hours. She'd never survive an ordeal as long as that. "Oh no," she moaned. "Here it comes again."

Arabella hastily dropped her wet cloth, and Esme grabbed her hand. The tidal wave came, swept her down and under, cast her up gasping for air. "I don't like this," Esme managed to say in a husky whisper.

"Never knew a woman who did!" the marchioness said cheerfully from the side of the bed. "All a lady can do is endure with fortitude, showing her well-bred nature in every moment."

Esme responded with flat profanity.

As the marchioness thought later, if she hadn't already known that Esme Rawlings was an appallingly ill-bred woman, she would have known from that moment on. The gel just had no idea how a lady behaved under duress.

## 27

### Sweet William

*G*iving birth in the presence of two elderly ladies of the *ton* was without a doubt the most uncomfortable experience of Esme's life. Arabella stood at her right, bathing her forehead every time one of the pains ended. Esme emerged from a swooping black wave of pain to find that Lady Bonnington, standing to her left, was exhorting her to greater efforts, and Arabella, not to be outdone, was instructing the midwife to hurry things along.

"There's no need to hurry things along," Mrs. Pluck, the midwife, responded with a glimmer of irritation. "The course of nature will do it. And Lady Rawlings has the hips for it, that she does."

"A little less conversation about my niece's hips, if you please," Arabella snapped. "There's no need to be vulgar."

"Arabella, you're a fool," Lady Bonnington announced with her usual politeness.

Esme took a breath, feeling the pain coming again. It was worse than she had ever imagined, rather like being scalded from the toes up. She struggled her way back out of the pain a moment later, dimly hearing Arabella's congratulations. Her aunt seemed to have decided that Esme needed applause after every contraction. And Esme definitely agreed with her. "Where . . . where's Helene?" she gasped at one point.

Lady Bonnington looked shocked. "Naturally, we sent her out of the room. The poor girl hasn't had a babe of her own, you know. This is enough to put her off for life."

"Oh no," Esme moaned. The next contraction was coming, sweeping up from her toes—

"Fortitude, darling, fortitude!" Arabella said, taking her hand even more firmly. Esme clutched her hand.

"You've got the hips for it," Mrs. Pluck said from the bottom of the bed. And then, "We're almost there, my lady. I told you this would be a ride in the park, didn't I?"

A ride in the park it wasn't. But Esme couldn't summon up the breath to argue the point. Instead she let the pain wrench her bones from their sockets, or so it felt. Arabella was alternating between putting a cool cloth on Esme's head and wrapping it around her own hand.

"All right, my lady," Mrs. Pluck said loudly. "Time to bring the little master into the world."

*Or daughter,* Esme thought, although she couldn't summon up the wherewithal to say so. But Mrs. Pluck was right.

Squealing, indignant, fat and belligerent, William Rawlings entered the world in a burst of rage. Esme propped herself on her elbows. There he was: dark red from pure anger, kicking jerkily, waving his fists in the air. Her heart turned over with a thump. "Oh, give him to me," she cried, pushing herself into a half seated position and reaching out.

"He'll need a good bath, and after that I will check all his toes and make certain that he is presentable," Mrs. Pluck replied, handing the baby to the waiting nursemaid.

"He seems to be a boy," Arabella said, ogling the baby. "My goodness, Esme. He's remarkably well endowed!" She giggled. "It looks as if he has two turnips between his legs."

"They're all like that," Lady Bonnington said with a tinge of nostalgia in her voice. "My son was just the same. I thought he was going to be a satyr."

"Just a minute, my lady," Mrs. Pluck said. "Just one little push now."

A few minutes later, Esme hoisted herself into a sitting position. "I'd like to hold my son, please," she said hoarsely. "Please—now!"

Mrs. Pluck looked up. "Everything in good time, my lady. After we—"

Arabella reached over and snatched the baby out of the nursemaid's arms. "Lady Rawlings wants to hold her son." She put him, rather awkwardly, in Esme's arms. He was still howling, fat little legs jerking out of the blanket.

"This isn't wise," Mrs. Pluck scolded. "It's best if the baby is washed within the first five minutes of its birth. Cleanliness is essential to good health."

"There's time for many a bath in his future," Arabella said, bending over the bed. "He's so plumpy, isn't he, Esme? And look at his gorgeous little toes!"

Esme had never felt anything quite like it. It was as if the world had narrowed to a pinhole, the size of herself and the baby. He was so beautiful that her heart sang with it. And yet he was remarkably homely as well.

"Why is his face so red?" she asked. "And why is his head this peculiar shape?"

"The course of nature," Mrs. Pluck answered importantly. "They all look like that. Now you'll have to give up the baby, my lady. We have just a few more things to do here."

But the baby had decided to open his eyes. Esme clutched him closer. "Hello there," she whispered. "Hello, love." He blinked and closed his mouth. His eyes were the pale blue of the sky on a very early morning, and he looked up at her, quite as if he were memorizing her face. "I know you think you're smiling at me," Esme told him, kissing his nose and his forehead and his fat little cheeks. "You just forgot to smile, didn't you, sweet William?"

"Are you naming him William?" Lady Bonnington asked. "I suppose that must be an old name in Lord Rawlings's family—his father, you know," she told the nursemaid, who looked blank.

William's eyes were sweet and solemn, trusting Esme to keep him safe, trusting her to nourish and protect him. For years and years to come. A chill of fear fell on Esme's heart. Benjamin, her own little baby brother, had died. Of course, it wasn't the same, but sweet William was so enchantingly dear. He frowned a little as a drop fell on his cheek.

"What is it, darling?" Arabella asked. "Oh no, the baby's getting wet. Shall I take him?"

"He's the most beautiful baby I ever saw," Esme said, hiccuping. "I lo-love him so much. But he's so little! What if something happens to him? I couldn't bear it!"

"She's having some sort of reaction to the birth," Lady Bonnington observed. "Takes some women that way. My second cousin twice removed went into a decline after her daughter was born. Mind you, that husband of hers was enough to send anyone into a decline."

Esme swallowed and dried her eyes on the sheet. "He has Miles's eyes," she said to Arabella, ignoring the marchioness. "See?" She turned William toward Arabella. "They have just that sweetness that Miles had. Miles's eyes were that same blue. And Miles is *dead*."

"But his son isn't," Arabella said, smiling down at her. "William is a fine, sturdy baby, with nothing fragile about him."

"I agree," Lady Bonnington said promptly. "I knew immediately that the baby was the image of your husband."

Arabella threw her a look of potent dislike. "Why don't you go transmit this happy news to your son, Honoratia?"

"I shall," the marchioness said, "I shall. And may I say, Lady Rawlings, that I am impressed by your handling of this entire delicate matter?"

Whether Lady Bonnington meant to refer to the process of giving birth, or that of identifying Esme's child's father, no one could tell. Mrs. Pluck took the baby, who promptly started crying again.

"He wants to be with me," Esme said, struggling to sit upright.

"He has a good healthy voice," Mrs. Pluck said, handing him to the wet nurse. "But the course of nature must take its course, my lady," she said, rather obscurely.

Helene had come in and was peering at the baby as the wet nurse wrapped him in a warm cloth. "Oh, Esme, he's absolutely lovely," she said.

"Does he look healthy to you?" Esme asked the nursemaid.

"Fat as a suckling pig," the wet nurse said promptly. "Now shall we see if he'd like some breakfast?"

She sat down and pulled open the neck of her gown. Esme watched as William turned to the nurse and made a little grunting noise. He had those great blue eyes open, and he was looking up at the nursemaid. From Esme's point of view, it looked as if he were giving the woman the very same blinking, thoughtful glance he had given her.

White-hot jealousy stabbed her in the chest. That was *her* baby, her own sweet William. "Give him to me!" she said sharply.

The wet nurse looked up, confused. She had William's head in position and was about to offer him her breast.

"Don't you *dare* nurse my baby!" Esme said, her hands instinctively clenched into fists. "Give me William this instant!"

"Well, my goodness," the wet nurse said. "You hired me, my lady."

"I changed my mind," Esme snapped. She was not going to have William think that anyone else was his mother. She would do everything for him that needed to be done, including feeding.

The wet nurse pursed her lips, but she brought over the child. "It doesn't come easily, nursing a child," she said. "It's quite painful at the beginning, and there's many a woman who can't master the art of it. And ladies don't have the breasts for it, to tell the truth."

"I have the breasts for it," Esme said with all the authority she could command. "Now, if you'll just tell us how to do this, I'd like to give William his breakfast."

"If you don't mind my being blunt," Lady Bonnington announced, "that very idea makes me feel squeamish. A lady is more than a milch cow, Lady Rawlings!"

"Oh do go on, Honoratia," Arabella said impatiently. "Don't you have something important to tell your son?"

Lady Bonnington left the bedchamber feeling a bit piqued. After all, Lady Rawlings was no relative of *hers,* and yet there she'd stayed, for all of three hours, counseling her to greater efforts. It was quite likely due to her efforts that Lady Rawlings had managed to get through the birth so quickly. But, on the other hand, she couldn't have hoped for a better outcome. Lady Rawlings herself had identified the child's father, and that was all there was to it. Sebastian would have to acknowledge himself free of responsibility now.

"He doesn't look a bit like you," the marchioness told her son with more than a twinge of satisfaction. "He's bald as a belfry, just like his father."

"Miles Rawlings had hair until a few years ago," Sebastian pointed out.

"You wait until you see that child," his mother said, rather gleefully. "He's the image of his father. You needn't feel a moment's anxiety about whether you have a responsibility to him. You haven't. Lady Rawlings started weeping the moment she saw him, because the child has her husband's eyes. There's no doubt about it. Miles Rawlings has a posthumous son."

Lady Bonnington paused and looked at her son. He seemed a little pale. "You're free," she said, rather more gently.

He looked at her, and the expression in his eyes shocked her to the toes. "I don't suppose she asked for me?"

"No," his mother said, shaken. "No, she didn't."

She bit her lip as Sebastian turned about without another word and walked from the room. Could it be that he was more entangled with this woman than she thought? No. But it seemed that she had underestimated the amount to which Sebastian had hoped the child would be his own. I'll have to get the boy married off as soon as possible, the marchioness decided. To a girl from a large family, a woman who wouldn't be loathe to have more than one child herself. Although if my future daughter-in-law shows the faintest interest in turning herself into a milk cow, I'll have to set her straight.

There are some things that would *never* happen in the Bonnington family. And that sort of ludicrously ill bred behavior was one of them.

# 28

## In the Library

*B*eatrix Lennox had made up her mind. She had dillydallied enough over the question of Stephen Fairfax-Lacy. In fact, she had given him far too much importance in her life. She had never had the faintest wish to invite a man to her bed twice; actually inviting one into her chamber was the best way she knew of to utterly blot out any future desire for his company.

Dressing to seduce Stephen took her all afternoon. At the end, she was certain that she was utterly delectable. She was scented and polished and curled and colored . . . every inch of her. She wore no corset, and no cotton padding; instead she chose a gown that offered everything she had to the world in a burst of pagan enthusiasm. It was of French silk, shaded in a subdued blue-green color that turned her hair to flame. It was daringly low, and ornamented with ribbons of a slightly darker shade.

There were very few covers at the table for dinner, of course. Esme apparently would not even rise from her bed for a matter of days or weeks. Bea paid Stephen almost no attention during the meal, allowing him to flirt as he wished with Helene while Earl Godwin watched with a sardonic expression. She had no wish to engage in a noticeable competition with Helene. After all, just the previous evening Helene had lavishly thanked Bea for her help in gaining Stephen's friendship. She would likely be somewhat startled if Bea snatched him back before her very eyes.

When she sauntered into the salon after supper, the earl and countess were, naturally enough, already hammering away at the piano. Stephen's eyes darkened when he registered her gown. No matter how censorious the man might be about her face painting, he liked that dress. There wasn't a man alive who wouldn't like it.

"You look delicious!" Arabella cried, holding out her hands. "Trust my own Bea to keep us from falling into country doldrums. If we spend too much time here, we're likely to stop dressing for dinner at all!"

Bea gave a faint shudder. The idea of wearing the same clothing through an entire day was intolerable.

"Bea," Helene called, looking up from the piano, "would you very much mind trying my waltz again? I would like to demonstrate it to Rees."

*Perfect.*

Bea turned around to find that Stephen was already at her side. His eyes were almost black, and she felt a surge of female triumph. Why *shouldn't* she woo if she wanted? Men had their way far too often in life, as it was. She dropped into a low curtsy, putting out her hand to Stephen. He bowed and straightened, kissing her hand. Then he paused for one second, gazing at her arm. Bea looked down. There was nothing odd about her arm. "Are you quite all right?" she asked.

"I had a sudden recollection of dancing with a young lady who shall remain unnamed," he said. "She left marks of white powder all over my coat."

Bea raised an eyebrow. "This white is all my own."

Their eyes caught for a second, and she let her smile tell him that the rest of her was just as white, and just as unpowdered.

Then the music began. Helene had curbed the waltz's frenzied pace somewhat. It still rollicked, though. Bea was shivering with excitement. Now that she'd finally got herself to this point, she couldn't imagine why she'd ever wasted the previous fortnight thinking about it. Wooing—wooing was like breathing, for her. Why hadn't she seen that? She smiled at him and let just a hint of the desire that was pounding through her body show. Just a hint.

He didn't respond, which was a little disappointing. All he did was swirl her into another series of long circles that carried them down the long length of the Rose Salon. Bea couldn't help it; the very feeling of his hand on her waist made her feel greedy. She edged closer. He seemed to push her away. Her heart was beating so fast that she could hardly hear the music.

"Have you joined the adoring hordes in the nursery?" Stephen asked.

And what would be the point of *that?* Bea wanted to shriek. Ladies such as herself never had children! They had men . . . not babies. She didn't want one anyway. William looked like a buttery little blob to her. The moment she peered at him, he started to cry, and the very sound put her teeth on edge. "I'm not very maternal," she said.

Stephen drew her into a sweeping circle. "I don't seem to be developing a paternal side either," he said, once they were straight again. "Helene is agog over that child."

Bea didn't want to talk about Helene. She had to get this done. "Mr. Fairfax-Lacy," she said, and stopped.

He bent his head, that dark head that was so beautifully shaped. "Yes?"

"If you would join me in the library, I should like to discuss a poem with you."

His eyes were inscrutable. Yet surely he knew what she was saying! *He'd* told her to woo, after all. She managed to smile, but it was hardly a seductive triumph. Then she just waited, heart in her throat.

"I would very much like to finish reading you a poem," she said steadily, when he didn't respond.

He raised an eyebrow. He looked ages older and more worldly than she. Perhaps he didn't feel the same sort of ravishing longing that she did. "The Barnfield poem," she clarified.

"Ah."

So when the waltz was over, she bid everyone good night and left the Rose Salon. She didn't look to see whether he followed. Because if he didn't follow, she was going to cry, and then she was going to pretend that none of this had ever happened. In fact, she'd probably go to London the next morning and stay with friends.

But he did follow.

She walked into the library, Stephen behind her. He was mesmerized by the way Bea's hips swayed. It seemed to promise everything, that little swing and sway. "Did you practice that walk?" he asked, lighting the lamp with a candle from the mantelpiece. He had the oddest feeling of disappointment. She had invited him to an impromptu seduction. What else had he expected when he'd told her to woo? She was, after all, just what she appeared to be: remarkably available.

He turned around and she was smiling, nestled into the arm of a high-backed settee like a wanton. "What do you think?"

"I think you're too damned practiced," he said bluntly.

Her smile disappeared, and there was something uncertain in her eyes. Almost diffident. He walked over. "You needn't look like a little girl denied a sweet. You can have any man you please."

"At the moment, I would like you." Trust Bea to go straight to the point.

Her hair had the sheen of a feverish rose. Stephen had never felt anything like the lust he had at the moment. And yet every civilized bone he had in his body fought it. She was a young, unmarried woman. He didn't succumb to such wiles. In fact, he realized with an almost visible start, he'd never *been* seduced. He had only seduced. It was a great deal more uncomfortable the other way around.

She turned from him and picked up the small leather book on the table. "Shall I start with the poem which gave everyone so much excitement?" she asked. There was a satin thread in her voice that made Stephen's entire body stiffen.

> *O would to God (so I might have my fee)*
> *My lips were Honey, and thy mouth a Bee.*

He couldn't stop himself. He drifted over to the settee. His will was strong enough that he didn't sit down, but he found himself leaning over the tall back, standing just at her shoulder. She looked up at him, a sparkling glance, and he found to his torment that this position merely gave him an excellent view of her breasts. They were a perfect white that had nothing to do with powder, not that snowy perfection.

> *Then shouldst thou sucke my sweete*
> *and my faire flower*
> *That now is ripe, and full of honey-berries . . .*

Stephen could just make out the outline of Bea's nipples, puckered under the frail silk of her bodice. He gave in, reached a hand over her shoulder, and wantonly, deliberately, took one of her breasts in his hand. There was a gasp, and she stopped reading.

But she didn't jump away or protest. That was disappointing too. What a fool I am, he thought. Why not just enjoy what is being offered?

Her breast was perfect. Somehow he'd thought it would be larger, fleshier. But it was flawlessly tender, an unsteady weight in his fingers.

" *'Full of honey-berries,'* " he prompted. His voice was rough and unsteady. He supposed dimly that her other lovers had been more debonair, probably, less—

He couldn't pretend this was normal behavior for him. Or normal desire, for that matter.

" *'Then would I leade thee to my pleasant Bower,'* " she said, and the quaver had moved from his to her voice. " *'Filled full of grapes, of mulberries and cherries. Then shouldst thou be my Wasp, or else my Bee, I would be thy hive, and thou my honey bee.'* "

He brought his other arm around her neck and took both breasts in his hands. She moaned, a throaty little sound, and dropped the book, arching her head back into the curve of his neck. He let his mouth play along her cheek. She smelled like lemons, clean and sweet, an English smell. Her ear was small and neatly placed against her head. In fact, her ear was like the rest of her: small, perfectly shaped, rounded, beautiful. He nipped it in anguish. Why did she have to be so—so beautiful and so available?

Her arms were tangling in his hair, pulling his head closer to her mouth. The small gasps that fell from her lips didn't seem practiced. They sounded wrenched from her throat. God knows the hoarse sounds he kept swallowing were wrenched from his own chest.

Her breasts seemed to swell in his hands, and he hadn't even allowed himself to move his hands. "Bea." His voice was hoarse and embarrassingly gruff. It sounded like an old man's voice.

This time he managed to speak clearly. "Bea, we cannot do this."

Her eyes closed, and her arms fell from his hair. He lifted his hands from her breasts—what if someone walked into the library? He waited a second, but she didn't open her eyes.

"Bea?" he asked. He was standing straight now, as straight as possible given the strain in his pantaloons.

"You may leave," she said. She didn't open her eyes.

"What?"

"I'm going to sit here and pretend that you aren't a stick-in-the-mud Puritan," she said. "I'm going to pretend that you actually had the courtesy to go through with the invitation that you ordered me to issue, if I remember correctly. Or is it a lack of guts that's the issue?"

"That's incredibly vulgar," he said slowly.

She opened her eyes. "Mr. Fairfax-Lacy, listen to me carefully."

She seemed to be waiting for a response, so he nodded curtly.

"I can be far more vulgar than this. I am a vulgar woman, Mr. Fairfax-Lacy." Her eyes were flashing, for all her voice was even. She was in a rage, and Stephen didn't know why that would make him feel better, but it did.

"Look at this, Mr. Puritan-Lacy!" she said, grabbing her bodice and pulling it down. Two perfectly shaped breasts, satin smooth, white velvet, fell free of her bodice. "I-am-a-vulgar-woman," she said, emphasizing every word. "I am the sort of woman who allows herself to be handled in the library by—"

He was at her side. "No, you are not." His voice was dry, authoritative and utterly commanding. In one split second he hauled her bodice so high over her breasts that it almost touched her collarbone.

She narrowed her eyes. "How dare you say what I am or am not?"

"I know you," he said calmly, although his hands were shaking. "You are no vulgar woman, Bea."

"Well—," she said, obviously about to rush into a hundred examples, but he stopped her with a kiss. They drank each other as if manna had fallen between them, as if kisses were the bread of life.

"You're worse," he said against her lips, a moment later. He felt them curve beneath his mouth, and he wanted her so fiercely that his entire body throbbed. "It must be tiring being so much worse than vulgar day and night."

She could not answer because his lips were crushing hers. And somehow his hands were back at her breasts. He brushed her nipple through the silk of her bodice, and she gasped.

"These must be your *honey-berries,*" he said in her ear.

"That's so vulgar," she said, a hint of laughter in her voice.

He yanked down her bodice, the mere inch that kept her nipple from the evening air, and flicked his tongue over it. She stiffened and clutched his shoulders so hard that he would likely have bruises. He did it again. And again.

"Stephen," she whispered. Her voice didn't sound so practiced now. It was ragged and hoarse.

Finally his mouth closed over her breast. She arched against him, shaking all over. He felt a stab of pure arrogance. She may have slept with other men, but he couldn't believe that she reacted to them like this.

Of course, that's exactly what every other man thought.

"I want to be *courted,*" he said fiercely.

"What's the difference?" she said. She sounded genuinely perplexed.

"I am not wooing you at this moment," Stephen said. "I am seducing you." He ran a hand up her leg, past the sleek silk stocking and the slight bump of her garter. "You need to learn the difference, Bea." His voice was rough with lust. His fingers trembled as they danced over the skin of her inner thighs, closer, closer—

She reached forward, pulling his hair toward her. "Kiss me!" she said, and her voice had an unsteadiness that sent his blood in a dizzying swirl.

So he kissed her, took her mouth with an untamed exuberance, at the very moment his fingers slipped into her warmth, pressed up and in with a strength that made her arch helplessly against him. She was ripe and plump, and it took every bit of strength he had to let his fingers drift where his body longed to be. To drive her mad, make her shudder under his hand even as he drank her cries with his mouth.

"This is seduction," he said to her, and his voice was raw with it.

He could feel the coil in her, feel the tension growing. She was so beautiful, trembling in his arms, coming closer and closer . . .

"Would you do this for me?" he said fiercely.

Her eyes opened. They were magnificent, drenched, beautiful . . . "Of course!" she choked. She reached out for him. "Please . . ."

"It's seduction."

"It's glorious."

He made his fingers still, just stay there, in the melting warmth. Then just as she was about to stir, he moved again. She gasped, and her body jerked against his. He stopped. And then pressed hard again.

"Stephen, don't!" she cried.

"Don't? Don't?" He let his fingers take a rhythm then. And allowed himself, finally, to return to her lips, beautiful dark and swollen, not with false colors but with kisses.

She was writhing against him now, panting little bursts of air, a scream building in her—he could feel it, could feel an answering shout in his own chest, a desperate longing—

She shuddered all over and clutched his shoulders so hard that he could feel her fingernails bite into his flesh, even through his coat.

And then she was pliant in his arms, a sweet, curved womanly body. He whispered into her hair. "That was a seduction, Bea."

There was silence in the library, and then she said, "I think I guessed that. At some point." The thread of laughter in her voice would always be part of living with Bea.

She didn't pull away from him, though. She stayed, nestled into his arm like a dove. He had to leave the room or he'd lose his resolve. Stephen had the sense he was fighting the greatest battle of his life: his own Enclosure Act. He had to enclose her, keep her, marry her.

And he had to make her understand that.

"I want more from you," he said into her ear.

She opened her eyes rather drowsily and smiled at him. His blood licked like fire at the look in them. "I'm amenable," she said sleekly.

"You don't know what I want," he pointed out.

She blinked. "Couldn't you teach me?"

"I want to be courted, Bea." He watched her carefully. "Not seduced, *wooed*."

"Do I have to consult a dictionary?"

"I hope not. May I escort you to your chamber?"

She was the most beautiful thing he had ever seen in his life, with her hair tumbling over her shoulders and a faint rosy color high in her cheeks. It took every bit of self-control he had in his body to leave her at her bedchamber door. But he was playing for keeps.

# 29

## *Spousal Relations*

*C*andles were being snuffed in bedchambers all over the house. Rooms were sinking into darkness, into the pleasant intimacy that welcomes a lover's step, a silent kiss, a whispered invitation. But Rees Holland, Earl Godwin, was hardly in a loverlike mood. He stared at the door to his bedchamber, grimly awaiting—

His wife.

And wasn't that an irony? That he should feel such a revulsion of feeling, such a disinclination to even speak to the woman, that he felt like dashing out of the house and saddling a horse on the moment? But there it was. She was a viper, Helene was. She could say the merest thing to him, and it would sting to the bottom of his soul for days.

And yet—he told himself again—he only wanted the best for her. Fairfax-Lacy wasn't a man to stand by her during a divorce. 'Twould ruin his career, for one thing. She was infatuated with the man, he could tell that. But it wouldn't last. Fairfax-Lacy was naught more than a smooth-talking politician, a silver-tongued devil, as his grandmother would have said. He didn't look at her with much desire, either. Rees had caught Fairfax-Lacy looking at Beatrix Lennox with real interest in his eyes.

That was the crux of it. He himself had been a damned failure as a husband to Helene. Not that she'd been any good as a wife. But presumably she was bedding Fairfax-Lacy, so perhaps it was only with him that she felt so—revolted. It was amazing to find that it still stung, years later. Even now, when he saw her, he had the impulse to put on a cravat, to cover any stray chest hair that might show. Because it *disgusted* her. She had said that again and again. Hairy beast, that he was.

Rees grimaced. What the hell was he even worrying about her for? She was a sharp-tongued little devil. Except he couldn't let her make the same mistake again. She needed to find a husband who'd be true to her this time. And Fairfax-Lacy wasn't the one. Not with the liquorish way he glanced at Lady Beatrix when no one was looking. He never looked at Helene that way. Oh, he was wooing her: teasing her with extravagant compliments about her moonlit hair and other such blather. But he didn't look at her with that smoky longing that a man looks at a woman he wants to bed. Can't bear *not* to bed, in fact.

And yet she was obviously planning to ask for a divorce. Presumably Mr. M.P. thought he could get an Act of Parliament allowing her to remarry. But if Helene married Fairfax-Lacy, she'd find herself with yet another unfaithful husband. He, Rees, had allowed her to go her own way and find a consort of her own. He'd given her her own life back. But Mr. Proper Fairfax-Lacy would never do that. No, he would dally with strumpets on the side, embarrassing Helene in public and private, but he'd never give her freedom to do the same.

There was a scratching on the door, and it silently swung open. Rees marveled for a moment: the doors in Lady Rawlings's house seemed to have been greased, they moved so quietly.

Helene looked rather like a silvery ghost. She was muffled up in a thick dressing gown, looking as drearily proper as any matron in all England. Rees had to admit that he was rather glad she had found a consort. The burden of being the only adulterous one in their marriage was exausting for his conscience.

"Forgive me for my informal attire," she told him. Her voice was cool, with just the faintest edge that told him that she expected him to be rude. Vulgar, even. She always thought he was vulgar.

So he bowed and settled her in a chair with all the manners he could summon to mind.

"I've come to ask for a divorce," she said abruptly, "but I'm sure you've guessed that."

"Has Mr. Fairfax-Lacy agreed to exposure as your consort?" Perhaps the skepticism in his tone was audible. "He will allow me to sue him for adultery?"

But she was shaking her head, perfectly calmly. "Oh, no, that might infringe upon his career. Stephen has a very important role in the government, in the life of the nation. We'll simply have to hire some man to stand in his place."

Rees didn't have to think hard to know that a writer of comic operas wasn't considered important to *the life of the nation.* "Shouldn't Fairfax-Lacy be in session at this very moment, if he's so vital?" he asked.

"Stephen is quite, quite exhausted by the ordeals of a recent parliamentary debate," Helene said, waving her hand in the air.

Rees thought sourly about exhausted men and their proclivities to entertain themselves with other people's wives. "Ah, exhausted. I see."

"You wouldn't understand, Rees. Stephen has a critical role in the House. He just finished orchestrating a tremendous battle against an Enclosure Act. That's when a rich man fences in land that was originally openly used for grazing by villagers. Stephen had to go against his own party!"

"I know what an Enclosure Act is," Rees said irritably. "And I fully understand that he is a worthy man."

"So it would be better for all concerned if we simply created evidence of my adultery."

"I don't see any reason for us to go to the tremendous expense of effecting a divorce," Rees said. Despite all his caution, he was starting to get angry. It was something about that martyr role that she played so well: as if he had ruined her life. Whereas it was more the opposite—she had ruined *his* life!

Her jaw set. "I don't wish to be married to you any longer, Rees."

"We can't all have what we want. And now you seem to have the best of all worlds, if you'll excuse a little plain speaking. You have the proper politician for a bit of kiss and tumble on the side, as well as the title of countess and the very generous allowance I make you."

"I don't give a fig for the allowance," she said. Her eyes were glacial.

"No, I don't suppose you do." He was losing his temper again. Damn it, but she had a way of getting under his skin. "Because if you did, you might actually buy some clothing designed to appeal to a man. How the hell does Fairfax-Lacy fight his way through that thing you're wearing?" He eyed her thick woolen dressing gown.

She raised her chin and squared her shoulders. She could have been wearing the mantle of a queen. "The allowance, the title—they're *nothing*. It's a baby that I want," she said. And to Rees's horror, her voice wobbled. Helene and he never, ever showed vulnerability to each other. It was beyond possibility that he should comfort her.

"A baby. I believe you told me that before," he said, giving her time to gather herself together.

Helene took a deep breath and leaned forward. She had to convince Rees: she simply *had* to. Never mind the fact that she had no intention of marrying Stephen. It took ages to obtain a divorce, and she could find someone else to marry during the process. "Have you seen Esme's baby?" she asked.

"Of course not. Why on earth would I venture into the nursery to peer at a newborn?"

"William is the dearest little boy that you ever saw," Helene said, trying vainly to convey the stab of longing that overtook her at the very sight of the baby. "His eyes are a lovely clear blue. And he looks at Esme so sweetly. I think he already knows who she is."

Rees couldn't stand children. They mewled, spit and vomited on a regular basis. They also created any manner of revolting odors without the slightest consideration for others in the room. Moreover, there was something about the slavish adoration in her voice that set his teeth on edge.

"A baby is unlikely, in your situation," he said bluntly. "You would do better to avoid the nursery, if a mere visit sends you into this kind of transport of emotion."

Helene had been smiling a little, but the smile withered immediately. "Why not?" she demanded. "And what precisely do you mean by *my situation?*" Rees was grateful to hear that her voice was not trembling now; she sounded more likely to garrotte him on the spot.

"You would do better to simply accept the truth," he said. "I have done so, I assure you. I have no hope of having an heir." Never mind the fact that he'd never wanted one. "I think it is far better that we simply accept our situation."

"And that is?"

"We're married to each other and, obviously, our marriage isn't tenable. But no putative second husband has presented himself. Fairfax-Lacy won't even stand by you during the divorce. Therefore, he's extremely unlikely to marry you afterwards."

"He would!" Her voice was shrill now, but Rees far appreciated shrill over teary.

"I doubt it. And frankly, my dear, he's eyeing that wanton little friend of Lady Withers's. So even if he did obtain an Act of Parliament allowing him to marry you—and I suppose, given his position, he has more chance of success than most men—he'd be as unfaithful to you as I am." Rees rather liked the way he had summed up their situation. "If you find a braver consort, I'd be happy to reconsider the idea of divorce," he added.

"Bloody hell!" She exploded out of her chair like one of those Chinese firecrackers he'd seen in London. "How bloody generous of you! You are the most stubborn, disgusting man in all England!"

"I think I am being perfectly reasonable," Rees said, staying right where he was. Surely husbands didn't have to follow that nonsense about standing up every time a lady did.

"Reasonable!"

"You would be happier if you simply accepted the situation," he said.

"You *bastard!*"

That caught him on the raw. "Don't you think that I would like something more?" he roared. He bounded from his chair and grabbed her by the shoulders. "Don't you think that I would like a real marriage? A wife I could love, could talk with, laugh with?"

For a second she shrunk away from him, and then she raised her head and glared. "Am I responsible for that? No! *You* eloped with me when I was barely out of the schoolroom!"

"I was barely of age myself," he said. "We were fools together, Helene, don't you see?" He gave her a little shake. "God knows I'd love to take back the moment I asked you to elope. I wanted—want—more from life than I have! I see Darby and Henrietta together, and I wish—" He turned away. There was no point in continuing this subject. He sat down, plopping into the chair with a sense of exhaustion that took his whole being.

There was silence in the room for a moment and then, with a faint rustle of wool, she sat down opposite him.

"So," she said finally, "you see your friend Darby and his new wife, and you wish for a more appropriate spouse. Someone as charming and beautiful as Henrietta, I gather. Whereas I see Esme's baby, and I feel equally envious."

"My only point," he said, feeling as tired as he ever had in his life, "is that at some point one simply has to accept what's happened. I made a mistake, and God knows I've paid for it."

"*You've* paid for it," she whispered, incredulous. He could see her small fists clenched in her lap. "I'm the one who lives to be ridiculed, to have everyone tell me about your—your opera singer. I'm the one who wants a child and will never be able to have one. I'm the one who can't even attract a man willing to face the scandal of marrying me! Your life is *perfect*. You have your music and your opera singer. And I don't believe for a moment that you really want Henrietta: she's not at all musical."

"I don't want Henrietta. I just want—I want what Darby has with his wife." Rees leaned his head back against the carved oak of his chair. "Fool that I am, I want a woman's companionship."

After that, they just sat there.

Helene didn't say anything about the light his comment cast on his relationship with his opera singer, the woman living in Helene's own bedchamber.

And Rees didn't say anything about the fact that Helene herself had admitted that Fairfax-Lacy didn't have the nerve to stand by her during a divorce.

There had been precious few acts of kindness in this particular marriage, but sometimes silence can be the greatest kindness of all.

## 30

### In the Midst of the Night

It was two o'clock in the morning, and Sebastian had only just managed to wave his mother off to her bedchamber. She had spent the evening babbling of balls and Almack's and other locales at which he was sure to meet an eligible wife. A fertile one, as she kept emphasizing. But he didn't want a wife, not even the fruitful woman his mother had set her heart on. Naturally, he couldn't visit Esme's bedchamber during the day. But now . . . was it late enough? Surely the child would be snug in the nursery, and that would leave Esme able to receive visitors. She'd been through an ordeal. He had to see her.

He walked up the darkened stairs feeling as cautious as a man rendezvousing with a new mistress. Esme's room was quite light due to a roaring fire in the grate. Esme herself was sitting in the middle of her bed, rocking back and forth, the baby in her arms. Her hair had fallen forward over her face, and she apparently didn't hear him come in.

He closed the door softly. "Esme," he whispered.

Her whole body jerked, and she stared up at him. She looked so exhausted and drawn that Sebastian swallowed. He knew birth was difficult, but my God, she looked as if she'd been through the wars.

And then he heard a thin wail. Esme shot him a look of pure rage, and turned to the child. Miraculously, the anger dropped away, and her face turned to an expression of pure adoration. She started cooing at the baby, and smiling at him, and dusting his little face with kisses. Naturally the child stopped crying immediately. Even more so when Esme offered him her breast. Sebastian sat down next to the bed and watched as moonlight washed over Esme's tumbling hair, her breast, the baby's little hand holding her finger as he suckled. Surely it was wrong to feel such longing to be part of the group. But he did. He wanted to climb onto the bed, to help position William at her breast, to . . .

To be there.

"He seems to be a good-natured child," Sebastian ventured, once Esme had tucked William over her shoulder and was patting his back.

Her eyes flashed at him. "He's very delicate. I shall have to be quite careful that he doesn't take cold."

Sebastian watched William's chubby legs kicking. "He is delicate?"

Esme nodded as William gave a burp.

"He sounds like one of the lads down at the tavern," Sebastian said. William looked at him with a beery expression. "He even looks drunk."

"He does not!" Esme said indignantly. "But Sebastian, don't you think he's the image of Miles? I knew he would be. I just knew he would be."

To Sebastian, William looked like most of the babies he'd seen in his life: bald, round and red. Yes, he looked like Miles. But then *all* babies looked like Miles.

"I have blue eyes," he said, unable to stop himself.

"Not that azure blue," Esme said. "And it's not the color that matters anyway. It's the way he looks at one, with such a deep sweetness . . . just like Miles. He's the sweetest boy in the whole world, aren't you?" And she gathered little William up into her arms and kissed him all over his face again. "Now he has to go to sleep," Esme said, looking expectantly at Sebastian. So he left.

She likely thought he would leave the house as well. But no. He would stay. And his mother would have to stay as well, like it or not. If the *ton* discovered the whereabouts of the notorious Marquess Bonnington, the presence of his stodgy mother would likely dispel some suspicion.

Or perhaps it wouldn't. He didn't really give a damn.

William slept most of the following day while Esme and Arabella hovered over the crib, pointing out the pink perfection of his toes, and the sweetness of his round tummy. Esme was convinced he already knew who she was. "That's a loving look," she told her aunt when William finally opened his eyes.

"If you say so," Arabella said.

"I know it. Do you think William is warm enough? I think his cheek is a bit chilled." She felt it with the back of her hand and tucked his blankets around him even more securely.

"I'll ring the footman for another log," Arabella said, going to the other side of the room. That was one of the things that Esme loved about her aunt. Unlike the nursemaid, who was annoyingly contentious, and even her own nanny, Arabella never questioned Esme's judgement.

Esme picked William up and put his little cheek against her own. It felt like the softest silk in the world.

"So your mother writes that she will visit at her earliest convenience?" Arabella asked, coming back and fingering the delicate embroidery on William's coverlet.

"I'm so happy about it," Esme said. "It was disappointing when she didn't visit during my confinement. But she can't help but love William."

Arabella cast her a worried look. "Of course Fanny will love William. But I just . . ." Her voice trailed off.

"Don't worry. William will enchant her."

Arabella took another glance at her niece's hopeful face and decided that she had to speak. "I'm worried for *you*, Esme. Your mother has suffered many disappointments in her life. She's not always as agreeable as she could be."

"I know that," Esme said instantly. She had always been aware that she was her mother's primary trial. "But William will make up for all that, don't you see? And of course, I'm going to be just the sort of daughter she always wished for. She won't have to be ashamed of me anymore."

"Yee-es. I certainly hope that's the way of it."

"But you don't believe it?"

"I'm afraid that you may be disappointed," Arabella admitted. "I shall *scream* at Fanny if she hurts your feelings. But, I just—"

"You mustn't worry so much. Truly, Mama has always wished me to be respectable, and now I am. I'm living in Wiltshire like the virtuous widow I am. What more could she want?"

"Fanny has a difficult nature. She has spent a great deal of her adult life berating you for one thing or another, and I never approved of it, never."

Esme gave her a rueful grin. "It's not as if I didn't deserve it. I'm the first to say that my reputation was precisely as black as it deserved to be."

"But Fanny was disappointed even before you grew into such a convenient whipping boy. When I was growing up with her, she was always finding fault with me as well. In fact, Esme, my sister Fanny is a bit of a malcontent. Your grandfather used to call her Miss Tart, because of the way she pranced around the house with her mouth tight, finding fault with everyone."

"I know Mama has had an onerous life," Esme said. She was tickling William through his blankets, and he looked as if he might start smiling any moment. "But perhaps having a grandchild will transform some of her discouragement, especially if he starts smiling. Smile, William! Smile for Mama! And he *is* beautiful. Even Sebastian said last night that—" She stopped short and turned around to find Arabella looking at her and shaking her head.

"A woman after my own heart," Arabella said. "I told you that living with a man was far more fun than living alone, didn't I?"

Esme bit her lip. "Sebastian only—"

"Never mind the details. What about Fairfax-Lacy? When are you planning to drop that pretense?"

"Not yet! Not until after my mother visits. The only reason she is making a visit is due to Lady Bonnington telling her of my engagement."

"In that case, I would advise that you wait until nighttime to entertain Bonnington again. Lord knows, if Honoratia Bonnington found out that her son was making secret trips to your bedchamber, and you still in confinement, she'd likely shriek the roof down."

Esme smiled a bit at that. "I'm not worried about the marchioness. It's Mother, of course, whom I would prefer not to realize that Sebastian and I have a friendship."

"Naturally," Arabella agreed. "We definitely do *not* wish for sainted Fanny to discover that you have a man visiting your bedchamber in the wee hours of the night."

"There's nothing *salacious* about his visits," Esme hastened to say.

Arabella bent over the crib again, and Esme couldn't see her face. "My first husband, Robbie, used to look at me the way Marquess Bonnington looks at you."

"I don't think I remember him," Esme said. "And Sebastian doesn't look at me in any particular fashion."

"Robbie died when you were a young girl. You likely never would have met him anyway. How he loathed your father!"

"Were you very much in love?" Esme asked.

"Too much," Arabella answered flatly. She turned around, and her smile was bright. "Never fall in love, darling. It makes farewells utterly dreary."

Esme didn't say anything to that nonsense, but just gave her a kiss.

"I can't be as angry at your mother as I'd like to be," Arabella said, with one of her lightning changes of conversation, "because I was so lucky with my first marriage, and she so unlucky. Robbie was a sweet-hearted man. He died laughing, you know. We were riding in the country, and he was laughing at something I said. He wasn't paying attention, and his horse caught a rabbit-hole."

"Oh, Arabella," Esme said, putting her arms around her.

"I only tell you because your memories of your father are undoubtedly as clear as mine," Arabella said. "That man never laughed a day in his life. Being married to him was a terrible hardship, for all your mother won't acknowledge it. Terrible. I was allowed to choose my husband, as I was the homely sister. But Fanny went to the highest bidder."

"Don't you think that William will assuage some of her grief?"

"I hope so, darling. I hope so."

## 31

## A Proposal

There was no saying when, if ever, Arabella might decide to return to London for the rest of the season. As far as Bea could see, Arabella spent every spare moment fussing over the baby's clothing and counting his toes. She and Esme hovered over that fat little creature as if it were made of spun sugar. Earl Godwin left; Lord Winnamore finally left as well. There was no one in the house to talk to, given that Helene and Stephen pounded away at the keyboard for hours.

Not that it mattered much, because all Bea could think about was the Puritan, and his wish to be *wooed* rather than seduced. Wooed. Whatever that meant.

She headed off down the lane to visit the goat. It was very cold, and the wind was sprinkling small white flowers all over the lane, almost as if it were snowing. It could be a pear tree losing all its blossoms; Bea had almost made up her mind to try to find a book identifying plants. That was how boring she was becoming.

When she rounded the bend, he was there. Bea slowed down. Wooing, wooing. She was no good at wooing. She was only good at seduction. Why didn't he understand that? Why didn't he know that she had nothing else to offer? She tramped up beside him and leaned on the fence without bothering to say hello. A large hand curled around her neck.

"Bea," he said. Why did he have to have a voice like that?

"Doesn't the Parliament miss you?" she asked aimlessly, trying to take her attention away from that warm hand.

"It doesn't seem that way. According to the morning paper, they just passed a law giving poachers seven years' hard labor. I keep thinking of an old man named Maidstone, who lived on our estate when I was young.

He was such a one, poached in my father's forest his entire life. It was an art to old Maidstone. My father sent me out with him to learn to shoot."

"I wish I could shoot," Bea said. "My father didn't consider it a lady-like pursuit."

"Perhaps I'll teach you."

The statement hung in the air between them. She finally risked a glance at him, and he was smiling at her.

"When you're my wife."

She suddenly felt the splintering wood of the gate under her fingers. "You are engaged already."

"You know as well as I do that the engagement is a temporary one, having naught to do with love nor even desire."

White petals had floated onto his dark hair. "I could never marry you. I thought you understood that."

"You must have misunderstood." He moved closer and looked down at her. His eyes were flames, telling her something. But the misery in her heart was beating in her ears.

"Men like you don't take wives like me," she cried.

"Am I too old?"

"Don't be a fool."

He smiled a little. "Too rigid?"

"Something like that. It would destroy your career."

"I don't care about my career."

"Who will save the poachers from seven years' hard labor?"

"Someone else," he said. "I will go home and take care of Maidstone's son, who is undoubtedly poaching every pheasant I have in the world."

"You can't marry me." It seemed imperative to make him understand. "I am—*ruined,* Stephen." Her face was wet with tears, and she didn't even know where they had come from. "Don't you understand that? And damn you for making me say it aloud! *Why* do you insist on being so cruel? I told you, you can have me!" Her voice broke with the humiliation of it. And the truth of it. He stared at her, eyes veiled. "You could have had me, anywhere," she said brokenly. "On the billiards table, in the library. Anywhere. You're some sort of debauchee, aren't you? You just enjoy tormenting me. You don't even really want me."

"No." His voice was hard. "That's not the case and you know it, Bea. I want you." He took her shoulders. "I want you more than any other man has wanted you. But I don't want only your delectable body. Or your mouth. Or even the direction to your bedroom door. I want more, Bea, and if you can't give it to me, I don't want any of it."

She stared ahead, and the goat's sharp little horns were blurred by her tears. "I wish things were different," she said. "I wish I weren't myself, or that myself was—"

"No! You don't understand. I want you with all your face paints, and all your sultry glances, and all your wicked poetry. I want you just as you are, Bea."

It was probably a tribute to her father that she didn't believe him for a moment.

She cleared her throat. "That is remarkably kind of you. I am honored, truly. Of course, I might be even more honored if you didn't already have a fiancée. But I appreciate your willingness to add me to the list."

"Stuff that," he said, and his voice was harsh and utterly unlike the smooth cadences that members were used to hearing in the House. "Don't *be* honored," he said fiercely. "Be my wife."

"I can't do that." She turned and faced him, head high. "I care for you too much. You may be exhausted by your position at the moment, but you will long for it after a few months. I don't see you spending your days fishing and befriending poachers, Stephen. After a month, even a year perhaps, you would yearn for your position back. And they'd never give it to you, *never*. Not after you married me."

"I disagree, Bea. I could marry you and stay in Parliament. But I want to resign. If I grow bored in the country, I'll find something to do. But not Parliament. I don't want to think about votes again. I'd rather think about you."

"Leave," she said tersely, hanging onto the splintered boards with all her might. "Just leave, Stephen."

The smile fell from his face.

"Please leave," she whispered.

## 32

## And Motherly Love, Part Two

*E*sme's mother arrived on a beautiful spring day, a week after her grandson's birth. Esme looked out her bedchamber window and there it was, rounding the bend before the road to Shantill House: a squat, ugly carriage that she remembered from her childhood. The family used to travel to and from London in it. The seats were made of slippery horse-hair and sloped upward. As a child, Esme constantly slid to the carriage floor, earning a scolding for her fidgety nature.

William was sleeping in her arms, his long eyelashes curling against his cheek. "I'll never make you ride in a carriage for hours," she whispered to him. And then rethought that promise. "Well, perhaps only if we make many stops."

Then she turned aside and rang the bell. "My mother has arrived," she told Jeannie. "I must change my clothing. I'll wear the gray morning gown with the white lace trim, the one with the small tippet. And I shall wear a cap as well, perhaps with a silver ribbon so it matches."

Jeannie looked surprised. "But, madam, that gown is half-mourning, and so heavy for this weather. Wouldn't you prefer to wear something more cheerful? Surely your lady mother will wish to see you more light-hearted. We don't even have such a thing as a silver ribbon in the house!"

"No, the gray dress will be perfect." Fanny had worn full mourning for two years after Esme's father died. The least Esme could do was appear to have a virtue, even if she had it not.

"Shall I take Master William to the nursery?" Jeannie said, once Esme was dressed in gray, complete with a lace cap but no silver ribbon.

"I'll bring him downstairs with me. I'm certain my mother is quite eager to see her grandson."

"Of course she is! And he's the bonniest boy that's ever lived. She'll likely cry with pure joy. I know my mother would."

When Esme entered the morning parlor, she found her mother seated with Marchioness Bonnington and Arabella. To Esme's relief, Bea was nowhere to be seen. Esme had a secret fear that her mother would take affront at the idea of staying in the same house with her sister's *dame de compagnie* and leave without delay.

She could see on the instant that Fanny and Arabella were already twitting at each other. They were seated opposite each other, and Arabella had the look of someone who has just delivered a magnificent set-down. Fanny was shaking her head sadly and looking at her younger sister as if she were addled. Esme hurried across the room toward them.

Fanny looked like an exquisite watercolor rendition of Arabella. Arabella's hair was ginger; Fanny's was a pale rose. Arabella's complexion was a tribute to French face paints; Fanny's face had a delicate bloom all her own. Arabella's face somehow just missed being beautiful, but Fanny had been acknowledged as flawless from the moment she'd toddled into her papa's arms.

"Mama, it is such a pleasure to see you!" Esme cried. "I've brought William, who is longing to meet his grandmother."

All three ladies looked up. Her mother gave her the melancholy smile with which she always greeted her daughter, a perfect blend of responsibility and disappointment. Impulsively Esme went to her knees beside her mother and folded the blanket back from around William's face so Fanny could see him. He was still sleeping peacefully, as beautiful a child as she'd ever seen. William was the one thing in life that Esme had done perfectly.

But her mother looked at her rather than at William. "Esme," she said, "I must ask you to seat yourself properly. We are not *en famille* here. There is no need for such boisterous manners."

Lady Bonnington leaned forward. "Please don't insist on convention on my account, Fanny dear. I find your daughter's affection for her child quite refreshing."

Esme rose and seated herself next to her mother on the settee. Fanny raised her eyebrows slightly and then finally looked down at William. For a moment she stared at him in utter silence.

"Isn't he beautiful?" Esme said, unable to stop herself. "Isn't he the most darling baby you ever saw, Mama?"

Her mother closed her eyes and put out a wavering hand as if to push William away. "He looks just like your brother," she murmured, turning her face away and shading her eyes. Her hand stayed in the air, shaking slightly with the strength of her emotion.

Esme bit her lip. "William doesn't resemble Benjamin so much," she ventured. "Benjamin had such a lovely cap of black hair, do you remember? Even when he was—"

"Naturally I remember every moment of my son's short life!" her mother broke in. "You do me great disservice, daughter, to suggest that I could forget the smallest detail of my little angel's face." She sat with her face shaded by her hand, overcome by grief.

Esme was stricken into silence. She literally didn't know what to say.

"William is quite an adorable child," Arabella said. There was a crackling warning in her voice. "And I do think that he has the look of his father rather than Esme. In fact, I would say that William is the spitting image of Miles Rawlings. Why don't you look at William more closely, Fanny?"

Esme's mother visibly shuddered. "I couldn't . . . I just couldn't." She waved her slim white hand in the air. "Please, remove the child. I simply am not strong enough for this sort of blow. Not today. Perhaps when I am having a better day."

"Of course, Mama," Esme said quietly, tucking William's blanket around his face. "I'll take him back to the nursery."

"Give him to the footman," her mother instructed, sounding a bit stronger. "I didn't come all the way to this house merely to watch you act like a servant."

Esme had never given William to one of the servants, but she handed him over without a murmur. She should have realized how much pain the baby would cause her mother. No wonder Fanny hadn't attended her confinement. The whole event was undoubtedly too distressing to contemplate. As she returned to the parlor, Esme braced herself for the look of disapproval that always crossed her mother's face. But it was, miraculously, not there. Esme blinked and almost stumbled.

"Do come here, daughter," Fanny said, patting the seat next to her.

Esme sat down next to her, careful to not allow her back to touch the back of the settee.

"We were just discussing how much your cap suits you," Fanny said. "I think you will find that a cap truly eases one's life. It does the necessary work of informing lecherous men that you are a woman of propriety and virtue. They never, *ever* make indecent proposals to a woman in a cap."

Arabella looked at Esme with a faint smile. "I've just told your mother that she needn't lend me one of hers."

Fanny ignored that. "And Lady Bonnington has been regaling me with tales of your fiancé's devotion. I must say, he sounds like an estimable gentleman. What a shame that Mr. Fairfax-Lacy stands to lose his courtesy title if the Duke of Girton's wife gives birth to a son. The Earl of

Spade, isn't he? Of course, the duchess may birth a girl. We shall have to hope for the best."

"Mr. Fairfax-Lacy doesn't use his title," Esme murmured.

But her mother swept on. "It would be even better were the earl to give up his seat in Parliament. The House of Commons is so very . . . common, is it not?"

"Mr. Fairfax-Lacy plans to resign his seat," Esme said. "He wishes to spend more time on his estate."

Her mother gave her a smile and patted her hand. "I'm certain that you can effect the earl's resignation without delay. I feel quite heartened by this news, dearest."

"I'm very glad to hear it, Mama."

"Perhaps you could marry by special license," her mother continued. "That would be by far the more respectable choice. No one to gawk, as would happen in a public ceremony."

"Choice? What choice does she have?" Arabella said, and there was a distinct jaundiced note in her voice.

"Whether to remain a widowed woman or marry Mr. Fairfax-Lacy immediately," Fanny said sharply. "Given our plans to rehabilitate dear Esme's position in society, I tend to think that immediate marriage would not be frowned upon. What do you think, Honoratia?" she asked the marchioness.

"While I am naturally eager to see Lady Rawlings settled in such a beneficial position," Lady Bonnington announced, "I do not approve of marriages within the first twelve months of mourning."

Esme breathed a sigh of relief.

Arabella gave her a wink. "You must be eager to find an appropriate spouse for your son," she said, turning to Lady Bonnington, "since he has returned from the Continent. I know there is no one of the slightest interest to him at *this* house party, but I am quite certain that you must have some thoughts on the subject."

Esme's mother stiffened. Clearly she had had no idea that her friend's disreputable son was even in the country, let alone in the very house in which she sat. "May I ask—" she said, her voice shrill.

But Lady Bonnington broke in. She was magnificently quelling, Esme had to admit. "Fanny, there is no one in the world who deprecates my son's behavior more than I do. But I decided he had been in exile long enough. He has naturally attended me here; as a dutiful son, he is engaged in accompanying his mother wherever I wish to be."

"But *this* particular household is surely not the appropriate place to be!" Fanny sputtered. "Given the events of last summer—"

"We do not speak of that," Lady Bonnington said with magnificent hauteur.

Fanny snapped her mouth shut.

Esme had to hide a smile. Perhaps she could learn something of Lady Bonnington's technique herself.

"The events of last summer were grievous for everyone in this room." Lady Bonnington gave Esme a little nod, and then turned back to Fanny. "You must understand, Fanny, that I have decided to keep that boy on a very tight rein. Where I go, he goes. I found London entirely too stuffy and tedious this season, and I decided to retreat to the country."

Fanny nodded. "I agree with you. It is far too early for the marquess to reenter London society. But must he be *here,* in my daughter's house?"

"No one could possibly question his presence, given that *I* am here," the dowager trumpeted.

"That is certainly true," Arabella put in merrily. "And now that you are here as well, Fanny, this party is positively taking on the air of a wake!"

"Your levity is repugnant," Fanny snapped. "My only pleasure in making this visit is finding that my daughter has changed so much." She patted Esme's hand. "You have become the daughter I always dreamed of."

"Yes, Esme has been remarkably silent, hasn't she?" Arabella put in.

"Silence is a virtue that few women understand. Believe me, a virtuous silence is a far greater blessing than the kind of impudent chatter that you consider conversation," Fanny retorted.

"You must ask Esme to tell you about her Sewing Circle," Arabella said, standing up and shaking out her skirts. "I am afraid that the very sanctity of this room is wearying to such a devout Jezebel as myself."

Esme felt an unhappy hiccup in the area of her heart. Fanny had leveled the same disapproving glare at her sister that she usually gave to her daughter. On the one hand, it was a pleasure not to be the target of her censure. But Esme didn't like to see Arabella slighted either.

"Aunt Arabella was a blessing to me during my confinement," she said after the door closed. "I don't know what I would have done without her."

"Really?" Fanny asked with languid disinterest. "I can't imagine what that light-heeled sister of mine could possibly do to help anyone. Except perhaps a womanizer. I doubt she would have any hesitation helping such a man."

Esme blinked. She had never before realized the amount of vitriol that her mother felt toward her sister. "In fact, Arabella was quite helpful during William's birth," she said cautiously.

"I knew you would see fit to reproach me for not attending you," Fanny said in a peevish voice. "When you see how much pain it caused me to merely look at a young child, I wonder that you would even bring it up!"

"I didn't mean to imply such a thing."

Lady Bonnington had been sitting silently, watching Fanny and Esme with a rather odd expression on her face. "I will do Lady Withers the credit of saying that she was a source of strength to Lady Rawlings during the birth. Much more so than I was."

Fanny shuddered. "*You* attended the birth, Honoratia? Why on earth would you put yourself through such an ordeal?"

"'Twas your daughter who went through an ordeal," Lady Bonnington pointed out. "I merely counseled from the bedside."

"Yes, well," Fanny said in a fretting tone of voice. "Naturally I am ecstatic if Arabella actually managed to summon up an ounce of family feeling. When has she ever thought of me? She simply made one short-lived marriage after another, and never a thought for my wishes in the matter."

"Aunt Arabella can hardly be blamed for the deaths of her husbands," Esme pointed out, and then wished that she hadn't opened her mouth.

"She drove them into their graves," Fanny spat. "I grew up with the woman, and I've always known what she was like."

Esme rose and rang the bell. "Why don't I ask Slope to bring us some tea," she suggested. "You must be exhausted after your long carriage ride, Mama."

"As to that, I've been staying a mere hour or so from here, at dear Lady Pindlethorp's house," her mother said. "The season is just too tiring for someone my age, I find. Lady Pindlethorp and I have had a perfectly lovely time in the past fortnight. We have so many interests in common."

Esme turned around slowly. "You mean you have been living at a short distance? But—but you could have come for a visit at any time!"

Fanny blinked at her. "Not until I was quite certain that you had reformed, my dear. I would never risk my reputation merely on dear Honoratia's assurance, although of course I took her advice quite seriously. No, indeed. I will admit that I had quite given up hope of your reformation, as I believe I mentioned in my letter. I always thought you took after my sister, although naturally I am pleasantly surprised to find you so much changed."

Esme's jaw set. I will *not* scream, she thought. She felt her face growing red with the effort of not lashing out at her mother. Lady Bonnington seemed to guess, because she quickly turned to Fanny and asked her if she would like to stroll among the roses in the conservatory.

"Only if I need not step a foot outside," Fanny said. "I'm afraid that my poor departed angel, Benjamin, inherited his weak constitution from me. I take a chill at the slightest *breath* of wind. I am virtually housebound these days, if you can believe it."

Esme curtsied to her mother, walked up the stairs to her chambers, and jerked the cap off her head so harshly that hairpins spilled on the floor. Throwing the cap on the floor didn't help. Neither did stepping on it. Neither did ripping off that horrible gray dress with its foolish little lace tippet that worked so well to give the wearer a nunlike air. None of it helped. She stood in the middle of her bedchamber, chest heaving with tears and pure rage.

She had achieved it all: the Sewing Circle, the respectability, her mother's approval, Miles's wishes—why did success make her feel so terribly enraged? And so terribly, terribly afraid, at the same time?

## 33

### In Which the Goat Eats
### a Notable Piece of Clothing

The irritating man hadn't left Shantill House, even after Bea had begged him. He stopped opportuning her and made no seductive moves. Instead he played duets with Helene, which left Bea embroidering on the other side of the room and trying not to think about the Puritan. She stayed away from him. No more flirtatious glances. No more flirtation, period. Certainly no more failed seductions.

It was late morning, and they were gathered in Esme's morning parlor. Arabella and her sister were conducting a genteel squabble; Esme was presumably in the nursery. Naturally, Helene and Stephen were practicing the piano. Bea sat by herself, stitching away on her tapestry.

When Slope arrived with the morning post, Bea looked in the other direction. It was foolish of her to wish that one of her sisters would write. They had never answered her letters, and she was fairly certain that her father was intercepting them. Surely Rosalind would have written. They were only separated in age by a few years. Rosalind was to make her debut next year, and Bea wanted so much to tell her—

Well, to tell her not to make her mistake. Or did she mean to tell her to follow her example? Bea kept thinking and thinking about it. On the one hand, it was grievously hard to turn down Stephen's marriage proposal on the grounds that by accepting, she would ruin his career. On the other hand, had she married whomever her father had seen fit to select as her husband, she would still have fallen in love with Stephen at some point, she was sure of that.

So Bea bent over her tapestry and surreptitiously watched the way Stephen leaned toward Helene, the way their shoulders touched as they played. What would it mean to him, to no longer be the estimable Mem-

ber of Parliament? Would he be happy? If he were married, would he give
up his mistresses, not to mention his supposed fiancée, Esme?

Helene received a letter. "I'm going from pillar to post," she told
Stephen. "This is from my friend Gina, asking me to visit her during her
confinement."

"I gather you refer to the Duchess of Girton?" Stephen said. And at
her nod, he added, "Cam, her husband, is my cousin."

Wonderful, Bea thought sourly. Splendidly cozy.

"She and the duke returned from Greece a few months ago," Helene
was saying, "and now they are living on their estate. Apparently Gina will
be having a child this summer." She made a funny, rueful face.

Bea bit her lip as Stephen put a comforting arm around Helene. They
had the intimacy of an old married couple.

"I can't even bear to look at William. Although I love him." The
agony in Helene's voice mirrored that in Bea's heart. Nothing more was
said, and after a moment Helene and Stephen returned to playing a Turkish march for four hands. Bea was sick of pieces written for four hands.
She was sick of everything that had to do with one prim countess and one
proper politician.

Abruptly she got up and walked out of the room. She might as well
visit the goat. She still kept a daily pilgrimage to the ungrateful beast, although she hadn't encountered Stephen again in the lane. He seemed to
be avoiding the goat, as well as her.

As she tramped down the lane, regardless of the mud clinging to her
boots, Bea was actually beginning to think that perhaps she *could* live in
the country. Some sort of wild rose grew over the hedges in the lane.
They were pale pink and hung down like faded curtains. For the first time
in her life, she had a sense of what happened in spring. A scraggly tree
next to the road had broken out all over in white buds. They stuck out
from the branches like the knotted ribbons on debutantes' slippers.

And there were daisies growing all up and down the lane. Impulsively
Bea started gathering them. Finally she took off her bonnet and filled it
with daisies. It hardly mattered if her skin colored in the sun. She could
powder it white, or powder it pink. The sun felt kind on her cheeks. Finally she reached the end of the lane and leaned on the pasture gate. He
was there, of course, the old reprobate. He trotted over and accepted a
branch Bea gave him to chew. Bea even walked in his pasture sometimes;
he had never again tried to chew her clothing. She pushed open the gate
and headed for the small twisted tree in the center. There were no daisies
in the pasture, of course. The goat presumably ate them the moment they
poked up their heads. But the tree was in the sun, and surrounded by a
patch of grass.

It was when she was sitting against the tree that she realized what she had to do. She had to go home. Go home. Back to her irate father, who wouldn't throw her out again if she promised to be a model of proper behavior. And back to her sisters. She missed her sisters. She didn't want to play the voluptuary role anymore, not after meeting Stephen. He made her games seem rather shabby and hollow, rather than excitingly original.

Without really thinking about it, she picked all the daisies from her bonnet and braided a daisy chain, a rather drunken daisy chain that had a few stems sticking out at right angles. It was just the sort she used to make for her little sisters. Perhaps she would ask Arabella to send her home tomorrow morning.

He was there, in front of her, before she even noticed his arrival. "How you do sneak up on one!" she snapped.

"You are the very picture of spring," he said, staring down at her.

Bea allowed him a smile. She rather fancied that compliment, since she was wearing a horrendously expensive Marie Antoinette–styled shepherdess dress that laced up the front and had frothy bits at the sides. Suddenly he dropped onto his haunches in front of her, and she blinked at him. His eyes were dark and—

She reached out and touched his cheek. "What's the matter, Stephen? Are you all right?" She forgot they weren't on intimate terms and that, in fact, she had hardly spoken to him in virtually a week.

"No, I'm not," he said, rather jerkily. "I've made rather a mess of my life."

"Why do you say that?" Bea asked, taken aback.

"Because I asked a lady to woo me," he said, and the look in his eyes made her knees weak. "Because I asked a lady to woo me, and she very properly refused. I was unfathomably stupid to ask such a thing."

Bea bit her lip. "Why?" Don't say that you never wanted me, she prayed inside. But there was that something in his eyes that gave her hope.

"Because I should have said, 'Seduce me. Take me. *Please.*' "

Bea supposed that was her cue to leap on him like a starving animal, but she stayed where she was. Her heart was beating so fast that she almost couldn't feel her own disappointment. Wasn't this just what she wanted? Of course it was.

"You see, I need her any way she'll have me," Stephen said. His voice had lost all those liquid rolling tones he used so well. It was almost hoarse. "Any time she'll give me. I don't care. I won't make any demands."

Bea couldn't quite meet his eyes. She fidgeted with the ribbon on her parasol, tilting it slightly so that she couldn't see his face. "I've decided to return to my father's house," she said almost inaudibly. He was silent, and all she could hear was her own pulse beating in her throat and the goat ambling away to the other side of the pasture.

"Am I too late, then?" he said finally. There was a bleakness in his voice that wrenched her heart.

She took the parasol and neatly closed it. He would always have a patrician's face. It was the face of an English gentleman, long chin and lean cheeks, laughter wrinkles around his eyes, tall, muscled body. He would wear well. She raised her eyelashes and gave him the most smoldering look she had in her repertoire.

He made a hoarse sound in his voice and pulled her into his arms so fast that her parasol flew into the air.

"Will you, Bea, will you let me . . ." He was plundering her mouth, and he couldn't seem to finish the sentence. Finally he raised his mouth a fraction of an inch from hers, so close that she was almost touching his lips. His voice was husky. "Will you seduce me, Bea? Or let me seduce you?"

She strained forward, trying to catch his mouth with hers, but he held back.

"Please?" The urgency in his voice awed her. "I was a fool to refuse you. I'll take anything, any little bit you'll give me. Of course you don't wish to woo me, marry me. But I'll take whatever you give me, Bea. Please."

She closed her eyes. One of the proudest gentlemen in the kingdom was literally, as well as metaphorically, at her feet. "I didn't mean that," she whispered, clutching his shoulders as hard as she could. "It's not that I don't wish to marry you—"

"Hush," he said, rubbing his lips across hers. "I know you don't want to marry me. I was a conceited fool to think you'd even consider me. But I don't care, Bea. Just—just seduce me, Bea."

She could untangle this later. At the moment she unwrapped her arms from his neck and smiled at him with the slumberous smile of Cleopatra. "But what if I lead you to do things that are less than gentlemanly?"

"You already have," he said. "This is absolutely the first time in my life that I have begged a young unmarried woman to seduce me."

"Oh, well, in that case," she said, with a gurgle of laughter. Then she settled back against the tree trunk and, looking at him, very, very slowly raised the ruffled dimity of her skirt. She was wearing gossamer silk stockings, with clocks, and her slender ankes were crossed. She pulled her skirts up just past her knee, so that Stephen could see the pale blue stocking, and its darker garter, and then the pale cream of her thigh.

She saw him swallow. "Bea, what are you doing?" he said, and the rasp in his voice was a warning.

"Seducing you." Her smile was blinding. He didn't seem to be able to stop staring at her legs.

"What if someone comes?"

"No one ever comes down this lane," she said blissfully. "It leads nowhere except to the goat. And you and I, Stephen, are the only persons who have ever shown interest in the goat."

Just as deliberately she uncrossed her legs and drew them slightly higher. Her skirt fell back against her thighs.

"And where is the damned goat?" he said hoarsely.

"The other side of the field." Her knees came a little higher, and her skirts slid farther down, exposing smooth, milky thighs.

"If I touch you, Bea, there's no stopping this," Stephen said, meeting her eyes.

Her heart tumbled in her chest. "I wouldn't want to stop you. I never have."

He put his hands gently on her ankles. "Last chance, Bea. Are you sure you wish to make love in a goat's pasture?" But she was laughing, and her eyes were shining. There was desire there, so that was all right. And obviously, she didn't mind the goat's pasture. So Stephen let his fingers wrap around that delicate little ankle, slide up the faint softness of her stockings. He stopped at the garters and untied them. They left angry red marks on her skin.

She was watching him with a half smile, but there was something uncertain there too, for all she was such an accomplished seductress. He smoothed the red marks with his fingers. "Why so ruthless with your poor skin?" he said, as he lowered his head and ran his tongue along the groove in her leg.

She gasped and squirmed in his hands. "It's particularly difficult to keep stockings this flimsy from collapsing around my ankles."

"Ah." He had his hands on both her knees now, and he pulled them apart. She resisted for a moment and then gave in. She was wearing some sort of fluttering gown that obediently fell back, as if it had been designed for outdoor games. Stephen ran a finger down the inside of her thigh. He stopped at a burst of lacy cotton, then ran his finger over all the fabric.

She visibly shuddered and reached for him. But he pushed her back against the tree and knelt in front of her, between her raised knees, and pressed his lips there, on the inside of a quavering knee. And then let his lips drift down, down smooth, ivory flesh.

And all the time his finger was running inquisitively over the white cotton between her legs, dancing a little surface dance that made her hips jiggle a bit. He could hear her uneven little *whoosh* of breath, and it made him feel a steely wave of triumph, and then a wave of lust so pure that he almost wrenched that cotton down—

"What do you call this?" he asked, and his voice came out hoarse. He put his hand between her legs, firm, and rocked forward.

"Oh," she said, and her voice seemed very small.

He ran his thumb under the frilly border. "This?"

"Pantalettes," she said, quivering all over.

He leaned foward and put a leg over her left knee so he was straddling her, and then he let that thumb sink, fall into sleek, hot folds. She had been lying against the tree as if she were too shocked to move, but that shudder woke her up; she reached out and pulled his head toward her.

Her lips trembled under his, and opened, and Stephen let his thumb take on the same rhythm as his tongue, although his chest felt like bursting for lack of air, or for the thumping of his heart in his chest.

Her eyes fluttered open, and she was beautiful. This close, her eyes had the green of a rock glimpsed at the river bottom, greeny blue, with small specks of light. All the more beautiful for being slighty glazed.

Suddenly she focused on him. "You seem to have forgotten that this is my seduction," she said. Her voice was such a deep purr that he almost didn't catch her meaning. But with one flip of her hip, she pushed his hand away and came up on her knees. Alas, her skirt fell down and covered her legs again.

He reared up so he was facing her. Then he very, very deliberately took his thumb and rubbed it over his lips. She gasped in shock, and he felt a throb of pleasure. She wasn't so jaded then. He licked his lips, enjoying the faint taste of her.

"Stephen!" she said. He grinned. But she was pulling at his neck cloth. She seemed to have some trouble undoing it, so finally he tossed it to the side and undid the placket on his shirt.

It was her turn then to inch that shirt up his muscled abdomen. Her fingers were everywhere, delicate, admiring. The shirt billowed past his eyes and disappeared. Now her fingers were at his waist. But she couldn't seem to undo the buttons there either. She looked so serious.

"I thought you'd make my clothes fly off like greased lightning," he said teasingly. But she didn't look up, so he pushed up her chin. "That was only a jest, Bea. In poor taste, to be sure, but a jest."

"I—" Her eyes were larger, not so passionate now. Stephen felt a pang of pure fear. She'd changed her mind. She didn't want him. He was too old.

"I'm afraid I'll disappoint you," she said.

"Never."

"I don't—I don't have as much experience as you might think," she said, staring fixedly at his waistband as she tried to undo it. The very feeling of her fingers fumbling around his pantaloons was driving Stephen crazy.

But once he registered what she'd said, he laughed. "I don't care what kind of experience you've got, Bea. All I want is you. You." He pushed up her chin again. Her lips were swollen with his kisses. "Oh God, Bea, you're so beautiful."

But she wasn't really listening. "You see, I did—that is, there was Sandhurst, but it was only once, and I'm afraid I didn't learn very much, especially as we were interrupted by Lady Ditcher. And then I allowed Billy Laslett, but I didn't truly enjoy it towards the end, and so I told him to go."

Stephen laughed. "Are you trying to tell me that the bold seductress herself didn't find the experience pleasurable?"

Bea blushed. "No, I did. Although I wish I hadn't."

"Why?"

"Because it would make me almost like a virgin, wouldn't it?" Her eyes were shadowed. "But I did—did enjoy it, up to a point. I haven't liked—well, that's irrelevant. I took another lover once too." The last came out in a rush of admissions. "So you see, I've had three lovers. But I never gave anyone a second chance, and I'm not certain that I actually *learned* very much, if you see what I mean."

Stephen threw back his head and laughed, laughed so hard that four starlings and a wren flew out of the crooked tree and wheeled into the sunlight. When he looked back, she was still there, blinking at him, looking a little defensive, extraordinarily lovely, and far too young.

"Bea, you are over twenty-one, aren't you?" he said.

"I'm twenty-three."

"Good. Are you trying to tell me that you won't let me have a second round? That one time with lovely Bea is all any man could hope to achieve?" He let his hands settle on her waist.

She blushed faintly. "No." But he could hardly hear her.

"Because I want more, Bea." He lowered his head and brushed his mouth over hers. She opened to him, willing and shuddering. "I'm going to take more," he told her.

Her eyes closed, and she wrapped her arms around his neck. "Take me, Stephen."

An invitation no man could refuse. He took over the job of removing his pantaloons himself. And threw off his boots and every other stitch of clothing he had on as well. She sat on the ground in front of him, mouth open.

He laughed at her. The sun was warm on his shoulders, and under her eyes he had that sense of his body that he only seemed to have with her. A sense of powerful muscle and a lean stomach. He came down on his haunches. She watched him in fascination, her eyes looking either at the powerful muscles in his thighs—or between them. He wasn't quite sure. But she seemed to like what she saw. That faint blush in her cheeks had turned rosy.

"I can't believe you're quite naked in the outdoors!" she said. She had her hand over her mouth, but giggles escaped.

"Your turn," he said, and her eyes grew serious.

"Oh, Stephen, I don't know . . . I wasn't thinking . . ." She kept squealing. But Stephen was very good at removing ladies' clothing, and so he had her dress over her head in a moment, and her chemise followed. She wore no corset, to his great interest. He left her only that flimsy little garment she called her pantalettes, a foolish little trifle of white cotton and lace.

The sun threw dancing spots over her ivory skin, skipping shadows of dappled color. Her face was quite rosy. She sat on the ground with her hands covering her breasts, for all the world like a timid virgin. Though of course, even an experienced courtesan might never have made love outdoors.

He kneeled just before her and put his hands over hers. "It's all right, love," he whispered. "Truly, no one will come down the lane."

"It's not that!"

He peeled one of her hands away from the alluring curve of her breast. They were perfect, rosy-tipped, uptilted, just the size for a man's hand. He bent his head and drew her nipple into his mouth, roughly for such a sweet bit of flesh. One hand flew away from her breast and curled around his neck instead.

He couldn't play this game much longer. It had been too long, weeks of longing for her, watching her secretly, watching her openly, dreaming of her. He swept her up in one decisive movement and then put her down gently on top of his jacket. As he kissed her, he let one hand shape her breast so she strained into his hand, and he let his other hand pull down that bit of cotton she called a pantalette.

She wasn't sure about that. "What if someone? . . ." but her voice was melting. He moved down, kissed her breast in passing until she squeaked out loud, until she writhed upwards, kept going further down her body until he found her. Until he had all that sweet, lemony flesh in front of him, and she was moaning, all deep in her throat and begging him, and begging him, and—

She reached out, grabbed his hair and yanked it hard. Bea could hardly breathe, because her whole body was on fire, but she knew there was a remedy here. There had to be. And his tormenting her was not going to be the answer.

"I want you," she said fiercely, having got his face where she could see it.

"It's your seduction, darling," he said. His lopsided grin made her heart somersault, and she almost forgot and just started kissing him again. Instead, she reached down and wrapped her fingers around him, and that did give her a shred of sanity. He was a great deal larger than Billy Laslett, and a great deal, well, firmer than Sandhurst.

For a moment she froze. What if this wasn't possible? Billy had been difficult enough. It was embarrassing to have been a party to that encounter. She had been phenomenally pleased when he'd stopped bucking about on top of her and taken himself away.

But Stephen was smiling down at her, and he seemed to know exactly what she was thinking. He unwrapped her fingers and brought himself forward, nudging her knee out of the way. Bea couldn't help herself. She arched up to meet him. But he was just teasing her, bringing her that hardness and taking it away again.

She may not have learned much, but she had learned one thing, because Billy Laslett had asked her to. . . . She brought her hands down from his neck and deliberately brushed his flat nipples with her fingers. He jumped and arched forward for a moment, deliciously hard. How could she ever have thought that—but this wasn't the moment for comparisons.

Instead, she gave him the same lazy, mischievous grin he gave her, and leaned forward and nipped him with her teeth. He groaned and drove forward. The rush of feeling was so exquisite that she flopped backwards and clutched his shoulders. And this time their eyes were serious.

"All right?" he said, hardly able to recognize his own voice.

And she nodded, clutching him so hard that he was going to have ten small bruises on his shoulders. He drove forward again. She cried out, unintelligible, the sound swallowed into the bright air. But it didn't seem to be pain she was registering.

He bent to kiss her, and she made startled, gulping sounds, as if she thought he might lose his balance if he tried to do two things at once. He finally managed to coax her mouth open, but she kept trying to speak.

"What is it?" he finally said, huskily.

"Nothing—oh! Don't stop *that!*"

Stephen smiled to himself. He pulled himself even higher and listened to her squeals floating into the meadow.

After a bit, he came up on his knees and caught her slender hips in his hands. She gasped and said, "No!" and then said nothing. So he taught her that if she lifted her hips to meet him, that was very pleasant too.

At some point she really did seem to have something to say, so he stopped kissing her. "Do you . . .", she was panting. "Do you—could you just keep going a little longer?"

He grinned, a fiendish grin. "I'm better at this than I am at billiards," he said. His voice was guttural, deep with desire. She was coming to meet him now, matching him. Her skin was gleaming with sweat in the sunlight. Stephen knew at that exact moment that his Bea had experienced no real woman's pleasure with those other lovers of hers.

She was a virgin, in all real senses of the word.

He felt as if the raw joy burning in the back of his throat might explode, so he simply tucked back, concentrating on showing the woman he loved that she didn't know a thing about making love. Great waves of passion kept swamping the joy. Far off in the distant recesses of his mind not occupied by the sweet undulations of her body, with the way she panted with surprise and the way her eyes were squeezed tight now, as if she were going somewhere that couldn't be seen, he was conscious of two things. One was that his buttocks had never been exposed to an English summer, and they were definitely beginning to feel as if a sunburn might be in the offing. And the second was that that infernal goat had stolen Bea's dress and galloped to the other side of the field with yards of white lace falling from its mouth.

But then even those bits of rational thought flew from him. He dove higher into her body, and she cried out, cries that spiraled, falling away into the bright air. Stephen ground his teeth and said hoarsely, "Come on, Bea, come with me!"

And Bea opened her eyes and saw him poised above her, outlined in the indigo blue sky, her beautiful, proper Puritan.

He stopped for a moment, bent his head and crushed his mouth against her. "I love you," he said hoarsely. "My Bea."

She arched up to meet him, heard his groan, lost herself in the prism of sunshine and pleasure that rained on her, spiraling through her arms and legs, driving her against his chest, telling her without words the difference between wooing and seduction.

# 34

## Yours Till Dawn

"Esme, what's the matter?" She was even whiter than when he'd seen her last, her face pallid and drawn. There was a gleaming trail of tears down her cheek. "Is William all right?" Sebastian sat down on the bed and peered at the babe. William looked just as moon-faced as he had last week. Long lashes brushed his cheeks, and he was snoring a little bit. Sebastian felt a funny sensation around his chestbone. He was a sweet-looking child, as children went.

"He's caught a cold," Esme said, her voice strangling on a sob.

Sebastian could see that she had obviously been crying for a long time. He put an arm around her shoulder and peered down at William again.

His rosy little lips opened in a snore.

"There! Do you hear it?" Esme said.

"He's snoring," Sebastian said. "Did Miles snore?"

"That's not a snore. He's caught a cold . . . probably inflammation of the lung," Esme said, tears rolling down her face. "Now I'll only have him with me for a few days at most. I knew this would happen; I knew this would happen!" Her voice rose to a near shriek.

William stirred. He could hardly move, he was wrapped in so many blankets.

"I think he's hot," Esme continued, and the broken despair in her voice caught Sebastian's heart. She put a trembling hand to the baby's head. "I keep feeling his head and one moment I think he's caught a fever, and the next he seems to be perfectly all right. What do you think, Sebastian?"

"I'm hardly an expert." He cautiously felt William's forehead. It felt sweaty to him. "Do you think he might be wearing a few too many blankets? There's quite a fire in here, after all."

"No, no," Esme said, tucking his blankets around him even more securely.

"Why don't you ask your nanny?" Sebastian asked, inspired.

"I sent her to bed. She's too old to be awake at night."

"The nursemaid, then? Surely you have some help at night."

"I sent the woman away. She just didn't understand babies. She didn't understand William, not at all. She never forgave me for nursing him myself, and she was always trying to bathe him in the midst of a cold draft."

"Oh," Sebastian said. He fished in his pocket and pulled out a handkerchief.

Esme wiped her eyes. "She kept talking about *strengthening* him. But William is far too frail to be exposed to drafts, or to the fresh air. Why, she actually wanted to take him outdoors! She was being grossly imprudent, and I had to tell her so."

She sniffed, and a few more tears rolled down her cheeks. "And then—and then she said that William was as fat as a porkchop and didn't have a cold at all. It was as if she'd never been around babies at all! Any fool could hear that William was having trouble breathing when he's asleep."

William snored peacefully. Sebastian looked closely at Esme and was shocked. All the generous lushness in her face was gone, replaced by a drawn exhaustion and a brutal whiteness. "Poor darling," he said. "You're all topped out, aren't you?"

"It's just that it's so tiring! No one understands William, no one! Even nanny keeps saying he's a brawny boy and I should just leave him in the nursery at night. But I can't do that, Sebastian, you must see that. What if he needed me? What if he were hungry? What if his cold worsened, or his blankets slipped?"

Sebastian pushed himself back against the headboard and then gently pulled Esme into his arms. She leaned back with a great, racking sigh, her head falling on his shoulder.

"He's a bonny lad," he said.

"Yes." She was utterly exhausted. He could see violet shadows under her eyes. Slowly he curled an arm around her and eased her back more comfortably against his shoulder. "Rest," he said softly.

"You shouldn't be here!" she said, sitting up again. "My mother—well, surely you met my mother at dinner. She's come for a visit."

Sebastian had decided not to say a word about Esme's mother. "She can have no idea that I'm in your chamber. Rest, Esme."

William snored on. After a few moments, Esme's long eyelashes fluttered closed and her body relaxed against his. Sebastian waited for a few minutes more, eased her back against the pillows, and gently took William from her arms.

Esme's eyes popped open. "Make sure you hold his head up," she said blearily. "Tuck in his blankets."

"I will," Sebastian said soothingly. "Lie down."

"You mustn't forget to prop up his neck," she insisted, but she was already toppling to the side, her whole body a testament to acute exhaustion.

Sebastian experimented cautiously for a moment and discovered what she was talking about. William's head seemed to be too heavy for his body. "I hope you outgrow this problem," he told the baby, walking over to the rocking chair by the fire. Perhaps it was just because the child was sleeping.

In the light thrown by the firelight, he could see two things. One was that William was definitely overheated. His hair was damp with sweat and his cheeks were rosy. But it didn't look like a fever; it looked as if four blankets were too much. He gently loosened some of the blankets, and it seemed to him that the baby was a little more comfortable. The second thing he noticed was that William did indeed look like Miles Rawlings. His eyes were closed, of course, but surely those were Miles's plump cheeks and Miles's rounded chin? Even the fact that William had no hair seemed evocative of Rawlings's balding state.

So Sebastian, Marquess Bonnington, rocked the baby in front of the fire and thought hard about how much he wanted the child to be his, because he hoped that if the child was his, Esme couldn't deny him fatherhood. But fatherhood wouldn't be enough anyway. He looked over at the utterly silent mound of womanhood in the bed. He didn't want Esme as a wife merely because she felt it necessary to give his son a father.

He wanted Esme to love him for himself, love him so much that she braved scandal. It was almost comical. How on earth had it happened that he, an excruciatingly correct marquess whose ideas of propriety were so rigidly enforced, had ended up asking a lady to disregard social mores, cause a scandal of profound proportions, and marry him?

And more to the point, how was he to get her to that point? He knew instinctively that it was no use asking her to marry him again. She cared only for William at the moment. Somehow, he had to bring her around to see him as a man again. And herself as a woman, as well as a mother. Sebastian rocked and thought, and William snored.

## 35

### *Lady Beatrix Entertains*

Since Bea had never allowed a gentleman to repeat the experience of bedding her, she had no idea whether she was expected to articulate a further invitation, or whether Stephen would take it for granted that he could knock at her bedchamber door. He had given no sign of his intentions over dinner. But fairness led her to admit that there was little he could have done, since he was seated between Arabella and Fanny. The two ladies spent dinner hissing insults around his shoulders, and ignoring his attempts at polite conversation. Bea's own enjoyment in the meal was dimmed when she distinctly heard Esme's mother reproach Arabella for allowing Bea to live in the same house with the *pure little soul in the nursery.*

Bea clenched her fists at the memory. Could she possibly marry Stephen? She, with her tarnished reputation and a malevolent influence that apparently extended to babes in the nursery? She dismissed the thought for the four hundredth time. Tonight was just another seduction, not a wooing. And she had dressed for that seduction—or undressed, howsoever one wished to put it. After all, her flimsy negligée was, well, flimsy. And she was painted, and perfumed, and curled to within an inch of her life. The only thing that seemed to calm her was applying another layer of kohl to her eyelashes, or adjusting the candles so that they fell on the bed *just so.* For a while she lay on the bed in a posture that displayed her entire body to its best advantage, but her stomach was jumping so much that she had to hop off the bed and pace.

There was nothing to worry about. The candles were lit, and she was perfumed in every conceivable spot that he might wish to kiss. She'd even placed a glass of water next to the bed, as she'd felt appallingly thirsty after their encounter in the goat pasture. But should she have arranged two glasses of water there, offering him one? Or would that look too rehearsed?

By the time the knock came on her door, Bea was more overwrought than she'd ever been in her entire life. "One moment!" she croaked, flinging herself toward the center of the bed. To her horror, the edge of her trailing sleeves caught the glass of water. It arched through the air, splashing water as it flew, and ended up on the bed next to her hip.

*"Damnation!"* Bea cried, under her breath. There was another discreet knock on the door. Of course Stephen didn't want to stand about in the corridor: what if he were seen by Helene, Esme or—a rather more terrifying possibility—Esme's mother?

"Enter!" she called hoarsely, rolling on top of the wet spot and positioning herself on her side with a hand propping up her head. Her hair was falling in the right direction to be enhanced by the pearl blue of her negligée, but she was uncomfortably aware of dampness soaking through the said garment.

He walked through the door looking as urbane and composed as if he often conducted this sort of excursion. Which, of course, he *did,* Bea reminded herself. Stephen was the man with two mistresses and a fiancée, after all.

"Good evening, lovely Bea," he said, closing the door and walking over to the bed.

Bea cleared her throat. "Good evening," she managed, with reasonable serenity. She looked surreptitiously down her body and was horrified to see that the silk of her negligée was apparently soaking up the water from her coverlet. Just at her hip there was a spreading patch of dark greenish–looking silk. Quickly she pulled the silk behind her and rolled onto her back so that her bottom covered the spilled water.

"And how are you, sir?" she said, smiling up at Stephen. He had seated himself on the side of the bed and was looking at her with a rather quizzical expression.

"The better for seeing you," he said.

What was that in his eyes? Bea wiggled a little. Her bottom was growing distinctly damp. Who would have thought there could be that much water in one glass?

He leaned forward and dropped a kiss on her forehead. "My word, that's a very elegant perfume you're wearing," he whispered against her cheek.

He was hovering above her. Perhaps she should give him a kiss? She brushed her lips over his, but he pulled back suddenly and sneezed. Bea sat up, realizing as she did so that she was now damp all the way to the small of her back. If she didn't change clothing, she would be sneezing as well.

"Excuse me," he said, bracing a hand on the bed and reaching into his pocket, presumably for a handkerchief.

Bea shivered. His shoulders . . . and the way his neck rose out of his shirt. Who would have thought Stephen Fairfax-Lacy was a symphony of muscle under all that linen? She was trembling, literally trembling, to take off his clothes again. She leaned toward him. "I missed you during dinner," she said. The naked longing in her voice was rather embarrassing. Why hadn't he given her a proper kiss?

He frowned, held up his hand and said, "Bea, your coverlet appears to be rather damp."

Bea bit her lip. "I spilled a glass of water."

"Ah." He bent close to her again and—sneezed. "I'm sorry," he apologized. "I'm terribly sorry to say that I—*achoo!*"

"You caught a chill in the pasture," Bea said, her heart sinking.

"Not I." He looked at her and smiled. For the first time since he entered the room Bea felt a rush of confidence. His smile said volumes about the cut of her bodice. She shifted slightly, just enough so the neckline fell off her shoulder.

The look in his eyes was dark and seductive. Bea quivered all over. Her knees suddenly felt weak, and her breath disappeared. A strong hand rounded her ankle, and the melting sensation crept up to her middle. He was on the bed now, leaning over her; Bea raised her arms to pull that hard body down on hers and—

He sneezed again.

"You *are* ill!" Bea said with anguish as he pulled away again.

Stephen almost wished he were. But there was no way he was leaving the room without tasting Bea's perfect little body. "It's the perfume," he admitted.

Bea's eyes widened. "*My* perfume?"

He nodded.

"One moment. I shall—" She scrambled off the bed and headed toward her dressing table and the pitcher of water that stood there. She began pouring water into a bowl.

Stephen swallowed. The backside of her negligée was drenched. The wet silk clung to the middle of her back, clung to the round curve of her ass, to a secret curve that turned inward, drawing a man's eye. He was off the bed in a moment, splaying his hand across that sweet bottom, eyes meeting hers in the mirror.

"Stephen!" she cried, shocked.

"Yes, Bea?" he said with a grin, his fingers slipping over the wet silk, letting the cool fabric rumple against his fingers, against the smooth skin of her bottom as he curved his fingers in and under. Silk met silky flesh and her head fell back against his shoulder. Stephen reached around her with his free hand and scooped water from the bowl.

"This may be chilly," he murmured, opening his hand on the smooth column of her neck. Her eyes flew open and she began to protest, but he had her now, wet silk over one breast, and wet silk below, and both hands slipping and rubbing. Her head fell back again and she made that little throaty moan he loved. It sounded different in a bedchamber than it had in the pasture: less thin, more deep with womanly delight. She was liquid in his arms, and the chilly silk was taking heat from her burning skin.

She turned in his arms, and her curious eyes, always so vigilant, so watchful, so wicked, were dazed. He kissed her fiercely and she begged him without words, so he cupped her bottom and pulled her hard against him.

But he couldn't concentrate because of the damn perfume, so he pulled the negligée over her head in a moment, took more water, and used his fingers as a facecloth. He started at her neck, at the smooth skin just under her ears, water dripping from his fingers, shaping her body, singing over her skin, licking kisses from his fingers. Over her collarbone, down her arms, back to her breasts, further down. . . . He was on his knees, and the water came with him, cooling her burning skin until he worked his way up her legs and there, then and there, his control snapped.

Bea was throbbing so much that she felt unable to speak or move. She hardly noticed when he picked her up and put her down on the wet part of the bed. She scarcely realized that he had shed his clothing. She was too busy twisting toward him. But then he was pushing her legs apart, and that dark head was there, and she was quivering, crying, pleading. . . .

Then he cupped her face in his hands and pressed his lips to hers, and she opened to him as gladly as she wound her legs around him, as joyously as she surged against him, with as much urgency as she shattered around him, waves of pleasure flooding to the very tips of her fingers.

# 36

## Because It Takes Courage to Admit a Mistake

*The following afternoon*

Marchioness Bonnington was having a most unusual sensation. It took Honoratia quite a while to identify precisely what it was: not an incipient warning of gout, not an attack of indigestion, not a premonition that rain would soon fall. It wasn't until the gentlemen had retired to take port and the ladies to take tea in Lady Rawlings's private sitting room that Sebastian's mother knew exactly why she had a queasy feeling in the back of her stomach. There was a chance—a slim chance, but a chance nonetheless—that she was Making a Mistake.

An odd sensation, Honoratia considered. One with which she, for obvious reasons, had very little familiarity.

Mistakes seemed to generate an oddly bilious sensation in her middle section. She had it every time she looked at Lady Rawlings, who had joined them for supper on the first occasion since her child was born. She was astonishingly beautiful, that girl. Her skin had a magnolia creaminess to it. The ripeness on those lips didn't come from a bottle. Overall, though, the marchioness thought that Esme Rawlings probably gained most of her appeal from her nature, from those clever, laughing remarks of hers. From the way her eyes lit up with pleasure when she mentioned her baby.

Fanny clearly did not approve of her daughter's nature. She visibly stiffened every time Lady Rawlings laughed. "Modulate your voice, my dear," Honoratia had heard her snap during dinner. "A lady finds little to laugh at in a strident fashion."

"I'm sorry, Mother," Lady Rawlings had said instantly. She was trying so hard to make this reconciliation a success. But Honoratia thought the chances were slim.

"I find that dress rather unappealingly low in the chest," Fanny announced as soon as the ladies seated themselves.

Lady Rawlings gave the bodice of her gown an uneasy little tug. "It's only because my bosom is enhanced by the situation."

"Yes, you have gained some flesh," Fanny said, eyeing her up and down. "Perhaps a brisk walk every morning. A diet of cucumbers and vinegar can be efficacious. Dear Mr. Brummell confided in me that even he has occasionally undertaken a slimming project."

"Oh, I couldn't do that," her daughter said with a smile. "Mama, may I give you a lemon tartlet?"

"Absolutely not. I never partake of sweets in the evening. And I certainly hope you won't take one yourself."

Honoratia swallowed a smile as Lady Rawlings quickly transferred the tartlet she was about to put on her own plate to that of Lady Godwin.

"Why should you not try a cucumber diet?" Fanny insisted. "I judge you to be in rather desperate need of a slimming plan."

"It's not advisable for nursing mothers to undertake such a drastic step."

Lady Bonnington had always counted herself dear friends with Fanny, but as it happened, this was the first time they had encountered each other at the same house party. It was a bit demoralizing to realize that after a mere two days, she already recognized the thin white lines that were appearing next to Fanny's mouth as a sign of temper.

"Helene, did I understand you to say that you are leaving us?" Lady Rawlings said, turning to Lady Godwin.

"I'm afraid I must," Lady Godwin said quickly, demonstrating that she too had come to understand the signs that indicated Fanny's impending attack of temper. "Gina, the Duchess of Girton, writes me that she is expecting a child and she would be grateful for companionship. I am planning to take a carriage in two days, if you have no immediate need for my presence."

"Nursing mother? That must be some sort of witticism you thought up to horrify me," Fanny said acidly, ignoring her daughter's diversionary tactics. "My stomach is positively turning at the very thought." And she looked it. Honoratia thought there was a fair chance that Fanny would lose her supper.

"Mama, perhaps we could discuss this at a later time," Lady Rawlings said pleadingly, putting her arm on her mother's sleeve.

She shook it off. "I shall not be fobbed off. And I am certain that these ladies are as repulsed by what you said as I am!"

Honoratia took a sip of her tea. When Lady Rawlings first demanded to nurse her baby, she had been repulsed, certainly. The very idea of allowing a child to munch from one's private parts was instinctively revolting. But then she had been in the nursery yesterday while Esme nursed William, and it was hard to reconcile that experience with her own repulsion.

"While I am quite glad to have utilized a nursemaid myself," she announced, "I do not find Lady Rawlings's actions distasteful."

Fanny flashed her a hostile look that had Honoratia stiffening. Didn't Fanny realize that she was of far lower rank than she, Marchioness Bonnington? Why, it was pure kindness on her part that kept the friendship intact.

"Be that as it may," Fanny said with frigid severity, "the majority of the polite world agrees with me. Are you telling me that the fleshy expanse of chest that you are exposing to the world is due to this unsavory practice, Esme?"

Lady Rawlings sipped her tea quietly. "Yes it is, Mama."

Honoratia had to admit, Esme Rawlings had backbone.

"Had I ever been blessed by a child, I hope I would have had the courage to be as excellent a mother as is Esme," Arabella put in.

Her sister turned to her with the lowering look of a striking serpent. "It was the will of God that you not be given children, and no more than you deserve!"

Arabella went pure white, rose from her chair and walked out. There was no sound other than a faint swish of silk and then the click of the door shutting behind her.

"That was most unkind," Lady Rawlings said, looking straight at her mother. "It was unworthy of you."

"I spoke the truth as I saw it."

"I would urge you to apologize to Aunt Arabella. She has a forgiving soul, and if you make haste, she may overlook your unkindness."

Fanny merely took a sip of tea. There was a suppressed air of triumph about her. "Now," she said brightly, "you must all forgive us for this unwarranted display of poor judgement. I assure you that our family is not generally so rag-mannered!"

But her daughter was standing up. "You will have to forgive me," she said to the company at large. "Mama, I know you will act as a hostess in my absence. I shall speak to my aunt." And she was gone.

Fanny turned to Lady Beatrix Lennox. "As my sister's *dame de compagnie*," she said with a sapient smile, "perhaps you would like to join her, given that my daughter seems to think that Lady Withers might be distressed?"

Lady Beatrix gave her a stony look and stood up, curtsying. "I can think of little that would give me greater pleasure."

"Now we can be cozy," Fanny said, once the door closed again. "I find the presence of impure women to be extremely trying on my nerves. One has such an impulse to help, and yet no help is ever enough. Once lost, a woman's reputation can never be recovered." She shook her head. "I fear it is all a question of nature. Clearly, my daughter inherited my sister's disposition."

That was the moment when Lady Bonnington discovered what it felt like to have Made a Mistake. She accepted a tart from Fanny while she thought about it.

Countess Godwin was a lovely, if rather pale, woman. Yet when she leaned forward, Honoratia caught her breath. In profile, the countess looked like an accusing angel, a stone statue of Saint Michael standing at the gates of Paradise with a sword. "I wish you to be the first to know," she said, speaking with great precision.

"Oh?" Fanny said, looking a bit uneasy.

"I am having an affair with your daughter's fiancé, Mr. Fairfax-Lacy. We enjoy each other in ecstatic union every night."

Fanny gasped. "What a thing to say to me!" she said shrilly.

"If it be sin to love Mr. Fairfax-Lacy . . . well, then sin I!" retorted Lady Godwin. She stood up. "I expect my presence will make you uncomfortable, so I shall leave."

Honoratia raised her eyebrows. There was something distinctly odd about the phrasing of Lady Godwin's parting shot. And as someone who'd watched many a marriage and many a sinful union, she doubted that Lady Godwin had ever experienced *ecstatic union*. Still, loyalty was an admirable quality, and Lady Godwin had it in spades.

Fanny had stopped looking horror-struck and was eating one of those lemon tartlets that she never consumed in the evening. They were left alone, two hardened old harridans with shining reputations and naught much else. Neither of them had had an illicit proposal in years.

Fanny patted her mouth delicately. "I wonder that you chose *this* house to retire from the season, dear Honoratia," she said. "I leave tomorrow at dawn to return to Lady Pindlethorp's house. I told Esme as much this morning, and now my mind is made up. You would be more than welcome to join me."

"Wouldn't you rather stay and make further acquaintance with your grandson?"

"It's far, far too painful. My daughter has no understanding of the grief I still bear every time I think of my dear departed son. And I am very much afraid that my initial qualms about my daughter's rehabilitation are entirely correct. I admire your generous nature, my dear, but you are far too optimistic. Are you aware that my daughter has no real idea whose child she birthed?"

"Certainly not!" Honoratia replied in her most quelling tone of voice. Surely—*surely*—Esme's own mother wouldn't repeat such a vicious piece of gossip about her own daughter.

Fanny took a bite of tartlet. "I queried her on the matter, most discreetly, you understand, through the post. She did not respond to my query, which speaks for itself, does it not? This tea is quite cold." She rang the bell. "As I said, I would be more than welcome for your company tomorrow morning."

Honoratia stood up. Fanny looked up, startled. Honoratia thumped her stick, and, sure enough, Fanny quailed with as much fear as any lazy housemaid. "You will *not* say a word to anyone about your grandson's patrimony," she ordered.

"Well, naturally, I—" Fanny said, flustered. "I only tell you as you are a very close friend!"

"From this moment, we are not close friends," Honoratia said, pulling herself even straighter. "In fact, we are not friends at all. If I ever hear a breath of scandal about your daughter or your grandson that has begun at your lips, Fanny, I shall ruin you."

Fanny stared up at her, faded eyes wide.

"Do I make myself clear?"

Fanny jumped but said nothing.

"Do I make myself clear?" Honoratia said, with the snap of a carnivorous turtle.

Fanny twittered. "I can't imagine why you would think that I would ever do something as ill-bred as gossip about my daughter's debased circumstances." Then she faltered, seeing Honoratia's expression. "I shall not!" she said shrilly.

Honoratia didn't bother with a reply. She just stumped over to the door and left Fanny there among the crumbs of lemon tarts and cooling cups of tea.

## 37

### Nights of Ecstatic Union

"And then I said that we spend every night in ecstatic union with each other!"

"Ecstatic *what?*" Esme asked.

"Ecstatic union. It was the only thing that came to mind. It *is* a rather odd phrase, is it not? And then I quoted a bit of the poetry Bea lent me, the part being a *sin to love*. Your mother was quite horrified, Esme." Helene looked triumphant.

Esme choked with laughter. She was sitting on her aunt's bed, arm wound around her aunt's neck. Helene was standing before them like a militant, raging angel. Bea was curled up on the little armchair to the side.

"You didn't have to do that," Arabella said damply, blotting a last few tears with a handkerchief. "Drat! I've taken off all my facepaint. I must look a veritable hag."

"You look beautiful," her niece said, giving her a squeeze.

"Fanny really doesn't mean to be so horrible," Arabella said. "She's had a most difficult life."

"Yes she does," Helene said firmly. "I'm sorry, Lady Withers, but your sister is a truly poisonous woman. And I'm sorry for you, too, Esme."

Esme looked up with a rueful smile. "And what a dreadful thing in a daughter to agree with you." But she didn't disagree either.

Arabella gave a last sniff. "I haven't cried for years," she said, "so I suppose I was due for a bout of tears. Fanny's comments generally don't distress me very much. But Robbie and I did so want children. I thought perhaps when he died . . . well, I didn't have my flux for months. And I thought that perhaps I carried a bit of Robbie with me." She gave another sniff. "But finally the doctor said that it must have been due to grief." She wiped away some tears. "What a wet blanket I've become!"

"You're *not* a wet blanket," Esme said. "You're one of the bravest people I know."

Arabella chuckled damply. "Well, that's a new compliment for me. Thank you, my dear."

Esme's own smile wavered. "And the dearest as well. No mother could have helped me more than you have, Arabella, nor a sister more than you, Helene." She met their eyes, and now they were all a little teary.

"I couldn't have loved a child more than I love you, dearest," Arabella said.

Helene sat down hard on Arabella's dressing table stool. "Do you still feel a great deal of grief due to not having a child, Lady Withers? If you don't mind my asking?"

Arabella gave her an unsteady smile. "It is not terrible, no. But it is a sadness to me, since I would have been delighted to be a mother. Yet just having the chance to be with William is very healing in that respect."

Helene pressed her lips together. "I want you all to know that I am going to have a child."

Unexpectedly, Bea, who'd been sitting silently to the side, yelped, *"What?"* And then clapped her hand over her mouth. "I'm sorry! It's none of my business."

"My dissipated husband returned to London still refusing to divorce me, and I have decided to have a child irrespective of my marital situation. If Rees wishes to divorce me after the fact, on the ground of adultery, I truly don't give a bean."

"Would you then marry Mr. Fairfax-Lacy?" Bea asked. The strain in her voice made all three women look at her.

"Stephen? No!" Helene said. "Stephen has no aspirations to my hand. Or bed, for that matter, although he was kind enough to pretend so before my husband." There was a pause. "Are *you* going to marry him?"

Bea swallowed and then looked to Esme. "Lady Rawlings has precedence."

Esme laughed. "I surrender my claim."

"Then I am," Bea said sedately. A smile was dawning on her face. "I *am* going to marry him."

"Bravo!" Arabella said, tossing her handkerchief onto her dressing table. "I knew the man was good marrying material. Didn't I tell you so, dear?" she said to Esme.

"I merely have to ask him," Bea put in.

Helene blinked at her. "Hasn't he asked *you?*"

"Not in so many words. He wishes to be wooed."

"What an extraordinary thing," Helene said slowly. "Do you know, I am coming to have an entirely different idea of how to behave around men?"

Arabella nodded. "If you wish to have a child, you will need to move decisively. That's why I married so quickly after Robbie died. I wasn't in love, wasn't even in my right head, I think now. But I wanted a child. Mind you, it didn't work for me, but it might well for you."

Helene nodded. "You may not wish to acknowledge me in the future," she said, looking at Esme. "I will create a tremendous scandal by having a child. Everyone in the polite world knows that I have no contact whatsoever with my husband."

Esme stood up and gave her a fierce hug. "You never deserted me, and I would never desert you. What would I have done without you and Arabella these past few months? Besides, I do believe I shall give up some of my aspirations to respectability."

"Thank goodness!" Arabella said, with a world of meaning in her voice.

Helene turned to Bea. "I trust you don't mind my saying that you are very inspiring. I mean to copy down that poem, if you don't mind. Perhaps I shall have use for it another day."

Bea grinned. "As long as you are not planning to direct your invitation to Mr. Fairfax-Lacy, you may use it as you please."

"How *are* you going to ask him to marry you?" Esme asked, fascinated.

Bea bit her lip. "I only just this moment decided to do so. I really don't know."

"Poetry," Helene said positively. "Obviously, you must use poetry."

Esme clapped her hands. "We'll have a small party tomorrow night, just amongst ourselves, and we shall complete the poetry reading that we began."

"That means I shall have to find an appropriate poem," Bea said. "I suppose I had better hie me to the library." She looked at Esme. "You didn't read a poem at our last such reading."

"I haven't such a pressing need as yourself," Esme said lightly.

"Humph," Arabella snorted. "That's one way of putting it."

Esme frowned at her.

"Well, you've got an eligible man visiting your chambers on the sly," Arabella said irrepressibly. "You might as well let him make an honest woman of you."

Bea's eyes grew round. "Which man?"

Arabella replied. "The marquess, naturally."

Helene laughed. "Oh Esme," she said, "you are truly Infamous Esme, are you not?"

"I most certainly am not," Esme said with dignity. But all her friends were laughing, so after a bit she gave in and laughed as well.

## 38

### The Poetry Reading

$\mathcal{M}$rs. Cable was rather scandalized to find that she was attending a poetry reading. But while inviting the Sewing Circle, Lady Rawlings
had noted that she herself intended to read from the Bible, and Mrs. Cable had decided that encouragement of such a devout practice was a
virtue. And if she was honest, she was finding the presence of the scandalous Marquess Bonnington rather enthralling. He was, well, *wickedly*
attractive. Mrs. Cable secretly thought that she'd never seen anyone quite
so mesmerizing: those dusky golden curls, and he had such a powerful
body! Although she hardly put it to herself like that. In truth, Mrs. Cable
had some difficulty dragging her eyes away.

There certainly was enough to see at this particular gathering. She
was absolutely certain that Lady Beatrix, for example, had reddened her
lips, if not worse. Naturally Lady Winifred was having the time of her life
trundling around the room with her dear friend Arabella. It was quite a
sorrow to see how susceptible Lady Winifred was to the lures of the fash-
ionably impure. And Mr. Barret-Ducrorq was almost as bad. He seemed
to be fascinated by Lady Withers, and Mrs. Barret-Ducrorq had had to
call her husband to heel quite sharply. Mrs. Cable looked with satisfaction at her own husband. He was sitting next to her, nursing his brandy
and looking stolidly bored. Mr. Cable had attended the reading only after
bitter protest; he did not consider poetry to be palatable entertainment.

Lady Rawlings clapped her hands. "For those of you who have recently joined us, we have been entertaining ourselves in the evening by
giving impromptu poetry readings. We shall have two readings this evening. First Lady Beatrix will read a piece from Shakespeare, and then I
shall read a piece from the Bible."

Mrs. Cable felt cheered. She must have had an influence on the young widow. Shakespeare and the Bible: what could be more unexceptional than that? Lady Beatrix walked before the group and stood in front of the fireplace. She was wearing a dinner gown of moss silk, in a bright rose color. Of course, the bodice bared far more of her neck and bosom than Mrs. Cable considered acceptable. But Lady Beatrix looked nervous, which Mrs. Cable counted in her favor. A young lady entertaining a group of distinguished guests ought to be fairly shaking with fright.

And, indeed, had she but known, Bea was literally trembling. She kept sneaking glances at Stephen, but he hadn't even smiled at her. There was nothing in his demeanor to indicate that he had spent virtually the whole of last night in her bed. "I have chosen a dialogue," Bea told the assembled company, "from *Romeo and Juliet.*"

"An excellent choice," Lady Bonnington commented. "I am very fond of Mr. Shakespeare's works. I don't hold with those who criticize him for frivolity."

"I suppose you need a man for your dialogue," Esme said. "Do choose a partner, Bea."

My goodness, but Esme's eyes had a wicked suggestiveness to them, Bea thought. It would serve her right if she chose Marquess Bonnington, if she stole Esme's supposedly unwanted suitor from under her nose. Naturally Esme was cushioned between the two most eligible men in the room. She had Stephen on her left and Marquess Bonnington on her right.

But Bea didn't chose Bonnington, of course. She turned to Stephen and gave him a melting smile. "Mr. Fairfax-Lacy, would you be so kind?"

His face gave nothing away. He came to his feet with easy grace and accepted the open book she handed him.

"We'll read from the balcony scene," she told him.

"Very good! Very good!" Lady Bonnington trumpeted. "I've always been fond of *'Wherefore art thou, Romeo'?*" She turned to her son. "Do you remember when we saw Edmund Kean perform as Romeo last year, dear?"

Sebastian frowned at her. He had the feeling that something quite important was happening and—more important—it looked to be the kind of event that might derail Esme's patently artificial engagement to Fairfax-Lacy. Lady Beatrix seemed to be a handful, but the way Fairfax-Lacy was looking at her, he was ready to take on the task.

Meanwhile Stephen looked down at Bea and felt as if his heart would burst with pure exhilaration. She was wooing him, his own darling girl had decided to woo him. He glanced down at the book. " *'But, soft! What light through yonder window breaks? It is the east, and Juliet is the sun.'* " His eyes told her silently the same things he read: She was his east, his sun, his life. But she hardly glanced at him, the silly girl, just kept looking at her book as if she might lose courage.

Bea gripped her book as if holding its pages would force her fingers to stop trembling. She was doing it: she was stealing him, taking him, ruining him . . . " *'Good night, good night!'* " she said steadily, " *'As sweet repose and rest come to thy heart as that within my breast!'* " She risked a look at him. The tender smile in his eyes was all she ever wanted in life. She took a deep breath and kept reading until there it was before her. She glanced at the group watching: met Esme's laughing eyes, and Helene's steady gray ones, Sebastian Bonnington's sardonic, sympathetic gaze, and Lady Bonnington's look of dawning understanding. Then she turned back to Stephen.

She had no need of the book, so she closed it and put it to the side. " *'If that thy bent of love be honorable,'* " she said clearly, ' *"thy purpose marriage, send me word tomorrow . . . '* "

But his voice joined hers as he held out his hands. *" 'Where and what time thou wilt perform the rite, and all my fortunes at thy foot I'll lay, and follow thee my lord throughout the world.' "*

"I will," Stephen said, smiling at her in a way that broke her heart and mended it again, all in one moment. "I will, Bea, I will."

"You will?" she asked with a wobbly smile, clinging to his hands. "You will?"

"What's that? Part of the play?" Mr. Barret-Ducrorq said. "Quite the actor, isn't he?"

"I will marry you," Stephen said. His voice rang in the room.

Bea's knees trembled with the shock of it. The smile on her lips was in her heart. She'd wooed a man. His mouth was hungry, violent, possessive, and she nestled into him like the very picture of—of a wife.

"Ladies and gentlemen," Stephen said a moment later. He turned, his arm snug around Bea. "May I present the future Mrs. Fairfax-Lacy?"

Esme was laughing. Marquess Bonnington bellowed, "Good man!" Even Lady Bonnington gave a sedate little nod of her head, although she quickly turned to Esme. "You would appear to have lost your fiancé," she observed. And then, "How fortuitous that your mother left this morning."

"Yes, isn't it lucky," Esme said, smiling at her.

Stephen pulled Bea away to sit next to him on the settee, where he could presumably whisper things in her ear not meant for public discussion. Esme straightened her shoulders. Her heart was hammering in her chest from nerves. "I shall read from the Bible," she said, picking up the book from the table and walking to the front of the room. It was Miles's Bible that she carried, the family Bible, into which she had written William's name. But she had the feeling that Miles approved, almost as if he were there in the room, with his blue eyes and sweet smile.

"It is a pleasure to see a young widow immerse herself in the Lord's words," Mrs. Cable said loudly. "I believe I have set an example in that respect."

"You're not a widow *yet*," her husband said sourly.

Sebastian was the picture of sardonic boredom. Obviously he thought that Esme was merely cultivating her Sewing Circle, quoting the Bible in the hopes of polishing her reputation. Esme swallowed. He was looking down at his drink, and all she could see was the dark gold of his hair. "I shall read from the Song of Solomon," she said. Sebastian's head swung up sharply.

" *'The song of songs, which is Solomon's,'* " she read, steadying her voice. " *'Let him kiss me with the kisses of his mouth: for thy love is better than wine.'* "

"Didn't she say that she was going to read from the Bible?" Mr. Barret-Ducrorq asked, in great confusion.

"Hush!" Lady Bonnington said. She was sitting bolt upright, her stick clutched in her hands. Her eyes were shining and—wonder of wonders—she was smiling.

Esme kept reading. " *'Stay me with flagons, comfort me with apples: for I am sick of love.'* "

Abruptly Sebastian stood up. Mrs. Cable was looking at him. Esme looked at him too, telling him the truth with every word she read. " *'My beloved spake, and said unto me, Rise up, my love, my fair one, and come away.'* "

He strode toward her, skirting his mother's chair, the settee, Mrs. Cable sitting in rigid horror.

" *'For lo, the winter is past,'* " Esme said softly, only for him. " *'The rain is over and gone; The flowers appear on the earth.'* "

He was there before her, taking the book away, taking her hands in his large ones. She looked up at him.

" *'My beloved is mine, and I am his: he feedeth among the lilies.'* "

His arms closed around her with hungry violence. A shudder ran through Esme's body as she lifted her mouth to his. How could she ever have thought that anything mattered more than Sebastian, her love, her deep center, her heart.

He tore his mouth from hers for a moment. "I love you," he said hoarsely.

Joy raced through Esme's body, sang between them. "And *'I am sick with love for you,'* " she said softly, repeating the beautiful old words of the ancient book.

Mrs. Cable's mouth snapped shut. She grabbed her husband by the arm and hauled him to his feet. "I am appalled!" she hissed. "Appalled!"

Lady Rawlings didn't heed her, crushed as she was into that degenerate marquess's arms. Mrs. Cable could see what had happened. She had lost the battle for the widow's soul, yes, and the devil had won. Lust and Lasciviousness ruled this house.

"We are leaving!"

She turned to go and found her way blocked by Marchioness Bonnington. "I pity you!" Mrs. Cable croaked, narrowing her eyes. "But perhaps your son is well matched by such a lightskirt."

"I daresay he is," the marchioness replied. There was something in her eyes that gave Mrs. Cable pause. "Surely you wish to give the happy couple your congratulations before you leave so precipitously?"

But Mrs. Cable had a backbone to match the marchioness's. "I do *not*," she said, fixing her beady eyes on Lady Bonnington. "And if you would inform your dissolute daughter-in-law that her services are no longer desired in the Sewing Circle, I would be most grateful."

The marchioness stepped back, something to Mr. Cable's relief. He was beginning to fear that his wife would actually pummel a peeress of the realm.

"I should be most happy to fulfill your request," Lady Bonnington said.

The smile that played around the marchioness's mouth so enraged Mrs. Cable that she didn't even realize for several hours that the rest of her Sewing Circle had not followed her from the room.

Alas, it was the demise of that excellent institution.

A month or so later, Mrs. Cable began a Knitting Circle drawn from women in the village, priding herself on bringing the Lord's words to illiterate laborers. Without her leadership, the Sewing Circle drifted into dissolute activities such as attending Lady Rawlings's wedding to the degenerate marquess. Society noted that Lady Rawlings's mother did not attend. But the smiling presence of Marchioness Bonnington, and the weight of her formidable power in the *ton,* established the marriage as the most fashionable event of the season.

Rather more quietly, Lady Beatrix Lennox married Mr. Fairfax-Lacy from her own house, with only her immediate family in attendance. It was rumored that her only attendants were her sisters, and that they wore daisy chains on their heads, which sounded odd indeed. The newly wed couple returned to London, and by the time that society really noticed what had happened, and with whom, the new Mrs. Fairfax-Lacy proved to have such powerful friends that hardly more than a murmur was heard of her blackened reputation. Besides, the Tory party quickly realized that she showed considerable potential as a political wife.

Helene, Countess Godwin, traveled to attend her friend the Duchess of Girton's confinement. Through the whole summer and fall she brooded on the child she was determined to have. By hook or by crook, with the help of her husband, or without him.

But that's a story for another day. . . .

# The First Epilogue

## Plump as a Porker

*E*sme started awake, as always, with a bolt of fear. Where was William? Was he all right? A second later she realized that what had woken her was a chuckle, a baby's chuckle. The curtains were open and early sunlight was streaming into the room. Sebastian was standing in front of the window, wearing only pantaloons. His shoulders were a ravishing spread of muscles. And there, just peeking over his left shoulder, was a tiny curled fist, waving in the air.

A cascade of baby giggles erupted into the room.

Sebastian was dancing William up and down on his arm. The question of chilly drafts leaped into Esme's throat. She never let William go anywhere near a window. But then . . . it felt as if high summer had come. Sebastian spun around and William screamed with laughter. He was sitting on the crook of Sebastian's arm, and he wasn't even wearing a nappy.

Esme's heart skipped a beat. She *never* took all William's clothes off at once!

But the baby was clutching Sebastian's hair and squealing. Sebastian obligingly bounced him up into the air again. Esme found herself looking at a stunningly beautiful man, all muscles and smooth golden skin, and tumbling curls.

And then, suddenly, she looked at William. It was rather like looking sideways and suddenly catching sight of oneself in the mirror without recognizing who it is. Because the naked man in her bedchamber was holding one of the fattest, healthiest, happiest babies she'd ever seen.

That was William. Her sickly, fragile son?

Esme's mouth fell open.

Sebastian still didn't know she was watching. He was holding William in the air and laughing up at him. Pudgy little legs kicked with delight. "You love that, don't you, son," he said. And every time he jig-gled William, the baby giggled and giggled. Until Sebastian nestled him back against his chest. It was when Sebastian was kissing William's curls that he caught sight of Esme's wide eyes.

He was clearly unsure of Esme's reaction to William's undressed state. "He loves it, Esme," he said quickly. "See?" And he tickled William's plump little tummy. Sure enough, William leaned back against his shoulder and giggled so hard that all his fat little bits shook with de-light. And there were many parts jiggling.

"He *is* healthy, isn't he?" Esme said with awe.

"He's a porker," Sebastian said.

"Oh my goodness," Esme breathed. "I just—I didn't—"

Sebastian brought William over to the bed. "I promise you that he's not chilled, Esme. Not in the slightest. I never would have removed his clothes if I thought he might take a chill."

William lay on the coverlet kicking his legs and waving his arms, gleefully celebrating freedom from three layers of woolens.

"It's summer, Esme," Sebastian said gently. "Roses are blooming in the arbor. And I do believe some exercise will do him good." He rolled the baby over. William squealed with delight and then poked up his large head inquisitively. "He's gaining some control over his neck," Sebastian said, looking as pleased as if William had taken a top degree at Oxford University.

Esme opened her mouth—and stopped.

The sun was shining down on the sturdy little baby's body, on his brown hair that was so like his father Miles's hair. Onto his unsteady head, blue eyes blinking up at Sebastian with precisely the sweetness that Miles had given to him.

And there, at the very base of his spine, was a small spangled mark. A mark that hadn't been there at his birth, but was indubitably present now.

"Sebastian," she said quietly. There was something in her voice that made him turn to her immediately. "Look."

Sebastian stared at the bottom of his son's spine and didn't say a word.

"What do you think?"

"I think it looks very much like the mark I have at the base of my spine," he said slowly. He looked puzzled rather than joyous. Then, after a moment, he laughed. "I was right! He may have suddenly become my blood relation, but I already loved him with every bit of my heart."

Esme looked up at him, eyes brimming. "Oh, Sebastian, what would I ever do without you?"

He stared at her for a moment, and then a little crooked smile curled his mouth. "I won't answer that, because it will never happen."

William rolled over, his naked little arms waving in the air. His mama and papa weren't watching him wave at the dust fairies playing in a ray of sunshine. They were locked in each other's arms, and his papa was kissing his mama in that way he had: as if she were the most delectable, desirable, wonderful person in the world. And she was kissing him back, as if she would throw away the world and all its glories merely to be in his arms.

William giggled again and kicked the air, scattering dust fairies like golden stars in all directions.

# The Second Epilogue

## In Which a Puritan Loses His Reputation

*J*t was high summer. The air was heavy with dust and smoke, and the streets smelled of ripe manure. The odor crept into the houses of the very rich, even into an occasion as grand as Lady Trundlebridge's yearly ball, where bunches of lavender could do nothing for the stench. "Paugh!" exclaimed the Honorable Gerard Bunge as he held a heavily scented handkerchief to his nose. "I cannot abide the end of the season. Even I must needs think of the country, and you know I loathe the very sight of sheep."

"I feel precisely the same way," his cousin, Lady Felicia Saville, sighed, fluttering her fan so quickly that it would have ruffled hair less severely tamed by a curling iron. "London is simply abominable at the end of the season." She straightened and snapped shut her fan, making up her mind on the moment. "I shall leave for the country tomorrow, Gerard. The season is over. This ball, for example, is unutterably tedious."

Gerard nodded. "Nothing left but the dregs of gossip, m'dear. Did you catch a glimpse of Fairfax-Lacy and his bride?"

"A doomed marriage," she said, with some satisfaction. Alas, Lady Felicia Saville was something of a personal expert on the subject. "A man of such reputation marrying the notorious Lady Beatrix!" Her high-pitched laughter said it all. "Do you know, I believe I saw Sandhurst earlier. Perhaps she will recommence her *alliance* now she is safely married. Given Lady Ditcher's interruption, I would say their encounter left, shall we say, something to be desired?"

Gerard tittered appreciatively. "You *do* have a way with words, Cousin. Look: Lady Beatrix is dancing with Lord Pilverton. She is rather exquisite; you can't fault Sandhurst for taste."

But Felicia had never been fond of musing over other women's attractions, particularly those of women like Lady Beatrix, who appeared to have a flair for fashion rivaling her own. "I should like to walk in the garden, Gerard," she commanded.

"My red heels!" he protested. "They're far too delicate for gravel paths."

"And far too out of fashion to protect. This year no one wears red heels other than yourself, although I haven't wanted to mention it." And she swept through the great double doors into the garden, her cousin reluctantly trailing behind her.

They weren't the only people to escape the stuffy ballroom. The narrow little paths of Lady Trundlebridge's garden were fairly heaving with sweaty members of the aristocracy, their starched neckcloths hanging limply around their necks. Stephen Fairfax-Lacy, for example, was striding down a path as if he could create a breath of fresh air just by moving quickly. Bea had talked him into giving up his pipe, and while he thought that it was a good idea on the whole, there were moments when he longed for nothing more than the smell of Virginia tobacco. Thinking of Bea, and pipes, he turned the corner and found himself face-to-face with—

Sandhurst.

Bea's Sandhurst. The man disreputable enough to seduce a young girl in a drawing room. The man who'd ruined Bea's reputation.

Sandhurst was a sleek-looking man, with his hair swept into ordered curls and a quizzing glass strung on his chest by a silver chain. He took one look at Fairfax-Lacy and didn't bother with prevarication. "I offered to marry her," he said, his voice squeaking upward.

Stephen didn't even hear him. He was stripping off his coat. There was a reason why he'd trained in Gentleman Jackson's boxing salon, day after day for the past ten years. True, he hadn't known what it was, but now he realized.

"Mr. Fairfax-Lacy!" Sandhurst squealed, backing up. "Couldn't we simply discuss this like gentlemen?"

"Like what?" Stephen asked, advancing on him with the slow, lethal tread of a wolf. "Like *gentlemen*?"

"Yes!" Sandhurst gulped.

"You forfeited that title a few years ago," Stephen said, coming in with a swift uppercut. There was a satisfying thunk of fist on bone. Sandhurst reeled back, hand to his jaw.

"Fight!" yelled an enthusiastic voice at Stephen's shoulder. He paid no mind. His arm shot out. A sledge-hammer, in Jackson's best manner. Sandhurst fell back, tripped, and landed on his ass. Stephen was conscious of a thrum of disappointment. Was the man simply going to stand there and play the part of a punching bag? He watched dispassionately as Sandhurst picked himself off the gravel.

There was a growing circle around them in the shadowy garden, calling to each other to discover who was in the fight, hushing to a whisper as the relation between the two men was explained. A voice bellowed from behind Sandhurst: "For God's sake, man, pull yourself together!" Others joined in, rather like a crowd at a cockfight. "Show yourself a man, Sandhurst! By God, you're nothing more than a nursling! A molly! A . . ." Stephen blanked the voices from his mind and watched his opponent, who was being goaded into a decent effort. He was pulling off his jacket with the air of a maddened bull.

I think, a nobber, Stephen thought. Yes, and then a left hook. And after that, he dodged a hit, feigned right, launched a chop at Sandhurst's jaw. Took one himself in the right eye—damn, now Bea would demand an explanation. The irritation he felt at that translated to his right arm: a leveller, and Sandhurst dropped to the ground like a fallen tree. Stephen nudged him with his foot to make sure he was completely out, looked up, and caught the eye of his hostess. She deliberately threw up her fan and said something Stephen couldn't hear to the lady beside her, who laughed shrilly and said, "It's what comes naturally after associating with the House of *Commons!*"

He was picking up his coat when he felt a hand on his arm. "Mr. Fairfax-Lacy," said Lady Felicia Saville, her voice sweet as honey. "*Would* you be so kind as to escort me to the house?"

Stephen bowed. Apparently barbarous—nay, common—behavior was the way to this gentlewoman's heart. "If you will allow me to replace my jacket," he said.

"Hardly the behavior of the prudent man of Parliament," Felicia laughed up at him as they strolled back toward the house, quite as if nothing had taken place at all. "You will be quite the man of the hour."

"I highly doubt that. I'm afraid Lady Trundlebridge did not appreciate my behavior." He didn't feel like a Member of Parliament. He felt damn near—exuberant.

Felicia shrugged. "You were defending your wife's honor. Any woman of sense must applaud you, sir!" There was a flutter of warmth in Felicia's stomach when he smiled at her compliment. Perhaps once Lady Beatrix returned to her wandering ways, she could comfort Beatrix's neglected husband.

Just inside the ballroom doors, Stephen bowed. "If you will excuse me, Lady Felicia, I shall locate my wife."

He walked away without a backward glance, leaving Felicia with her mouth all but hanging open. Why had she never noticed how muscled and attractive the man was? She turned to meet the curious eyes of one of her bosom friends.

"Did you see the fight itself?" Penelope squealed. "Is it true that he called Sandhurst a blathering blackguard?"

Felicia's eyes were still a little dreamy. "Now there's a man worth having," she whispered to Penelope. "He was like a medieval knight protecting his wife's honor. He *flattened* Sandhurst!"

"Do you think he means to keep it up?" Penelope giggled. "Unless marriage changes Lady Beatrix's nature, he's going to be a busy man."

Felicia was watching his dark head as he made his way to the other side of the room. "She'd be a fool to stray," she sighed.

Bea was growing a little tired. Her shoes pinched loathsomely, and thanks to an overly energetic waltz, Pilverton had left a damp patch from his hand on the back of her gown. She turned gratefully at the sound of her husband's voice, and then gasped. "Stephen! What on earth happened to you?"

But he was grinning. "Nothing important. Are you ready to leave, m'dear? It's damnably hot in here."

"Stephen!" Bea said, her voice rising. "You tell me this moment what you've been up to."

"Making a spectacle of myself," he told her obligingly. "Fistfight in public. Shouldn't wonder if my reputation for tolerant debate isn't *ruined*." He said it with distinct relish, towing her out of the ballroom as he spoke. "I think it's time to retire to the country."

"We can't go to the country yet," Bea said, stopping and looking up at him suspiciously. "The House isn't closing session for at least a week." His eye was growing darker by the moment. "Just *who* have you been tussling with? Don't tell me you actually resorted to blows over that Enclosure Act?"

He reached around behind her and opened the door to the library. When she was inside, he leaned against it and grinned at her. "Something of the kind," he drawled.

"Really!" Bea said, rather amused. "It's hard to believe that solid, respectable members of Parliament can bring themselves to violence." And then, "What on earth are you doing, Stephen?"

He had turned the key in the lock. "I'm not a solid, respectable member, Bea. I'm resigning tomorrow morning, and I won't stand for reelection either." There was a sound at his back.

"Someone wishes to enter," Bea observed. "Stephen!" For he was walking toward her with an unmistakably lustful glint in his eye. There was something tantalizing about the air of wild exuberance that hung around him. "Did you take a blow to the head?" Bea asked, her voice rising to a squeak.

"No," he said, and his voice was rich with laughter. There was a bang at the door. "It's Fairfax-Lacy," he bellowed. "I'm in here kissing my wife. Go make yourself useful by telling Lady Trundlebridge."

There was a sound of rapidly retreating footsteps, and then the room was quiet but for the faint hum of the ball continuing on the other side of the house.

"Stephen Fairfax-Lacy!" his wife gasped.

"I'm a madman in love with my wife." He had her now, cupping her face in his hands. "I do believe I shall make love to you at Lady Trundlebridge's ball, and ruin my reputation for once and for all." One hand slid to her breast, and that rush of melting pleasure that came at his slightest touch rushed down Bea's legs. He kissed her until she was limp, until he had backed her onto a couch, until she was gasping, pink in the cheeks, almost—almost lost.

"Stephen," she said huskily, removing his hand, which had somehow managed to get under her gown and was touching her in a flagrantly ungentlemanly fashion.

"Darling." But he was busy. The necklines of Bea's gowns were so useful that he didn't know why he'd ever thought they were too low. They were perfect.

She pushed at his shoulders. Something was prickling the back of her mind. "Stephen, with whom precisely did you fight?"

He raised his head and looked at her. His right eye was almost swollen shut, but the gleam of desire was there. He feathered his lips over hers.

"Stephen!"

"Sandhurst," he said obligingly.

Bea gasped.

"We were fighting over an Enclosure Act, just as you guessed. I'm like all those nasty sheep farmers, Bea. You're mine. I've enclosed you."

"But—but—"

"Hush," he said and kissed her again.

Bea looked up at him, and there were tears in her eyes. "Oh Stephen," she whispered. "I love you."

"Can we go home now, Bea? We've been in London for a month and have been received everywhere. I've tramped off to the House and listened to assinine debates. Our marriage didn't ruin my career. In fact, with the way Lord Liverpool looks at you, I stand to be named to the cabinet if I'm not smart enough to resign quickly."

She smiled at him mistily. "Are you saying I told you so?"

"With any luck, *I* just ruined my career," he said, kissing her. "Now may we leave London, please? Shall we go home and chase each other around the billiards table, and start a goat farm, and perhaps a baby, and make love in the pasture?"

Bea wanted to weep for the joy of it, for her luck in finding him, for the bliss of realizing he was right. He was *right*. She hadn't ruined his career. "Oh, Stephen," she said huskily, "I do love you."

"I made you woo me," he said, looking into her eyes. "I think it's time that I courted you, don't you think?" His arms closed around her, arms that would never abandon her, and never let go. "Flowers at dawn," he whispered into her ear, "daisy chains for lunch, champagne in your bath."

Bea swallowed hard so she wouldn't cry. "I love you," she said again.

"I think Romeo said it best," her husband said, brushing his lips over hers. "You are, indeed, *my love, my wife.*"

# A Note on Shakespeare and his Wilder Brethren

The last words of *A Wild Pursuit* were written by Shakespeare, and spoken by Romeo. I decided to close the novel with Romeo's farewell to his bride because Renaissance poetry is so important to this book as a whole. Bea uses *Romeo and Juliet* to propose to Stephen Fairfax-Lacy; Esme uses the King James version of *The Song of Solomon* to propose to Sebastian Bonnington.

But the book is also punctuated by works far less known than these two famed pieces of love poetry. Richard Barnfield published only two books of verse, which appeared in 1594 and 1595, precisely when *Romeo and Juliet* was likely first performed. For their time, both Shakespeare's play and Barnfield's poetry were shockingly original. Juliet's proposal to Romeo, not to mention the speech in which she longs for their wedding night to begin, both startled and delighted London audiences. *Romeo and Juliet* was a howling success; ten years later, young courtiers were still quoting the play to each other on the street. Its popularity is attested to by the fact that in 1607 a company of boys put on the stage a play called *The Puritan*, which contains a riotous parody of Juliet's balcony scene. Some lines from that play are used by Esme to poke fun at *Romeo and Juliet*, precisely as the original boy actors did back in 1607.

Richard Barnfield's poetry was, in a different fashion, as shocking as Shakespeare's portrayal of Juliet. The book that Bea brings with her to Esme's house party was an odd amalgam of love poetry and narrative verse. Amongst the various odes and lyrics Barnfield wrote are some of the most beautiful, sensual, and explicit poems written before the twentieth century. As you can perhaps tell from the reaction Helene has to reading aloud a Barnfield poem, neither Renaissance nor Regency readers were accustomed to expressing in public a wish that *My lips were honey, and thy mouth a bee.* I sometimes receive letters from readers contending that aristocrats living in the Regency period would have acted with propriety at all times, even in the privacy of their own bedchambers. I thought it well to present some poetry written over two hundred years before the Regent took the throne. Barnfield may have been one of the first Englishmen to put this desire in print; he was neither the first, nor the last, to express it.

# YOUR WICKED WAYS

## 1

## In Strictest Confidence...

18 March 1816

*The Countess Pandross to Lady Patricia Hamilton*

... my dearest, as to what you tell me of the exploits of Earl Godwin, I can only say that nothing will ever surprise me. The former Countess Godwin (who was, as you know, one of my very dearest friends) would turn in her grave if she knew that her son was entertaining opera singers in her house! And I shudder to think that one of these infamous women may actually be living with him. How his poor wife is able to hold her head high, I shall never know. Helene has always showed edifying composure, although I did hear a whisper—just a whisper—suggesting that she may request a divorce. I can't imagine how much *that* would cost, but Godwin must have at least fifteen thousand pounds a year and can probably afford it. At any rate, my dear, what I am truly longing to hear about are your plans for sweet Patricia's debut. Didn't you tell me that you were planning a ball for the weekend of the fifth? Mrs. Elizabeth Fremable tells me . . .

21 April 1816

*Helene Godwin, Countess Godwin, to her mother, currently residing in Bath*

Dear Mother,

I am most sympathetic to your distress over the continuing debacle of my marriage. I fully recognize that my decision to elope with Rees brought scandal into the family, but I would remind you that the elopement was years ago. I am equally aware that a divorce would be far more grievous. But I beg of you, please accept my decision. I simply cannot continue in this fashion. I am heartsick when I think of my life.

Your loving daughter,
Helene, Countess Godwin

22 April 1816

*Rees Holland, Earl Godwin, to his brother, a vicar in the North Country*

Dear Tom,

Things are all right here. Yes, I know that you are fretting over my infamous reputation, but you will simply have to overlook my slurs on the family name. I assure you that my sins are even more plenteous than your pious correspondents have told you. Women dance on top of the table in the dining room daily.

Yours with all proper sentiment,
Rees

22 April 1816

*Miss Patricia Hamilton to Miss Prunella Forbes-Shacklett*

Dear Prunes,

It is too bad of your mama to bury you in the country! When is she planning to bring you to town? I assure you that it is already very crowded here, and if one does not make an appointment, it is impossible to find a mantua maker who will even discuss a court gown. But Prunes, I met the most absolutely fascinating man yesterday. He is apparently quite, quite notorious—a veritable rake! I am not going to put his name here, in case my abominable little brother obtains this letter before I mail it, but he is an earl and his initials are RH. You can look him up in Debrett's. Apparently he threw his wife out of the house some years ago, and now lives with an opera singer! My mother (as you can imagine) was in a flurry of anxiety and told me later not to even think of dancing with him, as there is talk of a divorce. Imagine: me dancing with a divorced man! Naturally I shall do it if the opportunity ever presents itself . . .

23 May 1816

*Rees Holland, Earl Godwin, to Helene Holland, Countess Godwin*

Helene,

If you'd like to see me, you'll have to come to the house, as I'm trying to finish a score that's needed in rehearsal directly. To what do I owe this charming, if unexpected, pleasure? I trust you are not going to request a divorce again, as my answer will be the same as the last. I'll tell Sims to wait for a reply as I think it doubtful that you will find the backbone to enter this den of iniquity.

Rees (should I say, Your Darling Husband?)

23 May 1816

*Mr. Ned Suffle, Manager of the Royal Italian Opera House, to Rees Holland, Earl Godwin*

Without putting undue pressure on you, my lord, I must have the score of *The Quaker Girl* by the end of this month latest.

23 May 1816

*Helene Holland, Countess Godwin to Rees Holland, Earl Godwin*

I shall visit you this afternoon at two of the clock. I trust you will be alone.

## 2

## The Key to Marital Harmony

*Number 15, Rothsfeld Square*
*London*

The Godwin carriage pulled up before her former residence, but the countess did not emerge. The footman was holding open the carriage door, and the steps were down. But Helene was unable to force her limbs to move her forward, along the walk, into the house. She hadn't even looked at the house in years. She'd gotten in the habit of glancing the other direction should she visit a friend in Rothsfeld Square. It was easy enough to let her eyes drift away, or examine the lining of the carriage as if she'd never seen it before. Because if she did peer at the house, *her* house, what if she glimpsed what her former neighbors saw daily?

What if she saw the woman who by all accounts was living in Helene's own bed chamber, sleeping in Helene's bed, in the room next to Helene's own husband? A bitter taste of metal rose into her mouth. What then, indeed? She could only hope that Rees had abided by her request; it would be just like him to include his doxy in the conversation she had requested this morning.

Her footman was standing perfectly still. She could see him out of the corner of her eye, as curious as the rest of the servants about her unexpected excursion to this side of town. They knew she and her husband never met. Servants always knew everything. She rose, descended the steps, and walked up the path to the house. She held her head high, as always. It is not my fault that my husband is a reprobate, she told herself. It is not my fault. I will *not* accept the shame. Helene had spent a great deal of her time in the past few years refusing to accept shame. She was tired of that particular mental exercise.

The great house looked just the same, from the outside at least. One might have expected literal signs of the moral dissipation within: shutters askew or missing railings. But other than the need for a good polish on the brass, her house looked just as she had left it ten years ago. It towered above them, the highest in the square, home of the Godwins before Rees's father was born, before his grandfather became an earl, since the days when King James reportedly stopped by for a cup of the new extravagant beverage, tea, by which Rees's great grandfather had made his fortune. Even then, the Godwins were no merchants; that early Lord Godwin was an extravagant madcap courtier, who threw his entire inheritance into shares in the East India Company. His stroke of genius had turned a minor Stuart lord into the forefather of one of the most powerful families in England. Successive Godwins had augmented their fortune by shrewd marriages, and their reputations by political acumen . . . until the birth of Rees Holland.

Far from showing a flare for political life, Rees had occupied himself since reaching majority by attempting to shock polite society, and by writing comic operas of dubious artistic value. In both endeavors, he succeeded with flamboyant success. The very thought of it steeled Helene's back. It was no more her fault that Rees was the way he was, than it was his mother's for giving birth to him. A carriage clattered by and still no one had answered the door. Her footman banged the knocker again. She could hear it echoing away in the vast reserves of the house, but a butler did not appear. "Try the door, Bindle," she ordered.

Bindle pushed on the door and, of course, it opened. Helene marched up the steps and into the hallway and then turned: "Take the carriage around the Park, and return for me in one hour, if you please." The last thing she wanted was her carriage to be recognized.

So she entered the house alone. It was utterly silent. Rees must have forgotten their appointment. Not a servant was to be seen. Helene had to admit to a spark of satisfaction at that. A month or so after she left the house, most of the staff had decamped, informing all London of their displeasure at being witness to a troupe of Russian dancers practicing their art on the dining room table. Naked, or so they said. At the time Helene had been glad both to be vindicated in the eyes of her peers, and at the thought that Rees might be uncomfortable without adequate staff.

But naturally he wasn't. She wandered into the sitting room and it was abundantly clear that Rees was anything other than uncomfortable. True, there was some dust about. But the ornate and vastly uncomfortable sofa given them on their wedding by Helene's Aunt Margaret had disappeared altogether, likely banished to the attics. Instead the room was home to three pianos—three! Where a Hepplewhite secretary used to stand, there was a harpsichord. A grand piano blocked any view of the street. And a pianoforte stood at an awkward relation to the door, clearly plunked down wherever the movers happened to put it. Surrounding the feet of all three pianos were piles of paper: half-written scores, scribbled notes, crumpled drafts.

Helene's mouth twisted. Rees wrote music anywhere, and on anything. One couldn't discard a single sheet of paper due to his overwhelming fear that a brilliant phrase or a snatch of melody might have been scratched down and forgotten. From the looks of things, not a single sheet of foolscap had left the house since she did, and many reams had entered the door.

She sighed and glanced in the mirror over the mantelpiece. It was rather dusty and cracked in one corner but it showed her precisely what she wanted to know: all the trouble she had taken dressing was worth it. Her walking costume was made of a pale primrose fabric that made her hair look even lighter, almost white blond. Rees loved her hair. She remembered that. Her lips tightened. She remembered that, and a great deal more.

Helene walked briskly over to the nearest piano. She might as well see what frivolities Rees was concocting while she waited for her carriage to return. Unlike everything else in the room, the piano at least appeared to have been dusted. But Helene grabbed a handful of the haphazard compositions that were floating around her feet and used it to dust the stool, just in case. Then she threw the sheets back down on the ground, where they floated into a drift of foolscap. The layer of paper looked like a snowbank; her sheets floated down like fresh flakes atop an older accumulation.

The music on the piano was rather more than scrawled notes. It looked as if Rees's partner, Fen, had given him the text of an aria, a young girl's song about spring amidst the cherry blossoms. Helene snorted. Richard Fenbridgeton wrote all the librettos for Rees's operas, and he tended toward flowery exuberance. How Rees could spend his time with this twaddle, she didn't know.

Without removing her gloves Helene picked out the melody with her right hand. The melody was rather enchanting, tripping up and down until—*plunk*.

That had to be a mistake. It was utterly clear that he needed an ascending scale to an E-flat. He was making the girl sound like a dowager. She tried it again. Hum-di-de-la-la-*plunk*. Luckily Rees had ink wells positioned all over the top of the piano, so she stood up, pulled off her gloves, stuck the score atop the piano, and began rewriting. After a while, she started singing as she rewrote, taking huge pleasure in jotting sarcastic comments in the margins. The idiot kept pushing the poor girl into the lower register when she *had* to stay high or the whole pleasure of springtime would be lost.

Rees Holland was as appreciative as the next man of a curved female derrier, particularly when the possessor was clearly trying out his aria, just as he'd requested. It was hard enough to coerce Lina into singing for him; it was a true pleasure to find her engaged in the exercise on her own. He crossed the room in a few strides and clapped an appreciative hand onto Lina's sweet little bottom. "For this I'll buy you—"

But his promise turned into a strangled exclamation. The woman who jumped and spun away from his hand was no Lina.

"God above, I forgot you were coming!" Now she was facing him, Rees could hardly believe he'd made such a mistake. Lina was a plump little partridge, and his wife was a gaunt stick of a woman, with cheekbones that could cut you, if her eyes didn't first. They were narrowed at him in that way he detested.

"Helene," he said resignedly.

"I gather that charming greeting was meant for someone else?" If her eyebrow went any higher, it would dance right off her face.

"I apologize." As always, he felt a mantle of awkward, heavy resentment settle about him. Helene had a way of looking at him that made him feel like a great hog. A huge wallowing beast of some sort.

He turned away and sat down, ignoring the fact that she was still standing. To his mind, after a woman has poured the contents of a chamberpot over your head, one needn't stand on occasion anymore. Not that the chamberpot-throwing happened recently, but it wasn't the sort of thing one forgot.

She raised her chin in that way she had and sat down opposite him, as dainty and precise as a bloody little sparrow. He eyed her for no good reason other than because he knew it made her nervous.

"Lost more weight?" he finally said when the silence grew oppressive. He liked a ripe armful of flesh, and she knew it. Her lack of curves always used to be good for an outburst. But she ignored him, just twisted those thin hands of hers in her lap.

"I've come to ask you for a divorce, Rees."

He settled back into the corner of his settee. "Didn't my letter say not to bother? I haven't changed my mind on the matter."

When she didn't answer immediately, he added a sardonic comment that surely would drive her into a fury. "I find your request all the more surprising, since it appears that your future bridegroom has already changed *his* mind. The last time you asked me—April a year ago, wasn't it?—you wished to marry Fairfax-Lacy. But from what I've heard, he's up and married another, as the old ballad goes. So who are you wishing to marry now, Helene?"

"That is irrelevant to my desire to divorce you," she said, her voice disappointingly steady.

"I disagree. As I told you at the time, if you find a man brave enough to stand at your side during the proceedings, brave enough to allow himself to be sued as your consort, I will go through with it. For your sake. But if you haven't found such a man . . ." He paused. Her jaw was set in a manner he still dreamed about sometimes.

"Why not? Why can't you simply divorce me without knowing who I would marry?"

"Divorce would cost us thousands of pounds," he said, folding his arms over his chest. "I may look like a lackluster estate manager, Helene, but I'm not. Why in God's name would I put that drain on the estate when there's no point to it? Besides, remarrying would take an Act of Parliament. Fairfax-Lacy might have been able to obtain it, but there's few others with the same power. If you want to take a lover, take one. God knows, it will do you good."

He watched with satisfaction as color crept into his wife's porcelain cheeks. Damned if he knew why one of his primary pleasures in life was to get Helene to show some signs of life.

"I don't wish to take a lover," she said. "I merely want to rid myself of you, Rees."

"By means other than murder, I suppose you mean?"

"I'm willing to consider all options," she said coolly.

Rees laughed, more like a bark than a laugh. "You'll have to take a lover. *You* cannot petition on the grounds of adultery, only I can. Has someone already replaced Fairfax-Lacy, then?"

Her cheeks flared and she swallowed. "I could hire a man to stand as my consort," she said in a low voice.

"I see no reason for wasting substance on lawyers and bribes and the rest of it."

"I can pay that sum out of my dowry. And I'm quite certain that my mother would contribute a substantial amount as well."

"I don't give a hang whose money it is. There's no point to it, Helene! We married, and married we stay. I don't think it's such an uncomfortable life. After all, it's not as if I'm a dog in the manger, am I? Surely you can find someone in London to warm your toes!"

Helene barely heard him, barely listened as insult after calculated insult broke over her head. She just stared at him instead. Every time they were apart for a length of time, she managed to school herself into remembering only her husband's disgusting habits and his slovenly dress.

But then, when she saw him again, she couldn't help noticing the way his eyelashes cast shadows on his cheeks, and the fact that his lower lip was so full. The better to sneer at her, obviously. But then he had dimples in both cheeks and they offset how deep-set his eyes were. Oh, Rees wasn't beautiful. He had a broad nose, after all, and a shambling way of walking, and he was far too big for beauty. Simon Darby, now there was a beautiful man. Simon and Rees together were like Beauty and the Beast, except that God help her, she couldn't help but think the Beast was—was—

"Damn it all, Helene, I'm doing my best to drive you into a frenzy and you're not even listening," Rees said now, with obvious frustration. "I must be losing my touch."

"I don't care if you don't want to spend the money," she snapped, looking away from his face with a tinge of self-disgust. "I ceased to take your wishes into account quite a few years ago."

"There's my Helene," Rees said, leaning back again. "It throws me into a fidget if you don't snap back with a rejoinder. It's as if the sun didn't rise."

"Don't you see how much better it would be for both of us if we divorced and didn't have to snap at each other anymore?" she said. "We're at our worst around each other. I know I am. I turn into a veritable shrew and you—you—"

"My wife a shrew?" he said mockingly. "Never say so!"

Helene swallowed. Somehow she had to break through the barrage of mocking remarks he always threw at her. He had to listen. "We would both be better off if we were no longer married to each other."

"Can't see that it would make any difference. I'm quite comfortable as I am. I rather like having a wife around."

"You can hardly say that I'm *around*!"

"Your presence, ephemeral or otherwise, keeps the fortune-hunters away," he pointed out. "Were we to divorce, I'd have carriages breaking down before my railings every other day, with debutantes waltzing in here to play me their scales."

"But Rees," Helene said desperately, "I wish to marry someone else."

"Who?"

She was silent.

"Are you telling me," Rees demanded, "that you don't care who you marry, as long as you rid yourself of me?"

She nodded, a trifle jerkily. "Precisely."

He opened his mouth and shut it. "I can't imagine why we're having this conversation," he said finally. "I refuse to grant you a divorce." Rees stared at his wife in frustration. In general, he had no trouble understanding women. For the most part, he found them bland, foolish, and greedy in a petty sort of way for things like bonnet strings and silk stockings. But he had never made the mistake of underestimating his wife's intelligence.

"I should have left that house party the very moment I met you, back in '07," he said suddenly. "Young fool that I was."

"I wish you had," Helene said.

"But I didn't." Rees's voice had a harsh edge that surprised himself. "I still remember walking into the drawing room and seeing you playing the piano—"

She shook her head. "It was a harpsichord."

"Anyway, there you were, wearing a yellow sort of gown and playing Purcell's *Fairest Isle*."

"I had no idea you were so sentimental, Rees," she said with perfect indifference.

"I would hardly call it sentimental. I try to keep the image in mind because it encapsules the most crack-brained impulse of my life: asking you to elope with me."

He couldn't tell whether he was annoying her or not. Lord, but she had gained control since they were married! In those days, the merest comment would drive her to burst into tears and throw something at his head. He eyed her rigid, dried up posture and wondered if he didn't prefer the old Helene.

"It was hardly an impulse, Rees, given as we had known each other for some months by the time you asked me to marry you. But believe me, if I could take back my acceptance of your drivellingly insulting request, I would. It has ruined my life."

There was a heartfelt truth to her statement that silenced the witticism Rees was contemplating. He looked harder at his wife. She had dark shadows under her eyes and her hair was pulled up as tightly as it could be in those infernal braids she fancied.

"Is something the matter, Helene?" he asked. "I mean, something more than the usual?"

"You are." She raised her eyes, and the despair in them struck him in the chest. "You are, Rees."

"But why?" he asked, in honest bewilderment. "I'm far less scandalous than I was a few years ago, when I . . ." he paused and decided to skip over the Russian dancers, "when I was younger. I have never interfered with your doings. What could possibly be so awful about being married to me? I think it's a position that many women must envy. If you're lucky, I'll fall dead to the ground like Esme Rawlings's first husband, and you can become a rich widow."

That was a fairly lame joke, but surely it deserved a twitch of a smile.

"Honest to God, Helene, I simply don't see what's so objectionable about my being your husband. If I were requiring you to fulfill your wifely duties, I could understand." He stopped and the sentence hung on the air. He wished he hadn't brought up that old painful subject.

"I want a child," she said quietly. "I—I feel quite strongly about it."

"Still?" he said, without thinking. Helene was perched on the very edge of the couch, her delicate fingers clenched in her lap. There wasn't much that he liked about his wife's body, not really, but he always loved her hands. More fool he, he thought, remembering that he had been stupid enough to think that she would caress him with the same tenderness with which she caressed the piano keys.

A slight frown creased her forehead. "Yes, still. As I told you last spring. Why wouldn't I still wish for a child?"

When Rees was surprised, he generally spoke what he was thinking and regretted it later. "Because you're not exactly . . ." he eyed her.

"What?"

"Well, motherly," he said, feeling, belatedly, a distinct sensation of danger.

"Do explain precisely what you mean, Rees." She seemed to be speaking from between clenched teeth.

Rees resisted an impulse to check for breakable objects in her vicinity. He waved vaguely in the air. "Motherly . . . ah, fertile, fecund, you know what I mean!"

"Fertile?" He could hear her teeth grinding. "You venture to say to me that you think I am lacking in *fertility*? You have assessed my abilities, as if I were a sow you thought to buy at market?"

"Wrong word," he said, floundering deeper. "I only meant—"

"Yes?"

But Rees had woken to his own foolishness. "Why in God's name would you want a child, Helene?" Then he narrowed his eyes. "What am I thinking? Naturally you want a child because all your friends have children, don't they?"

"That has nothing to do with it."

"Esme Bonnington dropped that brat last spring," he said with deliberate crudeness, "Carola Pinkerton has a daughter, and there's Darby with a son. That pretty much covers your intimate circle, doesn't it? Oh, wait . . . I forgot the Duchess of Girton. She too has produced an heir, has she not?"

There was no color whatsoever in Helene's face now. He almost felt a gleam of pity.

"Gina's son was born last December. But I assure you, Rees, that my desire for children has little, if anything, to do with the good fortune of my friends."

Rees made a rude sound and stood up, wandering toward the piano. "That's garbage, Helene. Women are all the same. You want what everyone else has, and you'll go to any means to get it. Well, don't count on me. I refuse to petition for divorce. I see no reason to put myself through an experience so expensive and ruinous to my reputation—" he threw it over his shoulder—"aren't you pleased, Helene? I am finally gaining an aversion to scandal."

Just then something caught his eye. "What the hell!" He bent over the sheets of paper on top of the piano. His vicious little wife had clearly enjoyed herself by destroying his score. "What in the hell did you do here? That line must dip. You've turned it to a bloody orange seller's tune!" He spun around but the room was empty.

## 3

## *In Which Tempers Are Lost*

*Number Forty, Berkeley Square*
*London*

*A*fter women have been friends for ten years, or even one year, they can generally judge each other's state of mind from five yards. Esme Bonnington, sometimes known as Countess Bonnington and sometimes as Infamous Esme, counted herself a near scientist when it came to the nice art of reading emotion. When her friend Helene's braids were elegantly nestled on her head, without even a stray strand of hair to be seen, all was well. But today Lady Godwin's backbone was as rigid as if it had been welded in place, her eyes were narrowed to chips of ice, and—most telling of all—wisps of hair were framing her face.

"What on earth is the matter?" Esme asked, trying to remember whether she, Esme, had done anything to outrage Helene's sense of propriety. No. Since her second marriage, Esme quite prided herself on being about as scandalous as a cow. That meant Helene had encountered her husband.

With one chilly glance, Helene sent Esme's butler, Slope, from the room. "I was going to ask Slope to bring us some tea," Esme said with some disappointment.

"You can live without a lemon tart for at least another hour or so," Helene snapped.

Helene lived on the air, from the look of her. But Esme was used to solid nourishment, and having asked Helene for tea, she would like to partake. She rang the bell to summon Slope. "I would guess that you have asked Rees for a divorce again?"

"He won't even listen to me, Esme." Despair and anger battled in her voice. "He doesn't care a bean that I want a child."

"Oh, Helene," Esme said. "I'm so—"

"He laughed it off as a matter of competition," Helene interrupted. "He won't even try to understand what it feels like to watch other women have children and know that you are unable." Her voice caught on the last word.

"Men are insensitive brutes," Esme said sympathetically. "And your husband is among the worst of the species."

"Anyone's husband is better than mine! Do you remember when I told you after Miles died that I envied you your rapprochement, even if it was brief?"

"Of course."

"I meant it. I would give anything to have married someone like your first husband."

"Miles and I were far from an enviable couple," Esme pointed out. "When he died, we hadn't lived together in ten years. How can you envy a marriage like ours?"

"I don't envy your marriage. I envy your *husband*. When you told Miles that you wished to have a child, what did he do?"

Esme's eyes filled with understanding. "He agreed."

"And if you had asked him for a divorce?"

"He would have agreed to that as well," Esme said, swallowing a lump in her throat. "Miles was a truly amiable person."

"He was better than amiable," Helene said fiercely. "He was a kind person. He would have done anything for you, Esme, you know he would have."

"You wouldn't have liked being married to Miles, Helene. He was so placid, truly."

"*I* am placid!" The only argument one might have with that statement came from Helene's voice, a near shriek. "I would have—would have— oh, this is absurd! I don't want to argue over who has the worst husband. It's just that I want a child so much. I have for *years*! And now Carola has a perfect little daughter, and you only had to ask Miles in order to have a baby, and now Henrietta Darby, who didn't even think it possible to carry a child, has a son—" her words were lost in a torrent of sobs.

Esme stroked her arm. "I'm sorry, Helene. I'm so sorry."

"It's just not fair!" It burst from her like rain from a drainpipe. "I don't ever complain about my husband; you know I don't, Esme. But why did I ever, ever have to meet Rees Holland and marry him! Why didn't my mother stop me? Why didn't someone come after me when we eloped? Why did I have to end up married to an utter degenerate when the rest of you—you and Carola and Gina—all of you have taken your husbands back and they have been utterly decent about it?"

"Actually, my first husband is dead," Esme felt it necessary to add.

"That's irrelevant! Sebastian will probably give you five more children if you wish."

Esme had never seen her friend Helene show a stronger emotion than annoyance and once, when Esme had behaved appallingly, a sharp disgust. Helene's every motion and thought was effected with a maximum of grace and control. But now the intricate braids that graced the top of her head were tilting slightly to the side. Her pale blue eyes were blazing and her normally pale complexion was pink with rage and grief.

Still, Esme thought she ought to point out that her first husband Miles's death was hardly *irrelevant*. "That seems a bit harsh," she said cautiously. "After all, Miles would far rather be alive than—"

Helene cast her a look that stopped that proper sentiment in its tracks. "Save it for the Sewing Circle," she snapped. "Miles's death means that you didn't have to live with the man."

The reference to the Sewing Circle stung; Esme had had a brief-lived foray into respectable widowhood before making a scandalous second marriage, whereupon the righteous woman leading the Circle repudiated Esme's skills with the needle. "Miles and I may not have suited each other, but it isn't as if I disliked marriage itself. After all, I did marry Sebastian, and I live with him, very happily too."

"Cut bait," Helene said impatiently. "Can't we speak the truth in private? Men are a dreadful aberration of humanity: selfish, disgusting and forever rooting about looking for their own pleasures. Carola may well be besotted with Tuppy's dubious skills at fishing or whatever skills he claims to have, but will it last? There'll come a day when she'll realize that he's just like all the rest."

"Why, Helene, I had no idea that you felt this way!" Esme cried. "What on earth did you like about Miles, if you find all men to be selfish beasts?"

"Miles would have given you anything you asked for. He honored the vows of marriage. You wanted a child; he gave you one. You wanted him to leave the house; he did so. And he never bothered you again, did he?"

"No," Esme said, "yet—"

But Helene had risen and was pacing back and forth. "Rees and Miles are like night and day! Rees threw me out of our house years ago; he hasn't said a civil word to me since; and all of London knows the depths of depravity to which *he* has sunk!"

Esme had to admit the truth of that. "Miles did have a mistress," she put in.

"A quiet, respectable liaison," Helene said. "No hysterics on either side. Lady Childe is an indubitably respectable woman, and while I can hardly sanction such a liaison outside marriage, it's infinitely better than taking a woman of the streets and putting her into your wife's bedchamber. If one more person tells me how much they sympathize with me due to my husband's proclivities, I shall—I shall scream!"

Somewhat to Esme's relief, Slope appeared with a tea tray. He didn't seem to notice Helene's disheveled appearance, but then he was highly paid to overlook any sort of irregularity. Esme had hired him in the days when she was the toast of all London and doing her best to live up to a reputation as Infamous Esme.

"We'll think of something," she said consolingly, as she poured tea. "For one thing, Rees is far more likely to agree to divorce if you actually had a lover, Helene. How can he possibly sue you for adultery? You have one of the most irreproachable reputations in London. We have to change that before divorce is possible."

"It won't work," Helene said dully. "I know that you like creating these little scenarios, Esme. But I could hardly trick a man into my bed. The only person who has shown interest in years was Fairfax-Lacy. That came to nothing, and now he's married and probably Bea is in a delicate condition already!" She stood at the window, with her back to the room, but Esme didn't think she was admiring the view.

"You have to trust me," Esme said, trying to sound confident. "Didn't I arrange for Carola to bed her husband? Not to mention Henrietta and Darby!"

"You sound like some sort of vulgar matchmaker," Helene said, not turning around.

"I do not!"

"Yes, you do."

Esme pressed her lips together. She had a policy of courtesy toward sobbing women, although she was willing to bend the rule if needed.

Helene wheeled about and walked aimlessly to the other side of the room. "I will not be party to one of your absurd schemes. You think that you can manage everyone and everything, just because you're beautiful and you've always had your way and got whatever you wanted—"

"*I*? I have got whatever I wanted?" Esme threw policy to the wind. "You're the one who married for love, Helene, remember? So you made a bad bargain. At least you chose the man! I was married off to a man I'd danced with once and with whom I had exchanged exactly five words. A plump, balding man who may have been sweet but he certainly wasn't the answer to a young girl's romantic dream. You thought yourself in love with Rees when you eloped, if you remember!"

"Who cares how we got into our marriages?" Helene said, just as hotly. "If I was idiotic enough to elope with Rees, I've paid for that mistake in humiliation! Whereas you simply went your own way, and took whatever lovers you wished, and Miles never caused you a moment's worry. And then when you decided on a whim to have a child, he accommodated you immediately—not to mention Sebastian Bonnington's contribution!"

Esme could hardly remember being as enraged as she was at this moment. She jumped up and pointed a finger at her friend. "Don't you *dare* say that I decided to have my child on a whim! Don't you dare say that! I desperately wanted William. Otherwise I would never, ever have stooped to ask Miles to visit my bed, not when he was telling all and sundry that Lady Childe was the love of his life. I would never have done it!"

Helene narrowed her eyes. "I would undergo *any* humiliation to have a child—*any*! And you dare to complain because Miles loved Lady Childe more than you? Why the devil should he have loved you? You were unfaithful to him the very night before you reconciled! There was a whole nine months when you didn't even know whose child you carried, if you remember!"

Esme took a deep breath. She and Helene were friends; they had been friends for years. But all friendships end at some point. "I see no reason to discuss your views of my behavior further," she said. "I fully understand your opinion of me." She had gone from being burningly angry to icy cold. "Please do not hesitate to finish your tea. I am afraid that I have a headache and shall retire to my chamber."

"I didn't mean—" Helene said.

Esme cut her off. "Yes, you did mean it. And you clearly have been thinking it for a long time. I'm glad that you expressed yourself so clearly. Now we both know where we stand."

"No," Helene said flatly. She walked around Esme and sat down again. "I won't leave."

"In that case, I will." Esme walked toward the door.

"I apologize if I offended you."

Esme paused for a moment and then turned. "I am sorry as well, but forgiveness is hardly the issue, is it?"

"What did I say that was so terrible?" Helene said, looking her straight in the eyes. "One of the things I have always loved about you, Esme, is that you don't lie to yourself. You have never hidden from me the fact that you bedded Sebastian Bonnington the night before you reconciled with your husband, and therefore you initially had no idea who fathered William. Why would it wound you to hear that fact repeated by me?"

"You called my wish to have children a whim," Esme said, feeling as if Helene were stealing the ground out from under her feet. Just a moment ago she had been righteously furious and now—

"I shouldn't have said that," Helene said, her voice wavering a bit. "I only said it because I have so desperately wanted a child for years. I am sure that no one has ever wanted a child as much as I. I spoke out of jealousy. I'm sorry. You're my closest friend, and if you throw me over, I might as well jump in the river because—because—"

"Oh, for goodness' sake!" Esme said, walking back and plumping down next to her. "All right, I forgive you, you sharp-tongued viper!" She wrapped an arm around her.

"Rees always said I had the temper of a devil," Helene said with a wobbly smile.

"What temper? We've been friends for years, and you have always been calm, to my memory," Esme said in honest bewilderment.

"I have to be in control because I'm a true witch otherwise. Rees couldn't live with me. I threw a chamberpot at his head."

"You *what?*"

"I emptied a chamberpot over his head."

"My goodness," Esme said with some fascination. "I presume it was . . . in use?"

"He keeps a chamberpot in the sitting room so that if he has the urge to use it, he doesn't have to waste time visiting the water closet," Helene said wearily.

Esme shuddered. "That is truly revolting. Rees got what he deserved."

"So I try to remain collected. Otherwise I might throw plates at people's heads regularly."

"Thank you for the warning," Esme said with some amusement, moving the lemon tarts to the far side of the table.

"Not at you. But I doubt that I could live with a man at this stage in my life. I'm all of twenty-seven years old. I don't think I could put up with their disgusting habits."

"Sebastian hasn't any disgusting habits. And what does that make me, an old woman? I have twenty-eight years myself. Are you telling me that I'm too old to live with a man? Or that men aren't attracted to me due to my advanced years?"

"Don't be silly! You will always be enticing. I expect that men are even more attracted to your figure now that you've had a child."

"You've bats in your belfry," Esme replied. "I'm plump, and I know it."

"I'm like a board, all flat and dried up, whereas you are even more curvy than before."

"As you said earlier, cut bait. If my body curves, it only curves *out!*"

Helene stood up again and walked over to the window, wrapping her arms tightly around her chest. Finally she said, "I have to do something. I cannot go on like this."

The raw misery in her voice caught at Esme's heart. Sunlight was falling on Helene's hair, making it look like spun sugar, gleaming white-blond.

"I can't bear this life anymore," she said. "I'm warning you, Esme, I am about to create a far bigger scandal than Rees ever did with his tawdry little singer and his Russian dancing troupe. And it will all be his fault, the utter unmitigated bastard."

Esme blinked. "What are you thinking of?" she asked cautiously. "Do sit down, Helene."

"I'm going to have a child," Helene said, setting her jaw so that she looked as bullish as a Norse goddess. "I'm going to have a child, with *or* without a divorce. I've been thinking of nothing else for months."

"Are you certain that Rees won't—"

"Absolutely," Helene said, cutting her off. "I've spoken to him about divorce repeatedly. And why would he ever change his mind? He's cosily tucked up with that singer of his. Rees was never one to consult a book of etiquette on any matter, let alone in questions of marriage."

"I suspect you're right, but—"

"I have two choices, Esme: I can wither on the vine asking my husband for a divorce that he won't give me, or I can simply have the baby I desire, and let the devil take the consequences."

"It will be a terrible scandal," Esme warned her.

"I don't care. I literally don't care."

Esme took a deep breath and nodded. "In that case, we'll forget the whole idea of divorce and simply select an available man to father your child." Her imagination was already jumping to the task. "Neville Charlton has lovely hair. Or there's Lord Brooks. He has that gorgeous Roman nose."

"I wouldn't wish my child to have a father whose first name is Busick," Helene put in wryly.

"Excellent point," Esme agreed. "We'll just pick exactly the facial features and names that you would appreciate, and there we are."

Helene shook her head but didn't say anything, so Esme rattled on.

"Lord Bellamy has very broad shoulders, Helene. What do you think of him? And he has black hair as well. I'll make a list. For goodness' sake, it's not so hard to have a child. It only took me one night. Rees won't repudiate you once you're with child. He's a decent sort."

Helene snorted. "Decent? *Rees*?"

"Well, at any rate, he's far too lazy to repudiate you," Esme amended.

"He wants to make my life a misery for some reason," Helene said flatly. "It's the only explanation for his continued behavior toward me."

"Well, Rees is not a skinflint," Esme said. "He's one of the richest men in England, and he would hardly leave you and the babe to starve."

"The greater problem is that someone has to father the babe," Helene said. "With *me*." Helene's eyes were swollen and red; her skin was patchy from crying.

"This isn't your finest hour," Esme said consolingly, "but—"

Helene plucked at the front of her gown. "Esme, there's *nothing here!*" She waved her hand in front of Esme's chest. "Just compare you and me."

There was no question that Esme won that sweepstakes. Helene was wearing a very tightly buttoned walking costume that emphasized the fact that she had only the faintest, faintest curve in the front.

"Admit it," Helene demanded. "You haven't looked like me since you were fourteen years old!"

"More like twelve," Esme admitted. "But gentlemen are not only attracted to large bosoms, you know."

"They like curves. I don't want to get excited about impossibilities. I don't have curves. I can't flirt in that way you have, as if you were—"

"As if I were what?" Esme asked, bristling a little.

"Oh, you know, Esme. Promising them *things*. I can't do that. I loathed being in bed with Rees, what I remember of it. I can hardly look at a man as if I would want to do such a thing voluntarily!"

Esme bit her lip. Helene's marital relations had obviously been unpleasant. "You'll have to feign desire," she said bluntly. "Because it matters far more to a man that you desire him, than that you have a large chest."

"I'm not sure I even know how to do that. Stephen Fairfax-Lacy wasn't fooled for more than a few moments, to be honest. He could tell that I didn't really want to go forward with it."

"We'll work on that part later," Esme promised. "It's not hard to fool a man into thinking that you think he's Adonis himself, if you go about it the right way." She looked over Helene again. "First we have to order some new clothing."

Helene smiled, a tiny curl of her lips. "You can turn me into a blaze of fashion and it won't make any man wish to bed me."

"Nonsense! You are ravishing, darling. There's many a woman who would be more than grateful for that lovely hair of yours, not to mention your cheekbones. What we're going to do is advertise the fact that you are available for bedding. I'm afraid that men are rather slow and foolish when it comes to these things, and they rely on obvious signals, such as clothing."

Helene sighed and began wrapping her braids back into a stack on her head. "I'll have to just cover up my chest with a sign, then. *Available tonight*. Please inquire within."

# 4

## Of Song Birds and Strumpets

### Number 15, Rothsfeld Square

*A*lina McKenna was bored. Lord, who would have thought that the life of a courtesan was so tedious? There were more and more days when she would give anything for the frantic hither-and-yon of the opera house, to be back there, knowing that a line of gentlemen were at the stage door, just hoping for a glimpse of her. Of course, she hadn't been a prima donna, and she'd had less attention than the leads, but even so . . . Her eyes softened, remembering a certain Hervey Bittle who gave her a pair of blush-colored gloves and took her for a ride around Hyde Park. It was rather sad to think that these days she would never wear such poorly made garments.

Which reminded her precisely of her own situation. Naturally Hervey Bittle couldn't compete with a genuine earl, once Godwin had made it clear he was interested. All the other girls were mortified with jealousy, properly mortified. Especially when Rees whisked her off to his grand house on Rothsfeld Square and said she could have whatever she wanted in the way of new gowns, just as long as she'd sing for him when he wished. And bed him, naturally.

She brooded over that for a moment. He wasn't the first gentleman in her life, although it was hard to know if Hugh Sutherland, back in Scotland, really counted as a gentleman. Probably not. He was the son of a butcher, and people had called him Cow when he was a boy. But Hugh grew up well enough to catch the eye of a bored vicar's daughter longing to take her fine voice and flee to the city.

Ah well, Hugh was far in the past now. There was no need to wonder what her father would think of her now. He was surely praying every night for the safety of her soul, even without knowing she'd become a fancy woman. Lina pressed her lips together hard. She didn't like to think of her mama crying, but life was what it was. She wasn't made to live in that dreary old vicarage.

She glanced around her bedchamber. The only relief she had from the tedium of it all was when she summoned decorators. Perhaps she should change the appointments again. At the moment her bedchamber was hung entirely in blush silks, the color of the faintest damask rose. No, she'd leave it for at least a month or so.

She sat down at the dressing table, virtually the only piece of furniture left in the room from when Rees's wife lived in the house, and dragged a brush through her already shining hair. She felt dreary, properly dreary. Rees did most of his writing at night, and so he refused to go anywhere, not to a concert, not to a ball, not even to Vauxhall. It must have been months since he had taken her out of an evening. She couldn't go back and talk to the girls at the opera because she ended up feeling embarrassed by her circumstances, for all they envied her. And she missed it, oh, she did. All those cosy conversations about who had a pair of stockings without a run, and who had lost a garter on a dark night, and who might be chosen to sing. . . .

Lina's eyes darkened. *He* had taken her away from there. He could bloody well accompany her out the door.

Rees was in the sitting room, naturally. Lina walked in, distastefully aware of the papers brushing her ankles. It reminded her of walking down a street filled with rubbish. But Rees would no more allow one of those sheets of papers to be discarded than he would dress in a gown. The thought of burly Rees in a petticoat made her giggle and he looked up.

"Lina!" he said in that abrupt fashion he had. "Sing this phrase for me, will you?"

"Are these the words?" she asked ungraciously. "*I trip through the green woods, all covered with dew.* What is Fen thinking? That *trip through* is going to be very difficult, if not impossible, to sing."

"I don't give a damn about the words, or what you think of them," he said impatiently. "Just sing until you get to the end of the second page."

"I don't like the melody either," she said with some satisfaction, a few moments later. "The way that line drops to a lower register is a disgrace. It makes me sound like a hymn-singer."

Rees's lips set. "I particularly like that section of the line."

She was about to poke fun at the melody when she remembered that she wanted to go shopping. So she leaned against his shoulder instead. "Perhaps I sang it too quickly. Here, let me have another go."

This time she gave it her best effort. And since Lina had a voice that

rivaled that of Francesca Cuzzoni, the best operatic voice of the last century, her best was very good indeed. In fact, Lina pretty much thought that
she could make any plunking old tune sound better than it really was.

He looked happier now, which was all to the good. "It's lovely. I was
wrong," she cooed into his ear. "Rees, I should like you to accompany me
to Madame Rocque's French Trimming shop on Bond Street."

He twitched away from her kiss and was scribbling on paper again.

"I'll do whatever you wish . . . tonight," she whispered throatily,
leaning against him again.

This time he gave her a little shove. "I'm busy, for God's sake, Lina.
Go practice your tricks on someone else, will you?"

She narrowed her eyes. Madame Rocque made the most ravishing
creations in all London but to Lina's fury, she had discovered that if Earl
Godwin did not accompany her to the modiste, she was treated like ditch
water.

"I'll sing the entire aria for you after we return," she said, not bothering to add a throaty intonation. He hardly ever visited her bed anyway. In
fact, it had been months since he darkened her bedroom door, now she
thought of it. Rees's skills in that area weren't of a sort to keep a girl
awake at night wondering where he was.

He didn't say anything, just kept scribbling on his sheet.

"Three times," she said. "I'll sing that"—she swallowed the word stupid—"I'll sing your lovely new aria *three* times, Rees."

He shoved back from the piano and stood up with a sardonic look on
his face. "Since I'm obviously not going to be allowed to work until
you've gotten your way, we might as well go. Did you call the carriage?"

"How could I? Leke is nowhere to be seen," she pointed out. Rees had a
great deal of difficulty keeping servants. The butler, Leke, was the only servant who never left, but he kept his own hours and couldn't always be found.

"Damn it," Rees said elegantly, heading for the door.

Lina paused for a moment and very delicately, with just the tip of her
rosy finger, pushed his score off the piano so that it drifted into the scads
of trash wafting around her feet.

"Coming, dearest !" she thrilled, adding a little tremolo to give him a
frisson. Because it hadn't taken her long to realize that her personal ac-
coutrements did nothing for Rees Godwin. The luscious body and suggestive glances that had reduced Hervey Bittle to a stammering fool
hardly interested the earl at all. Witness the fact that she was living in his
wife's bedchamber as if she were a nun.

It was her voice that he had wooed from the opera house, and her
voice was the only thing that he really wanted in his house. More fool she,
to have been so blinded by infatuation that she didn't notice.

Oh well. Native Scottish practicality forced her to recognize that singing a few lines of music was infinitely preferable to being at a man's beck and call in the bedroom. It wasn't as if the earl had been any great shakes in the bed anyway. Mind you, he had a lovely body. But it was a matter of here, there, see you later.

Lina shrugged and headed out to the hall to join the earl. But first she nudged the libretto once more with her boot to make sure it was completely buried in paper.

Madame Rocque maintained an establishment at 112 Bond Street, an enclave that whispered money and screamed elegance, to Lina's mind. She took a deep breath the moment they walked through the door. There was nothing she loved more than the elusive fragrance that wafted through silk-draped rooms like this one. It was the smell of rich satin, of French perfume, of ladies who changed their clothing four or five times a day and thought nothing of ordering three bonnets to match a gown, or two gowns to match a favorite bonnet, for that matter.

The antechamber was made up to look like a lady's boudoir, complete with a dressing table lined with ruffle after ruffle of crocus-colored silk. The walls were hung with silk of the same dulcet yellow. To one side, an exquisite evening gown was hanging over the back of a chair, as if a distinguished beauty might waltz into her chamber at any moment and put it on. One of Madame Rocque's innovations had been her habit of making up each of her new models so that one could actually see a gown before ordering it.

Rees stuck out in the midst of this exuberant femininity like a sore thumb. He looked like the very worst kind of degenerate today, with his hair falling out of its ribbon, and too long to begin with. Not to mention that sulky lower lip of his. Yet his title was the only thing that truly mattered to Madame Rocque. Sure enough, with the earl stomping along at Lina's side they were ushered into an inner room the moment they entered the establishment, and by Madame herself. In the past Lina had been relinquished to a minion after being asked to wait in the antechamber for upwards of a half hour.

Madame fluttered about Rees like a rather weedy sparrow courting a hawk. If she wasn't such a fool, she'd realize that twittering like that would simply make his temper grow, Lina thought. He was like a child being told to wait for dinner. Madame had yet to greet Lina herself; she was obviously walking a delicate balance between desire for Rees's patronage and a lavish desire to make it clear to her, Lina, that she wasn't welcome.

All right, Lina could accept that. There were other modistes who would be ecstatic to gown the chosen mistress of Earl Godwin, given his thousands of pounds. But she wanted the best. To her mind, if she had to live with Rees, she deserved the very best, and that meant patronizing the establishment where ladies went.

So she sat down on a spindly chair upholstered in green silk and disregarded the way Madame Rocque was cooing over Rees. Perhaps she should refurnish her chambers in this green color. It would look like the first breath of spring in the woods behind her father's vicarage. Lina crossed her legs and swung her ankle gently. She was willing to wait.

As soon as Madame Rocque left the dressing room, Rees took out a piece of paper and began jotting down notes without saying another word to her. Madame Rocque's establishment was rather flimsily constructed, Lina decided. Even draperies of green silk couldn't hide the fact that the inner rooms were perfectly audible to each other. Two ladies in the next room were having a most interesting conversation.

"Men like to see an expanse of bosom," one lady said. She had a sort of honeyed, husky voice that Lina associated with stage actresses. She was an alto, a seductive, opulent contralto. Men must adore her voice: she could have made a fortune on the stage.

The other woman had a higher voice that was rather bell-like. In fact, it was rather like Lina's own, so she was probably a soprano. The soprano didn't agree with her friend, which was utterly foolish. Lina firmly agreed with the alto. Show a man a bit of bosom, and he'll blather himself into a frenzy. She cast a glance at Rees. He was the exception to the rule. She could have dropped her gown to her waist and he wouldn't notice, Lina thought rather bitterly. He had never shown much interest in her breasts, even in the first few weeks when he was so gratifyingly attentive.

And when they were in bed, well, she could have been in a dead faint, for all he caressed her. Lina was practiced at turning her mind away from depressing subjects, so she went back to the conversation next door.

The alto sounded a little exasperated. "How in the world do you think to catch a man's attention if you dress like a Puritan?" The soprano presumably was in need of a husband. She must be coming out of mourning, since her voice had far too much maturity for a debutante. At that moment Madame Rocque came burbling into the ladies' room—so that's where she was!—and Lina could hear the swishing of silks being held up.

The alto was obviously in charge. "We'll try that one," she said, sounding coolly approving. Lina memorized her tone. It was hard not to allow a note of pleading to enter her own voice when she spoke to Madame Rocque.

There was some rustling as the gown was cast over the soprano's shoulders, or so Lina assumed, and then the alto and Madame Rocque started cooing.

But the soprano cut through it decisively. "I look like an orange without its rind," she said firmly. "More so because this silk is quite an odd shade of yellow, Madame, if you'll forgive me saying so."

No doubt Madame Rocque had put her in one of her newest gowns, the ones cut low in the back and even lower in the front. They were being worn with bared shoulders. Lina, naturally, wanted one of those herself, ever since she'd read a description in *La Belle Assemblée*.

The alto was doing her best to convince her friend. "You look splendid—"

But the soprano seemed to have a practical turn of mind. "No, I don't. I look like a plucked chicken. There's no point to wearing a gown designed precisely to expose one's bosom when one hasn't that bosom to expose!"

She had a sound argument, to Lina's mind. There is nothing worse than a stringy set of shoulders. She looked rather proudly at her own plump figure. Mind you, boredom had made her rather plumper than she'd like to be, but it was in all the right places.

More to the point, Madame Rocque appeared to have chosen sides with the soprano. "I have another idea," she said in her heavily French accent. Lina was absolutely certain that accent was contrived. She'd had to study in order to rid herself of her Scots accent, and she knew how easily an accent could be faked. Likely Madame Rocque was really Mrs. Riddle from Lower Putney, Lina thought to herself sourly.

There was a moment's pause and she heard Madame say something curt to one of her assistants. A moment later there was a light knock at their door and a girl entered holding a gown, obviously the *same* gown, since it was orange. Lina's eyes narrowed. How many orange gowns could there be in this establishment? She expected to be served by Madame Rocque herself, not by a stammering girl clutching a gown that had just been rejected by another client. She had a mind to refuse to try the gown at all.

"Put on the damn thing," Rees growled at her. "I have work to do."

Lina took a closer look and changed her mind. The gown was lovely. The assistant began nimbly unbuttoning her walking costume.

Next door, Madame had returned with another costume. "This gown is a concoction that I offer only to my most daring clients," she said in her strident, Frenchified voice.

There was a moment of absolute silence in the room next door. Lina strained her ears. Was the soprano being offered something more daring than the creation she herself had just slipped on? Because if so, Lina wanted it as well. Not that the gown she wore wasn't lovely. It was precisely as described in *La Belle Assemblée*, and Lina fully intended to order one in primrose, and perhaps another in lilac. But—

"I couldn't!" That was the soprano. But she had the awed voice of a woman who clearly *could*.

"My lady, if you will just remove your chemise, and corset, I will put the gown over your head. I think you will be most pleased."

"Remove my corset? I would feel quite uncomfortable without a light corset," said the soprano. "I'm afraid that's out of the question."

Lina almost giggled. She had given up wearing corsets the moment she left Scotland. She heard some rustling, presumably the gown going over the soprano's corset.

The alto cleared her throat. "Glory be, Helene, you look—you look—"

"Exquisite, is it not?" Madame Rocque sounded extremely pleased with herself. "You see, when a lady has not quite the endowments that one would like—" she caught herself.

The soprano must be flat as a chessboard, Lina thought with some amusement.

"This style of dressing compliments the grace and delicacy of your form, my lady. It is sensual, enticing, and yet, as you see, there is nothing uncovered."

The alto laughed. She had a dark chocolate laugh, and Lina thought again that men must love that laugh. Proving her point, Rees raised his head to listen.

"It's utterly glorious," she said. "I think you'll have it in amber, Helene? Amber will suit your hair, and it's quite the rage these days. And perhaps in a shot silk as well, Madame?"

Madame Rocque's voice had all the satisfaction of a cat encountering a bowl of cream. "I would suggest just a delicate pearl border, Lady Bonnington, if you agree."

Rees had snapped to attention like a terrier confronting a mastiff. Lina cast him a curious glance.

"Do you like this gown, Rees?" she asked, twirling in front of him. A man would have to be a limp lily not to appreciate the way her breasts swelled from the crimped satin riband that wound its way over her shoulders.

He didn't even notice, just said, "That's my wife next door, for God's sake. My *wife*. With Esme Rawlings—Esme Bonnington now. Christ."

"What?" Lina said, hardly listening. Perhaps she would order the gown she was wearing in white, with black trim. That way men would instinctively look to the black ribbons outlining her breasts. She smiled and turned before the mirror again.

"That's my wife next door!" Rees hissed at her. "Take your pelisse. We're getting out of here."

This time Lina caught what he said. It was too delicious! She had been dying of curiosity about Rees's wife. The papers ignored the countess, never even reporting on her gowns. Had she, Lina, been Countess Godwin, she would have ensured that every costume she wore was reported in detail.

She deliberately raised her voice, knowing full well that her voice rang as clear as a bell and had the power to carry to the back of a theater. "Why Rees, darling, why such a hurry? Surely you can't wish to return home already?"

Rees narrowed his eyes at her and if she didn't have the fortitude of an elephant—and she did—she might have been almost afraid. But she'd learned long ago that Rees's bark was worse than his bite.

There was absolute silence next door, not even a whisper.

"I'm not ready to return to the house," Lina said. "Why this gown, even if it is a quite *odd shade of yellow*, is positively enticing, isn't it darling? Or . . ."—she let a teasing hint of delicious pleasure enter her voice—"is it the very delightful nature of the bodice that has inspired your wish to return home, Rees? And in the midst of the afternoon!" She giggled naughtily.

Rees had turned an ugly shade of dark red and Lina thought he was probably at the boiling point. Still not a sound next door. "Your manly enthusiasm is *so* gratifying," she cooed.

"Shut up!" he growled at her in a low voice.

"Of course, you may suffer from some competition once men see my figure in this gown!" Lina continued blithely.

He rose and was coming toward her. It was probably time to go but oh, what fun that had been! She hadn't had an audience in over two years. She pranced toward the door, pausing for one last second. "I hardly think, Rees dar—" But a large hand clamped over her mouth and Rees carried her straight through the anteroom and almost threw her into the carriage.

Alina McKenna hadn't gotten free of a dark and draughty vicarage, the cold fields of Scotland, and the windy corridors of the King's Theatre in the Haymarket without regular use of her not inconsiderable intelligence. That same intelligence suggested that she sit quietly in the corner of the carriage and not say a word about her walking costume, left behind at Madame Rocque's. Instead she spent the ride home examining the exquisite workmanship that made up the deep yellow gown she was wearing. The stitches were so small they could hardly be seen against the silk. She would send a message immediately requesting another of these gowns in a deeper color. She changed her mind about white and black. That was a bit garish. Perhaps amber.

Since amber was a fashionable color these days, or so she'd heard it said.

Quite the rage, really.

# 5

## Hair Today, Gone Tomorrow

$\mathcal{E}$sme had often thought that the only thing lacking to make Helene into a devastatingly beautiful woman was a little animation. Helene was always calm, always exquisitely polite, always . . . evasive.

Not at the moment.

"I cannot believe that I patronize the same shop as that doxy!" Helene snapped, eyes flashing with rage.

Madame Rocque rushed into a frothy waterfall of apologies, but Esme cut her off. "If you would be so kind as to bring a cup of tea to soothe Lady Godwin's nerves."

As Madame gratefully closed the door behind her, Esme observed, "I'm afraid the coincidence is not unusual. After all, Rees's mistress must be flush with money, and there is no more fashionable modiste in London than Madame Rocque."

Helene narrowed her eyes. "For the demi-mondaine, perhaps!"

"I have bought all my gowns from her for the past two years."

"She should maintain higher standards in her clientele." Helene shuddered. "That woman is wearing the yellow gown that I had on my body a mere moment ago. And Rees likely overheard everything we said!"

"Good," Esme said uncompromisingly.

"Good?" Helene's voice rose to a shriek. "What's good about it?"

"Perhaps Rees will wish to join the competition for your favors." Esme pointed to the mirror before which Helene still stood. "Look at yourself."

Helene swivelled. "The last thing I would want is for that reprobate to approach me." But she looked, obediently.

"You must remove your corset. The fabric is so fine that I can see the trim on your chemise in the back. But the gown is vastly becoming to you."

"Likely all the courtesans are wearing the same piece!" she said rather shrilly.

Esme shrugged. "You're getting a little priggish in your old age, darling."

Helene turned on her like a viper. "Don't you dare call me priggish simply because I am overwrought at being made fun of—humiliated!—by my husband's mistress. Lady Childe was never less than gracious to you, when you were married to Miles and she was his mistress." She collapsed into a chair. "The woman was making a game of me. Did you hear that comment about her bosom? Clearly, Rees has told her everything about our marriage."

Esme busied herself with looking into her reticule. She didn't want to make Helene embarrassed, but naturally she was longing for more details about her marriage. "What might he have told?" she said, trying to look utterly uninterested.

"Oh, that he—we—"

"Yes?"

"Bedroom details!" Helene snapped. "He has told his mistress of private events."

"I gather your marital intimacies were not all they could have been," Esme said delicately.

Helene stared at her. "How would I know? Listening to your jokes about bedding men, I have always felt as if we lived in two different worlds. No sane woman could possibly wish to repeat that experience. And yet you have *willingly* engaged in—"

"Bedding," Esme put in cheerfully, powdering her nose.

"How you do it, I shall never know," Helene said with stark conviction in her voice. "I found the experience repulsive. It's some defect in myself, no doubt. Rees said I was incapable of women's pleasure, if there truly is such a thing."

"But did it never occur to you, Helene, that perhaps the fault was with him? In my experience, men often try to cover up their own failures by blaming the woman in question."

"I fail to see what skill has to do with it." Helene seemed to have thrown her customary reticence to the wind. "It hurt. It hurt initially and then it continued to hurt, and I do think Rees was right in thinking that I simply am not suited to the act. And I have to say, Esme, I am much happier *not* having to perform those duties. It's very hard to countenance a man pawing me about in that manner. Last year, for example, I could not bring myself to allow Stephen Fairfax-Lacy any intimacies. I am not accustomed to it."

Obviously whatever happened between the bedsheets in the Godwin bedchamber was beyond repair at this point, so Esme reverted to practicality. "When do you think to wear your new gown?"

"If Madame Rocque can have one made up so quickly, I might wear it to Lady Hamilton's ball," Helene said.

"That's not for two weeks! Believe me, Madame Rocque will make you a gown with two days' notice at most, given what just occurred in her own establishment."

"But I'm working on a new waltz and it's going well. I don't want to lose my direction with this sort of foolishness." Helene rose and stood before the mirror again. "Do you truly think that I must discard my corset?"

"Absolutely."

"What will I do with my hair?"

"Why don't you wear it down?"

"It's dreadfully unfashionable," Helene said dubiously. She pulled a number of pins from her hair and undid her braids. When she was finished, she was surrounded by a shimmering curtain of hair falling, waterfall-like, to the top of her legs.

"Goodness," Esme said faintly. "It certainly is long, isn't it?"

"Braids make it a manageable length."

"It's exquisite."

"Rees loved it," Helene said, narrowing her eyes. "I do believe it was the only thing he liked about me. He—" She stopped. "I'll cut it off."

"Cut it off?" Esme was astounded. Helene's great woven mound of braids was an integral part of her regal, calm character.

Helene nodded. "All of it." She drew her hands through sleek masses that fell like cornsilk. "*Now.*"

"What?"

"Madame Rocque must have a pair of scissors," Helene said. She flung the door open. Madame had left a girl in the hallway. "Fetch a pair of scissors!" she commanded, and the girl fled.

"No!" Esme gasped. "You cannot do such a thing without forethought. We'll send a footman to request that Monsieur Olivier attend you this afternoon. Helene!"

Helene grabbed the shears from the girl.

"You!" Esme said, waving at the maid, who was standing, mouth agape, staring at the beautiful woman about to chop off her hair. "Send about to Monsieur Olivier, Number Twelve, Bond Street. Beg him to come here immediately, with kindest compliments of Lady Bonnington. Tell him we have a challenge for him. Did you get that?"

The young girl fled.

Even as Esme turned back to Helene, the first great sheaf of hair fell to the ground. And Helene was already hacking off another chunk.

"Oh lord," Esme moaned. "You never do anything by half measures, do you?"

"Why should I?" Helene said. She didn't look like a Danish queen now, remote and icy cold, but more like a belligerent English dairymaid. "Why should I keep all this hair? Do you know, it just occurred to me that I haven't cut it in the past because of some misguided sentiment leading back to Rees's fondness for my hair? Rees, who dragged his inamorata home so that he could have his way with her in the middle of the day? *Rees? The hell with Rees!*"

"Helene!" Esme gasped. She was quite certain that she had just heard the very first profanity ever to leave Helene's mouth.

"And the same to all of them!" Helene said gleefully, wielding her shears. "I don't care what men think of my hair, do I? All I want is their participation. Their cooperation!" She sliced off the last hank of hair and threw it to the ground. "There! What do you think?"

Helene's hair stuck out around her shoulders like the stubble from cornstalks left on a harvest field. She was shaking her head and grinning like a fool. "Oh, Esme, it's wonderful not to feel all that weight on my head. I had no idea! I would have done this years ago." A moment later she pulled Madame Rocque's gown over her head and began unlacing her corset. The corset hit the floor, followed by her chemise, and the gown went back over her head.

A mere ten minutes later, a sharp knock sounded on the door and Monsieur Olivier trotted into the room. He was small and round and very French. His own hair was pomaded and brushed in such a fashion that it rose straight from his forehead like the curl of a wave.

"Where is zee challenge?" he said, but his voice died as he caught sight of Helene.

To Esme's mind, if anyone could repair what Helene had just done to her hair, it would be Maurice Olivier.

He moved toward Helene, delicately kicking a sheaf of hair away with the toe of his boot. "I gather you committed this outrage yourself, my lady?"

Helene tossed her head and the chopped ends of her hair flew about her shoulders. "If you're going to be impudent about my hair, Monsieur Olivier, I shall summon another stylist."

"That would be your downfall," Olivier remarked, prowling about her for all the world like a stout tiger, who has cornered a pullet. "I am the only man in London who may—*may*—be able to recapture your natural beauty, my lady."

"What do you think of your gown now, Madame?" Helene demanded.

Everyone looked. Madame Rocque's creation was made of rose-colored silk, so delicate that it fell to the ground like a stream of water. It was formed of two layers, drawn tight under the breasts with silver ribbons. Halfway to Helene's knee the upper layer of silk was caught back by small clusters of embroidered roses. It had a fairly high neck, trim around the neck of a slightly darker color and short sleeves. In all . . . unexceptionable. Appropriate for a debutante, really. Except . . . except . . .

Except it was almost transparent.

Where two layers clung together, one could see nothing other than the outline of Helene's body, which was revealed to be slender but not angular. She had curves: her waist curved in, and her breasts curved out. The thin silk of Madame Rocque's gown hugged each of those curves in a way that revealed them to be deliciously rounded.

And then where only the underskirt was revealed, below her knees, one could see everything: Helene's delicate ankles, the garter holding up her stockings, the delicate shape of her knees.

Esme blinked. She suddenly felt fleshy and over-plump.

"I gather zat we are considering something of a major reconstruction, are we, Madame?" Olivier asked.

Helene laughed. "Something along those lines."

"Never fear," he said, clashing his scissors. "I am the only man in London who is up to zis challenge! Now, if you would have a seat."

Helene sat down. She was feeling a little bit daunted. She had spent so many hours—nay, years!—of her life tending to her hair: washing it, combing it, drying it endlessly before the fire. And in two seconds, it was gone. Truly, Rees was right when he said that she had a monstrous temper. More and more hair was flying to the floor. Helene tried not to look. She concentrated on the gloriously weightless feeling of her head.

"What are you thinking of doing, Monsieur Olivier?" Esme asked.

"We must be daring," he announced. "It is zee only way. Courage!"

"How daring?" Helene asked, feeling a qualm.

"Very daring! It is zee only way to recover your beauty. More audacious than Lady Caroline Lamb ever dared to be."

Esme giggled. "Really, Monsieur Olivier! Didn't that young woman chop off hair from . . . another place and send it to Byron?"

Helene looked at her, scandalized, but Monsieur Olivier just chuckled. "An indiscreet young woman, but she did have acceptable hair. It's been all of five years since I gave her that short hair, and now I'm tired of making frizzled ringlets, day in and day out. With luck you will start a rage, Lady Godwin, and I can shear off hundreds of tired curls in the next few weeks."

Helene tried not to look at the mirror. More and more of her hair flew from the scissors. An hour later, Helene didn't know whether to faint or applaud. Her hair was short now. Truly short. It clung sleekly to her head until her jawbone, where little wispy curls softened the angles of her cheekbones and emphasized her eyes.

"Oh, Helene," Esme said in an awed voice.

"Zhee looks spectacular!" Monsieur Olivier said in a smug voice. "Only I could have done this for you, Madame! You see, I have given you zee appeal."

"Appeal?" Helene said, still staring at herself.

"You look utterly delicious," Esme put in. "You are going to turn heads with a vengeance!"

"As long as I can turn one head, that's enough," Helene said, staring at herself. In truth, she looked like another woman: a bold, impudent, sensual sprite of a person.

"He will be yours!" Monsieur Olivier kissed the tips of his fingers. "Believe me, Madame, zere is no man in London who will not be at your knees!"

"Good," Helene whispered. "I hope they *all* are."

"Rees as well?" Esme said with an eyebrow raised.

"Only so that I can spurn him," Helene said firmly. "But yes, Rees as well!"

# 6

## With the Wave of a Wand

*Hyde Park*

"*A*nd then she said *what?*" Rees's friend Darby was utterly fascinated by the debacle of the dressing room.

"Lina announced, loudly, that I must wish to return home because I was overcome with desire at the sight of her in that gown, and had to have my way with her," Rees said gloomily. "Which is rubbish. I haven't been to her room in weeks. Months perhaps." Come to think of it, he couldn't remember the last time.

"Why on earth not?" Darby asked, startled.

They were walking in the woody part of Hyde Park, where one never saw the fashionable sort of gentlemen. Rees kicked a trailing strand of faded wild roses to the side but didn't answer.

Darby stopped and chose a coral bud to put in his buttonhole. He was wearing a morning costume of bronze broadcloth. The rosebud looked strawberry-pink against his chest, perhaps just a shade pinker than he would have desired.

"I don't know," Rees said. Darby wasn't looking at him, just shaking back his deep lace cuffs and examining all the rosebuds on the bush, so Rees knew he was burning with curiosity. You couldn't be friends since you were both in short coats without being able to read each other's minds. "The prospect simply isn't appealing anymore. I'd move her out, but I need her voice to help me with this opera."

"Appealing? Just when does making love to a woman with a body like Lina's lose appeal?"

"I must be getting old," Rees said, kicking a stick off the path. It hit a mulberry tree that dropped a glossy spray of water over them.

"For Christ's sake, Rees," Darby said, examining his shoulders to see whether the water had left stains. "Why we can't take a civilized promenade around the duck pond, I'll never know."

"I like it here. At least we don't meet any simpering matrons." They walked on.

"How's Henrietta?" Rees asked, after a bit. He liked Darby's wife immensely. In fact, now that he thought about it, his disinclination to knock on Lina's door had started around the time that Darby found Henrietta. Not that he desired Henrietta for himself, not that. He just wanted . . . he wanted the fire that burned between Henrietta and Darby.

Sure enough, a smile curled on his friend's lips. "She is being very cool to me at the moment."

"Why?"

"Because I'm a dandified fool," Darby said, without any sign of regret. "I wouldn't pick up Johnney after he'd been sick all over his crib and was wailing."

Rees gave an involuntary shudder. "Why on earth would she wish you to do such a thing?"

"The nursemaid had her half-day," Darby explained. "You know Henrietta dislikes allowing the servants to care for the children. So she was bathing the girls and we heard Johnney being sick. So I went to have a look, but of course I didn't pick him up, not while I was wearing velvet. I was just taking off my coat when she came running in, acting as if a few screams from the lad would be mortal."

Rees couldn't think what to say to that. He'd rather slay himself than pick up a child covered with vomit. "Doesn't Johnney seem to cast up his accounts rather frequently?" he inquired, more to be polite than anything else.

"Too much," Darby said. "He's seven months now. He'll never get married at this rate."

"Fortunate for him."

"So have you seen your wife since your near encounter in Madame Rocque's establishment?"

"No. But I gather I'll see her tonight."

"Don't tell me that you are venturing into polite society?" Darby asked, greatly entertained.

"Lady Hamilton's ball."

"Why are you going there? Debutante sort of affair, isn't it? We've declined."

"Because that wretched friend of Helene's, the one who married Sebastian Bonnington, wrote me a note and said that my wife intends to go to the ball specifically in order to acquire an heir, and that if I wish to join in the competition, I should make an appearance."

There was a moment of stunned silence. A chestnut tree dropped cream-colored petals on their hair and Darby didn't even notice. "*What?*"

"You heard me. Helene told me she wanted a child, but I had no idea that she would go to such lengths."

"She told you that she wanted a child? What did you say?"

"I told her that she ought to resign herself to the truth of the matter, which is that our marriage is not going to produce offspring," Rees said irritably. "It never occurred to me that Helene would decide I had given her carte blanche to put a cuckoo in my nest! This is *Helene* we're talking about here. From the way she's harped at me over the years, you'd think reputation was the most important thing in the world."

"My God," Darby said slowly. "She must have a crack in the upper story."

"She had that years ago."

"But she'll be ruined!"

"I can only think that she doesn't care about her reputation anymore." Rees kicked a rock across the path. "Perhaps I should have shown her more consideration. I would have divorced her, if she had made a convincing case for it."

"So you're going to Lady Hamilton's ball. . . ." Darby said, clearly still in shock.

"Have to, don't I? I've been thinking about it for two days, ever since I got the note from Esme Bonnington."

"And that's an odd thing," Darby put in. "Why on earth did Esme let you know of Helene's plans?"

Rees shrugged. "She didn't explain herself. But I can't let Helene bed just anyone and make the child into my heir. Tom is my heir, obviously, and while he seems to be rather slow in the marital department, presumably he'll get around to producing a child at some point."

"Yes, but—"

"I can't allow her to give me a cuckoo. But if she's that determined, I can"—he paused and considered his words for a moment—"be of assistance."

"So you'll—what *are* you going to do?"

"I'll tell her that if she wants a child that much, she'll have to take me. It's unfortunate that the process is going to be about as much fun as going to a tooth-drawer."

Darby blinked. "I didn't know it was that bad between you."

"In the bedchamber it was."

It was Darby's turn to stay silent. He couldn't imagine being married to someone under those circumstances. They walked along, and Darby decided that he would go home and lure Henrietta into their chamber for a little dalliance. They were in danger of forgetting how fortunate they were.

"I must be cracked myself," Rees suddenly said. "I'm actually thinking of trying to get her back in the house."

Darby gaped. "Going respectable in your old age?"

"Hell, no. I need help with the opera," Rees said grimly. "It's garbage. I was thinking of trading my assistance in creating offspring for Helene's help with the scores."

"Are things that bad with the current piece?"

"Worse. It's overdue by months, and I have nothing worth hearing. Nothing."

"Helene will murder you if you put it so bluntly," Darby said after a moment. "You'll have to emphasize the fact you want your children under your own roof. But what will you do about Lina?"

"She's bored to death with me. I'll give her an allowance so she needn't take another lover. She has a quite prudish streak, and I dislike the idea that she might have to take on a curmudgeon like myself."

One thing Rees hadn't told Darby was that he was going to the ball as much for Helene's sake as for his own. Who the hell would want to sleep with Helene? Likely she would be humiliated by discovering that gentlemen wanted a ripe little body and a come-hither manner when it came to dalliance. They didn't want a stiff scarecrow with a pile of braids bigger than a halo, and a reputation to match. True, Helene somehow inveigled Fairfax-Lacy to follow her about last summer, but then he'd up and married another woman within a few weeks. That can't have been easy for Helene.

It was almost amusing to realize that he was feeling both guilty and protective. Perhaps his wife's reckless wish to destroy her own reputation *was* his fault. If they were still living in the same house, this child business likely would have worked itself out in the normal way, years ago. And estranged though they might be, Rees couldn't stand the idea that his wife would be rebuffed at the ball. She was no Cinderella, after all, with a fairy godmother waiting in the wings.

He would just have to wave his own magic wand. He found himself grinning at that, and decided not to share the joke with Darby. They'd never been the kind of friends who sat around trading bawdy jokes and hawing with laughter. And it didn't seem polite, not in reference to his own wife.

# 7

## Undergarments Are Vastly Overrated

*H*elene wasn't sure she could do it. It was one thing to stand half-naked in a small dressing room, with Esme, Monsieur Olivier, and Madame Rocque enthusiastically applauding. But it was quite another story to appear in public wearing a costume not much heavier than a nightrail. Although the bottom layer of rose silk was just slightly darker than the top, individually, each layer was transparent. Helene's entire body was on display. The silk was so fine that it clung and then swirled, just barely concealing her most private areas.

The only saving grace of the whole situation was that her mother was paying a visit to friends in Bath. Helene could just imagine her reaction to Madame Rocque's gown. She would have locked Helene in the wine cellar rather than let her be seen in such a state. This gown didn't hide her lack of breasts; it put that lack on display for all to see. Color rose in Helene's cheeks at the memory of the only person who had seen her unclothed, in her adult life. Her husband had laughed out loud the first time he saw her breasts.

Rees's laughter had been the beginning of a disastrous night. They were on their way to Gretna Green but had stopped at an inn, as Rees had pointed out that her father would never bother to chase them. Of course, he was correct. It wasn't every day that the heir to an earldom elopes with one's daughter, and Helene's father was likely swilling champagne at home while his daughter waited in a bedchamber, fairly trembling with adoration for her almost-husband.

She had waited, and waited, and waited. But Rees had apparently decided to loiter in the tavern, and when he finally appeared in her doorway, he had to catch himself against the door frame so as not to fall down. She had giggled, thinking it all romantic. There was nothing Rees could do wrong: not this big, beautiful man who thought about music as much as she did. When he kissed her, Handel's arias exploded in her mind, aching, arching waves of sound stretching to the very tips of her fingertips.

Well, if their kisses were Handel, then the actual bedding was naught more than a Beggar's Opera. Because Rees pulled off her gown and then fell about laughing, finally asking whether her breasts had evaporated in the last rain. By an hour later, it was clear to her that the rest of her body was as unsuited to matrimony as was her chest. Helene dismissed the memory with a little shudder.

Saunders, Helene's personal maid, obviously didn't know what to make of her mistress's transformation. At the moment she was bustling about folding clothing, but she kept stealing glances over her shoulder. "Would you like me to make some nice curls in your hair, my lady?" she said now, waving a curling iron. "We could wrap a bandeau around your head and with just a few curls, it would look quite, quite—" Saunders couldn't bring herself to say *fashionable*. The fashion was for ringlets bobbing around one's ears, and Lady Godwin didn't have enough hair for even one ringlet.

Helene smiled and seated herself at her dressing table. "I like my hair as it is, thank you. Saunders, do we have any rouge?"

"No, my lady."

Helene bit her lower lip. Her cheeks were the color of a frightened ghost.

"Mrs. Crewe has a large collection," Saunders added. "Would you like me to fetch it?"

"Mrs. Crewe?" Helene said, picturing her mother's starchy house-keeper. "I don't believe I've ever seen Mrs. Crewe wearing face paints!"

"She confiscates them from the maids," Saunders explained. "No one is allowed to use paints in the house, of course. Once in a blue moon, when she's in a good mood, Mrs. Crewe takes out the basket and allows the downstairs maids to play about in the evening. Not that I've done so for years." Saunders had developed a strong sense of her dignity when she was promoted to personal maid five years ago.

A few moments later Saunders plumped a large wicker basket on the floor. "Oh my," Helene said, fascinated. She picked up a small tin box.

"Chinese colors," Saunders said importantly. "Too dark for you, my lady." She burrowed in the basket. "If I remember correctly, there's a box of red sandlewood in here. That Lucy, who only lasted a few weeks before she was let go for stealing Mrs. Crewe's own brooch, she had it. Likely nimmed it from her previous mistress, unless I'm much mistaken." Saunders held out a round box, enameled all over with pansies.

"The box is very pretty," Helene said uncertainly.

"I'll use a little on your cheeks," Saunders said. "We'll use the darker one, the Chinese colors, for your lips. And here's black frankincense. We can darken your lashes with this, and your eyebrows as well."

"My goodness, Saunders," Helene said, smiling at her maid. "I had no idea that you had so much facility with face paints."

Saunders was standing back and looking at her work. "I'm that used to seeing braids atop your head," she said slowly. "But shorter hair does make you look years younger. Everyone said so, below stairs."

"That's good," Helene said, cheered.

Saunders was expertly sweeping frankincense onto a brush. "Tomorrow you might wish to go to that perfumer, Henry and Daniel Rotely Harris, where all the ladies go. They'll make up colors just for you."

"Goodness," Helene said rather faintly, "I had no idea that was a possibility."

Saunders began wielding the tiny brush around Helene's eyebrows. Helene had to admit that the change was very dramatic. Her brows suddenly appeared as high arches, emphasizing her eyes.

"Now your lashes, my lady," Saunders said. "If you would just close your eyes, please."

Helene obediently did just as she said, and then almost gasped when she opened them again. Her ordinary gray eyes had been transformed into jewels: they looked green and seductive, like mermaid's eyes. And instead of her cheekbones sticking out like those of a hungry beggar, a delicate wash of color emphasized the heart-shaped triangle of her face.

"Oh, Madam," Saunders said, sounding awed by her own work. "You look ravishing!"

"Thanks to you," Helene said, smiling. She *could* do this. The face paints helped. The timid, skinny woman who wrote waltzes and was never asked to dance them was hidden behind the colors on her face. The pale, timid Helene who had cried when her young husband laughed at her breasts was behind a mask. *This* Helene had impudent, seductive eyes. This Helene wouldn't care a bit that her husband preferred women with udders rather than breasts. She walked across the room and the delicious feeling of thin silk made her feel like dancing. There was something about the way the silk caught between her legs as she walked and then swirled away that made her feel far more naked than when she rose from her bath.

It remained for her to take herself, her gown, and her determination to have a child . . . and let events take their natural course. Because Esme had promised, nay had sworn up and down, that the gown would do all the work and Helene could simply choose a father for her child from a bevy of suitors. And for the first time, Helene began to believe her. Courage rose in her. Men would like the way she looked.

"Will you wear the diamonds tonight?" Saunders enquired.

"I believe my rubies would suit this gown." Helene never wore the rubies set because they had belonged to her late mother-in-law, and she herself had never really felt like Countess Godwin . . . but the color would be perfect. The rubies settled around her neck with a delicious rosy glow. Saunders put ruby drops in her ears. Helene almost laughed with the surprise of seeing her own reflection, even as Saunders fastened rubies around her wrist. Could this glowing, beautiful woman be *her*, Helene?

At that moment there was a knock and Esme tumbled into the room. "Hello, darling! I've just come to—" she said and stopped.

There was a moment of extremely gratifying silence. Then:

"You are not to come within two feet of my Sebastian, do you hear? Not within *two feet*!" Esme squealed.

Helene made a little pout. It was the most delicious thing in the world to pout with cherry red lips, rather than her own pale pink mouth. "But Sebastian *must* dance with me at least once. We are attending the ball together, after all, and he's so handsome."

Esme was laughing. "I think not, my girl. I'm not letting him anywhere near you. However," she took a list from her reticule, "here are a few men with whom you *may* dance."

Helene dismissed Saunders. The last thing she wanted was the entire servants' quarters enjoying the contents of Esme's list, let alone discovering the reason for its existence.

Esme, meanwhile, had thrown herself into a chair and taken off her slippers. "It is so distressing," she said, revolving her slender foot in the air. "These slippers are deliriously beautiful but they already hurt, and I've only been in them for an hour or so. I shall have to dance barefoot, and that will offend Sebastian's sensibilities."

"I thought your husband was a reformed man, and no longer had any sense of proprieties," Helene said rather absentmindedly. And then, without waiting for an answer: "Esme, are you out of your mind? I can't lure Lord Guilpin into my bedchamber. The man is obviously searching for a wife. I myself saw him in Almack's the other week. The last thing he wants to do is dally with an aging, married woman!"

"*You* are no aging, married woman," Esme said. "You are about to be revealed as the most desirable woman in all London. And I like Guilpin's looks. Those gray eyes are very taking, don't you think?"

"I never gave his eyes the slightest thought."

"Well, you'll have to do so now," Esme said. "To my mind, Guilpin is tired of looking for a wife. We're well into the season, so he's seen all the young women being presented. More to the point, he's not dancing attendance on any of them, which means that he's quite likely to dance attendance on you instead. All three men on that list are debauched enough to lure you into a chamber at the ball and do what comes naturally to them. And each of them is both intelligent and reasonably good looking. That way, your child won't be born hunchbacked or hare-brained."

"I don't care very much about looks," Helene noted. "More important is that he know something of music. Just imagine if my child wasn't musical!" She looked horrified.

"Any child lucky enough to have you as a mother will undoubtedly end up horse-mad and unable to sing a note," Esme said, laughing.

Helene was still looking at the list, and she had begun to laugh as well. "Garret Langham? You mean the Earl of Mayne? The very idea of Mayne trying to tempt me into a side chamber is ludicrous. Half the women in London would like to bed him!"

"And the other half already have," Esme said smugly. "I being one of them. So I can tell you that Mayne's aristocratic nose is echoed with becoming size in other parts of his body, *and* he knows what he's doing."

"He's predatory," Helene moaned. "I couldn't allow such a thing!"

"Why on earth not? Mayne may be a wee bit rapacious, but I have only the most ravishing memories of our night together. And darling," she said, slipping her foot back into her slipper, "obviously poor Rees is a bungler in the bedroom. A night or two with Mayne and you'll feel entirely different about the whole experience of bedding. I'm quite certain he's very red-blooded. My mother-in-law informed me that red blood is the trick to conception, and she seems to know that sort of thing."

"Everyone is red-blooded," Helene told her, wondering if she should slip the little box of sandlewood into her reticule. If there was even a chance that Mayne would approach her, she would need ruby-colored lips for courage.

"There are matters of degree, I suppose," Esme told her vaguely. "Well, at any rate, Mayne may be a libertine, but he's not overly dissipated, and he happens to be between attachments. The very moment he sees you in that gown, he'll be dragging you into the library." She smiled fondly. "If I remember correctly, it was a library."

"Esme, you're married to Sebastian. You oughtn't to be sighing romantically over Mayne!"

"Of course I'm married to my darling Sebastian," Esme said with a wicked grin. "And I have every intention of dragging my libertine husband into a library if the opportunity presents itself. But marriage hasn't damaged my memory." She stood up and readjusted her bodice before the mirror.

"Mayne would never consider me." He was like a bird of prey— beautiful, untamable, and far above her head. Helene shook off the thought. She wouldn't want such an uncomfortably sensual companion. "You look absolutely lovely!" she said, looking at Esme in the mirror. "If only I looked like you, this whole escapade would be simple."

"This is the gown that you discarded," Esme said rather smugly. "I had it made up in violet. It only arrived this afternoon, but Sebastian was quite gratifyingly dumbstruck when I tried it on."

"I have no doubt," Helene said. Esme's black curls tumbled down in such a way that they promised to cover the lush expanses of breast barely confined by her gown, although they didn't quite do it. She looked back at the list. "Why on earth is Rees on your list?"

Esme wound her arm around Helene's waist and met her eyes in the mirror. "For practicality's sake. It would be considerably easier if you had a child with your own husband. I know Rees is an uncomfortable companion, and even worse, he's inept between the sheets. But should Rees show the inclination to drag you into a side room, you might want to give it some thought."

"You're out of your mind!" Helene said, shaking her head. "He would never consider such a thing, even if he were at the ball. Lady Patricia Hamilton is giving this ball for her daughter's debut, if you remember. Persons such as Rees and his inamorata won't be welcome!"

"The opera singer certainly is not," Esme said, "but Rees is. I asked Lady Hamilton to send him a card." She decided not to mention that she had also sent Rees a separate note.

Helene was frowning at her. "I may have jested about wishing to attract Rees, but truly, I was just funning. He's likely to burst with laughter when he sees me in this gown!"

"Now that," Esme said with satisfaction, "I truly doubt. He might puff up, of course, but it won't be a matter of humor."

Helene rolled her eyes. "Your puns grow worse and worse, Esme. Rees and I are *married*. Rees has never shown the faintest interest in what I wear, and the idea that he might drag me off to a side chamber in a surfeit of passion is laughable! In fact, I haven't heard of many husbands who have inclinations in that direction."

"My husband does," Esme said. "And we'd better return downstairs, Helene. I'm not sure that Sebastian and your Major Kerstings have much to talk about, since Sebastian is not fond of opera."

Helene let Esme walk down the stairs before her. Only a deranged woman would stroll through a door arm-in-arm with Esme. She lingered for a moment and looked at herself in the hallway mirror. A fire of determination went up her spine. She *could* do this.

She heard the low rumble of Esme's husband, Sebastian, asking a question, and the quieter voice of her escort, Major Kersting, answering.

If she didn't walk through the door, she was betraying all her dreams of having a child. She was dooming herself to living with her mother for years to come. More years. They had already lived together for eight years of her married life.

Helene straightened her back (which caused her breasts to point forward, she couldn't help noticing), and marched through the door.

# 8

## *Of Cravats*

"*H*e's at it again," Rosy shrieked, bursting into the butler's pantry. "Uncle John, the master called me a bad name!"

John Leke, butler to Earl Godwin and uncle to Rosy, looked up from the silver he was polishing. "There's names and names," he said. "The master may be one screw short of a dozen, but he's not ill-tempered. What did he call you?"

"Hell-begotten brat," Rosy said rather triumphantly. "And Mum said that I wasn't to stay in this position if I heard anything low. So I think I would do best to leave the house immediately."

"Why'd the earl call you such a thing?"

Rosy pursed her lips. "I needn't give any notice, Uncle John, not after such an objectionable thing was said to me. It's bad enough that I'm working in a house of *sin*, but to take abuse is more than a person such as myself need endure!"

Leke had known his niece since she was a mere bantling, and he took her dramatics with a grain of salt. Moreover, he and Rosy's mum had agreed that Rosy was a headstrong girl, and the better for working under her uncle's eye. "Now what did you do? I'm guessing that you earned the phrase the earl called you. What was it again?"

"Hell-begotten brat!"

"Nothing that I haven't thought myself," Leke said, eyeing her. Rosy was just fifteen, but her bouncing ringlets and saucy manners had started to bring entirely too much attention for her own good. The sooner they found her a solid husband, the better. "Rosy?"

Her pout turned sulky. "It's the master's own fault for not hiring enough staff."

"I'm in charge of hiring the staff," her uncle pointed out. "If we don't have many, it's because I won't hire the ones who aren't straight, and the others don't want to work in this house."

"Well, I burned his neck cloth, ironing it," Rosy said in a rush. "But if he had a proper valet, I wouldn't have had to go near an iron!"

"Bring him another cloth, girl. Step to it."

"There aren't any more!" Rosy moaned.

"What do you mean, there aren't any more? The man has at least five cravats. Mind you, in a proper household, he'd have upwards of two dozen."

"I ruined them," Rosy admitted.

"You ruined them *all*?"

"Honestly, Uncle John, I didn't know I was doing it! You know how untidy he always looks. I thought I'd better starch them. I did it just as mama does, with a cloth over them. Course the iron was sizzling hot, but I was thinking about not burning myself, and there was a terrible amount of steam, and then I don't like the smell of starch, so I just rattled through them as fast as I could—"

"You burned them *ALL*?" her uncle roared.

"They aren't exactly burned," Rosy protested. "The starch just put yellow streaks . . ."

But Leke was already bounding up the servants' stairs. He found the earl seated on a chair by the fire, scribbling on a piece of paper. He was tapping his finger against the armrest, looking as balmy as a breadbasket.

Leke gave a silent sigh of relief. Godwin didn't show signs of being driven mad by Rosy's ironing. "I am distressed to hear that your neck cloths have suffered an injury due to my niece's inept ironing, my lord," he said, bowing.

Godwin looked up, pulling his hand through his hair. He must have been dressing for the evening when he discovered the loss of his cravats; at any rate, he was wearing pantaloons. "Never mind about that," he said with his sudden smile. "My fault for not wanting a valet around the place, fussing with my clothes. Likely my neck cloths should go out of the house for laundering along with Lina's clothing. Could you send Sims out to buy a few more?"

"I'm afraid that the Christian & Sons have closed their doors for the night," Leke observed. It was at moments like these that he remembered why he hadn't yet deserted Earl Godwin, even when the rest of the household staff had fled like fleas from a dying dog. The man lived an irregular life, and one could not approve of the fancy piece living in the countess's quarters. But there was something disarming about Godwin, and he was far more reasonable when it came to household crises than many a gentleman Leke could bring to mind.

Rees grunted. "Well, if they're all closed, perhaps you could just pick out the least singed of those cloths, Leke. I can't say it really matters much to me."

Hell-born brat, indeed, Leke thought, turning over the cravats. Had Rosy confessed her ironing failures immediately, he could have bought more cravats, and no one the wiser. Instead, here was the master going out for the evening, and nothing to wear but yellowed cravats.

"I believe, sir, that if you tie a Mathematical with this pale pink cravat, the discolored starch will be inconspicuous. And may I offer my deepest apologies for this deplorable event?"

"Don't give it a second thought," Godwin said. "Does it have to be the pink one? I feel like a man-milliner in it."

"The white cloths are beyond use," Leke admitted. "I shall obtain new cravats at first light tomorrow."

"Right." Godwin bounded up from his chair and threw the cravat around his neck. Far from tying a Mathematical, he merely pulled it into a rough knot.

Leke restrained himself. He was no gentleman's gentleman; he was a butler. "Will Miss McKenna join you this evening?" he asked, backing toward the door as Godwin wrenched on a tailcoat in a russet color that clashed abominably with his pink cravat.

"No," Godwin said, folding up the paper he was working on and sticking it into the pocket of his waistcoat. "I'm off to Lady Hamilton's ball for her daughter."

No more needed to be said. The strumpet (as Alina McKenna was known to the staff) obviously wouldn't be welcomed by Lady Hamilton. Leke bowed and retreated back to the butler's quarters. But he was burning with curiosity.

Why was Rees Godwin attending a ball being given for a debutante? Could it be that he was the girl's godfather? Surely they would have heard something of that in the past.

"You *are* a hell-born brat," he told his niece severely. "I'm docking your wages to pay for those cravats, girl, and you're lucky to be a family member or I'd have you out the door in a twinkling!"

Rosy scowled but kept her silence. Neither the earl nor her uncle had noticed the little brown tinges around the cuffs of Lord Godwin's shirts, and she didn't want to push her luck.

# 9

## Of Great Acts of Courage

*Lady Hamilton's Ball*
*Given in Honor of Her Daughter Patricia*
*Number Forty-One, Grosvenor Square*

There are moments of great bravery in every woman's life. Helene had gathered from her friends that childbirth was one of those. She herself had exhibited a remarkably stupid form of bravery at age seventeen, when she agreed to elope with the heir to the Godwin earldom. But other than that one foolish act, there had been little cause for courage in her life. Until tonight.

Helene was fairly sure that there was no moment more terrifying in her entire life than when she removed her pelisse and handed it to one of Lady Hamilton's footmen. There she was: practically undressed in the antechamber of the house. The door behind her swung open and a crisp breeze went straight through two layers of silk. She could feel the chill all over her body, even parts which normally never felt a draft, such as her bottom. There was only one thing to be done, and that was to brazen it out.

Sebastian Bonnington put a hand under her elbow and said "Courage!" in his deep voice. Then he gave her a look of such deep appreciation that Esme elbowed him and said laughingly, "Isn't it lucky that I already warned Helene to stay away from you?"

But then Sebastian turned from Helene to Esme, and the look in his eyes when he looked at his beautiful wife was far more potent than mere appreciation. He dropped a kiss on her lips that was so indicative of passion that Helene turned pink. Just seeing it stirred envy in her heart and an odd wink-ling feeling in her stomach.

They were announced by Lady Hamilton's butler. Helene had the distinct feeling that she was an imposter, and as such, she should have a new name. Was she really still Lady Godwin, the prim, contained Lady Godwin who was just announced? But at first, no one seemed to notice any difference. Lady Hamilton was frazzled by the stress of her daughter's first ball; she smiled at Helene's hair and whispered a compliment, but didn't notice her gown.

But little by little, the news spread. It was almost as if she could see it rippling through the ballroom. Helene solemnly paced through a country dance with Major Kersting. He and she, who had always been so comfortable with each other in the past, were quite the opposite now. He kept fingering his narrow mustache, and when they were greeted by three gentlemen at the close of the music, he fled with a look of extreme relief.

Helene had never had more than one aspirant for a dance at the same time. The thrill of seeing three gentlemen before her went to her head like midsummer wine. None of the three were on Esme's list, alas. Moreover, Lord Peckham was out of the question. The man was married, although he preferred to ignore the fact, and she would never be party to causing Lady Peckham the distress that she herself had suffered due to her husband's infidelities. She raised a cool eyebrow at him and accepted the hand of Lord Ussher. He was a bit younger than she would have liked, but perhaps that meant his blood was redder.

But by the end of their dance, she had quite decided against Lord Ussher. For one thing, he had sweated through his gloves, and his touch was unpleasantly damp. For another, he appeared to be quite overcome by her gown; he kept glancing down and then wrenching his eyes back to her face as if he were a starving man faced by an apricot tart. *Tart* being the appropriate word, Helene thought with some amusement. But the truly crucial thing was that he was unable to follow the music, and trod on her toes several times.

When the music stopped, instead of three gentlemen asking for her hand, there were *seven*. They crowded around her, brown-eyed, blue-eyed, young and old: surely Mr. Cutwell was far too old? Helene smiled at them all, trying desperately to remember what she had heard about each. Did anyone here have an affinity for music? How would she know if they did? Presumably the only way to tell was to dance with each, and assess his ability to keep from stepping on her toes.

She put out her hand more or less at random. Some minutes later, she returned from dancing with the Honorable Gerard Bunge to find that the crowd that surrounded her now rivaled any that had ever surrounded Esme, even at the very height of her popularity as Infamous Esme. But this time it wasn't so difficult to choose a partner. For as she smiled at the circle, acknowledging their bows with the smallest inclination of her head, Garret Langham, the Earl of Mayne, effortlessly brushed the other men aside without even seeming to notice them.

Mayne had never paid Helene the least attention. Yet now he walked toward her as if they'd known each other their entire life. He looked the epitome of a London buck: his hair brushed into a perfect tumble of curls, his pantaloons sleekly following the line of muscled thighs, his eyes alive with a wicked combination of laughter and desire. "Lady Godwin," he said easily, holding out his hand. "I believe this is our dance."

To Helene's utter surprise, rather than babbling agreement, she found herself raising an eyebrow and looking him over from his hair to his glossy boots. It was a look that she had seen Esme give various gentlemen, and never thought to use herself. But it seemed to come naturally to a woman surrounded by men, all of whom were clambering, nay panting, for the same thing. A dance. Or (insisted Helene's common sense), a chance to lure her into a side chamber.

Mayne seemed unbothered by her survey, just waited with a little smile playing around his mouth, as if he had always known that they would be partnered, and he had merely waited for her to discard her corsets before telling her.

The thought hardened Helene's heart. He thought he could just *have* her, did he? Well, he could. But on her terms.

She stepped forward, and silk embraced her legs. The other men seemed to melt away. "Lady Hamilton has an exquisite Broadwood piano," she said, giving him a provocative smile from Esme's repertoire. Goodness knows, she'd spent enough of her time in the past six or seven years watching Esme seduce gentlemen. "Would you accompany me to the music room? I should like to play . . . *a tune.*" She lowered her eyes and watched him through her eyelashes.

He didn't show even a flicker of surprise. "That would be my pleasure," he said, holding out his arm.

Really, men were absurdly easy to seduce, if that was the right word. Last spring, she had invited Mr. Fairfax-Lacy into her bedchamber merely by reading a poem. Of course, the whole event hadn't turned out exactly as she planned, but the invitation itself was effortless.

Mayne was just as amenable as Mr. Fairfax-Lacy. They strolled into the music room; he closed the door behind them; she leaned against the polished wood of the Broadwood piano.

Surely he would lunge at her directly? But no, he strolled over to the sideboard and poured them each a glass of wine.

As he handed it to her, he said, "Lady Godwin, you are quite ravishing in that gown."

She said, "Thank you."

And he began kissing her. It was all quite effortless, really.

Five minutes later, he drew a teasing finger down her neck and stopped just at the edge of her bodice. It felt white-hot, as if his very finger blazed a trail on her skin. Helene drained her glass of wine, and Mayne promptly poured her another. Then he put his finger in the glass and put it back on her throat. Helene could feel her eyes growing wider as his wet finger slid across her skin, inside the frail silk of her bodice.

"I should very much like to escort you home," he said, his eyes blazing down into hers.

"Home?" Helene repeated. She was having trouble paying attention. One part of her was absolutely enthralled by his games with the wine. The other side of her (alas for her practicality!) was hoping that he wouldn't stain the silk. She wanted to wear this gown again.

"Yes, home," Mayne said, smiling down at her. "Your home or mine."

Helene gulped. She didn't want to take the man home, for goodness' sake! Didn't he realize that he was supposed to get the job done here and now? "Absolutely not," she snapped, and then realized she didn't sound very agreeable. So she put her hands on her hips and gave him one of Esme's curling, seductive smiles. "Why don't you just kiss me again instead?"

His eyebrow went up. "Why, Lady Godwin, you are growing more surprising by the moment," he murmured, bending to her lips.

Of course, he immediately started plunging about with his tongue. Helene had never liked that sort of kiss. To be honest, it reminded her of the marital act, and both things were just far too intimate for her. But she had to admit that Mayne seemed to be better at it than Rees ever was. His tongue felt rather delicate and enquiring, rather than bullishly trampling. Naturally, he wished to continue kissing long past when she, Helene, would have closed her mouth and moved on to other things. Her mind started wandering. What was it that Esme said she must do? *Be encouraging, show enthusiasm, and be intimate.* Intimate must mean use of his Christian name. Helene ran her hand up Mayne's shoulder and gasped, "You're so marvelous, Gerard!"

"Garret," he murmured. "And you, Lady Godwin, are a very interesting bundle of womanhood indeed." His hand was running down her back to her—to her bottom! Helene almost jumped out of her skin.

"No corset," he murmured against her cheek.

She shook her head.

"No chemise?" he suggested.

She shook her head again.

"A package wrapped just as I most like them," he murmured, and captured her mouth again. Helene stifled an inward moan. Wasn't he ever going to be done with the kissing? And, "Do call me Helene," she said, once she managed to get some air in her lungs. "Shouldn't you lock the door?"

"In a moment," he said. His hands were stroking her back. It felt rather as if he believed her to be a cat: up and down, his hand sliding against the sleek silk. Helene had to admit that it felt quite nice. Although he did end up touching her bottom quite a few times. The caress made her feel rather wiggly and pleasant, rather than outraged. She took advantage of a moment's pause to gulp her second glass of wine.

Really, she was quite getting into the spirit of the thing now, she thought rather dazedly. He kept kissing her ear. Well, nibbling it really. And although the thought of such an action wasn't very enticing, Helene felt it was something she could definitely live with. If only ear-nibbling gave one a child!

Time to give him some more encouragement. If he were as slow with the rest of it as he was with the kissing, she wouldn't get home until the wee hours of the morning. That was one thing she could say about her husband: he never wasted any time in the bed. "Gareth," she whispered into his ear, running a finger down the side of his cheek. He really did have a lovely lean cheek, and he smelled good too.

"Helene," he whispered back. "My name is Garret." There was something about the slightly husky tone of his voice that gave her the oddest feeling between her legs.

She was about to suggest that he hurry along, but she gasped instead. Because he scooped her up in his arms and carried her over to the couch in one long stride. A moment after that, she had almost forgotten that she wanted him to hurry. Because Garret, as it turned out, liked her breasts. Adored them, in fact. He said so, several times.

"They're perfect," he said, in his faintly husky accent. His hand ran over her bodice, again and again, shaping the silk against her nipple and running his thumb over it. Helene had to admit that it all made her feel most peculiar.

"Where is your accent from?" she said, and was surprised to hear her voice was slightly breathy.

"My mother was French," he replied. And then: "Helene, I believe it might be time to lock that door. Would you be agreeable if I were to do so?"

And Helene stared at him, knowing that her eyes were as big as saucers, and feeling that odd sparking queasiness between her legs, and whispered, "I would—yes, please, Garret."

He stopped for one second to kiss her again. Helene was thinking that perhaps kissing wasn't all *that* terrible, when there was a noise at the door and someone walked in.

"*Merde*," he said under his breath and pulled back. But he didn't seem terribly perturbed. "One moment, Cherie, and I will—" Mayne turned to look over the back of the sofa and his body stiffened.

"Who is it?" Helene said, wondering if she should stand up. She would be ruined anyway, once she had a child, so she couldn't bring herself to care overmuch about being caught kissing. Besides, as Esme said, half the women in the *ton* had kissed Mayne.

"Your husband," he said briskly, putting her on her feet. "Good evening, Lord Godwin," he said pleasantly. "Perhaps you were looking for your wife?"

And there was Rees, looking like an olive-skinned, brawling prize-fighter in comparison to Mayne's sleek elegance.

"Yes, I was looking for her," Rees snarled. "I'd be grateful, if you'd give us a moment to speak before you add my wife to the list you keep nailed to your bedside table."

For a moment, Helene thought there would be a fight. The air in the room seemed to have vanished, and the menace on Rees's snarling face was matched by the potent fury on Mayne's. Then she blinked. She had almost forgotten that Rees had relinquished any claim to being her husband, that in fact he had virtually ordered her to find a consort. *It'll do you good,* wasn't that what he said?

She put a hand on Mayne's arm. "Will you give me a moment to speak to my husband?" she said, giving him a significant glance. "I will rejoin you in a moment."

Mayne had gone white with fury and looked even more amazingly beautiful. Rees's ancestry was just as ancient, but his face looked as if all his ancestors were farmers rather than courtiers. "I dislike the idea of leaving you with a man who may not be able to control his temper," Mayne said.

She gave him Esme's liquorish smile, and this time it didn't even feel like Esme's—it felt like *hers*. There was something in the smile that thanked him for the tingling feeling she had all over her body. Thanked him and welcomed it again. "My husband is of little concern to me," she said softly, but not so softly that Rees couldn't hear it. "Although I thank you for your concern."

Rees moved backwards with mocking gallantry as Mayne started for the door. But Mayne stopped just beside him. They were of a height, and oddly enough, although Mayne's rippling muscles were so much more in evidence because of his well-fitting clothing, they seemed to be of similar body weights as well. But the comparison ended there. The Earl of Mayne was dressed with a Gallic flare; his neck cloth, for example, was an exquisite snowy white, tied in a complicated fashion. Earl Godwin seemed to have knotted an old kitchen cloth around his neck; the outline of an overly hot iron was face-out, for all the world to see.

"I suggest that you not exercise your temper overmuch," Mayne said, and the French tinge to his voice sounded truly dangerous now.

"The day I take orders from a dissolute frog like yourself is the day I go to my grave," Rees stated.

"I will excuse your passion on the grounds that you appear to have suddenly recognized that Lady Godwin is your wife," Mayne said with precision. "Although you have given very little sign of that in the past few years, and I believe you discovered it too late." Then he walked out.

Helene had to admit that it was a magnificent exit line. "What on earth are you doing?" she demanded of her husband. "You told me—"

"I know I told you to take a consort," Rees bellowed back at her. "I didn't tell you to spawn a child with one!"

"You know that I'm—*how do you know that?*" she cried.

"Your friend Esme was kind enough to inform me."

Helene felt a red-hot blaze of fury go up her body. Esme—Esme— had betrayed her? Esme, her closest friend in the world?

"I came to tell you that I won't allow it," Rees stated.

"You won't allow it," she said slowly.

"No. I won't allow it. You can't have thought clearly about the fact that any child you carry would become my heir. I can't allow that. Tom, or Tom's son, once he has one, will become the earl when I kick up my heels. I couldn't let a cuckoo take over the estate before Tom's child. It wouldn't be right."

"You're got nothing to say about it," Helene managed. Alarmingly, the fact that Esme had betrayed her was making her feel rather teary.

"I certainly do." Rees strolled over and locked the door. "I'd rather that people don't walk in on us at this moment, if you don't mind."

"I can't see that it matters," Helene said. Why had Esme done such a thing? She had been so close to having her baby, so close to success!

Rees was sitting down. "What are you doing?" she asked with patent scorn.

"Taking my shoes off," he said.

Helene's mouth fell open. "You cannot possibly think—"

"I certainly do. If I understood Lady Bonnington's message appropriately, you came to this ball precisely to find a man to act as stud for you. I'm as available as any other man in London, and a hell of a lot more in your style than the Earl of Mayne."

He pulled down his pantaloons and threw them to the side.

# 10

## *In Which Salome Begins Her Dance*

*The Yard at the Pewter Inn*
*Stepney, London*

Reverend Thomas Holland, known as Tom to friends and parishioners alike, hadn't been in London for years, but it looked just the same: dirty, crowded, and wretchedly poor. It was early afternoon, but it might as well be stark night for all the sunlight that made it through the sooty air. He got off the mail-coach and stretched his limbs, ignoring the ground-shaking thumps near him as stableboys pulled pieces of luggage from the top of the coach and tossed them to the ground. Shrieks echoed off the wooden walls of the Pewter Inn as passengers protested the ramshackle treatment of their belongings. Tom didn't care. He was mostly carrying books, and they wouldn't break.

Someone tugged on his coat and he turned.

"Would you like to buy an apple, mister?"

She couldn't be more than five years old. She had on a grimy pinafore but her face was clean, and the little collection of apples she carried in a basket seemed to be clean, too. "Where's your mum?" he asked, squatting down before her.

She blinked. "Would you like to buy an apple?" she repeated.

"Yes, I would. Shall I give the money to your mother?" He took the apple. "How much is it?"

"Tuppence," she said, holding out a small hand for the payment. There was a bruise on her wrist.

This is why he didn't come to London. He simply couldn't bear it. "Damnation," Tom muttered to himself. "Where's your mother, Sweetheart?"

She looked away again. But Tom had some practice talking to children in the village; he took her hand and said, "Take me home, please."

She didn't move. "I don't go places with men."

"And you're absolutely right," he said, dropping her hand. "Going home is not the same as going *places*, though, is it?"

She thought about this for a moment. She had a sweet, rosy little face, although her eyes were terribly serious. Tom had a familiar feeling, as if his chest-bone were pressing into his stomach.

"I don't go home until I sells all my apples."

Tom got out four pence, for which he received two more apples. There was almost a smile in her eyes: almost. Then she started walking away, so he tossed all three apples to a stableboy and asked him to keep an eye on his luggage. She didn't head out into the series of twisting little streets that surrounded the Pewter Inn, but straight around to the back and into the kitchen.

"I've told you not to come back in here until you've sold them all!" he heard someone say, as he pushed open the door.

A red-faced, middle-aged woman was standing in the middle of the kitchen floor, scowling down at the apple-seller.

"I did sell them all," the little girl said, giving the woman her money. "To him." She pointed at Tom.

The woman swung around and her face changed instantly from irritated to menacing. Tom almost took a step back, as she reached behind her and palmed an enormous rolling pin, as long and wide as his arm. "You get out of here," she ordered. "I've had your kind around here before, and we don't hold with them." She grabbed the girl and pulled her behind her apron. "Meggin is not going anywhere with you, no matter the money you offer!"

"I'm a vicar," Tom said, loosening his traveling cloak so that his collar showed. "I was merely worried about little Meggin being by herself in the posting yard."

"She's not by herself. The posting yard is safe enough. And I never heard that being a vicar stopped nobody from being wicked." Mrs. Fishpole had heard enough stories about the roguery of men in black to distrust the very sight of a collar.

"I'm not one of them, Madam. I'm from the North Country, though, and not used to seeing children as small as this earning their living. But obviously you are taking excellent care of Meggin, and I apologize for disturbing you."

Mrs. Fishpole narrowed her eyes. He was a good-looking man, for a vicar. Nice eyes, he had. "Whereabouts in the North Country?"

"Beverley, East Riding," Tom said cheerfully. The odd tightness in his chest was easing. "I've a small parish there. I'm only in London to visit my brother."

A huge smile spread across the woman's face. "Beverley, eh? I'm Mrs. Fishpole, Reverend, originally from Driffield meself, though I haven't seen it in years. So you must be in the Minster, isn't that what it's called? My dad took me to Beverley once when I was a youngster and we delivered a load of sand to the Minster. It's a beautiful church. I've never forgotten it. I do think that it rivals Paul's."

"Perhaps the sand was used when they were refurbishing the west transect," Tom said. "I'm actually not the reverend of the Minster, but of an adjoining parish, St. Mary's. Reverend Rumwald is the vicar of the Beverley Minster."

"Lord Almighty, is old Rumwald still alive, then?" Mrs. Fishpole's whole face had softened. "He taught me my catechism, he did. He used to come over to Driffield once a month, seeing as we didn't have a parish priest. Too small, we were."

"I'll give him your best," Tom said. "I'll tell him of your happy situation here, as cook in this excellent establishment. And about your lovely daughter as well." He smiled at Meggin but she looked away.

Mrs. Fishpole pursed her lips. "Meggin isn't my daughter. And she doesn't earn her living with these apples, either. I have to feed her from the servants' scraps."

"Meggin isn't your daughter?"

"No," Mrs. Fishpole said, pushing Meggin out from behind her skirts now that she seemed to be in no imminent danger. "Her mum was no better than she should be, I've no doubt. We found her here one night, all but set to have the child on me own kitchen doorstep. The poor woman didn't survive the birth, God bless her soul."

"In that case, Meggin is doubly lucky to have you," Tom said. "I shall have to congratulate Reverend Rumwald on how well he taught you the catechism."

But Mrs. Fishpole was looking at him like a dog that's found a string of sausages on a street corner. "And what if you had found Meggin in a bad situation, Reverend? What was you planning to do next?"

Tom hesitated. "I'm not certain."

"I expect you know of them charities, though, don't you?" she demanded.

"Something of them," Tom admitted, thinking that most of what he knew about London charities wasn't very cheerful.

"You take her!" Mrs. Fishpole said, giving Meggin a little push. The girl gasped and tried to dart behind her skirts again.

"What?"

"You'd better take her. She'll be better off in East Riding than here in London. We looked after our little ones, back home. Here, it's all I can do to keep her out of the way. And she's getting bigger, don't you see?"

"Yes, but—"

"You'll have to do it," Mrs. Fishpole said decisively. "I can't keep her safe anymore. She sleeps there, you see—" she nodded toward a heap of rags in the corner. "But she's getting on towards five now. I don't know how much longer they'll let her stay in the corner, and the older she gets, the more worry I have, to be honest."

Tom could see the truth of that.

"I've done my best with her. I've taught her thank you, and she's learned to say please as well. She knows the difference between right or wrong. I didn't want her turning out like her mum. So you can tell Rumwald that I did my charitable duty with her."

Meggin made another concerted effort to get behind Mrs. Fishpole's skirts and hide from Tom.

"It's not that I won't miss you," Mrs. Fishpole said, putting the rolling pin down on the counter and pulling Meggin around before her. "Because I will, Meggie. You know I will. You're a willing little girl, and you've always been cheerful."

Meggin was blinking very hard. "I don't want to go nowhere."

"You've never carried on and screamed the way some of them children do. But I can't keep you here, Meggie. It's not safe. And you know I can't take you home." She looked up at Tom. "Meggin used to live with me, but Mr. Fishpole died three years ago, and I went to live with my sister-in-law. Her husband doesn't want to take in an orphan, not given the circumstances of her birth and all."

Tom nodded and held out his hand. "Meggin, would you like to come with me to visit my brother? And then after a visit, we'll go home to my village, and I'll find you a family of your own to live with." And between now and then, he swore to himself, I will not even *glance* at the children sweeping the streets.

"No!" Meggin wailed, big fat tears rolling down her cheeks. "I don't go home with no men, I don't! I belong with you, Mrs. Fishpole." She ran at the cook, butting her head against her legs and wrapping her arms around her skirts, just as a hosteller burst into the kitchen shouting something about a sausage and fish pie.

Mrs. Fishpole ignored him, kneeling down on the none-too-clean floor. "I'll come see my old da in East Riding, and I'll see you as well. But I can't let you sleep in the kitchen anymore, Meggie."

"No one will see me," Meggin wailed. "I'll stay so small. And I didn't talk to *him*, I didn't! I'll sell all my apples to ladies after this."

"We needs more sausage pies," the hosteller broke in. "You don't want as Mr. Sigglet to have to come here. You know he doesn't like the brat."

Mrs. Fishpole picked up Meggin and held her against her chest for a moment. Her jaw was set very firmly, and Tom had the impression she would never recover from the mortification if she let a single tear fall. "If I'd had a daughter, Meggie, I'd want her to be just like you," she said. "Now you go with the Reverend here because he'll keep you safe. I can see it in his face. I want you to grow up to be a good girl."

"I won't!" Meggin cried. "I wants to stay here!"

Mrs. Fishpole handed Meggin to Tom. "You'd best go," she said roughly. "She's the most biddable girl usually." For a moment her face crumpled and then she spun around and screamed at the hosteller: "Go on then! Fetch me a sausage pie from the pantry. What are you, crippled?"

Tom held the struggling little body close and walked out of the door to the accompliment of a howl of despair from Meggin, who was holding out her hands and struggling to get free.

"I don't want to go!" she cried. "I don't want to be a good girl. I want to be a cook, just like you, Mrs. Fishpole!"

And then, heartbreakingly, "*Please?*"

After listening to the pounding on the front door for a good ten minutes, Lina decided that Leke must have given the servants the evening off. Finally she traipsed downstairs dressed only in a French negligee, hoping that it would be one of Rees's more prudish acquaintances so that she could watch him dither with embarrassment.

She carefully arranged her negligee so that the lace bits showed off all her best assets and pulled open the door with a flourish.

But it wasn't anyone she'd seen before. A man dressed in a dusty black cloak was standing on the doorstep, clutching a sobbing child and accompanied by a sulky ostler with two boxes on his shoulder.

"Who the devil are you?" she demanded, knowing exactly who he must be. Rees only had one relative in the world, after all, and the man had Rees's nose and mouth. But Rees never said that his oh-so-proper brother was married, nor that he was encumbered with a child. And he certainly never mentioned that the man was paying them a visit.

"Thomas Holland," he said with a bow. "This is Meggin, and these are my boxes, as I've come to stay with my brother. More to the point, Madam, who are you?"

At that moment, the child, who had been eying Lina's negligee with her swollen eyes, said in a choking wail, "I knows who she is! She's the Whore of Babylon, she is! Mrs. Fishpole told me all about her. You's lied to Mrs. Fishpole, and taken me to a house of sin!" She started screaming as loud as she could and kicking Rees's brother in the leg.

Lina raised an eyebrow. This looked as if it might be a most complicated situation. She opened the door further and stepped back. "I gather the vicar is returning home," she said sweetly. "If I'm the Whore of Babylon, wouldn't I be dressed in scarlet and purple? Let me see . . . if I'm the Whore of Babylon, wouldn't that make *you* John the Baptist?" She giggled and turned to go upstairs. "I suppose you can choose whatever bedchamber you wish, although I have to tell you that they are not as clean as one might wish. And I haven't any idea about the condition of the nursery."

She kept walking as she climbed the stairs, raising her voice above Meggin's howls. "Rees will return sometime this evening, and until then you shall have to entertain yourself."

"Where are the servants?" Rees's brother asked, sounding desperate.

Lina ignored the question, pausing on her way up the stairs. "I may not be dressed for the part, but I just realized that I *do* know what the Whore of Babylon would sing. Popish hymns, wouldn't it be? That's what my father would have said. Alas, I don't know any, so this will have to do." And she burst into a magnificent rendition of *O God Our Help in Ages Past*.

Tom stared up at her, stupefied. Even Meggin stopped crying. The music rolled off the walls. She had the largest voice that Tom had ever heard, a gloriously rich, velvety, dangerous voice. At the very top of the stairs she paused and grinned down at him, looking the picture of a godless wench, her body softly gleaming through peach-colored silk, hair rippling past her shoulders, ruby lips laughing. "This is my favorite verse," she announced. "Do pay attention. *A thousand ages in thy sight are like an evening gone. Short as the watch that ends the night, before the rising sun.*" She turned and kept singing, the words falling to them like silken rain as she walked away down a corridor.

"Blimey!" the ostler muttered. "There's a cracked-brained one, for you. Bedlam, this is."

Tom stood absolutely still, staring up the stairs. He felt as if he'd been poleaxed. He could feel Meggin pulling at his hand, and he was aware that the ostler wanted to be paid for tossing his boxes to the ground. But the only thing he could think of was that girl's rosy mouth, and the way she laughed, and the way her voice flew all the way to the rafters of the dusty antechamber, and (God forgive him) the way her hips swayed in that peach-colored negligee.

## 11

## *Marital Consummation*

"Well, for God's sake, Helene, it's not as if you'd be doing it for plea-sure. At least I won't give you a disease which, let me point out, is entirely possible if you dally with a Frenchman. Everyone knows that Frenchmen have the pox."

"Not Mayne," Helene said weakly. But in truth, she wasn't entirely sure what the pox was. It didn't sound pleasant.

Rees was down to his smalls now. "You get the pox from sleeping with the wrong sort of women," he said, quite as if he weren't unbutton-ing his most intimate undergarments in Lady Hamilton's music room.

"I will *not* do this with you!" Helene hissed.

"Why not?"

"Because I don't wish to!"

"You can't tell me that you were looking forward to doing the deed with Garret Langham," Rees said reasonably. "He may be a very pretty man, but you and I both know that your body isn't really suited to this sort of thing, is it?"

To her utter fury, there was no way to interpret his look but as honest sympathy.

"I'm sorry that Fairfax-Lacy went off and married Beatrix Lennox," he continued. "But can you honestly tell me that you two were happy in bed?"

Helene swallowed. There was something even worse about being comforted by one's husband than there had been in failing as a lover to Mr. Fairfax-Lacy.

"It's the devil and truly unfair," he was saying. "But don't you see, Helene? If you're that eager for a child, we might as well do the deed now and get it over with. At least it will be my child that inherits my estate. I couldn't make Mayne's child into an earl ahead of Tom's son."

Helene saw what he meant. She hadn't even remembered the existence of Rees's brother Tom. It wasn't fair to him.

"I'm not a very good earl," Rees said, "but damn it, I suppose you and I could make a child without too much trouble, and at least I would have done my duty."

Helene bit her lip. "Esme says it only takes one time," she heard herself say.

Rees put his hands on her shoulders. "Right. So would you mind giving up Mayne and allowing me to father the child instead?"

"All right," she said, swallowing. It was rather disappointing, but she knew perfectly well that once Mayne had reached a certain point, she wouldn't have liked it any more than she did with Rees, years ago. So what was the difference, really?

Then she realized that Rees was staring at her. "Your hair's gone," he said.

Helene tossed her head, and felt the pure glory of weightlessness again. "I cut it all off."

"And where did you get that gown? No wonder I found Mayne in here with you. That gown is a siren call to rakehells."

Helene resisted the impulse to cover her breasts with her hands. Mayne had said they were beautiful. "If you're going to laugh at my chest, why don't you get it out of the way immediately," she said coolly.

"I'm not," he said, his voice rather strangled with surprise.

Helene looked down at her gown. It was already crumpled by the exertions of the evening, so she needn't worry about taking it off and further exposing her inadequacies. "I suppose we might as well simply get it over with," she said, turning and walking back to the couch. "Are you going to remove your shirt?"

He followed her and stood looking at her as she lay down. "Are you certain that you wish to do this, Helene?"

She actually smiled. "Yes. I think you're right. It's such a relief not to have to pretend with you. I'm not going to enjoy this much, but I would be very, very grateful if we could make a child."

"I wish that wasn't the case for you," Rees said.

But Helene's eye had been caught by something else. "I'd forgotten that it was quite so large," she said faintly.

He blinked and looked down.

"Could we get this over as quickly as possible?" she said, feeling rather dizzy. She never liked pain.

Rees carefully lowered himself onto the couch. He didn't wear any kind of scent, unlike Mayne, who smelled faintly of some male fragrance. Rees was horribly careless about his style of dress, but he did bathe every day, and so there was always a combination of soap and, well, Rees.

He was just as heavy as she remembered. She wriggled a little in protest, and then gasped when she felt his hand between her legs. "What are you *doing*?"

"I just have to make sure—" his voice sounded very husky now. And his fingers—Helene gasped again. Little lightning strokes went down her legs. But then his fingers were gone and then he presented himself in their place.

He was braced on his hands, looking down at her. A lock of hair had fallen over his forehead. "I'll make this as fast as I possibly can, Helene. I'm sorry for the pain of it. I always was, you know."

"I know that," she whispered, tucking the hair back behind his ear. Rees wasn't all bad.

He started to push inside and Helene almost stopped him. But she bit her lip instead. Really, the fear was worse than the pain.

In fact . . .

In fact, the pain didn't really seem to be there. There was a feeling of stretching that wasn't entirely pleasant. But it wasn't really unpleasant either. He managed to push his way right to the back of her, and Helene couldn't help it; she wriggled again.

There was a scrabbling noise at the door and the door handle turned. Helene went rigid. She could hear a female voice raised in fury. "I'm certain that I left my reticule next to the harpsichord."

"I'm sorry, Madam,"—that was surely the voice of Lady Hamilton's butler—"if you will just come this way for a moment, I will look for the spare key."

"Hurry up," she hissed at Rees.

"Does it hurt very much?" he asked, not moving.

"Not so very much," she said, riddled with anxiety. "Rees, do make haste! The butler will return in a moment with another key."

"No, he won't," Rees said, and there was a thread of amusement in his voice now. "He said that to warn us to leave."

"Well, let's comply shall we?" Helene snapped. There was something about having Rees *there*, between her legs, that gave her the oddest feeling. It wasn't anything she had ever experienced before. She felt edgy, as if she wanted to move against him, though what an odd thing that would be! Everyone knows that gentlemen do all the necessary moving.

"All right," Rees said, and he seemed to be talking between clenched teeth. "I hope this doesn't pain you too much, Helene."

"It's quite all right," she said. "Just—just . . ."

But she lost track of that thought. For he'd withdrawn and then pushed his way slowly back against her, and it did the oddest things to her stomach. It felt quite—well—it wasn't good exactly. Helene clutched his shoulders and felt a huge bulge of muscle as he braced himself and lunged forward again. It seemed to be going fairly easily now, as well as she could judge it.

The only problem was a slight burning sensation—probably friction, as when two ropes are pulled together. It must be because he was going so quickly. That must be it.

"Almost there, Helene," Rees said, "sorry," and the guttural sound of his voice did it again, gave her that odd liquid feeling in her legs, a feeling that made her want to buck up against him.

At that moment Rees positively lunged toward her and Helene couldn't help it, a little cry flew from her throat. It wasn't due to pain. Then she braced herself because she remembered quite well that he would flop on top of her like a beached whale and she would lose all the air in her lungs, but he didn't.

"Oh God, Helene, did it hurt that much?" he said a moment later, putting his lips on her forehead for a moment. "I heard you cry out."

"No," she said, feeling queerly as if she were going to weep. "It didn't."

"You needn't pretend. That's the one thing that makes me a better choice than Mayne, remember?"

But Helene didn't say anything. It hadn't hurt. She couldn't say what it did feel like. He seemed to have shrunk, though, which was good. Rees withdrew and then sat on the edge of the couch to draw his smalls back on. He ran a hand up her slender thigh. "You have beautiful legs, Helene," he said, almost absentmindedly.

Helene raised an eyebrow. He *liked* something about her? Probably that was because she had made the right decision to keep her gown on and her bosom covered so that he wasn't faced with those laughably small breasts of hers.

"Thank you very much for the compliment." It was all a bit embarrassing. "I think I would like to go home," she finally said.

He yanked her gown down over her legs. "Wait here, and I'll tell the butler to summon my coach."

He unlocked the door and walked into the hallway. Helene could hear him brusquely telling the butler to fetch his carriage, as his wife wasn't feeling well. His wife! How odd it felt to hear him use that word. But, to tell the truth, she'd never felt more of a wife.

Wives were taken home in fits of exhaustion by their husbands; wives knew the deep pleasure of thinking that they might be carrying a child. . . . That night, Helene fell into bed with an ecstasy of happiness and anticipation.

## 12

### The Saint and the Sinner

"What in the devil's name are you doing here, Tom?"

Tom opened his eyes sleepily. He'd fallen asleep in the library, waiting for Rees to return home. "Came to visit you," he said, his words almost strangled by an enormous yawn.

"Well, you can take yourself home again tomorrow morning," Rees said with a ferocious scowl.

Tom had woken up by now and he watched his brother's back as Rees poured himself a glass of brandy.

"Do you want something to drink?" Rees tossed over his shoulder.

"No, thanks."

"How could I forget," Rees said, obviously between gritted teeth, "men of God don't drink or fornicate, do they?"

Tom bit back a rejoinder. It had taken him the five years since their father's death to decide that Rees wasn't going to visit him, so he would have to make the trip to London. But he'd forgotten what an utter bastard Rees could be when he wanted to. Which was generally when he was unhappy, as Tom remembered it.

"How's Helene?" he asked.

"Fine." Rees tossed off the brandy.

"Have you seen her recently?"

"Saw her tonight," Rees said, putting down the glass with a thump. "Actually, you'll like this, Tom, with all your sanctimonious views of matrimony. Helene's moving back to the house."

"I'm glad to hear it."

"I don't know if she will be," Rees said, turning around and giving Tom a wolfish grin. "I haven't told her yet. But I've decided to get myself an heir."

"An excellent provision."

"Since you look to be just as hen-hearted as you ever were," Rees said with brutal precision, eyeing Tom's collar. "I suppose you haven't done a thing about getting an heir for the estate. Unless you're planning to introduce me to a pious hymn-singing wife?"

Tom's muscles tensed and then he counted to ten. Just because their father delighted in pitting them against each other didn't mean that he had to play the game any longer. He couldn't tell from Rees's face whether he expected him to lose control, or not.

Instead, he rose. "I've taken the Yellow Bedchamber."

"How long are you planning to stay?" Rees asked, pouring himself another drink.

"As long as I wish to," Tom said with a flash of the old anger.

"Why did you come in the first place?"

"I'm staying until I find my brother again," Tom said evenly. "That would be the brother I had until I was ten years old. The brother I miss."

"I am your brother," Rees said, with a twist of his lips. "I can't say exactly when you turned into such a Holy Willie, but if you would put the transformation at ten years old, so be it."

Tom shook his head. "I became a priest at twenty-two, Rees. Ten years old is when our father first noticed me."

"Well, I'd prefer that you left," Rees said flatly. "Touching though I find your concern, it's going to be very tricky with Helene back in the house. I'd rather do the straight and narrow without my moralistic little brother poking his nose into everything."

Tom felt a slow burn in his chest and managed to count to seven. "I have never questioned your life. If you hear reprimands in your ears, they come from Father, not from me. And he *is* dead, Rees. You could stop trying to get his attention any day now. He hasn't the faintest idea that you have an opera singer living in mother's bedchamber."

There was a chilly moment of silence and then Rees laughed, except it sounded more like a bark than a laugh. "It must be enviable to understand the world in such a clear fashion, Tom. I never think about the old man anymore. Lina lives with me because I want her to. And she lives in mother's bedchamber because it's convenient to mine."

Tom snorted. "She lives here because you're still trying to make father spit fire and actually look at you. But the man is dead."

"I like Lina," Rees said softly, rolling her name off his tongue like a delectable sweet. "I gather you met her. And what did *you* think of her, little brother? Isn't she a luscious bit of goods?"

"Are you planning to toss her out the door tomorrow to make room for Helene?" Tom asked, not trying very hard to keep censure from his voice.

"That's the way of the world." Rees shrugged.

"Where will she go?"

"A dissolute man like myself doesn't worry himself with trifles, does he? Probably to the streets, brother. That way, if you were very lucky, you could whisk her off to some charitable home for wayward ladies."

"Your attempts to bait me are a poignant reminder of how much Father meant to you," Tom observed.

Rees narrowed his eyes. "So do give me the churchman's views. What *does* one do with a discarded mistress? Wait! I wasn't supposed to commit adultery, was I? How could I forget that little detail?"

Tom turned toward the door. "I imagine you know precisely where your Lina will go after you turn her out. I can't think why we need to discuss it." He paused and grappled with his temper for a moment. And lost. "I don't know how you can live with yourself, debauching a girl like that."

"I continue to do my best to live up to my family reputation. As do you. Couldn't you take that infernal dog collar off even when you were making a trip to the big bad city?"

"I *am* a vicar," Tom said, shrugging.

"I suppose if you removed the collar, you'd lose the authority to hand out moralities like sweets at Christmas, would you? I wouldn't want all that talent of yours to be wasted." Rees's eyes would have set the room on fire, were it physically possible. "I've just changed my mind, and it's all due to you, brother. I'll keep that poor debauched girl here even when Helene returns. She can stay in mother's bedroom, where she belongs. I need Lina close enough so that I can tup her at a moment's notice, wouldn't you say?"

Tom paused, hand on the doorknob. He could hardly speak, he was so angry. "And Helene?" he managed. "Your wife? I thought you planned to *get an heir*, brother."

"I shall," Rees said casually. "I'll put Helene on the third floor, up where the nursery is. That will nicely symbolize her role in the household."

Tom yanked open the door and stalked out. He doesn't mean it, he thought. He can't mean it. He's just unable to be himself. Damn Father. And when the Reverend Holland brought himself to use a word like damn, he really meant it.

Tom managed to make it into the hall and start up the stairs without going back and throwing himself at Rees until they hit the ground in a rolling pile of fisticuffs, which was exactly what his brother wanted him to do. Rees was never any good at talking out grievances; he preferred to rush into action. It was Tom who had given Rees his broken nose; Rees who had blackened Tom's eye not once but three times.

And it was their father who applauded from the sidelines, feeding the fire with judiciously placed little barbs that pitted his godly and his ungodly son against each other. Except they weren't that, they were never that.

I never wanted to be the godly one, Tom told himself. Not if it was at the expense of my big brother, who had to become my opposite.

He stuck his head into the nursery and looked in on Meggin. He hadn't been able to get her onto a bed. Finally he had given her a sheet and she had arranged it into a nest in the corner. She seemed to be sleeping peacefully, so Tom returned to his own room with a sigh. If things were different, he could have been the one nestled up to a songbird like Lina.

He couldn't quite imagine it. Dog collar or no dog collar, a woman like that would never want him.

## 13

### An Odd Household, Indeed

*R*ees stamped his way down to breakfast in a fit of irritation. Tom had to be booted from the house directly. The maddening comments he had made the previous evening stuck in Rees's mind like a burr. Rees actually found himself up in the middle of the night, wondering whether Lina's presence in his house had anything to do with their dead father, until he decided that Tom, as usual, was being overdramatic. Reading had addled his brother's brain, or so their father always—Father! What on earth was he doing even thinking of the man?

He pushed open the door to the breakfast room with a snap and then stopped short. Lina was sitting at the head of the table. Thank goodness, she appeared to have decided to dress herself this morning, instead of appearing in negligee, as was her custom. Even more startling, next to Tom was a small girl who looked to be his image.

"You didn't tell me that you had a child!" he said, staring at the girl and then at his brother. She had precisely the same sweet expression as had Tom when he was a boy. They were two of a kind; Tom had obviously sprouted a hymn-singing four-year-old, if there was such a thing. His mind spun: Tom, father of an illegitimate child?

"This is Meggin," Tom said, his hand touching the child's head for a moment. "She's not my daughter."

Meggin looked up at Rees. "I belongs to Mrs. Fishpole."

"Belong," Tom corrected her.

Of course. Meggin must be one of Tom's strays. It was always animals when he was young; one might have guessed that he'd move past livestock once he became a vicar. Rees walked into the room, nodding at Leke to give him a plate of coddled eggs.

"You have an excellent cook," Tom said cheerfully.

"I gather you have met my brother?" Rees asked Lina, dropping into a chair to her right. She nodded around a piece of dry toast. She must have decided to go on a thinning plan again, a move he usually deplored because it turned her into a shrew. Truthfully, though, if you compared Lina's and Helene's bodies, Lina did look a bit overly round. Not lumpish, exactly, but her waist must be twice the size of Helene's.

Rees had always thought that it was best to get over rough ground as lightly as possible. Brutal honesty had generally worked for him in the past, although not, he had to admit, with any consistency during his marriage. "I'll be bringing Helene back to the house later," he announced, without fanfare. Then he forked up some eggs.

"You can't have really meant what you said last night?" Tom said slowly.

Lina had dropped her toast. "Helene, your wife?" she gasped.

Rees would have felt a pulse of guilt, but he saw a fugitive gleam of excitement in her eyes. If he had been tired of Lina, she seemed to be positively blue-deviled with boredom. She would likely adore the idea of returning to the opera house with a large settlement in hand. He was perfectly well aware that he had been just as disappointing from Lina's point of view as he was from Helene's.

"I'm not putting you out," he said, taking another bite of eggs. When he was finished, he looked at Lina. "You won't even have to move rooms. Helene will stay on the third floor, in the room next to the nursery."

"I was planning to put Meggin in the nursery," Tom said. He shook his head. "What am I saying? Helene will never agree to this absurd plan!"

The memory of his wife's anguished face saying that she wanted a child—and a similar memory from over a year ago—flashed through Rees's mind. "Yes, she will," he stated.

"You're dreaming."

"I threw her out of the house. Now I'm taking her back."

Lina started to laugh. "You want me to stay in your wife's bedchamber? While she moves to the third floor? You don't know much about women, do you?"

"No. But I do know Helene."

"Why?" Tom demanded. "Why in God's name would she humiliate herself in front of all London society in such a way? I doubt very much that she's been pining for your presence."

He didn't say it with scorn, but Rees felt the pinprick all the same. "She wants a child," he said shortly, forking the eggs in his mouth as quickly as he could. He wanted this conversation over. The sooner he could go to Helene's house and take care of arrangements there, the sooner he could get back to work.

"I never heard of a woman wanting a child that much," Lina said. She had put down her toast. "The scandal will be tremendous."

"If Father was going to turn in his grave, this would do it," Tom put in. "Do you suppose if I showed you disturbed earth, you would stop trying to wake him?"

Rees just looked at him. "I need Lina in the house."

A flash of distaste crossed Tom's face.

"To sing what I compose," Rees finished calmly. He took the last bite of his eggs. "Where, might I ask, did Miss Meggin come from, Tom? And what are you planning to do with her?"

Meggin looked across the table at him. Now that he'd had a moment, he could see that she didn't really resemble Tom. Her eyes were light blue and utterly bewildered. She didn't seem to know what to do with her fork and kept putting it down and trying to eat eggs with her fingers.

"She sold me three apples," Tom said. "I shall take her back to East Riding and find a family to care for her."

Rees looked at the little girl. Her pinafore was stained and crumpled, and she didn't look terribly clean. "Have we any maids at the moment, Leke?" he asked the butler.

Leke was obviously listening with all his attention. This must be the most exciting morning of his life. "My niece Rosy, my lord."

"Of course, I'd forgotten Rosy. I hope she's better with children than she is with an iron. You'd better ask her to help us out with Meggin until my brother decides to return to his parish, which I dearly hope will be very soon." Rees shot Tom a look. "And Leke, send a message to Madame Rocque and ask her to send one of her assistants to measure the child."

"Lovely!" Lina said, "I should like Madame Rocque's current pattern book as well, Leke. Just think of the cosy times Lady Godwin and I shall have, pouring over *La Belle Assemblée* together." She laughed. "You're a fool, Rees."

"We need sturdy, serviceable clothing, not the kind of thing that—" Tom's eyes skittered over Lina's elegant morning gown.

"I'm sure they can provide whatever Meggin needs," Rees said with perfect indifference. He rose and bowed to the room at large. "I'm sure you'll all excuse me. I have to collect Helene. You should expect your mistress in the house by supper time, Leke."

But he was followed by a light swish of silk. "Surely you were wishing to speak to me, Rees?" The sarcasm in her voice pricked his shoulder blades.

Rees pushed open the door of the sitting room. "Right. We can speak, and then work on that aria."

Lina strolled before him. "I think not." She walked over to a couch graced by three towering stacks of paper and plumped herself on top of one of them.

"What are you doing?" Rees bellowed. "Get up at once! You're sitting on Act One."

"Mmm, what a pity," Lina said sweetly. "Don't worry, Rees. I shall restrain myself from the obvious joke about having had the trots."

Once again, he had underestimated a female's anger. Rees ground his teeth for a moment. He should just give Lina a payment and send her on her way. Boot out the mistress, get back into good odor with his saintly brother, bring his wife back into the house, spawn an heir . . . It felt as if the prison gates were closing about him.

"How much do you want?" he asked abruptly.

Her eyes narrowed but she said nothing.

"You know I'll give you a large settlement when you leave," he said impatiently. "But how much extra do you want to stay in the house for a few more weeks, at least until Tom goes home?"

She still said nothing.

He had the uneasy feeling he was missing something, but that was nothing new. He ran a hand through his hair. He didn't know why other men seemed perfectly capable of understanding women. He found Helene and Lina equally incomprehensible.

"You're tired of me," he pointed out.

She nodded at that.

"So the problem is staying in the house with my wife, then?" He turned away and the score waiting on his piano caught his eye. It was hogwash, no question about it. The awful feeling of failure dragging at his ankles just made him feel more stubborn, and more obstinate. If he wasn't writing comic opera, what was he? Nothing. Nothing more than every other self-satisfied pisser of an earl in this country. At least he made people laugh with his music. But the scores he'd written in the last year wouldn't do more than send people to sleep.

"What do you want, Lina?"

"Nothing you can give me," she said.

"I can—"

"This is not about money."

Rees ran his hand through his hair again. He knew that Lina had left the opera house for love of him. But Christ, that was two, almost three years ago. Surely she had time to get over her infatuation? It only took

Helene ten days. "I'm sorry," he said, turning around and leaning against the piano.

To his relief, she didn't look broken-hearted. "Why are you taking your wife back?"

"She wants a child. I need an heir."

"*You* are thinking about heirs?" Lina hooted.

Rees scowled at her. "I'm not getting any younger," he said coldly.

"Are you trying to tell me that you're suffering an old man's complaint, and that's why you avoid my bed?"

"No! No," he said more calmly. "We're finished, Lina. You know that."

She shrugged. "So why am I still here?" There was a faint bitterness in her voice that found its way straight to his conscience. "Why haven't you already set me up with a little house of my own and a snug allowance, to assuage your conscience until I find another protector? Or am I incorrect about the fate of a high-flung courtesan?"

"You're not a courtesan," Rees said.

Her eyes blazed scorn. "Only courtesans can be paid to humiliate themselves. I truly am curious, Rees. Why *do* you want a courtesan in your wife's bedroom, and a wife in the nursery?"

At the moment he wanted nothing more than for her to be gone. He shrugged. "An impulse. Obviously a stupid one."

"Afraid of your wife?"

She knew him far too well. "Absolutely not!" he snapped.

"Afraid of your brother, then."

"Bored at the idea of domestic bliss," he drawled. "After all, given the little scene you created at Madame Rocque's, I can always count on you to enliven the atmosphere."

"I won't do it," she said flatly. "You must be cracked to think I would. The woman will likely kill me, and she would have every reason to do so. I may have lost my virtue, Rees, but I haven't lost every crumb of common decency. I'm not staying in your wife's bedroom while she sleeps upstairs. I wouldn't enter the door while she's here."

"Don't make a Cheltenham tragedy about it," he snarled. "Go if you want to go."

But she just stayed there, her eyes glinting at him. "You told your brother that you wanted me in the house to sing your compositions. I think it would have been easier for both of us if you had clarified that particular aspect of our relationship some time ago."

"I know. I've been a bastard." He said it impatiently: he'd had this sort of conversation with women before and it didn't interest him.

"Well, if I'm to be here to sing for my supper," Lina persisted, "do tell me: just what do you have in mind for your wife?"

"She'll help with—" he stopped. Too late, he saw the trap.

"Help with the opera?" Lina inquired in a particularly sweet voice. "Ah, yes, we all know that the Countess Godwin is a brilliant musician, do we not? I thought there was something fishy about your sudden wish to beget an heir. But if we take your recent musical compositions into account . . . well, now I understand. So the countess will write the score, and I will sing the score, and you merely do your bedtime duty, is that it?" She laughed. "Your wife must be desperate indeed."

Rees was at her side with a snarl of rage that startled them both. "Don't you *dare* speak of Helene in that tone!"

She shook his hand from her arm. "I'll pack my bags."

Rees gritted his teeth. "If you stay and sing when I ask you to, I'll make Shuffle give you the part of the Quaker girl."

She paused, hand on the door.

"You are no courtesan, Lina. We both know it. What are you going to do with the rest of your life? There'll be no second protector for you."

Lina laughed briefly. "Not after what I've learned of men from you."

"You'll go back to the opera house, won't you? So how would it feel to go back with a lead part under your arm, *and* the part already learned? Six weeks at most," he said. "You can learn the Quaker's part by then. Hell, I'll even toss in a little of that coloratura that you do so well. And I'll clear it with Shuffle and the rest of the management."

There was a moment of silence.

"I'd rather have the role of Princess Mathilde," she said. "Not the Quaker girl. I'm no Quaker."

"You'd make an excellent Quaker. For all your beauty, there's a deep down Puritan side to you."

She pulled open the door. "Must be pretty far down. I haven't seen a twitch of it in years. I want the Princess."

He touched her arm. "It wasn't that bad, was it, Lina?"

She looked up at him, remembering how deeply she fell in love with the big, shaggy earl, his dimples and his abruptness, his burly body and his secret kindness. He was the one with a secret Puritan soul, if anyone. She shook her head. "It's been lovely," she said flippantly. "Nothing more than constant gaiety."

Rees had to let her go. What more could he say? What could either of them say?

# 14

## An Outrageous Proposal

*H*elene had a shrewd feeling that she would be besieged with morn-ing callers. No staid matron could chop off all her hair, put on a fla-grantly outrageous gown, and disappear from a ballroom with the Earl of Mayne, without every single female acquaintance she had in the world—and several whom she did not—developing a burning ambition to partake of tea at her house.

So she instructed Mrs. Crewe to prepare for callers and then put on a recklessly daring morning gown sent by Madame Rocque, so that she could entertain all those who might have missed her appearance the previous night. The morning gown was of a style with the gown she had worn to the ball: the cut of the bodice was almost prudish, but the fabric was so fine that it floated around her body, allowing every curve to speak for itself.

But she felt no pleasure in shocking her visitors. In the morning she had discovered that she had her monthly, and only the fact that she had already darkened her lashes prevented her from bursting into tears. It wasn't until she read the very first card brought in by her mother's butler that Helene shed her listlessness like a snake sheds its skin.

Her heart started beating quickly and her cheeks suddenly turned a pink that had nothing to do with cosmetics. "How could you?" she cried, the moment the door opened. She had been thinking about blistering Esme's ears ever since waking up.

Except Esme was followed by William, a plump, cheerful one-year-old. William didn't see the point of solitary walking; he trusted his nurse-maid, Ivy, to keep him upright while he tugged on her finger and pointed. And now he wanted to go to Helene, so Ivy walked him across the room. William had his father's golden hair and blue eyes, but that mischievous twinkle in his eyes was all Esme's.

"Hello, sweet William!" Helene said, holding out her arms. He let go of his nurse's hand and walked one step alone, toppling toward her like a falling star. She scooped him up and tickled him for a moment, and then kissed him all over his curly little head. He smelled wonderful, like bread-and-milk pudding and baby.

"This was very clever of you," Helene observed, giving William's mother a narrow-eyed glance.

"I know," said Esme happily. "I expect you've consigned me to the dungeon, darling, and Lord knows I deserve to be." She turned to Ivy. "I think William will be just fine with us for a short while, Ivy, if you'd like to greet Mrs. Crewe."

William's nursemaid curtsied and took herself out of the sitting room with dispatch. "Ivy is in love with one of my grooms," Esme said. "Now she'll peek out the door and drive the poor lad to distraction."

"How could you do such a thing?" Helene scolded, although it was difficult to sound severe when William's giggles filled the air. "How *dare* you tell Rees that I was intending to get myself with child?"

"It was the most practical solution," Esme said, looking not at all repentant. "I gave a lot of thought to illegitimate children two years ago. Miles and I hadn't lived together for ten years, and there he was in love with Lady Childe. But I decided finally that it made far more sense to approach my own husband than to bear an illegitimate child, and the same is true for you."

"You should have simply told me," Helene scolded. "As it was, I was positively mortified. You should have seen Mayne's face when—"

"No, wait!" Esme cried. "You mustn't describe what happened last night until Gina arrives. She said she'd be here early, and she threatened me with murder if I allowed you to begin the tale without her. We are both quite moribund with curiosity. And Helene, we must instruct your butler that you're not receiving for *at least* an hour. You do realize that all of London will be here this morning, don't you?"

"Of course I do," Helene said irritably. "Why would I be wearing this drafty garment if I didn't know that? Every scandal-mongering matron from here to York will be on my doorstep."

"Matrons!" Esme cried. "Who cares for such trifles? All the men in London will be here, which is why it matters that you look exquisite. Do you know, I think that lip color is more suited to you than anyone I have ever known? It makes your mouth look as ripe as a berry."

"You sound like the worst kind of flatterer. The foolish things were said to me last night! I danced with Gerard Bunge and he kept sighing, and saying that I looked like a tree-nymph in springtime."

"What a coincidence," Esme said acidly. "So did he."

At that moment, Harries announced the Duchess of Girton, Esme announced she was positively starved, and William fell over and bumped his head against a table, so the conversation proper didn't start again until Ivy had borne William downstairs for a consolatory pudding, and Harries had been instructed to bring sustenance, and deny entrance to anyone for one hour.

"Now tell me *all!*" Gina said gaily. The Duchess of Girton had beautiful green eyes and pale red hair. She could turn in a heartbeat from being the most composed, regal woman in London, to being doubled over with fits of wicked laughter. "Helene, darling, you look so elegant! I sent a message to Madame Rocque this morning for an appointment. After hearing about your gown from at least four different women last night, I want precisely the same. Although I promise to order it in a different color," she added.

Helene couldn't help smiling. "How is Max?"

Gina wrinkled her nose. "A despot. I do believe he's the only child in all England who doesn't sleep at night. Now he's teething, and he must have his mama at night or he screams so loudly that even the staff can't sleep. Cam says I must just leave him, and then he'll get used to Nurse, but I can't bear his cries."

"William howls his head off during the night sometimes," Esme said cheerfully. "I must be a very unnatural mother, because I leave him to Ivy."

"I wish I could do that," Gina said.

"Much more important," Esme told Gina, "is the fact that just before you arrived last night, Mayne swept Helene into the music room, and Rees came pounding after her, and the next thing I heard, Mayne had come out with a brow like thunder, as they say."

They both turned and looked expectantly at Helene.

"I got my monthly this morning," she blurted out.

"Oh, what a shame," Esme said softly, winding an arm around her shoulder.

"I'm a little worried that I may be barren," she said, and her voice shook.

"You are *not* barren," Gina said. "I was married for several months before I found myself in a delicate condition and"—she colored—"there was no lack of the necessary activity."

"The idea is absurd!" Esme said. "But I would suggest that you choose a more private setting for your next encounter with Rees."

"I live in anticipation," Helene said with a curl of her lip.

"I don't know why you're so preoccupied with the idea that Helene must reconcile with her husband," Gina said to Esme. "It's almost as if you wish Helene to return to her husband simply because you reconciled with Miles."

"Nonsense," Esme said tartly. "But Helene wants to have a child, and Rees is the obvious choice. If she finds herself in an interesting condition due to the efforts of some other man, who could say how Rees will react?"

"I don't even care," Helene said. "I would retire to the country and raise my baby."

"But I would miss you," Esme pointed out. "We would both miss you, and you would miss us. You would miss London."

"No, I wouldn't miss London," Helene said stubbornly. "I agree with Rees as far as that goes: the season is a dreadful waste of time. As long as I had both my pianos in the country, I would be completely happy."

"She's right," Gina said. "*You* were bored in the country, Esme. But the fact that you happily abandoned your Sewing Circle doesn't mean that Helene would feel the same. For one, I enjoy living on our estate."

"Be that as it may," Esme said stubbornly, "it's always better if a child's father *is* his father."

"Of course that's true," Gina admitted.

"And I'm the only one of us who has actually committed adultery," Esme said. "So I can tell you with some authority that it makes a person feel rather loathsome, after the fact."

"That may be true," Helene said, "but bedding Rees makes me feel just as loathsome, I'm sure."

Gina bit her lip. "You'll have to give us some details, Helene." And, when Helene said nothing, "You must, you absolutely must. Otherwise we'll never be able to decide whether you should return to Rees or look farther afield."

"Perhaps *I* should be the one to decide that!" Helene said tartly. But then she gave in. "Bedding simply didn't work for us," she said with a faint shrug. "I was disgusted, and he disliked the fact I am so thin. The pain didn't go away after the first time, the way it is supposed to. In fact, it only really started to fade after several months, and by then it was clear that our marriage was an utter disaster."

"Oh, poor you," Gina said, giving her a hug.

"It was very distressing at the time, naturally. But I have come to the conclusion that the bedding process is not for me, and I can't say that the fact causes me much grief."

"I'd be inclined to ascribe that to your husband's ineptitude," Esme said.

"I agree," Gina said, nodding.

Helene shrugged again. "It isn't worth discussion."

"Poor you," Gina repeated. "Well, I vote for the Earl of Mayne. Why should Helene be forced to petition her husband for a child? Rees is living with an opera singer, after all. I say that Rees deserves what he gets. And I also think that Helene should not be forced back into a situation that causes her pain and humiliation!"

"That's all very well," Esme said stubbornly, "but I still think that Rees, unpleasant though he is in bed—and out, for that matter—is the better option. I simply believe that Helene will feel a good deal more comfortable if her son actually *is* Earl Godwin, rather than being illegitimate. And if we think ahead, what of your son, Helene? How would he feel if he knew that he was really an illegitimate offspring of the Earl of Mayne, all the time he was carrying the title of Earl Godwin?"

"Perhaps I'll have a daughter," Helene pointed out.

"The fact is," Esme went on, "my little William has inherited the title of Lord Rawlings from Miles although he's really Sebastian's child. I don't feel right about that although I am persuaded that Miles would forgive me, under the circumstances. But it also means that Sebastian's eldest son won't inherit his title . . . it's all very complicated."

"I forgot that you were entangled in something of an inheritance mess yourself, Esme," Gina said.

"Luckily Simon Darby, who would have been Miles's heir, is so hopelessly rich that he says he doesn't give a pea about the inheritance or title. I actually think it's hardest on Sebastian."

"Miles was a decent, good man," Gina said. "And so is Sebastian. But Rees isn't. Oh, I know he's not a murderer or anything. But I don't think that he deserves very much consideration, given the way he has treated Helene. He threw her out of her house!"

"Let's change the subject, shall we?" Helene said, rather wearily. "The question is moot, for the moment anyway."

"Have I told you how much I adore your hair?" Gina asked. "Are you using lampblack to darken your eyelashes? Because I am an expert on the subject. The best product is resin. It's rather hard to find, but you can buy it in Haymarket."

"I have been using black frankincense," Helene said, perking up. "How does that compare to resin?"

There was a knock at the door. "An hour has passed, my lady," Harries announced. He was holding a salver strewn with cards. "Twenty-four persons have called and left their cards; one person just arrived. Shall I announce him?"

"Who is it?" Helene asked.

"The Earl of Mayne."

"Of course!" Gina said, clapping her hands.

When Harries had closed the door and gone to fetch their caller, Esme added quickly: "I do think that you should continue a flirtation with Mayne, for the moment anyway. Rees obviously responds to competition. Look at last night!"

"What about last night?" Helene said, wondering whether she should put on more lip color.

Gina answered her unspoken question by handing her a small pot of the color she had just put on her own lips. "Why are you beautifying yourself?" Helene said, taking the color. "You *are* married."

"I could say the same to you," Gina replied, grinning. "I would never even think of being unfaithful to Cam. But that doesn't mean that I have to look like a corpse in the presence of a man as delicious as Mayne."

"Thank goodness for that," Mayne himself said, strolling into the room. "I have a peculiar dislike of corpses in a lady's sitting room." He bowed elegantly. "Well, this is a true pleasure. Three of the most ravishing women in all London in one room!"

Helene couldn't help thinking that the earl had shown no sign of considering her ravishing a month ago. But it was hard not to appreciate his compliment. When he looked at her with those deep-set eyes, marked by straight black brows, Helene felt a thrill straight down her spine. He himself was, quite simply, ravishing.

"If you'll forgive me, ladies, I will play Prince Paris. Surely you three are Hera, Athena, and Aphrodite." He grinned down at them, and even Gina, who was starting to think that she'd left Max for rather longer than she wished to, felt a spark of pleasure. But then Mayne turned to Helene and gave her his madcap, suggestive grin. "As Paris, I award the golden apple to Aphrodite. Because she has been hiding her radiance for so long that it's burst forth with particular brilliance."

Helene raised an eyebrow, but Esme nipped in before her. "A tediously overwrought compliment," she said reprovingly. "Surely you can do better than that! Besides, I was labeled the Aphrodite when I debuted, and I would take it very amiss to find that I've been demoted to Hera."

"Every Aphrodite has her day," he said, twinkling at Esme. "If you ladies would allow me a private visit with Lady Godwin, I assure that I could wax far more eloquent."

"Well, I expect we shall have to give you free rein for your eloquence, Mayne," Esme said, rising.

He bowed and kissed the very tips of her fingers. "It's a pleasure to see you so radiant, Lady Bonnington."

Esme laughed.

"Good-bye, Helene," Gina said, pulling Esme toward the door. "No, don't worry, Mayne. You can kiss my hand next time." Giving him a con-spiratorial smile, she closed the door behind them.

Mayne turned around and looked down at Lady Godwin. She was faintly pink, and seemed to be examining her skirts with great curiosity. He sat down next to her on the couch, stretching out his legs before him. "I am enchanted to see you so unscathed by last evening's debacle," he said.

Helene could feel herself blushing so hard that her ears were going red. If only she didn't blush so much! "My husband and I are—are friends, Lord Mayne. Truly, there is little disagreement between us."

"That sounds remarkably refreshing," Mayne said, picking up one of her hands and running his thumb delicately down each finger. His grin re-ally was irresistible. Helene smiled at him a little shyly. She wasn't used to the heady pleasures of flirtation.

"Won't you call me Garret?" he said softly. "You did so last night."

Helene just knew that she looked unattractively pink in the face. "I apologize for leaving the ball after I informed you that we would meet di-rectly."

He turned her hand over and began brushing kisses onto the rounded part of each finger. "The occasion lost all interest after you left." He spread her hand against his. "How slender your fingers are, compared to mine. Musician's hands."

"Yes," Helene said rather uncertainly. Her heart was thumping quickly. Suddenly his fingers curled in between hers. "May I kiss you?"

Helene hesitated. He took that for a yes, and she caught one last glimpse of his dark eyes before his head bent and he brushed a kiss on her lips. And another. Another. His kisses were very sweet. Delicate. Helene relaxed. He had very large hands: without question he would be able to span one-and-a-half octaves.

"Do you play?" she said, against his mouth.

"All the time," he answered. He went back to his brushing kisses, without seeming to be in any hurry.

Helene found that she was quite enjoying it. Then she realized that perhaps he hadn't understood her question. "I mean, do you play music?" she asked.

"That too." He moved closer and put a finger under her chin to tip it up. "May I play with you?"

Helene could feel her heart pounding so hard it was likely visible through the thin fabric of her gown. That was the important question, wasn't it. And yet—she *couldn't* do anything of that sort. "It isn't the right time," she managed.

He bent his head again and his lips drifted across hers. She wouldn't mind if he tried to kiss her a bit more . . . intently. But he didn't. Instead his mouth drifted off to the corner of her lips. "Curiosity is my besetting sin," he said silky. "Also a ruthless wish to have things absolutely clear between playfellows. Is it not the right time because you are, alas, attached to that shaggy husband of yours, or is the issue a rather more ephemeral one?"

Helene opened her mouth to answer but he took advantage of it and slid inside. She found her arms around his neck without conscious volition. I don't like this kind of kissing, she thought to herself, rather wonderingly. But she liked Mayne's kiss. He was so debonair and restrained.

Finally Mayne himself drew back, and Helene was startled to see that he was looking at her with distinct hunger. No man had ever looked at her with that expression, although she'd often seen them looking at Esme that way.

"I want you, Helene Godwin," he said, and there was a dark throb in his voice that made Helene's legs feel weak.

"I couldn't—I've never—" she stumbled, and then pulled herself together. "I've never done such a thing before."

His hands were holding her face lightly. "You are so exquisite," he whispered. "Was I blind before last night?" His fingers ran over her cheekbones. "I must have been blind not to see your beauty."

"Thank you," Helene said awkwardly.

Then his mouth came to hers again, and this time it was easier; this time she sank more naturally into the circle of his arms, and her mouth opened up to his with a little gasp. And when he let her go, Helene found that her hands were trembling.

"I hope that you will give me a place in your life," Mayne said, and Helene registered the hoarse note in his voice with a feeling of pure triumph. "I generally do not think myself a fool," he continued, with a rueful tilt of his eyebrows. "But I've been a fool. In the last few years, I've ranged far and wide amongst the ladies of the *ton*, Helene. Frankly, I've stopped caring very much if a particular lady refused my attentions. And yet I find myself caring a great deal about your answer. And that is a truth."

Helene knew that he was, indeed, telling the truth.

## 15

*In Which Helene Finds Herself Unaccountably Desirable*

*H*elene was having one of the most thrilling mornings of her life. The Earl of Mayne had left her with her heart beating quickly, stooping over her for one second before he left and kissing her cheek. "You are utterly enchanting," he whispered.

Helene had grinned like a fool. No one had ever called her *enchanting*. Mayne had left only when the butler announced that there were fifteen ladies crowded into the library, and then he strolled out so slowly that everyone knew exactly why she was pink and slightly breathless. All of which gave her a sense of power that went to her head like fizzy wine.

She didn't even blink when he kissed Lady Winifred's hand, and complimented Mrs. Gower on her reticule. He was *hers*. He turned back, for just a moment, before he took his cloak from Harries, and she saw it in his eyes.

Thus Helene greeted her guests with the smile of an utterly confident woman. "How lovely to see you, Lady Hamilton!" she said. "Your ball last night was a remarkable success."

"Due to you," Lady Hamilton replied cheerfully. "There's nothing like a sensation to give one's ball polish. I came to thank you, my dear . . ."

And so it went. The whole morning was a series of delightful conversations. Even Mrs. Austerleigh's waspish comment that the Earl of Mayne was nothing more than a rakehell didn't disturb Helene. She knew as well as anyone that Mrs. Austerleigh was lucky to have gained the earl's attentions for one evening. She should have been happy with that, instead of lamenting his supposedly wandering eye.

"I find him a pleasant companion," Helene assured her. "Nothing more."

"But your husband!" Mrs. Austerleigh tittered. "Do you find *him* a pleasant companion as well? You could have knocked me to the ground with a feather when I saw Lord Godwin stride into the ballroom last night. I had to ask dear Patricia whether she actually invited him. An odd decision on her part, to be sure."

"Rees and I are comfortable together," Helene said cautiously.

"You must be!" Mrs. Austerleigh laughed shrilly. But her laugh broke off in midair as Rees himself strode into the room.

He ignored all her guests and walked straight over to her, with his usual lack of common courtesy. To Helene's mind, his behavior presented an eye-opening contrast to that of the Earl of Mayne.

"Rees," she said, holding out her hand for a kiss. It was a bit odd knowing that his legs were as muscled under those breeches as she had discovered last night. The very thought made her want to giggle.

"Helene," he said, "I must—"

But then he seemed to realize that fifteen pairs of eyes were watching him with keen curiosity. "Perhaps we could speak in private for a moment?"

"Alas, this is not a convenient moment," she said, her smile not slipping an inch. "If you send me a note, we could fix on a mutually agreeable time . . . next week, perhaps?" He frowned, probably thinking that she was acting like a recalcitrant servant.

Actually, Rees was making a rather unpleasant discovery that had little to do with servitude. He had forgotten, again, that this Helene wasn't the girl he married. He seemed to have to make that discovery over and over: he had married a hysterical, high-strung young girl, easily driven to tears by a few strong words. But in the last few years, she had utterly changed.

"I would prefer to speak to you now," he said. He turned and gave a hard-eyed stare to the madams twittering with each other, their teacups halfway up to their mouths, fairly trembling with curiosity. Finally Lady Hamilton put down her cup, hopped to her feet, and made a quick apology to Helene. The others followed suit like a flock of chickens running from a rainstorm.

"There," he said with satisfaction, when the room was empty. He strode over and sat down on a comfortable looking couch. There was a cup of tea in front of him likely not even tasted, so he drank it.

"You are revolting," Helene said, sitting opposite him. "I'll pour you your own cup of tea if you'd like some."

"I loathe tea," he said. But he was interested to hear from her voice that she wasn't really that angry with him. Perhaps tupping on a couch was the key to wifely good temper. He wouldn't mind a few more sessions, if they resulted in a peaceful household. She was wearing another one of those gowns like the one she wore last night. He could see the long line of her thigh. Suddenly his breeches felt a bit tight.

"Why are you here, Rees?" Helene asked him.

"I've come to bring you back to the house," he said bluntly. There were two cucumber sandwiches left, so he ate them. He'd been up since five in the morning, working on those damn orchestrations, and he was famished, even given the coddled eggs he ate for breakfast.

There was silence, so finally he looked up. Helene was looking rather amused.

"Don't tell me you actually think I'm taking you seriously?" she asked.

"You're my wife. I want you back. Tell your maids that I'll send over a couple of footmen to carry your boxes."

"You must be cracked!"

"No. Unless I'm much mistaken, we have decided to have an heir, and we may already have begun the process. Under those circumstances, obviously you have to move back into the house."

She shook her head. "I wouldn't move into that house for a million pounds. And you cannot have really expected that I would do so!"

"I know you, Helene. You'll want what's best for the child. And living in his family home with a father on the premises is by far the best." Darby had been absolutely right. He could see in her eyes that fatherhood was a potent argument.

"I see no reason why we should live under the same roof," she said.

"Because the child will be my son or daughter."

"Mine as well!" Helene snapped.

"Of course. I may be a rakehell," he said, unconsciously echoing Mrs. Austerleigh's condemnation of his rival, the Earl of Mayne, "but I'm growing old. I seem to be gaining some measure of responsibility towards my name."

"That's the first I've heard of it!" Helene scoffed. Then she asked the question Rees was rather dreading: "Is one to suppose, then, that you are planning to reorder your household to accommodate my presence? Won't that be a sacrifice?"

The delicate irony in her voice made his stomach churn. He picked up a half-eaten cucumber sandwich.

"Don't eat that!" Helene screeched. "It belonged to Lady Sladdington, and she has very bad teeth."

Rees shrugged. "Do you think they're catching?" But he put the sandwich down. "At any rate, no, I haven't."

"You haven't what?"

"Told Lina to leave the house." This was harder than he thought, now he was looking right at Helene. "I told Leke to clean out the bedchamber—the *large* bedchamber—next to the nursery for you."

"You must be joking," she said, staring at him with what appeared to be fascination.

"I'm not." This was the tricky part. "You want a child, Helene, am I right?"

She laughed. "Not under those circumstances."

"I want an heir as well. I hadn't really thought about it until you brought up the question, but now I realize that I do. Tom shows no sign of marriage; he's about as wet as a waterlily, and he's never shown any interest in women that I know of. If neither of us has issue, the title and the estate would revert to the crown, you know. My father was an only child and as far as I know, there aren't any far-flung cousins waiting for my obituary in the *Times*."

"Why would you care?" she asked. "You've never shown any interest in the honor of your name. The very suggestion is laughable."

"Well, now I do," Rees said, picking up the sandwich and eating it. Who cared if all his teeth fell out? Not his wife.

"This is all very well," Helene said impatiently, "but I fail to see that it has any relevance to the presence of a strumpet in my bedchamber, not to mention your absurd suggestion that I take over the nursemaid's quarters."

"You want a baby," he said shrewdly, meeting her eyes. "Don't you, Helene? All these—" he waved his hand at her "—these changes in your hair and dress, they're because you want a baby."

"Yes, although," she said with a little smirk, "they have compensations of their own."

"Mayne, I would gather."

"Precisely," Helene replied, noticing with appreciation that the idea seemed to irritate him. Esme had said that Rees was jealous and while Helene thought it was unlikely, the idea of causing her husband any sort of annoyance was too pleasurable to ignore. "Mayne was here this morning, and his attentions are most marked."

"If you have a child with Mayne," Rees said deliberately, "I'll make its life a misery. I will divorce you, of course. Did you know that I keep your dowry in the event that we divorce on grounds of adultery? How will you raise the child, Helene?"

Her heart was sinking, but she kept her chin high. "My mother and I shall live together, just as we do now."

"Now you have an extremely generous allowance from me," he snapped. "As a divorced woman, you will have to live in the country, of course, but I believe your mother's dower estate includes only this house in town. So you'll rent some small house somewhere. Your child will go to the parish school, if there is one, *and* if they allow bastards to attend these days. I'm not sure about that. I am certain that he will be ostracized though. And what if you have a daughter, Helene? Who will she marry? What will her life be like?"

She stared at him, lips pressed together.

"She'll live a life like yours, I suppose," he continued ruthlessly. "She'll grow old living with her mother—*you*. Except there won't be very much money, especially after your mother dies and the dower estate reverts to your father's cousin." He didn't feel good about what he was doing. She still hadn't said a word, but he remembered something else that had to be said.

"And don't think that Mayne will obtain an Act of Parliament to marry you," he added. "Even if he stayed with you through the divorce proceedings. The man may be rich, but he's slept with most of the wives of the men sitting in the House of Lords. They're just waiting for some miserable cuckold to up and shoot the man, and believe me, they'll pardon the offence as justifiable."

"Why?" she asked between white lips. "Why would you do such a cruel thing, Rees?"

"Because I want you in the house," he said coolly. "You're my wife."

"I'm not your property!"

"You're my wife," he repeated. "It's that simple. You merely need to decide how much you want that child. We made a dog's breakfast of our marriage, but we can surely pull ourselves together long enough to get this taken care of."

"You just want me to be wretched," she said flatly. "You must be out of your mind to even come up with this plan. Never mind my feelings about the matter: my reputation would be ruined!"

A great surge of resentment rose in his chest at the very mention of reputation. "Of course, your name is all important to you. It remains to be seen whether it's more important than having a child. And may I point out, Helene, that your reputation will also be ruined if you have a bastard with Mayne? All the *ton* will watch the two of you like hawks on a pair of frolicking mice."

She seemed to be huddling in her chair, and Rees had a terrible feeling, as if he'd wounded a bird in flight. He stood up to go, but he couldn't quite make himself leave. She looked like a wounded sparrow, all shorn of its feathers now that she'd cut her hair.

"This bombast on your part doesn't explain why you want me in the house alongside that woman," she said, looking up at him. "If indeed you want an heir, get rid of her."

"No." Rees knew he was being stubborn, but he didn't care.

"Then you wish it merely to force me to live in a house of sin due to some perversion in your character. You're a devil, Rees."

"It's no house of sin," he said brusquely. But he could feel a wave of guilt coming. "Tom arrived yesterday. We have our own resident vicar."

"Your brother Tom? What does he think of your domestic arrangements? And did you even dare to tell him of this scheme?"

Rees's lips twisted. "He's worked up some sort of idea that blames my father for all my excesses. He didn't seem to mind Lina too much, but he said you wouldn't come to the house."

"He's right!"

"And I told him," he continued, staring down at her with that fierce look he had, that seemed to look into her very soul, "that he had no idea how desperately you want that baby. Or am I underestimating you, Helene?"

"You're mad," she said, standing up. "You were always odd, and now you've gone stark, raving mad. I'm actually glad that we didn't manage to create a child yesterday, because I wouldn't want to pass on any sort of dementia."

"We didn't?" he asked, staring at her. "You already know?"

"Yes," Helene said, glaring back. She had gone from shock, to rage, to despair, and she was back to rage again. But threads of rational thought were stealing back into her mind. He was bluffing. He had to be bluffing. It wasn't truly in Rees's nature to act in such a cruel—nay, almost wicked—fashion.

He took her arm, stopping her from leaving the room. "How much *do* you want a child, Helene?"

"Enough so that I accepted the fact that it may look like you," she said coolly. "And enough to know that you're not the only man capable of making one."

"You would condemn your own unborn child to bastardy. She will hate you someday, when she has no one to marry except the local cowherd. Let's face it, it's not as if you and I would particularly enjoy being next door to each other anyway. Did you really want me able to enter your room at any hour of the day or night and slip between your sheets?"

She spat it at him. "Absolutely not!"

"Right. The chamber on the third floor is easily larger than my mother's room. You can fit a piano in there."

"That's not the point! I do not wish to spend even a moment under the same roof as your doxy, a fact which should be clear, even to a person with your *perceptive* nature."

"All right," he said. "We'll compromise. You live in the house until we conceive the child. You can come in secret, so there won't be any scandal. And then you can take the child and raise it elsewhere. Here, with your mother, if you wish. But I refuse to continue trailing around after you and stripping off my pantaloons in public."

"You could come here on occasion."

"I'm not going to waste my time flitting around to balls, and to my mother-in-law's house, trying to find my own wife. I have work to do."

"I don't spend my time flitting around to balls!" she retorted. "You know as well as I do that I spend most of each day here working on my piano. You could come here."

"I noticed an advertisement for Arrangements of Beethoven Piano Sonatas for Four Hands, by a Mr. H. G.," Rees said, distracted for a moment. "Are those the pieces you were working on last summer?"

She nodded. "I'm writing a waltz at the moment," she said. "Well, this has been an utterly enthralling conversation, Rees, but I really must—"

"I need you, Helene."

"*What?*"

"I need help." He said it jerkily, in the tone of a man who hasn't asked for help since he was eleven years old. "I have to put an opera on the stage next season, and I've only written a few songs that are even decent. I shouldn't have left the house this morning."

"That's not like you. I thought you poured out all that comic stuff as if it were dishwater."

There was a muscle working in his jaw. "Believe me, Helene, the stuff I'm writing now is worse than dishwater."

He met her eyes with the old flare of obstinacy and anger, but there was something else too. A plea? She frowned. "You need my help? How could I possibly help you?"

"I thought perhaps we could make an exchange. You've gotten better and better over the years. Whereas I've become pedestrian." He couldn't think how to frame it in proper terms. "If you can help me turn my score into something playable, I'd be grateful." It was clear how his gratitude would be expressed.

Helene felt her cheeks going pink. "That's—That's—" she spluttered. "Absolutely not."

He turned away, raking his hand through his hair. "All right."

Helene watched him suspiciously. He was giving up, just like that? He must not have wanted her help very much. And did he really think that she was a better composer than he?

"If you can wait nine months or so, until the opera is rehearsed and opens, I'll start coming over here whenever you want me to," he said, sounding extremely tired.

"Couldn't you possibly do so now?"

"I really couldn't." He was looking out the window, back to her. "I've dried up, Helene. I slave over the damn melodies, and they get worse every time I touch them. I lost most of last night due to the Hamilton ball. I can't afford to do that again."

"What part is *she* taking?" Helene said sharply, suddenly realizing something.

He looked at her. "The lead."

"So you need her in the house to sing the parts," Helene said, working it out.

"Yes."

"And for other reasons," she pointed out with a little edge to her voice.

He'd got his satirical gleam back now. "It's not as if you would like to do any recreational bedding, is it, Helene?"

"No!" It was madness. Utter madness. And yet, she couldn't bear the idea of waiting months. She'd already waited half her lifetime, or so it felt. If she were honest, there was also a small part of her reveling in the idea that he wanted her help. That he admired her music. Fool that she was.

"I'll do it for one month, and on one condition."

"What?" Rees was rather startled to find how much he wanted her to agree.

"You can't even *enter* that woman's bedchamber while I'm in the house. Not under any circumstances, Rees. Do I make myself absolutely clear? You are not going to parade from one bed to another. She can stay and sing, but that is all."

He looked at her, and for a moment she thought he was going to refuse. Bile rose in her throat.

But then he said, "I see no problem with that request."

"And no one can know that I've returned to your house," Helene commanded. "I'll inform my household that I'm traveling in the country. It's not as if anyone from polite society would think of paying you a call."

"No one ever comes to visit. But you would have to be a virtual recluse, Helene. And servants talk."

"Do you still have Leke?"

Rees nodded.

"Leke won't talk," Helene said. "You'll have to let anyone go whom you think might gossip."

He shrugged. "We haven't hardly any staff at the moment. There's Rosy, Leke's niece, a couple of footmen, and Cook."

"How you can live in such a pigsty, I don't know," she said.

"I'll tell Leke to expect you this evening then," Rees said, controlling his voice so that not even a trickle of pleasure came through.

"No. I'll arrive in a few days. What did you tell your singer?"

"The same thing I told you." He pulled open the door and told the butler to fetch his greatcoat. "Her name is Lina McKenna, by the way."

"What did Miss McKenna say of this scheme?" Helene demanded, dumbfounded to find that she was even considering such an action.

Rees shrugged. "Something about the two of you pouring over fashion plates together." He left Helene staring at the door.

# 16

## The Nature of My Sex

"What do you wish to do this morning?" Tom asked Meggin as they left the breakfast table. She didn't seem to have eaten much, although who knew what a child this age should eat? And why didn't he think to ask Mrs. Fishpole when her birthday was? He wasn't even quite certain how old she was. He'd have to return to the inn. How did children amuse themselves?

Meggin just looked up at him and didn't say anything.

"Would you like to have a bath?" he asked.

She didn't reply. It was rather irritating. Or it *would* be irritating, he quickly corrected himself, if she wasn't such a little girl. One couldn't be annoyed by an innocent orphan. Could one?

"What would you like to do today?" he said, rather more loudly. They were climbing the stairs. Meggin wasn't even pretending to pay attention. She was caressing the satiny finish of the stair rail as if it were a cat. What was needed here, obviously, was a female.

He paused. "Wait here," he instructed her and then turned around. Meggin was nothing if not obedient. She sat down on the stair and began stroking the stair railings.

Tom clumped down the stairs feeling extremely irritable. He'd been thinking about this trip for over two years now. He had planned to arrive at Rees's house, and—and there's the rub. Talk to him. Tell him he missed him? Their father's taunts rang in his ears just as loudly as they obviously still did in Rees's: expressing such an emotion would be girlish. How could he tell Rees that he missed his big brother, that he missed talking to him, that he wished they were friends? From what he could see, the only friend Rees had was Simon Darby, and that all went back to the days when Rees would flee the house and disappear to the Darby household for days.

Tom sighed. "Leke!" he shouted.

"Here, sir." The butler trotted through the green door, drying cloth in hand. "I'm just on my way to the employment agency, sir. I think we could use a few maids."

"Undoubtedly," Tom said, allowing faint irony to enter his tone. The corners of his room were festooned with cobwebs.

"Had I known of your arrival, sir," Leke said majestically, "I would have had your room prepared."

"Never mind that, where's your niece? The one and only maid? I need someone to care for the child."

"I'm afraid she has let us down," Leke admitted. "She's run back to her mum this morning. I'm sure my sister will send her back with a good ear-warming, but meanwhile, there isn't a woman in the house barring Cook. And Cook is not the sort to do any child-minding. Takes her position very seriously. After all she cooked for the Prince of Wales once; his lordship pays her one hundred guineas a year just to stay in the household."

"Bejesus," Tom muttered. One hundred guineas was nearly what he made as vicar, and more than most of his parishioners made put together.

He started back up the stairs. Cook wasn't the only woman in the house. Lina was a woman. Anyone except a blind man could see that. Halfway up the stairs, he passed Meggin and she got up without a word and started following him, for all the world like a curious kitten. At the top of the stairs he turned left and marched down to his mother's room.

The door opened immediately. "Well hello, Reverend," Lina said, smiling as wicked a smile as any self-respecting Whore of Babylon would give a bishop.

Tom felt that smile all the way down to his groin. No wonder his brother had thrown his wife out and moved Lina into the bedchamber next to his. God help him, he probably would have done the same. He gave himself a mental shake. She's a fallen woman. Someone to pity and succor, not lust after as if he were a common ruffian.

She had changed into a tight costume made of green velvet that buttoned down the front and made a man's hands itch to stroke it. A green velvet hat nestled on her glossy brown curls. All in all, she looked like an enchantingly naughty wood elf.

"I gather you like my walking costume?" she said, as he remained silent.

"It's delightful," Tom barked, embarrassed. Meggin had inched forward and was stretching one dirty finger toward the white fuzzy stuff that edged Lina's jacket. "I came to request your assistance."

Lina raised an eyebrow. "You'd better come in, then. These shoes are the very devil to stand in, and 'tis against the nature of my sex to stand, anyway."

Tom followed her, trying to sort that out. Why not stand? Could she possibly have meant a joke on a man *standing*? Or rather, parts of a man, standing? Surely not. He must have misheard. Perhaps she was simply referring to her shoes.

Meggin followed Lina into the room as closely as she could, still touching her jacket. "It's swansdown," Lina told her briskly. "You may touch it as long as you don't soil it."

"May I borrow your lady's maid until Leke hires a temporary nurse-maid?"

"I don't have a maid," she said, slipping into a seat next to the fire-place.

"You don't?" His mother had employed two personal maids.

"I had one when I first arrived, but I decided I could do without her. She didn't really approve of my situation." She wrinkled her nose. Her eyes were merry, and not at all bitter. "I always managed to dress myself at home, after all."

"Where is home?" Tom asked. "Do you mind if I seat myself as well?"

"A long way away, alas," she said, and it was as if a curtain fell over her face. "Now how can I possibly help you, Mr. Holland?"

"Meggin needs a wash, and I don't think she'll feel comfortable with me."

"Probably not," Lina murmured. She looked down at the little girl. "I suppose I could supervise a bath."

Tom was looking around the chamber. If he hadn't known it was his mother's bedchamber, he'd have never recognized it, hung with rosy silk as if it were the inside of a sea shell. It didn't look like a strumpet's boudoir, not that he had personal acquaintance with such a room. There weren't any portraits of naked gods and goddesses, or anything else to signal that Lina was a kept woman. Damn his brother, anyway.

Lina stood up, unbuttoning her jacket and tossing it on the bed. She wore a shirt of thin muslin, which made it obvious that she was graced with one of the most glorious bosoms Tom had ever seen, with a sweet lit-tle waist that curved in and then out. He had to take a deep breath. He hadn't had a woman since he became a vicar. It wasn't for want of desire, either, for all his father used to call him a molly. But a vicar who hap-pened to be the younger son of an earl, and possessor of a large private income inherited from his mother, learns very quickly to avoid conversa-tion with unmarried women unless he can countenance marrying them. He had a deep-down, abiding respect for the vows of marriage, and the vows he had made when he entered the churchhood, which prevented him from frivolous flirtations—or worse. I'm not in tune with the age, he thought ruefully. Lina's breasts strained in the thin muslin of her shirt as she bent toward Meggin and said something into the little girl's ear.

"Perhaps I will leave," he suggested. He had to get out of the room. One glance at his breeches and the oh-so-experienced Lina would know exactly how he was reacting to her presence. "I'll send a footman with a tub of hot water," he said, hand on the door.

He turned to watch, just for a second.

Lina had managed to coax Meggin's dirty pinafore over her head by giving her a swansdown tippet to hold. Meggin was stroking the tippet with an expression of utter bliss, and rubbing it against her face. Lina didn't seem to mind. She had got out a brush and was making a determined assault on Meggin's tangled curls. And all the time she talked, a low stream of chattering, joking conversation that continued even though Meggin didn't reply.

Her accent was unmistakable. Rees's little songbird, as he called her, was indeed from a long way away: Scotland. Tom stored away that scrap of information, and went to order a tub and buckets of hot water.

It was to be a council of war, if held in Helene's mother's elegant drawing room. Something along the lines of the Council of Vienna, Helene thought to herself, and Rees was their renegade Napoleon. If only Rees would go live on an island somewhere . . . Elba would be perfect.

She moved a plate of gingerbread cakes away from the edge of the table and fussed with the linens for a moment. At least she didn't have to tell her mother. Of course, she didn't *have* to tell anyone. She could change her mind.

Too late. Esme rustled into the room. She was supremely elegant, wearing a morning frock of Italian crepe with a painted border of shells. An exquisite little reticule decorated with the same shells dangled from her wrist.

"Darling, you just caught me!" she said. "I am on my way to Madame Rocque's establishment. And I mustn't miss my appointment; I have nothing to wear, and from what I hear, Madame Rocque is being barraged with requests, entirely due to *your* successes! I have no doubt but that half the women in London are hopeful that a gown fashioned by Madame Rocque will ensure them attention from the Earl of Mayne."

"That's a lovely gown," Helene said.

"I had to dress to impress," Esme explained. "I'm afraid that if I don't appear a veritable blaze of fashion, Madame Rocque will fulfill other requests before mine."

At that moment Gina rushed in. She looked the opposite of Esme; her hair was rather more disarranged than fashionable, and she was wearing a Pomeranian mantle that was supposed to be worn over a ballgown, rather than a walking costume. "I'm here!" she called. Then she collapsed into a chair. "Barely. I'm afraid that I find child-rearing a detriment to the normal business of paying morning calls."

Helene poured her a cup of tea. "I do apologize for summoning you both to my house at such short notice," she said apologetically.

"Never mind that," Esme said. "Tell us *all*!"

"Rees arrived after you left yesterday morning. He frightened away all my callers—"

Esme's deep chuckle punctuated the sentence.

"And told me that he wants me to move back into the house."

Esme's laughter stopped. "Really?"

"He wants me to move back into the house," Helene repeated, well aware that she hadn't exactly told the whole truth . . . yet.

"Oh, my goodness," Gina said with fascination. "What has happened to the rakehell husband himself?"

"He must be feeling his age," Esme said. "Perhaps he was infected by that odd malady called respectability."

"Not exactly," Helene said.

"What do you mean?" Esme raised an eyebrow. "I should tell you that Miles's reaction was just the same. When I asked him for a child, he said that he would move back into the house, and he would bid Lady Childe farewell. Which he did do," she added conscientiously, "although he and I never had the chance to live together again."

"Well, once again Miles and Rees are shown to be not precisely of the same caliber," Helene said, twiddling with the delicate handle of her teacup rather than meet her friends' eyes.

"How do you mean?" Gina asked. "I don't follow. How does Rees's request differ from Miles's?"

"Rees wants me to return to the house," Helene said, raising her chin. "But his mistress, Lina McKenna, will remain in the house as well. And those are the only circumstances under which he will father a child." She had decided to keep Rees's offer to engage in the business nine months in the future to herself. Her friends would undoubtedly argue for waiting, and if there was one thing Helene knew for certain, it was that she could not wait months.

A second later she took a deep breath and hoped that Harries was a good distance from the front hall so that he wasn't shocked out of the few strands of hair he had left by the shrieks issuing from the drawing room.

On the surface of it, Gina was the more furious. She literally turned red and spluttered, unable to put a complete sentence together.

Yet Esme was, in her own way, more dangerous looking. There was something positively terrifying about her expression. Helene wouldn't have been at all surprised if her black curls suddenly turned into snakes and she transformed into Medusa herself.

"The dissipated fiend!" Esme said between clenched teeth. "How dare he even suggest such a revolting thing to you. How dare he even say such a thing in a lady's—in his wife's—presence!"

"He dared," Helene said calmly. Having thought of nothing else all night long, she no longer felt any surprise over the occurrence. "Actually, it's quite like Rees, if you consider the proposition at length."

"There's no word to describe him!" Gina screeched.

But Esme was looking at Helene, and something in her eyes made Helene shift uneasily in her seat. "And just what did you tell him in reply, Helene?"

"That's hardly the question, is it?" Gina said. "The question is—The question is—" But she stopped and blinked at Helene. "Of course you said no."

Helene stirred her tea with a small silver spoon and then put it precisely to the side. "Not exactly."

"You cannot enter that house under those circumstances!" Esme said, her voice low and fierce. "I will not allow it."

"While your concern is endearing," Helene replied, "I am a grown woman."

"You wouldn't!" Gina gasped. "You'll be ruined. Absolutely ruined! And that's not to mention that the very idea is revolting."

"I agreed to his proposition, with certain conditions."

"Let's hear them," Esme said grimly.

"I shall enter the house for one month only, and no one is to know of my presence."

"Unlikely," Esme said. "It's bound to get out."

"Rees has few servants, and no callers. I shall take a hackney to the house and live as a recluse."

"This is all irrelevant," Gina said. "You can hide in the attics if you want to, Helene, but you're still entering the house—living in your own house—with a nightwalker!"

"She's not quite so repellent. I did meet Miss McKenna, if you remember. I judged her remarkably young, and certainly not practiced in her profession, if you can call it that. I do believe that she was, in fact, merely an opera singer before Rees debauched her."

"Yet a brief encounter with the woman was enough to send you fleeing into the country," Esme reminded her. "And now you are considering sharing a house with her? With your husband's *mistress*? Have you gone raving mad, Helene?"

"Perhaps. Sometimes I think so." Helene bit her lip hard. "I want that child. I will go to any lengths to have a child. Any lengths."

"Every sensibility must revolt against the notion!" Gina said, shuddering.

"True. I know it's a horrifying proposition. I would not have told either of you, except I could not imagine how I was to explain my ensuing delicate condition."

"Of course you had to tell us!" Esme said, crossly. "Lord knows, I certainly engaged in some deranged behavior myself in the past."

"Nothing like this," Helene said.

"True." Esme gazed at her in wonderment. "How you've changed, Helene! Just consider your customary severe attitude towards my wicked ways. Why, I've never had to develop much of a barometer of societal opinion because I could count on you to know precisely how little the *ton* would approve of an action. But now—"

Helene smiled. "Perhaps I'm doing this for the sake of our friendship. Now you need no longer feel like the wicked one between us."

"I think you're both missing the point," Gina broke in. "How are you going to get rid of her, Helene?"

"What do you mean?"

"I mean the strumpet, of course. How are you going to get rid of her?"

"Why should I?" Helene said, shrugging. "I did force Rees to promise that he wouldn't frequent her bed—"

"Ug!" Gina wailed. "I don't even want to *think* about that!"

"I apologize," Helene said calmly. "I am rather used to considering the whereabouts of my husband's mistress. For all I know, she's sitting at my dressing table as we speak."

"Gina's right," Esme said. "You'll have to get rid of the woman. It's the only way to protect your reputation. The moment she's out of the house, your presence there is acceptable. The gossips will, no doubt, be fascinated to learn that you've returned to the house, given the very public state of your separation from Rees, but reconciliation is certainly acceptable."

"And how on earth am I to dispense with Rees's mistress?"

"Perhaps she'll just leave," Gina said hopefully. "After she meets you, I mean."

"Nonsense," Esme said. "You'll have to buy her off, of course. How long has she been in the house?"

Helene put down her cup with a little clink. "Two years and three months."

"Oh," Esme said, clearly taken aback by Helene's precision. "Well, you will make her a persuasive offer. Monetary, of course."

"I suppose I could do that," Helene said, biting her lip. "I could use my allowance. I rather like the idea of using the money Rees gives me, as a matter of fact."

"And she will accept it," Gina put in. "No woman in her right mind would choose to live with Rees." She broke off. "That was inexcusably rude, Helene, please forgive me."

"True, none the less," Helene said with a smile.

"If you give her a goodly sum," Gina continued, "she'll likely return to whatever village she was from, and you need never think of her again."

"That would be . . . pleasant," Helene said. "Very pleasant. I will try to find an occasion to make such an offer."

Esme shuddered. "How you will survive in that house, I don't know. I think I would succumb to the vapors, and I don't have a sensitive constitution."

"I will not succumb to the vapors," Helene said, and the clear determination in her voice rang like a bell. "But I will return to this house in a delicate condition. I have made up my mind."

Esme shook her head. "I just can't get over how much you've changed, Helene. I feel like a character in that Shakespeare play, the one where the Bottom appears out of the woods with a donkey's head instead of his own: "Oh Helene, thou art changed! Bless thee, thou art translated!"

Helene smiled at her. "You're lucky that we are old friends, otherwise I should take exception to being likened to an ass."

"Well, if the head fits!" Esme said, laughing as she dodged a small cushion thrown in her direction.

## 17

*Trouble Comes in Many Guises*

It wasn't until evening of the next day that Tom truly understood just how much trouble he was in. The butler's errant niece had returned, thank goodness, and Meggin was tucked away in the nursery, still clutching Lina's tippet.

"She seemed to like it so much," Lina told him, "that I gave it to her. I remember quite well the joy I felt on first feeling silk next to my skin." The smile that curled her lips sent a stab of pure fire down Tom's legs.

He was indeed in trouble.

Rees had appeared only briefly at supper, laconically announcing that Helene would return to the house in three to four days. He bolted his food and went back into the salon, from which they could hear discordant fragments of piano music emerging.

That left Tom and Lina together. It was, literally, the first time he'd been alone with a woman in six years, since the night before he took his vows when he'd said good-bye to a certain Betsy Prowd. He looked up from his almond custard to find Lina's brown eyes fixed on him. She bewildered him. One moment she was a little brandy breasted songbird that looked as if it would nestle sweetly in one's hand; the next she was like a scarlet redbreast, shaking her feathers with all the insouciance of a *très-coquette*.

"What made you decide to become a priest?" she asked. Her voice was as clear and fluting as a bell. It made him wonder how it would sound calling his name, if they were in bed together.

Tom dragged his attention back to her face. "There was never really any question but that I would," he explained. "My profession was established long before I can remember. The church is a common occupation for the younger son of a nobleman."

"You wouldn't have chosen to go into the church on your own?"

"I don't know that I would have," he said slowly. "But that doesn't mean that I'm not happy now."

She wrinkled her nose. "Drafty old vicarage?"

"There are a few drafts, but—"

"Leaky roof in the springtime?"

"There is—"

"Far too many rooms to keep clean, and just one little maid, trundling about with blue fingers, and not enough money to buy coal!"

"No," he said startled. "It's not at all like that."

Her mouth curled into a teasing smile. "Have you heard the jest about the vicar who wandered into a bawdy house, Reverend?"

"I wish you wouldn't call me by my title."

"I apologize. In that case, Mr. Holland, have you heard the jest about the misinformed vicar?"

"No," he said in a measured voice. "Would I like it?"

Lina looked at the man before her. He was like a younger version of Rees, without the barbed tongue. He had the same tousled hair, and the same broad shoulders, but without the sharp edges. "Don't you like jests?" she asked, picking up a slice of hothouse peach and slipping it slowly between her lips. He was watching. This was more fun than she'd had since she left the stage.

"Yes, but not those that you're wishing to tell me," he said, calmly selecting an apple from the dish before them.

"And what kind are those?" she asked saucily.

"I suspect your plan is to tell me jokes not suitable for a vicar's ears," he replied. "But I know those jokes, and I don't find most of them funny. They're all to do with men making themselves like sailing ships and spending their main masts, and I can't say the subject interests me."

Lina burst out laughing. "I don't know any shipping jests, Mr. Holland."

"But undoubtedly your jokes are of the same caliber, Miss McKenna."

She tossed a grape into her mouth. "It's too late to save me, as they say, Reverend, so best leave the chastisement to your congregation. Why don't you think of your time in London as an education in improper pursuits?"

Tom felt a wave of black rage. She was so beautiful, so witty, so utterly charming: how dare his brother have taken her to his house and made her into a concubine?

She seemed to guess his thoughts. "I expect you'd like a full confession," she said with a little pout, "but you shan't have it. I will tell you, though, in case you plan to lambaste your brother, that Rees effected no corruption. To be frank, Reverend, I lost my maidenly virtue back in my own home village." Her eyes twinkled mischievously. "There are some of us who never agree with societal strictures. Haven't you noticed that yourself? I listened to my mama's dictates, but I couldn't picture myself marrying one of the boys I grew up around. And I couldn't see any good reason why I shouldn't bed Hugh Sutherland, if I wished to. So I did bed him, and then I turned down his request for my hand, and then I left. And I haven't any desire to return. I simply didn't fit in."

"I suppose you couldn't return now," Tom said, hardening his heart against her tempting gaiety. "'Tis base to be a whore, after all. It would cause your mother some grief."

Her fingers froze for a moment. Then: "Am I that name, John?"

"I see you know *Othello*. But why are you calling me John?" he asked, irritated beyond all control. He drained his glass of wine and poured another.

"You *are* John the Baptist, are you not?" she said. In the candlelight, the skin of her throat glowed a creamy delicate white. And her throat led down to sweet mounds of breast, looking like snow against the dull gold of her gown. "I rather think that young Meggin called it right," she said, and the husky amusement in her voice had deepened. "If I am the Whore of Babylon, perhaps I should serve as your temptation. Or have I got it wrong? It *was* John who was tempted in the desert was it not?"

"No," he said, "it wasn't. And I believe you know that as well as I do, given the rather surprising extent of biblical knowledge you've already demonstrated."

"Ah, it must have been John who lived in the desert for years. Now how long did you say that you'd been a priest, John?"

He met her eyes. Hers were deep pools of chocolate-brown mischief, and yet with a hint of vulnerability. That label *whore* had stung.

"I shouldn't have called you that word," he said. "I wished to hurt you. I'm sorry."

"It was very difficult to make my way to London on my own," she said casually, peeling herself an apple, her hands absolutely steady. "Do you know, I actually contemplated, one night, whether it was better to live poor or die in sin? But I chose to live poor, Reverend. Believe it or not, when I chose to move to this house, it was because I thought myself in love with your brother." Her smile was self-mocking now.

"I'm sure that he feels the same," Tom said, cursing Rees.

"No. He never did, although he might have experienced some sort of temporary infatuation with my voice." There wasn't a trace of self-pity in her voice.

"I—I'm sorry," Tom said finally.

She shrugged. "He's kind enough. He's a gentleman, your brother, for all that most of the nobility think he's a degenerate. He has rather wished I wasn't living in the house any time in the last two years, but he's caught by his own integrity, you see. He can't put me out because he's honorable, and he doesn't really want me in, because he's honorable."

"And do you wish to leave?" One of the candles was guttering, casting her half of the table into a shadow that hid the sparkle in her eyes and made her look as if . . . but he couldn't stand the idea that his cursed brother had broken her heart.

"I believe I shall return to the opera house in the very near future, and yes, I will welcome that."

"But do you like London? Has it been as enthralling as you hoped to find it, back when you were a girl in Scotland?"

"No," she said. "London is disappointing, like so many things in life. Don't you find it so, John?"

"On occasion."

"I find it so virtually all the time," she said almost dreamily. "Your brother is a prime case in point. Disappointing."

"I'm sorry," Tom said, feeling a surge of gratitude for his brother's shortcomings.

She stood up. "I am worn quite ragged with all this confession, John. I believe I shall retire."

He came to his feet, and walked to her side in order to escort her from the room. He stopped her with a touch on her arm, just as she was about to open the door. "Please don't call me John."

She looked up at him, and there wasn't a hint of sadness in her eyes; he must have imagined it. Instead, she came up on the tips of her toes and brushed her mouth across his. Tom froze.

"Don't do that," he said, and he was shocked by the roughness of his own voice.

She didn't seem to realize her own danger. She thought it was all a game. "Tempting the vicar?" she said pertly. "A crime, I'm sure. But I never could tempt *you* into sin, Mr. Holland. From everything Rees told me about you, back a few years ago when we used to converse, you are the perfect son."

Tom tightened his jaw and kept his hands at his sides.

"Always kind, always forgiving, always Christian. I suspect Meggin is not the first waif you've rescued. If I remember the stories correctly, you've never put a foot wrong, isn't that right?" She smiled up at him, as seductive a woman as he'd ever seen in his life. In fact, he had never seen anyone like her.

And just like that, he snapped. He put out his hands and drew her into his arms. His blood was pounding so that all he could hear was the roar of seawater in his ears. And all he could see was the tempting sweetness of her mouth.

It was the kind of kiss that brings drowning men back from the edge of death. He pulled her against him hard, relishing every inch of silky satin flesh, so giving to his hardness, so very unlike his own body. He even pulled her off her feet because he had to have her closer, all that soft, warm flesh. And she didn't protest; instead she melted against him, curling her arms around his neck, letting him ravish her mouth. After a bit, she started teasing him with her tongue until he growled and sucked her tongue into his mouth. She made a little noise, a funny little hoarse noise but it didn't sound like a giggle.

Still, that tiny noise reminded him of where he was. Of who he was. He put her back on her feet and tried to think of an apology. If there was an apology for that sort of behavior.

But she cut him off. "Am I to suppose that the Baptist has succumbed to temptation?" There was a trace of wonder in her voice, and the words seemed to hang on the air. For a moment, she stood there, staring up at him with her beautiful lips stung by his kiss and her eyes all lazy with pleasure.

Then she turned and was gone.

# 18

## *Dancing in the Desert*

*T*wo days later, Tom was fairly well convinced he might as well be John the Baptist. Lina made an excellent Salome: everywhere he turned, she seemed to be dancing, just like Salome before the King, and he had the feeling he was about to see his head on a platter. She left the room before him, and the only thing he could think about for an hour afterwards was the curve of her waist. She bent to pick up Meggin, giving him a view of the deep hollow between her breasts, and Tom could scarcely breathe for the hunger that swept over him. She smiled at him over the table, and her skin gleamed bronze in the candlelight. He wanted to lick it, all of it. And when she touched him lightly on the arm, and said cheekily that she had been practicing the dance of the seven veils, his whole body went rigid with the effort not to pull her into his arms and kiss her silliness into silence.

So he did the only thing he could think of: retreated to his bedchamber and prayed for help. At first, he prayed for guidance. Then he gave that up and started just praying for self-control. For help.

On Tom's third evening in London, Rees announced that he would begin to train Lina in some aria or other. Tom trailed into the sitting room after them even though he was conscious that an ice water bath was a better proposition. When Lina started to sing, his heart almost stopped from the pure beauty of it. Her voice fluted higher and higher, dancing in the rafters of the room.

"Her voice is incredible," he breathed to Rees, sitting next to him.

But Rees was frowning at his score. "Lina!" he said, cutting her off. "Try that last bar with the count as written. It's a dotted quarter and an eighth note, not two quarter notes."

Lina nodded, but her eyes slid to Tom's, holding him prisoner. She took a deep breath and began to sing again. For a moment it looked as if her breasts would surely topple from her bodice. Tom found himself tensing, as if to jump forward and protect her, shield her beauty—and from whom?

There was no one in the room but himself and her protector. His own brother. Tom felt a surge of primitive hatred, one that went back more than twenty years, a gift from their father. The old earl had reveled in creating divisions between his two sons. He whipped them with his taunts from the moment they were out of the nursery. Who knew why? From the distance of the five years since the earl's death, Tom rather thought that their father was afraid that they might present a unified front and rebel against him. Not that they ever had. Obedient as hunting dogs, they turned out exactly as he had prophesied. The earl had told Tom that he was too wet to marry, and that he would end up in a minor parish, unable to get his spineless self into a sufficiently political position to achieve a large parish. That was true enough. Tom couldn't seem to bring himself to flatter the right people, to grease the right palm, to take those steps that would have him rising toward being a bishop. The fact that he loved his small parish and his wayward parishioners wouldn't have mattered to their father.

"I suppose you'll marry one of those prim do-gooders who flock in churchyards," their father had sneered the day Tom fastened on his collar. "Thank God one of my sons has red blood in his veins."

Something died in Tom's heart every time Rees snapped at Lina, every time she took a deep breath and started singing again. If he was the man his father had prophesied, Rees was exactly the rakehell that their father had wanted him to be: a man of vicious habits, a man who would bring a young girl into his house and make her his mistress, a man who would force his wife to return to the same house.

Lina was singing the same bar for the tenth time. Her voice was not soaring quite as easily now. There was a little line between her brows, and she'd stopped throwing Tom teasing glances. Surely she was getting overtired.

"Damn it all," Rees bellowed, "don't you listen to anything I say, Lina? Read your score. That trill begins on E-flat, not G-natural. I shouldn't have to be your *répéteteur*, teaching you each aria note by note!"

She glared at him and her soft mouth trembled. Tom longed to spring to his feet and take her in his arms, but he stayed where he was. Lina was Rees's mistress. Not his to protect.

With very little emotion, she picked up her glass of wine and tossed it in their direction, stalking out the door.

"For Christ's sake," Rees muttered, shaking the papers he was holding, and paying no attention to the red splotches marring his shirt.

Tom wiped the wine from his face. "You drove her too hard. Do you have to be so brutal?"

"Stay out of what you don't understand," Rees growled.

"I understand that Lina has the voice of an angel," Tom said hotly. "Yet you keep shouting at her. I don't know why she puts up with it."

"She has to. I'm trying to prepare her to sing a lead role." Rees tossed the papers on a stool. "Lina has a gorgeous voice but she doesn't have the drive to be a great singer. If I don't prod her, she won't practice. You saw her. She pays no attention to the score, even when I'm standing before her, shouting the notes."

"You made her sing one phrase over and over!"

"She should be doing that on her own: over and over until she could sing it correctly in her sleep. But she doesn't want it enough." He rubbed some drops of wine from his forehead wearily. "I know you'd like to make me out to be some sort of miscreant, Tom. But in this case, I'm actually doing my best."

"I fail to see how shouting is doing your best."

"I've promised her the lead in my next opera. She's not ready, and she doesn't deserve it. But if I can somehow whip her into shape before the management realizes that she's inadequate, and perhaps even make her smooth enough so that she's a success—and that's doubtful—the victory might just carry her into another lead role. After that, it's out of my hands."

"Oh."

"You always see things in black and white." Rees was leaning his head back against the couch, staring up at the ceiling. "If I'm shouting at Lina, I must be evil."

"What about you?" Tom asked boldly. "Did you always know you were a rakehell, or did you have to be instructed in your wicked ways by father?"

"I suppose I received instruction," Rees said, sounding rather bored. He was still staring up at the ceiling.

"How well we both understood our orders."

Rees turned his head so that his eyes flicked over Tom's face. "Is that why you're here, then?" he drawled. "Are you sick of being the godly vicar, and you've come to the house of sin for lessons in titillation?"

"No!" Tom said, horrified to find that some part of his soul leapt at the idea. Could that be the truth?

"Good," Rees said, turning his head and staring back up at the ceiling. "Because for all Lina looks like a little strumpet, she's not."

"I would *never* treat her so," Tom said, and the memory of the way he had kissed Lina, the way he had pulled her body against him, lent urgency to his tone.

"I didn't mean to imply such a thing," Rees said, sounding utterly exhausted. "I'd better take a nap. I have to work all night."

"Is there anything I can do to help?"

Rees was already off the couch and heading for the door. "If you could keep Lina out of my hair tomorrow, I'd be grateful," he said over his shoulder. "She has an annoying habit of wishing to leave the house, and she expects to have an escort."

Tom sat there by himself for a while, staring at the washes of paper surrounding his boots and thinking about temptation.

But thinking about temptation, let alone praying for help, never seemed to help much when he was faced with the living, breathing woman herself.

He was walking down the corridor toward his bedchamber when she opened her door and slammed right into him. He drew in a deep breath. Her curvy, fragrant body seemed to leave an imprint on his skin.

"God's bodkins!" she said, pulling back. "How you startled me!"

He stared at her, and the desire in his heart must have been written on his face, because she turned a delicate rose pink.

"Lina," he said and his voice came out with a harshness that not one of his parishioners had ever heard. "If you don't want to be kissed, you should run back into that room of yours."

Instead, Lina raised her fingers to his cheek. "Kiss me, then," she said in a voice like velvet.

But he didn't, holding back due to a grain of wisdom, some shred of sanity.

"*Tom*," she added, using his Christian name rather than the bevy of labels she gave him. Not John the Baptist, not Reverend, not Mr. Holland. *Tom.*

His lips came to hers with the hot, insistent hunger of a starving man. And she succumbed to him with the same fervor, the silky touch of an arm around his neck setting his skin on fire. Even that fugitive touch made him understand for the first time in his life what a blessing it is for a man and a woman to be unclothed together. But he didn't—couldn't— think of that or he might sweep her straight to his chamber.

So he contented himself instead with a rough, demanding kiss. This wasn't the kiss of a timid vicar, the succor of the poor and the rescuer of wounded animals. This was the action of a licentious rakehell, a man driven by lust, a man who took no prisoners. His mouth scorched across hers, a merciless barbarian with his wild-eyed queen, a man who invaded first, and asked questions afterward.

Still, he was a barbarian in control of himself. He didn't let his hands roam. Instead he told her with every stroke of his tongue just what he'd like to be doing to the tender undercurve of her breast, to that sweet spot at the inside of her elbow, to the curve of her hips.

It was an endless kiss, because Tom knew under it all, that when the kiss was over, he would go to his chamber by himself. So the barbarian fought with himself, keeping his hand on the Barbarian Queen's back, never allowing himself even to pull her luscious body against his.

Lina had twined her arms around his neck, and her fingers were compulsively clutching his curls. Through the hot waves of desire that kept breaking over him and threatening to make him buckle at the knees, he realized that her breathing was quick and rapid. Her hands began to wander down his back, a path that threatened to erase Tom's control.

"Lina," he said in a hoarse groan, tearing his mouth from hers.

She didn't open her eyes. He wanted to see languorous pleasure there, so he dropped kisses on her eyes, trying to calm the pounding of his heart, giving her space to recover.

"Reverend," she finally said, her voice just a wisp of sound.

His heart dropped into his boots. Reverend again. He was *Tom* no longer.

"My name is Tom!" he said, and the roughness in his voice would have been, again, unknown to his flock.

"If I call you Tom," she whispered, finally opening her eyes and looking at him, "will you kiss me all night?"

He froze, his hands on her back. He was pretty sure that the agony in his body was echoed on his face. "I can't sleep with you," he said harshly. "Never mind the fact that you belong to my brother—"

"Your brother hasn't entered my bedchamber in months," she said, tracing his cheek with her fingertips. Her very touch burned his skin. "And not very often even before that."

"That's not the crucial issue," he managed. "I couldn't sleep with you, because I don't"—he gathered strength because it was truly one of the hardest things he'd ever said—"I don't believe in engaging in intimacies outside of marriage."

Could Salome have ever been so beautiful?

"Are not kisses intimacies?" she asked, her eyes searching his.

"Not inadvisable ones," he managed. Now her small hands were wandering across his chest. "But you are touching me inappropriately, Lina."

Her hands flew away, although she didn't look chastised.

He nodded and put her away. She didn't hear him say "God help me," because he was already halfway down the corridor toward his bedchamber.

# 19

## In Which the Household Gathers

*H*elene arrived at the house in a hackney. This time she didn't even bother having her maid knock on the door; she simply told Saunders to push it open. Saunders had been dumbstruck from the moment Helene informed her that she intended to return to her husband's house. Now she stared around the antechamber of the house as if she expected the devil himself to make his presence known by waving a forked tail around the corner.

"Where's the butler?" she finally asked in a hushed tone, for all the world as if they were visiting the Regent himself. Helene had taken off her pelisse and was looking around for somewhere to put it that didn't appear to be too dusty.

"Lord knows," she said. "His name is Leke, and he's not a bad sort. But I can't imagine how he manages to run this house with virtually no staff."

Saunders was beginning to see the dirt clinging to the corners of the entryway. Her lip curled. "Harries would keep the house clean, if he had to do it on his own hands and knees."

"No doubt we'll have to do a thorough cleaning of my room," Helene said grimly, heading up the stairs.

When they reached the next floor, Saunders paused, but Helene turned without a word of explanation and kept climbing. She hadn't told Saunders the unpleasant truth about Rees's refusal to dislodge the strumpet. It caused enough commotion when she announced she was returning to her husband. The truth was demented. *She* was demented.

No one seemed to understand that she wanted a baby more than anything else, more than her dignity. If she had to trade a brief period of humiliation for a lifetime with a child, then so be it. Besides, she was hopeful that the presence of Rees's brother—a vicar, after all!—would anoint the household with some level of dignity.

The chamber next to the nursery wasn't terrible. It was large, with windows from which one could just glimpse the trees of St. James Park. "Look at this, Saunders!" Helene said, looking out, "I didn't have this view on the second floor."

"I don't like it," Saunders said, stumping around the room and looking with distaste at the furnishings. "I don't understand why you're not in the countess's bedchamber, my lady."

Leke had obviously made an effort to fit out the room as befits a countess; Helene recognized the beautiful Turkish rug that used to adorn the back sitting room. The bed had obviously belonged to the nanny, but he had found a dressing table and a rather motley collection of furniture and arranged them into a lady's boudoir. Helene sat down on a velvet sofa. "There's another lady in that chamber, Saunders."

"Another lady?" she said. "Is it the earl's mother, then?"

"No. She is a friend of Lord Godwin's," Helene replied.

Saunders generally offered any comments in a consciously genteel tone of voice. But shock brought out her Bankside origins directly. "He never has that singer here while you're in residence!" she gasped. And when Helene nodded, she pulled open the door so violently that it slammed against the wall. "I'll find a hackney on the corner, my lady!"

"I'm staying," Helene said quietly.

"Never! You're addled!" Saunders stared at her, eyes large. "Your mother doesn't know of your husband's depravity!"

"I trust you not to tell her." Helene took a deep breath. "Saunders, I need to be here, and Rees's mistress is really irrelevant. We will stay only until I find myself with child. Do you understand? Then we return to my mother's, and no one the wiser. Remember, no one except my closest friends knows I'm in this house. Callers will be informed that I am indisposed."

She looked directly at Saunders. "Obviously, the scandal that would ensue from people knowing of my presence here would be staggering."

"I can't even imagine," the maid said, gasping a bit.

"I trust you. There's no one else I could entrust with the truth."

Saunders blinked rapidly and straightened her shoulders. "Well, my lady, of course I should never wish to fail your confidence in me. You can trust me, naturally, but—"

"I am counting on you," Helene said earnestly.

"But it's impossible!" she protested. "How on earth are you to speak to each other? How will you take meals?"

"I shall take most of my meals in my room," Helene replied. "And since I have promised to help his lordship with his current opera, I doubt that I shall have much interaction with Miss McKenna at all."

Saunders slowly closed the door. "Thank goodness we packed all those gowns from Madame Rocque." Madame had delivered a season's worth of gowns in the past two weeks, all constructed with the same principles in mind: weightlessness and a vivid display of Helene's slender form.

"I hadn't thought to wear them here," Helene said, startled.

"That you will," Saunders stated. "I'm not having a light-heeled wench come out more elegantly dressed than the countess herself."

"I've met Rees's friend, Saunders. She's very young."

Saunders narrowed her eyes. "Face paints as well."

Helene sighed. "In that case, we should probably begin unpacking, because Rees generally eats the evening meal at an earlier hour than we're used to."

In truth, she was only barely ready when a dull gong downstairs signaled the dinner hour. Helene looked at herself in the slightly cracked glass of a dressing table that Leke had obviously found in the attic and slung into her bedchamber. She had chosen a simple gown of white muslin, embroidered at the hem and around the sleeves with gold thread. Its great secret was that the muslin was as light as thistledown and constructed in such a way that the hem rippled out around her ankles, and even fell to a small train in the back that floated behind her. The bodice wasn't low, nor were the sleeves uncomfortably small. It was comfortable, airy, dignified—and yet, ravishing, as the Earl of Mayne might say.

Helene smiled at herself. Thinking of the way Mayne had called her *enchanting*, and then touched her cheek, she found the courage to go downstairs.

If the truth be told, Helene had had very little contact with strumpets. She knew they wore garish colors on their cheeks, and gowns that barely hid their nipples. She knew that they pleasured men. She had met Rees's opera singer two years ago, when Rees brought her to the opera and to their box. Helene shuddered at the mere memory. She had made stilted conversation with Rees, while Major Kersting conversed with the singer.

As Leke opened the door to the sitting room, Helene had to pause to collect herself. Lina McKenna had changed. This was no untried green girl.

Sitting next to Rees's brother was one of the most beautiful women Helene had ever seen in her life. Her hair was swirled on top of her head in a gleaming mass of brown curls; Helene felt an instant stab of pain for the loss of her own hair. Her eyes were glowing with intelligence, curiosity and laughter. And her evening gown was neither outrageously revealing nor did it exhibit more décolletage than might any young woman in polite society. But she was obviously endowed with a bosom that rivaled Esme's.

Helene nearly turned and ran straight back to her room. How could she sit in the same room with this ravishing creature—she, a dried up old stick? Why, if Miss McKenna were brought out as a debutante, she would have been judged a diamond of the first water.

But then Rees looked up and saw her. It was just a glance, but his eyes dropped from her hair to her toes. Helene couldn't read his reaction, but she didn't have to. He would be disdainful. Why should she care if she presented an unappetizing contrast to his mistress? After all, in comparison to the Earl of Mayne's sleek beauty, Rees's shaggy hair, great burly body, and all those heavy muscles were most unattractive.

She walked into the room and Rees's brother jumped to his feet and came toward her, holding out his hands. "Helene," Tom said, kissing her hand quickly, "you look exquisite."

She beamed at him. He had the same sweet brown eyes that she remembered from the first year of her and Rees's marriage. Truly, he was a very good-looking man: rather like Rees, except he was groomed and civilized. "It's lovely to see you again, Mr. Holland." And she really meant it.

"Please call me Tom," he said, squeezing her hands. "Are you quite certain that you wish to be here under these circumstances?"

She smiled again, but knew that this smile didn't reach her eyes. "Rees and I have an understanding," she said, turning to the couch.

Miss McKenna had risen as well. The better to show off her remarkable figure, Helene thought to herself sourly. "Lady Godwin," she said, dropping into a curtsy that would have sufficed when meeting the Queen, "may I say that it is a surprise to meet you?"

Helene nodded in reply. "I find myself in the grip of something like amazement as well." She could not curtsy to her husband's mistress; she simply could not. Instead she sat down and found that she was shaking. She gripped her hands tightly, in her lap.

"I'll bring you a brandy," her brother-in-law said in a low voice. "I'll be right back."

Helene never drank spirits, but she swallowed the whole glassful and concentrated on the burning liquid running down her throat. If she had had any idea that Miss McKenna was so beautiful, Rees would have had to drag her on the back of his horse before she agreed. When she met Rees's opera singer two years ago, Miss McKenna was a mere lass, a tongue-tied girl, whereas now she was formidable.

The brandy settled in her stomach, giving her Dutch courage. I can do this for one month, Helene told herself. One month, that's all. One month. She and Esme had decided that Rees had to be recruited to do his husbandly duty once a day. For a month.

Tom brought her another glass of brandy, and Helene drained it, sending another path of raw fire blazing down into her stomach. "Steady now," he said in a vicarish type of voice.

He truly was a sweet man. "What a shame that I didn't marry you," she said, with a little hiccup. "You have the same dark hair and eyes as my dissolute husband over there, and you would never—never—"

"Probably not," Tom said, patting her hand again. "But I don't know a thing about music either."

"Oh," Helene said. "That's a shame." She was beginning to feel altogether more cheerful. So what if her husband had a ladybird next to him on the couch? Why should it bother her? She could have had the Earl of Mayne or any number of others offering her compliments, if she so wished.

She got up with just the slightest stumble and walked back over toward the fireplace. "I forgot to say hello to you," she said to Rees.

"Helene," he said. Far from cuddling up to his mistress, he was scribbling on a piece of paper and looked utterly unaware of the tensions circling through the room.

Helene seated herself next to Lina, ignoring Tom's little gestures of anxiety. "We probably should discuss a few things," she said, trying very hard to remember what they were.

Lina's eyes were bubbling with amusement in a way that reminded Helene of Esme. *Not* that Esme was an improper woman. No. No indeed. She'd lost track of her thought again.

"I believe we should have supper now," Tom said, rather desperately. "Rees, why don't you summon Leke and tell him that we must eat?"

Rees shook his head without looking up. "Cook and Cook alone determines when the household sits to a meal. Leke will fetch us when the food is ready."

"That's a very nice gown you're wearing," Helene told Miss McKenna.

Miss McKenna blinked. I suppose, Helene thought to herself triumphantly, she expected me to be outraged, and now she doesn't know what to make of me.

"I think we should discuss Rees," Helene added, without waiting for a response. The brandy was giving her a lovely warm feeling of confidence. "If it is quite all right with you, I would like to borrow him once a day."

Tom was scolding his brother in an undertone. Helene heard him say, "Well, why didn't you tell me that she never drinks spirits?"

"From what I remember, I only need around five minutes of Rees's time," she told Miss McKenna. "That truly is a lovely gown, by the way." It was an odd color of orange that gave Lina's skin a tawny glow.

"Sometimes Rees is good for seven minutes," Miss McKenna said with just a hint of laughter in her voice. "I would give him the benefit of the doubt."

"Seven minutes!" Helene exclaimed. "How nice to know that one's husband has matured a whole two minutes in the past nine years."

"I like a man to have ambition, don't you?" Miss McKenna said, taking a sip of wine.

Suddenly Helene's eyes met those of her husband's mistress and they broke into laughter. Tom made a gulping noise. Rees looked up from his paper for a moment and shrugged.

"It shouldn't discompose your day at all," Helene said.

"I doubt that it will," Miss McKenna replied. "Your gown is also very lovely. Is it from Madame Rocque?"

"Indeed," Helene said. She decided not to nod again because it made her head feel quite dizzy. "I think I may have tried on your gown, but I looked a veritable scarecrow in it."

Miss McKenna's eyes had lost the sharp edge they had when Helene first entered the room. Helene found that now that she was used to Miss McKenna's startling beauty, she was taken aback by her composure. She was almost ladylike in her demeanor. If she hadn't known to the contrary, Helene would have assumed she was a rather formidable, if young, member of the *ton*. How very peculiar.

"How is your mother, Lady Godwin?" Tom said.

"Oh, she's very well," Helene said, with just the tiniest, ladylike hiccup. "But you might as well call me Helene. I am your sister-in-law, and after this, no one can say that we're not on intimate terms!"

Leke arrived at that moment. "Dinner is served," he said, in a voice of deep gloom. He had rather enjoyed the martyrdom of remaining in Earl Godwin's employ when the rest of the servants fled a house of sin. But even he was wondering whether this situation was too much for his sense of propriety. It just didn't suit his nerves to find a mistress and a wife sitting next to each other and chatting, for all the world as if they were bosom friends.

## 20

### *Inebriation Is Sometimes a Wise Choice*

*H*elene sobered up slightly during the meal. But only slightly. At some point she realized that even another sip of red wine was going to leave her with a pounding headache in the morning, but she ignored the thought. Best to get through the evening, and let the morning worry about itself.

Rees sat at the top of the table, scowling at a score he had carried into the room. The conversation, such as it was, was carried by Lina, Tom, and Helene. After Leke had removed the pudding, even that chatter seemed to finally wilt. Helene took a deep breath and turned to Lina.

"If you will excuse us," she said politely, "I shall return him in five minutes."

"Please, take seven," Lina said with a twinkle.

A little smile wobbled on Helene's lips. Was it too, too odd to feel respect for her husband's mistress?

"Rees!" she said, standing up.

He stuffed the paper into his pocket. "Right," he replied. He showed no sign whatsoever of giving a damn about Lina's and Helene's remarks about the brevity of his bedroom activities.

But instead of heading up the stairs, he walked across the hall into the music room—well, the room that used to be their sitting room and was now occupied by three pianos.

"Rees," Helene said, trailing after him, "what on earth are you doing?"

"I need to show you this score," he said impatiently, running a hand through his hair. "We'll get to the rest of it in a few minutes."

"I would rather do the rest, as you put it, *now*," Helene insisted. She certainly didn't want to lose the little curtain of inebriation that was making the whole evening seem rather funny. And she particularly wanted to blunt the experience of bedding Rees, even if it was only a matter of seven minutes.

But Rees had strode to the piano and was leafing through sheets of paper. Helene walked cautiously into the room. Paper swirled around her feet with the same dancing motion as the hem of her skirt. She tried kicking a few in the air. "How do you live with all this mess?" she asked.

"It only appears messy," Rees said with an obvious disregard for the truth.

Helene laughed. "There's no method in this madness." She kicked a few more papers into the air.

"Don't do that!" he said sharply. "And it is organized. Drafts are on the floor. The various acts of the opera are arranged on the sofa."

"Sofa?" Helene wandered over and discovered that the hideous sofa given to them by her Aunt Margaret was actually still in the room, although buried under high stacks of paper. "You must have most of the opera here, Rees. I don't know why you can't be ready on time."

"Namby-pamby stuff," he said, hunching his shoulder. "I haven't written a decent line in the last year." He played a few bars. "What do you think of this?" he said.

Even tipsy, Helene retained full musical capability. "I can't say I like it over much," she said, wandering over and putting her elbows inelegantly on the top of the piano.

"That's because you're hearing it out of context," Rees said. "Actually, it's one of the better pieces I have. Here, I'll play from the beginning."

He poised his hands over the keyboard and then let them fall. Helene allowed the music to pour through her and watched his hands. They were extraordinarily large and yet wondrously delicate in playing. Each finger tapered gracefully.

But when he stopped and looked up at her, Helene shook her head. "It sounds like a country ballad," she said frankly, "but not very interesting as pastoral music goes. Is it to be sung by a young girl?" Rees always wrote operas about young girls.

He nodded. "She's a princess who's run away and disguised herself as a Quaker girl."

Helene had long since learned to ignore the fragile plots that made up Rees's operas. "What's she supposed to be singing about at the moment?"

"She misses her lover, Captain Charteris. I'll play it again with the words, shall I? Fen did a good job on the libretto."

Rees had a dark, liquid singing voice as much at odds with his growling speaking voice as his elegant fingers were to his muscled body. *"While I'm waiting here in eager expectation, Always waiting for my lover to appear,"* he sang, *"In my fond and fanciful imagination, Every moment seems a year."*

"Florid Fen," Helene said with some amusement. "Move over, Rees." She sat down, nudging him slightly with her hip. "What would happen if you used an ascending scale when she was *always waiting*, and then dropped when it *seems a year*?" She tried it out on the keyboard.

Rees was frowning. "That doesn't sound very wistful."

"She needs to sound as if she's yearning, not as if she's counting the linens. Try this," and Helene started singing as she played.

Rees moved over enough to allow her plenty of room for her elbows, but not so much that he wasn't touching her hip. He liked Helene's hips, he had discovered. In fact, he rather liked her new style of dressing for that very reason. Who would have thought that Helene had such a delicate yet sensual curve to her? He remembered her as angular and almost bony. But she wasn't, not at all. She made other women seem over-fleshy.

She had stopped singing. "Sorry," Rees said. "Could you sing it again?" She turned and looked at him. That was another interesting thing about Helene. She was tall enough to look right into his eye when they sat together. And her eyes were a very curious color, a kind of gray that shaded into green. Like a cat's.

"Pay attention, Rees," she said, looking rather amused.

She sang again. "It's better," Rees said, his attention now back to the music. "But I don't think the ascending scale works."

"You need to give her a sense of longing," Helene said again. "There has to be something to mark the fact she's desperate to see her captain."

"Perhaps she's not desperate," he growled, scribbling in the notes she had suggested.

"Then why bother writing about her?" Helene said with a shrug.

Rees's hand slowed. Why indeed? That was the problem with the whole opera. The piece was set to open the opera season next year, and he didn't have more than five measures of decent melody.

"Because she's my heroine," he said, crossing out his line so violently that the foolscap tore.

"I guessed that. You always write about princesses, young ones in love."

"I have two heroines, and one is a Quaker girl, not a princess. But princesses are in fashion," he said. "Damn it, Helene, do you always have to be so critical?"

She blinked at him. She did have lovely eyes. They were rather like the surface of a stream, deep with a gold-greeny quietness.

"I didn't mean to be disparaging," she said. "I'm sorry, Rees. You speak so lightly of your own work that I'm afraid I took license."

"If anyone's going to criticize, it might as well be you," he said gloomily. "I know this is paltry stuff."

"Shall we look at it again tomorrow?"

"I expect. But it's like trying to turn horse manure into gold."

"It's not that bad!" Helene exclaimed. "There's a very sweet bit of melody *here*," and she played the phrase.

"Don't you recognize it?" Rees asked. "That's from Mozart's *Apollo and Hyacinth*. Stolen. There's not a bit of music in here that's worth the paper it's written on," he said savagely, pointing to the stack on top of the piano. "It's all claptrap."

Helene put a hand on his arm. He looked down. She had the delicate, pink-tipped fingers of a real musician, not a charlatan like himself.

"I doubt that very much," she said.

"You might as well believe it, since it's true," he snapped, getting up. He walked one length of the room, but the papers swirling around his boots bothered him so much that he stopped. "I suppose we might as well get the tupping out of the way," he growled. "I'm going to have to be up all night rewriting that score."

Helene was biting her lip. She had a beautifully plump lower lip, he noticed, as if seeing it for the first time.

"Are you sure you want to?" she asked hesitantly. "We could wait a day."

Suddenly he was quite certain that he did want to. "It's best to start as we mean to go on," he growled, striding to the door. "My room?"

"Absolutely not!" Helene said, running after him. She wasn't going to engage in any such activities if there was even the slightest possibility that Lina could overhear. "We'll go to my room."

A moment later they were standing in her bedchamber staring at the bed. "It's no narrower than the sofa at Lady Hamilton's house," Helene said, rather uncertainly. It was one thing to make plans with Esme to bed her husband once a day. It was quite another when his large body was standing next to one. It gave her an odd zinging feeling in the pit of her stomach.

"It'll have to do," Rees growled, pulling off his cravat. A moment later he was down to a shirt. Helene watched with some fascination. His legs were just as muscled as she remembered from Lady Hamilton's music room. It was rather mesmerizing to see the powerful way his thighs flexed.

"How do you take exercise?" she asked.

"I walk between my pianos. Aren't you going to undress?"

"Well, you still have on your shirt," she retorted.

"I thought you'd prefer it."

"Why?" Helene asked, wondering whether there was something about shirts that she should know. Perhaps gentlemen always wore their shirt in the presence of ladies.

"You dislike the hair on my chest," Rees pointed out.

"Oh," Helene said weakly, "I'd forgotten." How extremely rude she had been, all those years ago. She was so hurt and desperate to injure him that she would have said anything. "I'm sorry if I made inappropriate comments," she added. "I believe I was quite rude."

He just stood in the middle of the room like some sort of big jungle cat, watching her intently. "It's quite all right. I'm not wedded to my chest hair. Aren't you going to undress, Helene?"

"I can't undo this gown by myself," she said, turning about and presenting him with an elegant row of pearl buttons.

Rees began unbuttoning. Helene's hair curled into little wisps just at the nape of her neck. She wasn't wearing a chemise. He would never have thought that Helene—his Helene—would wear a gown without a chemise and, underneath it, a sturdy corset. Every newly opened button revealed skin the color of snowflowers in the mountains, skin as clear and delicate as a baby's cheek.

His fingers, Rees noticed with a flash of objectivity, were trembling. It was absurd to be excited about the prospect of bedding one's wife. One's *estranged* wife, he corrected himself. And the bedding was merely for purposes of procreation. The gown parted far enough now so that he pushed it forward, making it fall forward off her shoulders.

"You have a beautiful back, Helene," he said, startled to hear the little rasp in his voice. He had obviously gone too long without visiting Lina, if he was getting excited over one slender back, albeit with an elegant curve that made a man long to run his hands down . . . down.

Helene didn't know what to think of Rees's compliment. Last week he had said she had beautiful legs, and now she had a beautiful back as well? She clutched the gown to her bosom. But she could hardly cover up her breasts forever.

So she turned around and let the gown drop to the floor. He might as well see it all, although surely he could remember for himself.

For a moment he didn't move at all, just drew in a breath. There was something about his eyes that made Helene feel a bit better. It was only Rees, after all. What was she so worried about? She walked over and sat down on the edge of the bed, crossing her legs. She felt rather wicked, sitting naked in the presence of a man. Back when they were first married, they had conducted all intimacies discreetly under the sheets, and here they were, estranged, and she naked in front of him.

"Do take off your shirt," she suggested. It hung past his hips. She didn't care about his chest either way, but she was very curious to see whether her memory of last week could possibly be accurate.

Her memory was absolutely accurate. Helene felt a stinging tingle between her legs; it was as if her body had its own memory.

He strode over and gestured at the bed. Helene lay back, trying to quell a heartbeat of anxiety. It hadn't hurt last time. She simply had to believe that it wouldn't hurt this time as well.

"I suppose," he said rather tentatively, and then seemed to make up his mind. His hand went straight down between her legs. Helene nearly jumped out of her skin.

"What are you doing?" she gasped, and then realized she sounded critical. Esme had told her that no matter what, she couldn't sound critical or she might cause him to be unable to perform. And since the only thing she wanted from Rees was performance, she was determined to be encouraging.

He seemed to be—well, whatever he was doing, Helene had to admit that it felt—well, it felt . . . He took his hand away.

"You're not ready," he said to her. His hand lay on her thigh. It felt as if it burned into her skin.

Helene bit her lip and her heart sunk. Trust her body to have got it wrong, somehow. "What do I need to do?" she asked.

"God," Rees said, "you really don't have any idea what happens between a man and a woman, do you?"

"Well, of course I do," Helene said with some indignation. She pulled herself into a sitting position and drew up her knees so that she felt less vulnerable. "I was married to you, if you remember. I mean, I am married to you. And I have perfectly accurate memories of that year we lived together. Not to mention the fact that we reenacted the process last week."

"Nine years ago," he said slowly, running one hand down her shoulder. It felt good. She shivered a little. "That's a very long time to be without bedding." So she didn't sleep with Fairfax-Lacy last spring, he thought to himself, with a distinct throb of pleasure.

Helene smiled at him ruefully. "Yes, but as you yourself said, Rees, I'm not made for this kind of activity. I can't pretend that I missed it."

"I said a lot of stupid things," Rees said. He wrapped a finger and thumb around her wrist. "You're much more delicate than I remember."

Helene caught herself, about to say, *and you're much bigger*. But perhaps he would construe that as a derogatory remark. It might remind him of how she used to complain of being flattened by his weight.

He was running his fingers up her arm now, almost as if she were a harp. "Do you mind if I touch your breasts?" he asked suddenly, not meeting her eyes.

"But—do you want to?" she asked in astonishment.

"Very much."

"Then of course you may," she said, feeling as if she were granting him permission to smoke a cigarillo in her presence, or something equally mundane. A moment later that thought flew from her head. He touched her with the same passion and strength with which he touched the piano keys. Helene felt herself begin to tremble. It felt—it felt—odd. His fingers were sun-dusted, dark against the cream of her skin, curling around her breast. A thumb wandered across her nipple and she almost jumped out of her skin.

A little smile crossed his lips. "Do you like that?"

She opened her mouth but didn't say anything. What was she supposed to say?

He did it again, and again. "Do you like it, Helene?"

"Well," she managed, "it's acceptable." There was a sense of tension between them that made her unable to meet his eyes. She was naked. Naked! And he was caressing her breasts, almost as if she had the same—

The thought of Lina brought a chilly moment of sanity. "Do you think we could progress now?" she asked. She certainly didn't want Lina to think that she was taking up Rees's time or even, horror of horrors, deliberately detaining him in her bedchamber in order to win him back.

"Mmmm," he said, and there was something in his voice that made her whole body thrum.

This time she relaxed her legs and let him feel there without protest.

"I don't think this is going to work tonight," he said, after a moment.

Helene felt a wash of disappointment. "Why not? Is there something wrong? Can't you just go ahead?" she asked, hating the fact that she was almost pleading with him.

"Not without hurting you," he said, shaking his head. "I believe that's why bedding was so painful between us years ago, Helene. I didn't know enough to wait for your body to be ready for me."

She could feel tears pricking the back of her eyes. It was all her fault, her body's fault. "I don't mind if it's painful," she said earnestly. "Please, Rees. Please. It wasn't painful the other night, I promise!"

"I'm sorry, Helene," he said, standing up. "I just don't know very much about bedding ladies." He stared down at her. His hair had fallen over his eyes before. "You were my first, you know."

"First lady?"

"That too," he said, with a wry grin.

"I had no idea! You certainly didn't act as if it was a new experience. I thought you had slept with hundreds of women."

"I wanted you to think that, of course. Back then, I was trying to cover up every imaginable shortcoming by pretending they didn't exist."

"What shortcoming?" Helene said. She was trying to avoid looking at him. Even a glimpse of his muscled buttocks seemed to do odd things to her stomach.

"That I was a virgin, among other things," he said. His smile was sardonic. "I bungled your first time, Helene, and I'm sorry about that."

"I don't see what you could have done differently," she pointed out, liking the apology though. "From what I've heard, every woman dislikes the first time."

"Whereas men are supposed to love it," he said and there was a distinct tone of self-derision in his voice now.

"But you didn't," she said, saddened. "I'm sorry if I bungled my part in it."

He stood up and pulled on his shirt. "I should get to work," he said, obviously dismissing the whole memory from his mind. "We'll try again tomorrow night, shall we?"

"What is going to be different tomorrow?" Helene insisted, watching him pull up his smalls.

He didn't answer, so she persisted. "What's going to be different tomorrow night, Rees? We have to do this every single day in order to ensure conception."

"Every day, hmm?" A flash of amusement crossed his face.

"Unless you have some serious objection. Esme says there's no way to know what particular day is the right one, so we can't miss even one day this month or we might have to continue into next month. And if I disappear for two months people will think I've come down with consumption!"

He pulled on his boots and went to the door, then paused. "I'll speak to Darby tomorrow and ask him about bedding ladies. I've never been the sort to engage in that sort of conversation at the club and my brother—" he shrugged. "Sometimes I feel as if Tom must have been born in that black frock of his. We certainly have never discussed women."

"Thank you," she said, watching him leave.

## 21

### *Andante*

*F*our hours later, Helene realized that she was not going to be able to sleep. She had been staring at the ceiling for hours, thinking. One sentence kept sticking in her mind: Rees said he was going to ask Darby about *bedding ladies*. So what was so special about bedding a lady? What was different between her and Lina, for example? Why did *she* need special treatment? She just wanted him to do it, and get it over with.

Far downstairs, in the depths of the house, she could occasionally hear pings from the piano. Apparently Rees meant it when he said he was going to work throughout the night on that lackluster score of his.

Finally Helene rose and pulled on her dressing gown. He could damn well do to her whatever it was he did to women who weren't ladies. She marched down the stairs, her bare toes curling against the smooth wood. The house was so old that each stair dipped a bit in the middle, presumably from the tramping feet of Jacobean Hollands, making their way up to their wives' chambers.

Outside the music room, she paused. He was still working on the same piece but it sounded a bit more adventurous now. Finally she pushed open the door. He threw up his head immediately and stared at her. The room was lit by two candelabra perched on top of the piano. His hair was standing on end, and there were black circles under his eyes. He looked desperately tired and, somehow, defeated.

Helene gave up the idea of bedding on the spot. "Can I help?" she said, tightening the cord of her dressing gown and walking into the room.

He shook his head as if to wake himself up. "I think it's improving." He played the bit that Helene had heard outside the door. "What do you think of this?"

"I like it." This time it felt natural to nudge him over and sit down.

"What if you ended on D in alt? Can your soprano reach that high a note?" She played it again. "You could pause here on A-natural, and then either up or down to the D."

"Better the first time," Rees said. "It sounds a little florid with that triplet, but I like this minor chord." He pushed her hands off and played it himself. "Nice! You always were the better musician of the two of us, Helene."

"Not so," she said. "*You* write real music; I just play with notes. Real musicians don't spend months reworking Beethoven for four hands. They write original pieces, as you do."

He closed the top of the piano over the gleaming keys with a quiet click. "I write poppycock, Helene. You knew it, even back when we first married, before I'd had a single piece staged. You told me that I was doing nothing more than writing squeaky duets and that my harmonies were unremarkable."

"I didn't!" she said, startled. "I have never said such a thing, and I certainly don't think it either! Last year, for example, I didn't love everything in *The White Elephant*, but there were parts I thought were brilliantly conceived."

That lock of hair had flopped over his eyes again. He leaned against the closed piano keys and gave her a sardonic smile. She could see wrinkles at the corners of his eyes. "I can list precisely what you disliked in the *Elephant*. The tenor aria in Act One, the oboe and clarinet duet in Act Three, and the minor scale that opened the Finale."

"True," Helene said. "As I told you last year. But I also thought your delineation of character was dazzling. The repeated pianissimo high F's in the Duke's aria were exquisite. The sense of pandemonium during the thunderstorm, when the elephant is running loose, was brilliantly executed. And the soprano mezzo duet, as everyone in London undoubtedly told you, was a glorious bit of inspiration."

He raised an eyebrow. There was a self-mocking smile lurking in the depths of his eyes. "*You* never told me."

"I didn't—" She stopped. "I should have. I didn't think you cared."

"Did you really like the pianissimo F's?"

She nodded. "It was daring—but it balanced the second half of the aria perfectly."

"I never thought of it in quite those terms. But did you read the review in the *Gazette*?"

"Written by Giddlesheard, and he's a fool," she said contemptuously.

A slow smile was growing in Rees's eyes. "He loathed that section."

"More fool he." And: "My opinion matters to you?" she asked, still confused. The answer was in his eyes. And this was no time to stand by her pride, not in the darkness of the music room, with the candles making his hair look like coal touched with edges of flame, his eyes like dark pools. No time for dishonesty. "I have always known that you were the true musician of the two of us," she said. "I never thought you'd want me to praise you." She looked at her hands. "I just wanted you to think that I was clever."

He still didn't say anything. She finally looked up to find his eyes fixed on her face. He had beautiful eyes, with the thickest black lashes she'd ever seen.

"You wanted *me* to think you were clever," he repeated.

Helene raised her chin: in for a penny, in for a pound. "I listen to your operas more carefully than any other piece of music," she confessed. "Obviously, I couldn't go more than once. It would seem odd. So I listen for something—anything—I can say to you that will demonstrate my own . . ." Her voice trailed off. "I have been wretchedly ill-bred and ill-mannered," she said quietly. "I'm ashamed of myself."

Rees reached out and pulled up her chin so his wife's eyes met his, those astounding honest, green eyes of hers. "Did you truly like parts of the *Elephant*?"

"I loved it," she said flatly. "Everyone did, Rees. You know that."

"The hell with everyone. Did *you*?"

"Of course."

He dropped his hand with a bark of laughter. "Do you know how I write these scores, Helene? Do you?"

She blinked at him. "No."

"I sit here and I try something, and then I think, *What would Helene think of that?* And then I hear your voice saying that it's underwritten, or tiresome, or—sometimes—clever. Never exquisite."

"Oh, Rees," Helene said aghast. "I had no idea. None!"

"I know you didn't," he said with that little half-smile again.

There was an odd silence between them. "I feel like such an idiot," she said miserably. "Here I've spent the last nine years picking your music apart, just to make myself feel clever." She couldn't even bear to look at him; a sense of humiliation was growing in her chest.

"You have never been an idiot," Rees said. He pushed open the piano lid with a snap that made the candles flicker and dance. "What if I wrote this section in B-minor, then moved into D-major from the *Cantabile*?"

"Why a major?" Helene said, distracted from her self-loathing for a moment. She tried it. "Moving it to G-minor would make it even darker, more interesting."

"But I want a witty resonance there, not gloom," Rees said, pushing her aside in his turn and demonstrating.

Helene looked down at his powerful hands, then at his black hair, gleaming in the candles, at his powerful shoulders. It's all changed, she thought.

"You're not paying attention," Rees said. "Listen to this."

"Try it slower this time," she said. *Andante.*

## 2 2

### *The Vicar Falls in Love*

Tom arrived in the breakfast room to find it empty. He was not a man given to self-delusion; he knew perfectly well that his step slowed at the door because he didn't see Lina, not because of the absence of his growling brother, nor Rees's incomprehensible wife.

"Would you like a dish of kippers, Mr. Holland?" Leke inquired.

"No, thank you, Leke. Merely a cup of coffee and some toast, please." He couldn't bring himself to ask about Lina. "Has my brother eaten yet?"

"Lord Godwin is still in bed," Leke responded. "He was working at the piano quite late at night." After fussing for a moment with the dishes on the side table, Leke left, closing the door behind him.

Tom sat down and found himself wondering what Lina looked like in the morning, all sleepy and rumpled. Before he realized it, he was struggling with the impulse to run up the stairs and knock on Lina's door. In the general run of things, Tom didn't find himself faced with much temptation of the ungodly sort. His parish was small and such nobility as there were in Beverley attended the much larger and more majestic Minster Church. That didn't mean he was ignored by the local gentry: the younger son of an earl, with a good private living, would never be ignored. But the temptations offered by local damsels had not, so far, been much of a struggle.

Lina was another story.

I want her, Tom thought to himself. I want her more than I've wanted any woman in my life. And it's not just lust (although he was uneasily unaware that he was possessed by a feverish variety of that emotion, such as he'd never experienced before). But I want all of her, he reassured himself: that silly chuckle, her odd knowledge of the Bible, even those horrible jokes she keeps offering to tell me.

Very precisely he cut his toast into small squares. He'd spent a great deal of his life respecting his instinct. An unmanly thing to do, perhaps, but it had worked for him. Instinct had led him to take the healthy inheritance his mother left him and more than triple it with shrewd investments. Instinct had told him to return to London and patch things together with his brother. Instinct told him . . .

Lina was the one for him. She was wildly unsuitable for a vicar's wife. Marrying her would likely ruin the possibility of his ever being transferred to a larger parish. Moreover, if his local Bishop found out that he had married his brother's mistress, he'd be thrown out of his parish entirely. Marrying her would . . . marrying her was his only option, so why should he worry about the consequences? He finished his toast. If only he could just throw her over a horse and flee back to the North Country.

He didn't see Lina until afternoon. She didn't come to luncheon, and neither did Rees. And neither did Helene for that matter, although Tom could hardly blame her for taking meals in her room. He was surprised his brother's wife emerged at all. Finally, he was so tired of waiting around downstairs that he decided to visit Meggin in the nursery.

The moment he walked down the hallway, he heard laughter. Lina laughed with the clear, belly-rocking enjoyment of a child, not with the practiced thrills of a courtesan. Because she was not a courtesan, Tom thought to himself, pushing open the door. Her clear eyes could not lie to him. His brother—his own rotgut brother—had made her a kept woman, a mistress. Tom hated the truth of it. It made him feel as if a piece of steel was lodged in his chest.

Lina was sitting on a low stool next to the window and Meggin was standing behind her, drawing a brush through her long hair. Neither of them saw him for a moment. Meggin was utterly concentrated on watching the gleaming river of Lina's hair run by her brush, and Lina was saying, "so you see, Meggin, the miller didn't have any choice other than to send his three sons out to seek their fortune."

"Why couldn't they stay home with him?" Tom said, walking toward them. Lina looked up quickly, and there was a welcome in her eyes. "Good afternoon, Miss McKenna," he said, with a bow, and, "Hello, Miss Meggin." Meggin didn't even look up, just kept watching as if mesmerized, as her brush swirled through the silk of Lina's hair.

"Meggin, darling," Lina said, twisting about. "I think my hair is sufficiently groomed. May I ask you to brush my hair again later, please?"

A flash of real anger crossed the little girl's face and she reached out to grab Lina's hair and keep it in place.

"This afternoon," Lina said calmly, standing up and handing Meggin the swansdown muff.

Meggin blinked and began to brush the muff carefully.

"If you would ring that bell, Mr. Holland," Lina said, "Rosy will return to the nursery to take charge of Meggin."

Tom rang the bell. "Meggin," he said, turning back to the little girl, "would you like to go for a ride in the park this afternoon?"

She didn't look up or reply in any way.

"I thought perhaps you might like to see the lions in the Tower of London?" he tried again.

She still didn't look up, but she said something.

"What?" he asked.

"Izzat near the Pewter Inn?"

"No," he said.

Her mouth trembled for a moment and she went back to brushing the muff without a word.

At that moment, Rosy bounced into the room and so they left.

"Meggin is not happy," Lina said without preamble, after Tom closed the door behind them. "She speaks only in order to ask when she will see Mrs. Fishpole."

"I could take her back there, but only for a visit," Tom said rather helplessly. "Meggin was sleeping on a pile of rags in the corner, and Mrs. Fishpole's circumstances were not such that she could take Meggin in herself."

Lina walked down the hall. "So you rescued her? Just like that? Took her away without a second thought?"

"I had no choice," Tom said, feeling oddly defensive.

"Why not?"

"Because there I was, and Mrs. Fishpole said to take her, and so I—"

"But why were you there?"

"I saw Meggin in an inn yard, and I thought perhaps she was in an unenviable position."

"You meant to rescue her," Lina said flatly. "You meant to rescue her from the moment you saw her."

"It wasn't so simple," Tom replied, nettled.

"How many children *have* you rescued?"

Her hips were swaying before him in a way that made it hard for Tom to concentrate. "Not many."

"It must give you quite a glow of virtue." She walked into the library and tucked herself onto a couch, looking up at him.

Was her tone scornful? Tom felt a wave of irritation. "That has nothing to do with it," he said.

"Poppycock," she said flatly. "You vicar types are all the same. You enjoy wearing a halo, so you removed Meggin from the only mother she had ever known—Mrs. Fishpole. And that was a mistake."

Tom was conscious of a feeling of resentment. "Mrs. Fishpole couldn't keep her much longer. Meggin was sleeping on a pile of rags in the corner, and Mrs. Fishpole herself told me that she was worried for Meggin's safety. Do you understand what I mean?"

"Of course I do," Lina said impatiently. "So you galloped in like a knight in shining armor and took Meggin away, did you? It must have given you quite a pious glow, for an hour or two at least."

"It wasn't like that," he protested. "And why are you so scornful of an honest effort to help a child?"

"I'm not," she said. "But I am quite familiar with the godly sort rushing in to save people and doing it without forethought, and without the ability to admit that they may have been mistaken."

"So the mistake I made was to remove Meggin from Mrs. Fishpole, rather than Mrs. Fishpole from the inn," he said.

She nodded. "But surely you have thought of some pious justification for removing her so abruptly from her mother to counter my criticism?"

"Mrs. Fishpole is not her mother," Tom protested. But he'd never been one to deny a fair point. "You may be right. Although I do not agree that I did so merely for a sanctimonious bout of aggrandizement."

She wasn't looking at him anymore. Instead she was frowning and examining her fingernails. "We have to take her back."

Tom sat down next to her without asking for permission. "Meggin can't live in the kitchen forever."

"No, of course not," Lina said, throwing him an impatient look. "But she needs her mother. Mrs. Fishpole will have to find other circumstances. What a pity that Rees already has a cook."

"I suspect Rees wouldn't like a cook whose main facility seemed to lie in fish and sausage pie," Tom said. "Apparently he pays Cook one hundred guineas a year."

Lina gave up the idea of sacking Rees's Cook while he wasn't paying attention. "We have to do something. The poor little scrap: her eyes are like to make *me* start crying!" Lina never cried. That was a rule she set for herself the very first day she left home, when she got to London and discovered that her purse had been stolen and all her money was gone.

"I thought I would find her a family when I returned to East Riding," Tom said.

"Who would take in an orphan?" Lina asked. She had seen many so-called charitable people decline to give a farthing to a beggar.

"I could pay for her support."

"You? A vicar?" Lina laughed. "I can estimate how many pounds a year you earn, Mr. Holland. It's a wonder you had the money to come to London, let alone support an orphan!"

"How much do you think I earn?" he demanded.

"Of course, you may have money in rents, but your living is unlikely to pay more than two hundred pounds a year. An amount that would almost pay for this gown," she said, touching a fold of cloth.

Lina was wearing a crimson morning gown made in the Russian style, with white tassels on the shoulders. She looked adorable and utterly expensive. Tom had never had much use for the money his mother left him other than supporting charity, but now he sent up a fleeting prayer of thanks. Lina could be the best-dressed vicar's wife in the kingdom, if she wished. "The gown was a worthy purchase, in your mind?" he said, putting an arm on the back of the couch, but not touching her shoulder. "You certainly look lovely in it."

"Of course it was! I am particularly fond of the silk fringe, which is all the rage. One cannot step outdoors without a fringe this year."

"And would that gown cost more than I might give to a family to support Meggin for a year, in your estimation?"

She narrowed her eyes. "I despise that sort of trick, Reverend. Believe me, I'm an old hand at avoiding guilt. And I don't think much of you for trying it. I'm not one of your flock."

Tom grinned. "No more you are. A fact about which I am very sorry."

She shrugged. "You're a vicar. How else can you behave?" Suddenly she seemed utterly uninterested in him, as if he were no more than a tedious houseguest whom she was forced to entertain. "I shall ask Rees to support Mrs. Fishpole," she said. "He can more than afford it, and he never refuses any of my monetary requests." She said it flatly, without a gleam of triumph in her voice.

Tom looked at her until she finally looked away. This vicar with deep gray eyes was altogether disturbing. It's only his similarity to Rees, she had told herself the night before. For all Rees had never loved her, she had loved him. And here was the vicar, with all of Rees's unruly looks and burly body, but paired with eyes that felt as if they looked to her very soul. How annoying.

"Wouldn't you rather sell the gown?" he asked her.

"Given all your talk of my gown, I can only assume that you wish *me* out of the garment," she said; leaning back against the couch, she gave him her most enticing smile, the one she had practiced for hours.

He looked at her more intently than anyone ever had in her life; more intently than even her mama had looked when Mama knew full well that Lina had been stealing blackberries from Mrs. Girdle's garden. "That goes without saying," he said with a grin that made laughter lines appear around his eyes. "There's no man alive who wouldn't look at all those buttons and feel his fingers twitch."

Lina couldn't help but grin back, for all he was a vicar and she didn't like the species. "I thought a man of God was above such feelings," she said impudently. "Shouldn't you be upstairs praying for your soul?"

"Who told you vicars had no feeling?" he said, looking distinctly amused. "And my soul suffers nothing from loving you, Lina. You are as beautiful a creature of God as I've ever seen."

"Love?" she said, hooting. "Your tongue slipped there, Reverend!"

"No, it didn't," he said quietly. One touch of his hand on her cheek and she stopped her rather feverish laughter. He was looking at her that way again.

Lina felt a wash of nervous fear. "Did you hear the jest about the bishop who heard a noise in the night," she said, "but when he got up to see—"

"Hush," the vicar murmured, as he moved toward her, eyes intent on hers.

Lina knew why men had broad shoulders; it was so that one could clutch them when you couldn't see. And you couldn't see because the vicar—the vicar—had crushed his mouth against hers and he was kissing her in a way she'd never been kissed. Not by Hugh Sutherland, nor by Hervey Bittle, and never once by Rees Godwin.

"Are you"—she gasped some time later—"are you *sure* you're a vicar, Tom?"

He looked at her, and his eyes were glowing with something she couldn't quite recognize. "No question about it."

Well, she could have answered that herself. Look at the way he never touched her below her shoulders, although his hands had made havoc of Meggin's hairstyling. "You don't kiss like a vicar," she whispered. His lips were so beautifully shaped that she had to lean close again and taste him.

"And you don't kiss like another man's mistress. If I weren't a vicar," he said rather hoarsely, "you'd be in some danger, Lina."

Lina didn't see what *she* could possibly be in danger of. Sure, and she was a lost soul, they both knew that. The thought was a bit lowering. He seemed to read her thoughts.

A hand forced up her chin. "You're no strumpet, Lina McKenna," he told her.

"Just because you don't like the truth does not mean that you can command it not to be so," she said, managing a wry smile.

"I know it to be so," he said.

She had to marvel at the confidence in his voice. Men were like that. Her father was like that. Undoubtedly, he would welcome her back as a lost sheep . . . forgiveness is the Lord's, he would say.

"Doesn't it get tiring to be so good all the time?" she said, and the edge in her voice was half for him and half for her absent father.

He was running his hands through her hair, straightening out the tangles that he had put there. "Yes," he said frankly.

Her father never said such a thing. He was endlessly forgiving and loving, tiresomely understanding, tediously perfect. "Still, I suppose you have never broken one of your vows," she said sharply. "Not one of the Ten Commandments and their permutations."

Tom kept his hands sweeping through his Lina's glorious hair. He was learning something very interesting. "I haven't had much trouble with *Thou shalt not commit adultery*," he said mildly. "It's a good thing you're not married. I think I prefer, *Thou shalt love thy neighbor as thyself*." He paused and dropped a kiss on her head. "I favor adhering to *that* commandment, Lina. You are, after all, my neighbor."

She ignored his punning. "What about the question of fornication, Reverend? What of that?"

"Tom," he reminded her. "Fornication is not a sin I worry about."

"How can you say that?" she said sharply. "*You*, who wishes to unbutton my gown?"

He drew her close and said it in her ear. "Fornication is to couple with a woman whom one does not love. My temptation would be to make love before sanctifying our union. But it would be making love. Make no mistake about that, Lina."

She shook her head. "You're cracked, Reverend. It must go with the black frock."

"So who was the vicar in your life?" he asked.

"He still is a vicar," she corrected him. "My father. Reverend Gideon McKenna, County Dumfriesshire, Scotland."

She couldn't see him, so Tom let his grin spread across his face. She was a vicar's daughter, his rebellious little Lina. No wonder she talked so fluently of Salome. No wonder she hadn't succumbed to the greater sins of London, and fell only to the blandishments of his brother because she was in love with him. "What is your father like?" he asked, hardly daring to breathe in case she got up and ran from the room.

"Perfect," she said flippantly. "Absolutely perfect in every way."

"An unusual trait," Tom said, rather taken aback. "Do you find the rest of humanity sadly flawed in comparison?"

"Oh no," she said, shaking her head rather violently. "There's nothing more wearing than perfection. I hate it."

"What do you mean?"

"No matter what I did as a child, no matter what the crime, he understood and forgave me."

Tom was silent. Her experience was so very far from his own that he hardly knew what to say.

"I know," she said crossly, "it sounds heavenly, to use the appropriate word."

He pulled her onto his lap. Surely this didn't count as over-intimate touching. A second later he changed his mind as he realized exactly where her sweetly rounded bottom was nestled.

"Those commandments . . . *He* never faltered in adhering to them," she said.

Tom tried to take his mind off his body. Outside the window was a fat squirrel, his little paws holding up a nut like a communion wafer, his plump cheeks moving briskly as he peered in at them.

"The only problem with living with a saint," Lina said, "is that he always loves God more than you."

Tom tightened his arms. Surely it wouldn't lead to sinful intimacies if he kissed her ear. It was so exquisitely delicate, peeping from her hair.

"One year I was chosen to sing the lead in the village Christmas pageant," she said. "I was so proud of it. I was singing the role of the Angel Gabriel, you see, and had all the best solos. I practiced for weeks."

"I expect you were marvelous," Tom said, and was alarmed to hear the husky note in his own voice. He quit kissing her ear. Any moment now she would notice what she was sitting on.

"I might have been," she said. "But the night before the pageant my father caught me kissing Hugh Sutherland behind the kitchen door. He was horrified, naturally." She looked up at him with the most beautiful hazel eyes that Tom had ever seen. "He prayed for two hours and then told me that he had to take away the thing that I most wanted, because God had strictly forbidden lechery. So no Angel Gabriel."

"I'm sorry," he whispered, kissing her nose, and the corner of her eye, and the sweet bend of her cheek.

"But that wasn't really the whole of it. He thought I took too much enjoyment in the song itself, you see, rather than in the content of the words. From the time I was a small girl, he tried to teach me not to love my own voice, but to love the words I spoke or sang."

"Make a joyful noise unto the Lord," Tom offered.

"Psalm sixty-six," Lina said wearily. "That night he told me I couldn't sing Gabriel, and that he didn't want me to sing at all for six months. Not at all."

Tom held her tight. It was as if someone had tried to silence a songbird.

"I was frantic. My mother begged him. I think in the end he regretted it. But he couldn't admit to having made an error, because it was undertaken for godly reasons. He had made a vow to that effect, you see—that he wouldn't allow me to sing for six months for the good of my soul—and he couldn't break the vow, no matter the consequences, or the foolishness of it." She hid her face against his shoulder.

"After midnight I sneaked out of the house and lost my virginity to Hugh in the cowshed."

"Lucky Hugh," Tom whispered.

"And the next day," Lina continued, "I caught the mailcoach to London at five in the morning. I was determined to find a place where people would ask, nay, *beg* me to sing."

"Oh, sweetheart," he said, holding her even tighter.

"Kiss me again, Tom?"

"I don't know," he said, nipping her ear with his teeth. "I have this odd feeling that I ought to go upstairs and start making a series of wild vows so that I can break them all tomorrow."

"Later," she said, turning her face up to his. "I *do* like the way you kiss."

"Am I more adroit than Hugh Sutherland?" he said, his lips hovering above hers.

"Kiss me again, and I'll tell you," she said, just before he stole her breath away.

# 23

## *Talk of Marriage*

*Lady Griselda Willoughby's residence*
*Number Fourteen, Chandois Street*
*Cavendish Square*

"The point is, darling, you must get married. It's your duty to the name, etc., etc. Surely you can imagine the rest of the lecture without my having to take the trouble to spell it out." Lady Griselda Willoughby waved her hand languidly in the air.

"You are a lazy creature, Gressie," the Earl of Mayne told his sister, not without affection. "But you'll have no success bringing me to that point, even if you exerted all your energies."

"Well, I don't see why not. I quite enjoyed being married to poor Willoughby."

"I doubt you can even remember what he looked like."

"Nonsense," Griselda said, quite stung by the sardonic look in her brother's eyes. "It's only been ten years, you know, and I do declare that the very mention of his name makes me feel quite, quite *triste*." She caught sight of herself in the mirror that hung over the mantelpiece and arranged her face into a charmingly tragic expression. She was an enchantingly lovely woman of thirty years, who prided herself on looking at least eight years younger, and perhaps all of ten, by candlelight.

"You must have indigestion," her brother said rudely. "Willoughby was all right in his own way, but you were only married for a year or two before he popped off. And since you haven't shown any signs of fixing yourself in another marriage, I don't know why you'd wish the fate on me."

"*I* am not the question," Griselda said majestically. Then she rather ruined the effect by rummaging through her reticule and pulling out a screw of paper. "Although I might marry Cornelius. Do look at this, Garret! He has written me the most delicious poem."

"Cornelius Bamber is a fop," her brother said. "But if you can stomach the man's manner, I've got no objection to your marrying him."

"*My love is like to ice*," Griselda said dreamily.

"*And I to fire*," her brother put in.

"How did you know that?" Surprise actually brought Griselda to a sitting position, a rare event given as she thought her figure showed to its best advantage at a slight decline.

"On second thought, don't marry Bamber. A man paltry enough to borrow poetry from Spenser doesn't deserve your esteem."

"Piffle!" she said. "I never thought to marry Bamber. Is Spenser alive, a friend of Byron's, perhaps? It is the most delicious poem. I would like to meet him."

"Dead. Very dead. It's Edmund Spenser, and he was a contemporary of Shakespeare's."

Griselda pouted and threw the sheet of paper to the side. "To return to the point," she said, eyeing her brother. "You need to marry. You're getting doddering for the marriage market."

"I haven't seen any revulsion amongst my female acquaintants."

"That's because you don't know any marriage-minded mamas," she said.

He shrugged. "Why should I? A woman with a daughter to put on the market has no time for games."

"*You* need to think of something other than games as well," she said with asperity. "I'm the last to read you a lecture, Garret, but I haven't any children, and if you are uncivil enough to die and leave papa's estate and the title to those rubbishing offspring of Cousin Hugo, I shall never forgive you."

"I don't mean to," Mayne said. The profusion of rosebuds sprinkled around his sister's drawing room was starting to make his teeth clench. "I'll marry in my own good time."

"And how old will you be by then?" she said, giving him a clear, direct look that he tolerated only from her. For all their teasing, neither of them had ever been as close to another person as they were to each other. "I'd like you to have a babe while you're still able to throw the lad up on a horse yourself."

"I'm not that old!" Mayne said.

"You're thirty-four. You're been caterwauling around town for years now. You're dangerously close to turning into a joke."

His customary sardonic gleam was replaced by a flare of real anger. "Careful. You're getting dangerously close to insulting."

She took out a fan and waved it before her face. "I mean to be. You need a shake-up, Garret. At this rate, there won't be a matron in London whom you haven't slept with."

He had turned toward the fireplace and was scowling down into the unlit logs. Griselda bit her lip and wondered whether to keep talking at him. But he straightened and turned around.

"I suppose I could consider matrimony," he drawled.

"Good," she said with some relief.

"But not at the moment. I've something in train, and I've a mind to finish it."

Griselda knew well enough when there was no moving him. "Countess Godwin?" she said, with a raised eyebrow.

"Precisely."

"I heard all about it, naturally. I'd keep an eye out for Godwin, though. The man's not fully tamed, you know."

"He was civil enough when he found us in the music room together," Mayne said indifferently. "The problem is that the lady has disappeared. No one has seen her in days."

"Perhaps she's retired to the country, worn out by chopping off all her hair," Griselda suggested, giving her own blond tresses a loving pat. She shivered with fear when her ringlets had to be trimmed.

"Her household claims that she is taking the waters. But I went to Bath and there's no sign of her. Nor in her country house either."

"Goodness, you *are* all het up over this one," Griselda said, rather entertained. "Traveling all the way to Bath. Well, I can tell you precisely where she is!"

He swung around. "Where?"

"Hiding until her hair grows back. I didn't see the effect myself, but I am told that she made a Statement. And you know, Garret, one does rather regret a Statement the next morning. I certainly did, after I wore that Prussian gown with the blue ostrich feathers to the Queen's Birthday."

"Hiding where?" Mayne demanded. "I don't want her to hide. I thought her hair was delightful."

"You'll find her," Griselda replied, giving him a narrow-eyed glance over the pocket mirror she had taken out of her reticule. "Just get the whole business out of your way before the end of the season, will you not? I'd like to see you tie the knot this summer, and you'll need at least two weeks to choose a bride and ask for her hand."

Mayne suppressed a shudder. "I can't imagine I'll find a woman whom I'd wish to see every morning for breakfast."

Griselda was painting her mouth with a small brush. "Don't bother," she suggested. "After I learned that Willoughby was fond of eating calves' head pie for his first meal, we never ate together again. And our marriage was perfectly amiable, I promise you."

"I'll let myself out," Mayne said, bending down and dropping a kiss on his sister's cheek. "Prettying yourself up for Bamber, *soi-disant* Edmund Spenser, are you?"

"Naturally," she said, patting her cherry-red lips delicately with a handkerchief. "I am most looking forward to exposing his little scheme. You are *such* a useful brother, dearest. And you have such unusual talents! There's not another man in London who could identify that Spenser poem, I warrant you."

But the Earl of Mayne paid her compliment little heed. He had no interest in his own ability to remember poetry (he'd always found a love poem or two to be the greatest help in fixing a reluctant matron's affections, although he scrupulously granted the poems their proper authorship). He just wished he were cleverer at finding errant countesses.

It was positively infuriating. He couldn't get her out of his mind: that slender, fawnlike grace, the tender curve of her slim shoulder, the way her eyes seemed to take up half her face, the way her eyebrows arched high at the corners of her eyes, the way her hair—damn, but he hoped she wasn't growing her hair. A woman that beautiful had no reason to doll up her hair with fussy little ringlets, the way his sister did. Helene's hair had felt as sleek and slippery as water, gliding through his fingers. He wanted more.

Outside his sister's townhouse, the earl paused and adjusted the shoulder capes on his greatcoat before springing into the seat of his high-perch phaeton. If Helene were indeed hiding until her hair grew back, he thought with a grin, there was no reason not to afford her some amusement while in retirement. His smile grew as he considered the possibility. He never believed that story of Helene taking the waters, for all her household and friends had insisted on it. She wasn't the type of woman to sit around docilely sipping cups of water that smelled of rotten eggs. No, his sister was likely right. She regretted her hair, and she'd gone to ground like a partridge during a hunt.

With a flip of the reins, the earl started off decisively down Chandois Street. He could guess who might tell him where Helene was.

And he was a master at the hunt.

# 24

## *Come, Come, Come to the Ball!*

She and Rees had worked on the score until morning light started to creep into the music room; by then her headache was already in full force. At some point Saunders had crept into the bedroom and enquired whether she wished to rise, but Helene had waved her off with a groan. "Not until this evening," she'd said, wondering whether she would ever rise from the bed again without feeling the ground lurch under her feet.

When the door to her chamber opened at two o'clock, and brisk footsteps approached the bed, Helene wearily opened her eyes again. But it wasn't Saunders; it was Rees, standing next to her bed looking disgustingly healthy.

"Go away," she moaned, putting her hand to her brow like any self-respecting heroine in a melodrama.

"Time for you to get up," he said cheerfully. "I heard from Leke that you're not in the pink of health, so I've brought you Cook's remedy for a bad head."

Helene eyed the glass he held with great suspicion. "Thank you, but no. I never drink things that foam," she said with a shudder.

"Today you do," Rees announced, and without further ado, he grabbed her around the shoulders, hoisted her into a sitting position and stuck the glass to her lips.

"How dare you!" Helene protested, rather feebly as her head was reeling from the sudden movement. She tasted the drink. It was as vile as it looked.

"Drink every drop," Rees commanded.

"Why are you plaguing me?" she moaned.

"I've a new idea for the second act," he said.

Some women might think his excitement was adorable, the way his eyes were gleaming with exhilaration.

"It came from something you said last night, about the tenor aria in *The White Elephant*."

Helene had given up the battle and was struggling her way through the glass. At the end she pushed him away and flopped back onto her bed. She felt worse, if that was possible. "Go away," she said. "Please."

A footman staggered in carrying pails of steaming water, followed by a second with a tin hipbath. "Bit of a pity having to carry it all the way up here," Rees remarked. "I've had water piped into the water closet off my bedchamber, Helene. You'll have to take a look."

Helene covered her eyes and wondered whether she could have slipped into a long bad dream, without noticing. How could her husband think that she would overlook the presence of his mistress in *her* bedchamber and merrily investigate the plumbing arrangements? Maybe she was dreaming all of this, and she would wake up back in her own bed. But if it was a dream, why was her head hurting so?

Although . . . she had to admit . . . the pain seemed to be receding slightly.

"Do you need some help getting into the bath?" Rees said, looking perfectly prepared to jerk her from her covers and toss her into a steaming tub of water.

"No," she said wearily, managing to get her feet on the ground. "Get out of here, Rees."

"I'll wait for you downstairs," he said.

"I refuse to work on your score. I need fresh air."

"Where are you going to get that? You do remember that this house hasn't a garden to speak of, don't you?"

"I'll go to Hyde Park in a closed carriage," Helene said, abruptly remembering that all of London thought she was in Bath, taking the waters. "But I'm not sitting down at the piano, Rees, so you can just forget that idea."

"We'll go for a walk then," he said with unimpaired good humor. "Excellent notion. I can sing you the aria while we're strolling."

Helene put her head in her hands. "Out," she said hollowly. "Out, out, out!"

"I like your hair this morning," her husband said, giving her a wicked smile. "Especially the bit on top. The rooster crest is a nice effect."

"Out!" Helene said, lurching to her feet and glaring at him.

An hour later she trailed down the stairs, still feeling like a despairing heroine from one of Rees's operas, albeit one dressed in an exquisite blue walking costume that likely cost as much as a whole chorus's worth of Quaker costumes.

Rees was sitting at the harpsichord. He got up as soon as she entered. "The carriage is waiting and I've told Cook to pack a hamper, as you haven't yet eaten."

"I couldn't," Helene said faintly.

"Then I'll eat it," he said with a shrug.

"I had no idea that this part of Hyde Park existed," Helene said with fascination, a short time later. The grasses to either side of the little winding path had grown so tall that they touched the slouching limbs of the huge oaks. Daisies poked their heads above the seas of grasses like intrepid soldiers, fighting off nettles and thistles growing breast high.

"I've never met another soul here," Rees said. "All the polite sort prefer raked gravel paths."

Sometimes the oak trees bent down as if they'd been humbled, brushing their branches to the ground, and then suddenly they would fall back, leaving a patch of emerald grass, or a cascade of daisies. Twenty minutes later, Helene could no longer hear any din from the city at all, no sound of carriages, bells, or shouts. "It's like being in the country," she said, awed.

They rounded the bend and the trees trailed off again, forming another clearing. "How lovely," she said, walking into the middle of a lake of frothy white flowers shaped like stars and stooping to pick herself a flower or two.

When she glanced back, Rees was still standing on the path, his face unreadable. The sun fell relentlessly on his harsh face, on the lines around his eyes, the scowling eyebrows, the generous lower lip, those two dimples . . .

And Helene realized with a great thump of her heart that she'd never gotten over that first infatuation with him, that first blinding passion that had driven her out her bedchamber window and into his carriage, the better to make their way to Gretna Green.

She almost dropped the flowers she held, the realization was so blinding.

When Rees appeared at her side, hamper in hand and plopped himself onto the grass, squashing a hundred starflowers as he did so, Helene couldn't even bring herself to speak. She'd spent nine years telling herself that the brief infatuation that led to their elopement was a dream, a moment's blindness.

But it wasn't. Oh, it wasn't.

Numbly she helped Rees pull a tablecloth from the basket and load it with pieces of chicken, pie, fruit, and a bottle of wine.

She refused a glass of wine. "Hair of the dog," Rees said, "and very nice hair it is." He grinned at her. He had a chicken leg in his hand and was eating it like a savage. And he had that wicked look about him again, the one that made her think about the muscles hidden by his white shirt.

To her surprise, Helene found that she was hungry. She put a plate of chicken on her knee and began struggling to cut it properly.

"Don't bother," Rees said lazily. He was lying on his side, looking twice as comfortable in a bed of flowers as he did in a drawing room. "Just eat it, Helene."

She looked at him with disdain. "I don't eat with my fingers. I discarded that habit in the nursery."

"Who's to see? There's only you and I, and we're nothing more than an old married couple."

*Old married couple* implied comfort and ease, and she didn't feel any of that with Rees, particularly with the secret prickling awareness she had of his body. He had removed his jacket and rolled up his sleeves and one bronzed arm lay all too close to her. "It seems to me that you are always removing your clothing," she told him, eyeing him with distinct hostility. How dare he be so comfortable, while she was both overheated and hungry? Her beautiful little blue jacket felt altogether winterish with the sun shining on her back.

In answer, he sat up. Helene edged back. Rees was overpowering at close quarters. "Here," he said simply, holding the chicken leg to her lips.

"I couldn't!" But she hadn't eaten all day. Her stomach gave a little gurgle.

Rees laughed. "Go ahead. There's no one to see."

"You're here," she said mulishly.

"I don't count," he said, giving her an oddly intent look. "That's one of the nicer things about being married, I always thought."

She took a bite. The chicken was delicious, faintly reminiscent of lemon. "It's exquisite," she admitted, taking another bite.

"I pay my cook extremely well," Rees said, ripping off a little strip of chicken and bringing it to her lips.

There was a dark, velvety something in his voice that made the little coil in Helene's stomach grow tighter.

But he drew back. "My idea is that I'll stage the second act not in the Puritan village, but in the court," he said. "You see, the Princess has left her beloved, Captain Charteris, behind. I'm thinking of adding a subplot in which the captain is being wooed by another lady."

"So the captain would be the focus of the act?"

Rees nodded. "I had an idea for a tenor solo. I took the words from the solo Fen wrote for the little Quaker girl who's in love with the Prince."

"I don't know how you keep all these lovers apart," Helene said, amused.

"See what you think," he said abruptly. And then he began to sing. *"Love, you're the brightest of bubbles, out of the gold of the wine. Love, you're the gleam of a wonderful dream, foolish and sweet and divine!"* Rees had a pure baritone that washed over her with as much potency as that brandy she had drunk the night before. And his music was wonderful: light, foolish, unutterably heartwarming.

Helene put the plate to the side and leaned back on her hands. Rees was watching her as he sang, which made her feel edgy, so she closed her eyes and tried to concentrate on the music. He was using too many long portamento phrases: it would sound mawkish in a tenor range, though it was lovely in Rees's warm baritone. Somehow, without the drive of the last nine years to prove to Rees that she was intelligent, she couldn't think of another critique.

*"Come with me, come, come to the ball,"* Rees sang. The sunlight was warm on her eyelids. *"Flow'rs and romances fade with the day. Come in your beauty, fair as a rose . . . At the ball! At the ball!"* There was a finely tuned urgency in his voice, in the notes, a siren call that to miss the ball was to miss life, to miss love, to miss everything golden and beautiful.

Helene had to swallow a lump in her throat.

Now he'd reached the coda: his voice was deeper now, and slower, rather sleepy, but there was still that sense of deep urgency: *"Come, Come, Come to the ball . . . Romances fade with the opening of day . . . Come, Come, Come to the ball!"*

She didn't open her eyes when he finished, letting the emotion of it sweep through her, really enjoying Rees's music for the first time in years. Then the bright gold behind her eyelids darkened as his body blocked the sun. "Have I put you to sleep?"

At that, her eyes flew open, and she knew they were drenched and she didn't even care. "It was lovely."

He put a hand on her cheek. "Tears?"

She smiled, but the smile wobbled. "It was just so lovely. I've—I've missed your voice." She closed her eyes instinctively on seeing the look in his eyes and then his mouth was touching hers tentatively, just a brushing of lips.

How could she have forgotten how much she loved his kisses before they married? During her debutante year, they spent all the time they could retreating to the corners of ballrooms and talking of music, finding a piano and running through one of his compositions, and finally, when she knew him well enough, one of her compositions. And throughout it all, there was the thrilling matter of a kiss or two, stolen behind doors, taken in secret.

As to why they were so secret, who can tell? Her father was ecstatic that the heir to an earldom had formed an attachment to his gawky, plain daughter. "Why did we elope?" she asked now, weaving her fingers through his hair.

"I wanted you," Rees answered.

He was merely brushing his lips across hers. Helene hoped he wasn't thinking about how loudly she had proclaimed that kissing was disgusting, once it became associated with all the humiliation and pain of actual bedding.

Before those ugly times, before they eloped, her heart would become shallow and rapid at the mere sight of his mouth, and she dreamed of the moments he caught her behind a door and gave her a hard kiss. Those were the kisses of a boy, a boy without finesse and experience . . . at the time she thought he was the most potent and sophisticated lover who ever lived.

"Give me a real kiss, Rees," she said.

His hand was stroking her neck. It froze for a moment.

"Do you remember how you used to kiss me before we were married?" she asked.

"I must have been a beast, always pulling you into a corner."

"I loved it," Helene admitted.

"You never—"

"Ladies don't."

But Rees had clear memories of his wife refusing to kiss him with an open mouth, telling him he was disgusting to want such a thing. He hesitated. Their newfound friendship was so fragile and (although he didn't really want to think such a thing) important to him. Something about his wife made him feel, well, *whole*. He didn't want to frighten her off. To disgust her.

So she came to him. The wife who hated kissing opened her mouth and timidly, sweetly, begged for entrance.

Rees had always known he was no gentleman. And he'd known for years that he had no control around his wife either. Nothing seemed to have changed. He plunged into her mouth so violently that she toppled backwards into a bed of flowers and he came with her, his limbs tangling with hers, devouring her mouth.

All the while, some part of him was waiting for her to tear her mouth away, to push him away, to scream that he was depraved, disgusting . . .

But the only thing that happened was that slender arms wound around his neck and a slender body tucked itself into the hard curves of his body with such melting softness that he could barely stop himself from groaning with the pure delight of it.

Finally, he was the one who lifted his mouth from hers. "Helene," he said hoarsely. "You did say *every day*, didn't you?"

She opened her eyes, dazed. "Yes." Her voice was a whisper of sound. Perhaps he was crushing all the air from her lungs.

Of course he didn't move. Every inch of Rees's body was aware that he was cushioned between her thighs, his hardness pressing into her softness. But: "Am I too heavy for you?"

Her face was rosy, but her eyes had that clear honesty he loved. "I used to hate it when you lay on me," she said and stopped.

He propped himself on his elbows and dropped kisses on her high, arching eyebrows, on the edge of her eyes, on the delicate curve of her cheekbone. "Do you dislike it now?" he asked, carefully controlling his voice. His heart was pounding in his ribs, and it wasn't all a matter of desire either.

She had her eyes closed again. "No," she whispered, and to Rees's ears the little sound echoed around the glade with as much force as a shout.

Deliberately he thrust forward into the soft embrace of her thighs. A surge of blood went through his body so fiercely that he almost groaned out loud but caught himself. He didn't want to seem like an animal, grunting at his pleasure. "What about that, Helene?" he whispered, his lips slipping down to her slender neck. "How did that feel?"

Her hands were running feverishly through his hair and now one slipped to his shoulder. There was silence between them for a moment. Rees dimly heard the call of a bird in the distance.

She wasn't protesting. Cautiously he put a hand on her chest. She'd always hated his even looking at her breasts: he remembered that clearly enough. But last night she'd allowed him to caress them.

They gave in his hand with a movement that sent fire roaring through his blood. She had no corset on. Perhaps no chemise. His hands began to shake.

"Rees," Helene said, and there was an ache in her voice that startled them both. "Are you certain that you've seen no one in this forest?"

"Never, in five years of walking here," he said, looking down at her. Her face was flushed and her eyes were alive, glowing. "You can't be suggesting?"

Helene looked up at him and grinned. Esme had given her lots of instructions about little breathy moans, and cries of "Yes! Yes!" Esme had said nothing about smiles, or the laugh that seemed to be coming from deep in her stomach. "I don't feel like myself here," she admitted. "I feel—*wicked*."

His eyes were so dark that they sparkled like coal. "I like what you're doing," she said, tracing his eyebrow with one finger. "That—"

"Thrusting?" he said.

Her cheeks turned even pinker. "What a word!"

"Mmmm." Rees started unbuttoning the little porcelain buttons that ran up her jacket. He straightened, putting his weight on his knees. She lay under him like a slender nymph, the little twists of hair flying away from her forehead. "I like your hair," he said, to distract himself from unbuttoning.

"I thought you would hate it," she said, and there was an uncertainty in her voice that made him lean down and put a hard kiss on her lips.

"You look beautiful." Reverently he pulled the jacket open. She was wearing one of the muslin blouses that were so popular now, made of celestial blue muslin so thin that he could see the curve of her breast. He closed his eyes for a second, and then brought his hand to her breast.

She was watching him. "Do I look acceptable?" she whispered, holding herself perfectly still.

"Acceptable?" he said, and the word tore from his throat with a gutternal groan. "God, Helene, when have I . . ."

He seemed to lose track of the sentence, so Helene allowed him to help her out of the sleeves of her jacket. He didn't look at all as if he might laugh now. He was leaning over her almost as if—as if—and then his mouth closed over her nipple, covered by muslin as it was.

For a moment Helene was shocked into motionlessness. He was suckling her—actually suckling her, even though she was wearing a shirt. The shock of it sang through her veins like a trumpet.

"Rees!" she cried, and the sound floated away to the bird songs.

He jerked her shirt up, with such hunger that Helene swallowed another cry. Shutting her eyes against the sun, she felt as if liquid sunshine ran through her veins, as if her heart's blood thundered from the exquisite feeling of his mouth on her breast. She clutched his shoulders as hard as she could so that he couldn't move, couldn't leave, couldn't stop . . . But he left only to move his head to her left breast, and then his hand took up a tormenting rhythm, rubbing over her nipple hard and harder until she was twisting in his hands, her nails biting into his shoulders. Those hands could pick up any instrument, and coax an intoxicating melody from it, and it seemed she was no different.

So she didn't protest, not at all, not when he unbuttoned her skirt and there she was, naked in a forest glade. Not when his hand burned a trail down her stomach to her legs, and she—wanton that she felt—let him slip those fingers between her legs. The very touch of him made her shudder.

"Helene," he said. He'd taken his hand away, and the absence was almost painful.

She blinked at him. "Yes?" She had to clear her throat. "Yes?"

"I'd like to make love to you. Would that be all right?"

"Yes, yes of course," Helene whispered hurriedly, wishing that he hadn't asked her. "Did you speak to Darby?"

His eyes seemed oddly unfocused. "What? Why would I speak to Darby?"

Helene could feel waves of sobriety cooling her body. "You had a question about a lady's—" she stopped.

His face cleared. "No need," he told her, dropping a kiss on her lips. It felt so good that he lingered, hungrily, but his hands dropped between her legs. "See, Helene? See?" His fingers sank into her warmth.

She gasped. Instinctively her legs opened a bit and he slipped deeper. "You're ready," he whispered. "We didn't need any of those methods for ladies, whatever they are."

"Oh," Helene managed.

And then he was there instead of his fingers. Helene looked up at Rees. His face was dark with passion, jaw tight, and despite herself, despite the trembling pleasure she felt, she braced herself. There was no getting around the fact that bedding was something her body didn't do well.

Rees felt that rigidity as if her body was an extension of his own, and even though he hadn't entered her yet. "It will be all right," he said, swooping down for a kiss. But he wasn't sure, any more than she was. Would it be painful? By the end of the time they lived together, he was absolutely convinced that there was something about her body that prevented her from enjoying bedding. He'd heard of such things before.

She had her eyes closed tight. "It's been lovely so far," she said. "Go ahead, Rees. You enjoy this part."

He didn't move.

"Go ahead!" she commanded him, as fiercely as he told her to drink Cook's remedy, that very morning.

And so he did, cautiously, slowly, holding himself to an agonizingly slow pace.

Her eyes popped open. "It didn't hurt!" she said, obviously pleased.

"That's good," he said between clenched teeth. "Do you mind if I—"

"Oh, go ahead," she said, with a wiggle that nearly undid him. "It doesn't hurt a bit."

So Rees did. There was something missing though. He was flying, plunging into her tight warmth again and again, his vision black, not thinking of anything, except—

Except he wished that she found more pleasure from it. Helene lay under him with a little smile, and the very sight of her skin gleaming in the sun coming through the branches made him feel maddened, crazed. He slid hands under her hips and pulled her up.

Her eyes opened very wide and her mouth slightly parted. He searched her face, trying to see whether she found any satisfaction in what he was doing, but the roar of raw pleasure in his own ears racked his body, driving him forward. His vision went dim and he poured everything he had into her with a groan that burst from his lungs and echoed around the empty wood.

Two minutes later, Rees was lying on his back in the flowers, trying to force air into his gulping lungs, trying to stop shaking.

Helene was eating some chicken with her fingers, and chattering about how it *wasn't bad, not at all*, and *if it had been like this, years ago. . . .*

Rees put his arm over his eyes. Foolish of him, to want anything else. To feel there was something wanting there. Stupid. Emotional. He had his release, and that was all that mattered. Wasn't it?

# 25

## The Hunt Is On

*A*mbrogina Camden, the Duchess of Girton, was sitting in the garden of her townhouse, attempting to look regal. This wasn't an overly difficult proposition: Gina had a dignity and grace that made her a natural duchess. She was sitting bolt upright, her head carefully poised atop her spine, her pale red hair pulled back into a gleaming mass, the better to frame her beautiful facial bones. "How much longer?" she demanded of the man who had been scrawling sketch after sketch in black charcoal for the last two hours.

"Hush," the man said. And then, "Don't move, Gina, for God's sake!"

Gina quietly ground her teeth (duchesses do *not* show outside signs of irritation, even under extreme provocation) and straightened her spine again. If only Max's nursemaid would bring him down into the garden to play, he would certainly toddle over on seeing his mama and she could pick him up and end this tedious business of sitting for her own sculpture.

"One more moment," said the man, "this one is rather good. Lovely, in fact." There was a tone of ripe satisfaction in his voice. "I think I've got it, darling. What do you think?"

Gina hopped up and went around the man's shoulder to look. "No!" she said, on a rising shriek. "You promised, Cam! You promised!"

The Duke of Girton grinned at his wife. "What? You don't like the shell?"

"The shell?" Gina squealed. "Who cares about the shell? You've done me without a stitch of clothing!" She tried to snatch the piece of foolscap from him but he held it out of her reach.

"It will look lovely on the front lawn at Girton House," he said, his eyes sparkling. "I can't think of a better use for that pink marble that was delivered last week." With his free hand he caught his wife tightly to him.

"I won't let you," she promised, trying once more to grab the sheet of paper.

"It doesn't matter if you rip up this sketch," he said, lowering his other arm so she was trapped in the circle of his arms, and bending to kiss her neck. "I know your body, Gina . . . I could take a piece of clay from the riverbank and mold it in the dark, and people would call it exquisite." His mouth hovered at the corner of hers.

"You're naught but a rogue, to even think of sculpting your own wife without clothing." He smelled so lovely, and she *had* got up quite early to visit Max in the nursery, and her husband *did* have the most beautiful eyes, and his hands . . . "We're in public!" she scolded him.

"I could sculpt the curve of your bottom were I blinded," her husband said into her ear, sounding rather drunken. "Let's go upstairs."

"I couldn't," Gina said, enjoying herself immensely. "Max might come outside at any moment."

"He's in the nursery being bullied into eating far more rusks than he wishes for nuncheon." Cam had dropped the offending sketch to the ground and his hands were roaming freely. His mouth burned a trail across her cheek . . . Gina turned to meet his lips.

"Yes," she whispered, opening her mouth to him, to the charcoal and chalk, the wild man whom she married. His tongue slid slowly across her lips, came to her with a sudden passion that made Gina fold into his arms in helpless surrender.

"Your Grace," came a pompous voice.

Gina tried to tear her mouth from Cam's but he wouldn't let her, finishing his kiss, lingering there without regard for the liveried butler standing at a polite distance.

"Yes, Towse," Cam said finally, not looking up from her face. He was tracing the line of his wife's rosy mouth with a finger.

"Her Grace has a visitor," Towse said majestically, his eyes fixed on a nearby bush. "The Earl of Mayne."

"If Mayne thinks he's going to add you to the notches on his bedpost, he'd better think again," Cam said softly, and suddenly the urbane duke disappeared, replaced by a muscled wild man who had spent years in Greece and thought Greek husbands weren't overly savage when it came to protecting their women.

"Mayne is wooing Helene," Gina told him.

Cam thought about that for a second. "She could probably use his attentions," he said with a wicked grin. "I always thought she was a bit too sober for her own good."

"Cam!" Gina protested, an instant scowl appearing on her face. "I won't have my friends insulted by you or anyone else." She turned to Towse and called, "Please ask the earl to join me in the garden."

"I'll give you ten minutes with that seducer," her husband said, grabbing her slim waist again and pulling her back against his hard body. "Ten minutes only, Gina, and then you belong to *this* seducer."

Objections trembled on Gina's lips, and then she realized that there was no point to cutting off her nose to spite her face. She no more wished to deny her husband's provocative smile than she wanted to kiss the Earl of Mayne, be he the most seductive man in London or not.

"All right," she whispered. "Ten minutes." Even meeting his eyes, seeing that sweep of smoky eyelash, made her stomach curl.

"Don't be late," he said, and the urgency in his tone had nothing to do with ducal responsibilities.

The Earl of Mayne found the duchess clipping roses and looking rather flushed from her gardening endeavors.

"How delightful to see you," she said, smiling at him and holding out a delicate hand.

Mayne admired the lovely picture she made, pale red hair gleaming in almost the precise color of the blush roses she carried in a basket. "It's a shame that you're so happily married," he said, dropping a kiss onto her palm. "May I say that I would be very delighted should that circumstance ever change?"

She chuckled, and the low, happy sound of it jolted his loins. If he could find a woman like *her*, marriage wouldn't seem such an unenviable prospect.

"I suspect you have come to see me for reasons other than my supposed marital bliss," she said, but the smile curling on her lips left him in no doubt that *bliss* was likely the right word.

"In fact," he said, "I was hoping you could give me the direction of your lovely friend Helene."

"Are you and Helene on terms of such intimacy, then?" she said, eyeing him with obvious curiosity.

"She was kind enough to give me leave to use her Christian name."

The duchess obviously remembered the story she had been told to recite. "Helene has decided to take the waters," she said piously. "She finds herself exhausted by the season. I'm afraid that I'm not at liberty to give her address to anyone."

"Hmm," Mayne said. "I would have thought the countess was one to eschew ill-smelling medicines. And when I saw her last . . . she was in the very pink of health."

"Yes, well," Gina said, conscious that at least eight minutes had passed since Cam went upstairs, "I'm afraid that I can't give you her direction without betraying her confidence."

He sighed inwardly and took a billet from his breast pocket. "In that case, would you be so kind as to forward this to her?" he enquired.

She gave him a beaming smile and began walking rather quickly toward the house. "I shall give it to a footman immediately," she said, towing him along.

Two minutes later, Mayne found himself deposited, rather unceremoniously, outside the front door. He walked to the pavement and then paused, examining his watch fob until the Girton butler closed the door. The house, and indeed the whole street, were sleepily dozing in the unexpected heat that had struck London that morning.

The only sign of life was the servants' entrance to the left. As Mayne watched, a greengrocer dropped off an order of cabbages. He nodded to the footman standing beside his carriage. "We'll wait here a moment or two, Bantam." If he wasn't mistaken about the duchess's character, she would dispatch of business matters at once.

Indeed. A footman, smartly dressed in Girton livery, emerged from a side door. Mayne smiled to himself. The footman passed a note to a groomsman; Mayne smiled again. The groomsman trotted sedately down the street on a placid old horse, and never noticed that he was being followed at some distance by a coach with an insignia on the door. Mayne smiled and smiled. He only stopped smiling when he realized precisely where the note was delivered.

What in the devil's name was Helene Godwin doing at the Godwin residence? Why was she staying with her oh-so-estranged husband, to be blunt about it?

## 26

## Darling Girl

*H*elene's stomach gave an odd lurch when she walked into the library before dinner and saw Lina sitting next to Rees on a small settee. Her shock was likely due to revisiting her youthful infatuation with her husband. All the better reason to forget she ever felt the emotion in the first place. It had only taken an hour after they returned from the picnic for Helene to remember that her husband had a beautiful young woman sleeping in the room next to his.

"Champagne, my lady?" Leke said now, bowing. Helene gave him a nod of assent.

"I should like to go to Vauxhall tomorrow night," she announced in a high voice that almost cracked like shattered glass. "It's the only place I can think of where I can go without being recognized, and I simply cannot stay in this house day and night."

Lina looked up, startled, and Helene was gratified to see her spring further from Rees's side. It was a sad thing indeed when one was grateful for the good manners of one's husband's mistress.

"Don't have the time," Rees growled.

"Make it," Helene said, with a tone of pure steel in her voice.

Rees looked up from his papers. "What do you think I should put at the end of Act Two, when Captain Charteris has discovered the Princess in the Quaker village? All Fen has noted is 'musical number.'"

"Some sort of dance, I expect," Helene said, sipping her champagne. It was deliciously cold and icy, and made her feel almost as if she would sneeze.

"I could do a polonaise," Rees muttered.

"I'd do a waltz," Helene said. She would have wandered over to look at his paper, but she wasn't going anywhere near the couch, even if Miss McKenna was a frigid distance from Rees's hip now.

"A waltz? I have never written a waltz. Weren't you working on one last summer?"

That was the odd thing about Rees. He never forgot a passing word said about music, although he had never remembered her birthday, not even during the first year of their marriage.

"Yes," Helene said, finishing her champagne.

"How do you think the audience would take it?" he said, frowning. "I have quite a prudish contingent going to the Theatre Royal."

"When did you ever worry about shocking someone?" Helene asked. Rees's brother was taking Lina away to look out the far windows. That was diplomatic.

"You know I'm conventional. When it comes to music," Rees replied with a lopsided smile. Helene's heart skipped and steadied again. "Will you play me your waltz?"

"There's no piano here," she pointed out. And what if he didn't like it?

But Rees was standing up. "We'll go in the music room. Tom and Lina can dance for us. Tom!" he called. "You know how to waltz, don't you?"

His brother turned around. "No, I haven't the faintest idea how to waltz. The sight of their vicar trotting around the dance floor would likely give my parishioners apoplectic fits."

"My father used to dance once in a while with my mother," Lina said to him with a giggle. "Though not a *waltz*, of course!"

"Too fast for a vicar, isn't it?" Rees said with satisfaction. "I can't think why I didn't write a waltz before. Come on, Helene. Lina, you show Tom the steps. It's easy enough and there isn't a single member of your godly flock here to disapprove, Tom."

A moment later they entered the sitting room. Helene put her arm on Rees's sleeve. "Did you forget something?" she asked, nodding at the floor.

Rees stopped and stared at the ocean of papers as if he'd never seen them before. "We can't—" he stopped.

Helene picked up a sheet. It had three words scrawled on it: *night dances past*. She handed it to Rees and picked up another. It had three staves of cascading arpeggios.

"Unfortunately, we cannot dance on paper," Tom said, looking rather relieved. "It wouldn't be safe. Miss McKenna might slip and fall."

Lina rounded on Rees. "Why *are* you keeping all this garbage?" she asked. "Do you honestly think there's a good piece of music on the floor somewhere?"

He looked at her, his face unmoving. But Helene saw a spark of uncertainty in his eyes and cursed Lina inwardly. How dare she make him feel worse about his music than he already did?

"There might well be something marvelous here," she said quickly. "This piece is breathtaking and fresh, for example." She sang the little score she had picked up from the floor, adding a couple of minor aeolian triplets, for emphasis.

Rees snatched it out of her hands and then gave her a hard look. "Breathtaking after you got hold of it, perhaps," he said. But he didn't sound truly distressed.

"Supper is served, my lord," Leke said, appearing behind them.

Rees dropped both sheets back to the floor. "Right," he said briskly, standing back and allowing Helene, Rees, and Tom to pass before him. "You are spared the indignity of waltzing for the moment, Tom."

"Tell the footmen to clear up all this mess," Rees said to Leke, jerking his head at the floor.

Leke's jaw literally fell open for a second before he snapped it shut. "Yes, sir," he said hastily.

"I should like the room cleared by the end of our meal. And move that harpsichord to the side so that we have a dancing floor," Rees said, striding after his wife.

In point of fact, he was striding after Lina and Tom, but somehow he didn't think of it that way.

"I didn't know that waltzes had a song with them," Rees said with considerable curiosity. "Where did you get the words from?" He had picked up Helene's score and was looking it over. Her fingers itched to grab it back. In the middle of the sitting room, Lina was showing Tom the steps of the waltz with a certain hilarity.

Helene bit her lip. The part of her that was terrified of being exposed as a rank amateur was urging her to dash from the room. "I wrote the words as well," she said, watching his eyes move over the paper.

Once he looked up at her briefly, but he said nothing. Then he put the score back down in front of her. "I feel as if I have never understood you."

Helene's eyes dropped to her fingers, waiting on the keyboard to begin playing. "There's not very much to understand," she said, embarrassed.

"Shove over," Rees said, sitting down.

"*I'm* playing the waltz," Helene protested. But her body traitorously welcomed that broad shoulder next to her, the heat of his body.

"I'm going to have to sing it with you, aren't I?" he asked.

"I can sing it myself," she said, the color rising even higher in her cheeks.

"I thought there were two voices!" he said, picking up the score again.

"Oh, no," Helene replied. "It's only one. I never marked a change of voice."

"Well, you should have done so," Rees said. "Look, here's your first verse, ending with *Let me, lovely girl, embrace you, As would a lover his lovable bride*. That line repeats, right? *As would a lover his lovable bride*."

Rees never sang things with florid emphasis. Instead his deep baritone took Helene's rather simple lines and gave them a masculine flair that turned them incantatory. "It seems obvious to me that the next verse should be sung by the bride, not the groom: *So surrender ourselves to the delicious deception, Happily imagining what will never come to pass, Happily imagining what will never come to pass*. The male voice wouldn't want to emphasize the fact their embrace will never come to pass. The female voice might, though."

"I never thought of making it a duet," Helene said, staring at the words. "I would have to rewrite the fourth stanza."

"If it was a duet, they could sing the final stanza together," Rees said. "*What has wilted once, ne'er blooms again. Never will rosy youth bloom for us, again . . .* That's a bleak line, but it makes sense to have their voices intertwine."

"Let's try it," Helene said. Tom and Lina seemed to be ready. In fact, they were holding hands as if they were about to start a country dance, rather than a waltz. "Tom," Helene called. "Do you feel able to give this dance a try?"

"Of course," he said, turning to Lina so quickly that he almost tripped.

"Right!" Helene said, nodding at Rees. "There's a musical portion first. The song doesn't begin until I've repeated this section twice. I'll count to three," she told Lina and Tom.

Lina curtsied before the vicar and then his hand settled at her waist.

"This is dangerous," Tom said, almost under his breath.

"Ready," Helene called, dropping her hands to the keyboard. The music flowed around them sweetly, a languorous, swirling invitation to dance.

Lina knew exactly why Tom called waltzing dangerous, but she chose to ignore his meaning. "My feet are in little danger," she told him. "You dance very well, for a man who tries these steps for the first time."

"You may regret that confidence; I'm going to attempt a turn."

"Do," she said. "We ought to move right down the room."

He misstepped and narrowly avoiding trampling on her toes. "There, Lina," he said, laughing down at her. "Your feet *are* in danger!"

She giggled.

"I think if I hold you more tightly," he said to her, "we'll move better together. Would that be agreeable to you?"

"All right," she said, struck by an unexpected wave of shyness.

"I suspect our bodies are scandalously close," he murmured into her hair a moment later.

But she was too taken by the realization that she was—she truly was—in *danger* to answer.

Rees turned the page for Helene and gave her a nod, indicating he would begin the song. She nodded back and he launched into the first verse: *"Let me, lovely girl, embrace you, As would a lover his lovable bride."*

Helene could feel her cheeks growing warmer. Could it have been she who wrote of a lover *embracing* his bride? What was she thinking? It was her turn to sing. Her voice caroled high. She didn't have tremendous range, but she liked what she had, as the saying went.

Rees's darker growl took over again: *"Face to face with burning cheeks."* She could feel him watching her, so she kept her own eyes primly on her fingers.

It was time to sing together. *"What has wilted once, ne'er blooms again,"* she sang, high and clear, and Rees's voice twined into hers, in a sweet descant, lowered to his baritone range, *"Never will rosy youth bloom for us, again."* And isn't that the truth, Helene thought, rather sadly.

Rees took the last verse, repeating: *"Let me, darling girl, enfold you, As would a lover his lovable bride, as would a lover his lovable bride."*

"It's not *darling girl*," she objected, as she played the final coda to the waltz. "I wrote *lovely* girl."

"You want an expression of affection, not a point about her looks," Rees said. Then he lowered his voice. "Did you happen to notice how much my brother is enjoying your music?"

Helene raised an eyebrow as she played the final chord. "The vicar sheds his Roman collar," she said, rather absentmindedly. She didn't want to think about Tom.

"Let's try it again," Rees said. "This time, every other line with the male and then the female voice."

"That won't work," she objected.

"The song could echo the waltz itself, bringing a male and female body together," he said patiently.

Helene felt she must be going purple. What kind of an old maid—
even if married—was she, writing lascivious songs? "I didn't think of the
waltz that way!" she said.

"That's why the waltz is so improper," he said with a smile that made
her uneasy. "It simulates intimacy, Helene. Surely you recognize that."

"Well, of course," she hastened to say. "I mean, the man puts his arm
around the woman. That in itself is terribly unseemly."

"That's not the point," Rees said, sounding rather amused. "You
knew exactly what I'm talking about when you were writing that music.
Lina!" he called.

"Yes?"

"Will you play the waltz this time? Helene needs to get a sense of it
in her feet."

"Oh, I couldn't," Helene said, feeling as if the last thing she wanted
to do was waltz with her husband. A moment later, she found herself curtsying to Rees's bow. "This is *too* odd," she whispered to him, taking his
hand. His other hand went around her waist as snugly as if they danced
together all the time.

Rees had only asked Lina to play, but she started to sing as well. Helene almost stumbled when she realized what a beautiful voice her husband's mistress had. It hung in the air like honey, making the words
Helene had written sound infinitely better, wiser, more allusive.

Rees drew her closer to him and let the music move them across the
room, his leg advancing, and hers falling back. And all the time his arm
pulled her closer and closer until there was no air between their bodies
at all.

"Rees!" Helene hissed.

But the glint of amusement in his eyes turned her silent. Her gown
wrapped around his muscled thigh and then blew free as he turned her
with just a touch, in circle after circle after circle across the floor. She felt
dizzy. The music pounded in her blood and prickled between her thighs.
It danced in her feet and made her press closer to his chest.

"Do you see what I mean?" he asked conversationally. "The waltz
starts out with a bit of introduction, undressing, as it were. A bow here, a
flourish there. Then when the preliminaries are out of the way, the two
dancers begin, first rather slowly and then faster and faster—" He spun
her as he spoke. "The man holds his partner more and more tightly. They
are in a closed position, his arms around her body."

Helene frowned at him.

"You do know the instructions posted at Almack's regarding the
waltz, don't you?" he asked her.

"No." Why would she notice such a thing?

"The man and woman must be dressed decently." His eyes had a wicked glint.

She couldn't help it: she giggled. He swept her in a great circle. "I *think* they may be referring to a doublet and coat."

"Undoubtedly!" Helene said severely.

*"As would a lover his lovable bride,"* Lina sang slowly, and again: *"As would a lover his lovable bride."*

Rees glided Helene to a perfect halt on the last breath of the song.

"You dance very well," he said, blinking at her in an almost startled fashion. But he didn't wait for a reply. "There's one line that needs changing, Helene." He dragged her over to the piano and Lina hastily slid off the piano bench. "I don't think the line about *fires of our hearts burning out* is right. You should replace it with something more joyful."

"But that's what I meant," Helene insisted. "You may think the waltz is about bedroom matters, Rees." She said it in a sharp undertone so that Tom and Lina couldn't hear. "But I wrote a song about youthful love that fades and dies at the end of the song. So it starts with a great deal of enthusiasm and musical flourishes, but towards the end—"

"No, no," Rees interrupted. "That's far too disheartening. How would it be if you changed that line to something simpler and more cheerful?" He hummed the bar. "*Love into air?* No, that's no good."

"I don't want to," Helene said stubbornly. "I wrote the words, after all. They move from the lover's exuberance to the loss of those feelings."

He paused for a moment, suddenly struck. Then he looked at her sideways. "You wouldn't have put any of your life into this waltz, would you, Helene?"

She colored. "Of course not!" she snapped.

He stared at her for a moment and then put down the score. Of course she'd written it about their marriage, about the fire she felt in the heart—burning out. Suddenly his own heart felt like a charred, blackened cinder. "You're right. It's much better as it is."

"Shall we plan on Vauxhall tomorrow then?" Tom said, popping up at Rees's shoulder.

"Yes," Helene agreed, moving toward the door. "I'll send a note to my friends, and see whether either of them might wish to make up a party with us."

"I should be working," Rees put in.

"Nonsense!" Lina said with a laugh. "You work entirely too much."

Because there's nothing in my life *but* work, Rees thought. It had never bothered him before.

## 27

## Morning Calls

*Lady Esme Bonnington's Townhouse*
*Number Forty, Berkeley Square*

"*D*arling, tell all!"

Helene grinned. "I can't. I have to wait for Gina. You know she'll be outraged to miss anything."

"You can't wait," Esme moaned. "She's always late these days. It's the devoted mother in her."

"As if you aren't one," Helene pointed out.

"I am a perfectly respectable mother," Esme protested. "I see William at proscribed times, and I do not allow him to overtake my every waking moment."

Helene forbore to point out that a set of childish fingerprints, seemingly dabbed with blackberry jelly, had made an imprint on Esme's exquisite gown. Nor did she remind her friend that only last month Esme had left a dinner attended by the Regent himself, on receiving a message from William's nanny saying that he showed signs of a cold.

"Just tell me a few details," Esme urged, her eyes shining with curiosity. "I have not been able to sleep wondering what's happening to you."

Somewhat to Helene's relief, Gina burst into the room at that moment. "I'm so sorry to be late," she cried. "I simply could not get out the door." She fell into a chair. "Don't pause for courtesies, Helene! What about the opera singer? What is it like, living in the house? Can you bear it?"

Her two friends were looking at her with expressions of identical curiosity, as if she were a calf with two heads or some other miracle of nature. "It's not so terrible," Helene said cautiously.

"I've done nothing but think about it, and I'm fairly sure that I would have to flay her," Esme said with frank bloodthirstiness. "Is she simply awful? What does she look like? Is she one of those brandy-faced women whom one sees around the Exchange, or the fancy articles who haunt Vauxhall?"

"Actually, Miss McKenna is not at all like a common lightskirt," Helene replied. "She's quite beautiful, and I have to admit that if I had the faintest particle of feeling for Rees—and of course I *don't*—I would be jealous of her looks."

"How can you bear it?" Gina asked wonderingly. "I know you're estranged from Rees, but he's still your husband. Even if I were separated from Cam for twenty years, I could not see him nuzzle up to some light woman in my presence without feeling murderous."

Helene shrugged. "They don't show any signs of intimacy in my presence."

"Well, that's quite considerate of her," Esme said, sounding rather surprised. "Frankly, I would think that she too would find this a difficult situation. After all, she's been living in that house for what, three years?"

"She knows which side of the bread is buttered," Gina said. "Why should she feel any distress, considering that she still lives in the house? Helene is obviously a mere visitor—*to her own house!*"

Esme nodded. "Have you found a moment to offer her a settlement, Helene?"

"No," Helene said slowly. "I'm not sure I would feel comfortable doing so, to be honest. She is oddly ladylike."

"Pooh!" Esme said. "She's no lady!"

Helene was silent. The awkward truth was that she was only beginning to feel pricks of jealousy now. And they didn't have anything to do with the fact Lina was sleeping in the vicinity of Rees, either. It was her voice. She had *music*.

"I told Sebastian about Rees keeping his mistress in your bedchamber regardless of your presence in the house," Esme was saying, "and he said that if you would like him to draw Rees's cork or worse, he'd be happy to do so."

Gina was nodding. "I haven't told Cam, because he hasn't the self-control. He would set off immediately to pummel Rees. But just let me know."

"No, no!" Helene said alarmed. "Rees is going to be the father of my child. Besides, that would lead to someone finding out where I am. Harries has been informing all callers that I am taking the waters in Bath." She turned a little pink. "Apparently the Earl of Mayne has called seven times."

"Didn't you get the note I forwarded to you?" Gina said, with an impish grin.

"Yes, and I brought it with me," Helene said, pulling a note from her reticule. "Listen to this: *I understand you are in seclusion, perhaps for as long as six weeks. Surely you are in need of diversion? I am entirely at your service.*"

"What a shame you can't meet Mayne," Gina said. "It must be utterly deflating to be in the same room with the opera singer, if she's all that exquisite. Mayne only stayed in the garden with me for a few minutes, while requesting your address, but I will admit that his compliments were quite amusing."

"The man has exquisite finesse in all areas, including the bedroom," Esme put in. "So Helene, have things improved at all on that front in the past nine years?"

Helene blinked. She had never gotten used to Esme's frank discussion of matters that she had been brought up to ignore. "I've told Rees, as per your instructions, that we have to do it every day, and he doesn't seem to find the prospect too insufferable." Then she remembered something. "His mistress made a joke out of his only needing seven minutes of time with me."

"You and she are joking together?" Esme said, clearly stupefied.

Helene felt a flash of embarrassment. "I was rather inebriated at the time."

Gina patted her knee. "If I were you, I would stay inebriated for the entire month," she said. "And if Rees's mistress is cracking jokes about his poor performance in bed, I think we can assume that his abilities are not going to improve in the next few weeks. It's a true shame you can't carry on a flirtation with Mayne. At least he would keep your spirits up."

"I don't see why I can't meet him if I wish to," Helene said.

"It's not worth the risk," Esme said. "You would be worse than ruined if anyone discovered the truth. I really can't imagine the scandal."

"I'll think about it," Helene said, unconvinced. She was not truly interested in a flirtation with Mayne, but whenever she thought about Lina's voice it gave her a queasy sensation . . . perhaps a few of Mayne's practiced compliments would restore her confidence. "Are you both free to make up a party to Vauxhall this evening?"

"Alas, no," Gina said with real regret. "Cam and I are dining with a delegation from Oxford. I'm certain it will be excruciatingly tedious, but Thomas Bradfellow from Christ Church is making my brother a professor, so we couldn't possibly miss it."

"I'll come!" Esme said. "I wouldn't miss a closer look at Rees's strumpet for the world. No one even knows what she looks like, you know. Naturally, we've all heard about her, but who has actually *seen* her? I do believe that her brief appearance at the opera with Rees—and that was some two years ago now—was the first and last time he paraded her before the *ton*."

"She will be wearing a loo mask and domino," Helene pointed out. "I'm not sure how much you'll observe. But thank you for coming, Esme. Somehow the idea of the four of us forming a party seemed uncomfortably intimate."

"How is Rees's brother holding up, then?" Gina said. "I find it hard to believe that a vicar countenances the presence of a fallen woman, let alone escorts her to Vauxhall."

"This is the oddest thing I have ever heard of," Esme said, sitting back with an utterly fascinated expression. "And it certainly will be the most scandalous evening in which I have participated—and that in a long and misspent life. Who would have thought that our docile Helene would be party to a dissipated revel of this nature?"

# 28

## Secret Flirtations Are by Far the Most Potent

*M*ayne turned over the little billet doux with a feeling of potent satis-faction. It was a prim and proper white; it was not perfumed; it had no air at all of *assignation*. Why he should feel an overwhelming relief on receiving it, he didn't know. Probably had something to do with his sister lowering the boom on his head with her lecture about marriage.

Griselda was right, of course. He had to marry. But not until he had satisfied himself with the delicate body of Lady Godwin. He couldn't even imagine flirting with another woman until he sated himself with her.

The moment when an exquisitely dressed gentleman ambles from a closed, unmarked carriage to a hackney is so common in Hyde Park as to be unnoticeable. Mayne strolled over, knowing perfectly well that she was watching him from one of the little windows, likely savoring his strong legs. He was wearing pantaloons that were not quite in the newest fashion, as he found that ladies responded much better to the tight, knitted styles of last year. Not so out of date as to make him ridiculous . . . but en-ticing enough to make him appetizing.

To his surprise, when he paused in the door of the carriage, Helene was not peeking out the window. Instead, she was frowning down at what appeared to be a musical score. It wasn't until Mayne sat down opposite her and signaled the footman to close the door that she looked up.

Her reaction was all the more gratifying when she took in his ele-gance. Her eyes widened, just perceptibly. For his part, Mayne suddenly remembered that while he liked the look of stockinet pantaloons, they were damned uncomfortable when he encountered a beautiful woman. Helene was wearing a gown similar to what she had worn to Lady Hamil-ton's ball, even if it was designed for the daytime. And, significantly, she had taken off her pelisse. It lay beside her.

"It is indeed a pleasure to see you," he said. "I am particularly gratified, knowing that you are in seclusion from the rest of society."

Helene looked at him a little uncertainly. Seeing Mayne in the light of day, it seemed unlikely that such a man would wish to spend any time at all with her, let alone pay her compliments. "I do greatly desire to keep my presence in London undisclosed," she said.

The smile on his lips seemed to promise all sorts of things.

"I hope never to disappoint you in any way," he said softly, picking up her hand and putting a kiss on her palm.

Goodness! Helene had a sudden wish to fan herself with the musical score she held. Rees thought she had merely gone for an aimless carriage ride around London, and had thrown a score at her. Naturally, he could not countenance any time lost that could be spent working.

"Shall we drive into the country?" Mayne asked, his deep voice rolling over her like the finest chocolate sauce.

"I don't think we have time for that," she said rather nervously. "I must be back for supper, you see. I'm going to Vauxhall tonight."

"How interesting," he murmured. "With whom are you staying?" he said, turning her hand over and examining it closely, as if looking for guidance. She said nothing. "Your hands are exquisite," he continued. "I know I told you that before, but. . . ." He started kissing the tips of every finger.

Helene rather liked it. She put the score to the side. Truly, Mayne was very delicate in his approach.

"I would very much like to pay you a call," he said silkily, "if circumstances allow."

"Unfortunately, they do not," she said firmly.

He was kissing her fingertips. "Because you are staying in your husband's house?"

Helene gasped. "How do you know that?"

"Are you reconciled?" Mayne asked. "You see, I ask only the questions that have relevance to . . . us." His French accent seemed more pronounced than normal.

"Oh, no," Helene said hastily. But she could hardly explain. "It's only for a month. I'm helping him with his opera."

"His *opera*," Mayne repeated, clearly stupefied. "I didn't know you collaborated on his operas."

"We don't," Helene insisted, feeling more and more embarrassed.

Mayne sat for a moment, still holding her hand. "All of London is under the impression that Earl Godwin lives with a young woman," he said, finally. "I gather they are mistaken?"

"Of course they are mistaken!" Helene said firmly. "My husband has ended the friendship to which you refer." But she had never been a good liar.

He didn't bother to ask again. *"Appalling!"* he said sharply.

"No!" she said. And then, "That is, I don't mean to tell you anything!"

Unless Helene was very wrong, there was an unusual expression in Mayne's eyes—at least, she had never heard tell that the Earl of Mayne was a sympathetic man. People said he was hard, driven, debauched as her own husband. She bit her lip. What if he decided to ruin her? But the look in his eyes . . .

She was wrong. That wasn't sympathy. "Whatever it is that your husband has done to you," Mayne said with precision, "that made you return to him under such humiliating circumstances, I'm going to kill him for it."

The stark chill in his voice froze Helene's marrow. "He hasn't done anything!" she said, with a little gasp.

Clearly he didn't believe her. Who would have thought that the man known for bedding most of London had such a principled streak to him? "Rees hasn't threatened me in any manner at all," she assured him. "I am staying in the house of my own free will."

Mayne spoke through clenched teeth. "You needn't explicate," he said. "I'll free you from the bastard if it's the last thing I do."

"No, no!" Helene said, anxiety coursing through her blood. "I don't want to be freed, truly I don't! I like being Countess Godwin." She clutched his hand. "Can't you understand, Mayne? Rees and I are *friends.*"

"Friends?" his voice had a frozen edge to it. "A friend doesn't make his wife live in proximity to a whore!"

"I should think that you, of all men in London, would understand. You are known, after all, for consoling ladies whose marriages are something less than . . . ideal." Which was a nice way of saying he had slept with many married women, so who was he to cavil over married persons' behavior?

His eyes flashed. "There is no similarity whatsoever. I would never offer such an insult to any lady, let alone to my own wife."

"Rees and I are friends," she said again. "Don't you understand? We married years ago, and there's no feeling between us other than a mild friendship." She pushed away memories of very different feelings. She *had* to convince Mayne that she was in the house of her own choice or he would kill Rees. She could see it in his eyes.

*"Mild* friendship," he repeated. "But every feeling of yours must revolt from proximity to a strumpet."

Helene let a teasing little smile cross her face. "There's no strumpet in the house," she said with deliberate falsehood, knowing he didn't believe her for a moment. "Yet I do believe that you may have overestimated the sanctimonious side of my character, Lord Mayne."

"I feel as if you are changing before my eyes," he said, staring at her.

She shrugged, knowing that her breasts moved with a delicious, unsteady wobble when she did so. "I am Countess Godwin, and I prefer to stay that way. I am helping my husband with his opera because he asked me to do so. I do not feel a particle of feeling for him beyond that fact." She let her hand slide to Mayne's knee. "Naturally, I would be most distressed if you felt moved to imprudent action. I could never be intimate with a man who had injured my husband."

Helene felt quite pleased with herself. For someone who had judged herself as having no subtlety whatsoever a mere year ago, she was developing a finely tuned dramatic sense. Perhaps *she* ought to audition to play the lead in one of Rees's operas.

Mayne obviously couldn't quite figure out what was going on. She let her fingers stay for a moment on his knee and then pulled them away. "I shall be at my husband's house for a month only," she said tranquilly. "Naturally, after that point I shall reenter society. You do see how much I honor you with this confidence, my lord?" She leaned back against the seat and sure enough, his eyes flew to her chest.

"I am nothing if not discreet," he said promptly. "But, Helene—"

Helene didn't want to talk about it anymore. In fact, the only thing she really wanted was to retreat to Rees's safe, messy music room and forget about this whole conversation, but she could hardly throw Mayne out of the carriage. Not when he might spread the tale to all of London and ruin her irrevocably, or—worse—do some injury to Rees.

"Garret," she said softly, interrupting him.

He was no idiot. He had her hand again and was pressing kisses in her palm, although for some reason Helene now found it irritating rather than enjoyable.

"Yes, darling?" he asked.

"I must allow you to return to your carriage in a mere five minutes," she told him.

The light burning in his eyes almost made her uneasy. He looked as if he wished to gobble her up, like an ogre in a fairy tale. "I've never met a lady who had your refreshing attitude towards marriage," he said, almost hoarsely. "I feel as if I never lived before this moment. I've never met a truly honest woman."

Helene suppressed a rather irritated sigh and let him press more passionate kisses on her hand. Thank goodness, Rees had taken up the challenge of fatherhood before she engaged herself further with Mayne. She would have never been comfortable with his passionate conversation. It made her feel embarrassed. Rees's brusque comments were more her style, in truth.

"You will be the making of me," Mayne was saying. "I never thought there was a woman so genuinely honest. So—so candid."

Feeling a pulse of guilt, Helene smiled at him. Why on earth was she bothering with this folly? Hopefully by the time she emerged from Rees's house, Mayne would have forgotten all about her. Everyone said he had the attention of a butterfly.

He was kissing his way up her wrist now. It is truly quite odd, Helene thought to herself, how little I appreciate these kisses after yesterday's encounter with Rees. The very memory made her turn rather pink, and then suddenly she realized that Mayne had slipped from his seat and was sitting beside her.

"You blush like the merest lass," he was saying in a throaty voice, "and yet you have the sophisticated wit and intelligence of a grown woman. I didn't think there was a woman like you alive, Helene!"

That's because there isn't such a woman, Helene thought uncharitably. Surely she could dismiss him to his carriage now?

"You truly have no feelings for your husband at all?" he said, his lips dancing across her cheekbone.

"No," Helene said, trying to make her tone even.

"In God's truth, a woman after my own heart," he said, and captured her mouth.

The Earl of Mayne's kisses would never be called objectionable. They were so sophisticated and sleek, persuasive and delicate, that Helene didn't even mind them—much. It was just that she really wanted to get back to Rees. She had a thought about the score he had given her.

"I must go," she said, pulling back. And then added, "alas."

His eyes had turned very dark. In fact, he looked half out of his mind. "But when can I see you again?"

"I'll send you a note once I leave Rees's house," she said cheerfully.

"A month? I can't wait a month! Not now that I've found you!"

"Well, I'm afraid that you'll have to. I am utterly incognita, naturally enough. It would be appalling if the news got out."

"But what has that to do with us? You cannot think to live like a nun in that house for a whole month, when you could be meeting me discreetly?"

Helene quelled a vivid image of Rees towering over her in the park yesterday. She could hardly be more indiscreet.

"You're blushing again," he said, seizing her hand. "Come to me, darling. I have a little house in Golden Square, close to Piccadilly—"

"Absolutely not," Helene said sharply. "I do not engage in surreptitious behavior."

He looked a little confused, as well he might, given that she was currently acting in a remarkably surreptitious fashion.

"I mean," she amended, "that our friendship will be conducted utterly in the open. I shall send you a note and request your company once I return to society." With luck, by then he would have found another married woman and forgotten all about her.

"Of course," he breathed. "Honesty such as yours is dazzling."

"Precisely," Helene said, rather uncomfortably. She rapped on the door and her footman promptly opened it. "I wish you good day, sir."

Mayne descended, but then he looked back, as if he couldn't bear to leave. "Helene . . ."

But she motioned the footman to close the door.

Wasn't she thinking of a glissando at the end of the seventh stave? Perhaps it would have more effect repeated as an echo at the end of the fifteenth.

# 29

## *Vauxhall*

$\mathcal{T}$hey arrived by water. Tom sat in the rear of the boat, conscious of Lina quietly sitting beside him. She was always quiet when Helene was nearby, almost as if she were trying not to be noticed. He missed her throaty chuckle. But then—and the realization felt like a stab to the chest—perhaps her silence reflected pain, due to seeing Rees with his wife.

The waterman in the front pulled the boat through the waves with one mighty heave of his oars after another. The water was a lightless, lurid black, but rays from the lantern hanging at the prow caught drops sliding from the paddles, turning them silver, like black diamonds. There was a very un-vicarlike excitement in Tom's stomach. He had never been to Vauxhall; men of God didn't normally entertain themselves with such indecorous amusement.

As they neared the steps leading from the Thames he could hear a dim cacophany of noise, the sound of an orchestra in the distance, the humming sound of visitors, the calls of hucksters wandering the grounds. The boat docked before the entrance and they all traipsed through the door, emerging onto a broad walk. Dusk was drawing on quickly now, and the gardens that stretched as far as he could see were lit by gaslights strung through the trees. The lamps looked like small candles, burning uncertainly in a breeze, and certainly providing no proper illumination. No wonder Vauxhall had such a bad reputation, he thought. A young woman could easily get lost in the maze of paths, alone or with a companion.

There was a voluptuous smell in the air too, one that stirred all his senses. Helene's friend Lady Bonnington was exclaiming over the same scent.

"Evening primroses," her husband told her.

Lady Bonnington was wearing a cloak of deep green and a loo mask that emphasized her mouth. But Lina was an easy rival for her, less fleshy, less indecorous, far more beautiful, to Tom's mind. What was he doing, comparing two women's mouths? Had he lost himself, the securely proper self he had always been? Reverend Thomas Holland wasn't interested in comparing women's mouths!

His attention wandered again. Would he be Lina's companion? Would they lose themselves on a path, walking side by side?

"I've reserved a supper alcove," Rees said brusquely. "The fireworks are not until eleven o'clock, so I suggest that we visit the arcades." Then he grabbed his wife's arm and set off down one of the paths. Tom felt a bounding surge of happiness. Lina was his for the evening, at least. He put out his arm to her. Lady Bonnington and her husband had strolled directly after Rees, so they were suddenly alone.

Her large eyes looked almost frightened. "Are you all right?" he said with a sudden pulse of alarm.

"This isn't proper," Lina said in a low voice. "I don't feel right here, not with Lady Godwin. It was different before I met her. I thought this was all rather humorous, the wife who lived with her mother, and I in her bedroom. I must have been mad!"

"You're as much a lady as either of them," he told her.

"No, I'm not," Lina said, shaking her head. Her skin glowed alabaster clear in the light of the gas-lamp hanging from a tree above them.

"And yet, I think you are a lady by birth, are you not?" Tom said, deliberately ignoring the implication of her statement.

"That's hardly the point."

"You are a *lady*," he insisted.

She shrugged. "My father was well born enough. But I'm not any longer, and I don't feel comfortable with them. I don't."

"Your father?" he asked.

"Just as you said of your position," she said indifferently. "He is a vicar largely because he is the youngest son of a baron. The youngest of four, mind you. But that is beside the point, as the term *lady* has little to do with kinship, not really. I'm your brother's doxy, Tom, and I don't want to make up a party with his wife. It's not right. I'm ashamed that I ever agreed to Rees's scheme."

He pushed back the hood of her domino. Her hair caught sparks of light from the lamps and glowed a bronzed gold. Tom was conscious of deep happiness. He caught her hands and held them under his chin, kissing first one and then the other. "You're going to be my wife, Lina McKenna," he said.

She stared up at him. "You're mad," she said flatly. "As mad as your brother." She tried to turn and go, but he wouldn't let her. Then his arms slid around her and she stopped struggling.

"Where would you like to go, Lina mine?" he asked her, his lips skimming hers, tasting delight with restraint. "If you don't wish to join the others in the supper alcove, we shall explore the gardens on our own."

She blinked up at him, her eyes thickly fringed with lashes tipped with the same golden light as her hair. "How can we sit about and pretend to have genteel conversation in a supper alcove? I and your brother's wife? It's absurd!"

"You are a lady, as well as she," he said gently. "And even if that weren't the case, Vauxhall is notorious for being ripe with all sectors of society."

"I don't want to be one doxy among many," she said flatly.

"You're no doxy," he said, pulling her against him. He devoured her with that kiss, trying with every fiber of his body to tell her how he felt: about her, about the two of them, about their impending marriage.

She was cradled in his arms, breathing quickly, melting against him, joy in his arms. It wasn't until some five minutes later, when Tom looked up, breathless, his body on fire—

To meet the expressionless eyes of his brother. And behind Rees, the bright, inquisitive face of Lady Esme Bonnington, her mouth frozen in a silent "O."

For one long second, no one said anything. Then Rees said in an utterly normal voice, as if he'd seen nothing and cared for nothing, "Our supper alcove is to the left of the Pavilion, Tom." He turned and offered his arm to Lady Bonnington.

Lina was looking up at him with horror. "Was that who I think it was?" she asked. Her back was turned to the walk and she hadn't known of Rees's presence until he spoke.

"Yes," Tom said. His arms tightened around her. "Did you truly not wish to go to supper, Lina?"

She shook her head violently. Her lips were plump from his kiss; she looked young and utterly defenseless.

"Would you like me to take you home?"

She hesitated.

"I'll take you anywhere you wish to go," he said, tracing one of her eyebrows with a fingertip. "And my only payment is kisses. Would you like to go to the opera tonight? With me?"

Her eyes brightened, but then she shook her head. "I couldn't. What if someone saw us?"

"And what then?" he asked softly. "May I not accompany a beautiful young woman to the opera? I think I may."

"I'd like to go to the Pewter Inn," she said suddenly. "I'd like to meet Mrs. Fishpole."

"Mrs. Fishpole!"

"Yes." She smiled up at him. "Meggin is at home, Tom. I find it very hard to forget that she is alone in the nursery, albeit under Rosy's care."

Shame and wonder are infrequent companions, but Tom knew them both. "You'll be the better part of me, won't you?" he said, his mouth swooping down on hers again.

She pushed him away, but not very resolutely. It wasn't until some minutes later that a rather discomposed looking young lady and her companion hailed a waterman and told him they wanted the Westminster Stairs, for a hackney to the Pewter Inn.

"Of course, I'm going to find her!" the gentleman said irritably to his companion.

"Yes, but what if you can't?" she replied, untangling a long curl from an emerald necklace that she was rather unwisely wearing, given the famed presence of pickpockets at Vauxhall. "Can't we simply enjoy ourselves, Garret? According to the playbill, there's a Spectacular Pyrotechnical Display tonight. I do love fireworks. I don't want to spend the whole evening traipsing around these dark gardens looking for Lady Godwin!"

"She must be here," Mayne told his sister. "Just hush, Griselda. Perhaps we can find her in the supper room."

"I don't want to go all the way over there!" Griselda said in some alarm. "My shoes aren't designed for walking miles and miles, you know. Why don't we sit in the Chinese pavilion? She's certain to turn up. Everyone visits the pavilion; you know that. And if she doesn't, I'm quite certain that some other flame of yours will wander by, and you can amuse yourself."

Mayne drew a reckless hand through his elaborately casual locks. At the moment he didn't give a damn for the effect his valet had achieved after some thirty-five minutes of devout labor. "You don't understand, Grissie," he said with frustration. "Helene is different from the rest."

"Poppycock," Griselda said, making her way toward the Chinese pavilion, whose delicate spires made patterns against the London sky. "You may feel that way now, but it will wear off. Contain yourself, please. And do remember that you're a man on the cusp of marriage. All these extremes of emotion are so tedious."

She waved to the attendant, who took one look at Mayne and his sister and escorted them to a prime table where they could both see and be seen.

"There, you see," Griselda said with satisfaction once she had arranged her reticule, fan, gloves and shawl just as she liked them, and checked her emeralds in a small mirror. "You can snap up your little countess as she passes, and I do promise not to giggle at her shorn locks. Though I must say, darling, that I begin to wonder at your taste. All this enthusiasm for Helene Godwin? I remember her in school as being just too, too tedious. All braids, restraint and pale skin. And no more interesting on further acquaintance, I assure you, unless you have a passionate interest in music."

"You're quite wrong," Mayne snapped at her. He was a fool to have brought his sister. He itched to be out strolling the paths. At this rate, he would miss Helene. She was probably walking down a shadowy path, and he could be next to her, enticing her into meeting him at his little house in Golden Square.

"Here!" Griselda called, waving her reticule and hooting until Mayne longed to shake her. "It's Cornelius," she said. "Cornnneeelius!"

An exquisite sprig of fashion strolled in their direction, peering at them through his quizzing glass. His hair frothed above his forehead as if he'd been struck by curly lighting, but Griselda seemed to find nothing amiss.

"I thought you dropped that fop based on his poetic failures," Mayne remarked.

"Not yet," she said complacently. "I told him to write me another poem. Then I shall give the poem to you, darling, and we will discover who he stole it from. That is much more fun. What's to be gained from discarding the acquaintance?"

But Mayne had suddenly realized there was, indeed, something to be gained from the presence of Cornelius Bamber. "Good to see you, Bamber," he said rather shortly. "I would be most grateful if you would accompany my sister for a short time while I attempt to find an acquaintance."

"My pleasure," Bamber said languidly. "Who would not grasp at such a chance? She walks in beauty, like the night . . ."

"Didn't Spenser say that?" Mayne asked acidly. "Or wait, wasn't that Byron?"

Bamber ignored him, since he was in the midst of an elaborate bow that involved three or four hand flourishes, so Mayne strode off. He was conscious of a surge of desire at the very thought of Helene that felt like electricity going from his toes to his hair. He hadn't felt this way since he was a mere adolescent. With her clear, thoughtful eyes and her sophisticated, urbane view of men and women, Helene was his twin. A gloriously feminine, beautiful version of himself.

Behind him, his sister had been joined by Lady Petunia Gemmel.

They were squealing at each other in a way that promised Lady Petunia had brought a luscious piece of gossip to the table. That should keep Griselda occupied for an hour at least; the two of them were positively savage when they began running down reputations, particularly if the people being discussed were near and dear acquaintances.

*Helene* walks in beauty, like the night, he thought to himself. Perhaps Byron wasn't such a bad poet after all.

## 30

## *In Which a Songbird Develops Talons*

The Pewter Inn was bustling with every kind of coach that trundled the streets of London: phaetons, barouches, landaus, and even a chariot. Postboys were shouting and running in all directions. Just as Tom and Lina walked through the gates (over which Pewter Inn was spelled out in flaking silver letters), the mail coach careened in, narrowly missing the left column, which would have brought the whole gate down on their heads.

"Meggin offered me an apple as I descended from the mail," Tom told Lina. "She was trying to sell apples to the passengers."

Shrieks reverberated around them as the boys began their game of throwing all the passengers' luggage to the ground, including a crate of chickens that promptly burst open and sent fowl fluttering in all directions.

"I see what you mean," Lina said, holding Tom's arm rather tightly. "She's very small to find herself amidst all this—"

She didn't finish because Tom abruptly dragged her to the right to avoid a landau being backed through the gates by a fine young gentleman who obviously felt that lowly persons should give way before his vehicle, and not vice versa.

"The kitchen is around the back," he said, taking Lina to safety under the covered walkway that ran around the yard.

Lina looked up and said something, but he couldn't hear it, due to the fracas (the owner of the chickens had taken in very bad part the fate of his chicken-coop, not to mention his fowl, who were comfortably roosting on the second-story balcony). So Tom shook his head at Lina and just brought her around the path that Meggin had taken, leading to the kitchens.

But when they walked through the door, Mrs. Fishpole had been replaced by a hatchet-faced individual wearing a dirty white apron. He had a bad-tempered look about him, as if he'd toss a pot of boiling water at the slightest provocation.

"No gentry coves in the kitchens," he growled, giving a ferocious stir to a pan of pale gray water, graced with a few bobbing vegetables. "Get around the front then, where your sort belongs." Without looking at them again, he grabbed a wine glass from the table and sucked a long draught of red down his throat.

"We're looking for Mrs. Fishpole," Tom said politely, removing his hat. "I wonder if you could tell me when she might be on duty again."

"Never, and that'll be too soon," the man growled, pouring himself another swig of wine. "Now be off with you. She weren't owed any wages, and if she's taken off without paying your tick, it's nothing to me."

"We merely wish to find her direction," Tom explained. "She owes us nothing."

But the man turned back to his pot as if he weren't even going to bother to answer. A potboy dashed in, calling "Mr. Sigglet, Mr. Sigglet! Mr. Harper has arrived for his regular and wants the fish and sausage pie as always, what should I tell him?"

"Tell him that the harpy's gone this afternoon, and left me without a fish pie to my name," Mr. Sigglet snarled. "He'll eat vegetable soup and be glad with it, or he can take himself off somewhere else. I'll have another cook by tomorrow."

He swung around and waved the wooden spoon so that greasy drops flew, landing on his beard and hair. "You all can make your way out of here," he said. "That Fishpole has done a bunk on me, left her job without a word of warning, and all to go back to her family. Who would have thought the woman had a family? Family!" It was clear that Sigglet, at least, had no faith in the institution.

Without another word, Tom drew Lina backwards out of the kitchen; he was a little worried that Sigglet would lose his patience and launch vegetable soup in their direction.

"Where could she have gone?" Lina asked. "Oh, this is the worst of all situations!"

"No, it's not," Tom replied, hating the look of distress in her eyes. "It means you were right. You were absolutely right, and I was a blunderhead not to consider other options."

Lina shook her head. "No, *you* were right. That inn yard is no place for a little girl. And what sort of a mother could Mrs. Fishpole be, if she up and leaves her position without a word of warning? Meggin needs a reliable family."

He cupped her face in her hands. "Hush, you," he said, grinning down at her. "Mrs. Fishpole quit her position because she's gone to find Meggin. All she knows of me is that I'm the vicar of St. Mary's Church in Beverley. Her family lives a few counties over. And that's where she's gone; I'll bet my last shilling on it!"

She was so beautiful that he had to kiss her. And the kiss was so delicious that they likely would have kept kissing all night, bundled up in their loo cloaks and leaning against the back wall of an inn, except Lina had an idea.

"She only just left the inn this afternoon, Tom," she said, rather breathlessly. "Perhaps Mrs. Fishpole hasn't set out for the North Country yet. Perhaps we could find her in London."

For a moment he didn't catch her meaning. His whole body was aching to make her his. "Will you marry me?" he asked rather thickly.

"No," she said. "Let's go find Mrs. Fishpole!"

"Not until you agree to marry me," he said, pulling her back against him.

"I could never marry a vicar!" The horror in her voice was genuine enough.

"Can we pretend that I'm not a vicar?" he asked.

"Ah, but you are."

"If I weren't a vicar, would you marry me?"

She hesitated.

"If I were the cook in this lovely establishment?"

"No!" she giggled and he had to kiss her for the impudence of it.

"If I were a mere country gentleman, living on an estate—because I do have an estate, Lina. And rather more than one maid, I promise you that."

"Estates have nothing to do with it," she said and there was a distinct chill in her voice. "I'm not interested in marriage."

"Not even to me?"

He looked down at her in the light of the one whale oil lamp that lit the back of the inn, and Lina's heart felt as if it turned over. Tom was so inexpressibly dear. And so beautiful too, with his dimples and deep-set eyes, and the masculine strength of him that made her feel—well, he wasn't at all like her ethereal, spiritual father. It was hard to believe that they were both vicars, to tell the truth.

"Perhaps if you weren't a vicar," she said reluctantly.

He dropped a kiss on her lips. "I love you."

Lina blushed, and she hadn't blushed in three years. "You're a fool, to be sure," she muttered, brushing away his hands. "Now, shall we find Mrs. Fishpole, or not?"

Without waiting for an answer she marched back through the dingy door into the kitchen. Tom strode after her. He entered the kitchen to find Lina with her hands on her hips and an air of command that he'd never witnessed on her face before. "You'll tell me Mrs. Fishpole's direction immediately," she was saying in a clear voice, "or it will be the worse for you."

"Pshaw!" Sigglet said, and spat on the ground for emphasis.

Lina opened her mouth and sang one high, ear-piercing note.

"God in heaven!" Sigglet gasped. The glass in his hand shattered. Splatters of red wine joined the grease clinging to his beard and hair.

"I wish to know Mrs. Fishpole's direction in London," Lina said conversationally, "or I shall stroll into your public room and give a free performance. Do I make myself absolutely clear, Mr. Sigglet?"

He was eyeing her with a kind of malice that made Tom step closer. Sigglet's eyes shifted to him, and Tom eased back his cloak, the better to give Sigglet an unadorned view of his muscled body.

"She lives in Whitechapel, on Halcrow Street," he gabbled. "I don't know the number, so you can break all the glasses in the house before I can tell you."

"No need," Lina said with a tranquil smile. "We shall find out the house ourselves, thank you very much, Mr. Sigglet."

She turned to leave, Tom protectively at her heels. Then she paused at the door. Sigglet had taken to swigging wine straight from the bottle.

"I did want to tell you," she said sweetly, "that I fear a little glass may have flown into your soup. Although"—she eyed the gray water with distaste—"it may add flavor."

Sigglet curled his lip. "Complaints! All I ever gets is complaints!"

Tom pulled Lina out the door.

## 31

### *Lessons in Love…and Rage*

They seemed to have lost the others. Rees wanted Helene to see Roubiliac's statue of Handel, so they had left Esme and her husband watching Indian jugglers. There was a stiffness in Lord Bonnington's behavior toward Rees that made Helene quite uncomfortable although Rees, characteristically, didn't appear to have noticed. To her relief, Tom had whisked Lina off to another area of Vauxhall.

"I simply can't get over the fact that your brother shows no disinclination to—" but Helene stopped, realizing that it was hardly polite to point out just why a vicar might not wish to wander Vauxhall with a fallen woman. Under the circumstances.

But Rees, naturally, waded directly into the subject. "My brother is showing a striking desire to shepherd Lina from place to place. All with the purest of motives, naturally."

"It seems odd for a vicar," Helene commented.

"Perhaps he's bent on reforming her. Actually, I'm not sure Tom ever really wanted to be a vicar. My father had him staked out for the church before he could walk, and he did seem suited to the task. But now he seems changed."

"Do you think that he might give up the profession?"

"Hard to tell. The whole piety and charity business comes naturally to him."

"He's a good man," Helene said with reproof in her voice.

"Exactly," Rees replied, unperturbed. "A far better man than I."

"You're a good man too," she said, slipping her hand under his arm. Then she looked up to find him grinning at her.

"Is this my shrewish wife speaking? Wife? Wife? Wherefore art thou? A changeling has taken your place!"

"All right," she said, with an answering smile. "You're a horrible person who occasionally has good moments. Most of which take place at the piano."

"I'm learning," he said. "I have a great deal to learn."

"What do you mean?" They were approaching a large hedge, from within which emerged the sounds of an orchestra tuning its instruments.

"Handel is inside," Rees said, steering Helene toward an arch cut in the shrubbery, "likely shuddering at the sounds around him. I'm afraid that the Vauxhall Orchestra is not going to achieve fame any time soon."

"But what did you mean by learning?" Helene persisted. "Are you thinking in a musical sense?"

"No," he said. And showed no inclination to continue.

Helene let him seat her on a marble bench before the statue, and then said, "Honest to goodness, Rees, you must be the most frustrating conversationalist alive! What on earth did you mean by that comment?"

"Something Tom said to me."

Rees sprawled out next to her on the bench, muscled thighs clearly outlined by snug pantaloons, his arms carelessly flung on the back of the bench. Helene quickly looked away from his legs. The very sight of them—and the memory of him standing over her in the pasture, quite unclothed—made her feel hot and prickly.

"Yes?" she said encouragingly. Unfortunately, her gaze had alit on his hands, and that made her think of the way his fingers curved around her breast, and the way he bent his head to the same place, kissing her almost—almost reverently. She shifted uneasily in her seat. It was mortifying to be looking forward to Rees's daily bedding. That couldn't be the case. She must be delusional.

"Well?" she snapped, suddenly irritated. "Either you're learning or you're not. Out with it!"

He turned to her, distinctly amused. The dimples in his cheeks had deepened and there was laughter in his eyes. Other people might have called his face expressionless, but she—

Helene took a deep breath. "Rees?" she said between clenched teeth.

"My father handily arranged his sons into two categories," he said, dropping his head back so that he could look up into the wilderness of black tree limbs curling into the night sky above them. "I was the sinner, and Tom the saint."

"Well, that seems fairly acute of him," Helene said a bit snappishly.

"Yes, but I begin to think I am less of a reprobate than he believed," Rees said. "I find it rather tedious, to tell the truth, Helene."

"Sinning?" she asked, disbelieving.

"Yes, sinning. And I begin to think that Tom is finding the saintly life just as tedious," Rees continued.

"Well, I certainly don't see any sign of your finding your life tedious!" Helene said, and then wished she could take the words back. He was watching her, so she carefully examined Handel's booted, marble toes.

"I don't find it tedious when I'm with you," he said suddenly.

Helene had to suppress a smile. "We hardly engage in *sinning,*" she pointed out.

"That's just it," he said, and his hand began tangling in the little wisps of hair at the back of her neck.

Helene looked straight ahead, unable to turn her neck and see his expression.

He stood up, and his tone was utterly normal, as if he hadn't said something that turned her world upside down. "Shall we take a promenade?"

Helene rose and took his arm. They walked for a time in silence until he said, "I didn't mean to bring our conversation to a standstill with a disconcerting revelation. Lord knows, my father was probably right." There was something tired in his voice that made her stumble into speech.

"Do you think that—that you might, that some of your actions during our marriage might have been due . . ." her voice trailed off.

"No question," he replied. "I eloped with you rather than get married in a proper fashion, in order to irritate my father although I've only recently come to understand this. And Helene, sometimes I think your exit in a coach and the Russian dancers who then graced the dining room table were directed to the same man."

Helene bit her lip. "We were not happy together, and that had little to do with your father."

"I was a bastard about it, though," he said. "I had no idea how to talk without being insulting. No one in my family simply talked. We still don't."

There was something in his crooked smile that made her heart ache, so she tried to think of a light, clever thing to say. And came up empty. "Shall we turn here?" she finally asked, in desperation.

The walk into which they turned seemed much dimmer than the one they had traversed; the gaslights strung in the trees were few and far between now, and shadows stretched like sleeping beasts across the path.

"This is Lovers' Walk," Rees said.

"Oh," Helene said faintly. They walked on, until they hadn't met anyone for at least ten minutes. The din of the Gardens proper seemed very far away now, and the orchestra couldn't be heard at all. Suddenly there was a popping noise and great flowering bursts of color splayed over their head.

"We can watch the fireworks from here," Rees remarked, pulling her into a little recessed alcove graced with a marble bench.

He sat down next to her and bent his dark head back to watch lights burst and tumble in the sky. Helene watched him instead, until he turned and met her steady gaze.

"I haven't bedded you today," he said, in an absolutely conversational tone, as if they were discussing the weather.

Helene gasped and looked quickly down the path. "Don't say such a thing out loud!" she scolded. "What if someone heard you?"

"So what?" Rees grinned. "I'll bet I'm not the only man thinking hungrily about bedding his wife."

Helene's face was hot. He was *hungry* for her. That was an . . . interesting thought. No one had ever been hungry for her before.

Rees took off her loo mask and pushed back the hood of her cloak. The night air felt like a caress on her cheeks. Over his shoulder the London sky flew with sparks, as if the great fire of '66 had come again, as if a conflagration of huge proportions had seized the sky and was making kindling of the clouds.

Helene had made up her mind that pushing off her hood was the only intimacy Rees was allowed. It hadn't passed her notice that her husband took to marital intimacies in the outdoors like a duck to water. She certainly wasn't going to add to the dismal reputation of Vauxhall Gardens by allowing herself to be intimately handled in Lovers' Walk.

At first he just kissed her. But could one call it *just*? Something about the way his tongue plunged into hers made her body burn to be near his. Yet when his hand strayed treacherously close to her bosom, Helene pushed him away. He kissed her so hard that at first she didn't notice his hand stealing up her leg, trailing a delicate, fiery caress toward her knees, and only belatedly squealed and pulled away. He followed her, and somehow she ended up half lying on the bench, with him laughing over her, pulling her cloak open and trapping her arms.

"It's only your cloak, Helene!"

"We're in public!" she said, struggling. "Anyone could see us."

"No one has come this way in a good ten minutes." His eyes were black against the sky and the feeble gaslight.

She licked her lips and the heavy droop of his eyelids suddenly became even more pronounced. "One could almost suppose you think that I haven't noticed what you're—you're doing," she managed. For one large thumb was rubbing over her nipple in a way that made her legs tremble.

"Do forgive me if I have disconcerted you," he said tranquilly, taking his hand away. Her nipple stood out against her light gown, and their eyes met as she glanced down. "I wouldn't like to do anything that you didn't enjoy, Helene." His voice was as low as a cello, and as seductive too.

She opened her mouth, but couldn't lie. His smile was pure wickedness. And the sigh that came from her lips when he put his hand back on her breast was pure delight. Yet Helene did not lose sight of her initial thoughts on the matter.

"This is all very well," she said—or rather, gasped—some time later. "But you are not going to bed me in Vauxhall Gardens, Rees, you are not!"

"I'm not bedding you," he said. He had rearranged herself and him so that she was lying across his lap, her body laid like a feast before him. One hand held her tightly against his chest, but the other—

The other wandered. From her breast, with an increasingly rough stroke that made the breath catch in her throat and her body arch toward him. To the sleek line of her leg, skimming under her gown, walking his fingers up her thigh so slowly that she started shaking all over and had to hide her face in his shoulder.

"What are you doing?" she moaned.

"Just playing," he said, and it seemed to her that his voice was more strained than it had been.

"With what?" she managed, with a fair degree of logic. For his hand had reached above her garter now, and he was swirling little circles on the skin of her thighs.

"With your body, Wife," he whispered into her neck.

"And what if someone comes by?" she demanded.

But he was bending over her and just as his lips captured hers, his fingers slipped into the sweetest space of all. He swallowed her cry with his mouth, and the next, and the next . . . Quieted her struggles with his body. For it didn't seem to him that she really knew what she wanted.

"No," she cried sharply, "you mustn't . . ." but her voice disappeared into a wave of pleasure that coursed through her body. He could see that well enough.

"If I hear anyone coming," he told her, "I'll simply drape your cloak over you."

"No!" she said tremblingly, but he tried a little flick of his finger, and was rewarded with a squeak of delight, and after that she stopped worrying about passersby, other revellers not enthralled by fireworks.

It took a bit of experimentation. Rees had never given much thought to women's pleasure. They were there; he was a rakehell, a take-what-you-want-and-leave type of man. He'd known that since he was a youngster. And nowhere in the training of a rakehell did it say anything about touching women for their pleasure.

Nor did it say anything about allowing one's own body to burn with a fierce fire without respite, or feeling oneself shaking with passion—and all from touching a woman.

Not any woman. From touching Helene.

Her face was tipped back in the crook of his arm now, so that every time she came to herself enough to protest, he could swoop down and silence her with his mouth until she succumbed again.

In the first year of their marriage, he told her, with an edge created by his own sense of rage and failure over the whole business of bedding a wife, that her body must be unable to experience women's pleasure. And so warring in Rees's soul was a battle between passion and self-loathing. For Helene's cheeks were tipped rose and her eyes unfocused; her willowy body had turned to plush in his hands, and she was urging herself against his hand, murmuring incoherent things, her breath as ragged as his own.

But, as he said, he was learning.

It took a while, but finally he thought he had a rhythm, a pace, a cadence like a waltz that seemed to drive her farther and farther from logic, and more and more into an incoherent series of little breaths that were like the most beautiful music he ever heard in his life, a medley of "Rees! No! Yes!" and "Oh, oh—" and finally, "Rees!" And then she arched against him, her body shaking in his arms. Rees buried his face in her hair. Self-loathing stopped warring with passion, and was replaced by something infinitely more tender, and more terrifying.

For Helene, it was as if a crescendo—a whole fanfare of trumpets— took over the sweet, arching sounds of a concerto and blew free and clear in the air, the sound tearing to the utmost ends of her fingers, again and again, music crashing over her head so that she was utterly lost in its grip and Rees's warm steady body was her only fulcrum in a spinning world.

And for the Earl of Mayne, who rounded the turn in the path a split second before, recognizing immediately the moonlit gleam of Helene's hair, and then just as suddenly the silver gleam of said moonlight on a slender leg, and finally, with a bitter blow that he felt to his chest, realizing that his Helene, *his* countess as he had imperceptibly started thinking of her, was shaking in the arms of her husband.

That same husband for whom she felt only mild friendship.

He turned without a sound and walked away, the black sweep of his cape sending stray leaves on the path into a lackadaisical spiral in the air.

Honesty is overrated.

Rage, on the other hand—rage has a good deal to be said for it. Rage coursed through his body with a black inevitability that left a bitter taste in his mouth. She was no more than a woman, like all the rest: faithless, dishonest. No more knowing in her understanding of men and women than any other woman.

Worse, actually. Taking her pleasure wherever she found it, apparently. Masquerading in society as a virtuous matron while she stole off to her husband's house to enjoy whatever attentions he had not given to his resident doxy.

With a faint objective edge, Mayne realized that he was literally shaking with rage. You're a bit out of hand, he thought to himself.

It's only a nuisance, that's all.

Another woman . . . just another woman. Nothing new there. And if she was rather more devious than many of the ladies he had bedded, that was hardly something for him to grieve over.

He was almost back to the Chinese Pavilion when he saw Lady Felicia Saville prancing toward him, waving her fan and chattering to one of her more foolish friends. Lady Felicia was notorious for two things: her unhappy marriage and her waggling tongue.

His pace slowed to that of a panther.

"Oh, Mayne," Felicia called, as they came into sound of each other. "Your sister awaits you at the Pavilion, sir." But he was moving toward her with a concentrated light in his eyes that she had only seen directed at other women. Felicia gulped. Could it be that Mayne—Mayne!—was finally going to approach her? She had quite despaired of the idea, and yet sometimes she felt as if his lovers were an exclusive gathering to which she had not been invited. And Felicia loathed that idea.

She turned to her friend Bella. "Darling," she said behind her fan, "do make an excuse to return to the Pavilion, will you? As a dear friend?"

Bella looked at her sharply and then at the earl, walking toward them with a little smile on his beautifully cut lips.

"Only if you visit me first thing in the morning!" she said, fluttering her fan as if a sudden tropical breeze had blown through London.

"Without question," Felicia said. She lowered her fan and smiled at Mayne. He didn't seem to notice Bella drifting away, slowly so that she could catch Mayne's greeting.

"I feel as if I never saw you before," he said, and his voice was dark and suggestive. "Do walk with me, Felicia."

"Into Lovers' Walk!" she said with a titter. "Dear me!"

But he tipped up her chin and brushed a kiss across her lips. "Only if you quite, quite wish to," he said, as his mouth came down to hers.

Mayne found it rather disappointing that when he strolled past the secluded little bench where the deceptive countess and her hell-born husband had been, they had disappeared, and so missed the sight of Lady Felicia Saville clinging to his arm, her cloak thrown off and her bodice slipping to the point of indiscretion.

There was a disappointing lack of revenge about it. He wanted to see Helene's eyes widen; he wanted her to know—absolutely *know*—that he had decided she wasn't worth waiting a month for.

He wanted her to know that he had never believed her in the first place. Never. He'd known immediately that it was all a Maygame, that talk about *mild friendship*. He had never believed her. He wasn't taken in.

Yet it wasn't until he was rather expertly, if with a dismaying lack of interest, sampling Lady Felicia's charms, that he realized just how to make Helene Godwin understand that he never, for a moment, believed her nor considered waiting for her to leave her husband's house.

"Felicia," he said, his voice as syrupy smooth as devil's broth.

"Yes?" she said, her voice quite steady and clear. Alas, Felicia was finding the famed Earl of Mayne rather less enthralling than she had been led to believe. But there you are. Reality, particularly when it pertained to men, was always rather disappointing.

"I heard the most dismaying piece of news today," he said into her ear, easing her bodice back over her breast.

"No, what?" Felicia asked, instantly revived.

So he told her. As her eyes grew bigger and bigger, he brought her to her feet and brushed a few spare leaves from the back of her cloak, and then they began their stroll back toward the lightened areas of the Gardens.

For Mayne understood as well as anyone that his duty, that evening, was to accompany Felicia wherever she wished to go, whispering intimately into her ear, and making it quite clear to all her acquaintances that she was one of his chosen lovers.

And Felicia didn't have to think twice to know what her duty was, since it came as naturally to her as breathing. She almost began trotting in her haste to return to her friends.

"I just can't believe it!" she kept saying, half to herself and half to Mayne. "I've never *heard* of such a thing!"

Garret Langham, Earl of Mayne, smiled down at her. Had she the perspicuity to notice it, she would have seen a murderous gleam in his eyes.

No one crossed Mayne.

No one.

## 32

### Mother Is a Relative Term

"*I*'m just not certain that we should have brought Meggin," Lina said quietly, as she, Tom, and Meggin climbed out of the coach onto Halcrow Street the next morning. "What if this is a disappointment?"

"If Mrs. Fishpole is here, she'll wish to see her," Tom said again. "And look at Meggin!"

Meggin had been like a child transformed, ever since they told her after breakfast that they were going to find Mrs. Fishpole. She was dressed in an enchanting little pinafore and gown, with a pelisse to match. She was clutching Lina's fur tippet, even though it was far too warm for that sort of clothing. But it wasn't her external appearance that mattered; it was the way her eyes were glowing and her little body was rigid with excitement.

Halcrow Street must have been in the district of London devoted to the cloth-dying trade, because everywhere they looked there were huge tubs of bubbling reddish or bluish water and women dumping in armfuls of old clothing. Each load would send a choking cloud of colored smoke into the air, adding to the pungent stench of rotting vegetables and horse dung.

Mrs. Fishpole wasn't hard to find. An old man dozing in the sun nodded across the street. "Number Forty-Two, she's at," he said. "Though I do hear tell that she's leaving Londontown and going back to somewhere else. I don't know but what she might have left already." And: "I thank you kindly, sir," as he tucked the coin that Tom gave him into an inner pocket.

They walked up three flights of stairs to the very top level. Meggin was clutching Lina's hand fiercely and Lina—for the first time in years— found herself praying. "Please let her be there," she said to that silent presence whom she used to know, but had put away with her childhood things. "Please, please, please, let Mrs. Fishpole still be here."

Tom knocked on the narrow door, while Lina and Meggin stood behind him on the stairs. There was no answer. Lina clenched her teeth and prayed harder. Tom knocked again, louder, and this time they heard the noise of feet approaching. Finally the door snapped open.

Mrs. Fishpole wasn't wearing a white apron anymore; she was dressed from head to foot in gray bombazine, and a shabby bonnet was jammed rather precariously on top of her hair. Her eyes widened and she opened her mouth, but at that moment a sturdy little body scrabbled past Tom and butted the gray bombazine skirt. And then it was just a flurry of tears and exclamations.

"My fiancée, Miss McKenna, told me the truth of it," Tom explained, a good five minutes later. They were all seated around Mrs. Fishpole's sister-in-law's table, there being no sitting room or extra room of that nature.

Mrs. Fishpole had Meggin on her lap and her arms around her as if she would never let her go. "I can't believe I did that," she kept repeating. "I must have been out of me mind. Clear out of me mind. Mr. Sigglet had been carrying on about the child, and then you appeared, and it seemed like Providence. But I knew within two minutes that I'd made a mistake. And then I was too late." Her arms tightened around Meggin until it looked as if she might suffocate the child. Not that Meggin seemed to mind. Lina's fur tippet, which she had carried with her every minute of the day and even slept with, was forgotten on the floor.

"Too late," Mrs. Fishpole kept repeating. "I'll never get over it in my life, I won't. I ran out into that street like a demented woman, but no one could tell me where you'd gone. I'd given my Meggin away, and I didn't even remember your name for sure. Not even your name!"

"I'm truly sorry to have caused you distress," Tom said.

"Well, as to that, you shan't have her, of course," Mrs. Fishpole said, narrowing her eyes and looking as if she wished that she had her giant rolling pin at hand. "I've left my position, and I'll care for Meggin myself."

"Mr. Holland made a mistake," Lina said, smiling at Mrs. Fishpole. "But he meant no harm to you or Meggin."

"I can see that," Mrs. Fishpole said grudgingly, "but you shouldn't as taken her," she told Tom.

"I gather you were planning to travel to the North Country to find Meggin?" Tom asked. "May I enquire whether you wish to continue to East Riding now that you two are reunited, or will you find another position in London?"

"I'm going back," Mrs. Fishpole said decisively. "I've given it a lot of thought over the past few days. London is no place for us. I'm going back and I'm taking Meggin with me. She's to be Meggin Fishpole now, and anyone who says differently will have a taste of my tongue."

Lina was nodding encouragingly. "That's a marvelous plan," she said warmly. "Meggin is a very lucky little girl to have you as a mother, Mrs. Fishpole."

Mrs. Fishpole was blinking rather rapidly. "As to *mother*, well I never thought to be such a thing. But I suppose—"

"You are definitely Meggin's mother," Lina said cheerfully.

Meggin peeped out from the iron circle of Mrs. Fishpole's arms like a sparrow waiting for a plump worm.

"I believe that Father Rumwold in the Minster Church is in need of a housekeeper who can cook," Tom said, not thinking it necessary to add that Father Rumwold had never had a housekeeper and showed few signs of needing one. "You would be an excellent candidate. If you are interested, I could send a note, suggesting your services to the father. It's a small household, just himself and two clerics." And, he thought to himself, Rumwold is just the sort to enjoy a good fish and sausage pie.

"I'd be grateful," Mrs. Fishpole said with a sharp nod. "I've never done any housekeeping, but I wouldn't mind putting my hand in."

"Excellent," Tom said, scribbling a note for Reverend Rumwold and giving it to Mrs. Fishpole. "May I pay for Meggin's passage to the North Country, Mrs. Fishpole? I feel responsible for the distress that I caused both of you in the past few days."

"As to that, I won't say no," Mrs. Fishpole said. "Things are a bit tight, and I meant to borrow some from my brother-in-law, but he's not a ready man."

"It's my pleasure," Tom said. Lina was kneeling next to Mrs. Fishpole's chair and saying something in Meggin's ear without disturbing her snug place on Mrs. Fishpole's lap. The little girl was smiling and then Lina put something in Meggin's hand and closed her fingers around it. Mrs. Fishpole didn't notice; she was busy pushing back all the money Tom had given her except one guinea.

"This'll be enough to get us to East Riding, and I thank you for that. I'm not taking any charity, not if my name's Elsa Fishpole. Meggin and me will make our way with what we have, and a deal of hard work, and that'll be enough. Right, Meggin?"

Meggin looked up at her and then suddenly burst into tears.

"We'll be fine," Mrs. Fishpole told her roughly. But she was rocking her back and forth with a manner that belied her curt words. "No crying, now. We Fishpoles don't cry."

Lina and Tom finally tiptoed out of the room with whispered farewells, as Meggin seemed to be bent on proving that sometimes Fishpoles, especially the little ones, did cry. And cry.

"What did you give Meggin?" Tom asked curiously, when they reached the street and climbed into their hackney again.

"My ring," Lina said.

"Your ring? What ring?" Tom asked.

She shrugged. "A ring your brother gave me."

"He gave you a *ring*?" Tom hardly recognized his own voice. That was the voice of a man about to commit homicide against a member of his family.

Lina touched his arm. "Only when I dragged him into a shop and demanded it," she said, smiling up at him.

"Oh."

"It was a pretty little emerald, though," she said cheerfully, "and since Mrs. Fishpole does not know my name nor my direction in London, she will have no way to return it to me. Therefore, I would guess that she will swallow her pride, sell the ring, and be able to set herself up with some comfort in Beverley."

Tom felt a reluctant smile curl his mouth. "You've solved it all, haven't you?" he said. "You knew I'd done the wrong thing taking Meggin away; you forced Mr. Sigglet to give you the proper directions; you found a way to give some money to Mrs. Fishpole when I utterly failed in that respect. You are going to be a superb vicar's wife."

"Hmmm," Lina said. "Perhaps, if I chose to be." Then she stretched up and for the very first time, under her own initiative, gave him a kiss.

# 33

## Because Rees Is a Very Good Student

*H*elene burst into the music room looking as vividly happy as Rees had ever seen her. He took one glance and went back to his score, pounding out a cello accompaniment to the Captain's aria he wrote yesterday. He didn't look up until she stuck something in front of his eyes.

"Do you know what these are?" she burst out.

"Flowers." He played the first few chords again. They sounded pedantic. Perhaps they would flatten the exuberance of *Come to the Ball!* Perhaps he should try oboes instead of a cello.

"Not just any flowers," Helene said, pushing him over on the piano stool. "I had them on my bedside table, ever since"—she seemed to be turning a little pink—"since we walked in the woods, day before yesterday."

"Yes?"

"And Saunders just told me that they are Star of Bethlehem flowers!"

Rees looked at the wilting starflowers. He vaguely recognized them, but the fact was hardly interesting. "Do you think that oboes are too windy to accompany the Captain's aria?" he asked her.

Helene paused and cocked her ear as if she were listening to silent oboes. "I'd try cellos," she said finally.

"That's what I thought," Rees said with some relief. He played the first few chords again. A three-cello accompaniment would be right.

"Rees, you're not listening," Helene insisted.

"What?" he snapped. "I'm busy. I can't accompany you upstairs at the moment, if that's what you want."

"These are Star of Bethlehem flowers," she insisted. "Saunders just told me that if a woman lies on a bed of Star of Bethlehem, she'll have an easy childbirth."

"We're hardly at that stage yet," Rees said, trying to keep his mind on the sounds of invisible cellos.

"Not yet," Helene said, and the happy note in her voice made Rees want to smile. The sound of cellos died. He put a hand on her back, pulling her snugly against him.

"So would you like to do our daily bedding?" he asked, dropping a kiss into her hair. She smelled faintly of flowers herself.

"I've already asked Leke to have the coach brought around," she said.

"What?" He had started nuzzling her neck and wasn't paying much attention.

She jerked away. "Rees! There's no need for that sort of thing. We aren't in the right place."

He blinked. Yes, there is, he thought. But no. Their bedding was only for conception. Only for children. He reached up and pulled her back. "You're my wife, Helene," he said. "I'll kiss you whenever I want. And I want. We weren't in the right place last night either."

For such a practical woman, who eschewed caresses unless quickly followed by a practical bedding, for practical reasons, she melted into his arms with a gasp and a sigh. In less than a second, the blood was raging along his veins. It was as if the cellos had leaped from his script and began a fiery sarabande.

Rees was just starting to think about easing Helene over to the couch when a voice said from the doorway, "The coach is at the front door, Lady Godwin."

"Oh!" Helene gasped, jumping away from Rees so quickly that he toppled toward the piano bench and slammed his knuckles. "Yes, Leke, we're coming!" she called.

"Helene, it was raining this morning." Rees shook his hand, trying to get his wits together. How on earth could a mere touch of her lips turn him into a bumbling adolescent boy, all raging lust?

"Good thought," she said. "I'll instruct Leke to place a blanket in the carriage."

"That wasn't—" but she was gone, darting from the room.

Rees rubbed his chin. He had bathed, but not shaved in the morning; shaving seemed like too much work since he'd been up half the night working on the tenor aria. And he'd forgotten to send a note around to Darby, although he thought he was working out the problem on his own. What would he ask? *How does one tup a lady?* It sounded absurd.

Helene reappeared in the doorway. She looked like a graceful little linnet, her beautiful hair ruffled by his hand, her lips stained ruby by his kiss.

"Will we have to make our way to the wood every day?" he asked warily, receiving a glowing smile in return.

"Perhaps."

The woods were different this afternoon, soft and rain-soaked. They walked along, Rees inspecting the little spigots of water dripping off the oak leaves. The sky was distinctly gray. "It might rain," Rees said, thinking about just how uncomfortable cold rainwater would feel on his ass.

Helene ignored him. "Look at that fat redbreast!" she said. "He looks just like a plump squire scolding a recalcitrant stableboy."

Rees gave the bird a glance and it flew away instantly. The truth was he didn't want to return to Helene's narrow bed. He didn't want to wait that long. He was burning, from head to foot, with the desire to get Helene's clothes off and feast on that lovely body of hers. See her long pale legs spread under him again, hold a breast in his hand so that only a rosy nipple peeked between his fingers, slip another hand under her bottom . . . He walked faster, blanket thrown over his shoulder.

The clearing looked very different today. All the starflowers were shut up, which turned the space to a muted green, very drowsy and wet looking.

Helene paused. "Do you think that it counts if the flowers aren't open?" she asked.

"Of course," Rees said, plowing into the meadow with no regard whatsoever for the water stains that instantly blotched his pantaloons. She was hesitating on the edge of the path, so he said, "You do want to have an easy childbirth, don't you?"

"Well, yes, but it's just a superstition."

He threw the blanket on the ground and went back and picked her up. She put her arms around his neck and smiled at him. Rees almost shook his head. Could it be that he was in a dream? Was this his sharp-tongued, hateful wife, the one who called him an animal and made him feel ten times more clumsy and idiotic than anyone else? She had her arms linked around his neck and she was rubbing her lips against his and then she slipped her tongue—

He put her down quickly and started throwing off his clothes. "Be careful, Rees," Helene cried. "It's so wet here, and you just threw your coat onto the grass. It'll be soaked."

A moment later he stood before her, all that broad, muscular body hers for the taking. Helene had never felt more dainty and feminine in her life. Without speaking, and without taking her gaze from his body, she pulled her morning gown over her head. She had deliberately chosen not to wear a walking costume. Instead, she was wearing one of her light, floating pieces from Madame Rocque.

Rees made a hoarse sound in his throat and sank to his knees in front of her. Helene blinked. What a nice gesture. He had never gone on his knees, even when he asked her to—

The thought was lost in a squeak. "What are you—what—Rees!"

Helene's whole body contracted down to a small area between her legs. She could do nothing but stand there, weak-kneed, mind blurred. It was a sin, what he was doing. She was sure of that. Some sort of sin, if not a crime. And yet she couldn't hold onto any particular thought. They drifted into her head and then he would lick her again, sending a racking wave of fire down her legs, and the thought would disappear.

"This isn't—" she began. He put his hands on her bottom and pulled her closer. The sentence whirled away, lost in a moan.

"I don't think—" she began again, but his thumb had found its way there too, and now her knees finally did buckle and he lowered her to the ground, kneeling over her, his hand still moving.

"One doesn't do that to ladies, does one?" she gasped, even as her body writhed under his hand.

"No," he said briefly.

She closed her eyes and a delicious smile spread across her face, and then she opened her legs even wider. "Good," she said softly.

"Helene," Rees said hoarsely, a few moments later. She wasn't listening. He slid in slowly. He'd thought a lot in the middle of the night, about how to turn Helene-in-Vauxhall into Helene-in-his-bed.

He pushed in, a little way, and she clutched his shoulders.

He pulled out. Slow, that's what he'd decided to do. Very slow. She was, after all, a very delicate lady. If he just kept everything slow, perhaps she'd feel some pleasure.

So he did. Belying the jokes of his mistress, Rees had full control of his muscled body. He'd just never seen the point of prolonging the experience. But now he propped his elbows on the ground and slid in and out as if he had all day. At first she just lay there the way she had the last time they tried this.

But after a while, she opened her eyes and said, shakily, "Rees, are you almost done?"

"I'm afraid not," he managed between clenched teeth.

Her hand tentatively touched his back, slid down toward his buttocks and he involuntarily lunged toward her. And was answered by a moan. Her face was growing pink.

He waited, and waited. Her fingers were wandering over his back, caressing every ripple of muscle. She asked him again, gasping, if he were almost done, and he shook his head. And then, as if she didn't even realize what she was doing, she started moving a little. Tipping her hips up to greet him. Rees let himself go a little harder, thanked by a cry that broke from her lips.

He went a little faster, and even harder . . . Helene's breath was coming quickly and her eyes were dazed; she'd stopped caressing him and he could feel her fingernails biting into his shoulders. Then she started turning her head from side to side and straining against him.

"Come, Helene," he said hoarsely, praying for strength.

Finally, when he couldn't last any longer, he reared back and slid his hands under her sweetly curved bottom, pulled her toward him and thrust into her with all his strength, a broken groan coming from between his teeth.

And then Helene opened her eyes and looked at him and said, in a tone of the greatest surprise, "Rees?"

Rees knew perfectly well that he was an idiot where women were concerned. But on the other hand, he knew his wife. He'd never seen that particular look on her face, but he knew it.

He pulled her even higher, even harder, and she started shuddering and crying out. Rees closed his eyes in silent thanks, and relinquished his control utterly. They came together with desperate urgency, with rough tenderness, with one last fierce kiss.

Rees remembered, dimly, that his wife didn't like to be flopped on. So he withdrew, and then rolled over onto his back.

It was only then that he realized they had traveled off the blanket. A cradle of wet flowers felt delicious on his heated back.

"I did lie on a bed of Star of Bethlehems, didn't I?" Helene said dazedly.

Rees felt a drop of rain on his nose and then one on his cheek. Helene's slender leg lay next to his, milky white against the green leaves. She had the look of a child who had just experienced her first ice, an astonished, almost blinded look of pure joy. He knew instantly that he would spend the rest of his life trying to give her that particular pleasure.

He rolled toward her, one hand slipping to her leg. "Since childbirth is all taken care of," he told her, "perhaps we should ensure that the previous steps are successful, hmmm?"

In the end, quite a few drops of cold rain fell on Rees's ass, just as he had feared.

But he didn't really notice.

## 34

### *Disaster!*

$\mathcal{T}$he elegant carriage that drew up before Number Fifteen, Rothsfeld Square had barely come to a halt when two ladies tumbled out, shawls flying behind them, hair all a whirl, a glove left on the floor of the carriage. Leke opened the door just in time to stop it being shoved in his face, only to find himself confronted by an army of two Amazons demanding to see the countess.

Helene was curled up in the library, trying very hard to concentrate on the score she held in her hand. Rees was thumping away on one of the pianos. More than anything she wanted to go into the room and bump him over with her hip and—and just sit there. Next to him.

I can't do that, she told herself. He must work. *I* must work. What if we added a French Horn to this section? she asked herself. What indeed?

The door burst open. "Oh, my goodness," Helene said, jumping to her feet. "Esme! And Gina! What on earth are you doing here?" It wasn't time for morning calls; they were over hours ago. And it wasn't yet time to ready oneself for supper, even if they had made plans to dine together, which they hadn't. To this point, the three friends had delicately avoided the fact that Helene couldn't receive callers, given Lina's presence in the house.

"Disaster!" Esme cried. "Helene, did you tell the Earl of Mayne that you were staying in this house?"

"No," she said. "But he knew—" She stopped, horrified. "I asked how he knew and he didn't tell me, and then I forgot to press the point."

"Do let me into the room!" Gina said, pushing Esme forward and shoving the door shut behind her, only narrowly missing Leke's nose. He had been on the verge of offering refreshments, but instead he retreated to the servants' quarters for a think. And then he ambled over to the Number

Eighteen, Rothsfeld, because the butler in that establishment, by the name of Watts, knew everything worth knowing.

In the library, Helene sank into the armchair she had just vacated, feeling as if her legs had lost all strength. "He promised he wouldn't tell anyone," she said. And then, "Surely he didn't!"

"He did," Esme said grimly, sitting down opposite Helene. "Since you didn't tell him yourself, he must have bribed the footman who forwarded his note to Gina."

"It's all my fault," Gina said. She was stark white and looked anguished. "I'm so sorry that I ever, ever passed on Mayne's note to you. He's naught more than a cad!"

"Cad!" Esme cried. "That doesn't half cover it. The man's an utter bastard, and if anyone's to blame, it's myself. *I* put him on the list I gave to Helene; *I* sang his praises between the sheets!"

Helene's lips felt numb. "Blame is surely not the point," she said. "May I ask what the Earl of Mayne has done with his illicitly obtained information?"

There was a moment of silence. Helene faintly heard a plink-plinking coming from the music room; Rees must have switched to the harpsichord.

"He told everyone," Esme said, finally. "Last night, at Vauxhall."

"He was at Vauxhall?" Helene gasped. "I never saw him!"

"Neither did I. But he was there, because Felicia Saville is citing him as her source of information."

"Felicia Saville?" Helene asked numbly.

"I would guess that she's paid twenty morning calls today," Gina said quietly. "And all circling around two topics: the Earl of Mayne and his magnificent endowments, and your scandalous activities."

"Mayne and Felicia?" Helene was unable to conceive the breadth of the scandal that must be spreading about herself, so she fastened on the lesser matter.

"Felicia would appear to be his latest *inamorata*," Esme said with distaste, "though how he can put up with all that mindless gabbing, I don't know. Helene, do you think that you might have insulted Mayne in some way? I don't mean in the least to defend the man, but he's acting like someone bent on revenge. I'm told he put a bet in White's that—" She stopped.

Helene looked at her. "What did he bet in White's?"

"Sebastian was likely mis—"

"What did he bet in White's?"

"It had to do with the portion of the night that Rees granted to you as opposed to his mistress," Esme said.

"Obviously not a real bet," Helene said slowly. "He wrote in the betting book only in order to spread the scandal."

"I agree," Gina said. "But I don't think we have anything to gain by sorting through what insult he may or may not have suffered. We have to figure out what to do."

"What are people saying?" Helene asked. "Don't give me a watered down version, Esme. We've been friends too long for that."

"You're ruined," Esme said, her eyes bleak. "I find it extremely unlikely that any woman of good reputation will receive you in her house ever again. Unless we do something."

"Do something? Do something? There's nothing to do." Helene leaned back in her chair. She could feel her pulse beating in her throat in a way that threatened to make her stomach flip over. But she wasn't hysterical. She, Helene, never became hysterical.

Gina was sitting bolt upright, lips pressed together. "There has to be some way out of this," she said fiercely. "There simply has to be. What if we make our own calls, and maintain that Mayne is a liar?"

Esme shook her head. "No one will believe us."

"What if Rees challenges Mayne to a duel?" Gina demanded.

"Duels are against the law," Esme began.

But Helene cut in, "and I don't want Rees fighting a duel. He'd never win against Mayne. I doubt he knows how to pick up a pistol."

Esme looked at her in disbelief. "I thought you cared nothing for Rees. If the truth be known, none of us are to blame for this situation except for that bloody husband of yours. Why *did* he force you to come here, with his mistress in residence? What on earth did he hope to gain from it?"

"I don't know," Helene whispered. "I should never have consented to do it."

No one wanted to agree with the obvious, so they just sat for a moment.

"Will you still receive me?" Helene asked, looking from one to the other. She was starting to feel a little shaky.

"Don't be a fool!" Esme snapped. "We're going to work this out, somehow. Maybe I'll send Sebastian to duel with Mayne."

"Or I'll send Cam to simply beat him senseless," Gina suggested. "Cam could tie him up and force him to recant. And break his nose in the process," she added with a relish that belied her reputation for duchess-like behavior.

Helene managed a smile. "Rees can pummel Mayne just as well, if that's needed. But no one would believe Mayne if he recanted now. The damage is done. I'm ruined."

"Where *is* Rees?" Esme demanded.

Helene shook her head. "I want to know what I'm going to do, first."

"Rees's reputation was already in shreds," Gina said with stinging emphasis. "Yet it never stopped him from attending a *ton* party, should he so wish."

"There's no use crying over the unfairness of life," Esme said with equal sharpness. "We have to think of a way out of this. Think!"

# 35

## A Sibling in a Righteous Fury
## Is a Terrifying Sight

"*I* don't like it, Garret," Lady Griselda Willoughby said, her voice as sharp as the edge of a knife. She was standing in his study, looking the very picture of enraged femininity in a gown of pale blue sarsanet, trimmed with white lace.

Mayne looked up from his writing desk and scowled at his sister. "No one likes it, Griselda," he observed. "There's something remarkably distasteful about the whole affair."

She walked closer and then began pulling off her pale blue gloves, finger by finger. "That's beside the point," she said, slapping her first glove onto the table.

"I hardly think so," he said dryly.

"If there's anything distasteful here, it's you," his sister retorted. Her second glove slapped onto the polished mahogany of his writing desk.

Mayne's features set into forbidding lines. He may have been thinking something of that sort himself, but he wouldn't take the same from a younger sister. "I apologize if I offended you in any way," he said with an air of chilling *froideur*.

"You behaved like a shabby cad," Griselda cried, unconsciously echoing Gina's indictment. "I'm ashamed of you. And I'm even ashamed of *me*, for being your sister!"

Mayne stood up. "For God's sake, Grissie, don't you think—"

She pointed a finger at him. "Don't you dare call me Grissie, you—you—degenerate! I have no idea what happened between you and Helene Godwin last night, but I can only assume that she sent you packing. And for you to turn from practically panting at the mere mention of her name—because you were, Garret, you know you were—to spreading vile rumors about her is *low*! Low and unworthy of you!"

"She lied to me," Mayne forced out, walking to the mantelpiece.

"Wait!" his sister said contemptuously. "Do I hear the sound of violins wailing? So you've never lied, is that it? You—who've made a name for yourself by sleeping with half the married women in London? You dare reproach a woman for lying?"

Mayne turned around. The injustice of it had occurred to him in the middle of the night, but he hadn't known that his little sister would agree. "I didn't know you thought this of me," he said, lips stiff.

"I love you, Garret," she said, picking up her gloves in an ecstasy of irritation and slapping them down on the table again. "You know that. I love you more than any other person on this miserable planet. But that doesn't mean I'm blind to you. You have to marry because you're becoming more and more a fribble and less of a man of substance. It seems as if you spend all of your time wooing married women, and then when you've got them in the palm of your hand, you dance onto the next woman. Why, Garret? Why?"

He stared at her. "I don't know."

"Exactly! I think you're bored. And boredom is making you do shabby things."

"I—" But what defense did he have, exactly? He felt shabby. He wouldn't have put that word on it, but he'd had a smutty taste in his mouth ever since he woke up, and a leaden sense in his belly.

"All right, I'll marry," he said hollowly, walking over to the fire and sitting down, ignoring the fact that Griselda was still walking around the room like a demented vixen.

"Of course you'll marry!" she snapped.

"You can just chose someone and I'll marry her."

"Not until you've solved the mess you've made," she said sharply. "You know I love to gossip, Garret. I'm thought of as a gibble-gabbler, and I am one. But I'm not vicious. Helene Godwin would never have gone to that house of her husband's, not with a strumpet in residence, unless he forced her to do so. You should have seen that as clearly as I! I've no objection to jabbering about a woman—or a man, for that matter— who chooses to blacken his or her reputation by imprudent behavior. But I would never palaver about a woman forced by her husband into detestable action, *never!*"

Mayne felt really sick now. He'd forgotten his first reaction to hearing that Helene was staying in her husband's house. "She said—she said he didn't force her to stay there."

"You're a fool! I've known Helene for years, and if you didn't even see the monstrous Puritanical streak in her, what did you see?"

"I don't know," Mayne said, pulling his hand through his hair.

"Godwin forced her into that house, and into the presence of his mistress—" Griselda shuddered. "I can't imagine how humiliating that must have been for her. And you—*you* break her confidence, and all because she doesn't choose to join the long line of women who've graced your bedsheets!"

Mayne's teeth were clenched. "You've made your point," he said, hearing a roaring sound in his ears. "You're right."

Griselda opened her mouth—and shut it again.

"The point is," she said after a moment or so, "what are we going to do to change things?"

"There's nothing that can be done," Mayne said through bloodless lips. "I've ruined her. I could let Godwin kill me in a duel, I suppose."

"Don't be a greater fool than you already are!" Griselda snapped. "I may be extremely annoyed with you, but you're still my brother and I won't have you shot by that degenerate. This is all *his* fault, at the base of it! We just need to *think*. Think!"

# 36

## Great Minds, etc.

$\mathcal{J}$t is a fact long established about the human race that when a great many fine minds assert themselves to the same task, solutions are found with astonishing rapidity. At some point, a clever group of primitives came up with the wheel; a group of housewives bent on retail therapy discovered that metal disks work for bartering just as well as do chickens; a few fishermen managed to extract Napoleon from lazy exile on Elba.

And so it was.

When Lady Griselda Willoughby was announced at the Godwin residence, Helene looked confused, but Gina, who knew the precedence of every living member of English peerage, said instantly, "That's Mayne's sister. Show her in, Leke."

It was during Griselda's rather flurried and apologetic entrance that Esme suddenly said, "I've got it!"

Griselda instantly dropped her rattled explanation that Mayne was waiting penitently in her carriage, and said "What?"

"I think it will work," Esme said slowly. "We just need the cooperation of one person."

"Who?" Gina said breathlessly.

"Mayne will do it," Griselda said firmly. "My brother will do anything that needs to be done."

"Not Mayne." Esme looked at Helene. "It's your husband's . . . friend. We need her."

"For what?" Helene asked.

"She has to marry," Esme said decisively. "Become respectable."

"I don't know if Mayne will wish to go that far," Griselda said, feeling a sudden flash of panic. "He does mean to marry, but—"

"No, I don't mean she should actually marry someone," Esme said. "But she has to pretend to be married. Helene, would you mind very much if we asked the young lady to join us?"

"Join us?" Griselda squeaked. To tell the truth, she'd never been in the room with a kept woman. It was a good thing that she'd left Mayne in the coach. He had an uncompromising streak when it came to his little sister's acquaintances.

"I don't even know if she's in the house," Helene was explaining. "We don't exactly—I have no idea—" she foundered to a pause.

"I shall enquire," Gina said firmly. "What is her name?"

"McKenna," Helene said. "Miss Lina McKenna."

The three women sat in utter silence, listening to Gina sending Leke off to request that Miss McKenna kindly join them in the library.

Griselda found herself rather disappointed, to tell the truth. The young woman who was ushered through the door by Leke some ten minutes later was nothing like what *she* imagined a Bird of Paradise to look like. Miss McKenna had soft brown curls, and large eyes. She was beautiful, in a young sort of way. But she didn't look debauched, and she certainly didn't look as if she was—well—spicy. Naughty. Any of those rather exciting words that one associated with strumpets. Mostly, she just looked painfully nervous.

"Miss McKenna," Esme said, having made sure that the girl was seated. "I am afraid that the news of Lady Godwin's residence in the house, in tandem with your presence, has created rather a sensation amongst London society."

Miss McKenna gasped and looked to Helene. "They found out?"

"She's ruined," Esme confirmed. "No one in polite society will ever receive her again." Her voice was quiet but merciless.

Miss McKenna swallowed. "I'm sorry," she whispered. "In God's truth, I am so sorry."

Helene found a smile wobbling on her lips. "It's hardly your fault. I think we have universally come to the agreement that the fault lies directly at the door of my reprehensible husband."

Griselda was rather interested to note that Helene showed no sign of loathing her husband's mistress. Perhaps Mayne was more acute than she had given him credit for. Helene was, indeed, an unusual woman.

"I did not wish to remain in this house," Miss McKenna said looking only at Helene, "and I'm ashamed that I ever agreed. I only did so because Lord Godwin offered me the lead in his next opera."

Griselda was feeling more and more confused. The supposed strumpet spoke like a lady, albeit a Scottish one. Griselda could hear a burr in her voice. And she wasn't even wearing rouge, for all Griselda could see. How could this woman be a self-respecting *élégante*? Helene didn't seem to have shed a single tear over the fact she was ruined, but Miss McKenna was obviously biting her lip to keep back a flood.

"You do not have the manner of a common woman," Esme commented.

"No," Miss McKenna admitted.

"How many of Lord Godwin's acquaintances have you met frequently, since becoming his mistress, enough so that they would recognize you instantly?"

Miss McKenna's face washed with color. "Almost none," she whispered. "Mr. Darby. Mr. Forbes-Shacklett. Oh, and Lord Pandross, but he hasn't been to the house in months."

"Simon Darby and Pandross won't present a problem; Rees can shut them up. Are the Forbes-Shackletts in town?" Esme asked Gina.

"I don't think so," Gina said slowly. "Lady Forbes-Shacklett was going to present her daughter this year, but then the family went into mourning, and I believe they remained in the country."

Esme drew a deep breath. "I think it's possible." She turned back to Lina. "I am sure you are aware how remorseless society will be to Lady Godwin. Her children will be shunned, should she have any. She will have to live in the country. She will lose her friends. How can we risk the reputations of our own children, by continuing to fraternize with a woman of her sort?"

Gina opened her mouth indignantly, but Esme silenced her with one glance.

Lina was trembling. "I am sorry," she said miserably. She had never felt so wretchedly ashamed in her entire life. "I'll leave the house immediately. I'll never—"

"I should like you to do something for Lady Godwin first," Esme interrupted. "There is only one way we can overcome this scandal. We must be so brazen that no one could possibly believe the truth." Esme turned to the others. "May I present to you Rees's third cousin, four times removed, recently widowed and come to London for peace and quiet?"

Gina's mouth fell open; Helene flinched; Griselda said, "Of course!"

"Third cousin?" Lina gasped. "Of Lord Godwin?"

Esme nodded. "From this moment on, you are a little-known relative from the country. No one has seen you as yourself, remember. No one is at all clear about what Rees's famed mistress actually looks like. We will announce that the mistress long ago departed. Rees had a distant connection staying here, and Helene joined the household temporarily, to act as a chaperone."

"Are you certain that everyone will believe us?" Helene asked, dawning hope in her voice.

"Obviously, we have to parade Miss McKenna before the *ton*. But I think that one occasion, if well handled, will suffice to silence the gossip. No one could possibly believe that the four of us"—she nodded to Lady Griselda—"would ever countenance being in the presence of Rees's mistress, let alone bring about the presentation of such a woman to the *ton*."

A little smile curled Griselda's lips. "And I know precisely who would best effect the presentation of this distant relative. My brother may have acted the fool last night, but now he can put his dramatic ability to work in our favor."

# 37

## *Siblings Are Sometimes Quite Similar*

*N*aturally, Rees was pounding away at one of his pianos when Tom found him. He seemed to be playing the same set of chords over and over again. Tom walked over to the piano and stood next to it until Rees looked up.

"Where's Helene?" Rees asked, by way of greeting. "I haven't seen her this morning."

"I have no idea," Tom said. "I shall be leaving for St. Mary's tomorrow, Rees."

His brother blinked up at him and his hands finally slowed on the keys. "I had gotten used to having you in the house."

Tom thought to sit on the couch, but it was stacked with paper. He pulled over a stool and sat on that instead. "I need to return to my parish. I intend to speak to the bishop about leaving the priesthood."

Rees was caressing the piano keys with long fingers, although he made no sound. "I would surmise that your change of profession is due to Lina?"

Tom lost his blaance and almost toppled from the stool. "I—that is, yes."

"How does Lina feel about you?"

"She refuses to marry a vicar," Tom said, wondering if he should apologize for taking Rees's mistress and decided that he needn't. "Perhaps I will be able to change her mind. It will take me some time to extract myself from the church, but I would like to marry her immediately."

Rees raised an eyebrow. Tom had the unnerving sense that their father was sitting before him. He'd never realized before how much Rees took after the old earl.

"I had the impression," Rees said slowly, "that although you were enjoying a glimpse of life outside the parish, you would return to your church."

"I miss my congregation, and I miss being a priest," Tom said, feeling almost as if he were confessing to a weakness. "It's who I am, after all these years. But Lina doesn't wish to marry a man of the cloth." He tried not to sound as if he were defending a weakness. Rees was *not* their father, only an elder brother.

"What will you do if the Bishop grants your request and removes you from the parish?"

"Likely work with abandoned children," Tom said promptly.

"You're a better man than I am," Rees said. "You know, Father was proud of you, for all he didn't express that particular emotion."

"Expressing contempt came far more easily."

Rees was silent for a moment. Then he said: "I'm proud of you, Tom. You're a good man."

Tom watched him scowl down at his keyboard, and felt a rush of affection, although it would never do to express it. "So will you forgive me for stealing your mistress?" he asked.

"It was her voice, as I expect you've realized," Rees said, ignoring his frivolous question. "I heard her sing, and I couldn't think about anything except getting that voice into the house so that she could sing for me." He smiled in a crooked kind of way. "I was a right bastard. It only took me a month or two to realize it, but it was too late."

"I wouldn't have met Lina if you hadn't brought her here," Tom said, and the very idea chilled him. He did want to stay a vicar, but only if he had Lina to keep him laughing, and warm his bed, and stop him from turning into a sanctimonious ass.

Rees played one key. The sound hung on the air, melancholy and fading. "I suppose I can lure Madame Fodor from the Italian Opera House to play Lina's part. It will suit her voice very well." And then, looking at the keyboard: "I am going to ask Helene to remain in the house."

"To remain in the house—or to stay with you?" Tom asked gently.

The smile on Rees's mouth was rather grim. "She has a great deal to forgive me for."

"You're lucky she loves you so much, then," Tom said.

Rees's eyes flew to Tom's, and then he looked away without comment, standing up. "I need to find Helene and play this phrase for her."

Tom stood up as well and then, to his utter surprise, Rees pulled him into a rough hug. He didn't say anything; Rees was never one to use words when there was no need. Tom followed his brother from the room without another word between them.

He was free. Free to tell Lina that she had to marry him. Free to take her away.

As Rees stepped into the hallway, Leke came out of the library. "The countess has just asked for you," he said, holding open the door.

Tom stopped. "Where may I find Miss McKenna, Leke?"

"In the library," he replied.

They strode into the room looking, had there been a mirror appropriately placed, extremely like their father. Yet another glance would have revealed that they were far more like to each other, than to their father.

# 38

## Snippets of Conversation Overheard in London During the Week

"*I*t's your penance," Lady Griselda Willoughby told her brother with some satisfaction. "If you have to endure a month or so of wretched bibble-babble, it will teach you to be more particular in your attentions. For goodness' sake, I may find Helene Godwin rather tedious, but I grow faint with ennui if I am unlucky enough to drift into the sound of Felicia Saville's voice. And believe me, you can hear her voice halfway across a ballroom!"

Her brother's answer was unintelligible; Griselda just smiled to herself. She had no need for an interpreter when it came to males and their childish dependence on profanity; after all, she had been married for all of a year, God rest his soul.

"You cannot leave the Church. I won't allow it!"

"For you. Only for you."

"I won't allow it!"

"But you said you didn't wish to marry a vicar." The said vicar's eyes burned down at his companion. "It never occurred to me that I could be anything other than what I am. But I could do so, for you. The only person I would ever give up my vows for is you, Lina."

"My name isn't Lina," she said, stumbling a little. "It's Alina. But my mother always called me Lina."

"You're my Lina now," he said into her ear. "And if what I do for a living would come between us, I'll do something else."

"I don't want you to relinquish your vows. You wouldn't be happy."

"The only thing that would make me unhappy is losing you."

"Then make me a vicar's wife, Tom."

There was nothing to overhear for a while and then, "You *will* keep me from becoming as perfect as your father, won't you, Lina?"

"I don't think that's a problem," she said with a giggle. "Take your hand away!"

He groaned. "Lord, I wish Rees would return with that Special License."

"Are you sure?" There was a hesitancy in her voice that rung his heart.

"I've never been surer of anything in my life," he told her. "Never. Listen—I'll make a vow so that I can break it for you!"

"Don't be silly!" she scolded, laughing.

"I vow to God himself that I will never kiss your breast."

And she, whispering, with a rosy blush, "You won't?"

"God will forgive me for breaking my vow," he said, his lips tracing the very edge of her bodice. "He can see into my heart and knows that I love you with every bit of my soul. That's the most important vow."

"I love you the same," she said, and then his lips did slip below her bodice—but only for a moment or two.

Mr. Holland, vicar of St. Mary's, was a man of considerable self-control, and considerable patience.

The portly Bishop of Rochester viewed the young couple before him with keen interest. "I only have the slimmest acquaintance with your father," he said to Miss McKenna. "I knew him at Cambridge, oh, many years ago, that was. He was quite the rapscallion, your father!"

That seemed to surprise Miss McKenna.

"Indeed," Bishop Lynsey assured her, with a belly laugh that made his vestments shake as if a tempest had struck the environs of Rochester Cathedral. "They do say that rascals make the best churchmen, you know! Well, mum's the word on that. He's an excellent man, your father, an excellent man. And you couldn't do better than marry Mr. Holland, my dear. I can see your father's influence in your choice. I'm only sorry that your family can't be with you. But I do understand the urgency of young love, even such an oldster as I."

He gave the bridegroom's elder brother a sapient look. It would be nice if that ne'er-do-well, Lord Godwin, were moved by the words of the marriage ceremony into conducting his own affairs with more propriety. It was surprising to see the earl and countess standing beside each other; Lynsey had heard gossip that suggested the two hadn't even spoken for years. But here they were, looking as married as can be. Well, the ways of God are mysterious indeed.

Still, he beckoned the married couple closer. It would do them good to hear the words of the ceremony since, if he remembered correctly, they had trotted off to Gretna Green in a harum-scarum fashion and married over the anvil. Likely two or three words in the whole ritual, if one could even call it that.

"Dearly beloved," he began with a fine flourish in his voice, "we are gathered together here in the sight of God, and in the face of this congregation"—he smiled encouragingly at Earl Godwin and his wife—"to join together this Man and this Woman in holy matrimony, which is an honorable estate . . ."

"You're awfully quiet."

"That was a very sweet ceremony, didn't you think?"

"Mmmm."

"I believe I shall retire to my chamber."

His hands stopped. "Weren't we going to work on the étude before bed?"

"Rees!"—rather exasperated—"I'm exhausted. We can think of this in the morning." And then, "What are you *doing*?"

"Taking you upstairs," he said. "I'm going to carry you over the threshold."

"*What?*"

"I never carried you across the threshold of the house ten years ago, Helene, so the bedchamber door will have to do. I have a mind to pretend that I'm going to walk into an inn bedroom and find you there."

She had her arms around his neck, and he was climbing the stairs. "Are you going to laugh at my bosom then?"

He stopped. "What?"

So, in the way of wives, Helene reminded the earl that on seeing his wife's breasts for the very first time, he had suggested that she might have shrunk in the rain.

Repentance is an emotion that can be expressed in many different ways. Rees was not eloquent. He wasn't good at tossing off debonair little phrases or comparing his wife to roses or jewels.

So he did the very best he could. He took his wife into his bedchamber, pulled her gown over her head, revealing a pair of breasts whose pale pink perfection instantly fired his loins, and then fell backwards, flat on the floor.

"What's the matter with you?" the countess asked with some curiosity, walking over to peer down at him.

"I've fainted from the beauty of your breasts," he said, grinning up at her lasciviously.

And then, as she giggled, large hands circled her ankles and crept up her legs. "I'll make up for my stupidity, Helene," he said, kissing his way up a slender thigh. "I'll make it my daily chore to praise your breasts. Even before I touch the piano."

As one musician to another, Helene could tell when she'd received the greatest compliment of her life, although nary a rose nor a jewel was mentioned.

# 39

## The Plot Unveiled

*L*ady Felicia Saville gave one, and only one, ball each year. The night before the event she often couldn't sleep. There was so much to worry about: would Gunter's deliver half-melted ices, would the champagne punch be sufficient, would her husband appear reasonably sane or utterly cracked? The last question was the most pressing. The year after they married he informed a large and amused audience that he was actually the child of a black-tipped ewe, and then there was the occasion when he insisted that his horse was a blood relative. Over the years, she had realized that his particular form of mania was less disagreeable than it could have been, but it did require forethought to make certain that he did not regale the ballroom with tales to rival those of Aesop.

But this year was different. Last night she had slept like a baby. The ball would be easy, because Mayne would be by her side.

Contrary to his usual custom, and quite contrary to what she herself would have expected, he was still showing her marked attention. It was the most delightful and unexpected pleasure of her entire life. They had been *intimates*, as one might say, for exactly one week, and his ardor showed no signs of cooling. Felicia had to hug herself for the pure joy of it. Everyone wanted to know her secrets. How could *she*, Felicia Saville, hold the attention of a man known to flit from woman to woman like the proverbial butterfly?

Felicia frowned over her morning hot chocolate. Frankly, she hadn't the faintest idea how she was keeping Mayne's attention. It wasn't as if they shared scintillating conversation. Nor were they terribly intimate with each other in private, if the truth were known. He certainly kissed her with a great deal of finesse, but then he muttered phrases about respecting her too much to overstep, and carried the business no further.

Which was rather disappointing. Felicia's marital partner, after all, was past hope in that area. After one night in which he shouted *tally-ho!* in an intimate moment, she banished him from the bedroom.

She was beginning to think that perhaps Mayne had never slept with any of the women he accompanied. Perhaps the women in question were so enchanted by his attentions—and their reputations so enhanced by his presence at their side—that they told no one their relationship was unexpectedly chaste. If that was the truth of it, Felicia was perfectly happy to continue the tradition. In fact, in the last week, when her friends kept noting that she was looking particularly becoming, she had given one and all a twinkling glance that put her renewed looks at Mayne's bedstead. The truth, after all, was hardly important in these situations.

With a shrug, she finished her hot chocolate and dismissed perplexing thoughts about Mayne's continued attentions. She was beautiful enough, wasn't she? Or at least, she would be, once she finished the four-hour dressing process that would ready her for the ball tonight.

She was three hours into the ritual, bathed, perfumed, painted and powdered, but only half-dressed, when a footman informed her maid that the Earl of Mayne wished a brief word, if she were available. A smile curled on Felicia's lips. Oh, this was even better than she could have imagined! She cast a look at herself in her dressing room mirror. She hadn't yet put on her evening gown. She was wearing stockings of the palest rose silk, tied above the knee with a silver garter. Her chemise certainly covered her flesh adequately, and its edging of rose lace would entice any man alive.

"I'd like my corset," she ordered.

Felicia's lady's maid, Lucy, rushed forward with her corset and laced it tightly over her chemise. Yes! That was perfect. Now Felicia's breasts swelled enticingly and her waist looked to be the span of a man's hand. She had never done such a risqué thing as entertain a gentleman in her dressing room. Not even her husband. Mind you, Saville had never shown the slightest interest in joining her during the dressing process.

Her maid began tucking tiny rosebuds high into a coronet on her head, from which hung precisely four ringlets. Felicia reached out and applied more color to her lips. "He may come up," she said coolly, as if she entertained gentlemen every day of the week. "And Lucy, you may go. Return in a half hour, if you please, as I shall need to finish dressing with some dispatch."

Lucy could be counted on to gabble to all the maids in attendance at the ball tonight, Felicia thought happily. She tweaked one curl forward over her shoulder. She did have a long nose, but really, she was remarkably well preserved. It must be her beauty that tied Mayne so closely to her side.

There was a knock and the man himself strode into her bedchamber. Felicia almost gasped. Her chamber was all frothy lace and pink ribbons; in contrast, the earl looked like the very personification of sleek masculinity. Tonight he was dressed with supreme elegance, in a coat of smoky blue that outlined the breadth of his shoulders and gave his hair the sheen of a raven's wing. He looked utterly male and (had Felicia the wits to perceive it) rather dangerous, as if some subtle rage were driving him forward.

"Darling," he said, bending down and dropping a kiss on her cheek so that their eyes met in the mirror. "This is an honor that I didn't expect."

Felicia tilted her head back, the better to show her neck. Her mother had once called it a trifle long, but Felicia disagreed. A graceful neck was a never-fading virtue. "You are always welcome by my side, even in the most intimate of circumstances," she purred.

Somewhat to her relief, he didn't take up the obvious suggestion, but just smiled and brought over a chair for himself. Felicia could hardly contain herself at the sight of the two of them in the mirror: he so beautiful, so potent, so devastatingly powerful. And she, leader of the *ton*, exquisitely dressed . . . Their coloring was quite perfect together.

"I need your help," he said, bending close to her ear as if he couldn't resist kissing it.

Felicia shook with excitement. "Anything!" she said eagerly, and then contained herself, adding languidly, "of course, darling, whatever you request."

"I seem to have made a small mistake," he said, "in the matter of Lady Godwin."

Felicia blinked. "You did?"

"You are the only woman powerful enough in the *ton* to salvage my disastrous follies," he continued, tracing her ear with his lips. And his hands . . . Perhaps Mayne *did* bed all those women. Perhaps he was just saving himself, building her anticipation for the moment when he would besiege her virtue. Felicia shivered a bit at the thought.

"If there's any way I can help," she said rather absentmindedly. It was hard not to gaze at the two of them in her mirror as if she were at the theater, watching one of those Restoration comedies from the last century. But his actual comment had finally sunk in. "I doubt I can do much to salvage Lady Godwin's reputation, Mayne."

"Do call me Garret," Mayne said, trying not to breathe deeply. The woman had practically papered herself in rice powder! He was like to sneeze, if he didn't watch himself.

"My pleasure," she sighed.

"It appears that Lady Godwin had returned to her husband's house merely in order to chaperone Godwin's brother's fiancée," Mayne told her. "The girl is a tender little Scottish vicar's daughter, if you can believe it, and doubtless horrified to hear that she's been mistaken for a strumpet."

Felicia sat straight up in her chair with the air of a fox scenting a rabbit. "You don't mean it!"

Mayne nodded. "I've made an ass of myself," he said, pulling a face of laughing mock repentance. "Blotted my copybook."

"And what's your excuse?" she asked, fluttering her eyelashes at him.

"Something about Lady Godwin irritates me," he admitted. "I'm afraid that I didn't bother to corroborate my impression that Godwin was still living with an opera singer. Now I feel, naturally enough, culpable."

"I share your feelings about Lady Godwin," Felicia agreed. "And now that she looks for all the world like a shorn lamb, I positively shudder to look at her. Her hair *was* her only beauty, you know."

Mayne's lips tightened, but his companion simply trilled on. "Goodness me! Are you quite, quite sure about the Scottish fiancée, Garret darling? I mean, that she's the daughter of a *vicar*?"

"Alas."

"Well, I shall do my best," Felicia told him. "I shall inform everyone. But you know how it is!" she tittered. "Once a rumor starts, it's impossible to stamp out. It's not as if we *know* this Scottish girl, after all."

Mayne moved behind her. One hand slipped down her throat. "You blind me," he said softly. "Truly, you do." He bent over and kissed her cheek. This was the tricky bit; Felicia might well take offense at his presumptuousness.

"I invited them to your ball," he said softly.

Was that the tip of his tongue touching her throat? Felicia swallowed. "You did what?" she asked quaveringly.

"I took the enormous liberty of inviting the Scottish miss and her fiancé to your ball," Mayne murmured against her throat. His hand had wandered down and was tracing the shape of Felicia's breast. "They will be accompanied by the Godwins, naturally enough."

"Her fiancé," Felicia said, trying vainly to keep rational. "Godwin's brother."

"He is a vicar himself, if you can believe it," Mayne said, tasting her skin as if she were made of the finest cream. "The brother, I mean."

Felicia noticed that he had a white streak on his cheek from the rice powder she had shaken over her bosom. But he didn't seem to notice the taste on his lips.

"A vicar and a vicar's daughter," she said dreamily, winding her arms around his neck. "A match made in heaven."

"Just as are you and I," he said sleekly. "Will you forgive me, then, for the impertinence of inviting guests to your ball?"

She smiled at him, a smile that combined chastisement and permission. "After tonight, Lady Godwin will be received in every house in the land," she assured him. "And the Scottish girl as well. I think we know each other well enough, Garret, that I might allow a few . . . *impertinences?*"

"Just what I longed to hear," he said. His smile, in the mirror, was meant both for her—and for his conscience.

# 40

## Come to the Ball!

*E*lsewhere in London, others were preparing for the same occasion. Lady Griselda Willoughby was delicately applying a black patch to the right of her cherry-colored mouth; she had decided that her newest fashion would be to ape the ornaments of her Jacobean ancestors. She wore a gown with a small train, and the tiniest suggestion of a ruff. The Duchess of Girton was having a rather less peaceful time dressing, as her little boy kept wandering through her dressing room. He had just learned to climb down stairs backwards, and therefore he spent most of his time eluding his nursemaids and unerringly finding his way to his mama's chambers. Lady Esme Bonnington was even further behind in the process, as her husband Sebastian had appeared in her room with an urgent request, and what with one thing and other (some of which involved unbuttoning rather than buttoning), she hadn't even put on a stitch of clothing yet.

But the most assiduous preparations were taking place at Number Fifteen, Rothsfeld Square. Monsieur Olivier had been to the house and left again: Lina's glossy brown curls were now a shadow of their former self, thinned, curled and starched into rigid little ringlets that dangled about her ears.

"I'm so sorry!" Helene said again, staring at the glass. "He went too far! What will Tom say?"

But Lina couldn't stop smiling. She didn't give a fig for the demise of her hair. "It will grow back," she said.

"Do you think I ought to add more freckles, or am I overdoing the effect, Madam?" Saunders asked, stepping back.

Helene looked at the mirror and gave a faint shudder. Lina had sprouted a multitude of freckles. First Saunders painted them over the bridge of her nose, which was all very well. But then she went farther afield and now there were battalions of brown speckles marching along Lina's forehead, making her look far older than her years.

"I'm sorry!" Helene said again.

"Don't be," Lina replied. Their eyes met in the mirror and Lina knew that she didn't have to say the rest of it out loud. She would never stop being grateful for the gift of Tom.

Saunders was mixing a little red sandlewood with chalk. As she painted it onto Lina's lips they took on a slightly palsied air, as if the color had leached out of them.

"Well, that should do it," Lina said cheerfully. "No self-respecting opera singer would look like this."

"No, indeed," Helene said with some satisfaction. "You look—you look—"

"A proper fright," Lina finished.

"Not so terrible. Countrified, perhaps?"

"I *am* a country vicar's wife," Lina said, and there was a note of joy in her voice.

"Now for the gown," Saunders said. She returned from the wardrobe with a gown reverentially laid over her arms.

Two minutes later, Lina was swathed—positively swathed—in white lace.

"Perhaps it's overpoweringly innocent," Helene said dubiously. She had picked out the pattern and fabric herself, ordering it from a *modiste*, Madame Pantile, whom she'd long heard was liable to make ill-fitting and over-trimmed clothing. And Madame Pantile had certainly lived up to her reputation. Every inch of Lina's gown was trimmed with blonde lace, or point lace, or bunches of white ribbon.

"Are you certain that the wreath isn't too much?" Lina said, showing the first signs of uneasiness.

"Oh no!" Helene said. "I consider the wreath a stroke of genius! Who but Madame Pantile could have designed a wreath made of silver oak leaves ornamented with heron's feathers? At least . . . that's what she told me they were. Who would have thought that heron's feathers were quite so tall?"

"My head will topple to the side if I'm not very careful," Lina said, demonstrating her predicament.

"Excellent. You need to look awkward while dancing."

"That won't be a problem," Lina commented. "Wearing shoes that are too large makes it extremely difficult to be graceful."

Helene beamed. "That was a clever notion of Esme's, was it not?"

\* \* \*

The night was going as well as Felicia could possibly have hoped. Mayne was at her side just enough so that her friends and her enemies couldn't help but notice his devotion, and yet he wasn't there so much that she felt constrained in recounting every detail of his physique and technique to her friends. Her husband was off in the card room, apparently acting in an appropriate manner. The ballroom was an utter crush. In all, the only thing missing to make her ball discussed throughout those boring fall months was a Sensation.

Something had to happen. An elopement, a betrayal, an argument. Something! She glanced around the room. What a pity it was that Esme Rawlings had married Lord Bonnington. Infamous Esme could always be relied upon to create some sort of a sensation, but now she had dwindled into positive respectability. There she was, dancing with her husband and it must be for the third time, at least. That was a scandal, to Felicia's mind, a scandal of hideously boring proportions.

At that moment there was a bit of a flurry at the door, and Felicia turned with relief. Perhaps the Regent had decided to—no.

Who on earth could it be?

A grotesquely bedizened girl, with plumes so high they were likely to be set alight by the candelabra hanging from the ceiling, had appeared at the top of the short flight of stairs leading to the ballroom. Felicia didn't recognize her escort but there, behind her, was Earl Godwin so that must be—

There was a titter in her ear. "Famous, my dear! Your ball is going to be notorious!" The Honorable Gerard Bunge suddenly appeared, for all the world like a jack-in-the-box in amethyst stockings, if such a thing existed. "That must be the vicar's daughter, or rather, the strumpet as Mayne had it!" He reeled slightly from the force of his own giggles. "Could be Mayne's going blind if he mistook *that* one for a Bird of Paradise!"

"She's rather an eyesore, is she not?" Felicia said with amusement. "Come along, Bunge. I must greet her, you know."

At the tap of a hostess's fan on their shoulder, her guests fell away before her, leaving Felicia a full view of the uncultivated lass whom Mayne, *her* darling Mayne, had insulted. And what a mistake that was! Felicia had rarely seen such an ungainly, rustic girl as the one clumsily curtsying before Lady Bonnington.

"You'd better make haste," Bunge said in her ear, as they expertly made their way through the crowded room. "She just poked the Duke of Girton in the eye with those plumes. How could Mayne ever have thought this one was a fashionable impure? They wouldn't have let her in the door of the opera house!"

Felicia held out her hand languidly. The country miss bobbed an inept curtsy and gabbled something. Felicia backed away as quickly as she could, to avoid being struck in the face by her waving plumes.

"I must say, this is quite a surprise, to see you in the presence of Lord Godwin," she said aside to the countess. "I thought you two were quite, quite adverse to being in each other's company."

"Oh, we are," Helene Godwin said cheerfully. "But I couldn't allow Mrs. Holland to come to town without a chaperone."

"Mrs. Holland!" Felicia exclaimed.

Lady Godwin clapped a hand over her mouth. "Oh no, I let the truth out! Well, the fact is that Mr. Holland, my brother-in-law, married his fiancée this morning. But we didn't want to announce the news until the happy couple has informed her father, in Scotland. He is a vicar, you know, and I believe he hoped to marry them himself. So you *must* promise not to tell anyone, Lady Saville!"

Felicia nodded, already planning the three or four acquaintances who would be lucky enough to hear the news first.

Lady Godwin drew a little closer. "The dear girl was so *devastated* to hear of the rumors flying around London—you do know what I mean, don't you?"

"A crime!" Felicia whispered back, ignoring the fact that she herself had been instrumental in spreading most of those criminal rumors.

"Yes, I do agree," Lady Godwin said. "You know, Lady Saville, you or I may chat about a matter of interest that occurs in the *ton*, but we would never make something up out of whole cloth! And I'm afraid that is just what the Earl of Mayne must have done. Why, everyone in London knows that my husband dismissed his mistress months ago."

Felicia nodded vigorously. "I had heard the same myself, from a number of people," she assured the countess. "Mayne has much to answer for!"

"Dear Mrs. Holland is happy now," Lady Godwin said. "All's well that ends well, after all. And who could possibly think her a woman of ill repute after seeing her endearing little face?"

"Who indeed?" Felicia murmured, suppressing a shudder as she watched the new Mrs. Holland stumble her way through a country dance.

"Marriage solves so many problems," Lady Godwin commented. "Now she and my dear brother-in-law can go back to the country, and she can simply forget this unpleasant little episode."

"And you, my dear?" Felicia said, returning to a more interesting topic. "Do you think to remain in your husband's house, or will you return to your mother?"

"Well . . . just for *your* ears only, Lady Saville—"

"*Do* call me Felicia!"

"Felicia," the countess repeated. "What a lovely name. The truth is, I haven't quite made up my mind! For some things, you know, husbands are a necessary evil."

Felicia nodded, although to be sure, she couldn't think of a single one of them.

## 41

### *The Seduction*

Floating through the house, up the stairs, came fragments of melody. He was playing the same piece over and over, the madrigal from Act Two, she thought.

Finally Helene got up and put on her serviceable dressing gown, tying it tightly around her waist. It was a good thing there were so few servants, given the number of nights she had spent tiptoeing around the house inadequately dressed.

The candelabra on the piano were burning quite low. They cast a pool of light that made the polished surface of the piano look clover-yellow, and tipped Rees's eyelashes and curls with fire. She walked forward. Her robe made a gentle hushing noise as it dragged through the sheaves of paper that had again accumulated around the piano.

His head jerked up immediately. Without speaking, without taking his eyes from hers, he rose from the piano.

Helene was experiencing, for almost the first time in her life, the heady intoxication of being a siren, a *séductrice*. She pushed the ugly, white dressing gown from her shoulders as if it were made of flowing silk, let it catch on her elbows so the fabric framed her body. She'd left her night rail on her bed.

Rees took one step toward her and then Helene started to walk toward him. It was as if the candlelight drew her into its circle; as she came closer to him, her body turned to flame itself, heat racing up the back of her legs.

He seemed mesmerized. She slowly walked forward until she stood in the circle of light that made the rest of the room fade away into obscurity, as if there were only the two of them in the world.

Still without saying a word, he wrenched off his shirt. The swirl of air made the candles bend and dance. Golden tongues of fire swept over her body, over his chest. She couldn't remember why she thought chest hair was so revolting, years ago. Compared to Mr. Fairfax-Lacy's hairless chest, Rees looked ruggedly masculine, with a kind of burly strength that made her feel weak in the knees. His heavily muscled chest rippled when he moved, making her breasts tingle to be crushed against him.

She let a little smile play on her lips, and then she dropped the dressing gown entirely, allowing it fall to her feet.

The next second he was there, one arm under her neck and another under her knees, scooping her up and taking her over to the sofa. With a terrific swirl of paper, all the drafts and parts and pieces of the opera swooshed to the floor.

"I don't want to be treated like a lady," Helene said, but he was kissing her.

*Kissing her.* His tongue plunged into her mouth as if she were *terra incognita*, new land, and he an explorer. And she, rather than feeling any kind of revulsion, gasped and said, "Oh," and then said, "Rees," and then said . . . nothing. One of his hands was holding her head tight against his. But the other was sending trails of fire down her spine, roaming her body with hungry violence.

Helene had her arms wound around his neck, but she wasn't a lady. Not tonight. She tore her mouth away. "How did Lina make love to you?" she said, her voice oddly hoarse.

Rees pulled her back. "Who cares?" he said before crushing her against him again, capturing her mouth and pulling them both into a whirlpool of desire and trembling sensation.

"I do," Helene gasped, when she got her breath back. "I do."

Rees let her pull back slightly. "It was nothing compared to you. Nothing." The rasp in his voice told her it was true.

"It's not that," Helene whispered back. "I want to know how to give *you* pleasure, Rees. Not—not like a lady. May I touch you?"

His eyes were pitch dark in the candlelight. "Lina never touched me," he said, his mouth wandering hungrily over her skin.

"I want to," Helene said, her voice quivering as his mouth closed over her nipple. "I—" but she lost the thought as her body arched toward his, her hands clenched in his hair, a moan flying from her lips.

"Do you want this?" he growled, sucking harder, so that she shuddered under him, gasping, unable to speak. One of his hands curved under her body, jerking her up against the leg wedged between hers, making her cry out with pure pleasure.

But she still retained some small crumb of sanity, enough to twist suddenly in his arms and end up lying on his body. "I want to be just as wicked as you," she whispered, raw desire speaking in her voice like velvet. "I want to make love like one of those Russian dancers who performed on my dining room table."

He smiled at that, that sardonic crooked smile that she loved, so she had to kiss him. It was different, bending her head to him rather than the other way around, having that powerful body under hers. It made her feel even more sensual, if outrageously strumpet-like. Part of her simply couldn't believe that she was straddling him, naked, where anyone could see her.

"Do you see whether I turned the key in the door?" she asked shakily, when he let her mouth go.

He was lying back, his hands roaming over her breasts, a rough caress that made her compulsively shudder and bite her lip to stop a moan. He obviously didn't give a damn about the door. *I'm starting to think in swear words,* Helene thought with some wonder.

She started to get up to check the door, but his hands captured her.

"Didn't you say that you were going to touch me?" he asked, and the silky pleasure in his voice sent a wave of fire through her belly.

She bent down again, feeling an incantatory mix of possession and desire. It came out of her mouth like a vow, although she hadn't been thinking of it that way. "You are *mine*, Rees. If anyone is going to touch you, it's going to be me. From now on. So if you wish me to touch you the way Lina did, you'll have to teach me."

He stared at her and she couldn't tell what he was thinking, but all he said was, "Lina was a lady, Helene."

Helene could feel a smile of utter delight curl her lips. She shouldn't be so shallow. But she was.

She slid off his body and kneeled beside the couch. He turned slightly, and there he was, all of him, muscled, golden skinned, dusted with hair that teased her skin into delirious heat. Just the sight of him made Helene want to pull him down to her so he would crush her with his weight, with his fierce, tender wildness.

Instead she licked his shoulder. His skin tasted like salt and faintly, like soap. Just as he had the night before, she whispered, "Do you like this?"

And as he had the night before, he said, rather hoarsely, "Yes. Yes, Helene, yes."

Tentatively she reached out and touched his nipple. It was flat and round, and looked like a copper penny. His muscles rippled at her mere touch. She did it again, a little more firmly, and then rubbed her thumb over him, the way he did to her. He made a hoarse noise that sent a surge of triumphant joy through her, so she bent her head and licked him. His hands clutched her shoulders. Slowly Helene wandered farther afield, discovering that she could make him tremble by gently dragging her teeth across his chest, that a ragged sound came from that chest whenever she suckled his nipple, that his entire body grew rigid as she made her way south.

"I'm not sure that you—" he said, and it sounded as if he were speaking between clenched teeth. Helene grinned to herself. She felt as if she were the most practiced courtesan in all London, and besides, it was too late for him to stop her.

The merest touch of her lips made him shudder convulsively. So she teased him, just as he had teased her. "Do you like this?" she said, laughter spilling into her voice.

"Yes," he gasped. "God, Helene!" He was clutching the sofa cushion beneath him. His body arched toward her.

"This?" she said. She had discovered that dragging her fingernails across his stomach seemed to drive him mad. She was really enjoying herself now. "And what about this?" she whispered, her voice a liquid thread of honey.

But it was too much. With one lunge, Rees pulled her up on top of him so she fell forward and down, onto him, her mouth an almost comical "O" that turned to a cry as she sank, all wet, sweet, warm, onto him. But it wasn't enough, it wasn't enough, so he flipped her over, and the last of the sheets of paper scooted onto the floor.

Then he drove into her in a way that replaced the last bits of laughter in those beautiful eyes of hers with a blurred desire, changed all that teasing to a panting, wanton cry that made him drive into her harder and harder, gritting his teeth against the glory of it. She was so beautiful, his Helene, delicate and supple in his arms, twisting up against him with little gasping moans.

The pleasure of it curled through Helene's body, streaks of heat pooling between her legs and then curling out toward her toes. Her hands sought purchase and found his muscled buttocks; she clutched him to her and he came to her harder in response, and it was building, she couldn't stop it, the curling was turning to streaks of fire.

She opened her mouth and nothing came out but a whimper, a scream, an echo of his name. . . . He came to her hard and looked at her face, at the passion in her eyes, and the faint sheen of sweat on her forehead, at the way she was looking at him, and lost all control, plunging into her body as if he were a man possessed, until her cry was answered by his, his shudder answered by hers, finally . . . his caress met by hers, finally, his lips on her forehead.

And when his weight came to her, she didn't feel suffocated. But he remembered and rolled sideways, off the low couch straight onto a snow-bank of paper, bringing her with him.

"Rees!" Helene protested with a weak giggle.

But he kissed her silent, and then said, "Quiet, love," and there was something aching in his voice that made her feel as if she might cry, so she had to bury her head in his shoulder and pretend to be sleepy instead.

He knew though. "I've been a fool, Helene," he said into her hair.

She bit her lip but said nothing.

"I never ever really wanted her, you know. I think Tom is right. I made an ass of myself because my father told me years ago that I would. I didn't even enjoy those Russian dancers."

"You didn't?" She pulled back her head and looked up at him.

He didn't smile. "I must have drunk two bottles of brandy a day for a month after I made you leave the house. It didn't help though. Nor did having a bunch of tarts cavorting on the table. I just couldn't figure out why I felt so sick all the time."

Helene held her breath.

"I was in love with you," he said slowly, his hands cupping her face. "But I couldn't admit it, not to you, not to myself. I just kept trying to get rid of you, and then feeling sick about it."

"I love you," Helene whispered. "I never stopped."

"How could you?"

She smiled at that. "I'm a fool, I suppose."

"You are," he agreed bluntly. And then, "Even when—even when I brought Lina into your chamber?"

"Oh, I didn't think I was. I kept telling myself that I was indifferent to you. But it hurt."

"I'm sorry."

"Were you—were you in love with her?"

He shook his head. "Never. She knew it too. I wanted her voice, you see. We stopped all sort of bedroom things a year ago, from pure lack of interest."

"I wish I hadn't said such cruel things to you," Helene said, dismissing Lina and the Russian dancers forever. "I do love your chest and every hair on it."

"I think I feel more than love for your chest," he said rather dreamily. "It's like an obsession. I shall have to compose a *canzonette*, To My Wife's Breasts."

"Silly," she said. And then, "I shouldn't have been cruel about your music, either."

"Nor I so dismissive of yours," he said.

She hesitated, and then, "I think . . . I think we may both write better with the other's help."

His arm tightened around her. "I know that is true for me, but I doubt there is anything I can add to your gift, Helene. Of the two of us, you are the brilliant musician."

"Not so!" she protested.

His lips traced a quarter note on her cheek. "I write at the peak of my ability when you are near; what more could a man want?"

"We have gifts of different kinds," Helene said slowly. "You are a genius at expressing emotion and creating a character, Rees. All I'm good for is doing a piece of music itself, with no story. *You* saw what my waltz was about, after all. I hadn't even noticed, though I wrote it."

Rees chuckled. "That was when I really started to wonder whether there was the faintest chance that I might be able to keep you in the house forever. When I saw that waltz."

"Scandalous, isn't it?" Helene actually felt proud of it.

"Worse than Russians on the table," he said. Then he sang: *Let me, dearest wife, embrace you, As would a lover his lovable bride . . .*" But he stopped singing to kiss her.

*"Face to face with burning cheeks,"* Helene whispered sometime later.

But her husband was kissing his way down her body, and she couldn't see his cheeks anyway, so she threw away the thought.

Much later, Helene lay against her husband's heart and listened to the steady beat of her life and her future.

She felt sleepy. Rees was already asleep. So the earl and his countess fell asleep, in a bed of opera scores, of discarded musical notes and florid lyrics, while the candles guttered on the piano.

It was morning when Leke opened the door and surveyed the room. By then, its occupants had vanished. Anyone less accustomed to Earl Godwin's organization methods might have noticed nothing amiss.

But Leke stood in thought for a moment or two, staring at the crushed papers piled high around the sofa, and then, even more intently, at a thick white dressing gown tossed to the floor next to the piano.

He left with his regular measured step, a garment neatly folded over his arm, and a smile curling the edges of his mouth.

# 42

## In Strictest Confidence...

18 January 1816

*The Countess Pandross to Lady Patricia Hamilton*

... I assure you, my dearest, that I am as startled as anyone. But it is quite true. Earl Godwin is positively lavish in his attentions, and you know that for a man like that to show any courtesy at all, particularly to his wife, is quite out of the way. The opera singer is definitely a thing of the past, and it's rumored that Countess Godwin is carrying a child, so perhaps all this attention he pays her has to do with the question of an heir. Men are so absurdly attached to the idea of reproducing themselves. Of course, it may also have to do with her part in that opera he's just put up, *The Quaker Girl.* The newspapers have all called it a triumph, although shamefully I haven't found time to see it yet. I told Pandross that if we don't attend this week I shan't be able to go anywhere in public, because darling, it is *all* that anyone is talking about. Almost, I envy you for your snug country life. You'll have to see it the moment you return for the season. The waltz scene is apparently scandalous, and yet I was told in the *strictest* confidence that Countess Godwin wrote the waltz herself, if you can believe it.

I do agree with you regarding your disappointment with Patricia's debut year. But have you noticed that this sort of thing happens more and more? I find that girls are not shot off until their second or even third year, so I would counsel you ...

19 January 1816

*The London Times: Music on the Town*

*The Quaker Girl*'s popularity continues. On Wednesday last it was necessary to throw open disengaged boxes to the public, in order to accommodate the crowds demanding admission. This opera is widely regarded as the finest work of Earl Godwin, and the most exquisite example of *opera buffo* yet produced on the English stage. There are those who compare it more than favorably with works of Mozart. Lord Godwin's vocal music appears to us not only of a high rank, but of a different order from that of almost every other composer. We venture with some diffidence to characterize it, in order to record the impressions we receive from it, by saying that he expresses passion, and excites sympathy in his viewers, in a manner not seen by us for many years. The waltz scene, of course, continues to be a popular favorite; evidence of which can be seen in the fact that in recent weeks Lady Sally Jersey has allowed this waltz, and this waltz only, to be danced at Almack's.

22 January 1816

*Rees Holland, Earl Godwin, to his brother*
*St. Mary's Church, Beverley, in the North Country*

Dear Tom,

Things are all right here. Yes, the opera appears to have been a success. Helene's waltz has created an enormous sensation and is being danced all over London. I'm glad to hear you both are well. I miss you, old sobersides that you are. Rees.

25 January 1816

*Miss Patricia Hamilton to Lady Prunella Scottish, née Forbes-*
*Shacklett*

Dear Prunes,

I'm so glad to hear that you are back from your wedding trip, and believe me, I want to hear about *every moment*. My mama is convinced that I shall end up an old maid, so I must needs hear of your exploits before I wither on the vine. On that front (although I tell you this, obviously, in the *strictest confidence*), I have received several billet-doux from Lord Guilpin! We danced several times during the season, but I didn't think he was in the least interested in me. But then we met quite by accident while riding in the Park and since then . . . I know I should not be accepting correspondence, but it is too, too delicious . . . At any rate, Prunes, I am not quite so distraught as my mama over the possibility of my withering on the vine, as you can imagine.

We just came up to London to see a performance of Earl Godwin's new opera, *The Quaker Girl*. My mother was positively galvanized with curiosity; everyone is talking of the piece. There is a waltz in Act Two that is the most romantic piece of music I've ever heard. I thought I might faint, and my mother turned quite pink! You must go to the opera the very first chance that you . . .


28 January 1816

*Rees Holland, Earl Godwin, to Helene Holland, Countess*
*Godwin, delivered by her maid*

If you come to the music room, I have something I want to show you.

Rees


28 January 1816

*Helene Holland, Countess Godwin, to Rees Holland, Earl*
*Godwin, delivered by a footman*

I've had a visit from Doctor Ortolon. Do you think that Star of Bethlehem blooms in September?

Your wife


28 January 1816

*The Butler's Daybook, as kept by Mr. Leke*

That hamhanded footman James, the one I hired last week, was knocked over by Lord Godwin when his lordship exited rather rapidly from the music room and dashed up the stairs. James insists that his wrist is sprained.

# Epilogue

*Five Years Later...*

*A Small Hunting Lodge*
*Belonging to Earl Godwin*

*R*ees was tired. He and Helene had stayed up half the night, playing around with a bagatelle for four hands, and now he was trying to compose a letter to Snuffle at the Royal Italian Opera House that would explain why he didn't plan to write an opera for next year's season. He and Helene were—he paused and cocked an ear. Far off down the sunny stretches of lawn, he heard a faint shriek of laughter. And then a call from his wife. "Rees! The river!"

Without a second's pause, Rees shoved back his chair and started running. Laughter that bright and that mischievous meant only one thing: little Viscount Beckford had managed to escape his nanny and his mama again, and was heading for the stream at the bottom of the garden. The river barely topped Rees's ankles; it was more of a rivulet than a river. But the danger was there.

Rees's long legs had him at the bottom of the garden in precisely three seconds, followed at some interval by his wife, waving a towel.

Sure enough, Wolfgang Amadeus Holland was standing fully dressed in the middle of the stream. Small blue butterflies were fluttering around his legs, startled from the grass and buttercups that lined the riverbank.

"Wolfie, out with you!" Rees bellowed, splashing in after him. "Haven't I told you a hundred times that you're *not* to go in the water unless Mama and Papa give you our express permission?"

Wolfie's eyes shone with pure joy. "Oh, let me go, Papa, let me go! Look what I found!"

He uncurled a singularly dirty little fist. He held a tiny, emerald-green frog. Rees stared for a moment, and let the fear and anger drain away. Then he bent down to examine the tiny prisoner.

When Helene made it to the riverbank, there were her two favorite men in the world, the smallest in water up to his thighs, and the other with river water washing about his boots, looking for all the world as if they were conducting a biology lesson. And, of course, neither of them had the faintest interest in the fact that their clothes were being ruined by river water.

"Wolfgang Amadeus!" she shrieked, sounding precisely like a fish-wife down at the docks. "Get out of the water this very instant! Rees, how could you let him stand there in that brook!"

Husband and son spun about, their faces mirroring the same expression of guilt and surprise.

"I'm very sorry, dear," Rees said, scooping his son up onto his arm. "You see, Wolfie found a rather fascinating amphibian."

Helene narrowed her eyes at him. "You didn't let him pick something up from that filthy water!"

"Papa's holding it!" Wolfie piped up, as his father put him down on the bank. His mother started rapidly stripping off his wet clothing and drying him with a towel. "Look, Papa, water is coming out of the top of your boot."

Helene couldn't stay angry any longer. "So what did you find, love?"

"A frog, a tiny, tiny, tiny, frog. Papa has it in his hand so it can't hop away. I'm going to keep it in my bedroom."

Helene shook her head at her husband. "A frog in the bedroom?"

"Two frogs and a snake lived in my chambers for one entire summer. The crucial thing is to make it clear that the snake can't share his bed."

"You two are so much alike!" Helene groaned. "Look at you; your boots are ruined!"

He grinned down at her. "Your fate is to be surrounded by men who don't give a fig for fashion."

Wolfie wasn't paying attention. Still naked, with an unhappy frog clutched in his hand, he decided to make a dash for freedom, back up the lawn to where his baby sister was dozing in the shade of a huge elm tree. Naturally he wouldn't get far. He was unclothed, and his mother was always worried that he would take a chill, although he never even got the sniffles.

Boys didn't.

He trotted up the lawn naked as a peeled apple. But when he looked back to track his pursuers, his mother was locked in his father's arms, and neither of them was watching him.

He knew as well as the next person that once those two started kissing, there was no stopping them. The only thing worse was when they were sitting at the piano together. Or sitting at the piano *and* kissing.

So Wolfie pranced happily after a sky-blue butterfly. He was naked and meadow grass tickled his toes. He had a frog in his hand.

Could there be more joy in the world?

# A Note on Waltzes, Operas and Musical Exceptions

When I decided to create a heroine who was a musical composer, Clara Josephine Wieck Schumann, likely the foremost female composer of the nineteenth century, was the model I had in mind. Clara was born in Germany in 1819, and lived until 1896. One of her most extraordinary works was written very early in her life, a waltz for the piano: this is the piece that I have given to Helene. When she was still a teenager, Clara fell in love with a fellow musician, Robert Schumann. They married and had eight children. Yet hers was not the life of a conventional mother in the 1800s. She performed and wrote music throughout her life; she made nearly forty concert tours outside of Germany.

If Helene is unique for the Regency (she supposedly wrote her waltz just before Clara was born), Rees is equally ahead of his time. Rees's opera, *The Quaker Girl*, is, in fact, an Edwardian musical comedy, composed by Lionel Monckton. The lyrics were written by Adrian Moss and Percy Greenbank (including the lovely song, "Come to the Ball"). *The Quaker Girl* opened at the Adelphia Theater in 1910. In the early 1800s, when Rees was supposedly writing, comic opera was flourishing in England. The first so-called ballad opera was John Gay's *Beggar's Opera*, performed in 1728; its direct descendants were operettas by Gilbert and Sullivan.

Those of you who are actual musicians must forgive my inadequate attempt to describe lives bounded by and expressed in sound. Composers seem to hear language as a series of notes; I tried to give a sense of relationships defined by lyric. My failures are all my own, but I received tremendous help in learning about the lives of eighteenth-century musicians from my marvelous research assistant, Frances Drouin, and I learned of Clara's waltz from a brilliant lecture given by Professor Sevin H. Yaraman of the Fordham University Department of Art History and Music.